❧ THE ❧ ❧ BEST-LOVED SHORT STORIES OF *Jesse Stuart*

selected and with commentary by
H. EDWARD RICHARDSON

with an Introduction by
ROBERT PENN WARREN

McGraw-Hill Book Company

New York   St. Louis   San Francisco
Toronto   Hamburg   Mexico
London   Sydney

1 2 3 4 5 6 7 8 9 DOC DOC 8 7 6 5 4 3 2

ISBN 0-07-062305-8

LIBRARY OF CONGRESS CATALOGING IN PUBLICATION DATA

Stuart, Jesse
Best-loved short stories of Jesse Stuart.
I. Richardson, H. Edward (Harold Edward),
1929–   II. Title.
PS3537.T92516A6 1982   813'.52   82-15264
ISBN 0-07-062305-8   AACR2

Book design by Roberta Rezk

We are grateful to The Jesse Stuart Foundation, Morehead, Kentucky, for
granting us permission to reprint all the stories in this collection.

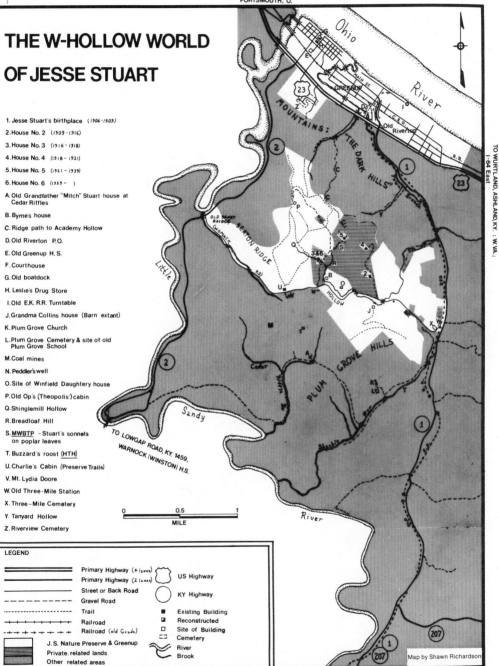

THE W-HOLLOW WORLD
OF JESSE STUART

TO SOUTH SHORE/FULLERTON, OLD McKELL (MAXWELL) H.S., PORTSMOUTH, O.

1. Jesse Stuart's birthplace (1906-1909)

2. House No. 2 (1909-1916)

3. House No. 3 (1916-1918)

4. House No. 4 (1918-1921)

5. House No. 5 (1921-1939)

6. House No. 6 (1939-)

A. Old Grandfather "Mitch" Stuart house at Cedar Riffles

B. Byrne's house

C. Ridge path to Academy Hollow

D. Old Riverton P.O.

E. Old Greenup H.S.

F. Courthouse

G. Old boatdock

H. Leslie's Drug Store

I. Old E.K. R.R. Turntable

J. Grandma Collins house (Barn extant)

K. Plum Grove Church

L. Plum Grove Cemetery & site of old Plum Grove School

M. Coal mines

N. Peddler's well

O. Site of Winfield Daughtery house

P. Old Op's (Theopolis') cabin

Q. Shinglemill Hollow

R. Breadloaf Hill

S. MWBTP – Stuart's sonnets on poplar leaves

T. Buzzard's roost (HTH)

U. Charlie's Cabin (Preserve Trails)

V. Mt. Lydia Doore

W. Old Three-Mile Station

X. Three-Mile Cemetery

Y. Tanyard Hollow

Z. Riverview Cemetery

TO WURTLAND, ASHLAND, KY.; W.VA.; I-64 East

TO LOWGAP ROAD, KY. 1459, WARNOCK (WINSTON) H.S.

0   0.5   1
MILE

LEGEND

Primary Highway (4 lanes)
Primary Highway (2 lanes)
Street or Back Road
Gravel Road
Trail
Railroad
Railroad (old Grade)

US Highway
KY Highway

■ Existing Building
▣ Reconstructed
□ Site of Building
▭ Cemetery
〜 River
〜 Brook

J.S. Nature Preserve & Greenup
Private, related lands
Other related areas

Map by Shawn Richardson

TO ARGILLITE, CANE CREEK (LONESOME VALLEY), GREENBO LAKE/LODGE, GRAYSON, I-64 West

Contents ❄❄❄

Youth

Part 3

The "Strange and Powerful" Characters of W-Hollow

Part 4

The Human Comedy

Part 5

Epiphany

Part 6

Introduction ✻ ✻ ✻

I<small>N MY LATE TEENS</small> and early twenties I wrote, sporadically, at a group of poems under the general title of "Kentucky Mountain Farm." I knew farms well enough, but the ones I knew, of all classes, were along the Tennessee line north and west of Nashville, far from the Appalachians of my pure imagination. Fortunately, my imaginary mountain farm did not require much realistic documentation, for it was not until many years later that I grew acquainted with the world of my mountain in hard fact; but by the early 1930s I had known my first Kentucky mountaineer, who had actually set the bull-tongue plow into that romantic and rock-ribbed earth. That mountaineer was Jesse Stuart.

I was then in the very beginning of my teaching career, at Vanderbilt University, and Jesse appeared there in graduate school after, I seem to remember, Lincoln Memorial University. No doubt the graduate school made its own deep impression on Jesse, and he absorbed it for his own purposes, for his eyes and ears missed nothing, even as he was reading the books strange to him. But it is certain that he made an impression on Vanderbilt. For instance, a paper assigned in one class (under Dr. Edwin Mims, I think) caught hold obsessively of Jesse, and he simply couldn't stop writing it. In a way, I suppose, he was discovering himself and his own special world, and Doctor Mims had no class paper but a big book on his hands—and a book having little to do with Victorian Poetry (or whatever it was the class was involved in). But Doctor Mims saw that here was something remarkable and strangely eloquent—a book about life in the mountains. And what had set out as a little class paper ended up as one of Jesse's earlier published books. This is only one example of Jesse's capacity to absorb, somehow, the world outside him into his own private, inner world.

Jesse took one of my classes at Vanderbilt in the academic year of 1931–1932, but what I remember most is that we also became friends—in walks now and then in woods along the Cumberland River, in the white-washed shack where I lived out in the country, and hoed my Depression garden, and where, I seem to remember, we occasionally mixed Golden Pond firewater with ice. (Or was that with somebody else?) And there was my office, and the shade of campus trees. So he allowed me provocative access to, or at least glimpses of, the inner world he carried with him.

He was a tall and very muscular man, brown-skinned and with eyes that seemed constantly alert to anything in the world about him, physically proud and, I must say, slightly superior in tone to most others, including my 160 pounds and five feet ten-and-a-half inches.

I remember the afternoon in the gymnasium when I was lying belly-down on a diving board for a breather and he passed by and grabbed the calf of one of my legs and remarked, "Not a bad leg for a little man." But his amiable contempt was a small price to pay for gripping anecdote and strange poetic turn of phrase, and the shadow of his past.

That one year was the only extended acquaintance I had with Jesse. The last time I saw him, in spite of a few suggestions that I come to Greenup County, was toward the end of World War II when I encountered him in Washington, looking strangely out of place in the blue of a Navy lieutenant. By that time he had long since, except for that patriotic inter-ruption, gone back to the world of his origins, the place where his imagina-tion and feelings throve best. This was being proved clearly enough by the books and magazine stories I read, each as it appeared.

This present collection provides us with examples of most of the kind of work to be found in those books and magazines. I miss a story now and then; for instance, "Love," which in a few paragraphs creates a memorable impact, with a temper somewhat different from that of most of his work. But here are "The Storm," "Dark Winter," with its grimly heroic stoicism and final burst of spring, recalling a similarly memorable piece, "Spring Victory," not in this collection. With a different tone, less of human warmth and toughness of fiber, but clearly belonging here, are "Nest Egg" (Jesse's first story, I believe), and "Saving the Bees."

Another, very different strain also appears in Jesse's work. There is violence, brutality, pitilessness, and even a kind of humor, now and then, based on such qualities. In spite of Jesse's personality, not infrequently tinged with sensitivity and poetry, he is related—as his world is related—to the tradition that reaches to Mike Fink (as we have him in *The Last of the Boatmen*, by Morgan Neville), the David Crockett saga, A. B. Longstreet's *Georgia Scenes*, and the subhuman outrageousness of Sut Lovingood, created by George Washington Harris. In fact, it is a streak that survives from the frontier on to the humor or violence of some back-country worlds today. The breeze from the American Arcadia has always had a peculiar stench mixed with the odor of spring blossoming. Certain items in this collection make it plain that the author knew more than the rugged virtues and sweet romance of his world. There is the inhumanity and painful comedy in "A Land beyond the River," "Sunday Afternoon Hanging," and "Another Hanging" (the last mentioned not in this collection). Here is a deliberate repudiation of ordinary human sympathy and pity, the comedy of anguish—the crowded, pushing, half-drunken, sex-ridden series of public hangings, one after another, from the "hanging elm." Strangely enough, we sense the primitive brutality that can be transformed into stoicism, courage, endurance, fidelity, and even love.

Jesse Stuart knows the beauty, virtue, and romance of his world. But he knows its bestiality and comedy, too.

Robert Penn Warren

Jesse Stuart at an autographing party in 1935 honoring Man with a Bull-Tongue Plow.

Out of Mountain Shadows: Growing Up in W-Hollow 🕷🕷🕷

Part 1

The Storm

About the story:

Jesse Stuart was born August 8, 1906, in a log cabin on the summit of a hill overlooking W-Hollow to the north and Shacklerun Valley and the Little Sandy River to the south. He has described it as "a lonely spot," a place of "silence" or of "wind." On silent nights the boy could hear the sounds of water in the Cedar Riffle Branch flowing down to the Little Sandy, but if the wind were blowing through the pine trees the water could not be heard. The closest town of size is Greenup, Kentucky, the county seat of Greenup County on the Ohio River, two miles north in a straight line from W-Hollow and separated by a ridge of bony hills. W-Hollow and W-Creek take their names from their shape. Jesse Stuart's father made his living first, so the boy remembers, as a coal miner, but it was dangerous work; and even though he owned no land then, he preferred to clear new ground and till the soil for his family's food and shelter. Jesse and his older sister, Sophia, moved with their parents down to the center of the middle prong of W-Creek in time for their new baby brother, Herbert Lee, to be born November 2, 1909.

Jesse's father, Mitchell Stuart, and his mother, Martha Hylton, were about as different as two people could be and still love each other. "Mick" Stuart, as he was known, was five feet seven inches tall, weighed an average of 130 pounds, had blue eyes, a long nose, and a strong, booming voice. He was Unionist, Republican, and

Methodist. Mrs. Stuart, "Sal" as he called her, was five feet eleven inches tall. Feminine and slender in her youth, she had crow-black hair, which grayed quickly in her middle years; she put on weight, as well. She was of a Confederate heritage, a Democrat, and a Baptist. Mr. Stuart could not read and could barely write his name, but Martha Stuart had gone through the second grade and had a natural interest in books and learning, and was known by her neighbors as being remarkably resourceful around the house. "Dad was fast, very quick," the author remembers; "Mom was just a little bit on the slower side . . . about opposites." Often his parents differed over trivial things, but sometimes the differences grew into anger and got out of hand. One time in particular, "My mother and father had . . . a long quarrel. This one . . . lasted about three days. My mother did most of the quarreling. . . . It was the old quarrel of the Union and the Confederacy. . . . Neither of them would give an inch. I will never forget the sad day in our young lives when my sister . . . and I . . . were old enough to understand when Mom said: 'Mick, I've had enough. I'm leaving you and forever, too!' "

Internal evidence marks the genesis of the story in April, 1912, when Jesse Stuart was six years old. The events lay dormant in his mind until early November, 1937, when he was on a Guggenheim Fellowship to Scotland and was returning across the English Channel to Dover from a month-long tour of northern Europe. A strong wind had blown up and nearly swept some of the passengers from the deck, but while people shouted, "Storm! Storm! Storm!" Jesse Stuart sought a writing pad. "I knew there was something about a storm lodged in my mind over many, many long years. 'Storm' . . . I didn't like to think about it! But now I had to write that story." Once he ran through the rain to the ship's railing to "feed the fish," the only time he was ever seasick. Then "I returned and finished my story just about the time we reached Dover in Kent, England."*

*   *   *

*Jesse Stuart's "The Storm" was first published in *Household,* Vol. 41 (Jan., 1941), pp. 4–5, 9, reprinted in Jesse Stuart, *Tales from the Plum Grove Hills* (N.Y.: Dutton, 1946), pp. 81–91, and in the Mockingbird ed. (N.Y.: Ballantine Bks., 1974), pp. 51–58. It was also reprinted in Martha Foley, *Best American Short Stories of 1942* (Boston: Houghton Mifflin, 1942), pp. 303–312. According to Professor Hensley C. Woodbridge, *Jesse and Jane Stuart: A Bibliography* (Murray, Ky.: Murray State Univ. Printing Services, 1979), p. 79, the story up to 1979 had been reprinted in the United States and Canada a total of five times. Further references to this useful source will be indicated by the shortened title *Jesse Stuart Bibliography*; and I wish to credit Professor Woodbridge's valuable work here and now for all information on publication and reprints of Mr. Stuart's work referred to in this edition of his short stories. Quotations are from H. Edward Richardson, unpub. biography of Jesse Stuart; from Jesse Stuart/ H. E. Richardson, Interview #7, W-Hollow, Greenup, Ky., Sept. 2, 1978; Interview #8, Sept. 3, 1978; Interview #9, Sept. 15, 1978; and from Mr. Stuart's unpub. ms. "The Storm, by Jesse Stuart," in the Jesse Stuart Collection, W-Hollow, Greenup, Ky.

"I CAN'T STAND IT any longer, Mick," Mom says. "I'm leaving you. I'm going home to Pap. I'll have a rooftree above my head there. Pap will take me in. He'll give me and my children the best he has."

Mom lifts the washrag from the washpan of soapy water. She washes my neck and ears. Mom pushes the warm soft rag against my ears. Drops of warm water ooze down my neck to my shirt collar. Mom's lips are drawn tight. Her long fingers grip the washrag like a chicken's toes clutch a roost-limb on a winter night.

"We're different people," says Pa. "I'm sorry about it all, Sal. If I say things that hurt you, I can't help it."

"That's just it," Mom says as she dips the washrag into the pan and squeezes the soapy water between her long brown fingers. "Since we can't get along together, it's better we part now. It's better we part before we have too many children."

Mom has Herbert ready. He is dressed in a white dress. He is lying on the bed playing with a pretty. Mom gave him the pretty to keep him quiet while she dressed me. It is a threadspool that Pa whittled in two and put a stick through for me to spin like a top. I look at the pretty Herbert holds in his hands. Herbert looks at it with bright little eyes and laughs.

"Mom, he has the pretty Pa made for me," I say. "I don't want him to have it."

"Quit fussing with your baby brother," Mom says as she puts my hand into the washpan and begins to scrub it.

"Pa made it for me," I say, "and I want to take it with me. I want to keep it."

Pa looks at the top Herbert has clutched in his young mousepaw-colored fingers. Pa moves in his chair. He crosses one leg above the other. He pulls hard on his pipe. He blows tiny clouds of smoke into the room.

"You're not going to take all the children and leave me alone!" he says.

"They are mine," says Mom, "and I intend to have all three of them or fight everybody in this hollow. They are of my flesh and blood and I gave them birth—and I remember—and—I'm going to hold them." Mom looks hard at Pa as she speaks these words.

"I thought if you'd let Sis stay," says Pa, "she'd soon be old enough to cook for me. If it's anything I hate, it's cooking. I can't cook much. I'll have a time eating the food I cook."

"Serves you right, Mick," says Mom.

"It doesn't serve me right," says Pa. "I intend to stay right here and see that this farm goes on. And if I'm not fooled an awful lot, you'll be back, Sal."

"That's what you think," Mom storms. "I'm not coming back. I do not want ever to see this shack again."

"It's the best roof I can put over your head," Pa says.

"It's not the roof that's over my head," Mom says. "Mick, it's you. You can be laughing one minute and the next minute you can be raising the roof with your vile oaths. Your mind is more changeable than the weather. I never know how to take you, no more than I know how the wind will blow tomorrow."

"We just aren't the same people," Pa says. "That's why I love you, Sal. You're not like I am. You are solid as a mountain. I need you, Sal. I need you more than anyone I know in this world."

"I'm leaving," Mom says. "I'm tired of this. I've been ready to go twice before. I felt sorry for you and my little children that would be raised without a father. This is the third time I've planned to go. Third time is the charm. I'm going this time."

"I'm ready, Mom," says Sis as she climbs down the ladder from the loft. "I'm ready to go to Grandpa's with you."

Sis is dressed in a blue gingham dress. Her ripe-wheat-colored hair falls over her shoulders in two plaits. A blue ribbon is tied on each plait and beneath the ribbons her hair is not plaited. Her hair is bushy as two cotton-tails.

Pa cranes his autumn-brown neck. He looks at Sis and blows a cloud of smoke slowly from his mouth. Pa's face is brown as a pawpaw leaf in September. His face has caught the spring sunshine as he plowed our mules around the mountain slope.

"Listen," says Pa, "I hear something like April thunder!"

Pa holds his pipe in his hand. He sits silently. He does not speak. Mom squeezes the washrag in the water again. Now she listens.

"I don't hear anything," says Mom. "You just imagined you heard something."

"No, I didn't," Pa answers.

"It can't be thunder, Mick," says Mom. "The sky is blue as the water in the well."

Pa rises from his chair. He walks to the door. He cranes his brown neck like a hen that says "qrrr" when she thinks a hawk is near to swoop down upon her biddies.

"The rains come over the mountain that's to our right," Pa says. "That's the way the rains come, all right. I've seen them come too many times. But the sky is clear—all but a maretail in the sky. That's a good sign there'll be rain in three days."

"Rain three days away won't matter much to us," says Mom. "We just have seven miles to walk. We'll be at Pap's place in three hours."

"Listen—it's thunder I hear," Pa says loudly. "I didn't think my ears fooled me a while ago. I can always hear the foxhounds barking in the deep hollows before Kim and Gaylord can. Can't beat my ears for hearing."

"I don't hear it," says Mom as she takes the pan of water across the dog-trot toward the kitchen.

"You will hear it in a few minutes," says Pa. "It's like potato wagons rolling across the far skies."

"Third time is the charm for me," says Mom as she returns from the kitchen without the washpan. "Ever since I can remember, the third time has been the charm for me. I can remember once setting a hen on guinea eggs. A blacksnake that you kept in the corncrib crawled through a crack to my hen's nest. He crawled under the hen and swallowed the eggs. He was so full of eggs that when he tried to crawl out of the nest he fell to the ground. I saw him fall with his sides bulged in and out like wild frostbitten snow-balls. I took a hoe and clipped his head. Then I set my hen on goose eggs and soon as they hatched my old hen pinched their necks with her bill like you'd do with a pair of scissors. I set her on her own kind of eggs—and she hatched every one of the eggs and raised all her biddies. Third time was the charm."

"See the martins hurrying to their boxes," says Pa. "Look out there, Sal! That's the sign of an approaching storm."

The martins fly in circles above our fresh-plowed garden. They cut the bright April air with black fan-shaped wings. They chatter as they fly—circle once and twice around the boxes and alight on the little porches before the twelve doors cut in each of the two big boxes. Martins chatter as they poke their heads in at the doors—draw them out one and chatter again—then silently slip their black-preening feathered bodies in at the small doors.

Mom looks at the long sagging martin boxes—each pole supported by a corner garden post. Mom watches the martins hurrying to the boxes. She listens to their endless chatter to each other and their quarreling from one box of martins in the other box.

"Listen, Sal—listen—"

"It's thunder, Mick! I hear it."

"Will we go, Mom?" Sis asks.

"Yes, we'll go before the storm."

"But it's coming fast, Sal, or the martins wouldn't be coming home to their nests of young ones like they are. Are you going to take our children out in a storm? Don't you know as much as the martin birds?"

I know what Mom is thinking about when she looks at the martin boxes.

She remembers the day when Pa made the boxes at the barn. She held the boards while he sawed them with a handsaw. She remembers when he cut the long chestnut poles and peeled them and slid them over the cliffs above the house. They slid to the foot of the mountain like racer snakes before a new-ground fire. She held the boxes when Pa nailed them to the poles. Mom helped him lift the poles into the deep post holes and Mom helped him wrap the baled-hay wire around the poles and the corner garden posts to hold them steady when the winds blew. I'd just got rid of my dresses then and started wearing rompers.

Mom turns from the front door. She does not speak to Pa. She walks to the dresser in the corner of the room. She opens a dresser drawer. She lifts clothes from the dresser drawer. She stacks them neatly on the bottom of a hickory-split-bottomed chair. She looks at the chair.

"I know what Mom is thinking," I think as she looks at the chair. "She remembers when she grumbled about the bad bottoms in the chairs and Pa says: 'Wait till spring, Sal—wait until the sap gets up in the hickories until I can skin their bark. I'll fix the chair bottoms.' "

And when the sap got up that early spring in the hickories, Pa took a day off from plowing and peeled hickory bark and scraped the green from the rough side of the bark and laced bottoms across the chairs. I know Mom remembers this, for she helped Pa. I held the soft green, tough slats of bark for them and reached them a piece of bark as they needed it.

Pa fills his pipe with bright burley crumbs that he fingers from his hip overall pocket with his rough gnarled hand. His index finger shakes as he tamps the tobacco crumbs into his pipe bowl. Pa takes a match from his hat band and strikes it on his overall leg and lights his pipe. I never saw Pa smoke this much before at one time. I never saw him blow such clouds of smoke from his mouth.

"The sun has gone from the sky, Sal," Pa says. His face beams as he speaks. "See, the air is stilly blue—and yonder is a black cloud racing over the sky faster than a hound dog runs a fox."

Mom does not listen. She lifts clothes from the dresser drawer. She closes the empty dresser drawers. Mom never opens the top dresser drawer. That is where Mom puts Pa's clothes.

"Bring me the basket, Shan," Mom says.

I take the big willow basket off the sewing-machine top where Mom keeps it for an egg basket. When I gather eggs, I put them in this basket.

"Where will Pa put the eggs, Mom?" I ask.

"Never mind that, Shan," she says. "We'll let him find a place to put the eggs."

Mom stacks our washed and ironed clothes neatly into this big willow basket. I see her looking at this basket. I remember when Mom told me how long it took Pa to make this basket. It was when Sis was the baby. Every Saturday Mom and Pa went to town and took this willow basket filled with eggs and traded the eggs at the stores for salt, sugar, coffee, dry goods, thread, and other things we needed.

"Listen to the rain, Sal," Pa says. "Hear it hitting the clapboards!"

Big waves of rain driven by puffs of wind sweep across our garden. We can barely hear the martins chattering in their boxes now. Their chattering sounds like they are hovering their young birds and talking to them about the storm.

Mom has our clothes in the big willow basket. She has Herbert's dresses on top of the basket. Herbert is asleep now. He does not hear the big rain-drops thumping the dry-sounding clapboard roof. It sounds like you'd thump with your knuckles on the bottom of a washtub.

Mom walks to the door. She looks at the clothesline Pa made from baled-hay wire. He carefully put the pieces of wire together so that they wouldn't hook holes in the clothes Mom hung to dry. Mom watches the water run along the line and beads of water drop into the mouths of the fresh spring-growing grasses. The clothesline is tied to a plum-tree limb on one end and a white-oak limb on the other. There is a forked sour-wood bush that Pa cut and peeled for a clothesline prop between the plum tree and the white oak. It is to brace the clothesline when Mom has it loaded with the wet clothes.

The rain pours from the drainpipe in a big sluice into the water barrel Mom keeps at the corner of the house. "You won't wash my hair in rain water any more," says Sis. "Will hard water keep my hair from being curly, Mom?"

"I don't know," says Mom.

"You used to say hard water would hurt my hair," Sis says.

"I don't care whether Mom washes my hair in hard water or not," I say. "I'd as soon have it washed in well water as in water from the rain barrel."

Mom walks from the front room to the dog-trot. She looks at the rock cliffs over the mountainside. I know Mom remembers holding the lantern for Pa on dark winter nights when the ewes were lambing in these cliffs and they had to bring the baby lambs before the big log fire in the house and warm them.

Mom looks at the snow-white patches of bloodroot blooming around these cliffs. She sees the pink sweet Williams growing by the old logs and rotted stumps on the bluffs. Mom is thinking as she looks at these. I know what she is thinking. "Mick has picked bloodroot blossoms and sweet Williams for me many evenings with his big rough hands after he'd plowed the mules day long around the mountain slopes. Yes, Mick, bad as he is to cuss, loves a wild flower."

Mom walks from the dog-trot into the big kitchen.

"Aren't we going to Grandpa's, Mom?" I ask as I follow Mom.

"Bad as it is raining," Mom answers, "you know we're not going."

"If we go, Mom, who'll cook for Pa?"

Mom does not answer. She looks at the clapboard box Pa made for her and filled with black loam he gathered under the big beech trees in the hollow back of the house. Pa fixed this for a nasturtium seed-box for Mom. Pa put it in the kitchen window where it would catch the early morning sun.

"I have my little basket filled with my dollie's dresses," Sis says as she comes running across the dog-trot to Mom. "I'm ready too, Mom. I'm not going to leave my doll. There won't be anybody left to play with her. You know Pa won't play with her. Pa won't have time. Pa plays with the mules and pets them and calls them his dolls."

"Yes," Mom says, "your Pa—"

The sky is low. The rain falls in steady streams. The thin tender oak leaves, the yard grass, the bloodroot, sweet Williams, and the plum-tree leaves drink in the rain. They look clean-washed as Mom washed my face, hands, neck and ears.

"God must have turned his water bucket over so we couldn't get to Grandpa's, Mom," I say.

It never rained like this before. It's raining so hard now we cannot see the rock cliffs. We cannot see the plum tree and the clothesline wire. We cannot see the martin-box poles at the corners of the garden.

"It's a cyclone, Sal," says Pa as he walks across the dog-trot into the kitchen. "I told you a while ago when I saw the martins making it for their boxes a storm was coming. Now you see just how much sense a bird has!"

"Yes, Mick, I see—"

"What if you had taken little Herbert out on the long road to your pap's place—a tree with leaves as thin as they are this time of spring wouldn't have made much of a shelter and there aren't any rock-cliff shelters close along that lonesome road."

Mom looks at the dim blur of wood-ash barrel that Pa put under the big white-oak tree where Mom washes our clothes. Pa carries the wood ashes from the kitchen stove and the fireplace and puts them in this barrel for Mom. She makes lyesoap from these wood ashes.

"Don't talk about the road," says Mom.

"Where is my pretty, Pa?" I ask.

"Herbert is asleep with it in his hand," Pa answers.

"When we go to Grandpa's I'm going to take it with me. Pa made it and I intend to keep it."

Damp cool air from the rain sweeps across the dog-trot.

"The rain has chilled that air so," says Pa, "a person needs a coat."

Through the rain-washed windowpane, Mom sees the little bench Pa made. Mom and Pa would sit on this little bench at the end of the grape-arbor and string beans, peel potatoes, and shuck roasting-ears. They sit here on the long summer evenings when the katydids sing in the garden bean-rows and the crickets chirrup in the yard grasses. Pa smokes his pipe and Mom smokes her pipe and we play around them. We hear the whippoor-wills singing from mountain top to mountain top and we hear the martins chattering to one another in their boxes. We see the lightning bugs lighting their way in the summer-evening dusk above the potato rows—and we hear the beetles singing sadly in the dewy evening grass.

"The sun, Mom," I say. "Look—we can go now."

Pa looks at the red ball of sun hanging brightly in the blue April sky above the mountain. It is like a red oak ball hanging from an oak limb by a tiny stem among the green oak leaves. A shadow falls over Pa's brown, weather-beaten face.

"The third time," says Mom, "that I've got ready to go. Something has happened every time. I'm not going."

"Aren't we going to Grandpa's, Mom?" Sis asks.

"No, we're not going."

"What will I do with my basket of doll clothes?"

"Put them back where you got them."

Pa puts his pipe back in his pocket. His face doesn't have a shadow over it now. Pa looks happy. There is a smile on his September pawpaw-leaf-colored face.

"Come, Sal," says Pa. "Let's see if our sweet potatoes have sprouted yet."

Mom and Pa walk from the kitchen to the dog-trot. They walk up the bank where Pa has his sweet-potato bed. Pa has his arm around Mom. They walk over the clean-washed yard grass as green and pretty as if God had just made it over new.

"I think the potatoes have sprouted," I hear Pa say.

Sis starts upstairs with her basket of doll clothes and her doll. I go into the front room to see if Herbert has my top in his hand. It is my top, for Pa made it for me.

Nest Egg

About the story:

"Could you put into words how you developed this love for the land," I asked Jesse Stuart, "your country here?"

He did not answer quickly. He looked at the burning apple log in the fireplace, pursed his lips, and scratched his head. His hair was closely cropped, thick and iron-gray. As he began to talk, he was up on the edge of his chair, and I wondered how the fire kept from burning his face. "You know, the land never fed you as it has fed me. When the land fed all these people long ago, it was different. We loved it and we needed it. I always loved to rub the tree, touch its bark. My father loved the land. It is father to me. . . ."

"What is your earliest memory of the land?"

"The hills. It has always been the land—wild plums, poplar trees, red birds, mules, geese. I hunted eggs down the creek. Our chickens laid eggs away from the chicken house—under the ferns and rock-cliffs, in hollow logs and stumps and the pawpaw groves. . . ."

Back then the Stuarts churned milk for butter and gathered eggs. These farm products they took to market in Greenup, usually to barter for "things that we couldn't make or raise on the farm . . . like salt, pepper, coffee, and sugar." While searching one day for hens that laid eggs in nests in the woods instead of in the chicken house, he found one old Sebright hen nesting "in the pawpaw grove where she was sure I couldn't find her." Young Jesse counted twenty-two eggs in her nest. When he told his mother about what he had found, she said, "Jesse, gather those eggs before that hen sits long enough to spoil them." As he returned, the hen jumped off her nest and ran away clucking. He took all the eggs, then thought a moment. "I hated to rob this hen of all her eggs. I put one egg back so she would find it when she returned to the nest. But I never dreamed what a remarkable chicken this hen would hatch and raise. And I never dreamed at that moment that this chicken would become the hero of the first short story I'd ever write."

The locale of the story is the four-room log house at the center of the middle prong of W-Creek, where the Stuarts lived from 1909 to about 1916.

"Right in the backyard," the author said, "still stands the white-oak tree where old Nest Egg . . . roosted. . . . "*

* * *

"S HAN, I DON'T WANT to tell you the second time to break that hen from sittin' on a nest egg," Mom said. "I don't have enough hens to spare to let one sit on a nest egg."

"Why don't you put more eggs under her, Mom?" I asked. "I never saw a hen that wants to sit on a nest like she does."

"It's too late in summer," Mom said. "She'd hatch off a gang of little chickens in dog days and they'd die. Now you go take that nest egg from her nest."

"All right, Mom," I said.

The wilted grass was hot beneath my bare feet as I walked across the carpet of wilted crab grass to a patch of pawpaw sprouts. I followed a little path into the pawpaw sprouts where the white agate sun had wilted the pawpaw leaves until they hung in wilted clusters. When I approached the nest, the old Sebright hen raised her wings and clucked. I thought she was tryin' to tell me to stay away. And when I started to put my hand back under her to get the egg, she pecked my arm in three places faster than I could wink my eyes. Each place she pecked me, my arm bled.

I don't blame her for sittin' in this cool place, I thought. I don't blame her for fightin' over the egg. She laid the egg.

Since Mom had asked me to take the nest egg from the nest, I ran my hand under her and got the egg and put it beside the nest. And when she started rollin' it back under her with her long hooked bill, I left the pawpaw patch.

"Did you take the egg out'n that nest?" Mom asked me soon as I reached the house.

"I took it out this time, Mom," I said. "Look at my arm!"

"That hen's a mean old hussy," Mom said.

That week hadn't passed when Mom called her chickens around the

*Jesse Stuart's "Nest Egg" was first published in the *Atlantic Monthly*, Vol. 173 (Feb., 1944), pp. 85–89, reprinted in *Tales from the Plum Grove Hills* (N.Y.: Dutton, 1946), and in the Mockingbird ed. (N.Y.: Ballantine Bks., 1974), pp. 164–172. Jesse Stuart/ H. E. Richardson, Interview, W-Hollow, Greenup, Ky., Nov. 19, 1966, later pub. in H. Edward Richardson, "Stuart Country: The Man-Artist and the Myth," *Jesse Stuart: Essays on His Work*, eds. Mary Washington Clarke and J. R. LeMaster (Lexington: Univ. Press of Ky., 1977), pp. 8–9. Other quotations are from Jesse Stuart/ H. E. Richardson, Interview #9, W-Hollow, Greenup, Ky., Sept. 15, 1978, and from Jesse Stuart, "Author's Introduction" to "Nest Egg," *A Jesse Stuart Reader* (N.Y.: McGraw-Hill, 1963), pp. 3–4. Woodbridge, *Jesse Stuart Bibliography*, p. 71, lists a total of four reprints of "Nest Egg" through 1979.

corncrib and fed them shelled corn. Since we lived in the woods and our closest neighbor lived a mile away, hawks, hoot owls, and varmints often caught our chickens. Once a week Mom called them to the corncrib to feed and count them.

"Shan, the old Sebright hen's not here," Mom said. Mom knew her chickens since we had such a variety of mixed chickens there were hardly any two with the same color of feathers.

"I guess something's caught 'er," I said.

"With her bright feathers she's a flowerpot for a hoot owl," Mom said.

Twenty-one days had passed when I saw this old Sebright hen goin' up the hill toward the woods with one little chicken. The nest egg had hatched. I didn't tell Mom what I had seen. I'd let her find out for herself. The old Sebright never came to the corncrib when Mom called our chickens to the house to feed and count them. She lived alone in the woods with her one chicken.

August passed and September came. The leaves had started to turn brown on the trees. I was out huntin' for a hen's nest when I heard a hen cackle, and I looked in time to see our old Sebright hen and her one chicken that was growin' tall and well-feathered disappear into the brush. I was glad to know that they were still alive and I wondered when they would come to the house. And this was a secret I kept from Mom and Pa.

It was in early October that Pa had finished cuttin' our late corn. He had come across the ridge and followed the path down the point to our house. When he reached the house, Mom was callin' our chickens to the corncrib to feed and count them.

"Sal, this reminds me of something," Pa said. "It must've been two miles back on the ridge, I either saw a Sebright hen with a young chicken with her 'r I saw a pheasant and a young one. They flew through the brush like wild quails before I could get close!"

"Did you take that egg from under that old hen that day?" Mom turned around and asked me.

"I did, Mom," I said.

"I don't want you to lie to me," Mom said.

"I'm tellin' you the truth," I said.

"I guess I saw a couple of pheasants," Pa said.

It was in late November, when the worms and bugs had gone into the ground for the winter, that the old Sebright hen came to the corncrib when Mom called the chickens. Hunger had forced her to come down from the high hills with her young rooster. She was very proud of him; though he was nearly as tall as she was, she clucked to him as if he were still a tiny chicken that had just come from the egg. When one of the hens came close to him, she flogged the hen.

Mom looked at Pa and Pa looked at Mom. They didn't say anything at first, but each stood there lookin' at the old hen and young rooster and then they looked at me.

"But, Mom, I did take the egg from her nest," I said.

"Where did you put the egg?" Mom asked.

"Over in the grass beside the nest."

"Didn't you know an old sittin' hen will roll an egg ten feet to get it back in the nest?"

"No," I said.

"There'll be bad luck among our chickens," Pa said.

"We're havin' enough bad luck already," Mom said. "I can't raise chickens as fast as something catches 'em. I missed eight in September and eleven in October. Since the trees lost their leaves so the hoot owls could see the chickens, I've lost seventeen this month."

"We'll lose more now," Pa said. "I'd put that young gentleman in the skillet and fry 'im if he wasn't sich a fine-lookin' young rooster."

"Don't do it, Pa," I said. "She's had a hard time raisin' 'im."

"Pap had this same thing to happen when I was a little boy," Pa said. "Before the year was over he lost every chicken he had with the cholera. They died in piles."

I didn't want to say anything to Pa, but I didn't see why a hen's sittin' on a nest egg and hatchin' it and raisin' her chicken had anything to do with the cholera. I wanted to beg him to keep this young rooster that I called Nest Egg. Pa must've forgot about killin' 'im and fryin' 'im, for November and December came and passed and Nest Egg still ran with his mother.

Nest Egg wasn't six months old when he started crowin'. Now he was much larger than his mother. He was tall and he had big legs and little straight spurs that looked like long locust thorns. His mother still ran with him and clucked to him, but he didn't pay his mother much attention. He would often stand lookin' at the spring sun and never bat his eyes. He had a mean-lookin' eye and a long crooked bill that looked like a chicken hawk's bill. He didn't look like his mother. Pa said that he was a cross between a Sebright and a black game. He had almost every variety of colors. I thought he was a mongrel rooster—a mixture of many breeds.

We had five roosters at our house; all five of them ran Nest Egg. They'd run him and flog him. Once our black game rooster, War Hawk, just missed Nest Egg's hawk-shaped head with his long, straight spur that had killed four of our roosters. But Nest Egg outran War Hawk. He took to the brush cacklin'.

"He won't always be a-runnin' you, Nest Egg," I said while War Hawk boasted to the big flock of hens around 'im.

Durin' the spring months we seldom saw Nest Egg. He kept a safe distance away from the house. He stayed away from the five old roosters who fought him every time he got near one's flock of hens. But once Mom was huntin' a hen's nest in the woods and she saw a chicken hawk swoop low to catch a hen. She saw Nest Egg hit the hawk with all the power he had. Mom said he tore a small wind-puff of feathers from the hawk. Mom told Pa about Nest Egg's fight with the hawk.

"He's a-goin' to make a powerful fightin' rooster," Pa said. "Any rooster that's game enough to hit a hawk has good metal."

And Pa was right in his prediction about Nest Egg. In early June we saw him a-runnin' Big Bill, our gray game rooster. In late July he whipped Red Ranger, our red game rooster. In July he whipped Lightnin', our black Minorca rooster. Three days later, he whipped our "scrub" rooster that was mixed with many breeds of chickens. We called him Mongrel. He had whipped all the roosters but War Hawk.

"If Nest Egg can stay out'n the way of War Hawk's spurs," Pa said, "he'll whip old War Hawk. He's a young rooster that's run over hills and scratched for a livin' and he's got better wind."

It was in the middle of August when Nest Egg came down to the barn. He tiptoed, flapped his wings, and crowed in the barn lot. This was War Hawk's territory. It was the choice territory War Hawk had taken for his flocks of hens. Not one of our roosters had dared to venture on War Hawk's territory. Maybe, Nest Egg had come down from the hills to challenge War Hawk's supremacy. Since he had whipped Big Bill, Red Ranger, Lightnin', and Mongrel he wouldn't be chased by War Hawk. He was a year older now and he felt his youth. He was ready to fight. And when War Hawk heard another rooster crowin' on his territory, he came runnin' with a flock of hens following 'im. He challenged young Nest Egg for a fight.

At first War Hawk and Nest Egg sparred at each other. War Hawk had fought many fights and maybe he was feelin' out his young opponent. They stuck their heads out at each other and pecked, then they came together with all their might and the feathers flew. Nest Egg hit War Hawk so hard that he knocked him backwards.

Again they struck and again, again, again. Each time the feathers flew lazily away with the August wind. Then War Hawk leaped high into the air and spurred at Nest Egg's head. His spur cut a place in Nest Egg's red comb. That seemed to make Nest Egg madder than ever. He rushed in and grabbed War Hawk by the comb and pushed his head against the ground while he flogged him with wings and feet. When Nest Egg's bill-hold gave away, he left a gap in War Hawk's battered comb."

War Hawk was gettin' weaker. But he leaped high into the air and spurred at Nest Egg's head; Nest Egg dodged and the spur missed his head. That must have given Nest Egg an idea, for he leaped high in the air and War Hawk leaped high to meet him. War Hawk caught Nest Egg's spur in his craw, which ripped it open. War Hawk fell on the barn lot where he had seen others fall. As War Hawk lay dyin', Nest Egg stood above him on his tiptoes and crowed. He was the new king of our barn lot.

Nest Egg's victory over War Hawk spread among our neighbors and many of them asked to bring their roosters to fight Nest Egg.

"He's not the fightin' stock," Pa told them. "He's only a scrub rooster. I don't like to fight chickens, but if it's a pleasure to you, bring your roosters around."

In September he killed Warfield Flaughtery's great Hercules game rooster that had never lost one fight in fifty-three fights. Hercules had whipped War Hawk. Two weeks later he killed Warfield Flaughtery's young game rooster, Napoleon. In early October he killed Eif Nippert's red game rooster, Red Devil; two days later he spurred Ennis Sneed's gray game rooster, Big Bee Martin, blind in both eyes. Later that month he pecked a hole in a hoot owl's head that had caught one of our hens. Before January he had killed nineteen roosters and one hoot owl.

"He's some rooster," Pa said. "But he's sure to bring us bad luck."

Pa was offered fifty dollars for Nest Egg by a man from a showboat on the Ohio River. He watched Nest Egg kill his twenty-fifth rooster before he offered Pa the money.

"He's bad among my other roosters here," Pa said. "They used to make him live in the woods; now he makes them live in the woods. But I don't want to sell him."

"That's a big price, Mick," Mom said. "You'd better take it."

But Pa wouldn't sell him. Finally, the man from the showboat offered Pa seventy-five dollars. Then he said he wouldn't offer him another dime. He started back toward town, turned around, and came back and offered Pa a hundred-dollar-bill, the first hundred-dollar bill that any of us had ever seen.

"I still won't sell 'im," Pa said.

Then the man went away and Mom was mad.

"Hundred dollars is a lot of money, Mick."

"I like that rooster," Pa said. "I'm not a-sellin' 'im."

Anybody would like Nest Egg if he could've seen him strut about the barn lot with fifty hens around him. He had nearly half the flock followin' him. When Nest Egg wanted one of our other roosters' hens, he just said something to her in his language and she followed 'im. And now when Mom called our chickens to the corncrib to feed and count them, she found that our flock was gradually growin'. This was the first time since we had had chickens that our flock had increased without our raisin' chickens or buyin' them. Mom couldn't understand how the number had grown. She saw several different-colored hens among our flock.

In February our flock increased seven; in March it increased twelve; in April it increased twenty-seven; in May it had increased thirty-two. In the meantime, Nest Egg had fought seven more fights and had killed six of the roosters; the seventh finally recovered.

In May, Warfield Flaughtery came to our house with his mule and express wagon.

"Mick, have you got some extra hens in your flock?" he asked Pa.

"Think we have, Warfield," Pa said. "How many did you lose?"

"About sixty," he told Pa.

"Would you know your hens?" Pa asked.

"Shore would," he said. "Call your hens to the corncrib."

"You're not right sure the hawks, hoot owls, and varmints didn't take some of them?" Pa asked.

"I'm sure they didn't," he said. "A two-legged varmint got 'em."

"Do you mean I stole your chickens?" Pa said.

"Not exactly," he grunted.

"They must've come to my rooster," Pa said.

"They didn't do that," Warfield said as Pa called the chickens and they came runnin'. "They wouldn't follow that scrub rooster."

Warfield and Pa were mad. Mom heard them talkin' and hurried to the corncrib.

"Then take your hens," Pa said. "Here's a coop. Catch 'em and put 'em in it."

Mom stood by and didn't say anything until Warfield got Nest Egg's mother. Mom made him put her down.

"You're a-takin' hens that I've raised," Mom said.

But Warfield insisted that he wasn't and kept takin' our hens until he had sixty. Then he hauled them away on his express wagon. He must have told others about our havin' his chickens. Jake Hix came and claimed thirty of our hens. And Pa let 'im have 'em. And then Cy Pennix came and wanted fourteen. We knew that Cy didn't even raise chickens and Pa wouldn't let 'im have 'em. Pa and Cy almost had a fight, but Pa told 'im to climb on his express-wagon seat and get outten the hollow fast as his mule could take him. Wiley Blevins, Ott Jervis, and Jot Seagraves came and claimed our chickens. "Who do you think I am," Pa asked them, "a chicken thief?" Pa showed them the way back down the hollow and they told Pa that he would be sorry.

"That rooster's a-bringin' us bad luck," Pa said. "These men live from one to three miles from us. Nest Egg is goin' back into the hills now since worms are scarce here. And he meets with other roosters and their flocks and he steals the hens. God knows I'm not a chicken thief. It's that good-lookin' rooster Nest Egg that the hens all take to. He tolls the hens here."

In June the four neighbors that Pa had chased away had indicted Pa for stealin' their chickens. Pa was branded as a chicken thief for it was printed in the *Greenwood County News* about his bein' indicted by four men. And before the trial was called in August, Warfield Flaughtery came back with his express wagon and hauled away forty-six more hens; Jake Hix came and claimed seventy. He said all his hens had left, and Mom said our flock had increased more than a hundred. Warfield Flaughtery and Jake Hix had always been good neighbors to us, but Warfield's roosters had always killed our roosters before, and now Nest Egg had killed two of his best games and he was sore at us over it. Pa asked him if he'd been summoned for a witness in the trial, and he told Pa that he and Jake both had.

Pa was tried on the indictment made by Cy Pennix. The courthouse was filled with people to see how the trial ended since there'd been much chicken stealin' in our county. We proved that Cy Pennix didn't even have any chickens—that he had just claimed our chickens but did not get them. And Pa came clear. Then Wiley Blevins' indictment was next to be tried. And when Wiley said that he would swear to his chickens' feathers, Judge Whittlecomb threw the case out of court. Since Warfield Flaughtery and Jake Hix had claimed and had taken their hens, saying they knew them by the colors, they got scared at the decision made by Judge Whittlecomb and they hauled the chickens they had taken from us back before sunset.

"That Nest Egg's a wonder," Pa said. "Our flock has doubled and he's killed fifty-one roosters. He's just a little past two years old."

But boys threatened me when I went to the store. They threatened me because Nest Egg had killed their roosters. And neighborhood men threatened Pa over our rooster. Once Pa got a letter that didn't have a name signed to it and in it was a threat to burn our barn. He got another letter and the man said he was a little man, that he would meet Pa sometime in the dark. He said a bullet would sink into a chicken thief in the dark same as it would in the daytime.

"I didn't know as little a thing as a rooster could get people riled like that," Pa said. "I didn't know a rooster could turn a whole community of people against a man."

Cy Pennix shook his fist at Pa and dared him to step across the line fence onto his land. And Warfield Flaughtery wouldn't speak to Pa. Tim Flaughtery hit me with a rock and ran. And often Pa would get up in the night and put on his clothes and walk over to our barn. He was afraid somebody would slip in to burn it.

"I feel something's a-goin' to happen soon," Pa told me one day in September. "This can't go on. Our flock is increasin' day by day. Look at the chickens about this place!"

There were chickens every place. Even our old roosters had increased their flocks with hens that Nest Egg had tolled to our house—hens that could not join Nest Egg's ever increasin' flock. When we gathered eggs, two of us took bushel baskets. We found hens' nests under the ferns, under the rock-cliffs, under the smokehouse corncrib, in hollow logs and stumps—and once I found a hen's nest with twenty-two eggs in it on top of our kitchen behind the flue. An egg rolled off and smashed on Pa's hat is how come us to find the nest. We had to haul eggs to town four times a week now.

One early October mornin' when Mom called our chickens to the corncrib to feed them, Nest Egg didn't come steppin' proudly on his tiptoes. And that mornin' he hadn't awakened Pa at four o'clock by his six lusty crows. I missed my first day of school to help Pa hunt for Nest Egg. We looked around the barn. We scoured the steep hill slopes, lookin' under each greenbriar cluster and in each sprout thicket. We looked every place in Nest Egg's territory and were about to give up the hunt when we walked under the white-oak chicken roost between the barn and house. We found Nest Egg sprawled on the ground beneath the roost with several hens gathered around him cacklin'. A tiny screech owl was sittin' on Nest Egg's back, peckin' a small hole in his head.

"Think of that," Pa said. "A rooster game and powerful as Nest Egg would be killed by a little screech owl no bigger than my fist. A hundred-dollar rooster killed in his prime by a worthless screech owl."

Pa reached down and grabbed the owl by the head and wrung its neck. "I can't stand to see it take another bit from Nest Egg's head," he said.

I stood over Nest Egg and cried.

"No ust to cry, Shan," Pa said. "Nest Egg's dead. That owl fouled 'im. It flew into the chicken roost and lit on his back when he was asleep. It pecked his head until it finished 'im."

"But I haf to cry," I said, watchin' Pa take his bandanna from his pocket to wipe the tears from his eyes.

Dark Winter

About the story:

The house at the center of the middle prong of W-Creek was to carry pleasant memories of idyllic days in young Jesse Stuart's life. Nearby is the site of a well-remembered pasture where the daisies were white and the wild roses pink. Once he hunted there for the milkcow, Gypsy, through saw-briar clusters and small pines, whose needles were weighted with "dew drops . . . like little lumps of polished silver until the sun lifted them skyward in ribbons of mist." That day he found the smart old cow in the alder bushes, shunned by the biting flies, and he drove her to "the big bushy-topped white-oak that didn't shade anybody but Gypsy, my mother, and me." While Martha Stuart milked the cow, the boy lay on his back and looked through half-shut eyes at the blue sky and "changing leaf pictures." It was a happy time, this world of pastoral contentment, "and I loved everything about it."

Yet, the tragedy of his four-year-old brother's death, along with Mitchell Stuart's chance to sharecrop on a two-thirds instead of a three-fifths return brought about the family's third move, taking the Stuarts to the head of W-Hollow, then the last log house up the last prong of W-Creek. It consisted of two log rooms joined by a connecting area, standing at the juncture of Shinglemill Branch and the final prong of W-Creek. It was "the most desolate place I have ever seen. . . . Every room of this house leaked through the roof. Behind the old front log room then was a log kitchen, and the connecting area was called a 'dog-trot,' or an 'entry.' " Situated deep in the forested hollow, the 1844 log shack inspired the author to write in what was probably more truth than hyperbole that "Owls hooted from the dark timber at midday."

This third home of the Stuarts at the head of W-Hollow is the locale of the story "Dark Winter." Many details of the piece have their counterparts in reality. Greensburg is Greenup, of course, and Doctor Frederick was based upon Dr. Henry Morris. Mom, "tall, sinewy, dark as a pawpaw leaf bitten by frost, her straight black hair, her white teeth there in the dim-lighted room," is as clearly Martha Stuart as "Pop" is Mitchell Stuart. The author has recorded in his personal story *Beyond Dark Hills* that his father "took sick" following the 1917 growing season when "Our corn rotted in the cold wet ground. . . ." The graveyard in the story, which the boy felt uneasy passing in the night, is Three-Mile Cemetery, located on a steep hill where the W-Hollow Road leaves State Highway 1. The family horse, Fred, and the family cow, Gypsy, were real enough, too, as well as the resourcefulness of the mother and her family caught in the midst of difficulty, right down to the details of making peck, half-bushel, and bushel feed baskets from the riven splints of little white-oak trees. The death of Jesse Stuart's infant brother, Martin Vernon, April 17, 1918, is all too prototypically tragic and real.

Although the Stuarts lived in this third log house only three years, the author would in 1939 return to it with his wife, Naomi Deane Norris of Greenup, and it would become the nucleus of their now remodeled and many-times-enlarged permanent home. The front living room of original logs remains intact, although its walls are now graced with books, *objets d'art* relating to a lifetime of distinguished publication, and memorabilia from round-the-world literary lectures. In an interview during which he was asked if "Dark Winter" were autobiographical, Jesse Stuart replied, "The baskets were made right there . . . in that old living room. . . ."*

* * *

"**Y**OUR POP is dyin'," says Mom, "you'll have to go after the doctor. It is a long way to send you, but you are all the one I have to send. You'll have to go to Greensburg tonight. Saddle old Fred and go and bring the doctor back with you. Your Pop can't die and leave me with all these children. There are four mouths to feed, not much to feed them on and a dark winter here."

Here lies Pop in bed. His face is flushed red, the red color there is in an October red-oak leaf. He kicks the cover, the heavy home-made quilts and he says: "They ain't never been nothin' in this country like this influenza. It's a plague and I believe I'm a goner. Has to be somethin' to thin us out, I guess. If it ain't one thing it is another. Get me a doctor, son. We ain't got the money tell him, but if he will come the cow will stand good, or the horse or both of them. Money don't matter when a body wants to live."

*"Dark Winter" originally appeared in *Head o' W-Hollow* (N.Y.: Dutton, 1936), pp. 67–92, reprinted (Lexington: Univ. Press of Ky., 1979), pp. 67–92. Woodbridge, *Jesse Stuart Bibliography,* p. 58, lists two other reprints through 1979. Jesse Stuart, "Angel in the Pasture," *Esquire,* Vol. 51 (June, 1959), pp. 49–50, orig. pub. in *The Year of My Rebirth* (N.Y.: McGraw-Hill, 1956), pp. 11–14. Jesse Stuart discusses circumstances of the family's move to his third childhood home in *God's Oddling: the Story of Mick Stuart, My Father* (N.Y.: McGraw-Hill, 1960), pp. 23–24. For a word picture of the place, see Stuart's *Beyond Dark Hills* (N.Y.: Dutton, 1938), pp. 38–39. Jesse Stuart/ H. E. Richardson, Interview #4, W-Hollow, Greenup, Ky., July 16, 1978.

Mom comes to the door with me. She takes a piece of pine kindlin' and sticks it between the forestick and the firebrands and gets a tiny blaze with a tiny black smoke swirlin' up. She lifts the lantern globe and touches the kindlin' fire to the wick. She lowers the globe and wipes off a speck of mud with the corner of her checked apron. I can see Mom, tall, sinewy, dark as a pawpaw leaf bitten by frost, her straight black hair, her white teeth there in the dim-lighted room. I can see the tears roll down her cheek without the curve of her lips for cryin'. Pop back in the bed, kickin' the quilts with his feet and fightin' them with his hands.

Our house is far away from all other houses. We cannot see the smoke from another house. We are so far away our chickens cannot meet and mix with our neighbor's chickens. Pop used to say that we always wanted to stay that far away. "When you live so close to a neighbor your chickens mix, take care, you are goin' to have a fallin'-out." Mom didn't want to move to this place. I remember Mom cried when we moved here. We thought we could do better by payin' one-third rent and have some bottom land down between the hills, than we could by payin' two-fifths grain rent and farmin' all hill land. We give one shock of corn and fodder now and take two ourselves. We used to give two shocks of corn and fodder and keep three out of every five. If you clear the land of briars and sprouts and hoe the corn and know how hard it is to raise, you will know then that there is a difference in sharecroppin', if you give one-third grain-rent or if you give two-fifths. That is why we moved to this last house in the Hollow. And Martha Smith told Mom before we moved, "Mrs. Powderjay, that house is hanted. I'll tell you that before you go. No family has lived there more than two years. They was a woman that killed herself in that house. She got tired of livin' because she didn't have anybody to talk to. One day when her husband was out in the field she hung herself from the upstairs window with a sheet fastened to the bedpost and to her neck. You'll never be able to live there. Lights are seen all around the house at night. There are two graves under a plum tree in the garden. You will hear all kinds of noises there. They ain't a house in a mile of you and the foxes come right in and get your chickens in broad daylight."

Now, we are here, Pop down in bed with the influenza, our crops failed last year in the craw-dad bottoms and we haven't anythin' to go on for the winter. That is why Pop got a job on the railroad section and walks four mile to and from his work, eight miles a day and ten hours work, to keep us goin'. And Pop is bed-fast.

The tiny bright flame flickers under the lantern globe. I set the lantern on the floor, put on a slip-over sweater and overall jacket over that to cut the November wind, put on a pair of rabbit-skin mittens and a sock cap that I stretched down over my ears. Mom ties a scarf around my neck. I walk over a white field of snow to the barn. It crunches beneath my brogan shoes. The stars are pretty in the deep blue winter sky. They twinkle coldly up there in the heaven. The wind hits my face keen as a razor blade and it bites the skin on my face like tiny mouse teeth. Fred is prancin' in his stall. He has never laid down on the warm bed of cornstalks yet. I go into the stall, lift his bridle from the harness rack, blow my breath on the bridle bits and warm them so they won't take the hide off his tongue. I put the bridle on Fred, knock off a few dirty flakes of mud with the currycomb, put on the saddle blankets and the pads, throw on the saddle and girt it tight for the long rough ride. I lead Fred out of the barn, pat his neck, for he is my friend tonight, and he must take me over a long rugged path. He must be fast and sure-footed, an art hill horses learn sooner or later and an art already perfected by mountain mules.

I am in the saddle. I do not need the lantern. When the moon turns dark I may not be able to follow the path without it. I tie it to the saddle. It is too cold to hold it in my hand. I blow out the tiny flame. I have matches in my pocket to relight it with if the moon goes down before I get back. I rub Fred's neck and say to him: "Now, boy, let's go. A straight piece of road. Slow here, Fred boy. Slow. Slow. Slow. It's a bad place. Take it easy." The stars are in the sky above me. The bull bat screams. I can hear the hoot owl laughin' under such cold moon and such cold sky filled with stars. I have to pass a graveyard and I am afraid of a graveyard at night. There are the white tombstones among the briars and brush that loom wiry and black above the snow. There are the broken-top trees at the edge of the graveyard and the old iron fence bare of snow. And I think, "What if Pop has to come here and sleep in this quiet place with only the wind to blow over him and the bull bats to try to wake him with their screams and the hoot owls to sit up there in bare chestnut tree tops and laugh all night over nothin'."

Fred gets his breath hard. He is wet around the saddle. I have to hold a tight rein. He is wiry and wants to tear up the mountain path. The snow crunches beneath his feet. His breath is loud as a wisp of wind in a tangled patch of briars. Over the ups-and-downs and around the steep shoulder of the mountain, I am on my way to Greensburg. We'll be there in another hour. I wonder how Mom is making it with Pop and Mary and Barbara and Finn. I left a warm fire burnin' and a light from the big fireplace that danced all over the room. It was a light different to the light of the stars. I love to ride beneath the stars on a winter night. My toes are not cold. I wiggle them in the yarn socks Mom made for me. I'll not get cold. I talk to

Fred and pat his neck: "Fred, you can take it, boy. Be careful your feet don't slip. Good old boy." The wind whips through the leafless trees and through the dead grass. It is such lonesome wind. I love to hear it, but it makes me think of Pop back there in bed and no doctor.

And I think: "If Pop dies, Mom and me can get along. I plowed old Fred a few furrows last year. Pop let me try it when we was plowin' in the oats and he said I done right well for a boy of ten. I'll stay with Mom and do my best. She said for me to bring a doctor and I am goin' to bring one if I don't get home till noon tomorrow."

I can see the lights from the little town. I am on the mountain ridge over it and soon I'll be goin' down the snake path to it. I can see the houses lighted. I'll go down a-past the old Rigley barn, out past the old stave mill and into Doctor Frederick's office. He is the doctor Mom wants. She says he's the best doctor in town for she has seen him save so many women's lives. I'll get Doctor Frederick.

Fred pauses, slips, throws his body this way and that to keep from sittin' down. He is goin' down the steep snake path. The ground is frozen and there is a sheet of snow on the frozen ground. It makes it bad for Fred, for he is slick-shod and his shoes are not corked. Snow balls on his feet. I get out of the saddle, take a stick and knock the frozen balls of snow-ice from his feet. I jump back in the saddle and he walks down the mountain better.

We dash out the street to Doctor Frederick's office. I jump down, throw the bridle rein over the gate post and run in the house. Doctor Frederick is tall, swarthy, and lean. He meets me. I say, "Can you go out in the Hollow to Mick Powderjay's house tonight?"

Doctor Frederick says, "Who is sick?"

"Pop's got the influenza," I say to him, "and Mom said tell you to come whatever you done, that she didn't have the money when you come, but we had a horse and cow and you could have either one of them or both of them if it took that much. Pop is awful sick. He's kickin' the covers and goin' on somethin' awful."

"It's a awful late hour to get in that Hollow tonight, Sonnie," says Doctor Frederick.

"I can't help that," I says, "Mom said for you to come and for me to bring you. I'll have to bring you. I won't leave till you go."

"I can't get my car in that Hollow. I'd head into the ditch some place. Roads are as slick as glass and they's so much doctorin' to do. That flu is everyplace. Wait till I get a sup of my cough medicine."

I don't say it to the doctor, but it smells to me like pure old whisky.

"Now you go on," says Doctor Frederick, "and ride your horse to the mouth of the Hollow and I'll be there about the time you get there. I can drive that far. You can get me another horse and I'll ride on in the rest of the way."

He corks the cough medicine and puts it in his overcoat pocket. I run out of the office, leap into the saddle, and snatch the rein from the gate. I am off with the wind. I ride with the wind. And I say to myself as I ride, "I got the doctor, I told Mom I would. Pop won't die. Pop can't die." I hear the car comin'. I have just been here about five minutes. I don't have another horse. We are not goin' to ride Fred double. The doctor can ride him and I'll walk. Doctor Frederick is not able to do much walkin'. It must be past midnight now. The car chugs up to the old bridge. Doctor Frederick gets out, puts coffeesacks over the engine and gets his pill bag.

"Where is the horse for me to ride?" he says.

"This is the one for you to ride," I say. I untie the lantern from the saddle. The moon is goin' down. It must be far past midnight. It is gettin' dark. I light the lantern. Doctor Frederick climbs into the saddle. I hand him the pill bag. We are off up the Hollow. I follow the horse.

"This is a devil of a place for a man to live," says Doctor Frederick. "You can't get in and out. It's dangerous for to ride into a place like this and road so slick this time of a winter mornin'."

Gray clouds scud the sky. The owls keep laughin'. The bull bat screams. The wind whips through the roadside briars like drawin' saw teeth across a rock. The road is dark. I get in front of Doctor Frederick and light the way with the lantern. I am warm enough to throw off my sweater and jacket and go in my shirt sleeves. It is hard work walkin' through the snow and keepin' ahead of the horse. But the doctor is goin' to see Pop. Pop must get well. What will we do if he doesn't? What can we do? I can hear the crunch-crunch of the snow beneath the horse's feet. I can hear the creakin' of the saddle. I can hear the horse gettin' his breath. I can hear myself gettin' my breath. But I cannot hear Doctor Frederick gettin' his breath. If I could though, I would carry him in myself to see him get Pop well.

We go past the Powell place. The only way I can tell it is the Powell place is by where they leave the jolt wagon set in the woodyard. The snow is fallin' again. It is turnin' warmer. Rabbits have eaten the bark sixteen inches high on the sassafras sprouts. That is just how deep the snow is goin' to get. The rabbits know more about it than we do.

The house is in sight. I can see the light in the window. Mom has never gone to bed. "Yonder is the house, Doctor Frederick. We are here. We are here! A doctor for Pop! I told Mom I'd fetch you. She'll believe me now."

Doctor Frederick gets down off the horse. He is stiff, to see him get down out of the saddle. He is tall, pale, and stiff with long legs and long bony arms and big joints and veins in his fingers. The snow preeks softly by the saddle bag—big white flakes, one can see in the lantern light.

"Welcome in, Doctor Frederick. I have never been so glad to see you. Mick is rollin' and tumblin' back there in the bed and just me with him back here. The children are all asleep. It is so lonesome here and Mick so sick."

"A body about pays for all they get out of life," says Doctor Frederick and he uncorks his cough medicine and takes a swallow. "If it wasn't for my cough medicine I couldn't keep going."

He goes back to the bed where Pop is. I sit before the fire and mend up the brands. I hear him say: "Mick has the flu. It's something like the old-fashioned grippe."

Mom says, "It's killin' a lot of people now, ain't it, Doctor?"

"Yes, a few," says the doctor, "but we all got to die someway and some-time. I'll do my best. You give this medicine every hour and this every two hours and he'll be some better after daylight. It's hard to tell who'll get over a thing and who won't."

"Now about the pay, Doctor," says Mom, "we'll pay you when we can. We have a horse and cow, some chickens and our meat in the smoke house and what little dab of furniture you see here in the house——"

"Stop such talk," says Doctor Frederick, "I've been doctoring in the Powderjay family twenty years and I've never lost a cent yet."

The chickens are crowin'. It is four o'clock. I sit by the fire and punch the dyin' embers with a hooked-end poker. A tiny flame leaps from the embers. My work is not done yet. I have to take Doctor Frederick back to his car at the mouth of the Hollow.

"Wait a minute, Doctor. You cannot go until I make you a biler of hot coffee," says Mom, "I know you are feelin' sort of drowsy after bein' up nearly all night." Mom goes to the kitchen and brings the coffee pot in the front room and sets it on the wood embers.

"Won't be long till the coffee will be a-bilin'," says Mom. "It is a cold clear frosty mornin' out with a lot more snow on the ground and a little coffee won't go bad with you."

"I could stand a cup all right," says Doctor Frederick.

We can see that Jack Frost has carved many beautiful things on our window panes, many more beautiful things than we have in the house. He has carved a castle out of the frost with windows and a sky above and trees around the house. Beyond the Jack Frost carved windows we can see a white world and plenty of frost in the air. The air is thin and cold as ice. It whistles around the eaves of the house. The chickens still sit on the black-oak roost, clutchin' the bare branches of the tree with their toes. Their feathers are all ruffled. The barn is white. The creek is a white sheet of ice, all but the riffles where the water ran too fast to freeze.

Doctor Frederick likes the coffee Mom makes. I like it too. It tastes good. It is warm to the stomach. He drinks one cup. "Another little taste of that coffee and I'll be on my way to the mouth of the Hollow."

Mom puts cream and sugar in the coffee. "That is enough cream, Mrs. Powderjay. That will be enough sugar." Pop is sleepin' in the bed in the corner of the room. The firelight is dancin' to the far end of the room. It shows the color of the pieces in the quilt that is spread over Pop's bed.

I go to the barn and slip Fred a bundle of can-fodder blades and eight ears of corn. He rolls the corn in the box and eats. Slobbers roll from his lips. Then he mixes with bites of corn, cane-fodder blades. It does not take Fred long to eat. And when we come back from the trip to the mouth of the Hollow I'll spread out a bundle of corn fodder for old Fred on the snow. He eats a quick meal now so we can get the doctor back.

The snow crunches beneath our feet. The snow is frozen. The wind bites the fingers and stings the face. I walk behind Doctor Frederick. Fred slips on the snow and ice. He is a big horse. He carries the doctor with ease. Frost has gathered on the hairs of his chin. They look like little silver spikes. The white breath goes from Fred's nostrils like streams of fog. This is a cold mornin'.

"I'll be back once a week," says Doctor Frederick "till your Pa gets better. You meet me here each Wednesday at six o'clock. If he gets worse, come and get me at any time."

He gets in his car. I leap into the saddle and Fred trots back up the Hollow. He is goin' toward the barn. Fred goes faster toward the barn than he does away from it. I come back to the house, take the bridle and saddle off Fred, put him in the barn lot. Then I get a bundle of corn fodder and spread it on the clean white snow. Fred nibbles the fodder and the wind blows his tail till the hairs tangle like a bunch of saw briars blown by the wind.

"Winter is here," says Mom, "and we don't have meal to make us bread. We don't have enough feed to last us for the horse and cow and chickens and hogs. Our feed will play out before March. Mick back there in the bed sick. God knows what will become of us. Doctor Frederick is a mighty fine man. I've knowed him ever since Barbara was born. He'll do all he can for us. He knows he'll get his money."

Mom walks before the fire and stands. She puts tobacco in her pipe, pushes it down with her forefinger and dips it down among the embers. Mom sucks the stem and blows the blue smoke out into the room. When Mom is worried she smokes hard. She sucks the long pipe stem hard and fast.

We have for dinner corn bread and milk and beans. For supper we'll have beans, milk and corn bread. We have our cow Gypsy. We raised our corn and we raised a good pole-bean crop. The bunch beans hit too, those that we planted out of the swampy bottoms. I can see the sun come over the high hill that lines in the Hollow, the hill so high that its shoulder cuts into the sky. There are streaks of sunlight runnin' from the sun like streams of blood. I can see the bushy-topped pines silhouetted against these streams of red sky-blood. The world is so big. What lies beyond these hills? Days come and go beyond them. Winds whine over the snow and the dead grass. Pop's face is white as the snow. He never talks much. He takes medicine and stays in bed. Mick Powderjay is gettin' to be a pile of skin and bones.

Today we haul wood with old Fred off the hill. Mom puts on a pair of Pop's overall pants. She picks up the double-bitted ax and says: "Come on, son. We got to get wood today." We go up the hill, through the briars and sprouts till we come to the timbered top of the hill. Here is where the fire ran through the woods last Spring and killed the trees. See the tall skeletons silhouetted against gum-leaf sky! See them tall and darin' in the wind with white coats of sap-rotten on their bodies. See my mother cut one with an ax! She can swing the ax like a man, tall, sinewy, strong as the hills that she has lived her days among. Strong and solid as the hills that have given her birth.

Chip-chop. Chip-chop. Hack-hack. Hack-hack. One, two, three, four. One, two, three, four. Hick-hack. Hick-hack. One, two, three, four. Hack. Hack. Hack. Hack. One, two, three, four. Hack. Hack. Hack. Hack.

"I'd like to know what is holdin' that tree," says Mom. She has a big notch chipped out of one side, a notch pretty as any woodman can make with an ax, pretty as the notch the rabbit makes on the young sassafras sprout, or the muskrat makes on the elder bushes it cuts for a dam. The wind blows against the tall tree skeleton that is lodged up in the winter icy wind. I can see Mom look up at the tree. I had better get Fred back out of length of the tree. It may fall a different way than it is notched to fall. One lick. It goes lumberin' to the earth. The snow flies up like dry powder when the skeleton kicks up its heels.

I bring Fred up to the tree. I unhitch the trace chains and loop them to single tree, clevis the single tree to the drag chain, and hook the drag chain around the butt of the tree. I get on Fred's back so I can rein him through the bush with the bridle. I say "Get-up." Dirt flies, dirt mingled with snow and leaves from powerful feet as they grip the earth with the weight of his huge sorrel-colored body, his flaxen mane and tail. The brush snaps and the drag begins to move. It bends down the brush and the briars and makes a path to the wood yard. I unhitch the drag chain so that it will slip from under the log, undo one of the trace chains so that there will be length enough for him to snake the single tree and log chain back and they won't hit his heels. We follow the road back that the log of wood made. It is a dry seasoned-out black oak. It will make good stove wood and good firewood. I go back and Mom says: "Two more for you. I'm slayin' these trees. I can keep you busy." Mom can cut the trees better than she can drive the horse through the brush. I can drive the horse better than I can cut the trees. I haul all afternoon to the wood yard off the tall hill back of the house. It is the hill we do not go beyond. It is the hill that only the sun goes beyond, the wind and the wild geese.

Wood is in our wood yard piled high. Mom and I fix us a rack by drivin' two stakes X-wise across a chunk of wood. We lift the ends of the light logs into the X and saw them off. Mom can use a saw better than I can. Snow fell on the logs in the wood yard last night and we sweep it off today with a broom-sage broom and saw up the logs. We have a tall pile of stove wood and firewood. "I'll teach you to work, Son," says Mom. "If you don't get sick we can make it."

Pop has to lie in bed. His face is not like it was when he followed the plow and burned the brush and was always sayin': "Come along with them sprouts, Shan. I'll soon be up with you." And Pop would be right behind me, plowin'. Color would be in his face. Strength would be in his arm.

He would talk to Mom and laugh and say, "This'll bring the best corn that ever growed out of God's green earth this season." That was Pop. He was like a sprig of wild honeysuckle. Cut him down and he would grow again. But now he lies in bed and takes medicine. He does not talk. There is not the color of sunshine in his face. The dead oak-leaf color is all gone. His face is the color of gray ashes where the brush pile has been burned. Pop cannot tell Mom to work. He does not know that she works. He cannot care.

"Our table is run down," says Mom. "We must have money. We are out of salt, sugar, coffee, lard. We are plum out of everythin'. I used to help Pap make split-bottomed feed baskets. I can do it myself. You go to the hill and cut me the prettiest little white-oaks that you can find. Bring them down to the barn. Cut the white-oaks that don't have a limb on them. You can't rive splits through knot holes. They just won't rive."

I take a pole ax and go to the woods. I find plenty of white-oaks that are the right size without a limb on their pretty slender straight bodies. I cut through the frozen wood with my ax, then I drag them down to the barn. We build a fire in front of the barn and we heat the white-oak till the sap runs from them. Mom splits them with an ax, then she rives them with a fro and knife. She whittles down the pretty white clean splits. Then she whittles out ribs and handles for the basket skeletons. She weaves the skeletons. Then, around the bones of the skeleton she works with the pretty splits.

We make three sizes of baskets. We make peck-sized feed baskets, half-bushel split-bottomed feed baskets and bushel split-bottomed feed baskets. "You are to sell the baskets," says Mom, "and get in the timber and I'll make them. Sell the peck baskets for twenty-five cents, the half-bushel baskets for fifty cents and the bushel baskets for one dollar."

I go to Mart Pennix's house and I say, "You want to buy a basket, Mr. Pennix?"

"A basket! Let me see! What kind of baskets do you have?"

"Feed baskets."

"Let me look at them."

He takes a basket and looks it over, feels of its ribs, looks at its weave and he says: "That basket is built for service and not beauty. I'll take a half-bushel basket and one of your bushel baskets. I need the half-bushel basket to carry corn to the fattenin' hogs in of a mornin' and the bushel basket to nubbin the calves from." He takes the two baskets to the corn crib and I put the dollar and half-dollar in my pocket to take home to Mom. I go from one house to another. I sell the baskets. The farmers buy them. I do not tell who makes them. I just sell them.

I go to the mouth of the Hollow and get the doctor once a week. I carry up water and split kindlin' and feed the stock and help Mom with the baskets. I ride Fred to town and get the things Mom has to have. At night Mom, Barbara, Mary, Finn and I sit before the log fire and listen to the wind howl around the chimney and the eaves. The smoke often comes out onto the floor and Mom will say: "That is a sign of fallen weather. We are goin' to have more snow. The rabbits has gnawed twenty-two inches high upon the sassafras sprouts and we are goin' to have twenty-two inches of snow."

Mom will say: "There's not anything here I am afraid of but them graves out there under the plum tree. It is not the snow I am afraid of, not the work about the place, but I am afraid to pass them graves at night. Just to think them little children buried out there under that snow in our garden. When spring comes I'm going to fix them graves up. If them was children of mine buried out there and somebody lived in this house, I would want them to fix up them graves and keep them fixed up. Put flowers on them. I can't stand to see a grave go back to nothin' but a forgotten place."

Pop doesn't seem to get much better. The flu has gone. The fever has gone. Pop is left weak and white. He lies in bed without any color in his face, a heap of skin and bones, and takes medicine. He never talks. He never laughs anymore like he used to laugh. I hate to see Pop in bed. I hate to think he'll have to rest in a bed of dirt like the two children rest in a bed of dirt under the plum trees in our garden. Doctor Frederick does not come once a week now. He comes once every two weeks. He says Pop's constitution is weak and that it might be spring before he is able to stir again if he is able then.

The snow holds to the earth. November has passed, December, January, and it is February now. The snow is twenty-two inches deep in places. I take old Raggs and hunt the rabbits. They cannot run through the snow. I just walk up and pick them up. They are lean to the bone. I hate to kill them when they are so easy to catch. They are a beast of prey. They are good to eat and we need meat. I pick them up in the deep snow. I dig them from the water seaps. I track the possum to his den and dig him out. I catch the skunk and trap the mink. I put their hides on boards and let them cure. It will mean money to us and we need money. We owe the doctor for comin' to see Pop. We have to pay the doctor. If Pop dies we will have to pay the doctor and buy a coffin for Pop too. And then, you cannot fool me, there is goin' to be another one at our place. I can tell now by lookin' at Mom. She is not lean as she was in the early winter, nor does she swing an ax like she did then. We have supplied the country with baskets. We have eighty dollars saved to make a crop in the spring. That is a lot of money for us. We'll come again in the spring though hard luck has hit us now.

A woman comes to our door. She walks over the snow, a heavy woman with a big clean face and a wide laugh, her blue eyes dancin' behind heavy glasses. She comes to the door and she says, "Does Mrs. Powderjay live here?"

Mom goes to the door. She says, "I am Mrs. Powderjay."

The woman says: "I'm working with an organization, Mrs. Powderjay, that can be of some assistance to you if you are interested. I learn that you are in needy circumstances and I observe that you are."

"Well," says Mom, "I thank you for your kindness, Mrs. Hamptin, but we have made it this far and we can make it on. I brought these children into the world and married this man. When I'm not able to work and none of the rest is able to work, then you can take care of them with your organization."

Mrs. Hamptin gets up and leaves the room. I can see her wobble across the foot log, past the well box, turn the curve to the right of the point, past the apple trees that stand bare and black on the snow-clad wind-swept hill.

"We'll sink or we'll swim together. I married Mick Powderjay and I'll stand by him and my children till Death parts us. I'm not goin' on the County either. What is a person that will go on the County? I'd work my finger nails off and toe nails off before I'd go on the County. That's what that woman was after. She was goin' to put us on the County. She'll do it over my dead body. I'd plant corn till the middle of July before I'd go on the County."

Our chickens freeze to death and fall off the roost. We find one and two under the roost every mornin' stiff as a frozen piece of dirt. We find dead birds around the fodder shocks. We find dead quails and dead rabbits. Life is dyin'. The winter is so severe and dark. Clouds scud the sky. Big flakes of snow fly through the crispy wind. The sun comes out somedays and it is weak as a copper plate in the top of a chestnut tree. It doesn't have any more power than the copper plate for it doesn't begin to melt the snow. We have not seen the ground unless we dig down through the snow to see it since last November. Barbara says to me, "Shan, wonder how the land will look when the snow goes off the hills again and the trees get green and Pop gets out of bed and walks around like he used to?"

When our chickens and guineas freeze to death we carry them to the wood house and make tiny wooden coffins for them. We put them in the coffins and carry the coffins up on the bank above the kitchen and make graves for them. We shovel away the snow with a corn scoop and then we dig down through the frozen ground with a coal pick. We shovel out the frozen clumps of dirt, bit by bit, then we put the boxes in each little grave and Barbara preaches a sermon about them goin' to Heaven and leavin' the cruel fields of snow and the cold wind that knows nobody and cares for nobody. We put the frozen lumps of dirt back on the tiny poplar-plank coffins, crumble the dust in on them, then we scoop back the snow and leave the dead chickens and guineas in a world of silence beneath the snowdrifts. Often their craws at death have been flat.

We keep as many as forty rabbits hanging on a joist in the smoke house and let them freeze. The meat is better after they freeze. It will soon be too late for rabbits. It will soon be matin' time and the heavy snow is still on the ground. We see the weak sun come up in the icy winter heavens and go down beyond the hills the way the wind blows. We do not go beyond these hills. We do not know if people die beyond like sheep, if the birds freeze to death and the chickens die and the crops fail. We do not know for we have not been beyond the barriers. We see the sun go beyond and we hear the wind.

"Pop is gettin' better," Mom says. "I can see some color comin' back to his face. When the sap revives in the spring tree, new blood will revive in him. He'll need a good tonic of wild-cherry bark, may apple, slipper-elm, yellow root and sassafras boiled together. That will be good for his constitution. Wait till spring comes back and he'll come out of that bed." Mom is givin' Pop boneset tea now. She goes down beside the creek and finds the old boneset stems. I dig down and get the roots from the frozen earth. "When new life comes back to the turtles, the terrapins and the snakes, and sap goes through trees anew, then blood will flow through your father's veins and he'll come out of that bed." Pop drinks the tea every day.

February is goin' day by day beyond the barriers of hills with the settin' sun and the wind that blows that way. Winter has been so long this year. We have not seen the ground. Winter is dark, though the sun comes up durin' the day and the moon and stars gleam down on a world of snow at night. The sky reddens at sunset like streaks of ox blood fringin' out from a ball of fire where the sun was and each spangle jinglin' with the green top of a mountain pine silhouetted against the sky where the high hills shoulder to the sky.

Pop says: "Spring will soon be here. I would love to be out now cuttin' wood and puttin' it in ricks and clearin' ground. This is the time to start clearin' ground, now while the snow is still on. It is a good time to work. My ribs and hips are bout to cut through the slats of this old bed. I have been like a coldblooded black snake waitin' for the spring. I have been here the winter long in a dream. I am feelin' better now. I want to eat." And Pop asks about this hen and that hen, if they have frozen to death and how we have got along with the wood the winter long.

Mom says, "Wait a minute, Mick Powderjay," and she goes into the kitchen. Where the flue goes up in the kitchen loft, Mom lifts up a board and brings her pocketbook. She comes up to the bed. She takes out of the pocketbook, one by one, eighty one-dollar bills. Pop's eyes get as big as saucers. "Where did you get all that money?" he says.

"Never mind that, Mick," says Mom, "but we made it honest. Me and that boy right in there." And Mom puts it back in the pocketbook and this time she saunters off toward the smoke house like a hen huntin' a nest. Mom will keep the money long as she can. She knows what is goin' to happen to her. She did not know what was goin' to happen to Pop. I can see Mom is not as active as she was and she is not shy before me anymore. She talks often to Mary and Barbara.

Mom goes to the barn with me. While I feed the horse she milks Gypsy. Gypsy won't let a man milk her. She follows Mom all over the barn lot. Fred follows me. I pat his nose. Gypsy is only givin' a quart of milk at a milkin'. She will be fresh in April, but she is goin' dry too soon. We do not have enough feed to feed Gypsy all she wants. Our feed is scarce. We are buyin' sixty shocks of fodder from Broughtons for ten cents a shock. I will haul it to the barn over the snow on a fodder sled with old Fred. That will take six of our dollars.

The sun is up today. Water drips from the eaves of the house. Icicles melt into water and drip-drip from nine in the mornin' till three in the evenin'. White clouds scud the sky. Winter has started breakin' up. Warm thaw winds blow through the bare Kentucky trees. One can feel them, warm soft winds, winds that remind one of rain. There will be rain and freeze and thaw and rain and freeze again. But spring is comin'.

"Mom," I say, "are we goin' to rent this place again and farm next year like we did last year?"

Mom says: "We are goin' to rent this place again if we can rent it and we don't find a place that is better. We failed last year on the bottoms. Craw-dads et up the corn. This year ought to be a dry season and the bottom ground hit and we'd raise a couple of cribs of corn. We'll put in some hill land and not take any chances on a season. I must see Mr. Woodrow before very much longer and have him draw up a artikle. We want it in paper with strangers so they won't be no trouble if me or your Pop would drop off."

Little Finn and Mary went upon the hillside today. It has been Finn's first trip out of the house winter-long. Mary was upon the hill when we buried the chickens and the guineas in the snow. The snow is melted off under the pine tree up above the kitchen. Barbara, Mom, and I go up under the pine tree and we put our feet on the ground. Here the pine needles feel soft from the weight of twenty-two inches of snow. The long winter is breakin'. There is a smell of dampness under the pine tree. It is a cold dampness. Finn jumps up and down and he says, "Goody, goody, goody, ground—ground—ground."

Today trains of crows have flown back among the bare trees searchin' for old corn rows and for places to build. They coupled off and searched among the tall trees on the south hill sides.

The earth looks today like a spotted hound dog's back. There is only clumps of snow here and there and the swollen streams run blue spring water. Spring has broken. Birds have come, the sparrows to the martin boxes and the wrens to the rag sack and tin cans in the smoke house. Robins, lapwings and jays have come back. It is the time to look over the land for next year's plantin'. Crows fly over carryin' sticks and mud. Pop is out of the bed. He walks across the floor, thin as a sack of bones, white as the petal of a needle-and-thread in June. "I am like a old black snake comin' to life," says Pop, "I thought the old Master was goin' to call me, but He has left me for another summer, another spring."

Mary comes in today and she carries a spring of greenbrier leaf. "The first green of spring," says Mary. It is the first green of spring that I have seen.

"Poke green ought to be a-comin' out," says Mom. "I'll have to get out and get us a mess of greens around the edges of the rich clearing." I see the windflowers comin' out to bloom. It is March. The land smells clean and sweet. The land is good to smell.

Mom sends me to the store. I bring back seed potatoes. I get feed for the cow and the chickens and the horse. I get food for the family. I get what Mom tells me to get. Mom is goin' to have a baby. I know it. I don't know what we will do without Mom. I don't think Mary knows about Mom. Barbara knows though about Mom. Barbara is old enough to know. We can see Mom walk out by herself. She will stand and watch a bird buildin' a nest. She will listen to the redbird sing from a bare poplar twig.

Weeds are comin' back to the south hill slopes. Once again the sheep bells tingle on the high hills. The air is cool. The percoon is in bloom and the blue violets bloom by the old stumps and stacks of rocks in the pasture field. Butterflies flit to the water hole for the cows. Spring is here. I know the spring is here. It is middle of March and I start to clear two acres of hill land to put in corn. I must cut the briars and sprouts and windrow them up the hill so they'll be easy to burn when time comes for spring burnin'.

Our chickens pick the green pepper weeds that grow by the barn. Our hound dogs go out and run the foxes by themselves and tree the possums and hole the rabbits. Pop says: "Don't hiss them dogs on a rabbit this time of year. The rabbit might be a old she about to have youngins. Be mighty careful. If it hadn't been for me, old Fleet would a-catched a old she rabbit up there in the old apple orchard yesterday. She holed it in a little piece of log that she could a tore open in a few minutes longer with her mouth. The log saved the rabbit till I got old Fleet away."

Today the grass is green, flutterin' in the wind. Mom takes a garden hoe out under the plum tree that is beginnin' to put out green buds. I can see her rake the graves with a hoe and fix little pieces of broken dishes and blue vases on the graves. Mom smokes her pipe. I can see the blue smoke in the blue March wind. It goes in a stream upward from her long-stemmed clay pipe. She chop-chops with the hoe and works around the headboards. She pulls away the dead grass. She cleans the stubble from the springs of fresh springin' flowers. Mom is not supposed to work now.

When I go out to clear ground after the work is done around the barn, I can see Mom comin' down the path smokin' her pipe. She comes to the clearin' and she says: "If I could only be in here with you things would be different. It will be different when your Pop gets well enough to work again. I am makin' him drink that bitter yarb medicine. It will do him good. He is feelin' better now. He is walkin' upon the hill. But his strength ain't come to him yet like it will come to him. You have been a good boy to work this winter and you ain't been no place but to town and right back. I am goin' to make you some shirts and some pants and buy you a better pair of shoes and start you and Barbara and Mary to Sunday School next Sunday. You are growin' up like heathens back here in this land that God has about forgot."

And Mom will pick up a brush I cut down with an ax and pile it on the windrow. She will pick up another and another and she will say: "I wish I could be out here with you. I love the spring. I love to dig my hands into the dirt, just to think of the days I have worked with your Pop—right by his side all day long and loved it."

It will not be much longer until Mom will have to quit work. She will have to go to the house for a while. I know how she loves the dirt, the wind, the sun. She loves the out-of-doors. She does not care for the house and she cares less to lie in bed. But Mom loves the trees, the briars, the wind, the grass, the wild flowers, and the stars. I have seen Mom saunter off to the woods and watch the lizard catch flies from the side of an oak tree. I have seen her find a birds' nest and would not touch the birds with her hands. She said the ants would eat them if you did. I have seen her sit out on the hills among wild roses and watch the white clouds in the June sky drift beyond the barrier of dark green hills that enclosed the Hollow like an iron rim that shouldered to the heavens. I know Mom does not like to lie in bed.

Our chickens cackle under the apple trees and wallow in the dust under the corn crib. We have a pretty flock of hens left after the cold dark winter. They lay eggs and we sell the eggs and buy coffee and sugar. "Did you know our chickens has got the limber neck?" says Mom, and she carries a young hen from the barn whose neck goes first one way and then the other. "These chickens is gettin' to somethin', maybe maggots. Somethin' them old hounds has carried in." Mom gets some turpentine and puts it in meal dough, spices it with red pepper. She fixes it in a crock.

"Catch all the chickens and put them in the cow shed and let's dope them and save all we can," says Mom. "It's maggots in their craws. That hen died. I cut her open to see what was wrong. Maggots was workin' out of her craw. Spring is here and these hens are after worms in the early spring. Dogs has carried somethin' in here. I smell it. Maybe it is that instead of the cold damp smell of winter leaves that comes in the early spring when buds begin to swell and life starts all over in the plants again."

I catch the hens and put them in the corn crib. Mom goes to the crib and I hold them while Mom puts dough down their throats. Pop hobbles to the corn crib. "That's bad luck to have to lose all them pretty chickens this time a year when a body needs them most. You can't save them when they once get maggots."

"We can save part of them," says Mom, "and if we had got to them in time we could have saved them all. I tried the turpentine on the maggot I cut out of the hen's craw and the maggot didn't last five seconds. It's gettin' the turpentine in their craws in time. Hurry it up and hand me the chickens."

I hand them fast to Mom and I hold their bills open. Mom puts gobs of turpentined and peppered dough down their necks. The hens shake their bills, crane their necks and walk off when I throw them back out the crib door. Mom says: "Here is one it's too late to fool with. She is nearly dead. She is sufferin'. She won't last much longer." She puts them in a group on the crib floor. They can't lift their heads. Their necks are limber. They sit there and quak, quak.

"Now," says Mom, "put these sufferin' chickens out'n their misery. Put them in a coffee-sack and carry them up there in the Hollow and take a ax and cut their heads off. That is quicker death than to let them die here the way they are. Don't be long about it."

I take the hens, one by one, put them in the coffee-sack. I take my pole ax. It is all I can do to carry the hens at two loads. They are not heavy. They are not fat. I take them upon this hill at this pine tree. I get a block of wood and I take them out one at a time. They cannot get away. I put their limber necks across the block and cut off the heads. I dig a big hole under the pine tree and throw in all their bodies and their heads and then I shovel in the yellow dirt. I pile rocks over the hole.

As I go back to the house I smell somethin' that Mom says she has smelled. It is not the sour damp winter leaves throwin' off scent to the spring wind. I follow the way the scent comes. I see the green flies swarm from the grass in the yellow spring sun. Here it is. It is an old horse knee one of the hounds has carried in. The maggots are a-workin' alive on it. I gather broom sage and pile over writhin' yellow-nosed worms. I strike a match and they shrivel up and squirm before the quick thin heat, more than leaves do when they burn in midsummer heat. I will not tell Mom. She will want me to get rid of a good possum hound. Mom has saved over half of the chickens with her remedy of turpentine and red pepper.

I get the potato patch plowed down in the rich dirt by the barn. This week is the time to plant the potatoes, for it is in the light of the moon. They will grow big and at the top of the ground Pop says, and will be easy to dig. The signs are in the skies. We must plant them to get a good yield of Irish potatoes.

Pop slices the potatoes to drop into the hills. I furrow the ground with long deep straight marks. Barbara covers the potato eyes with a hoe and Mom drops them. It is late March, the sun is yellow in the blue spring sky. It is the time to work. It is the time to plant potatoes. Mom says, "I have to go to the house, Mick."

Pop says, "Son, jump on that horse as quick as you can and get a doctor. Don't ask no questions, but go. Get Doctor Frederick if you can."

I unhitch Fred from the plow, throw off the harness in the potato patch and without a saddle I stride the mountain trail the way I went after the doctor for Pop on the cold winter night. Up the Hollow, around the slope, past the graveyard where the saw briars and the sprouts are greenin' now and will soon hide the tombstones. I go over the hill, around the ridge, and down to the town in full gallop except for the uphills. "Doctor Frederick, get out home soon as you can. Mom is sick. Maybe you know what is the matter with her," I say to him.

He jumps in his car. When I get home he is there. Mom has a little boy. Another brother for me and Finn. He is so small. He was born before the doctor got there. He does not weigh two pounds. Mom looks at him and laughs and we gather around the bed to look at him. Finn says to Doctor Frederick, "You got any more babies in that pill bag?" Doctor Frederick laughs.

Mom says: "The dresses that I made up there on the hill for him are all too big. He's the least baby I ever saw. I'll have to pin him to a pillow. I'll lose him in the bed." I remember seein' Mom sit out in the woods makin' little dresses and when I come around she put the work up. Now, I understand. "I hate to hear him cry," says Mary, "he goes like a mouse a-squeakin'. Let me carry him, Mom. Let me take him out to our playhouse under the walnut tree. He ain't big as my baby I got Barbara made for me."

"I'll keep him here," says Mom, "he's so tiny. Little ears and little tiny fingers. A little tiny cry. A little tiny mouth. But ain't he pretty?"

We want to play with the baby. "The doctor didn't bring Mom that baby," says Mary. "I heard him cryin' before the doctor come. Mom got that baby some place else."

Barbara is tall, slender, with two pretty rows of white teeth, eyes blue as the March sky, with hair the color of dyin' wheat straws. She cooks for us now. She burns the bread. She gets our dinner today. Mom says, "Shan, you go out in the smoke house and look in the coffee-sack of rags where the wren builds and lift up the rag to the left of the nest and get my pocket-book."

I go out and get the pocketbook. It is just where she says it is. I hand it to her. "How much do I owe you, doctor?"

"Ten dollars for the trip," he says.

She counts him out ten one-dollar bills. The doctor put them in his pocket. "We'll get you that other bill soon as we get on our feet a little."

I go to the field and clear the ground. Pop comes 'n' helps me a little. I can see that Pop's color is comin' back. He eats more now. He feels better. Mom is doctorin' him now. He is takin' Mom's yarb medicine. I cut a sprout down. Pop throws it on the windrow. I cut a swath of briars with the scythe. Pop forks them on the windrow. The sun is above us. The wind blows by us. We hear the wind. We see the sun. It is spring. We love to work in the fields. But I do miss Mom. She does not come these days and smoke her pipe and say: "I wish I could be out here. We'd do things."

Three days and Mom sits up in the bed and rips up the baby's dresses, cuts them down and makes them to fit. Barbara can't make a dress. She can make a paper doll dress for Mary's rag doll. She can't make a dress for my tiny brother. He is not big as a doll. Mom keeps sayin': "I'm tired of this bed. I'm comin' out of here. I can't stand it any longer." In four days Mom is up. She is workin' in the house.

"You can't get out of bed," says Pop, "you are out of bed too soon. You should stay in bed ten days and you ain't been in bed but four days."

Mom does not answer Pop. Mom will do the way she pleases. She pleases not to lie in bed. She walks out in the garden now and makes a lettuce bed and plants some early potatoes for summer use. Mom sets the hens. She marks the eggs with bluin'. She plants flowers in the yard. She is up and goin' while Mitchell sleeps.

April is here. Sun is pretty in the sky. Green is back to the hills. Gypsy picks the tender sprigs in the pasture. Birds sing and the hens' combs are red. They cackle in the woods. The crows fly over. They caw and caw. They carry worms to their young hidden back on the steep slope in the dense cloud of pine fingers that wash the wind on the mountain side. Pop is behind the plow again. His face is gettin' red like a rooster's comb. I am clearin' the hill land to be sure of good croppin' this year.

Mr. Woodrow rides his bony mare up where we are workin' and he says: "You sure are gettin' along well to have all the trouble you have had. Is there anything I can do for you?"

Pop says, "Not now, Mr. Woodrow."

"Well, we didn't put it in the artikle we drawed up, but I'll give Shan several days work along since he's got big enough to plow. I'll give him twenty-five cents a day and you and your horse a dollar and a quarter. Twenty-five cents for the horse and a dollar for you."

"Funny," says Pop after Mr. Woodrow leaves, "that a horse gets less than a man just because he is a brute and he does so much more than a man."

I get a day now and then when I have time. I work for Mr. Woodrow. We work from sunrise in the mornin' to sunset. I take the quarter home to Mom. Pop works the same way and so does poor Fred. He comes in at night a horse of a different color. His sorrel hair is the color of a wet blue cloth, slobbers hang from his lower dropped lip and there is a white thick lather between his hind legs.

"Mitchell don't grow a bit," says Mom; "if he grows I can't tell it. He ain't strong like my other babies. I am afraid. Somehow, I fear. I dreamed last night that Mitchell played with a lot of babies up there on the hill under that oak tree. I couldn't climb the hill to get him. I had to stay at the foot of the hill to watch him."

We plant the corn in the fields Pop has plowed. I'll soon have the two acres of hill land cleared. We'll burn this off and not plow it. We'll just double-furrow the weedless soft new ground after the fire runs over it and plant it. We'll plant beans in with each hill of corn and drop a few pumpkin seeds in the soft loamy places and around the old stumps.

Pop is plantin' corn. I am ready to fire the new ground. April the nineteenth here and the new ground not ready to plant. I see Mom comin' down the path to the clearin'. She is wringin' her hands and cryin'. I can hear her. Pop stops the horse, "What in the world is the matter?"

"Mitchell is dead. I can't go back into that house. Mitchell is dead."

Pop leaves Fred hitched to the plow. I run off the hill. We go to the house.

"I found him dead," says Mom, "on the sheet. He's never been like my other children when they was babies. He's dead! He's dead! I can never stand to go back in that house. He died in that house."

"You must take it easy," says Pop; "that's got to come some time or the other. And it has come to him before he knows the world like you and me knows it. He is better off than we are."

The Finneys and the Martins come to sit up with us. Our work stops. We go to town and buy a tiny coffin, one so small a person could carry it. "He must be put away nice," says Mom, "not in a home-made coffin, but in one bought with pretty linin'. We can pay for it. He must be dressed in a pretty robe."

Mom does not sleep while the coffin is in the house with Mitchell in it. She goes and looks at him and the tears fall. "The dark winter behind," Mom says, "now it is the spring and death in the spring when the world has changed so." Mom drinks coffee, black coffee without cream or sugar. She slips out and saunters beside of the creek that flows swollen and blue from recent spring rains. She will smoke her pipe. She will not smoke in the house in front of the Finneys and the Martins.

"He must be buried on land that Pap owns," says Mom, "he's the only blood kin I got that owns any land. I don't want him to sleep like these little children out here in this garden. Pap's land is same as my land. We'll haul Mitchell there. He'll not be on a stranger's land. He cannot be buried there."

It is tomorrow. Fred hitched to Mr. Woodrow's spring wagon leads the way through the April mud. It is April 21st. I remember. Mom and Pop ride side by side through the drizzlin' April rain. They ride in the buggy next to the spring wagon bearin' a little box. We go to Grandpa's place five miles away. It is noon and we are there. The grave is ready. It is a little grave with heaped-up yellow dirt under a pine tree. Grandpa shows us the way upon the hill.

There is a little crowd here. Mitchell does not know about the world. He rests in the dirt of the world. We leave him on the hill, a part of us, my father, mother, my brother, and my sisters. We leave him a part of the Kentucky earth. It is strange to leave one on a hill to sleep so long, one that you have seen breathe and move tiny fingers and blink an eye and cry like a little squeakin' mouse.

The horses race back over the April roads. We are tryin' to beat another rain. The skies have been clouded all day. "See the sun," says Mom to Pop as they ride back together, "first time today that I have seen the sun."

Uncle Fonse Laughed

About the story:

By the autumn of 1921, the Stuarts managed to build the first house of their own on Mitchell Stuart's fifty-acre farm. Actually, Jesse Stuart and his Grandfather Nathan Hilton did all of the masonry and most of the carpentry. Before moving into the first home of their own, Martha and Mick Stuart saw the birth of their seventh child and third daughter, Glennis Juanita. Now living were their five children—Sophia, Jesse, Mary, James, and Glennis.

At that time, the homeplace was the center of the Stuarts' lives. His mother and sister "canned hundreds of quarts of wild blackberries, strawberries, dewberries, and raspberries . . . corn, tomatoes, and apples, and made apple butter and pumpkin butter." His father, Grandpa Hilton, James, and he raised sweet and Irish potatoes, corn for livestock and fattening the hogs; and some went to the mill to make meal for cornbread. Wheat—cradled, shocked, and threshed—was ground into flour for home-baked bread. "I never tasted bread baked in a bakery until I was sixteen years old. For breakfast we had two big pans of biscuits and a small pan of spare 'biscuit pone' so we wouldn't run out of bread."

Sometimes relatives or neighbors would drop by to visit and "to take dinner with us." The Stuarts and Hillmans were good friends, and the parents and children enjoyed their visits through the backwoods to each other's places. Using the name "Tillman" for Hillman, the author wrote of the simple joys of neighborly sociability, good food, "tastebud cigars rolled out'n homemade tobacco," and life lived down close to the soil.

Jesse Stuart's first-person narrative and the speech of his characters rise out of the Kentucky hill tradition, as Professor Ruel E. Foster has observed, "with great naturalness and conviction." Here, as examples, the ground is "meller as meal," a good friend is "an old pup," a hefty wife jokingly complains that her husband "just plagues me to death," tobacco is described as "the fragrant weed" or "the blessed weed," a lazy and flighty neighbor is "that hirm-skirm piece of a man," a youth is cut with "a hawk-billed barlow knife," and Pa is "nervous as a sumac leaf in the wind." Early in the author's publishing career, now spanning more than a half-century, George

Marion O'Donnell wrote that Stuart "has never lost his identity as a member of his own community and a resident of his own section." The "vigorous narratives" of Stuart's people may contain "horror and pathos . . . that special kind of lusty, somewhat macabre humor" comparable to Erskine Caldwell's, but they also contain "a great deal of beauty and zest in this way of life." They possess "a racy dialect which enters into the whole texture of the writing." But in addition to these qualities, there is "the heroic quality, now almost lost from our literature . . . ," and "the most important thing about Jesse Stuart's stories . . . that they are always entertaining."*

*   *   *

HE WASN'T no akin to us. He was just a good friend to Pa. I remember when Pa would say to Ma: "Get every big pot on today, every little pot, every dirty pot—every clean pot. Fonse and Effie's coming over and bringing all the youngins." Then I'd see Pa just tickled to death—a smile on his thin brown lips from ear to ear. He would grab the ax and start to the woodyard. He would get a pole of wood and put it on a block. He would whack off a stick at a lick. He would cut two arm loads of dry stovewood. Mom would take a chair with her apron full of soupbeans. She would lift them from her apron and blow the chaff from them as she let them fall from her hand into a crock. It took plenty of beans when Uncle Fonse brought the family over to see us.

I can remember seeing the mule straining at the Tillman family express right down at the yellow bank below our house. He would stop, pant, wiggle his ears—then try again. He would pull the express about two cornrows wide at a time coming up the bank slonchways. Uncle Fonse would holler at Pa: "Good a mule, Mick, as ever was hooked in the harness. Never have to touch this mule with the withe." Pa would say: "Fonse, you old lazy devil you—why don't you get out and walk up the bank?"

Then Fonse would laugh and Pa would laugh and slap his knees. And the mule would pull again up the bank—the yellow clods of dirt a-flying from the hoofs—the foam spattering from the nostrils—white breaths of air going from the nostrils and spreading out thin on the blue air.

*H. Edward Richardson, unpub. biography of Jesse Stuart, Ch. II. Jesse Stuart, in *God's Oddling* . . . (N.Y.: McGraw-Hill, 1960), pp. 65–67, sets the background for his story, "Uncle Fonse Laughed," orig. pub. *Esquire*, Vol. 6 (Sept., 1936), pp. 32–33, 182, 184, 186; reprinted for the third time in Jesse Stuart, *Come Gentle Spring* (N.Y.: McGraw-Hill, 1969), pp. 195–209. Ruel E. Foster, *Jesse Stuart* (N.Y.: Twayne, 1968), p. 80. George Marion O'Donnell (review), "Jesse Stuart's Folk Tales," Nashville, Tenn., *Banner*, May 31, 1936, clipping in Jesse Stuart, Scrapbook #3, p. 16, Jesse Stuart Collection, Murray State University, Murray, Ky. All Jesse Stuart Scrapbooks referred to here are contained in this collection and will be indicated by the initials "M.S.U." in subsequent references.

When the mule would make it with his heavy load to our yard, Fonse would get out and he'd slap Pa on the back and Pa would slap Fonse. They would go around and around: Pa would say: "How are you, you old turkey buzzard you?" And Fonse would slap Pa on the back hard enough to scare us children for Fonse was so much bigger than Pa. Fonse would say: "How are you—you little game rooster you?" And they would laugh—Uncle Fonse's red face beaming in the sun—his blue eyes twinkling—his heavy jaws bobbing up and down on his wattled neck. Pa would say: "You're getting dough-bellied, Fonse. You ain't doing enough running up and down the hills. Maybe you're getting more to eat than I'm getting. My old woman won't feed me only when I got company. That's why I wanted you over here today." Then Uncle Fonse would hit Pa on the shoulder and Pa would laugh.

Aunt Effie would start in the house with all seven of the children. Pa would say: "Finn, you take your Uncle Fonse's mule out to the barn and give him seven ears of that good white corn and some of the clover hay." Well, I would unhook the traces, and do up the lines on the hames—take the mule from between the shafts and feed him hay and corn that our mules couldn't get. We were saving it for tougher plowing days. But Pa didn't have anything that was too good for Uncle Fonse's mule. Finn and me we had fists that made his boys stand around. Pa said once: "Why don't you call his boys Cousin Bill, Cousin Charlie, Cousin Henry and the girls Cousin Effie, Cousin Martha, Cousin Grace and Cousin Fleece."

We never said anything to Pa but we thought he was better to Uncle Fonse's boys than he was to us. We didn't like it. We put the rocks to Bill a couple o' times out in the cowpasture. Brother Finn peeled a pine tree right above Bill's head when he was running toward the house. Uncle Fonse's boys were afraid of us. We couldn't get 'em into the woods to play with us. Finn would say: "Them boys ain't no kin to me. I don't like 'em. Pa can't make me like 'em. I'll peel the bark off'n one's head with a rock when I get a chance."

Aunt Effie would go in the kitchen where Mom was. She would say: "Now let me help you right along with the dinner Mrs. Powderjay. Let me blow the chaff out'n the beans. Let me peel the taters. Let me do something." Mom would let her peel the taters. She was so fat and to stir around in the kitchen between the stove, the safe and the kitchen table and the woodbox, she'd get to wheezing a getting her breath. Mom would tell Pop when she left: "I just can't stand that wheezing. It is like catching a young mouse in a trap. It run all through me. I can't stand a mouse screak in the kitchen. So, I put Effie to peeling taters. She's so fat. She can't hardly get around in her fat. I don't see how she can cook for seven brats that eat as much as hers eat. Pon my words—I thought mine could eat. But it's just a drop in the bucket the way her youngins eat."

We would get Uncle Fonse's boys out as far as the smokehouse to play with us. We would play fox and dog. We kindly liked the little girls—they wasn't our cousins and we didn't want them to be. We helped them make playhouses behind the smokehouse. Sister Clara, Belle, and Sophie wouldn't like to see us play with Uncle Fonse's girls all the time—carry them the biggest arm loads of moss and broken dishes—but we did. We were the men and we watched over the house and kept away the Indians that were hiding behind the trees out in the pasture—out there among the pines.

Before dinner was ready—Pa and Uncle Fonse would sprawl down in the floor. They would wallow on the floor and talk. Pa would say: "Fonse what makes me and you such big fools? We ain't no kin are we?" Uncle Fonse would say: "We got good fences between our farms, Mick. We pay our debts. We take time off to go and see one another like them old folks used to do when we was boys back in Flint County. . . . We ain't no akin unless Pa's fox hound run a fox across the creek back yander on Gimpson creek in Flint County and your Pa drunk of the waters below." Then Pa would laugh and laugh. He would say: "Drunk of the waters below," and slap Uncle Fonse on the shoulder.

Pa would say: "Something I'm forgetting, Fonse. . . ." He would get up and bring a couple of tastebud cigars rolled out'n homemade tobacco by Pa's own hands. Uncle Fonse would lay there in the floor and look to the ceiling and laugh. He would say: "W'y you'd forget your head, Mick, if it was loose." And he would laugh. He would lay there in the floor with Pa. They would smoke their long cigars and look to the loft and blow smoke at a spider on a web. "Make that sucker sick up there, Fonse. A dime you can't do it." Uncle Fonse would blow smoke toward the spider on the low loft. It would fidget around on the little white strands of the web. It looked like it was looking over the edges of its mountain at the deep canyon below—at the big devils on the floor where the clouds of strong smoke were coming from.

Pa and Uncle Fonse would talk about farming. Pa would say: "I'll raise the best corn in the country over there in that new ground. Awful freeze we had this winter will make the ground meller as meal. I'll get some good taters out'n that ground too. You watch me this year. I'll raise more corn than you—you old pup. You beat me last year. But I'm going to lower the boom on you this year." Uncle Fonse would say: "You ain't going to beat nobody. Your wife might." And he would laugh and Pa would laugh. Uncle Fonse's neck wattles would shake like a turkey gobbler's red wattles.

Mom would come to the door. She would say: "Dinner is ready, Mick. Call the youngins." Pa and Uncle Fonse would jump up from the floor and Pa would go out and holler like he was blowing a foxhorn: "Dinner youngins—come to it. Yaho! Yaho! Dinner is ready! Come to it youngins if you want any." Well, we'd come running from behind the smokehouse and from the woods like chickens coming to the corncrib of a morning for corn. We would run in to get dinner. It would be late on Sunday when Mom and Aunt Effie would get dinner.

We didn't have to wait for a second table. Mom would say: "Put two tables together so everybody can eat." And we'd all eat together.

Uncle Fonse would say: "Pass me a little sugar for my coffee, please." Pa would hand him the salt. Uncle Fonse would be busy. He wouldn't notice. Uncle Fonse would say: "Three spoonsful of sugar to my coffee and if it ain't sweet enough I have Effie to dip her little finger in it." Pa would be trying to hold back a laugh so Uncle Fonse wouldn't catch on. And when Uncle Fonse would take the drink of coffee, Pa would stand up at the table and laugh at Uncle Fonse running to the door. All of us children would laugh at Pa and Uncle Fonse. Mom would say: "Pon my soul, Effie, I do believe there is two of the craziest men in this country. I believe we got 'em." Mom would laugh. Aunt Effie would shake in her fat and laugh. Then Uncle Fonse would say: "I take better care of my woman than you do though, Mick. I feed her better. Your woman is poor as a snake. She don't get nothing to eat only when I come over." Then Uncle Fonse and Pa would start laughing again.

"We got the two craziest men in the world," Aunt Effie would say to Mom. "Fonse just plagues me to death. When we go down the road in the express to town, Fonse hollers something at everybody. They stop and look at us in that old express setting upon that little hug-me-tight seat till we get out of sight." Aunt Effie would shake in her fat laughing at Pa and Uncle Fonse. Pa would say: "Want so-more sugar for your coffee, Fonse? You'd better let Effie stick her little finger in it the next time." Then Mom would start laughing.

After dinner Pa and Uncle Fonse would light their tastebud cigars. Mom and Aunt Effie would get their long-stemmed clay pipes. They would get homemade tobacco out'n the oatbox where Mom always kept her tobacco. They would fill their pipes—shove the tobacco down with a forefinger—light their pipes with a piece of rich pine kindling. I'd take it to the stove and light the kindling from the kitchen stove fire. And big clouds of smoke would go up from our table. It would be hard for us to get our breath around the table. I would say: "Bet I never smoke when I grow up. I hate the old stinking stuff." Pa would say: "Got the bluff on our youngins, ain't we Fonse?" And Fonse would say: "That boy ain't no Powderjay if he don't smoke the blessed weed when he grows up. Comes by it honest you know—his Ma, his Pa, and all his Uncles and Aunts on both sides used the fragrant weed—a blessing to all mankind."

After Pa and Uncle Fonse would smoke, they would walk out in the pasture. Mom and Aunt Effie would put my sisters and Uncle Fonse's pretty little girls in the kitchen to washing the dishes. I would come in and offer to dry the dishes. Mom would try to get me to help my sisters. But I never would do it. I'd say: "I ain't going to do no girl's work. I'm going to work outside with Pa. Ain't getting me in no kitchen." Mom and Aunt Effie would take their chairs out in the yard and put them under the peach tree. They would smoke their pipes and blow the blue smoke into the pretty spring wind. I can see it going to the sky in tiny swirls. I can see Pa and Uncle Fonse—Pa, little and spry—Uncle Fonse, big, square-shouldered and fat—walking slowly out the pasture path—talking, laughing, whittling.

We would play fox and dog over the hills. We would forget about Uncle Fonse's boys liking Pa and him liking them. We would forget all our troubles and play. We would quit throwing rocks at each other. Uncle Fonse's boys liked my sisters and I liked their sisters and Finn did too. We got along all right—running in the sunlight—jumping over the creeks—laughing, playing, shouting, screaming under the sun. It just seemed like the time was too short. Uncle Fonse and Pa would come back around through the pasture—around the path under the pines by the hog-pen. Pa so little and thin—Uncle Fonse so short and heavy. They would come whittling, laughing, talking. I could see Pa slap Uncle Fonse on the shoulder. Pa would say: "Fine day this has been, Fonse. Come again and see me." And Uncle Fonse would say: "I ain't never coming to see you again till you bring Sall and all the kids and come to see me, Mick. Now this has been twice on the straight I have been to see you. You got to come to see me next time."

Well, Brother Finn and Uncle Fonse's boy Bill would have the mule out and hooked to the express. I can see the mule standing in the blue wind by the hollyhocks—switching his tail in the bright blue wind at the flies. I can see the sun the way it went down over Lonesome ridge dragging a patch of red clouds behind it. I can see Pa and Uncle Fonse and Mom helping Aunt Effie into the express. They would put a chair by the express stirrup. Aunt Effie would step on a rock—from that up in the chair—from the chair to the stirrup and from the stirrup to the express bed. And when she got up to the chair, Pa, Uncle Fonse and Mom would all be ahold of her to keep her from falling. "I don't want to break a bone at my age," Aunt Effie would say.

"And if my wife gets any more pounds," Uncle Fonse would say, "she going to break a seat. I'm going to put a good hickory chair up there in the front for myself." And Uncle Fonse would laugh again and say: "I feed my wife. Now look at your wife there, Mick—thin as a beanpole." Uncle Fonse would slap the mule's back lightly with the lines and say: "Get up! Get up there, boy! Guess I got all the youngins."

"Come back again," Pa would say.

After they would leave Pa would say: "I tell you Sal, they don't make a better neighbor than old Fonse. Of course, he don't belong to my Party nor my church. I can't help that. He can't help it. He's just what he is and I am just what I am. But he's a good neighbor as a body ever lived by. It's good fences that we got between our places that make us good neighbors. You remember we couldn't get along with that hirm-skirm piece of a man that used to live over there. I built my part of the line fence and couldn't get him to build his. He would just brush it—keep throwing more brush on it. Cattle is smart these days on them brush fences after they've been used to barbwire. So his cattle kept getting in and eating up devilish nigh everything I had planted in the ground. Since Fonse has moved over there and bought that place we don't have any more trouble."

"But you all are the craziest-acting men I ever saw get together," Mom would say, "I don't care if he does belong to the Forty Gallon Baptis and you are a Slab Baptis and you belong to one Party and he belongs to the other. You all just plague women folks to death the way you lay around in the floor and go on about this and that."

Pa would say: "I popped it to him out there in the pasture when we's out there a looking at my cattle. I ast him some questions he couldn't answer about Resurrection. They've got some funny beliefs in his church. Them Forty Gallon Baptis is a funny church. And I sure did get him about his Party. Then he popped it to me about my Party and the Slab Baptis. Even jumped on me about my fox hound. He said the night out there when old Gun Powder led that pack of hounds that I put moonshine in sweet milk and give it to him. He'll have that going all over the country. Devil can't uptrip that man."

"You beat all men I ever saw," Mom would say.

"Something heavy in my coat pocket."

And when Pop pulled it out it was a tack hammer Uncle Fonse had made for Pop and slipped it in his pocket. "What do you know about that, Sal! Look here what old Fonse has made for me. He heard me say I needed a tack hammer and he made me one. He can make anything in the world he wants to make in a blacksmith shop and just think what I used to slip in old Fonse's pocket. I used to slip a dead bird in his pocket every week. I'd do it and he'd come to me and he'd say: 'Funny thing, Mick. I find a dead bird in my left coat pocket every week. It is some kind of a token.' I would laugh and say: 'You are just a dreaming. You don't find no bird in your pocket.' He would say: 'Oh, yes, I do. I know I ain't that crazy. I remember what happens to me. I remember too, that I don't put the bird in my own pocket. I reach down in my pocket. It is there—a dead bird. There's something strange about a dead bird. It is a strange token of some kind.' Yes, I put the birds in his pocket—and he gives me this fine tack hammer—big enough to draw nails with from the old planks."

Time will go on as time will. New people will be born into the world. The old people go from the world and give place to the new. Children grow up and babies are born. And the world goes on. There is not any turning back the hand on the clock. Time is in a swift race—it keeps running and running and it never gets anyplace. I could see the gray hairs come to Pop's head. He was getting older. Uncle Fonse was getting older. I remember when we made the blackberry wine and had it in a churn in the smokehouse, how Pop and Uncle Fonse went into the smokehouse. They walked in straight as sourwood saplings. They come out bent over and swaying like windblown willows by the creek. Uncle Fonse wasn't laughing when he said to Pa: "Mick, we ain't young as we used to be. But this old heart is young, Mick, even if the old body is getting old." Uncle Fonse was holding to the corner logs for the smokehouse and helping Pa around by the shoulder. . . . No, time is a thief that comes in the daylight, the moonlight—sunlight. He steals what that can never be brought back. He is a thief that cannot be jailed. There is not a jail big enough to hold him, nor money enough in the world to bribe him. But not a thief of time could keep Pa and Uncle Fonse from bringing the families together for a big dinner once and twice sometimes each week. Not even a thief of time could stop them from laughing and argying—They were against time. It didn't matter. They went laughing freely with the wind. Growing older had made them younger in a world where one sees joy, sorrow, has music, life, love, tears—where life is before one—life so big, so great—high as the skies are high—deep as the earth is deep.

I remember how Pa laughed at the table that morning. He said to Mom: "Pour me another cup of coffee, Sal. You remember how I got the salt in old Fonse's coffee that day for dinner here. Well, he tried to get a good one on me yesterday. I went over there to see him about my boy Finn and his boy Bill—You know how they are since they got to running together. He can't get no work out'n Bill and I can't get no work out'n Finn. I heard they'd been plum up there at that bad dance hall where them Perkins boys got cut the other night. So I says to Fonse: 'Fonse, ain't they something we can do about our boys running around together the way they do?' Fonse was getting in the express then. Had the mule all trigged up. Had red tassels on the bridle. Had brass rings on the hames for the check lines to run through and snap into brass rings on the bristle bitts. So, Fonse says to me: 'You take care of the boys, Mick. I won't be here to take care of them after tomorrow night.' And I says: 'Why, Fonse—you're not skipping the country, are you? Ain't stole no sheep—broke no bank—shot no man have you?' And Fonse says: 'No, I ain't done nothing I'm ashamed of. I am just going to die. It's my heart. The whole thing was pictured to me in bed last night. I saw the whole thing.' And Fonse, he just laughed and laughed. He thinks he's got a good'n on me. And when he started driving off, I says: 'Where are you going, Fonse?' 'Going to town to have the James boys to make my coffin tomorrow.' And he drove off down the road. He was laughing. And I was laughing. You know how Fonse acts. I can see old Fonse going yet—the mule trotting down that piece of sandy road by the pear trees. I can hear the creaking of the buggy wheels. And it all just kindly went through my mind that I'd have to slip another bird in the old boy's pocket. But instead of a bird this time I got a ground mole with baby hands. I'm going to slip it in his pocket. I'll pull a rich 'n on old Fonse. . . ."

Finn went to town the next day. I remember when he came in he said to Pa: "You know I believe Uncle Fonse is going crazy. I was over to see Bill awhile ago and Uncle Fonse was up on the hill cutting briars and sprouts off a little knoll. He said he was going to die tonight. Had the James boys to make a coffin out'n planks he's had seasoning in the barn for ten years. He's said he didn't want no undertaker's fancy-coffin. Said he wanted a coffin made out'n them oaks back of the barn. That's where he got them planks from ten years ago when Bill Ulling had that mill back there in the head of the hollow. He had a couple of trees cut and sawed into heavy planks. He had his coffin made out'n them very boards. While I was over there he got down in his coffin and tried it out. 'It is just a fit,' he said. Bill is a laughing at his Pa. Aunt Effie is a crying. The girls are crying. Aunt Effie said: 'He is either telling the truth or he is going crazy. And they ain't never been a Tillman gone crazy to the extent of my knowings yet.' He don't act to me like a man that is going to die. He won't tell how he knows."

I remember how Pa laughed. He said: "He's pulling a good one this time. He's got it up his sleeve to have some fun. If he's going to die, old Fonse would make his own coffin. He can make a hammer, make nails, wagon wheels, guns, smoothing irons. He can make anything he wants to make. He surely can make a coffin."

Pa went to bed that night. The wind howled through the green hickories at the end of the porch by Pa's bed. I remember seeing Pa get out of the bed in a night shirt. He looked at the moon and the stars in the heavens. He walked across the dewy grass barefooted. That was strange for Pa. Pa is a solid man. He is hard to move to tears. But Pa was in trouble. I heard him come to the bed. He got Mom up from sleep. He said: "Sal, I am troubled about Fonse. I can't sleep. I hear the death-bells ringing in my ears. I have tried to sleep. But I can see a wooden box in front of me. Get out of the bed and make a biler of strong coffee."

Pa put on his clothes. He walked to the barn and to the pigpen while Mom was making the coffee. I knew he went to the pigpen for the shoats squealed when Pa went past. The cows mooed when he passed them sleeping in the dewy grass by the barn-gate. Pa was in trouble. I never saw him act like this only once before in my life. That was the night Brother Finn got cut at the square dance and they brought him home all slashed up with a hawk-billed barlow knife. I heard Mom call him to get his coffee. And I heard Pa lumber through the house. I heard him pull his chair up to the table. I heard him say to Mom: "I am going over to Fonse's place just as soon as I've got light to travel by. I know something has happened. I have seen Fonse. I have heard him laugh. I know what I am saying is true. You know he said to me once when we's out in the pasture: 'Mick, you ought to be in my church. To prove to you we are right, if I die first you'll hear me laugh out there in the little pine grove where we always went on Sundays to talk and whittle by that salt-trough. If you die first I'll go out there and see if I can hear you laugh or speak to me first. And we'll see who's right—the Slabs or the Forty Gallons—' And I says to Fonse: 'It's a go, Fonse. You laugh to me. I'll know that old crow laugh you got.' And I would know it in Halifax too if I was to hear it there. So, I went out to the pine grove this morning. I've just come from there. I heard old Fonse laugh. I know it was his voice. Lord, I know his voice. I know that laugh. I know it was his laugh. It wasn't the wind. It wasn't the rustle of the green leaves. It was his laugh. I am trembling like a leaf in the wind."

I saw Pa cross the hill. It wasn't a good day. He told me to feed the hogs and not harness the mules till he come back. I saw him going up the path to the top of the hill. He walked beside of the good barbwire fence Uncle Fonse and Pa built. I saw him go between the wires and disappear among the green sassafras sprouts—wet with dew. They would soak Pa but he didn't care. Mom said: "It is a funny thing the way them men act. Maybe they're both going crazy. Your Pa is about crazy this morning. He drunk six cups of strong coffee. He says that something has happened to your Uncle Fonse. He says he knows that something has happened. Said he heard Fonse speak to him from the pine grove out there where they go on Sundays to talk and whittle. He said it wasn't the wind. He said it was Fonse. But wonder if it wasn't the wind in the pine needles? Wonder if it wasn't something besides Fonse? How could it be Fonse there so soon?" And Mom went to looking off into space. It kindly scared me. And I said: "Mom, there is something funny about the whole thing. I know I am right. I saw Uncle Fonse cutting the sprouts off a place to bury him on yesterday. He was having the James boys to make his coffin. He got down in it and tried it out. He said: 'It's just a fit.' I remember it well. I know that I am not dreaming. I come on up the road. I met Ben Ulling and told him about it. Ben said: 'He's either got a communication with the sperit or he's losing his mind, I-jacks, one.' I come on up there at that sweet apple tree blow Aimes' barnlot and frailed me some sweet apples with a crooked limb. I remember it as if it had just happened. I was not dreaming."

When Pa walked down the hill, Mom run out to meet him: "What has happened to Fonse?" Mom said. Pa just walked right down to the porch. He almost fell on the edge of the porch. He was quivering like a leaf in the wind. "Fonse is dead as a piece of dirt," said Pa. "He died last night sometime. I was there just a few minutes ago. I took the mole along to slip in his pocket. But he was dead. The family is all crying and going on something awful. I didn't stay. I couldn't stay. Fonse, there so quiet—not laughing! W'y he laughed when he was going to have the James boys to make his coffin. I thought he was joking. He didn't care to die. He laughed quietly into the arms of Death. I've always thought God would want a man that could laugh no matter what church he belonged to . . . Fonse there so quiet, so silent. He didn't speak to me. I couldn't stand it."

Mom shed tears. "What will Effie do now," Mom said, "with all that family of children? She can't keep 'em in grub the way they eat. Place not paid for with all them good fences around it. One thing Fonse believed in was a good fence between him and his neighbors. . . . Poor Effie, No way to turn back time. It just keeps slipping up on a body like it slips up on the flower and a stalk of corn. Everything has a season—even to man. God wanted Fonse to do something else—maybe to make fences in Heaven. Maybe, God wanted to hear him laugh."

Pa went about silently all day. He would walk to the pine grove, then to the house. He would watch a crow fly over. He would look at the growing corn. He would watch the white clouds float over. Pa would not turn his hand to work. He would not let us work. He did not go back to Tillman's house. Pa stayed at home all day. He was nervous as a shoemake leaf in the wind.

"Just to think about it all is a funny thing," said Pa, "life is so strange. To think about it all the time would make a man lose his mind. Fonse has left the earth. He was a good man—tended to his own business. He owned his land. He took care of his family and sent his children to school. He went to church. He believed in God's workings through the sperits. He didn't belong to the right Party but he belonged to the one he thought was right. Fonse Tillman was the kind of a man the country is built on. Yet, God called him out of this life. He left men in it not worth powder and lead to kill 'em. I just don't understand it. And tomorrow!"

"Yes, tomorrow, at two o'clock," said Mom, "right back of the house on that old poor point up there where the blackberry briars and the saw-briars take the place. That is where they will plant Fonse. That is where he wanted to be planted—up there where he used to tend corn. I remember seeing him go around that hill behind the mules. I can't forget it."

I remember the day at two o'clock. Yesterday never caught up with tomorrow. We were there. The crowd was there. The hill was lined with people. Pa said to Mom: "See what the people think of Fonse. Respected in life. Respected in death. Look at this crowd here. It's the biggest funeral I've ever seen among these hills. I have to help carry him up the hill to the grave. I don't know whether I can make it or not." I remember seeing Pa. He walked over the old corn rows—puffing and blowing under the corner of the heavy box. The crowd followed up the hill. We passed under Fonse's heavy-fruited apple trees.

The crowd stood there with heads bowed and heads bare. The check lines were slipped under the box—the heavy box was lowered into the earth and the check lines slipped from beneath it. I remember the tears that flowed down Pa's brown cheeks. I remember the cries of Uncle Fonse's children and Aunt Effie. I remembered they were not my real aunt and uncle but Pop and Mom taught us to call them uncle and aunt and they taught their children to call Pop and Mom uncle and aunt.

I remember the farm that Uncle Fonse owned. I remember the roses in bloom in the woods not far from where Uncle Fonse was buried. I remember how they waved in the wind—how the mountain daisy gently swayed on the hill where Uncle Fonse would sleep—the old furrows where he had plowed that time would soon blot out and leave the land level as a yard. I remember the silent crowd that left the hill—the wind overhead in the apple tree leaves.

Before my eyes were the eternal Kentucky hills. The crow flew over them. The buzzard sailed high above them. Among them men and women worked for their bread—knew the change of season. They saw life ripen sweetly and sourly with the years. They saw the flowers bloom in their season—die in their season. But even among these hills eternal in their great beauty of lilting green leaves in the wind—no one could stop time. No one could deny Uncle Fonse knew he was going to die. He had his coffin made himself. He cleared off his ground to sleep upon. Now he rests in that vast silence—under the sighing of the wind—the passing of the white cloud in the heavens—under the bloom of the rose and the mountain daisy and the swift wing of the crow. He lies in eternal Kentucky hills that if they were alive and could speak they could tell greater stories than any man of life, love, death, darkness, gloom, despair, the communion of the spirits. They could tell stories of many a carcass that does not sleep in a grave. They could tell unbelievable stories to make a book stalwart as a mountain.

Saving the Bees

About the story:
Growing up in W-Hollow, Jesse Stuart found time for games and mischief. He and his cousin, Glen Hilton, and Aaron and Ed Howard climbed trees in the valley of the last prong of the hollow. They used to "stick sticks back in hollow places and chase flying squirrels out . . . and make them fly." They also had a kind of wild peach tree racing game. The idea was to find wild peach trees in bloom—worth ten points. It was a running game, and Jesse Stuart wrote, "I like to think I ran faster than the wind blew." In late March and early April he would run ahead to espy the "pink blossoms blooming in the cool winds. . . . " The stark nudity of leafless trees intensified their beauty for the mountain boy. He liked to hear the others behind him, "breathing hard with their tongues out," and he gloried in shouting, "I've found another one. . . . In a cove near a white oak. . . . My tree." Then he would go on, never stopping for a second look.

"Big Aaron" Howard, the largest and oldest of the boys, was the leader of the W-Hollow gang. It was he who had pitched all sixteen innings of the Plum Grove School upset over Greenup High School, and his fictional counterpart emerges as a prominent character in several of the "Shan stories" Stuart was to write about the boys' teenage prankishness. In "Saving the Bees," Big Aaron is described as a sixteen-year-old with "big arms and a bull-neck." His hands are "hard as rocks," and "He has a heavy beard on his face." By far "the stoutest boy" in the Plum Grove hills, he intends "to free . . . the honeybees in this country," reasoning they "don't have liberty anymore." The boys, including Shan-Jesse, agree with their leader's sense of injustice at the slavery of the bees. In a series of Twainian adventures, the boys spirit away hive after hive of the bees—fifty in all—and hide them. At one time the boys are sprinkled with buckshot, and the shots "fall like rain," but they escape. Their last night of theft is characterized by a wild ride on a stolen Old Line Special handcar, adding zest to their thievery with painful bee-stingings and nearly disastrous gun-shootings. Baffled outrage grips the Plum Grove citizens, causing more than one to remark, "I'll tell you the world is going to hell."

Asked about "Saving the Bees," the author replied, "It was really *the stealing* of the bees. . . . " Asked further if it would be accurate to say that ninety percent of the stories came out of *his* life and out of facts, he responded, "I believe it would."

In reviewing the volume in which the story was first collected, Milton Rugoff wrote of "Saving the Bees" in the New York *Herald-Tribune* as "a Tom Sawyerish yarn of boys who sally forth nightly with true adolescent chivalry to steal and set free all the imprisoned honeybees in this neighborhood. The manner is robust, the humor broad."*

*   *   *

"**C**OME OVER HERE, Shan," says Big Aaron to me. "I've got something I want to tell you." I walk over across the creek to a rock cliff. Ennis Shelton, Little Edd Hargis and Dave Caxton are standing beside of Big Aaron Roundtree. Big Aaron is smoking his pipe. Ennis, Little Edd and Dave are smoking home-rolled, hawk-billed çigarettes.

"Now, Shan," says Big Aaron, "we are going to save the honeybees in this country. We are going to try to free them. The honeybees don't have liberty anymore. Look up in your yard! Your Pappie has six stands of them back of the woodyard. Look at the stands of bees my Pappie's got—twenty-six of them over on the bank from the house under the pines! Look at the honeybees that old Willis Dials has! Look at the bees Kenyons have upon the Old Line Special. Look at the bees Uncle Fonse Tillman's got and old Warfield Flaughtery! Boys, we've got to do something about it! Are you willing to jine us, Shan? If you tell anything it won't be good for you! If you are ever caught saving bees and you are whipped because you won't tell on the rest of us—you let them whip you until the blood runs out—and you never tell! Can you be that kind of a soldier?"

"I can," I says. "I'll do all I can to save the bees. We ain't going to take my Pappie's bees, are we?"

"We are going to take your Pappie's bees and my Pappie's bees," says Big Aaron. "We don't have any respect for any person's bees. We are going

---

*H. Edward Richardson, unpublished biography of Jesse Stuart, Chapter II. For Jesse Stuart's friendship with the Howard boys and Glen Hilton, his cousin, see his *Year of My Rebirth* (N.Y.: McGraw-Hill, 1956), pp. 141–142. "Saving the Bees" was first pub. in *Esquire*, Vol. 13 (Jan., 1940), pp. 104–105, 108; orig. collected in *Men of the Mountains* (N.Y.: Dutton, 1941), pp. 226–247, reprinted in Jesse Stuart, *Save Every Lamb* (N.Y.: McGraw-Hill, 1964), pp. 117–138, and *Men of the Mountains* (Lexington: Univ. Press of Ky., 1979), pp. 226–247. That the Howards were real people who lived in W-Hollow Mr. Stuart made clear in our interview, W-Hollow, Greenup, Ky., Nov. 3, 1978. Jesse Stuart/H. E. Richardson, Interview #41, W-Hollow, Greenup, Ky., Sept. 15, 1981. Milton Rugoff, "As Fresh as a Mountain Stream" (review), New York *Herald-Tribune*, March 16, 1941, clipping in Jesse Stuart, Scrapbook #7, p. 22, M.S.U.

after all of them. We are going to take the bees back to the woods. We are going to set them free. It is a big job but we can do it. Every man must fight to the last. He can't get cold feet. If he is shot at—he can't let that bother him. He must grab the bee stand and run anyway. The bees must be put back in the woods—let them grow wild again. It's got so in these parts you can't find a wild bee tree anymore. It is a shame to coop bees in boxes and sawed-off logs and make them work their lives away for a lazy bunch of people. We won't have it!"

The water drips from the roof of the cliff. It drips on my ear and tickles it. The ferns hang over the front of the cliff. There is a pile of ashes on the floor of the cliff with burned-brown rocks around the ashes. There is a wire wrapped around a splinter of rock above and hangs above the ash pile. It has a hook on the end of it to hold a pot. There are chicken feathers around the rocks. Back in one corner of the cliff is a .22 rifle. Beside the .22 rifle is a .32 Smith and Wesson pistol. Beyond the drip of water is a big pile of dry oak leaves.

"Boys, this cliff can be our home," says Big Aaron. "It is our hide-out. We can work from here when we are saving the bees. We can have chicken any time we want chicken. We can have honey any time we want wild honey. We can have Irish taters and sweet taters any time we want them. Show me a house here that ain't got a tater patch beside of it. We have a cup here to catch our water from the drip in this cliff. We have a good oak-leaf bed. All five of us can sleep in the oak leaves with our guns beside of us. This cliff is back from the road and the ferns nearly hide the front of it. It just looks like the green hillside. No one would know that a cliff is here un-less he would come over here, push the ferns back and look in. If he ever does that he'll be batted in the face so hard he'll never do it again."

"When will we meet, Big Aaron?" asks Ennis Shelton.

"Be here tonight when you see the moon come above the pines on the Flaughtery hill," says Big Aaron. "You be here, Shan. Don't pick up no stranger and bring 'im along either. You come straight to the cliff. All of you boys be here on time. It is in the light of the moon now and the moon ain't goin' to waste no time nohow gettin' to the top of that pine thicket on the Flaughtery hill."

"We'd all better be gettin' home to get our suppers now," says Dave.

Big Aaron hides the pistol and the rifle in the leaves. He walks under the cliff—pushes back the ferns and sticks his head out. "Everything is clear, boys," he says. He leads the way out. We follow Big Aaron. He is sixteen years old. He has big arms and a big bull-neck. He can pull the plow in the field like a horse. His hands are hard as rocks. He has a heavy beard on his face. He is the stoutest boy among the Plum Grove hills. He can lift 7 x 9 crossties and load them on a jolt wagon. He can shoot a sparrow's head off with the .22 rifle from the top of the highest tree. He says he can save all the bees among the Plum Grove hills.

I leave the boys at the forks of the road. I go up the creek home. I eat my supper, carry in stove wood, kindling—draw up water for the night from the well under the oak tree. I milk two cows and strain the milk into the crocks on the big flat rock on the smokehouse floor. I am ready to go to the cliff. I turn to walk away. "Where are you goin', Shan?" asks Pa.

"Fox huntin'," I says. "I'm goin' out with Big Aaron Hargis to hear his hound pup run."

"Just like me," says Pa, "when I was your age. I loved to hear hounds. Go out and lay around all night on the cold ground. That's the reason I'm so full of rheumatics today. But you go on and live and learn like I have. I still love to hear the hounds."

I walk down the hollow to the big road. I turn down the big road—down to the big sycamore. I look up the road and down the road—I cannot see anyone coming. I run across the rocks at the foot of the bluff. I run down behind the trees. I climb up the little path to the cliff. I can hear voices within. I climb up—part the ferns—the boys are all under the cliff. I look toward the Flaughtery hill—the big moon is coming up behind the trees. Its face is red—it is blushing like a young boy that watches things from behind the trees.

"You're here," says Big Aaron. "Now Shan Powderjay—remember if you ever tell anything, the rest of us will down you and cut your tongue out. That is the jail sentence for a tattle-tale among us. We have a job to do and we must do it. You fellars follow me tonight. We're goin' after Willis Dials' bees. I've been past his house today. I know where he keeps his bees. I know a little path that leads up the bank to the bee gums. You fellars just follow me."

We follow Big Aaron down the hollow. We do not go along the road. We follow the creek bed. We wade the water. We come to the big white-oak at the forks of the W-Hollow and the Three-mile road. We take to the hill. We follow a fox path over the hill to the Old Line Special railroad tracks. We can see the big log house upon the bank above the railroad track where Willis Dials lives. "See the bee gums in the front yard, boys," says Big Aaron. "There are five of them. There are five of us. The bees ain't working now. Stick little pieces of wood in their holes so they can't come out. Lift them easily. You won't get a sting. I'll get the first bee gum. You just watch me. Do as I do."

Big Aaron slips up the bank. He takes little sticks and stops the two little holes where the bees come out of the gum. Then he lifts the gum to his back. He walks down the bank. No one whispers. Each of us stops the holes where the bees come out with little sticks. We get our bee gums on our backs—we follow Big Aaron up a little path to our left around the Plum Grove hill. After we get away from the yard—a dog comes out and barks. He barks and barks. "Don't be afraid, boys," says Big Aaron. "He ain't no bitin' dog. He's one of them barkin' dogs that never bites. Come on with your bees."

"Lord, but this is a heavy load, Big Aaron," I says. "I don't know whether I can carry it or not. Sweat has popped out all over me."

"You ain't no man," says Big Aaron, "if you can't carry a bee gum loaded with honey and bees." My bee gum is a cut of a hollow log with boards nailed on the top and bottom. It is black gum and it is heavy.

"I'm about all pooped out with my load too," says Dave Caxton. "Sweat is streaming in my eyes until I can't see the path. I'm wet as a river with sweat."

"Follow me," says Big Aaron. "I've got the heaviest bee gum of all you. I got a cut from a hollow beech-log. It's the heaviest wood in the world. I'd hate to think I couldn't carry one cut of saw-log." We follow Big Aaron down the cow-path and up the Jackson hill. We follow slowly to the top. We are getting our breaths like spans of mules pulling a jolt-wagon load of crossties out of W-Hollow. Big Aaron reaches the top. He sets down his bee gum, "Here's the top, boys," he says. "Now we'll smoke before we go down the other side."

We reach the top of the hill. We put our burdens down. The bees are mad within the gums. If they could get out they would sting us to death. But we have them fastened in behind the little sticks. We roll our cigarettes in brown sugar-poke paper. We fill the papers with crumbled, home-grown tobacco. Dave takes a dry match from his hatband. He strikes it on his teeth. He lights our cigarettes. We stand in the moonlight and pant and blow smoke toward the red-faced moon. The cool wind from the high hill-tops hits us. It dries our sweaty clothes. It cools our faces.

"Let's finish our job," says Little Edd Hargis. "How much futter we got to go?"

"Just under the hill," says Big Aaron. "I've got the place picked. It's safe for the bees."

We throw down the stubs of our cigarettes. We twist the fire out'n them with our shoes. We pick up our stands of bees. We walk down the hill be-hind Big Aaron. We walk down to a locust thicket. There is a groundhog path back under the locusts. Big Aaron bends down and walks back this path. We follow him back to a little open space where he puts the bees down. "Ain't this a safe place for the bees," says Big Aaron. "Look what a purty place for them! See, I got one bee gum here already. I got one of Pap's and brought it here. He ain't missed it yet."

Big Aaron has come already and put rocks down for us to put the bee gums on. He has made foundations for many stands of bees. We place the bee gums solidly on the rocks. "When you get 'em fixed on the rocks," says Big Aaron, "jerk the sticks out and come away and leave them. They'll think they are at home in the morning. They'll work just the same as they've always worked. They are at home out here. They are away from everybody. They have come home to the hills where they used to be."

We place the bee gums on the rocks. We slip the sticks out of the holes. We slip back down the path—over the hill to the hollow. We cross the creek, climb the bluff to the rock cliff. "We are back home," says Big Aaron as he goes under the curtains of ferns to the good leaf bed. Big Aaron sprawls out on the leaves. Little Edd puts the .32 on a shelf of rock. Dave unstraps his rifle. He lays it on the shelf of rocks. We sprawl out for the night. "Our work is done for tonight," says Ennis. "I'm glad it's done too. I looked every minute to see fire flash from a gun when we's getting them bees. It ain't safe where there's a lot of house dogs around."

"Don' talk about it now," says Big Aaron. "You'll get me skeared after it's all over. Forget about it now. Our night's work is done. Go to sleep and dream."

I dreamed that Willis Dials saw me steal his bees. I thought he run me with a corn-cuttin' knife. I was just keeping out of his way. He was just barely touching me with the knife but I would jump out of his reach. His little black eyes looked like balls of fire. He had a pipe in his mouth and his lips were snarled. When he struck—I jumped and the knife just touched me. I could feel blood running from my face and neck.

"Get up all of you," says Dave. "It's Sunday morning—hear the Plum Grove church bells ringing. Get out'n that drip of water Shan. You've rolled over under the drip. Your shirt is wet." Dave laughs and laughs.

"That made me have bad dreams," I says. "I thought Willis Dials was after me all night. He was cutting at me with a corn knife. I could feel the blood running down my neck and face."

"Well, boys," says Little Edd, "we had a good fox chase last night. Let's all go home to breakfast."

We crawl out of the cliff—walk to the forks of the road. We part at the forks. I walk up by the sweet-tater bottoms to the house.

"Your Ma left breakfast on the table for you," says Pa. "She's gone to Sunday School. Hurry up and eat breakfast and help me do up this work. You can tell me about your fox chase then."

"All right, Pa," I says.

I eat my breakfast. I walk out where Pa is. I help him milk the cows and slop the hogs. I tell Pa about the big fox chase we had. Pa says he must have slept like a log for he didn't hear the hounds and that he always listens for them. I tell him if he didn't hear them it was his own fault for our hounds really put the fox over the hills.

When Mom comes from Sunday School she says: "Mick, did you know somebody took all of Willis Dials' bees last night? Took five stands from him. Said he saw them leaving with them. Said he shot five times. Said they had a wagon over on the road and loaded the bees on the wagon and run two big black horses hard as they could tear up the road with all his bees in the backend of the wagon. Preacher preached this morning about it. People are coming in here and stealing honeybees! Did you ever hear of sicha thing?"

"Must a-been hard up for honey," says Pa. "I'm forty-five years old and I never heard of people stealin' honeybees out'n a yard. I've heard o' men findin' bee trees on another farm and slippin' in and cuttin' 'em without permission but I never heard of thieves brazen enough to walk in a man's yard and carry his bees to a wagon! I don't know what this world's a-comin' to——"

"It ain't comin'," says Mom—"it's goin'—and to the Devil it's goin' fast. We ain't had sicha thing happen at Plum Grove for years. Betsy Roundtree was talkin' about it as we come back across the hill. She says she puts the fear of God into Big Aaron. I tell her I know that my boy will never steal—never—whatever he does that's onery—stealin' won't be a part of it."

Everybody talks in the community about Willis Dials losing his bees. We hear about how Willis shot at them—how they took to the wagon and drove the big black horses up the road—their feet striking fire from the rocks. We hear all sorts of tales. We do not talk about it. We listen to the others talk. I go to Prayer Meeting on Wednesday night at Plum Grove with Mom. Big Aaron is at Prayer Meeting. He comes to me and says: "We fox-hunt tomorrow night. Be at the cliff by moonrise. We go to Flaughtery's tomorrow night. We got to get his bees. He ain't got but four bee gums. Ain't much but enough to pay us for our trouble."

Thursday night we call our dogs—meet at the crossroads. The dogs take to the hills to start the fox. We go to the cliff. When the hounds are bringing the fox across the hollow by Warfield Flaughtery's house and his dog runs out and barks at the fox hounds, we slip upon the bank back of War-field's house—we plug the bee gums with sticks. We load them on our backs. We walk away. Little Edd carries the pistol and the rifle. We walk down the creek to the big sycamore, then we turn to our right. We walk up under the pines where the moonlight falls almost as bright as daylight. We put the bee gums down to rest, wipe sweat and smoke. We roll our cigarettes in the brown sugar-poke paper. We smoke and sit silently under the pines in the moonlight. We get up, twist the fire out of our cigarette stubs with our shoes. We move across the hill to the place under the locust thicket where we keep our bees. We place them securely on the foundation rocks—pull plugs out of the holes. Warfield Flaughtery's bees now have their freedom. We go back to our cliff for rest. Big Aaron gravels some of Warfield's sweet taters from the ridges in the bottom by the sycamore tree. We stick the taters in the bottom in the ashes under the cliff. We build a fire over them. We lie down on the leaves on the far side of the cliff for a little rest. The fire will burn down—the embers will roast our taters. When we awake, our breakfast will be ready. We'll eat a bite of breakfast and go home. We know our Paps are listening to our hounds bring home the fox.

"Breakfast, boys," says Big Aaron—"wake up to a good sweet-tater breakfast."

I watch Big Aaron rake the roasted sweet taters from the ashes. He peels the bark from one. He eats the golden-colored roasted sweet tater. "Better than honey," he says—"you fellars get up and taste o' one."

I get up from my bed of leaves. Little Edd, Dave, and Ennis get up. We get roasted taters from the ashes—peel the bark from them. They are warm and sweet. "I read," says Big Aaron, "where George Washington's soldiers et roasted sweet taters and went barefooted at Valley Forge in the winter time. I'd hate to think I couldn't stand as much as they could stand. People just don't know what good grub George Washington's soldiers had to eat. I ain't gone barefooted in the winter time but I've gone in swimming when I had to cut the ice and that didn't bother me a bit."

"That ain't nothing, Big Aaron," says Ennis—"we've all done that. Talk about something we ain't done while we're here at the breakfast table."

"We ain't got my Pap's bees and Shan's Pap's bees," says Big Aaron—"but we will get them if we keep our health. Boys, we'll hear a lot about somebody's getting Warfield's bees. Just say we saw that team of black horses goin' out'n the hollow about twelve o'clock—say we saw the driver slapping the horses with the lines."

"That's it," says Ennis. "He's the man Willis Dials saw gettin' his bees."

"It'll be a joke about how many liars we have at Plum Grove," says

Little Edd, "if they ever find our bees. They'll know then about the black horses." Little Edd talks with his mouth filled with sweet tater.

"It's time boys we's getting home," says Dave. "I've got to work in the terbacker field today."

Big Aaron picks up the sweet-tater bark. He puts it in a little pile and covers it over with leaves. "Remember," says Big Aaron, "we meet here Saturday night at seven o'clock—rain or shine or no moon. Now we must all get home and help our Mas and Paps." Big Aaron sticks his head out from under the ferns. He crawls out. We follow him down the bluff—across the creek and up the road. At the forks of the road I leave them. They go up the creek and I go up the Right Fork home.

"Now, Mick," I hear Warfield say, "my bees are all gone. All four stands are gone I tell you. I've found tracks down to the road—a lot of big tracks and little tracks. I can't track 'em no further. I heard dogs barking last night. The fox hounds run the fox right across by my barn. My dog barked and barked. I never thought anything. Now my bees are gone."

"Shan, Warfield lost all his bees last night," says Pa.

"Yes," says Warfield, "I lost my bees. Just keep bees to get honey for Ma and me. We live alone around there and ain't never had anything bothered in the last sixty years. I'll tell you the world is going to hell. I never heard of thieves taking bees before."

"W'y Mr. Flaughtery," I says, "we were back on the ridge last night and we heard a man driving in the hollow. When we walked down to the beech-tree footlog we saw a pair of black horses hitched to a wagon—the driver stood up like a ghost and whipped his horses with the check lines. We saw the fire fly from their hoofs as they left the hollow."

"The same damned thief," says Warfield, "that got poor old Willis Dials' bees. Old Willis wasn't seeing things. He actually saw the thief. I heard that Willis stung him with a few shot. I heard Sol Perkins found blotches of blood on the turnpike. Looks like if that thief got hot lead once he'd be afraid he's going to get it again."

"You can't lock from a thief," says Pa, "and you can't bluff one with bullets. You just haf to get 'im. Put him under the sod is the only cure."

Warfield goes home. I go to cornfield with Pa. I think about when Saturday night comes. "What if someone shoots me? What if someone shoots Big Aaron? I don't want to sleep under no ground. I want to live. Maybe, we'll make it somehow without getting shot."

It is Saturday night. I call Pa's hound dog and my hound pup. I walk down the Right Fork to the hollow. I turn left, walk down the road to the sycamore tree. The dogs leave me and take to the hills. I walk across the creek, climb the bluff up to the cliff. I hear voices. The boys are waiting for me. I crawl under the ferns to the big room under the cliff. The lantern is dimly burning.

"We have a hard piece of work before us tonight, Shan," says Big Aaron. "Uncle Fonse Tillman has one bee gum. He has it around from the house, chained around a big beech tree and the log chain is padlocked. We haf to have that stand of bees. I've brought a cross-cut saw and a meat rind. We'll grease the saw until you can't hear it run—saw the tree off above the bee gum and slip the chain over the stump. We'll fool the old boy. It's a prize bee gum. He ain't robbed it for four years. He's afraid of his bees."

"We ain't afraid," says Little Edd. "I'm beginning to feel like I'm a man if I am shot tonight."

"Let's go," says Big Aaron. "Don't anybody talk. Shan, you help me saw the tree down. You are tall and you can reach above the bee stand and saw and it won't tire you."

We follow Big Aaron out of the cliff. We follow him up across the hill back of the cliff. Big Aaron follows a cow path to the top of the hill. We see the fox hunters' fire on the ridge. Big Aaron cuts down under the hill through the briars and brush—we follow him—we cut back up to the ridge road on beyond the fox hunters' fire. We walk down the point to Uncle Fonse Tillman's little log house. Big Aaron leads us to the beech tree. He runs the meat rind over the saw. We start sawing. The saw slips through the wood like a mouse slips away from a cat. There isn't a sound you can hear ten steps away. "The chain takes up a lot of the sound," says Big Aaron. Our saw eats through the green beech tree. It falls through the night air with a slash—not a dog barks at Uncle Fonse's house. We lift the padded log chain up over the clean smooth-topped stump. Little Edd plugs the bee gum. Big Aaron puts it on his back. We walk back over the hill to Big Aaron's Pap's house. I carry the log chain and the padlock.

"I know Pap's bees," says Big Aaron. "I know where he keeps every stand. We haf to work all night, boys. I'm going to carry two light bee gums at one load. You boys can take one apiece. We can carry all of our bees at five loads."

"You can't carry two stands at one load," says Ennis.

"The hell I can't," says Big Aaron. "You ain't never seed me really put my strength out. I can just about carry three to the top of that hill over yander."

We chain two stands together for Big Aaron. He picks them up with ease. He walks away. We plug our stands of bees. We walk down the hill to the road. We climb the hill under the pines. We rest on the ridge and smoke. We pick up our loads and carry them down under the hill to the locust thicket. We place them securely on the foundation rocks. We take out the plugs. We walk back the little path that leads us to our city of bee gums.

"Now, boys," says Big Aaron, "we got four loads to carry from home and a load of bees over at Shan's Pap's place. It will take us all night to do this. We'll haf to work fast. We can't walk across Warfield's tater ridges at the bottom by the sycamore tree. We'll make a path and they'll track us. We'll come up the hill at a different place everytime. Let Pap track us down to the road. There's a lot of wagon tracks. He can't go no further."

We follow Big Aaron. We carry the second load. We carry the third load. We carry the last load. We carry away all the bees that Alec Roundtree has. "This will hurt Pap an awful lot," says Big Aaron, "but he has hurt the bees an awful lot. He went into the wild woods and took them from their homes in the trees. Now we take them back and leave them in the wild woods—a place so wild the hoot owls holler in the daytime."

"It's two o'clock in the morning," says Ennis, "and daylight comes soon. Do you suppose we'll have time to carry Powderjay's bees away before daylight?"

"We got two hours," says Big Aaron—"I can carry them away by myself in that time. Come on you fellars. You ain't no tireder than I am. I'm goin' to bring two stands over this time. I'm taking the log chain to wrap around them. Shan, you lead us the best way to your bees."

We walk up the hollow with our plugs to stop the holes. Our bees are beside the road. We just walk along—our dogs are running the fox. There is not a dog at the house to bark at us. We plug the bee stands. Big Aaron chains two together—loads them on his back. We get a bee gum apiece and we follow Big Aaron. Little Edd carries the pistol in his hand to shoot if we see somebody coming up the road. "Little Edd, just shoot to skear 'em a little," says Big Aaron. "Put the bullet fairly close and they'll tear out."

We hurry down the road. We cut across the meadow beyond the big sycamore tree. We take to the pine woods on the hill. The moon is down, down. The way is dark. We follow Big Aaron up the hill. He sweats and groans beneath his load. We reach the top of the hill. We are wet with sweat. We are tired out. "Last time tonight," says Big Aaron. "Let us have a good smoke."

"Who—who who are you?" says a voice near by. We never move. We do not speak.

"Who—who who are you?" says the same voice.

The wings of a big owl swoop over us. We can feel the cool air from its wings.

"Did you ever hear a hoot owl speak that plain?" says Big Aaron. "My heart was in my mouth. I thought it was Pap. I thought we's goners. Lord, but how thankful I am. Let's get the bees over and put them with the rest of the bees. This will make us forty-two stands of bees." We pick up our loads again. We walk over the hill to the locust thicket. We place them securely on the foundation rocks. We unplug the stands and walk down the little path we have worn under locust trees.

"Let's all go home and go to bed," says Big Aaron. "Remember we saw that team of horses about twelve o'clock again last night when we followed the fox hounds from the Flaughtery Ridge to the Powderjay Ridge. All tell the same tale. We're going to hear about this and not from Sunday School. Pap will be one mad man in the morning."

I leave the boys at the forks of the road. I am so tired I can hardly get home. I worked all day in the terbacker field—I carried bees all night. I am tired. I can sleep all day if there's not too much war going on in the hollow. I walk home—barely crawl to my bed upstairs. I just get my shoes off and fall across the bed. I'm all pooped out. "Lord," I think, "I'm glad I didn't get shot. I'm thankful to the Lord and I would pray to Him but I've been out taking bees and the Lord wouldn't listen to my prayers." I fall asleep.

"I'm robbed, Mick Powderjay," I hear Mr. Roundtree say. "They got my bees last night. Seventy-five gallons of honey stole from me last night. Lord, how I'll miss that seventy-five dollars! Took every bee gum I had— stripped me clean."

"Well I'll be damned," says Pa—"I never noticed that. All my bees are gone too. Look up there won't you! I'm robbed too! My God—look won't you! Thieves have come right inside my yard and took my bees!"

I get up—put on my clothes and go down. I walk out where Pa and Mr. Roundtree are standing. "Pa, did you say somebody got our bees last night?" I says.

"Look for yourself," Pa says. "I couldn't believe my eyes when I first saw it. Got all of Alec's bees last night."

"What?" I says.

"Yes," says Alec, "I've got Big Aaron out tracking this morning. Said he saw a span of black horses leave the hollow last night about twelve o'clock. Said the driver was layin' the buckskin to 'em and the fire was flyin' from their hoofs! Said the driver was leaning back and holding the check lines like a tall ghost."

"I saw it with my own eyes too," I says.

Uncle Fonse Tillman comes down the hill. He walks with a cane. He comes down to our yard—just ripping out oaths and cavorting. He waves his cane into the air. "Some thief got my only stand of bees last night," he says. "I had them chained to a beech tree. They cut the tree and slipped the chain over the stump—took chain, padlock, and bee gum. I'll kill him if I ever find him. I'll kill all the thieves connected with it." He pulls a long blue .44 from the holster and twirls it.

"We ought to swing 'em to a limb," says Pa, "if we can get 'em. We'll take the span of horses to pay for the bees."

Pa, Uncle Fonse and Alec Roundtree swear and stomp the ground. Pa puffs a cigar faster than I ever saw him puff one before. "A damn dirty shame," he says. "I've lived here all my life and this has never happened before. Somebody from a-fur has to come in to steal our bees."

Big Aaron comes up the road. "Pa," he says, "I've tracked them to the road. I see fresh wagon tracks. I can't track them no further."

"They're gone," says Alec Roundtree. "All my bees are gone."

"Mine too," says Pa.

"And my bee gum, log chain, and padlock's all gone," says Uncle Fonse Tillman.

"I've said," says Pa, "you can't lock against a thief. The best way is to fill his hide so full of lead it won't hold shucks."

I walk across the yard with Big Aaron. "We meet at the cliff next Tuesday night," says Big Aaron, "to set the last of the bee gums free. We're going up the Old Line Special to Kenyon's place. I've looked the place over. I've got plans. We'll set them free."

"I'm getting afraid," I says. "Look at these men. Listen to them cuss and watch them stomp their feet!"

"Yes, Pa smiled when he cut down the wild bee trees," says Big Aaron. "He can't remember how the bees stung him trying to keep him from robbing them and taking them out'n the woods. Now Pa cusses around because they have gone back where they belong. Shan, you be ready Tuesday night. All this will blow over—besides, we're goin' beyond the Plum Grove hills to get these bees. We're going up the Old Line Special!"

Tuesday night I walk down to the cliff. Everywhere we go we hear wild tales about people's seeing the bee thieves—dressed in white—driving big black horses. People shooting at them and they were hit by bullets and there was blood along the road. We laugh about it. We know what big lies can get started while we work to save the bees.

"Now boys," says Big Aaron, "we go to Jake Reek's place. He has a handcar beside the Old Line Special. See he is a track man and uses the handcar. He has it padlocked but there's a crowbar there. We can pry the chain off. We can put it on the track and ride up the rails to Kenyon's.

They live beside the railroad track. We can put the bees on the handcar— come down to Plum Grove in no time and carry the bees back on the hill."

"That is great," says Ennis. "We'll get to ride the handcar. Won't that be fun!"

"It won't be fun goin' up the Old Line Special," says Dave. "We haf to pull uphill. But comin' back we can coast all the way to Greenupsburg. Just turn the levers loose and let 'em work up and down—just watch that one don't crown you on the head."

Big Aaron leads the way. We follow him to Jake Reek's house. We walk down the path to the railroad. The handcar is settin' beside the railroad track. Big Aaron goes over in the weeds. He comes back with a crowbar. He puts it behind the chain and yanks against it with all of his strength. The lock flies open.

"Let's set 'er on the tracks, boys," he says. "Let's go to Kenyon's place and get the bees. The bees are in the orchard way out in front of the house."

We lift the handcar on the track. Little Edd hunkers down. He takes care of the .22 rifle and the .32 pistol. Big Aaron and I pull on one side— Ennis and Dave pulls on the other. The wheels grind against the rails. The cool wind hits our faces. We are off up the two streaks of rust—around the curves hard as we can go—into the Minton Tunnel—through it like a flash— out into the moonlight on the other side.

"Boy, I'd like to own a handcar," says Dave, "and just go places on it. I like a handcar. It's a lot better than walking over these old hills. I don't mind to free the bees when we can go like this. Come on and let's use more elbow grease."

"Just as you say," says Big Aaron. "everybody pull and let's travel."

"Ah, where you goin' on the Blue Goose?" a man hollers to us.

"Don't answer him," says Big Aaron. "Poeple over here go on this hand-car after the doctor. He thinks somebody is sick. Just keep pulling."

We don't answer.

"Pow. Pow. Pow. Pow." His gun barks at us. "Pow. Pow. Pow." The bullets wheeze all around us.

"Cut down on 'im Little Edd," says Big Aaron. "He's started this with us."

Little Edd empties the .32 pistol at him. We hear him run to the bushes screaming.

"You's nipping fer 'im Little Edd," says Dave. "Good work, boy. When they start this shooting with us we're ready."

Little Edd holds the rifle ready if he shoots again. I stop pulling the handcar to reload the pistol.

"I'll get 'im with this rifle if he tries that again," says Little Edd. "I'm a dead-eye Dick with a rifle."

Now we pull up to a switch and a big white house on our left.

"Right here," says Big Aaron. "Take it easy now, boys. Get the plugs, Dave, and let's go over and get the bees."

We walk over under the apple trees. We plug the stands. There is not a whisper. Every man knows his duty. He picks up a stand of bees. He carries them to the car.

"Three stands left," says Big Aaron. "Shan, you and Dave come with me to get them."

We walk back under the apple trees. We start to pick up the bees. The house dogs let out a yell. We grab the bees and run to the handcar. We put them on. Kenyon's door flies open. A man stands in the door—dressed in white. He turns an automatic shotgun loose at us. The bullets fall like rain. We crowd on the handcar. We start moving and Little Edd brings down a dog with the first crack of the rifle. He shoots at the other dog—he whines, yells and runs to the house. "Just skint him," says Little Edd. "I'll plug that door the fellar's just closed."

"Don't do it," says Big Aaron. "This is a gun country—more than the hollow we're from. Let's go down the track—pump the handcar even if it is down hill. Go faster than the Old Line Special's No. 8 ever pulled her passengers."

We turn the handcar loose. You can hear it a mile riding the two streaks of rust. "Pow. Pow. Pow." Somebody shoots from the bushes. Little Edd empties our .32 at the sound of the pistol. We keep moving. A bee stings me on the leg. One stings Big Aaron. They are stinging all of us. A plug is out of a hole or a bullet plugged a hole in one of the bee stands.

"We'll be there in a few minutes," says Big Aaron. "Just keep going until we get in front of Jackson's." Before we get to Jackson's I get nine bee stings under my pants leg. Big Aaron gets six, Dave five, Little Edd thirteen and Ennis don't get a sting. We pull down to Jackson's—put the brakes on—slide the car forty feet on the rusted rails.

"Off everybody," says Big Aaron. "See the bees coming out at the side of the bee gum. That fellar back yander put a hole through the bee gum with a .44. Glad it was the bee gum and not one of us. We are safe. We'll leave that stand here and take to the hills with the other seven."

"Dave, you can carry two, can't you?"

"Yes," says Dave. "I'm scared to leave that'n. Rope two together for me."

Dave takes two stands. Big Aaron takes two. The rest of us take one each. We go up the Jackson hill. We walk fast in the moonlight. We walk up the hollow, twist to our right until we come to the locust thicket. We put the bee stands solidly on the rocks—pull out the plugs and leave the bee city.

"Forty-nine stands now," says Big Aaron. "Just lost one stand. We'll never do nothing with them now. Let's run back to the handcar. We may be able to get the car back to Jake Reek's place. If it wasn't for all the bees on it we'd take a ride tonight on that car. I do love to ride it."

We run through the brush like a pack of fox hounds. We follow Big Aaron. He leaps the briars and brush and we leap them and go under the fences. We go back to the handcar. Big Aaron kicks the stand of bees off. There's not many bees in the stand. They are all over the handcar. We get on the handcar and start back up the track. We pull hard and fast through the tunnel—over to Jake Reek's place. The bees sting us. We do not care. We have the handcar back. We pull it from the railroad track—put it where it was—fix the chain and padlock back just like they were. We walk over the hills home and rub the places where the bees have stung us.

"It's all over now, boys," says Big Aaron, "for we have saved the bees. Any man that tells gets his tongue cut out by the roots. Now go to your homes. We won't meet at the cliff until all this trouble blows over. Now let's all play mouse and go to his own house."

"Shan," says Mom, "did you hear about somebody gettin' the handcar over at Jake Reek's place? Said there was a swarm of bees on it the next morning down around the cogs. Said when the men started to pull it, the bees nearly stung them to death. Said a lot of wild men had the car out riding it and shooting at men along the road. Shot Mel Spriggs in the leg. Said he hid in the brush and plugged one or two men as they come back. Went up the road and got all of Kenyon's bees. Said Mr. Kenyon pumped lead at 'em until he's black in the face. Said he really filled 'em with shot but they just kept going."

"Lord," I says, "what else is going to happen around here?"

"I'll tell you what's going to happen," says Pa. "We've got the thief. Enic Spradling was squirrel hunting around on the Jackson place the other day. He found forty-nine stands of bees. It tallies all but one stand. We've lost fifty stands. You wouldn't believe old Jackson would take all them bees, would you? Well, he has."

"Why he's a sick man," says Mom. "I heard he had the consumption."

"If he's got any consumption," says Pa, "it's the cornbread consumption. We can't get him on a bee thieving charge. The Government's got him. Got him for selling moonshine whisky too. W'y he's a bad man. Old Judge April-May-June (A.M.J.) Canter is going to put the cat on him. He'll be on the next soldier train that goes to Atlanter, Georgia. You're going to have to go over there and get our six stands of bees someway. Alec Roundtree is going to send Big Aaron after his. This has been a hard thing to believe. Old Lonesome just sit over there on the hill and acted like he didn't have a bit of life in him. Look what all he's done. Just turned out bad in the deestrict. Let this be a lesson."

"All right, Pa," I says. "I'll get Big Aaron. We'll go for the bees."

"Don't forget to look for Uncle Fonse Tillman's log chain and padlock either," says Pa.

"I won't," I says. "I think we'll be able to find it."

Mahalia "Big Haley" Mullins, probable prototype for Sylvania in the story "Sylvania Is Dead." The photograph was taken in Tennessee sometime about the turn of the century.

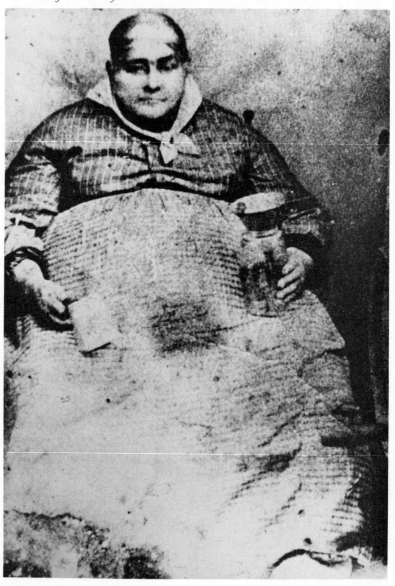

The Old People 🎋🎋🎋

Part 2

A Land beyond the River

About the story:

To state that the protagonist of Jesse Stuart's "A Land beyond the River," Big-Sandy Bill Frazier of the iron jaws and mullein-leaf-gray eyes, known by the epithetic jingle "Big-Sandy Bill who's never died and never will," is a descendant of that remarkable host of water dogs, riverboatmen, and rafters westering toward the trans-Mississippi in fulfillment of the Manifest Destiny of America is to state the obvious. Obvious, too, is his linkage with the likes of the archetypal riverman, Mike Fink, who knew the ways of the river as well as his enemies and handled both with equal dispatch.

Yet, "A Land beyond the River" was "a lived story and one told to the author." When Jesse Stuart was principal of McKell High School in the spring of 1936, a handsome blue-eyed blonde woman, whom he gave the name of Mary Frazier Jordan, dropped off her son and daughter and entered his office. Something was on her mind, there were tears in her eyes, and during the ensuing hour in his office she told him of her frustration in trying to write the story of her family, but she could not write it. The story involved the tragedies of marital infidelity and a double murder. "Mr. Stuart," she told him, "you can write the story yourself. If you sell it for money you can take all of it. I don't want money. I have all the money I need and want. I just want this story written and published like it happened."

He thought it was "a great story." She gave him the details and he took notes. When he asked about any possible family repercussion she said:

I don't care if there is. . . . But I don't think there will be for so many years have passed since my father killed Jim Hailey and brother Hilton was killed by Lester Shy. My dear brother, as fine-a-looking man as ever was born in Kentucky—big, tall, broad-shouldered, handsome—died at twenty-eight. My mother, now an old woman, was twenty-eight when my father killed Jim Hailey over her. Jim Hailey was only thirty-one. They were young people then with lovers' troubles. Young people, too, when brother Hilton was killed over his wife. I guess there will always be trouble of men getting killed over beautiful and attractive women. . . .

As Mrs. Jordan told the story, she continued to weep loudly.

I felt a little disturbed [at] having her crying aloud in my office when I was the only person in the office with her. Weepingly, she told me the story of her people, how they had lived on the Big Sandy and the Ohio Rivers all their days—more than a century. They had been pioneers on the Big Sandy and had lived there when "the gun was the law" and now on the Ohio River where guns were used but they were not the law. . . . The way she described the feelings she had when her father Big-Sandy Bill killed Jim Hailey over courting her mother—I couldn't forget. I was deeply stirred. I began to shed a few tears myself. . . . She had given me the story and it was my story now. She told me about seeing the blood on the floor and smelling the gunpowder when her father killed Big Jim Hailey and about smelling gunpowder and seeing blood when Lester Shy had killed her brother Hilton in his own home. . . .

It was a story of "river people," boat people, and "all were from well-to-do or wealthy people as compared to others around them. . . . And the ones I knew personally of Big-Sandy Bill's descendants were intelligent and handsome people who went to horseracing in Kentucky and Ohio, bet on horses, and as far away, in earlier years as Las Vegas to gamble." As she talked, Mrs. Jordan frequently interrupted herself to insist, "And, Mr. Stuart, you know we are a good family. We have pride. We live well. We're respected. We're intelligent. And we have integrity." He wanted to say, "Yes, Mrs. Jordan, but stories are lived by the people in top families as well as those on the lower rounds of the human totem pole. Stories are everywhere among all people who live, breathe, eat, drink, and propogate their species." He could have said this and more, but he remained sympathetically silent in order to get the facts down for fictional use.

That night he went home and began writing the story, taking time out to eat a delicious evening meal prepared by his landlady at Fullerton/South Shore, Mrs. Forrest (Lillian) King. He wrote on into the night and finished

the story about "four o'clock in the morning." The most significant change
he made was in point of view: "I let a son, Don, tell the story instead of
their daughter Mary.... I thought it would be more effective if a son told
it, then I wanted to disguise the story all I could and protect Mary should
the story be published and read by people in this area."

The following January, 1937, the story appeared in *Esquire*, and "in
early March ... all hell broke loose at home." One of the Frazier men, for-
merly a good friend of Jesse Stuart, wrote him a disturbing letter asking,
"Why had I resurrected old family tragedies that had lain dormant these
many years? Why did I blow breath into their nostrils to make them live
again? He also warned me against even stepping on any of the property his
family owned." Mrs. Jordan "looked sadly at me but never said anything."
Copies of *Esquire* sold out and newsstands ordered more. The story became
"the talk of the community." Amateur historians commended him on his
accuracy, though daily he tried to escape involvement. One man, "in love
with Hilda Thombs, Hilton Frazier's widow" and vengeful toward the
proud Frazier family, smilingly informed the author he had bought fifty
copies of *Esquire* to distribute "to people who count," for, he declared, "I
want to wreck that overbearing Frazier family."

Only when the school year ended and Jesse Stuart left for a year abroad
on a Guggenheim Fellowship could he clear his mind of the story. "I had
never had one of my stories to cause so much trouble and talk.... I longed
for peace again. I found it three thousand miles from home."*

* * *

M Y POP was the best water dog that ever rode a raft of logs from
the Levisa Fork down the Big Sandy. He was the captain
of a crew of water dogs. He got the job because he could holler the loudest,
and shoot the straightest. Pop was a big man with iron jaws and mullein-
leaf-gray eyes. His hair was the color of a yellow-clay clod. His arms were
big and where the sleeves were torn out of his shirt his big muscles rippled
up like where wind bends down the grass in the yard and when the wind
passes over it the grass comes up again. Pop was the strongest man on the
Big Sandy. People called him Big-Sandy Bill. Nobody along the Big Sandy
would call him a water dog and get by with it either. He shot at them till
they got out of sight. If they shot back at him from the woods he'd just

---

*"A Land beyond the River" was first published in *Esquire*, Vol. 7 (Jan., 1937), pp. 36–37,
166, 168, 171–172, 174, 176, reprinted in *Plowshare in Heaven* (N.Y.: McGraw-Hill, 1958), pp.
36–60, and in *Come Gentle Spring* (N.Y.: McGraw-Hill, 1969), pp. 143–163. The quotations are
from Jesse Stuart's unpublished manuscript, "A Land beyond the River, by Jesse Stuart," in
the Jesse Stuart Collection, W-Hollow, Greenup, Kentucky.

stretch out on the raft of logs and answer them long as he had a shell. And Pop always kept plenty of them.

I can see Pop now going down the Big Sandy on a raft of logs—a long train of rafts. I can see Pop standing there waving his hand from the front raft showing the boys the way to dodge the shoals and follow the current— great trains of logs—pine, poplars, oaks, beech, ash, maple, chestnut—great mountains of timber in them days on the Big Sandy and God knows it was the roughest place in Kentucky. Everybody carried a gun. Pop made all his men on the river carry a gun. They couldn't get a job unless they had a gun and a pole with a spike in the end of it. They had to be men who could jump from log to log like squirrels—good swimmers, too, or they'd better stay off the Big Sandy. It's filled with swirl holes and shoals and mean currents that twist log trains into the banks and then you have to wait forever to get a flood to clean the log jams up—a flood in March or April—sometime in the spring. No man that worked on the Big Sandy that had any raising would ride a raft of logs and let a fellow call him a water dog. Pop give his men orders to shoot the first man down in cold blood that called them water dogs.

God, but them was awful days on the Big Sandy. A lot of people didn't like Pop. One day when Pop and his crowd was passing through Evans—a little town on the Big Sandy—some fellow called Pop a water dog and he swum to the bank, went up in the town, and run the fellow around the square pouring the hot lead at him. Pop would a killed him but the Law come down and told Pop to get back on the Big Sandy where he belonged.

I remember how we used to hear about Uncle John Hampton and them old men that lived on the river till their hair got white. I remember how we used to hear how they'd shoot a man every now and then and they wouldn't try them for the killings. These fellers would come out and mess with the river men. They didn't like the water dogs. Pop was a water dog and Pop wasn't afraid of the devil. He'd come home and take his guns off his belt and have Mom to fix him a bite to eat and then he'd go right back to the river. Pop loved the Big Sandy as every man that lives on that river loves it. Pop was known from the Levisa Fork to the Gate City down on the Ohio River where the Big Sandy gives up her logs to a bigger river. Everybody called Pop "Big-Sandy Bill who's never died and never will."

Every spring Pop would stay away from Mom. It would be in the rainy season when the logs would have to be floated down the Big Sandy. Pop would never get to come home and stay with us. We'd watch the river day and night for Pop. He had a fox horn he'd blow when he's coming down the Big Sandy and Mom would have a basket of fine grub waiting for Pop about the time he'd come down the Big Sandy. We'd run down to the river and Hilton would take it out to Pop in a john-boat. And Mom would write Pop a letter and have it in the basket. That's all she'd get to say to Pop was what she could say in that letter. Pop would take the basket and grab the letter before he would the cake and fried chicken. His big hand would grab the little letter. He would read it and tears would come to his eyes. Then he would turn and start cussing at the men and tell them to watch the train of rafts—for a mile up the river or more. Pop would read the letter. Then he and his men would eat the chicken and cake. They would walk the raft of logs up to Pop, one at a time while the others watched the rafts. They were afraid to leave the rafts. It was easy to ground a raft of logs on the Big Sandy—river so crooked flowing around the mountains like a blacksnake in a briar patch.

I remember when my sisters, Clara and Grace, and I—we used to stand out on the bank of the Big Sandy and watch the big rafts go down. We'd watch to see if the raft belonged to Pop—if it was Pop or any of Pop's men. We could see the blue water from the house for we lived right upon the bank on the Kentucky side. We lived under a patch of big oaks and my brother Hilton kept his fishing poles hooked under the oak roots right in the yard. He kept his nets further down on the river. He fished from a split-bottom chair in the front yard. We'd lived in this house all of our lives and Pop said his pop had lived here all his life and raised him and his sisters and brothers here and his pop's pop on before his own pop had come from old Virginia and raised his family here. Our house sagged a little in the middle, but it wasn't the house so much we loved as it was the Big Sandy! We fished in its waters. Pop rafted logs on its back. We went riding on it in our john-boats. To us the Big Sandy was a brother and he was a bad brother at times especially in the spring after the mountain rains. I used to read in my old primary geography about the Don River in a far-off land called Russia and I always thought the Big Sandy in my country was something like the Don River in Russia. The Don River had its Cossacks that rode horses and fought; the Big Sandy had its mountaineers that rafted the logs and fought one another. Big men and tall men with sun-tanned hard iron faces and heads of shaggy hair that never was covered with a hat. And I saw mountains in a far-off land in Italy that come down to the blue waters—high rugged hills covered with trees—that looked something like the mountains that come down to the Big Sandy on the West Virginia side; on the Kentucky side there were fields of corn back on the mountain slopes and in the narrow valley. It was a pretty country. We loved the mountains and the Big Sandy.

Jim Hailey ran the next biggest raft train on the Big Sandy—the next biggest to Pop's. He worked as many men as Pop. He had nine men. Pop and Pop's men didn't like Big-Sandy Jim and his water dogs. They would pass Pop and his men when they was coming down Big Sandy with a raft of logs and Pop and his water dogs would be going back. They wouldn't call Pop anything but they didn't speak. Big-Sandy Jim would just grin at Pop. All Big-Sandy Jim's men would just grin at Pop and Pop's men and keep their hands on their pistols. Big-Sandy Jim's horses always beat Pop's horses at the Evans races every spring, too. Pop bet last spring and lost all he'd made on the river. Pop's not afraid to bet even on a horse he's not sure of. He would say: "I'll take his damn bet. It's a good one even if I lose from that low-down river rat. The Big Sandy River is disgraced to have a thing riding its back like Big Jim Hailey. If ever I get a chance—something he's got agin me—" Then Pop would cool down and smoke his pipe and twist his hands on his knees.

One night in April I saw a light hanging out in our yard. Mom slept in the room next to the river downstairs. She slept there alone. Hilton and I slept in the north room across the hall from the girls upstairs and they slept in the south room just across the upper dog-trot. I got out of bed and run down and told Mom there was a light on our back porch. I run down the stairs and I broke into Mom's room. She was up in bed. She was wide awake.

I said, "Mom, there is a light on the porch. What's it doing there?"

Mom said: "Go on back upstairs and tend to your own business. I had to draw a bucket of water from the well. I lit the lantern and I forgot to blow it out."

Mom got out of bed and walked out on the porch. Mom hooked the bale from off the nail, lifted the half-smoked globe, and blew out the quivering blaze. She walked back in the house, and it was light enough until I could see her. She went back to bed, pulled up the cover. I could not understand. There was light enough in a quarter-moon for Mom to go to the well and get a bucket of water. The girls and Brother Hilton never did wake up.

I told them about it the next morning and Hilton said, "W'y, you've been dreaming, Don. Never was a light on that porch. I was awake a long time last night. I looked out at the West Virginia mountains; I saw them in moonlight. I looked at the river and thought of all the times I'd swum it and of all the pike I'd caught from it and the jack salmon. I just laid there last night and listened to that old river flowing—the moan of the water and the wind in its willow banks. I thought of Pop, wondered where he was on this old river with a raft train of big logs. . . . That's what I want to do some day: I want to follow the river like Pop only I want to run a boat on the Big Sandy and let the whistle do my hollering. . . . Don, I was awake far into the night last night, dreaming, dreaming but with my eyes open. That's a fact, Don. I never saw a light."

And then I thought: "I could not be dreaming. I went downstairs. I remember stepping on the steps. I remember the broken step with the knothole in it. I remember it sagged with my weight. I remember hearing the wind out there in the oak tops. I remember how the light scared me. And I remember going in Mom's room. I remember the words she said to me. That she had used the lantern going to the well and forgot to blow it out. And how she told me to get back to bed. I remember Mom getting up in her nightgown. I remember how pretty Mom looked to me when I went back up the stairs. When she went out and got the lantern she looked so tall and straight. Her hair—pretty and golden as corn silks in an August wind—was loose down her back. Her eyes, big and blue, flashed in the lantern light. I remember. I surely was not dreaming."

And the next night I thought I saw the light again and I was too sleepy to go downstairs and see. I just don't remember. I thought I was going; maybe I went to sleep dreaming I was going down to see about the light. And maybe I just dreamed about the lantern the night before. No one can remember a dream not knowing it was a dream. But I remember the night and the stars, night around the house and the stars over the Big Sandy. I thought about Pop and wondered where he was on the river. Pop traveled nearly two hundred miles on the Big Sandy with the log rafts.

Grace and I were out in the swing on the oak tree in the front yard that day when we saw Pop and his men pulling up Big Sandy in a john-boat. They had gone down the river to Gate City with a raft train of logs. I would swing Grace awhile and she would swing me from a split-pole swing that was fastened with a horseshoe to a limb in the oak tree. We could swing out over the river and look down on the Big Sandy. Our house faces the Big Sandy River. All the houses face the river instead of the road. All the houses on the West Virginia side of the Big Sandy face the river instead of the road. We face one another. And when I swung out over the river and saw Pop coming up the river I told Grace to catch the swing and hold it. She held the swing and I run into the house and told Mom, "Mom, Pop is coming. Pop and his men are coming up the river."

Mom run out in the yard. Pop was the first to get out of the big john-boat and tie it to a willow.

He said, "Get out, you fellers, and we'll shade awhile and eat before we mosey on up the river."

Pop led the way up the bank. His beard was out long on his cheeks and chin. His hair fell down on his shoulder, hair the color of a dry yellow-clay clod in August. I wouldn't tell Mom but I thought Big-Sandy Jim Hailey looked better than Pop. He did go shaved. He had a clean face. He wasn't a big man like Pop and he wasn't near as hairy as Pop and didn't look as mean as Pop. Pop's men all looked mean. All had hairy faces like Pop: just a hole in the hair on their face for their mouths that worked when they talked and their eyes flashed blue, black, and gray under heavy ledges of hair. They had big pistols belted around them and they walked up our bank to the house like they owned the Big Sandy.

Pop grabbed Mom and kissed her.

Mom said, "Ah, them old beards, Bill. They don't become you one bit. You look awful in them."

And Pop said, "Honey, they ain't no razors out there on the Big Sandy when a feller has to live for three and four days on a log train. Has to sleep on a raft—catch a wink when he can and when the Big Boy's mad can't catch a wink of sleep. That's what's happened now. Had rain on the head o' Big Sandy and the river is just a-foaming like a mad bull."

And Mom said, "I didn't get the basket to you as you went down. Didn't hear the horn and I'm so sorry, Bill—I had chicken aplenty for you and the men."

And Pop said, "And we missed the chicken too. I thought I saw a light on the porch. That was Thursday night. And I wondered what it was doing there. I thought maybe it might be Hilton that had come from his nets and then I knowed he's got eyes good as a crow's eyes, and I just wondered about that light."

And Mom said, "I don't know anything about a light on that night."

And then I thought: "Well, maybe I was not dreaming. Maybe I did see the light. I dreamed it or saw it, one of the two."

And Pop said, "We saw a light here, didn't we, boys?"

And the men—all nine of them squatted around over the green grassy yard—said: "Yep, we saw a light."

Mom never said another word and Pop said, "Honey, fix us a bite to eat and we'll be getting on up the river. Another big train of logs waiting to be rolled in. Got to get them to the Ohio by Sunday."

I can see Mom, Clara, and Grace yet. They went into the kitchen, put a fire in the stove. They put on every pot. It took grub for ten river men where they'd been eating cold grub on the river. The table looked like it would feed twenty-five men. I remember the steam from the chicken and dumplings. I remember the white chicken dumplings going in at their hairy months. I remember how they'd never ask for anything but just reach over the table and if they couldn't reach a thing one would say, "Damn it, Zack, can't you give a body a lift to the dumplings? Can you hand over the beans there? What the hell do you think this is, your birthday?" And they just went on like this and Pop would say, "By God, boys, not so goddam-much cussing around over my grub."

And Mom and Grace would just get out of the dining room and let them have it. They'd clean every plate and sop them out. They'd come out with eggs in their whiskers and gravy all over their vests, picking their teeth with goose quills they carried for that purpose, and they'd light up a long green cigar apiece and pat their stomachs and stretch and make it back for the boat. And we'd see them far up the river. We'd see Pop wave good-by to Mom.

It seemed like Pop just come and went and Mom went about the place hunting for Pop. And the days just come and went—spring on the Big Sandy when the trees leafed along its rippling blue waters—and then the rains and the muddy waters and then blue waters again with mountains that come down, mountains of quivering green clouds of leaves. Then would come a dry season when white clouds would float in the West Virginia and Kentucky skies and the water would get low and a raft of logs would run on a shoal. Water would get low and the river bottoms would look white in the sun. Mare-tails would float in the sky. Pop would wipe his sweating brow and say: "Mare-tails in the sky. Sign of rain in three days." Butterflies would flit along the Big Sandy and water moccasins would sleep along the banks on a log and just plump in the water when they saw the raft coming. Turtles wouldn't move—there were so many of them. And they had been in the Big Sandy so long and knew as much about the river as the men and the snakes.

Another night and I dreamed I saw, or went to sleep dreaming I saw, a light downstairs and a man get out and come up the bank. I dreamed that it was Pop. I just don't remember. But I thought this or I dreamed this: "Now the other time I didn't go down. I don't know whether it was a light or whether I just dreamed it. Tonight I'm going down and see."

But I didn't go down and see. I must have just dreamed it was Pop back to see Mom but he hadn't been gone up the river but three days. He didn't have time to be back.

I told Hilton about it and Hilton told Mom the next day.

And Hilton said, "Don, you must be having nightmares. I never saw a thing and I just sleep right across the room from you."

But it seemed to me like there was something. I just felt it. Something bothered me. It was something very strange. I thought of Pop on the water.

I wondered where Pop was and if he'd shoot at anybody for calling him a water dog. I just know Pop would kill a man and do it quick. We don't know but we heard once Pop and a feller quarreled over a bottle of licker and they agreed to shoot it out. So they turned their backs, each one holding a pistol of the same kind with the same number of cartridges in it, and they walked so many steps apiece—ten, I believe—and turned and started shooting. Pop got the feller. That was when Pop was a young man, though. Pop's got a big scar on his wrist. We heard there was where he got it. He never told us. We don't know.

When Pop come down the river with the next train of logs and blew his horn it was on a pretty day—sun high in the sky—and Mom just piled in all the grub she had cooked in a basket that she always kept waiting for Pop and the men about the time for them to get back. And Hilton took the basket out in the john-boat. He brought a letter back to Mom. And Pop said in the letter: "Elizabeth, when I was going up the river old Jim Hailey was coming down with a train of logs. He was on the front raft with a white shirt on. He was all dressed up and on the river. And when he passed me he just looked at me and laughed and laughed and the men all laughed and looked at me. I'm not for taking such foolishness. I thought once I'd tell my men to fire on them after I'd bumped Jim off for the signal to start. I thought I'd redden this river to the mouth with their blood. I don't know why he's got the laugh on me. You know the only laugh us river men have on one another is when we get the other man's money playing poker, outshoot or outholler the other feller, or take the other man's wife. This is something Big Jim ain't done to me, can't do to me, and never will do to me long as my pistol will bark." I found the letter in Mom's room. I read it.

Pop and Big Jim both were down the river now. Big Jim had been down the river five days. He'd had time to get to Gate City with his log train. Pop had just passed. He would be down the river at least a week. The next day we saw Big Jim at the head of his big john-boat with a white shirt on and he looked toward the house. Mom was not in the yard. We didn't wave at him. We had been taught to hate Jim Hailey from the day Pop could tell us a word about him. He's getting mighty friendly to us. Pop ought to have been here when he waved. Pop would have killed him like he would shoot a rabbit.

It was five days before Pop got back up the river and we told him Jim Hailey passed and waved at us.

Pop said, "He's getting too smart of his pants. That lowdown vile water rat!"

Pop said to Mom, "Fix us a basket of grub and we'll take it to the boat.

We'll mosey on up the river. We don't have time to stop long. A train of logs is waiting us up on the Levisa Fork."

Mom and Grace fixed a big basket of grub. Two of Pop's big hairy men took it down to the boat. The rest of the crowd followed. I remember seeing them grabbing into the basket as they pulled away up the Big Sandy; I remember seeing the boat dip and swerve as they hogged into the basket.

Eleven more days and I remember. It was night and a full moon was up. Was I dreaming when I heard a shot fired? I heard a scream! It was not the wind among the oaks this time, the wind that blows from the Big Sandy. It was gunpowder. I smelled it. Hilton and I jumped out of our beds. The girls rolled out on the other side the dog-trot. I heard them.

"Who was that that shot?" hollered Hilton, and we run downstairs.

"You low-down vile skunk of a water rat, may God send your soul to hell—trying to break up my home," said Pop and he kicked a man lying on the floor bleeding and he held Mom's hand. "Goddam you and your kind—roast in hell, damn you—and you, Elizabeth, what do you mean! That's what the lantern's been hanging out for and what this sonofabitch has been doing wearing a white shirt on the river! Stopping to see my wife. . . . You children, get back up them stairs, every last one of you! . . . No man that is true river man on the Big Sandy can wear a white shirt and go clean-shaved on a log train—that's why you done it, you lousy river rat. I'd throw you in the river but you are not worthy to pollute the water with blood of your kind!"

Pop was standing over a man on the floor. I could see from the stairs the gun Pop was holding and the blue smoke leaving the barrel.

"Don't shoot Mom!" said Clara, screaming.

"Oh, I fooled you," said Pop to Mom. "I've been smelling this rat ever since he laughed at me when we passed on the river. I just went up to Evans with the boys. I sent them on. I slipped back and waited for the lantern. I saw the boat let a man out. I saw them anchor a boat that they ran in from the log train—ah, yes—and that's why the lantern has been out—a signal that I am not here. I happened to be here tonight! And you, damn you—"

And Pop kicked the man on the floor—kicked him over, and he kind of drew up one of his legs like a swimming frog, moaned, and his head fell over on the floor. His breath sizzled and he lay there perfectly still. We could see the white shirt and the blood down the front. We didn't go all the way up the stairs. Mom there holding to Pop and crying, just bawling on his shoulder, and all us children crying like we'd take fits. All scared to death, too. Lord, that smell of gunpowder and smoke! And Pop there—the big bearded iron-faced man that he was—his shirt torn, his hairy body in the light of the lantern and the moon that hung above the river! Lord, what an awful time it was.

Hilton got on the mule and rode for Sheriff Lakin to come and get the dead man out of the house. Pop told him to. He held Mom in his arms.

"For one cent," Pop said, "I ought to blow out your brains for being with Jim Hailey. Jim Hailey! My God, Jim Hailey with my wife—well, he'll never be any more."

We went upstairs and went to bed. Mom and Pop stood together by the dead man on the floor. Blood had run a big stream and dripped through a knothole in the floor. Mom was holding to Pop and crying, "Bill, spare my life for my children. I'll never do this again. I didn't love Jim Hailey—I love you—you was gone so much. You was always on that river. You never stay with me. You leave me. A woman can't be left so long as you leave me." And Mom sagged to the floor crying, almost into spasms.

Sheriff Lakin came. He put Big-Sandy Jim Hailey in the express, took Pop to Evans, and Uncle Jake went Pop's bond. Pop had to appear in one of the biggest murder trials that there ever was on Big Sandy. People talked about us. They talked about my mother.

When I would go to school the children would say "Don's mother had a man killed over her. She ain't no good, for my mommie said Don's mother wasn't no good." And the children wouldn't play with Clara, and Grace either. The big boys would say things to Hilton at school and he would fight. They would talk about Mom.

Mom never left the house. She never went to see a neighbor. She would sit out under the oaks and smoke her pipe, her blue eyes gazing steadily at the waters that flowed forever past our door—through drought and freeze, summer, winter, autumn, and spring. The waters of the Big Sandy kept flowing on and on and boats passed and big rafts of logs in the spring and corn in the fall went down by barge loads to the mills at Gate City. Mom would talk to herself and look at the river.

Pop went back to work on the river. Pop went back to the log trains. He kept two guns on him now. Once Pop was shot at from the bushes and the bullet hit Tim Zorns in the arm after it had gone through a bunch of men and just glanced off Pop's spike pole. It left its mark right in front of Pop's heart. And word was sent to Mom: "We are going to kill old Big-Sandy Bill—he ain't died yet but we guess he will."

They took us to the trial for witnesses. They asked me to tell about the light. And I told them I didn't know whether I'd dreamed it or whether I saw a light. But it was one of the two. The whole house was crowded with people and Pop's men that worked on the log train with him was right there with their hands on their guns waiting for Big Jim's men to start something. They were all there and the Law was there but the Law would a had a time if one shot had been fired.

Mom told that she didn't love Big Jim and he didn't love her, that she had told him to get away and stay away and he wouldn't do it. And that he come there that night with a gun and said if Pop ever come while he's around there he'd kill Pop. So Pop beat him to the draw.

And somebody said in the back of the house, "That woman ought to go to a limb. Having men killed over her."

And the tears come into Mom's eyes. She just sat there and waited for the lawyers to ask her questions. And they asked her a God's plenty. They asked her how many times Big Jim had come to see her. And a lot of stuff like that. And Pop just sat there mad as a hornet. He looked like the very devil was in him.

The jury was out awhile—about an hour, I guess—and when they come in the foreman of the jury said, "Murder in self-defense." Pop come clean of the charge.

There was all kinds of cussing around the courthouse. And one fellow says to Pop, "See that sign up there on the courthouse? Reads 'God is not mocked. Whatsoever a man soweth that shall he also reap.' And you, Big-Sandy Bill, will reap a bullet in your own heart. Kill a man over your vile wife. Oh, we are going to get you. I am a Hailey. I have not washed my hands with you yet. I am a second cousin to the man you murdered. There are many of us left yet."

And Pop said, "Bring on all your damned Haileys. There are many Fraziers yet in these mountains. Bring 'em on and shut up—bring 'em on and be damned. I love my wife. Or I would have killed her right there! I would kill another man over her."

Pop walked out down the road to the wagon. Mom never lifted her head out in the crowd. They were all looking at her.

When I would go to school the children would not play with me. They would whisper to each other about me. I would go home and go upstairs to my room and cry and cry. I couldn't help it. They would talk about my mother, and I would hear them say at school, "I'll bet Charlie Hailey gets Big-Sandy Bill. He's a-laying for him. He's going to kill him. He's gone longer now on Big Sandy than any other man has ever gone to kill a good man over a woman. Big Jim Hailey's men must not have anything to them to let him be killed like this and then not do anything about it."

I would hear all this. And to think Pop was back on the Big Sandy! I would think this: "I can see Pop. He is on the floor. He, too, has on a white shirt. He is bleeding at the heart. A stream of blood runs from his heart to a knothole in the floor. It runs down the knothole. Pop works his leg like a frog that's swimming. He turns on his back. He moans. His last breath sizzles. He is dead. Pop is dead. Pop, a mountain of a man, one unafraid of men and the river, but Pop is dead. A bullet went into Pop's heart from the dark. His heart was easy for a bullet as any man's heart. Now Pop is no more than a dry clod of yellow clay in August. Pop is dead."

Mom would turn the coffee cup in the morning after she had drunk her coffee. She would say, "I see the river; I always seé the river. I can see a dead man floating down the river." Then Mom would scream. She would get up and go out in the yard. She would sit down in the chair where Hilton sits and fishes. She would sit there and look at the river. It was the valley where we had lived for more than a hundred years, ever since the first white settlers had come to the valley. Now we would have to leave the valley—not that we were afraid to die—we would have to leave. Mom would have to leave. When a woman in the hills meets another man, she and her girls for generations are doomed. We would have to go to a new river.

Pop stopped the john-boat at the willows. He got out and threw the chain around a willow root. He walked up the bank holding to the oak roots to pull his heavy body up the bank. Mom was out in the chair under the oak trees.

Pop said, "Timber is growing scarcer in these mountains than ever before. Things just don't work like they used to. I got the whole river to myself now and I don't want it. Big Jim is gone and God be thanked for the riddance. But we are going to have to leave this river for a new river. Hilton cannot do any good on this river because he is your son. No one will ride his boat. Grace and Clara will have a hard time marrying a respectable man because they are your daughters. We'll have to go to a new river. Let's pack on a barge all the things we have and pass through Gate City and go down the big Ohio and land where there are hills on the Kentucky side. We must have hills coming down to the edge of the blue waters. We will be lost without the hills."

I remember packing things that afternoon and putting them on the barge. We took all we had and put on the barge. Pop's men helped us load. Big hairy men would carry big loads down the bank. They would sweat and work, their guns in their belts. We got all our belongings and left down the Big Sandy—not anything to pull the barge. It floated down the river that we had known all our lives—the river that had carried Pop so much up and down on its blue bosom—sheltered by the tall mountains and the green timbered slopes, the high jagged cliffs near the tops of the mountains where the mountains shouldered to the skies.

We looked back to our house on the bank. The sun was on the other side of it. We could see the oak trees and the swing between us and the sun. We could see the willows and the well gum and the barn. We could see the sun moving down over the green hills we had seen so many times.

And Pop looked back and said, "Well, old river, it's good-by." Pop steered the boat—it floated along. And Pop would say, "I know this river like a scholar knows a book. I know every shoal in it and almost every snag. It is like a person to me. I know even how its heart beats. I've been over it since I was seven years old. And I've started down the other side of the hill."

Mom would say, "I hate to leave this river. I've loved it all my days. Lived on it since I was a little girl. All my people lived on it in these mountains. I was born here, raised here, and I've never been any place else in my life. I learned to swim in this river. I first dived in this water. Lost a comb from my hair and I jumped down after it. I got it, too. But now we leave."

And Mom looked at the water, blue rippling in the sunlight, water pretty and flecked with little whitecaps. We moved down the river. Night came and a pretty moon and we kept floating, floating to the new river.

The next morning we passed through Gate City and onto a broad river of blue rippling water. One man stood on the bank at Gate City and I heard him say to another man, "Look at them Big Sandians, won't you, on that barge. Going down the river like a lot of them here lately to find a pot of gold."

We floated down the Ohio all that day and till a moon came up that night. The moon was up in the sky. And Pop said, "Must twist her in to the bank and wait for morning. Here is where we stop. I have been here and found this place. I come on down here after I brought the last log train down the Big Sandy. See these mountains on the Kentucky side. Over there is a town in Ohio. It is Radnor. We can boat between Lowder, Kentucky, and Radnor, Ohio. A lot of Kentuckians work over there in town and they must cross the river."

We moved from the barge to a house overlooking the Ohio. It was a pretty house with maple trees in the yard. There are no mountains in Ohio. We could see the town. Pop started to build a boat. He called it the *Hilton Frazier* for my brother Hilton. He would start it to making trips across the river. My brother Hilton would pilot the *Hilton Frazier*. He was learning to be a pilot now at a boat down the river between Anderson, Ohio, and Vanlear, Kentucky. He was working without pay. He didn't get to fish in the river and swim like he used to when he was free as the wind on the Big Sandy. Now he was a water dog. He had followed our people, the Fraziers.

Mom would turn the coffee cup and she would say, "No women here to talk. I cannot see the Big Sandy in this coffee cup. I see a wider river. I see more money. I see my daughters married to steamboat captains and boat-owners. Life looks so much better now."

And then she would go out under the maple tree and watch the boats pass with barges on the Ohio. Great loads of coal and sand and steel. But Mom would look for logs. We never saw the log trains on the Ohio we saw on the Big Sandy and we never saw the men with guns around their belts we'd seen back in the mountains. And the man that got to run a crew of men didn't get his job by being able to holler the loudest either. He got it when the old got too old to do the job if he was of blood kin and next in line. That's the way it works on the Ohio.

Pop built the boat. Pop saved some money on the Big Sandy. "A Frazier is never without money," people would say on Big Sandy. "Them Scotch-men can live on a rock."

Pop said, "Now, this boat will break us or make us. It just depends on how the town on the other side of the Ohio grows. If it does much growing we'll not be able to handle this business in a few years."

First the steel mills came to Radnor, Ohio. Then the shoe factories came. Kentuckians went over the river to work. The days passed and the gold poured into our hands. When a man paid his fare in pennies to brother Hilton, he would throw the pennies in the Ohio right in front of their eyes. Brother Hilton grew to be big like Pop and he was a pilot first and then captain of the *Hilton Frazier*. Pop made a new and bigger boat and we ran two boats across the river.

The years passed. The days passed into months and the months into years. We grew to be men and women. We learned to love the Ohio as Pop loved the Big Sandy. Pop never went back to the Big Sandy. He would say, "Elizabeth, we'll live here together until we die on this river. They can take us back to the Big Sandy and bury us in the old churchyard where we was borned and raised."

When Pop got on the Ohio River he shaved the whiskers off his face. Pop didn't look like he used to look upon Big Sandy. We remember how he worked there. He worked yet. He would swim to the middle of the Ohio River and catch a boat that had broken loose somewhere upon the river. Pop was still a water dog. Gray hair on his head didn't matter. He worked and told the men what to do. Money come in and plenty of it.

Pop built another boat with a dance hall on it—a fancy boat—and called it the *Elizabeth Frazier*. And Brother Hilton piloted it up the Big Sandy with the calliope playing. He stopped at Gate City and gave a big dance. Had his old-time band right on the boat. No one remembered Elizabeth Frazier. They remembered Big-Sandy Bill Frazier that shot Big Jim Hailey. But a young man in a blue suit with a cap, white cuffs, a black tie, and bright buttons on his suit took the boat up Big Sandy. He went right up Big Sandy with the music, stopping at every town for a dance. He went right in with the music playing "My Old Kentucky Home." People shed tears to see the big boat and to know this nice-looking captain was old Big-Sandy Bill's boy that left the river years ago over killing a man over his wife. People danced on the boat and had a good time. Horses scared at it and broke the tongues out of the wagons. And children ran from the banks of the river afraid of the big boat. People would say, "Big-Sandy Bill's boy, Hilton Frazier, captain of that boat. They say Big-Sandy Bill's made money like dirt since he left here. Made barrels of money and got rich down on the Ohio. Had a bad wife, though. Remember that trial? It's been about twelve years ago—you remember, don't you?"

While brother Hilton was up to the Levisa Fork—the only man to ever put a boat that far up the Big Sandy and the biggest boat that ever plowed the waters of the Big Sandy—a big rain fell and the water raised. It got so high the smokestack on the boat couldn't go under the new bridge that spanned the river right above Evans, Kentucky. Brother Hilton had to lay up twenty-four hours. The Government paid him three hundred dollars. He told the people that spread over the Big Sandy River valley, "W'y, Hilton Frazier is a big enough man that when his big boat is delayed the Government pays him." And the Big-Sandians went on the boat and talked to Hilton and asked about old Big-Sandy Bill Frazier when the boat stopped at the town and the calliope played "Old Kentucky Home."

At home Mom turned the coffee cup after she finished drinking her cup of coffee. And she said, "I can see Hilton. Hilton is dead. Hilton married. Hilton, dead. My first son! I can see the gun. I can see it spitting smoke." And Mom screamed. She said, "I tell you when you sow the seeds of life you reap the seeds of life. When you sow the seeds of death, you reap the seeds of death. Things come home to you on this earth. There is not any getting around it. I'll reap what I sowed on Big Sandy. There is not any escape. I can see it here. I know it is coming regardless of the money we have and the three boats we have."

Hilton told Mom, "Mom, I am going to marry Hilda Thombs. Her people are river people. They've been on the Ohio for three generations. Her grandpa used to run the old Grey Steamer here fifty years ago. I love her. I make the money. I am going to marry her."

Hilton did marry Hilda Thombs. She was a pretty girl. She looked like Mom used to look. She was every bit as pretty as Mom. And when Hilton married her, he started running a boat from Hardin, West Virginia, to Cincinnati, Ohio. It was bigger money for brother Hilton. He ran the *Elizabeth Frazier*—one of the big passenger and freight boats—on the Ohio. We would be out and wave when he passed. He would always whistle and whistle for home. Mom was proud of her boat and Hilton running it on the Ohio.

Old Jink Hammonds tipped Brother Hilton off: "Hilton, do you leave a light hanging on your porch on every Thursday night? Is that a signal you leave?"

One night, I remember, Mom had read the coffee cup that night and she said: "I see a dead man. I see him bleeding. It is Hilton."

And Grace said: "Mom, you think too much of Big Sandy. That is over. Forget about it. Coffee grounds are coffee grounds. They don't mean a thing."

Hilda and Hilton just lived a stone-throw from us. Mom said, "The other night I saw a lantern swinging at Hilton's house. If I did not I was dreaming. It looked to me like a lantern."

The boat whistle never moaned this night on the river. It always whistled before. Hilton slipped to the house.

There was a lantern on the porch. Lester Shy, captain of the *Little Ann*, beat Brother Hilton to the draw. Mom heard the shot. She screamed. She jumped out of the bed.

"I told you," said Mom, "Hilton is dead. Hilton has been killed."

We jumped out of our beds. We ran over to Hilton's house. Hilton was on the floor. Blood was spurting from his heart onto the floor.

Pop was along. "Oh, my God," said Pop. "Oh, God—I remember."

Mom was screaming. "You will reap what you sow," said Mom. "I was twenty-eight when this happened on Big Sandy. Hilton is twenty-eight."

Mom fell to the floor screaming. She had her hand in the little stream of blood running from Hilton's heart. Lester Shy had gone.

"He'll be brought to justice," said Pop, "Big Sandy justice where each man is his own law. I'll bring him to justice. I still can shoot."

"No, you won't," said Mom. "We have just reaped what we sowed. I've thought this was coming all the time. I have expected it. You'll lay your gun down. You'll not shoot any more. Enough has been done already without any more killings and heartaches in a world where you and I are growing old. We are growing out of the world. It is not leaving us. We are leaving it."

Hilda was down beside of Hilton. She was screaming, "I have caused it all. It has been my fault. Hilton has been away so much. God knows a man on the river is never with his wife. If I'd been on the boat with Hilton." And she would scream.

And Mom took her by the shoulder and said: "Take it easier than that, Hilda. No use to cry now. It is all over. I believe I understand."

I could smell the gunpowder. It smelled like it did that night on Big Sandy, the night I was a lot younger than I am now. I remember the stream of blood that night and how Big Jim moved his leg up like a frog. I saw brother Hilton do the same thing. I wonder why a man shot through the heart always does it. Grace and Clara just having one fit after another over the death of Hilton; they, too, heard his last breath go like a sizzle of wind, and he fell limp. His whole huge body relaxed and would be relaxed for-ever—Hilton, so much like Pop, his hairy arms, his color of a clay-clod hair, his big body stretched on his own floor in death and the killer gone free to kill again.

The *Elizabeth Frazier* did not make its regular trip on the river. It hauled the clay of its young Captain Hilton Frazier up the Ohio and through Gate City. Pop was piloting the boat. Pop can take a boat anyplace. A flag was floating at half-mast from the boat. We passed through Gate City and onto the waters of the Big Sandy.

"I used to know every snag in this river," said Pop, "but I guess it's changed as my hair has changed in the years I have been away. It seems like home to me, this little river where it takes more work to make money, more skill to pilot a boat."

Mom never spoke. Her eyes were swollen. We stopped at the little house we left. The oak tree in the yard, where we had played, we anchored to one of the oak trees. We carried the casket up the steep bank to the house where the funeral would be preached that night. The old men that used to work for Pop—that used to river-rat with him—would come back. They would be there. They would come from the mountains.

Mom walked into the house. She saw the old stains of blood upon the floor. Mom screamed and started to sink to the floor. Clara caught her.

That night, mountain men, huge men—tall and bony with steel-bearded faces—filed up the path from the river. Women came with them. Women lean and tall, dressed in long flowing loose dresses and with shawls around their shoulders, came up the bank with their men. I slipped into the room where Hilton was in his coffin. I had played on the river with Hilton, the river whose water washed him to cleanse him for burial; I had talked to him. I knew him as intimately as I know a stalk of corn in the garden.

I went in the room while the crowd was gathering in to hear Brother Ike Strickland preach the funeral. I went up to where brother Hilton was laying a corpse. And I said, "Speak to me, brother Hilton. Speak to me about the river. Tell me about the Big Sandy. Did you know you was back at the old

house on the Big Sandy? Speak to me—oh, speak to me, brother Hilton—"
The wind came through the window and moved his hair and ruffled the
window curtain. "Uncle Jake lives here now. Do you know it? You remember him, don't you, Hilton?"

But not a sound came. I could see the moon and the white clouds in the
sky. I could see the Big Sandy up between the two mountains, a ribbon of
silver fading away between two rows of willows, far up between the mountains.

I could hear them in the other room crying. I could hear them singing,
"There's a land beyond the river, that they call the sweet Forever." The
moon was high above the Big Sandy and the wind was blowing through the
window. Hilton lay there with his lips curved like Pop's, just like he wanted
to say something. I could see the tombstones around the church where we
used to go to Sunday School and church, the place where all of Pop's people
are laid after they left the Big Sandy.

Tomorrow we'll take Hilton there. He'll be laid there among his kin that
have followed the river, have been shot and shot others, those who have cut
the timber from the mountain slopes and cleared the valley. That is where
Hilton will sleep. The Big Sandy will flow not far away; one can hear it
murmuring from the church where Hilton sleeps for it is not a stone's throw
away. It knows the dreams and holds the dreams of three generations of
Fraziers now sleeping in this Big Sandy earth.

Men of the Mountains

About the story:

In this story, Pa and his son Shan go through the drought-stricken hollow to see with their own eyes the graves Flem Simpson has dug for himself and his wife. Mountain men receive "tokens" of death and prepare for it. "Never heard of one missing it," says Pa. Later the story ripples with grim humor as deaf Flem yells up from the grave he is trying on for size: "Say it louder, like Gabriel is going to do when he blows his trumpet." When I asked Mr. Stuart in a recent interview to comment on the factual basis of "Men of the Mountains," he said:

> STUART: . . . I'll tell you where they [the Simpson family] lived. Remember when you come up the road [Highway 1] where you turn off this lane [W-Hollow Road]? . . . You come straight off the road when you come right down over the hill [going out]. It's the first house on the left. . . . On the way back toward Greenup.
>
> RICHARDSON: [Making a note]. Flem lies down in his grave and says, "I just fit—see, boys. . . . How do I look down here, boys?"
>
> S.: [Grinning]. He scared them to death. . . .
>
> R.: Did you see this?
>
> S.: No, but I talked to the boys. They were Wade and Bobby S———.
>
> R.: Flem says he's going to stay in the grave "until Gabriel's trumpet," and he's got seven barrels of salt, four for him and three "for the old woman's [grave]." He says, "We're going to keep like a jar of apples till the judgment." Now, did this really happen?
>
> S.: I couldn't have made that up. I've just been lucky with material.
>
> R.: How did you come to write this story?
>
> S.: Well, I couldn't escape it. Not a story like that. A man, my neighbor, digging his own grave. . . .

The book in which "Men of the Mountains" was first collected as the lead story and for which it provided the book's title was destined for distinction. A telegram to Stuart at Riverton, Kentucky, invited him to come to New York, expenses paid, to receive the 1941 Academy of Arts and Science Award of $500.00.*

* * *

Behind the sun and before the sun in misty rays of light are the hills eternal where mortal men are laid—the trees mark their resting places now and the briars—the mountains are their tombs eternal. Men wrought of mountain clay and stone and roots of mountain trees—eat plants from the mountain earth and hear the music of mountain wind and water—men live among the mountains, curse the mountains, love the mountains, plant corn among them and lift the rocks and cut the timber—have seasons to fail and see the dry hard rocks point to the skies—men of the mountains unafraid of the cruel mountains, the homey mountains that give them scanty food and take them home in the end to sleep a while.

"FLEM WAS ALWAYS A GOOD WORKER," says Pa, "and a good man. I hate to hear that—poor old Flem—digging his own grave and him just fifty-six years old. W'y he's the same age I am and I'm not ready to leave this old world yet. Much as we talk about being unafraid to die when we go to getting up in years then's the time we want to live. We watch each precious day. Poor old Flem. We got to get over there and see if we can help him any. Do that much for a good neighbor."

Pa puts on his little gray hat. He walks out of the house, pulls out a package of red-horse and puts his brown fingers in at the head of the half-opened package of sweet scrap tobacco. He brings a wad of brown cut-up in the tips of his fingers to his mouth, shoves the scrap in, shoves it back properly. Then he takes a twist of home-made from his pocket so strong that it smells in the July heat. He twists off the end and shoves that into his mouth with his thumb and index finger, tamps it in like you tamp a fence post.

"Got to take a little sweet terbacker with the home-made any more," says Pa. "My ticker ain't good as it used to be. That's what the years bring a man. That's one way I know I'm not the man I used to be. Can't take my terbacker like I ust to could take it. W'y I chawed home-made—the strongest taste-bud that we could grow and I never thought a thing about it. Look at me now. Have to buy sweet terbacker and do a lot of mixing."

The July sun is hot—hot as a roasted potato. The wind, in dry burning sheets, moves slowly over the land and rubs the dry bellies of the poplar

*"Men of the Mountains" was first published in *Scribner's Magazine*, Vol. 100 (Oct., 1936), pp. 57–61, collected in Jesse Stuart, *Men of the Mountains* (N.Y.: Dutton, 1941), pp. 13–26, reprinted (Lexington: Univ. Press of Ky., 1979), pp. 13–26. Jesse Stuart/ H. E. Richardson, Interview, W-Hollow, Greenup, Ky., Aug. 19, 1978, pub. in H. Edward Richardson, "*Men of the Mountains*: An Interview with Jesse Stuart," *Adena*, Vol. 4, No. 1 (Spring, 1979), pp. 11–12.

leaves—their green throats rattle. Pa walks slowly down the path, a dry line of dirt, a cow path where there is no grass at all.

"A awful drouth," says Pa. "Don't know what the poor people are going to do this winter for bread and corn and feed for their stock. God Almighty only knows about a season any more. We never know—I've spent my life here among these hills and the older I get the less I trust the seasons. Can't get seasons any more like we used to get. Used to just go out and plant the corn and work it a couple of times—awfullest corn crops you ever saw popped out'n the ground. Land was a lot better then—but we had a season.

"Lord, look at these brown acres—look at the corn. By-the-grace-of-God I'm ashamed for a man to go through my field. Bumble-bee corn—a bumble-bee can't suck the tassels without his starn-end rubbing the ground! Look at the hills—once the land of plenty—the land of good crops—bone-dry—kick this dust with your toe and see how hard it is for yourself. It's going to be awful hard on poor old Flem to dig his grave through such hard dirt."

The dust is flying from where Pa is kicking with the toe of his shoe. I can smell the dust. I would rather smell wilted horse-weeds—that pig-pen smell they have—any old day as to smell July dust from a Kentucky mountain road—dust that has settled on the blackberry briars and sassafras sprouts— the red-mouse-eared sassafras sprouts that are coloring in the drouth. Lean cattle on the hill—seven cows to forty acres of grassed hillside and cows lean as rails. Buzzards sailing up over wilted trees—buzzards looking down on pastures and old rail-piles. Buzzards always know when the fires run through the mountains and burn terrapins to death, the lizards, the frogs, the snakes. Their crisp bodies turned to the sun, around them the black ashes flying in the wind. Buzzards high above in the blue heavens, high in the winds, coasting with wings spread, coasting, coasting and peering. They know when the drouth comes to the high bony hills where life is hard for man and beast.

"That hill over there," says Pa, pointing to a sag of corn that fits into a lap between two hills, "w'y old Flem cleaned that up for me when you was just a boy. Old Flem took his three boys in there—just little shavers then— and dogged if he didn't clear that land. He'd taken them little boys and clear land all through these hills. That Flem was a worker. What I mean he was a worker. Great big raw-boned man, so deef he couldn't hear the wind blow. That's all I didn't like about him. Had to get right up close and holler in his ear. Then he had that eye where some man back in Carter County hit him with a rock and his eye stays open all the time. Can't get the lid down. It looks right funny to see that eye standing wide open like a snake's eye.

That's what a man gets for fighting with rocks. Mountains full of rocks, and men fit with them before they ever fit with guns. Look at poor old Flem—old at fifty-six. Just my age. I get around just fine—if I just had a new ticker——"

Buzzards search the mountains—circle low down to the wilted trees. Snake marks are across our paths—long trailer-marks in the sand. Birds fly about and chirrup with a disconsolate wail.

"Poor birds are hunting water," says Pa, "poor birds. I'd rather see a man in trouble. He can help hisself more."

Pa swishes the sweat from his red forehead with his index finger and it drops in a straight line of fast-shooting white beads as he slings his hand. It hits the dry sand and sprinkles it—water to the dry earth—the bitterness of sweat to the parching lips of the earth. "Whoo-ee-ain't it hot," says Pa. "Never saw anything like this in my life. Hottest time I ever saw. Drouth. Birds dying and them buzzards up there just waiting for us all to die."

We leave the hollow road and turn to the right. We walk up this avenue of wilted weeds, of wilted trees, of brown corn-field rocks gleaming in the sun and lazy wilted corn—starving to death for water—standing in the dust down between two sweeps of hills—slanting back against the sun-scorched buff-colored clouds. We smell the burning weeds, the dying corn, the wilted sweeps of saw-briared hills and gloomy arms of scorched pine trees, the weeping fingers of the sourwoods. When we have reached the head of this little hollow, we cross the gap and go down the neck of the next hollow where Flem lives—right on the old John Kaut farm where all that big timber used to stand.

"We'll soon find out about this grave-digging," says Pa. "Son, that kindly bluffs me. When it comes to digging graves—it ain't very long. I've seen too much of it happen. These old men get the warning—they nearly always know—never hear of one missing it. But just to think of old Flem being the one called—who'd a ever thought about that? Just can't tell where the tree is going to fall, but where the tree does fall there is where the tree is going to lie——"

Flem's house is in sight—a house made from the rough oak planks and slabs from where the saw-mill used to set when it cut the giant oaks into slivers—a house there in the sun—the July Kentucky sun high in the burnt-up clouds. Windows in the house like burnt holes in a brown quilt, the color of seasoned-out lumber, brown against the wind—sweltering in the sun—the resin running from the pine knot-holes—smelly, tasty, bee-colored in the sun. Smoke coming from the rough-stone flue—smoke, thin smoke and light-blue against the wind, fat puffs of smoke with big bellies in the sun—going out with the wind—in all directions over the hot dog-tongued earth. Palings around the garden with fruit jars sunning—stone jars and glass jars and rag-rugs out on the palings to sun. Hoes with their goosenecks hung over the palings, a scythe, an oat cradle with one broken finger. Wilted corn on the mountain slopes above the house—a whole mountain of wilted corn—each stalk of corn crying for water. And the wilted arms of the corn—whispering—whispering—to the hot wind.

"Look in the garden," says Pa, "look at Flem's garden. Burnt up alive just like our garden. Look at them little tater vines. Bet you can gravel down there at them tater roots and you won't find taters bigger than a marble. Look at them cabbages. Looks for the world like wilted pusley to me. Look up that mountain—look at Flem's lean cows—and them buzzards. See them! There they are—always right around where the milk cows are trying to find grass to eat—right above the cows they snoop aroun' in the air. Why don't a buzzard wait for a buzzard to die?"

We walk in at the gate—a lean-to gate that we open and it shuts itself, weighted with a chain and plow-points—and up to the house. We smell the resin on the pine boards—scent of pine. We love the smell of pines in the spring, but the smell of pine on a hot day, the smell of pine, molted pine, wormy wood—we have to hold our noses. Around the house in the blistering heat—the smell of the wilted ragweeds—the poor wilted lady's finger and forget-me-nots drooping—the scent of pinks and iron-weeds in August.

"Hello," says Pa, "how are you, Flem." Flem does not hear. Pa goes up and he hollers in Flem's ear: "Hello, Flem. How are you!"

Flem laughs and he says: "I'm so deef can't hear nothing no more. Ain't heard the wind blow for years. The only way I can tell when the wind blows is to see the brush moving and the corn moving. It's awful to be deef. You'll never know till you get that way. When did you come over, Mick?"

"Just come," says Pa, getting up and hollering in Flem's ear. "Just come over through the hot sun and the whole air is filled with buzzards."

"Filled with buzzards," says Flem. "I'll be dogged. Sign of dead stock. Sign of deaths. Don't get me though. I got the hole dug to catch me. I'm looking for this thing."

Flem laughs. One of his eyes squints, the other eye can't, for the lid is stiff—stands open like a snake's eye—he never takes that eye off you. Flem is a big man, has a belly big as a nailkeg, doesn't have on any drawers—you can see a big white patch of belly where his blue shirt has worked up from his overalls. When Flem laughs his belly bobs up and down—up like a hand under dough lifting it up—down like a hand over dough beating it down. His hair is gray and stiff as wires in a brush—hair that won't lie down nor sit up nor do anything. It has a little crown in it—a twisted place in the bristled stuff. He has heavy eyebrows like ferns on the edge of a rock cliff.

"Wear number ten shoes," says Flem. "I see you got a mighty little foundation, Mick." Flem laughs and his belly works up and down. I see Flem's little pipe-stem hairy legs with the big feet to hold them down.

Pa says, "I got little feet. I wear eights." Pa laughs and pulls out his tobacco. He tamps it into his mouth, the sweet with the bitter, then reaches some to Flem.

"Thank you," Flem says, "I don't chaw my terbacker. I smoke it." Flem takes out a leaf of home-made tobacco, crumbles it in a little red corn-cob pipe, strikes a match on his pants leg, and wheezes as he sucks the long dry stem. Long streams of thin smoke come from Flem's mouth—thinner than the air and bluer.

"My ticker ain't good as it used to be," says Pa, hollering in Flem's ear, "that's why I got to take a little sweet with the bitter any more. Can't take it like I used to take it. Getting younger every day, too."

Flem says: "Huh—yes—ahh. Huh."

"God," says Pa, "he's the deefest man I ever tried to talk to. He's about got me winded. You try to talk with him a while. Let's get him to show us his grave."

Hodd is Flem's boy, twenty-two now, with two rows of black broken teeth, freckles on his face, patches of unshaved beard growing here and there, a straw hat on his head, a blue shirt on his back with two dark blue stripes on the back where his overall suspenders have not let the sun fade the blue out, overalls torn at the cuffs into ravelling ruffles.

"Hello, Hodd," Pa says, "will you talk to your Pa a little for us?"

"I'll do my best," says Hodd. "Pa's deef as a rock in this hot weather and deef ain't no name for it. Just sets around—can't do nothing—can't talk to nobody. He's got his grave dug—guess you know about that."

"Heard about it," says Pa.

"Well, he has," says Hodd, "and he's got Ma's grave dug with his. Right beside his. Ma's taken a cry every day since he's done it. She says it's the sure sign when a Simpson digs a grave. He's not much longer for this world."

Flem just sits on his rocking chair and rocks. Life doesn't have any noises for him, he can't hear the jingle of the harness any more nor the sound of the hoe and ax nor the barking of fox-hounds.

"Tell Flem," says Pa, "that I want to go back there where he has got them graves dug. Tell him I want to see them." And Hodd hollers in Flem's ear.

"All right, we'll go," says Flem. "About three miles back there. But we'll go."

Flem leads the way up the path. Pa walks second. Hodd is third and Ott comes out. He says: "Where you going, Hodd?" And Hodd says: "We're going to Pa's graves out here on the hill. Come along with us."

Ott comes up the hill. He is tall, thin at the hips, with twisted legs and a hairy chest, unbuttoned shirt, a partly bald head with hair thin as timber on a hill where the fire has run over it year after year. His lips turn down at the corners like the curve of a horse-shoe. He says: "Uhuh—ahh——"

And he walks up the path, his legs working strong and fast. We move on toward the graves, the sun high on the mountain above us among the burned-copper clouds. Flem is easily winded, walks with a stick. He gets his breath like a snoring hog sleeping in the sun. Sweat drips from Pa's face. He slings it with his forefinger from his forehead, and he wipes among his scattered wire-stubbled beard with his red handkerchief.

"Ma is worried plum sick," says Ott, "the way Pa has done. He tried to get me and Hodd to come back here and help him with the graves. We wouldn't do it. Me to dig my father's grave and my mother's grave. No. I just couldn't bear it. W'y he's been coming back here and working one hour at a time for the past five weeks. He brings that crazy boy of Mort Flannigan's back here. He comes with Pa. He laid down and had Mort's boy to mark him off—right back yander on the Remines pint."

Lazy July wind seeps out of the brush. It is soft and hot. It runs fast then slow. The scent of the corn—corn sweltering in the heat on the slope to our right—corn ready to tassel—corn so small and twisted. The mountain path is slow and twisting and the wilted leaves hang in pods in the July sunlight. Sweat runs from my face, from Pa's face, from Hodd's, Ott's, and Flem's faces. Flem is in the lead, setting the walking pace. It is slow as the slow smelly wind that comes out of the brush. The buzzards are above the mountain tops, flying in circles over the pasture slope where the lean cows pick the brown grass, grass that would burn quick if Flem would throw down a lighted match-stem.

"Ma's been just crying her eyes out," says Ott, "about Pa. Corn in the ground for another year. Pa is going to die. We know he's going to die. Nothing we can do about it. He says he's going to die. Ain't worked none this summer. Ma says she hates to die and leave little Effie, the baby girl you know, just twelve now. Just us three left at home. All safe, Ma says, but Effie and she says there's so much weakedness in the world she hates to die and leave her."

It seems like we are climbing to the sun, the sun that crosses the earth, in the region of the hill man's destiny—great backbones of ridges where the crow flies, where cows wither on the bone on the dry summer grass and where buzzards circle low. Men of the mountains growing old. Pa growing old at fifty-six—mixing sweet tobacco with strong. Flem Simpson growing old and his autumn not here. His grave is dug.

"W'y," says Pa, "Flem ain't but from March to June older than I am. I am still getting around and I've worked as hard in my day as any man."

"Yes," says Hodd, "but you wasn't hit in the head with a rock like Pa. That's what got Pa. You know about that fight. He's been a peaceful man ever since. He communes with the Lord often—gets out at night and communes with the Lord."

"Lord, I'm hot," says Pa, wiping the sweat from his face.

"No hotter than I am," says Hodd. "Look at Pa, though, he's still wiggling like a young weaned calf—big in the middle and little on both ends. . . . . Soon be at the top of the mountain."

The sun is high in the sky—high among the mountains, the color of a red sand-rock—floating—floating—heat below is dancing to the tune of grasshopper in the weeds. Heat on the fields of wilted corn on the mountains where the earth is baked in a big brown pone. If rain was to hit the baked earth, rain wouldn't soak down for a while—it would go up in steam. Great brown sheets of earth—wilted mountains of leaves—green clouds of leaves—clouds, wilted and drooping.

"Let the old men get their wind," says Hodd, as we top the mountain. "Won't be so bad now—it's about all going down the hill now."

Pa wipes the sweat from his face and moves faster and faster as the road on the mountain ridge goes down a knoll and up another knoll to the Remines point.

"Coming in sight of where I'm going to be laid out to rest, boys," says Flem, "just right over the pint here in these chestnut oaks. Nice quiet place out here away from the houses—back like the woods was when I was a boy."

We walk over the hill—here are the graves—two graves dug under the chestnut-oaks—twin graves—side by side. "Here they are, boys," says Flem. "Will show you this one is a fit for me. The other one is a fit for my wife. Prudy just comes to my shoulder you know. So when I laid down to measure her grave I had to make allowances. I measured from my shoulders down. But I just laid down here and had Mort's boy to measure me on the ground. He was a little scared, but he helped me here with these graves with tears in his eyes."

"God," says Pa. "Hodd, ask your Pa what made him do this. I didn't believe he had any graves out here when he told me. I thought he was just a funning me a little . . . Poor old Flem."

Pa sheds some tears. He remembers Uncle Fonse Tillman and the strange way he knew about his approaching death—now another one of Pa's comrades passing away and acting the same way about it. "A funny thing," says Pa. "I believe Flem knows what he's doing. Flem is a goner from these mountains. Gone to sleep among them forever and that before the winds of falltime blow."

"I just fit—see, boys," says Flem as he gets down in his grave and lies down, "a little wide here in the middle but it won't be when my oak-board coffin fits in here. Most people dig a hole to fit the coffin and order the coffin to fit the man. I'm making my coffin to fit me and digging the hole first." Flem's head is against the earth and he says, "How do I look down here, boys?"

He looks up at us and laughs, his belly shaking. Then he looks through the wilted leaves of the chestnut-oaks above his grave at the molten copper clouds that halfway secure the sun—hot clouds—clouds without rain. His one eye, the snake-eye, looks glassy from down in the grave. The other eye is squinted.

"Good place to be when a man is tired," says Flem, "no more worry about bread, land to tend, and pasture for the cattle. No more worry—out here where the fox-horns will blow and maybe I can hear them then. All troubles will be over, Prudy by my side, and we'll sleep here till resurrection day. A good place to sleep—right here on the mountain-top."

It touches Pa to hear Flem say this. Pa says to Ott: "Guess you'll have to run the farm when your Pa dies. Sure did pick a good place to be buried. I'd hate to dig my grave. Don't believe I could. Even if it is cool away from all the heat we been having. I just wouldn't like it."

Flem is still down in his grave. "Come on out of your grave, Pa," says Hodd. Flem can see Hodd's lips working but he can't tell what he is saying.

"Say it louder," says Flem, "like Gabriel is going to do when he blows his trumpet."

Hodd hollers as loudly as he can, down into the grave: "Come on out of your grave, Pa."

"That's more like it," says Flem, "more like the trumpet I'm going to hear on resurrection morning, when time shall be no more, and these fifty-six years ain't going to be a drop in the bucket. Help me out of my grave, boys."

Pa gets him by one hand and Hodd gets him by the other.

"I want to live where there's not any time. Then I can farm and lift rocks and cut sprouts the way I want to with a strong set of arms and a strong set of legs. We'll have seasons and crops. That's what I want and not this awful sun to burn up the crops——"

Flem comes from the grave and starts to get down in Prudy's grave to show us the length of it. "Oh, God," says Hodd, "don't get down in Ma's grave. No need of that—I don't want to think about Ma coming to this lonely place when she's always liked to go to town on Saturdays where she could see people. Ma don't like fox-horns. Has to be buried way out in these lonely woods."

"I'm ready to go," says Flem. "Can't farm any more. Don't have the legs—don't have the arms. Can't see as well. Can't talk to people. I'm in the way. Can't trade like I used to trade. Country is changing. Government telling me what to do—how to plant the mountains. Tell me I can only raise so many hogs and a lot of stuff like that. It's getting time for us old men who ain't used to that to die, Mick. God Almighty sent this drouth on such people as that. Won't let us plant—won't let us have what we want—we've always had that—even under a Republican, much as I hate that Party. I tell you, I'm tired and ready to sleep. I told the Master I was ready and I'd like to bring the old woman along with me, too. I told the Master she was ready—she'd been with me all through life and I wanted to be by the side of her in death."

Tears come in Pa's eyes. Hodd looks to the waters of the Little Sandy and keeps his eyes away from his father. Ott looks at me and I look at Ott and then at Pa. The Little Sandy River winds slowly down among the hills, down among the wilted clouds of leaves—a brown muddy river—curled like a snake crawling through the briars. Giant oaks tremble in the wind. Leaves flutter in the hot July wind.

"Great place to be buried," says Pa, "here among these mighty hills. They'll get me in the end. Oak roots will go in to old Flem. He'll go back to the mountains and only a tree some day will mark where he is buried."

Flem says: "Come down here a minute, boys. Got something I want to show you." We follow Flem down under the hill—just a little way down under the rim of the hill to a rock cliff—where lichen is bluish-gray and dying—the sourwoods lean over and twist their slender bodies groping for the light.

"Come in here," says Flem. "Look here, see these barrels of salt—seven of them—four for me and three for the old woman. The children can take care of themselves. I'm going to have four barrels of salt dumped in on my oak-board box—and three dumped in on the old woman's. We're going to keep like a jar of apples till the judgment. Going to keep right here on this mountain till resurrection day, looking fresh as two lilies. We're not going to be a couple of skeletons coming out of the grave. We're going to come out of there—the whole of us just like we went in. Salt around us and oakboards from our hills—buried on our mountain-top where only the fox-horns blow and the wind and the hound-dogs bark—w'y we'll keep forever."

"We got to get home and feed," says Pa, "got to be going. Come over, Hodd, you and Ott—come over when you can. Come over, Flem," says Pa, hollering in his ear. "Come over and see me before you change worlds. After you get out of here you won't be at a place where we can neighbor like we used to neighbor."

"I want to get around to your place and Hankas's place before September and see all you boys once more," says Flem, "then I'm ready for my rest. No drouths then, no crop failures, and people telling me what to raise and how to raise it. I'll still be a Democrat, though. You can't change a mountain Democrat or a mountain Republican."

"That's right," says Pa, "you know me. I'll be a Republican in Heaven or in Hell. But I like you Flem because you are what you are and a good neighbor. I hope we get to neighbor again in other mountains."

We walk up the hill—we take the near cut across the spur home. The path is dry and white as a crooked dogbone. Pa walks in front. Pa's shirt is wet with sweat as a dish-rag—sweat has come through the crown of his hat in places. We see the sun sinking—we look back at the vast hills, timber-covered, the great green clouds of wilted leaves that dry-rustle in the wind, and the houses down in the valley. "A good neighbor," says Pa, "a good neighbor if I ever had one on this earth."

Sunday Afternoon Hanging

About the story:

"It was as much fun to see a hanging them days as it is to see a baseball game nowadays here in Kentucky." Fittingly, one of the old people tells his grandson "a little about this hanging business in Kentucky" in the days before it "Just kept a-gettin'... easier till they didn't hang 'em at all." In the old days, "When they used to kill a man everybody got to see it and laugh and faint, cuss or cry, do just as he damn pleased about it." The old man proceeds to relate "how it was... before the days of baseball.... every Sunday of the world after church was out. We could hardly wait to get to the hanging." He tells of how two Sixeymore brothers and three other men murdered old Jim Murphy and his wife. Even though the murderers were careful to throw their victims' bodies into the dark waters of the Little Sandy at night, a fisherman got them out down at Cedar Riffles, for "nature don't hold things and uphold dirty work." The murderers were caught and everybody got to witness their suffering at the hanging. "Boy, you suffer for what you do in this old world," the old man tells his grandson. "Talk about men suffering before they died."

The grandfather spares no details for the faint of heart in describing all aspects of the hanging: the last menus of the murderers, the county-made coffins, the size and appearance of each murderer, the excursion boats bringing curious and jolly folk—men, women, children, and babies—to the hanging, the various horse-drawn conveyances, the band and its music, the atmosphere in a time when a hanging was a politically popular act, each murder's public "confession" and the crowd's reactions, and the expertise of hangman Bert Blevins whose knots "always flew up in the right place and hit 'em one on the jaw and broke their necks." As he does frequently throughout the frantic action, the old narrator here intrudes his presence to comment, "Bert was a whiz on this hanging business." As each of the five murderers is brought forward, the narrator savors every detail, reporting each confession with no verbal whitewashing: Dudley Toms' fear as "he kinda broke down," Freed Winslow's "struggling for breath and glomming at the wind with his hands," Work Grubb's being scared "not one iotum," Jake Sixeymore's "a-laughing" as he asked for "a pint of Rock and Rye to

stick in my hippocket for old Satan and a good homemade twist," and Tim
Sixeymore's salutation commencing, "Gentlemen bastards and sonofabitches. . . ."

Jesse Stuart said that both his mother and his landlady at South Shore,
Mrs. Forrest King, told him stories of the old hangings that occurred when
they were young. People would get "all dressed up to go to [a] hanging";
the author explained, "that's the way they dressed." They went by "excursion boats or by train"—anyway they could get there. Mrs. King herself as a
young woman went on a train to a hanging. Even schools "turned out to go
to that hanging. A special train took them. It was like going to an all-state
game . . . [or to see] Northwestern and Michigan. All these old hangings
were that way. The people dressed up in the best clothes and they came
from miles and miles on horseback to . . . the hanging. And they had to quit
hauling them with mules to the gallows [finally]. Mules and horses would
scare and run away. They hauled them with cattle—oxen."*

* * *

B OY, YOU DON'T KNOW anything about it. Let your grandpa tell
you a little about this hanging business in Kentucky. You set
around here and talk about the hot seat for a man that kills another man in
cold blood. Hot seat ain't nothing. People can't go and see a body killed in
the hot seat. Just a little bunch allowed in to write up a few of the poor
devil's last words. When they used to kill a man everybody got to see it and
laugh and faint, cuss or cry, do just as he damn pleased about it. It used to
be that way here in Kentucky. Now let me tell you, there's no fun to giving
a man the hot seat or giving him gas or a lot of stuff like that, giving him
the pen for life. Didn't keep 'em up there and feed 'em for life when I was a
boy. They took 'em out and swung 'em to a limb and people from all over
the country came to see 'em swing.

Let me tell you how it was. That was before the days of baseball. People
came for forty miles to see a hanging. We had one every weekend in Blakesburg for the people to come and see. You know that's how Blakesburg got
the name Hang-Town. God, I remember well as if it was yesterday. Used to

*Jesse Stuart's "Sunday Afternoon Hanging" was originally published in *Esquire*, Vol. 7
(April, 1937), pp. 48–49, 200–202, reprinted in *Plowshare in Heaven* (N.Y.: McGraw-Hill, 1958),
pp. 97–112. A similar and equally fine story by Jesse Stuart, told from a boy's point of veiw, is
"The Hangin' of Willard Bellstrase," *Esquire*, Vol. 18 (Nov., 1942), pp. 44–45, 143–145, reprinted under the title "Another Hanging," in *Tales from the Plum Grove Hills* (N.Y.: Dutton,
1946), and in the Mockingbird ed. (N.Y.: Ballantine Bks., 1974), pp. 125–134. Also reprinted
in Malcom Cowley, ed., *Great Tales of the Deep South* (N.Y.: Lion Lib. ed., 1955), pp. 183–192.
The source of Mr. Stuart's remarks on the factual and historical background for his hanging
stories is our interview, W-Hollow, Greenup, Ky., Sept. 15, 1978.

be an old elm in the lower end of town where they hung 'em. It was upon a little hill where everybody could get an eyeful of the man they swung to the elm limb. Pa and Ma and me, we used to go every Sunday of the world after church was out. We could hardly wait to get to the hanging. It was as much fun to see a hanging them days as it is to see a baseball game nowadays here in Kentucky. God, do I remember the old days. I was just a boy then but I remember it just like it was yesterday. I can see the crowd yet that gathered at the hangings, and all the hollering you ever heard in your life it was put up at one of them hangings when a poor devil was swung up to the old elm limb.

That old tree just fell three years ago. God Almighty got rid of it. Must a been some of them innocent men they swung up there and in Heaven they got after God Almighty to do something about that tree. And God Almighty got rid of it. He looks after his people. He'll do a lot too, I guess, of what his angels in Heaven wants him to do. Son, I am an old man and I believe I know. Well, of all the trees in the lower end of Blakesburg, the old elm where they hung all them men was the only one the lightnin' hit and split from limb to roots. Tree must have been five feet through the middle, too. And don't you know the people wouldn't burn a stick of that wood in their stoves and fireplaces. They just rolled it over the bank into the Ohio River and let it float away. People was afraid that if they burnt it they would be haunted the rest of their days.

You've heard about poor old Jim Murphy and his wife gettin' killed that time. I know you've seen the hickory club they've got over there in the Blakesburg Courthouse with poor old Jim's tooth stuck in it—that hard white hickory club—no, don't guess you did see it. The 1913 flood got up in the courthouse and carried it off. Had poor old Jim's tooth in it. See, here is the way it was. It happened up there in Sand Bottom. Right up there where that foul murder happened two years ago when that old strollop and that man tortured the little girl to death with a red-hot poker. Foulest things that have ever happened in this country have happened right up there in Sand Bottom. To go on with my story. A bunch of Sixeymores up there then. God, they's rotten eggs too. Well, there was two Sixeymore brothers well as I remember, a Dudley Toms, a Winslow, and a Grubb into that scrape. The Sixeymore brothers planned the murder of these two old people for their money. They had heard by a woman that went there and cooked for them that they had eleven hundred dollars hid in a old teakettle in the pantry. Well, the Sixeymore brothers—Tim and Jake—promised Freed Winslow Jim Murphy's mules if he would help kill him and his wife. They promised Dudley Toms the two cows and Work Grubb his thirty acres of land if he would help kill them.

They went to the little log house down by the Sandy River one dark rainy night when there was no moon. It was in the dark of the moon. They had the whole thing planned. They thought that if they killed the old people and throwed them in Sandy in the dark of the moon the bodies would never come to the top of the water. So they cut a hickory club; Tim Sixeymore cut it with a poleax up on Flint Sneed's pint, up where the old furnace used to be. People used to go there and see the stump. It all come out in Tim's confession before they swung him. They cut the club—all went there that dark night. Jim made a chicken squall and old man Murphy—game man as ever drawed a breath of wind—run out against his old lady's will. She said: "Somebody to kill us, Jim. Don't go out there." You know how a woman can just about tell things; God gives 'em the power to pertect themselves just like he does a possum or a horse. They can almost smell danger. Old Jim run out and—whack—Sixeymore hit him in the mouth with the hickory club. Killed him dead as a mackrel. That one lick finished him. He just walled his eyes back and died. Then all five of the men went in where old Lizzie Murphy was a settin' before the fire smokin' her pipe and she said: "Give me time to pray once more to God Almighty." She begged to pray but they didn't give her time. Dudley Toms said the hardest thing he ever tried to do was to kill that old woman and her a-beggin' to just get to pray to God Almighty just one more time. He hit her over the head with a fire shovel, and to make sure she was dead he beat out her brains with the shovel. Then they carried them down and throwed them in the dark waters of Little Sandy on that dark night. But nature don't hold things and up-hold dirty work. That water give up the dead bodies down at Cedar Riffles. Some fishermen caught them there. And Dudley Toms didn't know that there was a speck of blood left on his hatband. But there was. See, there's always a clue. Can't do a thing like that and get by with it, not even if the law is on your side. Boy, you suffer for what you do in this old world. Talk about men suffering before they died. I was right there at the hanging. Everybody in the county came to it. It was the biggest hanging we ever had. Had a hanging of five that Sunday. Hung these five and they was the kind of fellows the people liked to see swing to a limb. Was a lot better than just going out and getting somebody for stealing a horse and hanging him, or a man for abusing his wife; somebody like that hardly had enough against him to hang. I've seen many a poor devil hang over almost nothing. Today he wouldn't have to go to jail for it. Used to hang him for the same thing. The people wanted a hanging every week and the sheriff and judge had better have a hanging at least once a month or they would never get elected again. If they didn't have hangings often enough the people would go to them and say, "Look here, you'll not get my vote next time if this is the way you intend to do. Lay down on the job, never have a hanging. Damn poor Law. You'll never be elected again."

Well, the day these five men was hung I was just a boy. I remember it just like it was yesterday. I was up to the jail that morning after the confession and saw them getting their breakfast. Jailer Wurt Hammons said: "Boys, eat hearty. This will be your last grub here on this earth. The devil will serve your breakfast tomorrow morning. You have the chance to have anything that you want to eat that I can get for you."

Well, the Sixeymore boys took a stewed turkey apiece and a biler of black coffee without sugar or cream. Dudley Toms wouldn't eat a bite. Tim said to him: "Hell, take your hanging like a man. Go to the gallows on a full stummick. Get that much off the county before you die." Work Grubb took twelve hard-fried eggs and a pint of licker to wash 'em down with. Winslow took fried eggs and licker—don't remember how many eggs and how much licker. But that is what they had for breakfast. Well, the county carpenter, Jake Tillman, had the county make coffins for them. He was hired to make the coffins for the men the county hung. He had five good county coffins made—took their measurements and made them to fit. Had one awfully big for Tim Sixeymore. He was six feet and seven inches tall and weighed some over three hundred pounds. Biggest man I believe I ever saw. He wasn't dough-bellied either. Weighed a lot and was hard as the butt of a shell-barked hickory. His brother was about as big and powerful. God, old Tim was a man and not afraid of God Almighty hisself. God would have to watch him at the jedgment bar. If he got half a chance he'd do something to God Almighty.

I remember the two excursion boats that come down the river that day to the hanging and the one that come up the river. They was just loaded with people hollering and waving handkerchiefs around the deck. There was a double-decker come up the river with a load of people. And of all the people that ever come to Blakesburg they were there that day. Mules tied to the trees along the streets—not many houses in Blakesburg them days but there was a thicket of trees through the town. Wagons of all descriptions. Hug-me-tight buggies—them things had just come out then—people looked at the new contraption and quarreled about the indecency of men and women riding in them little narrow seats all loved up. Said they ought to be hung for an example for doing it. And there was a lot of two-horse surreys and rubber-tired hacks and jolt wagons there that day. Jolt wagons with whole families riding in wagon beds full of straw. People and people everywhere you looked. Never was such a crowd in Blakesburg as there was that day. Little children crying and dogs that followed the wagons to town out fighting in the streets and the horses neighing to each other and rearing up in the collar, mules biting and kicking each other! It was the awfulest time I ever saw. If a dark cloud would a riz over that town I would a swore the world was coming to an end. But it was a pretty day for a crowd and for a hanging. Sun in the sky. June wind blowing. Roses in bloom. One of the prettiest days I believe I ever saw. The reason that I remember it so well was that they hung 'em at sunup. Some of the people had come all night to be there in time to see the hanging in the morning.

Well, the band got there. You know they always had a band at the hangings to furnish the music. Had a seven-piece band at this hanging. Always before we just had a drummer, a pot beater, and a fifer. About everybody likes a fife. It puts madness in their bones and bodies and helps drown the screams of the women and the fighting of the dogs and the whinnying of the horses. The band had on the gayest suits you ever saw for this occasion. Just like a political rally where they used to butcher five or six steers to feed the people. These band players had on bright yaller pants and red sashes and peagreen jackets and them old three-cornered hats. God, but they did look nifty.

Well as I remember the band struck up a tune that day. It was "Dixie." Some of the horses broke loose and took down through the town but the people let 'em go. They stayed still for the hanging. It was the biggest thing we'd had in many a day. Horses broke loose without riders on them and took out through the crowd among the barking dogs, running over them and the children. People didn't pay any attention to that. It was a hanging and people wanted to see every bit of it. They didn't care if a child did get run over so it wasn't their own. And it took five or six sheriffs; they had big guns on 'em to keep any fights from starting and they wore bright yaller jackets. Lord, all the people there. And you could always tell a mountaineer them days from the back country. He always had the smell of wood smoke on him and barnyard manure. Big bony devils! Hairy as all get out! Never would shave their bony faces!

I remember seeing the first horse and express come into sight. Dudley Toms was sitting on his coffin with a rope around his neck, the hangman's knot alread tied. Bert Blevins always did that for the county. One of his knots never did slip. It always flew up in the right place and hit 'em one on the jaw and broke their necks. Bert was a whiz on this hanging business. And when the horse come in sight and Dudley was a sittin' up there on the coffin—God, the people nearly tore the limbs out of the trees with their jumpin' and screamin' and they had that big shell-bark hickory club that Tim hit Jim Murphy with back there the night he made the chicken squall.

That had just been three weeks before. They really brought men to justice back in them days when they had to have someone to hang every Sunday after church. Screams was so loud that you had to hold your fingers in your ears. Here was that big shell-bark hickory club held up in the air by a big man while Dudley stood on his coffin and made his confession. They wanted to hear it. They wanted all out of a hanging that there was in one.

At first Dudley Toms wouldn't talk. The jailer said, "Tell them, Dudley. They want your confession before you give it to the devil. We want it first-handed here. You can give it second-handed to the devil." And Dudley he stood up there on his coffin while that horse—a new one they was breakin' in to haul men to the gallows—he just ripped and snorted.

And Dudley said, "First time I ever killed anybody. Was hard to kill Lizzie Murphy with that shovel. But I had to do it. No use to cry over spilt milk. I hate like hell to hang. I do. But I'd rather do it right now and see what all this after death is that I've heard so much about. I hate to die. But take me out of all this—take me out!" And he kinda broke down.

Well, they unfastened his hands from behind him so they could see him kick and pull on the rope with his tongue turnin' black and hangin' out of his mouth. They just made him stand on the coffin and they tied the rope that went around his neck to the rope that was already fastened to the old hangin'-tree and just drove the wagon out from under him while the band struck up a tune. I'll never forget seein' him swing there and kick—that expression on the dyin' man's face. The band was a-playin', the children a-screamin' because it was the first hangin' a lot of them had ever seen. Some of the women started shouting. Never saw anything like it in my life. But Dudley's kinsfolk was there to get him. Some of the women fainted and they just had a couple of barrels of water there so they could throw cold water in the faces of the fainting women. That's what they done. Had boys hired right ready to throw water on the faces of the fainting women or the fighting dogs when they got in the way of the hangin'.

The next to ride up was Freed Winslow. He was up on top of his coffin and the horse that hauled him wasn't so afraid of the suits that the band-men wore. The horse had been to many a hangin'. Well, while the kinsfolk was claimin' the body of Dudley Toms, Freed Winslow was standing on top of his coffin making his confession. It was a fine confession, too, if there was ever a good hangin' confession made. Said Freed Winslow: "Ladies and gentlemen, I have made peace with my God. I am not afraid to die. I prayed all night last night. I been prayin' ever since I got in this mess. That very first night after I helped do this killing I saw so many devils around my bed that I had to get up and light the lamp. They was cuttin' all kinds of shines. They even run across my stummick. God, it was awful. I hope to

meet you all in Heaven where there ain't no devils to run across your stummick and grin at you. Good-by, folks. Sorry for what I have done and I
hope you won't hold it against me. I ought to die."

So they put the knot over his head and drove the wagon out from under
him and he fell off his own coffin and the band struck up a tune. While he
was in the air struggling for breath and glomming at the wind with his
hands, the band players kept pumping harder. That fife kept screaming
above the cries of the women. Talking of fainting of pretty girls. They sure
did faint. Freed Winslow was a handsome man. There his tongue went out
of his mouth. His face black. His curly hair flying in the wind, black as a
frostbit pawpaw in the early fall, and he died strugglin' just like a possum
struggles for breath after its neck has been broke under a mattock handle.

The next to come up to the hang-tree was Work Grubb. He was thought
to be a fine man in the neighborhood. He was a-ridin' on his coffin, hairiest
man you ever saw. Looked like one of them men in the days of old with all
the beard on his face. He looked kindly like he was ashamed when the
wagon rolled up under the tree. I never can forget all them knotholes in his
coffin. Bet he wasn't more than under the ground till the water started
seepin' and the dirt and these worms started crumbling through these
knotholes. Well, the band struck up a tune and the people screamed. Just
like a man when he makes a score nowdays in baseball. It was a score with
death then. The band had to play while the people screamed and waited for
his confession. He waited calmly as I ever saw a man waiting for death. He
wasn't scared, not one iotum. He just waited and when the people screamed
till they were hoarse he stood up on his coffin and said, "What I got to say
to you is: Go on and kill me. Remember the killer pays. I was guilty and I
deserve to die but you don't deserve to kill me."

One old fat snaggle-toothed woman up and hollered, "You won't get
pore old Uncle Jim Murphy's thirty acres of land, will ye? Might get some
hot land to farm in hell. Say they've got a lot of desert land down there!
And she just hollered and laughed at the condemned man going to the elm
limb.

Well, the band struck up "Dixie." And the wagon drove out from under
him soon as the rope was fastened. And Work swung there with his thin legs
dangling in the air. Didn't use a cap on their faces in them days. People
wanted to see their faces while they was dyin'. The band played while he
dangled at the end of the rope and clutched for thin air. Of all the cries that
ever went up from the people it did there. Then Doc Turner went up and
stopped the swinging body and put his hand on the heart. He said, "He's
dead. He's gone to the other world."

The next they brought up on the wagon was Jake Sixeymore. He was a-laughing. They asked him if he wanted to make any confession. And he laughed and said. "All I want is a pint of Rock and Rye to stick in my hip pocket for old Satan and a good homemade twist. He's going to have hell, with me and my brother Tim both with him. We'll both want jobs and we'll get into it. I want to get on the good side of him first. I'm not a damn bit sorry over anything I've done. Just one life to live, one death to die, something beyond or nothing beyond and I'll hold my own any goddam place they put me. So, swing your goddam rope to me soon as you give me that half-pint of Rock and Rye and that twist of Kentucky-burley terbacker."

"Sure thing," said the sheriff. "Give it to him. I'm afraid it's the last he'll ever get."

So the fellow just give one of them big horse-pints with just one little dram taken out of it. He give him a twist that looked as big as my arm at the elbow. He took it, thanked the fellow in the gray with the long handle-bar mustache and dough-belly that shook as he walked, and then he said, "I'm ready, gentlemen. Pull your goddam rope."

Well, the crowd was kindly quiet for a few minutes, then the band struck up a tune. And he was riding on the highest wagon and the highest coffin. The rope broke his neck the first crack. Of all the screams! His tongue just come out of his mouth, a twisted tongue, and where he bit it, it was bleeding. God, what a sight. And his face black as a pawpaw leaf. He swung there low against the ground, the limb sagging and the rope swinging. Doc Smith run out and put his ear to his heart. He said, "Dead man. He is in the other world by now or gettin' mighty close."

Well, people—just his old dad and mammy there in their rags. God, I felt sorry for them. I couldn't help it. Had two boys there that day to hang. They took him off in the coffin and carried him a little ways and put him down in the grass. They waited for Tim to die so they could haul them both to the same double grave on the same wagon. Her gray hair flying in the wind, him a mountain man with the smell of wood smoke and cow manure on him. He had shed tears. He was a man stout as a rock. His sons were no stronger-looking than their old white-haired father.

Well, the last wagon come up there that day. It had one of the biggest coffins I ever saw on it. The biggest man I ever saw was riding on top of that box. His big hands looked like shovels folded up there on his chest. He looked mean as the devil out of his eyes. They were black eyes and they had beads of fire shining from them. You could see them from the crowd. His hair looked like briars around a stump: a big mop of it, and it looked like a comb had never been run through it in his life. Clay still on his knuckles where he had worked in the mines. He'd kill and he'd rob and he'd work. He was a great worker. Could do as much as four ordinary men and lift more than any two men in the mines. Lord, he was a sight to look at. He looked like a mountain man. He could eat the side of a hog's ribs at one meal and a whole pone of corn bread and drink a gallon of buttermilk. He could eat three dozen fried eggs and drink a whole biler of strong coffee. Now he was facing the gallows. He just set there like a rock. I heard one old whiskered man with a willow cane say: "Now, if he confesses all his guilt we'll get a good confession."

The band struck up a tune. "Dixie," I believe. Nearly played it and "Old Kentucky Home" to death that day. It was one of the songs. And the people started screaming. It was the last one of the five and they just tried to see how much noise they could make. God, it was awful to hear. I remember his pore old mother fainting and how they dashed two buckets of cold water in her face. I remember the tears that come from his pore old pap's wrinkled eyes . . . it was a sight to see! I have often wished I'd never seen it. God, it was awful to think about.

When the band stopped the sheriff said, "Let's hear your confession, Tim Sixeymore."

Well, that great big man got up and stood on his coffin. And he looked like a giant to me. Great big devil, unafraid of the whole crowd.

And he said, "Yes, I've got a big confession to make. I got plenty to tell you bastard men and wench women, goddam you!"

You could a heard a pin drop there that day till some strange dogs started fighting and then the babies started crying. Well, they throwed water on the dogs and got them stopped and the women started nursing the babies and got them stopped. If they didn't want to nurse, the women just made 'em nurse. And they soon stopped crying. They wanted to get the whole confession.

"Gentlemen bastards and sonofabitches. Women wenches and hussies and goddam you all. Get this, the whole crowd of you that's come here to see me hang. I've done a whole hell of a sight more that I ought to hang for than this. But you—you come here to laugh at a man that meets death. All I got to say is goddam every blessed one of you and I hope to hand every one of you a cup of water in hell. You low-down brindle house-cats, come here to hang a man when he ain't done a single damn thing to you. I've killed seventeen men, raped five women, stole more than I can tell you about. Got a good mother and a good father. Don't hold a thing against them, you lousy bastards and wenches and young babies that nurse your mother's milk. This will be something for you to tell the generations about yet to come. And that is not all. I planned to kill Jim Murphy and Lizzie Murphy. It was all my work and yet all these fellows had to die. I hope God Almighty burns this sonofabitchen tree with lightning before another hundred years roll by. Poor devils without a chance. Die for you to laugh at and see struggle on the scaffold. Die for you to laugh at as you would a chicken fight. You low-down cowardly sonofabitches. Now laugh at me. I'll show you, by God, how a man can die. I'm not a bit afraid of whatever is to come. I'll be ready soon as I get one more good drink of Kentucky whisky and a chaw of terbacker in my jaw. Then you can give me the rope, goddam you. Strike up your goddam band. You people whoop and holler as much as you damn please, you low-lifed lousy bastards. I can whip any four fair-fisted in the crowd. Will fight you right up here on top of my coffin. Want to try it, any of you? None—"

There was silence in the crowd. Not a voice was lifted.

"Well, then, give me a drink of licker and a chaw of terbacker and I'm ready for the Happy Hunting Ground."

The sheriff stepped up and give him a drink out of a full horse-pint and give him a chaw of his own twist of terbacker. I'll bet twenty men offered him a drink of licker but the sheriff took charge because it was his duty under the sharp eyes of the Law.

When he got the rope around his neck I remember he said, "Look here, you bunch of wenches. Let me show you how to die. I'll hope to give your tail a couple of kicks in hell. I'll just get there first. So long, you goddam bellering crowd."

Well, a lot of the old men held their heads. The women sniffed and the band struck up the last tune, they thought, for the day. But it wasn't the last tune. They put the rope around his neck and tied it to the rope in the tree, and drove the wagon out from under him. Well, he just snapped that rope like it was twine and laughed till you could a heared him for a mile. The limb swayed with him, too. No well rope would hold him after it was wore the way it was, hanging so many people. Somebody went and got another rope. It was a brand new rope. And they fixed a new rope up in the elm and caught another limb so the two of them wouldn't give. And the seventh time, the rope held him. Well, the sheriff had to arrest his father and mother. They started fighting in the crowd. They's lots of people started taking it up for them and if they hadn't got him hung when they did it would have been a pitched battle by three o'clock. People started taking sides. You know what that meant in them days.

It wasn't long before the band started playing a retreat. It must have been Napoleon Bonaparte's retreat or some big general's—maybe George

Washington's. That was what happened at the end of the hangings. Had to have some soft music to soften the people up a little bit. God, it had been an awful day. Women pulling hair and shouting and praying, singing, screaming till you couldn't hear your ears. God, Kentucky used to have her hangings. And that was the biggest one I ever saw in Kentucky. Lauria and Kent Sixeymore riding on their sons' coffins. Lauria was a-setting on the end of one and Kent was a-setting on the end of the other. It was a sad thing to see. Pore old man and woman! Their hair white as cotton fleece flyin' in the spring wind, the dogs a-barking and a-fighting. And the band, just about petered out on fast music, started playing that slow soft kind. People almost in tears! Big day was over. People getting at the little restaurant where it said, "Good lodging for a man and brute and a glass of licker and a night's lodging for a quarter." People trying to get something to eat. Women and children hungry and old skin hounds running up to the back porches to slop barrels and fighting over them. People fighting in the streets. Wagons going out of Blakesburg with the dead. No wonder they call that place Hang-Town! It was a hang-town. If you could just a seen, Son, that crowd a-breaking up and leaving. It was a sight. People getting acquainted and talking about the hanging, talking about their crops and the cattle and the doings of the Lord to the wicked people for their sins. That was the biggest hanging I ever saw. Used all them two barrels of cold water on the fighting dogs and the fainting women. When the crowd left, all the gardens and flowers had been tromped under. Town looked awful and limbs broke out of the trees where people couldn't see out of the crowd and climbed the trees and got up in them like birds! God, but it was awful!

Then a little later on they got to building a scaffold an' just letting a body see their bodies before they dropped down into a trap door and a saw-dust bottom. They even put a cap over their face till people couldn't see their faces. Just kept a-gettin' it easier and easier till they didn't hang 'em at all. Got to having baseball games instead and then people got bad in these parts. Law got to be a joke! Something like it is now. Give 'em just as easy a death as possible, like the hot seat. They used to let 'em hang in Kentucky!

Sylvania Is Dead

About the story:

There can be little doubt that in his steady growth toward mastery of the short story genre, Jesse Stuart absorbed the literary tradition of the tall tale and southwestern humor, so popular as American settlers along the frontier moved ever westward. In Stuart's stories one may discover echoes of the down-east yarns of Seba Smith, of A. B. Longstreet's *Georgia Scenes,* and of the colorful works of John Phoenix, Mark Twain, Bret Harte, Sut Lovingood, and T. B. Thorpe. Ruel E. Foster observes in his biocritical study *Jesse Stuart* that "Stuart picks up the tall-tale element in his story 'Sylvania Is Dead.'" Yet, although the story advances boldly enough toward the hyperbole of tragicomedy, its sources are so authentic that Stuart chose to render them naturally and convincingly, letting them shine through his unusual subject. The result is a truer naturalistic impression, a richer texture, and a deeper verisimilitude than those achieved in the greater mass of the works of southwestern humor.

The Southern Appalachians of America possess many cultures with many truths—social truths such as isolation and prejudice, to be sure, but also codes of behavior, dialect, humor, and idiosyncracies that balance the nether side of human society. The locale of "Sylvania Is Dead" is authentic and the same as that of Stuart's novel, *Daughter of the Legend* (1965), published nearly a quarter of a century after the story made its first appearance. As a student at Lincoln Memorial University in Harrogate, Tennessee, from 1926 to 1929, Jesse Stuart had heard regional anecdotes about a mysterious race of people known as the Melungeons. He returned to the eastern Tennessee region several times after his graduation, and in the fall of 1934 devoted the space of a three-part series entitled "The Melungeons: America's Strange Race," to his then regular column, "Fragments from Nothing," published in the Greenup (County, Ky.) *News.* The Melungeons, the young columnist wrote, comprise "approximately one-third of Hancock County," but the Melungeons had then settled on the mountaintop of Newman's Ridge "in preference to the fertile Clinch River valley which winds below them and is followed on each side by unbroken mountain ranges" of the Cumberlands. The name, literally "New Man's Ridge," was bestowed upon the area of the strange race "about the year of 1790 by the few white settlers there." Their territory was then bounded generally by three villages, Stuart wrote, "Mulberry Gap and Sneedville, Tennessee—and Ewing, Virginia."

Jesse Stuart first published the source for his fictional character Sylvania in the second of his three-part series:

> When seven-hundred-pound Halley Mullins' little ninety-five pound husband died—the runt of the race—she had the funeral preached at home rather than by the grave-side. She was too big to get out of the door and she never bothered about having the door sawed out so she could get out and walk around the side of the mountain to his funeral. She had a reason for not having the door sawed out. She had the funeral preached in the house and while the preacher was saying a few words over Skinny and how much he would be missed in the community—Hall[e]y Mullins covered the whiskey barrel over with an oil cloth to keep the flies away from the auger hole. But just as soon as the preache[r] was through with his sermon, Halley had the cloth removed and she treated all the funeral crowd—especially the pallbearers. They had difficulty carrying Skinny to the grave.
>
> When the officers came to arrest Halley Mullins for selling whiskey—all they could do was arrest her. They couldn't get her out the door—and if they had sawed the door out—there was no way they could have gotten her down off the mountain. And if they had gotten her down off the mountain, they would have had to make the jailhouse door wider before they could have gotten her into the jail.
>
> When Halley Mullins died—they tore the stone chimney down at the end of the house and took her out the hole it left. Her home-made coffin was too big to get out the door. And it was easier to tear down the chimney, too, than it was to saw out the door. It required less labor and skill.

In adapting the local material to fiction, Stuart compressed the funerals of little Skinny and "Big Haley" Mullins into her funeral alone and kept Skinny alive as a grief-stricken husband for a more intense character focus and dramatic effect.

Should any doubt arise as to the authenticity of Sylvania's prototype, evidence provided by attorney Henry R. Price of Rogersville, Tennessee, who wrote Mr. Stuart shortly after *Daughter of the Legend* was published, should erase all skepticism. Referring to the author's "splendid work," Price wrote in part,

> ... I wanted to pass along a copy of a photograph of Big Haley Mullins, surely Sylvania in your book.... I have been closely associated with the Melungeons for many years and have a sincere feeling for them.
>
> I hope you will enjoy ... the photograph which, incidentally, is a copy of an old picture found among the papers of an elderly friend of mine who died in Sneedville some time ago. The old picture was inscribed "Mahalia Mullins."

The photograph on p. 72 depicts "Big Haley" Mullins holding a mug in one hand and a fruit jar with a funnel in the other. To her left the viewer may discern a spigot at the end of a barrel.*

* * *

"Iᴛ's ᴛᴏᴏ ʙᴀᴅ about Sylvania," Bert Pratt said as he caught hold of a sassafras sprout and pulled himself another step. Lonnie Pennix was behind.

"Durn this old coal pick," Lonnie said. "If I didn't have it I could make it all right."

"I got this long-handled shovel and broadax and I'm making it all right," Bert answered from above. "You're a lot younger than I am. You ought'n be grumbling."

September was here and the leaves were falling from the oaks and beeches. The backbone of the mountain was gray and hard as the bleached bone of a carcass. The buzzards floated in high circles and craned their necks.

"Funny thing about a buzzard," Bert said. "He knows when anything dies in the mountains. I've often wondered if a buzzard could smell."

"Must be a buzzard can smell," Lonnie answered.

"What do you say we blow a minute before we get to the top," Bert said with his breath getting shorter. "I'm about pooped out. We just didn't think about the heat nor the cold when we ust to climb this mountain and get moonshine from Sylvania, did we? I've come over this old mountain many a night, drunk as a biled owl. Come right down here over these rocks with a couple o' big jugs strapped on me. Had a pistol in each hand shooting to hear my pistols crack."

The two men started again to climb the mountain. Their shirts were wet as sweat could make them. They were sticking to their backs.

"I could wring my shirt out and hang it on a grapevine to dry," Lonnie said.

---

*"Sylvania Is Dead" first appeared in the *Commonweal*, Vol. 37 (Oct. 30, 1942), pp. 31–34; reprinted in *Plowshare in Heaven* (N.Y.: McGraw-Hill, 1958), pp. 73–83. Stuart recapitulated the story in his novel *Daughter of the Legend* (N.Y.: McGraw-Hill, 1965), pp. 191–211. Ruel E. Foster links the short story to the tall-tale tradition in his biocritical study *Jesse Stuart*, pp. 84–85. Jesse Stuart's columns "Fragments from Nothing" treating his topic "The Melungeons: America's Strange Race" are in the Greenup (County, Ky.) *News*, the publication dates of which can be determined with general accuracy from internal evidence to be most likely October–November, 1934, clippings in Jesse Stuart, Scrapbook #4, pp. 26–28, M. S. U. Mr. Henry R. Price's letter to Mr. Stuart, from Rogersville, Tennessee, is dated April 21, 1966, and contains a copy of the photograph reproduced here; these items are in my correspondence file.

"Take it easy, Lonnie, and get good footholts on the sand rocks," Bert answered.

"Look at the buzzards again," Lonnie said as he pointed to a cloud of circling buzzards.

"Whooie! At the top at last," Bert said. "I'd rather walk twenty miles on level ground as to climb that baby."

"When I see the shack, I have sad thoughts about poor old Sylvania," Lonnie said. "You could trade Sylvania a pistol fer licker when you didn't have the money. You could trade her corn, leather britches, beans and turnips, fer pistols, clothes, butter, eggs, ham meat, sow middlins, lard, flour, and corn meal."

"Look out there, Lonnie, at that crowd, won't you!" Bert said as he stood and looked toward the shack. "How did they ever get up this mountain?"

The mules and horses were tied to the garden palings and to the little blackjack saplings in the front yard. Many of the horses and mules were bareback and many had saddles on them. Overhead the buzzards circled low.

"Shoot into the buzzards, Lonnie, and shoo 'em away."

"Don't reckon the crack of my pistol will disturb the peace of the funeral as much as the buzzards will. Up there in the air pilfering around where they ain't got no business."

Lonnie pulled the pistol from his hip holster. He leveled it toward the turkey buzzards and pow-powed five times.

"Shooting around here and my wife a corpse." Skinny ran from the door of his shack and shouted, "Getting the mules and horses skeered to death! It ain't good manners, boys!"

"Just shooting away the buzzards, Skinny," Lonnie said. "See 'em taking off the mountain yander. Brought one down fer I saw 'im flopping among the black-oak tops."

"That part is all right, boys," Skinny answered. "Buzzards are a perfect nuisance in a time like this." Skinny walked back inside the shack.

The men had brought their picks, broadaxes, long-handled shovels, and corn scoops to dig the grave. They had brought handsaws, axes, hammers, nails, foot adzes to make the coffin.

"I tell you Sylvania is a big woman," Woodbridge Spears said. "Just six hundred and fifty pounds. She's never been out'n that house since she was a little girl. She married Skinny, a little hundred-pound man, and she has lived all her life in there with him. Her pap and ma moved out to let her and Skinny have the house. If they'd moved Sylvania out they'd had to tear the house down. They didn't bother about doing that."

"But she'll have to come out'n there today," Remus Wolf said. "God knows how we'll get her out. Might haf to tear the house down. Might haf to saw the door out bigger."

"Might just take the floor up and bury her under the floor," Estill Valence said. "We'd just have the furniture and the barrel to move out."

"We can't do that," George Fannin answered. "Skinny might want to jump the broom again. He wouldn't want his first wife buried under the floor."

"You're right, George," Remus said. "It would cause a lot of disturbances afterwards."

"We don't want no disturbances," Bert said with tears in his eyes. "I've come here and got moonshine when the country was dry as a bone. I was right here when the Revenooers was atter Sylvania. They come and bought some from her barrel and then showed her the Badge. She just laughed at them. 'You'll haf to get me out'n the house first,' she said. 'Atter you get me out'n the house, how are you goin' to get me down off the mountain?' All they could do was pour out a barrel of good licker. It wasn't no time until Sylvania had the barrel replenished and we were going back again."

The saws and axes were clicking up at the barn. You could hear the men talking and laughing as they worked.

"I'll bet that coffin is four feet wide across the bottom."

"Looks big enough for a whole family."

"We'll never get it through the door."

"Purty black-oak wood we're makin' this coffin out'n. Some say black-oak ain't as good as wild cherry."

"Just put the two in the ground fer fence posts, gentlemen, and see which lasts the longest."

"Right out under the pine where Pap and Ma are buried is where I want you to dig my wife's grave," Skinny said. "Bert Pratt, you take charge of it. It's the only place up here where there's dirt enough to sink a grave."

"I'll sure attend to it, Skinny," Bert said.

Bert walked in front with a broadax and a long-handled shovel on his shoulder. Men followed him carrying picks, mattocks, long-handled shovels, and short-handled shovels across their shoulders. They followed Bert out the mountain top, across a little sag where Skinny had a corn patch. They walked over to the tallest pine in the grove. Under the tall pine were two graves with sandstone tombstones hewn out with broadaxes.

Where Skinny had marked the place for the grave, Bert started digging.

"I'd do anything fer old Skinny," Bert said to the men. "He's in bushels o' misery just now."

"I'd do anything fer him too," Rodney Fitch said. "There never was a better woman than Sylvania. When she sold you a gallon of moonshine you got a gallon of unadulterated moonshine and not two quarts of moonshine with a quart of water and a quart of carbide all stirred up well and shook before drinking. I don't know what we'll do without her. We won't have no market fer our corn."

"They say," Tom Hankas said as he let his pick fall against the hard mountain earth, "that you'll never miss your mother until she's gone. I say we'll never miss Sylvania until she's gone. She's been a mother to all of us."

One crew of men worked hard and fast digging the big hole. Then they got out and rested and another crew took their places and worked until they got tired. Then the third crew of men took the tools and worked until they got tired. Then the first crew came back and replaced the third crew.

"We got a lot of dirt to move before high noon," Bert reminded the men as he sat under the pine and fanned his hot face with his cap.

The lazy wind blew over the mountaintop. Leaves swarmed in the wind. Leaves fell into the grave the men were digging for Sylvania. Buzzards flew above the shack while Flora Fitch and Vie Bostick worked in the shack and prepared Sylvania for burial.

"It's getting high noon," Skinny said. "Time the boys had the grave dug."

"We got Sylvania ready fer burial," Flora Fitch said, standing in the door of the shack. "We dressed 'er in that flowered silk dress she got married in."

"She allus wanted to be put away in that dress," Skinny said.

"I see them coming from the barn now with the coffin," Vie Bostick said.

"Coffin looks like a young house to me," Lonnie Pennix remarked.

Skinny walked out to the new coffin. He looked at the black-oak wood gleaming in the sun.

"It's a nice job, boys," Skinny said as his bony hand tried to shake it.

"Took six of us to carry that coffin from the barn down there," Amos Chitwood said. "Black-oak wood is powerful heavy."

"It'll take twelve of us to carry Sylvania to the grave, then," Bert Madden said.

"The boys have the grave ready," Lonnie said. "See 'em coming out the ridge path."

"Looks like they've all jumped in a rain barrel," Flora said. "They are all so wet with sweat."

Skinny walked inside the shack.

"The grave's ready," Bert said, wiping sweat from his beardy face with a red bandanna, then squeezing the sweat from the bandanna with his big hands. "Had a time getting through that dry ground. I had to plug five buzzards, too. Hope I didn't skeer you none."

"A little shooting is not goin' to bother us none," Flora answered. "What's a-going to bother us is when we start to take Sylvania out'n the house."

"Can't we saw the door bigger?" Rodney Fitch asked.

"Just as well take one side the house out by the time you make the door big enough to take that coffin out," Vie Bostick answered.

"The chimney nearly kivvers one end of the shack," Bert said. "Why can't we just tear it down? Won't take long."

"Bert, ask Skinny about it," Rodney Fitch said. "Tell 'im that's the only way to get her out."

Bert went inside the shack to speak to Skinny. The crowd of sweaty men waited outside. They held their working tools in their hands. The yard was filled with people. They stood and looked at the new coffin and talked about it. The horses and mules tramped around the blackjack saplings and fought the flies. The mules heehawed and laid back their ears and bit at the horses.

"I tell you men it was a job to get Sylvania ready for burial," Vie said. "It'll take six powerful men to put her in the coffin."

"We'll get 'er in all right," Rodney Fitch said.

Bert came to the door.

"Boys, tear down that chimney," he said.

Bert was the first to climb the wall. Lonnie climbed after him. They stood on the clapboard roof and rolled the rocks off the chimney. Lum Tremble reached Bert up a coal pick. Bert pried the rocks loose from the daubing where they were stuck.

"Soon have it done, boys, the way you're raining the rocks down here," Rodney Fitch said. "Stand in the clear, fellers, and see that the rocks don't roll on your toes."

The chimney was lowered to a flat pile of cornfield rocks. The hole was big enough to take the coffin through.

"All right, boys, let's take the coffin in and get Sylvania," Abraham Pitts commanded.

Three men got on a side and one on each end of the coffin. Over the chimney rocks they tugged it into the shack.

"Set 'er down easy, boys, on these poles now," Abraham Pitts said. "Don't ketch anybody's finger now. Take 'er easy . . . down . . . down . . . easy . . . down."

The coffin was placed on three poles. The poles were placed on rocks so the men could get their hands under the poles. Sylvania was upon the bed now, a great heap in a flowered dress.

"About six of you strong men lift her," Bert ordered.

Bert took his handkerchief from his pocket and wiped the tears from his eyes. Many of the men shed tears. The women stood and looked on. They could not begin to lift Sylvania. They strained their backs trying to roll her into the big flowered dress they had spliced so it would fit her.

The men, one ahold of each leg, one ahold of each arm, one at the head and one at each side, lifted her from the bed. "Easy, easy now, boys—easy—easy—easy—" It was a bad place to lift, and hard lifting, but they placed Sylvania in her coffin.

"Couldn't a made a better fit," Lonnie Fitch said.

"It was my wife's dyin' request that she didn't have her funeral preached nor no songs sung," Skinny said. "See that barrel over there! It's the last my wife made. It's all fer you, boys. There's the dipper over there. What you can't finish today you can finish Monday when you come back to hep me make my new chimney."

"Fellers, I'm a little thirsty," Bert said. "Let me to that dipper."

"She kept us wet through the dry season," Rodney Fitch said.

"It just takes another dipper to cool my throat," Lonnie said. "I'm hot as a lizard in a new ground fire."

The thirsty men stood around the barrel and drank like cattle around a water hole.

"I patronized Sylvania in life and I'll patronize 'er in death," Bert said. "Take your last long look at Sylvania, boys, while Lonnie gets the nails and the hammer."

The men looked at Sylvania. Strong men, tanned by the sun where their flesh was not hidden by beard on their faces, looked at Sylvania and wept. They pulled handkerchiefs and bandannas from their pockets and wiped their eyes.

"Just a lot o' drunk men crying," Rodney said. "It'll be awful before we get her to the grave. They'll all be crying. Ought to a had the licker last."

"Who is conducting this funeral, me or you, Rodney?" Skinny asked. "I'm doing what Sylvania requested. I'm going through with it if they all get down drunk."

"Ouch, whooie, that damn big-headed hammer," Lonnie yelled. "I couldn't hit the side of a barn with it. Lord, I nearly mashed the end of my finger off trying to drive that nail."

"Let me have the hammer," Rodney requested. "I can still drive nails. Hit some people with a sour apple and they get drunk. They can't take their licker."

Rodney shaped the coffin lid and spiked it down while the men looked on.

"My poor Sylvania is gone forever," Skinny cried.

"Come away from that barrel," Bert demanded. "Do you fellers want to get down drunk and leave the corpse in a shack that has the end out'n it? Get under these poles! What do you think today is, your birthday?"

Two men got under each end of the three poles. "Get in front, Rodney," Bert ordered. 'I'll get behind and tail the coffin."

Fourteen men were around the black-oak coffin. They walked slowly out at the end of the house where they tore the chimney down.

"Just like picking up a house with the family in it," Rodney groaned as they walked across the yard and out the ridge path toward the pine. The crowd was noisy now. The men were laughing, talking, and crying. The women walked behind as the men carried Sylvania to her grave. Before they reached the fresh heap of dirt under the tall pine tree, Bert pulled his pistol from his hip holster and shot into a cloud of buzzards.

"Easy—easy—easy—take 'er easy, boys," Bert said. "Don't mash no fingers."

They lowered Sylvania's coffin by the big pine where the dirt was piled high.

"You got the plowlines, ain't you, Oggle?" Skinny asked.

"I got five pair of plowlines," Oggle Fox answered.

"Put two big poles across the grave," Bert ordered. "There they lay already cut."

The men carried the green hickory poles and laid them across the grave.

"All the rest of you back to your places now," Bert ordered. Let's lift the coffin onto the poles."

"Let's wind a minute," Efi Turnstile said. "I'm about gone."

"Wish I was planted by 'er side," Skinny screamed.

"No use to feel that way, Skinny," Lonnie consoled him.

"Take it easy, Skinny," Bert said.

"Wish I could," Skinny answered.

"Eif, you've had time to get your wind now," Lonnie said. "What do you say we lower this coffin, men? Get the plowlines under it. Two get hold of the end of each line."

The men placed ten plowlines under the coffin.

"Ready now, boys!" Lonnie said. "Heave ho! Heave ho! Heave ho!"

"Let's pull these poles from under the coffin," Bert ordered. "Four men to each pole."

The men took the poles from under the coffin while twenty men held it up with the plowlines.

"Let 'er down," Bert ordered.

The big coffin dropped slowly while two men strained at each end of ten ropes. They pulled the ropes from under the coffin. It was all over.

"May God rest Sylvania's soul," Bert said, wiping tears from his eyes with his red bandanna.

Two men took Skinny toward the shack while clouds of gray dust swirled above the busy shovels. There were words of condolence in the lazy wind's molesting the dry flaming leaves on the mountain.

This Farm for Sale

About the story:

Of the large groups of English, Scottish, and Scots-Irish ancestors that settled the Appalachian highland, Jesse Stuart wrote, "They were not prison-
ers, debtors, ne'er-do-wells, or castoffs from the seaboard settlements, as
some rumors have reported them to be. They were the most aggressive of
the aggressive pioneers, brave with dreams and visions, who had come from
the Old World of the British Isles to establish new homes and a new country
in a wilderness." And they loved their land, were proud of the land in both
a personal and a communal sense, as Jesse Stuart has expressed it in this
lyric song:

> *My land is fair for any eyes to see—*
> *Now look, my friends—look to the east and west!*
> *You see the purple hills far in the west—*
> *Hills lined with pine and gum and black-oak tree—*
> *Now to the east you see the fertile valley!*
> *This land is mine, I sing of it to you—*
> *My land beneath the skies of white and blue.*
> *This land is mine, for I am part of it.*
> *I am the land, for it is part of me—*
> *We are akin and thus our kinship be!*
> *It would make me a brother to the tree!*
> *And far as eyes can see this land is mine.*
> *Not for one foot of it I have a deed—*
> *To own this land I do not need a deed—*
> *They all belong to me—gum, oak, and pine.*

But sometimes even the old people may forget how deeply attached they
are to the land. In the presence of a natural hill poet like Stuart's character
Melvin Spencer, who made his living selling real estate in general and spe-
cializing in small hill farms in particular, even Uncle Dick and Aunt Emma
Stone, who owned a century-old place on the Tiber River, were mightily
tempted to exchange their birthright for money.

"When I decided to write this story," Jesse Stuart said, "I felt that the
telling of it would be more effective if it were told firsthand rather than
from an onlooker's point of view. Thus I used the device of the first person

singular in the character of Shan, who spends his summers with Uncle Dick and Aunt Emma and his cousins." But the art of telling the story aside, its facts and the human elements were real enough. Sometimes "Melvin Spencer's way with words," the author wrote, "backfired. . . ." Or as old Uncle Dick, seeing his farm for the first time through other eyes and knowing what he saw was worth more than money, says, "I didn't know I had so much. . . . I'm a rich man and didn't know it."*

* * *

"THIS TIME we're goin' to sell this farm," Uncle Dick said to Aunt Emma. "I've just learned how to sell a farm. Funny, I never thought of it myself."

My cousins—Olive, Helen, Oliver, and Little Dick—all stopped eating and looked at one another and then looked at Uncle Dick and Aunt Emma. When Aunt Emma smiled, they smiled, too. Everybody seemed happy because Uncle Dick, who had just come from Blakesburg, had found a way to sell the farm. Everybody was happy but me. I was sorry Uncle Dick was going to sell the farm.

"This farm is just as good as sold!" Uncle Dick talked on. "I've got a real estate man, my old friend Melvin Spencer, coming here tomorrow to look the place over. He's goin' to sell it for me."

"I'd like to get enough for it to make a big payment on a fine house in Blakesburg," Aunt Emma said. "I've got the one picked out that I want. It's the beautiful Coswell house. I understand it's up for sale now and no one's livin' in it!"

"Gee, that will be wonderful," Cousin Olive said. "Right on the street and not any mud. We wouldn't have to wear galoshes all winter if we lived there!"

"I'll say it will be wonderful," Helen said, with a smile. "Daddy, I hope Mr. Spencer can sell this place."

I wanted to tell Aunt Emma the reason why no one was living in the Coswell house. Every time Big River rose to flood stage, the water got on the first floor in the house; and this was the reason why the Coswells had built a house on higher ground outside Blakesburg and had moved to it.

---

*Jesse Stuart, "Up the Branch," *This Is the South*, ed. Robert West Howard (Chicago: Rand McNally & Co., 1959), p. 221. The poem is Jesse Stuart Sonnet #7, *Man with a Bull-Tongue Plow* (N.Y.: Dutton, 1934), p. 6. Jesse Stuart's "This Farm for Sale" was first published in *Progressive Farmer*, Vol. 69 (Nov., 1954), pp. 19, 56–57, 114–116; reprinted in Jesse Stuart, *A Jesse Stuart Reader* (N.Y.: McGraw-Hill, 1963), pp. 130–140. Jesse Stuart remarked on the circumstances out of which he wrote "This Farm for Sale" in his *"Author's Introduction," A Jesse Stuart Reader*, pp. 130–131. Professor Hensley C. Woodbridge's *Jesse Stuart Bibliography*, p. 81, indicates that this story has been reprinted through 1979 eleven other times.

And this was the reason why they couldn't keep a renter any longer than it took Big River to rise to flood stage. But this wasn't my business, so I didn't say anything.

"Mel Spencer will come here to look this farm over," Uncle Dick said, puffing on his cigar until he'd almost filled the dining room with smoke. "Then he'll put an ad in the *Blakesburg Gazette*."

"What will we do about the cows, horses, hogs, honeybees, hay in the barn lofts and in the stacks, and corn in the bins?" Cousin Oliver asked.

"Sell them, too," Uncle Dick said. "When we sell, let's sell everything we have but our house plunder."

It was ten o'clock the next day before Melvin Spencer came. Since he couldn't drive his car all the way to Uncle Dick's farm, he rode the mail truck to Red Hot. Red Hot is a store and post office on the Tiber River. And at Red Hot, Uncle Dick met him with an extra horse and empty saddle. So Melvin Spencer came riding up with Uncle Dick. And I'll never forget the first words he said when he climbed down from the saddle.

"Richard, it's a great experience to be in the saddle again," he said, breathing deeply of the fresh air. "All this reminds me of another day and time."

Oliver, Little Dick, and I followed Melvin Spencer and Uncle Dick as they started walking toward the Tiber bottoms.

"How many acres in this farm, Richard?" Melvin Spencer asked.

"The deed calls for three hundred, more or less," Uncle Dick said.

"How many acres of bottom land?" he asked Uncle Dick.

"I'd say about sixty-five," Uncle Dick replied.

We walked down the jolt-wagon road, where my cousins and I had often ridden Nell and Jerry to and from the field.

"What kind of land is this?" Melvin Spencer asked. He had to look up to see the bright heads of cane.

"It's limestone land," Uncle Dick bragged. "Never had to use fertilizer. My people have farmed these bottoms over a hundred years."

Then Uncle Dick showed Melvin Spencer the corn we had laid by. It was August, and our growing corn was maturing. Melvin Spencer looked at the big cornfield. He was very silent. We walked on to the five acres of tobacco, where the broad leaves crossed the balks and a man couldn't walk through. Then we went down to the river.

"My farm comes to this river," Uncle Dick said. "I've often thought what a difference it would be if we had a bridge across this river. Then I could reach the Tiber road and go east to Blakesburg and west to Darter City. But we don't have a bridge; and until we go down the river seven miles to Red Hot where we can cross to the Tiber road, we'll always be in the mud. I've heard all my life that the county would build a bridge. My father heard it, too, in his lifetime."

"You *are* shut in here," Melvin Spencer agreed, as he looked beyond the Tiber River at the road.

"Now, we'll go to the house and get some dinner," Uncle Dick said. "Then I'll take you up on the hill this afternoon and show you my timber and the rest of the farm."

When we reached the big house, Melvin Spencer stopped for a minute and looked at the house and yard.

"You know, when I sell a piece of property, I want to look it over," he told Uncle Dick. "I want to know all about it. How old is this house?"

"The date was cut on the chimney," Uncle Dick said.

Melvin Spencer looked over the big squat log house with the plank door, big stone steps, small windows, the moss-covered roof. Then we went inside, and he started looking again. That is, he did until Uncle Dick introduced him to Aunt Emma and Aunt Emma introduced him to a table that made him stand and look some more.

"I've never seen anything like this since I was a boy," Melvin Spencer said, showing more interest in the loaded table than he had in the farm.

"All of this came from our farm here," Uncle Dick said.

I never saw a man eat like Melvin Spencer. He ate like I did when I first came to Uncle Dick's and Aunt Emma's each spring when school was over. He tried to eat something of everything on the table, but he couldn't get around to it all.

"If I could sell this farm like you can prepare a meal, I'd get a whopping big price for it," he said with a chuckle as he looked at Aunt Emma.

"I hope you can," Aunt Emma said. "We're too far back here. Our children have to wade the winter mud to get to school. And we don't have electricity. We don't have the things that city people have. And I think every country woman wants them."

Melvin Spencer didn't listen to all that Aunt Emma said. He was much too busy eating. And long before he had finished, Uncle Dick pulled a cigar from his inside coat pocket, struck a match under the table, lit it, and blew a big cloud of smoke toward the ceiling in evident enjoyment.

He looked at Aunt Emma and smiled.

"The old place is as good as sold, Mother," Uncle Dick said with a wink. "You're a-goin' to be out of the mud. We'll let some other woman slave around here and wear galoshes all winter. We'll be on the bright, clean streets wearin' well-shined shoes—every blessed one of us. We'll have an electric washer, a radio where we won't have to have the batteries charged, a bathroom, and an electric stove. No more of this stove-wood choppin' for the boys and me."

When Uncle Dick said this, Olive and Helen looked at Aunt Emma and smiled. I looked at Oliver and Little Dick, and they were grinning. But Melvin Spencer never looked up from his plate.

When we got up from the table, Melvin Spencer thanked Aunt Emma, Cousin Olive, and Helen for the "best dinner" he'd had since he was a young man. Then he asked Aunt Emma for a picture of the house.

Aunt Emma sent Helen to get it. "If you can, just sell this place for us," Aunt Emma said to Melvin Spencer.

"I'll do my best," he promised her. "But as you ought to know, it will be a hard place to sell, located way back here and without a road."

"Are you a-goin' to put a picture of this old house in the paper?" Uncle Dick asked, as Helen came running with the picture.

"I might," Melvin Spencer said. "I never say much in an ad, since I have to make my words count. A picture means a sale sometimes. Of course, this expense will come from the sale of the property."

He said good-by to Aunt Emma, Olive, and Helen. Little Dick, Oliver, and I follwed him and Uncle Dick out of the house and up the hill where the yellow poplars and the pines grow.

"Why hasn't this timber been cut long ago?" Melvin Spencer asked, looking up at the trees.

"Not any way to haul it out," Uncle Dick told him.

"That's right," Melvin Spencer said. "I'd forgot about the road. If a body doesn't have a road to his farm, Richard, he's not got much of a place."

"These old trees get hollow and blow down in storms," Uncle Dick said. "They should have been cut down a long time ago."

"Yes, they should have," Melvin Spencer agreed, as he put his hand on the bark of a yellow poplar. "We used to have trees like this in Pike County. But not any more."

While we walked under the beech grove, we came upon a drove of slender bacon hogs eating beechnuts.

"Old Skinny bacon hogs," Uncle Dick said, as they scurried past us. "They feed on the mast of the beeches and oaks, on saw-briar, greenbriar, and pine-tree roots, and on mulberries, persimmons, and pawpaws."

When we climbed to the top of a hill, the land slanted in all directions.

"Show me from here what you own," Melvin Spencer said.

"It's very easy, Mel," Uncle Dick said. "The stream on the right and the

one on the left are the left and right forks of Wolfe Creek. They are boundary lines. I own all the land between them. I own all the bottom land from
where the forks join, down to that big bend in the Tiber. And I own down
where the Tiber flows against those white limestone cliffs."

"You are fenced in by natural boundaries," Melvin Spencer said.
"They're almost impossible to cross. This place will be hard to sell, Richard."

Then we went back down the hill, and Melvin and Uncle Dick climbed
into the saddles and were off down the little narrow road toward Red Hot.
Their horses went away at a gallop, because Melvin Spencer had to catch
the mail truck, and he was already behind schedule.

On Saturday, Uncle Dick rode to Red Hot to get the paper. Since he
didn't read very well, he asked me to read what Melvin Spencer had said
about his house. When I opened the paper and turned to the picture of the
house, everybody gathered around.

"Think of a picture of this old house in the paper," Aunt Emma said.

"But there are pictures of other houses for sale in the paper," Uncle Dick
told her. "That's not anything to crow about."

"But it's the best-looking of the four," Cousin Olive said.

"It does look better than I thought it would," Aunt Emma sighed.

"Look, here's two columns all the way down the page," I said. "The
other four places advertised here have only a paragraph about them."

"Read it," Uncle Dick said. "I'd like to know what Mel said about this
place. Something good, I hope."

So I read this aloud:

*Yesterday, I had a unique experience when I visited the farm of Mr. and Mrs. Rich-
ard Stone, which they have asked me to sell. I cannot write an ad about this farm. I
must tell you about it.*

*I went up a winding road on horseback. Hazelnut bushes, with clusters of green
hazelnuts bending their slender stems, swished across my face. Pawpaws, heavy with
green clusters of fruit, grew along this road. Persimmons with bending boughs covered
one slope below the road. Here are wild fruits and nuts of Nature's cultivation for the
one who possesses land like this. Not any work but just to go out and gather the fruit.
How many of you city dwellers would love this?*

"What about him a-mentionin' the persimmons, pawpaws, and hazelnuts!" Uncle Dick broke in. "I'd never have thought of them. They're
common things!"

*When we put the horses in the big barn, Mr. Stone, his two sons, his nephew, and I
walked down into his Tiber-bottom farm land. And, like the soil along the Nile River,
this overflowed land, rich with limestone, never has to be fertilized. I saw cane as high*

as a giraffe, and as dark green as the waves of the Atlantic. It grew in long, straight rows with brown clusters of seed that looked to be up against the blue of the sky. I have never seen such dark clouds of corn grow out of the earth. Five acres of tobacco, with leaves as broad as a mountaineer's shoulders. Pleasant meadows with giant haystacks here and there. It is a land rich with fertility and abundant with crops.

"That sounds wonderful," Aunt Emma said, smiling.

This peaceful Tiber River, flowing dreamily down the valley, is a boundary to his farm. Here one can see to the bottoms of the deep holes, the water is so clear and blue. One can catch fish from the river for his next meal. Elder bushes, where they gather the berries to make the finest jelly in the world, grow along this riverbank as thick as ragweeds. The Stones have farmed this land for four generations, have lived in the same house, have gathered elderberries for their jelly along the Tiber riverbanks, and fished in its sky-blue waters that long—and yet they will sell this land.

"Just a minute, Shan," Uncle Dick said as he got up from his chair. "Stop just a minute."

Uncle Dick pulled a handkerchief from his pocket and wiped the sweat from his forehead. His face seemed a bit flushed. He walked a little circle around the living room and then sat back down in his chair. But the sweat broke out on his face again when I started reading.

The proof of what a farm produces is at the farm table. I wish that whoever reads what I have written here could have seen the table prepared by Mrs. Stone and her two daughters. Hot fluffy biscuits with light-brown tops, brown-crusted cornbread, buttermilk, sweet milk (cooled in a freestone well), wild-grape jelly, wild-crab-apple jelly, mast-fed lean bacon that melted in my mouth, fresh apple pie, wild-blackberry cobbler, honey-colored sorghum from the limestone bottoms of the Tiber, and wild honey from the beehives.

"Oh, no one ever said that about a meal I cooked before," Aunt Emma broke in.

"Just a minute, Shan," Uncle Dick said, as he got up from his chair and with his handkerchief in his hand again.

This time Uncle Dick went a bit faster as he circled the living room. He wiped sweat from his face as he walked. He had a worried look on his face. I read on:

Their house, eight rooms and two halls, would be a show place if close to some of our modern cities. The house itself would be worth the price I will later quote you on this farm. Giant yellow poplar logs with twenty- to thirty-inch facings, hewed smooth with broadaxes by the mighty hands of Stone pioneers, make the sturdy walls in this termite-proof house. Two planks make the broad doors in this house that is one-hundred-and-six years old. This beautiful home of pioneer architecture is without modern conveniences, but since a power line will be constructed up the Tiber River early next spring, a few modern conveniences will be possible.

"I didn't know that!" Aunt Emma was excited. "I guess it's just talk, like about the bridge across the Tiber."

After lunch I climbed a high hill to look at the rest of this farm. I walked through a valley of virgin trees, where there were yellow poplars and pine sixty feet to the first limb. Beech trees with tops big enough to shade twenty-five head of cattle. Beechnuts streaming down like golden coins, to be gathered by the bacon hogs running wild. A farm with wild game and fowl, and a river bountiful with fish! And yet, this farm is for sale!

Uncle Dick walked over beside his chair. He looked as if he were going to fall over.

Go see for yourself roads not exploited by the county or state, where the horse's shoe makes music on the clay, where apple orchards with fruit are bending down, and barns and bins are full. Go see a way of life, a richness and fulfillment that make America great, that put solid foundation stones under America! This beautiful farm, fifty head of livestock, honeybees, crops old and new, and a home for only $22,000!

"Oh!" Aunt Emma screamed. I thought she was going to faint. "Oh, he's killed it with that price. It's unheard of, Richard! You couldn't get $6000 for it."

Uncle Dick still paced the floor.

"What's the matter, Pa?" Oliver finally asked.

"I didn't know I had so much," Uncle Dick said. "I'm a rich man and didn't know it. I'm not selling this farm!"

"Don't worry, Richard," Aunt Emma said. "You won't sell it at that price!"

I never saw such disappointed looks as there were on my cousins' faces.

"But what will you do with Mr. Spencer?" Aunt Emma asked. "You've put the farm in his hands to sell."

"Pay him for his day and what he put in the paper," Uncle Dick told her. "I know we're not goin' to sell now, for it takes two to sign the deed. I'll be willing to pay Mel Spencer a little extra because he showed me what we have."

Then I laid the paper down and walked quietly from the room. Evening was coming on. I walked toward the meadows. I wanted to share the beauty of this farm with Melvin Spencer. I was never so happy.

Youth

Part 3

Split Cherry Tree

About the story:

"Split Cherry Tree" was originally published in *Esquire* in January, 1939, and since then has been credited with more than thirty reprints, including French and Israeli editions; it is the most frequently reprinted of all Jesse Stuart's more than 460 published short stories of record. The author also has received more letters on this story than on any other, numbering by his own reckoning in the thousands.

The genesis of this story goes back to his years as principal of McKell High School from 1933–1937. One of the salesmen of school supplies who came by his office told him a story "about high school boys climbing a cherry tree and splitting a branch from the tree and the high school principal's keeping them after hours because he didn't have money to pay the farmer for his tree." What excited the salesman most was "how the boy's father came to the high school with a pistol to shoot the principal over keeping his son after school, [a] father who didn't believe in microbes until they let him look into a microscope at some tartar he had taken from his teeth. This convinced the father that teachers and [the] principal in the high school were right and he was wrong and behind the times." The salesman was a pleasant older man of imposing size "with a shock of white hair," and he often retold the story on subsequent calls, the author said, "until it had become a fixture in my mind." He never planned to write the story because it did not seem "colorful or compelling enough" to set down on paper.

Yet, while on his Guggenheim Fellowship in Edinburgh, Scotland, on a winter night of 1937–1938 in his room at 8 Viewforth Gardens, his mind reached back across the Atlantic to his homeland. It was a long dark night because "Scotland is on a latitude with Alaska and the shortest day of the year in Scotland has about twenty-two hours of pitchblack darkness and two hours of light and then darkness again. . . . I couldn't sleep all of these long nights. So, I wrote about all the ideas I'd jotted on paper, even if I didn't think too much of them." And so he wrote "Split Cherry Tree," not really valuing it much, although his typist, an elderly Scottish spinster named "Miss Penny," did like it.

One explanation of the story's continuing popularity may lie in its point of view, that refreshing universality of youth looking with puzzlement at the world of adult values and responsibilities and perceiving through the transforming experience of education the old verity of familial pride, initiated by the homely assertion of Dave's Pa in telling Professor Herbert, "We don't want somethin' for nothin'," and then staying on with his son after school and helping him sweep the floor to repay the debt of the split cherry tree. As successful as the story is, the author had his reservations, which in retrospect may serve as a commentary on his own astonishing artistic negative capability. Had he identified too closely with his subject? At any rate, he declared, "One of the unfortunate things about this story . . . is . . . I let the high school boy who had split the limb from the cherry tree tell the story. Young readers thought I was that boy when I went to high school. They thought his father who came with a gun for the teacher was my father. I'm glad my father never knew this. He was the most pro-schoolteacher of any man I ever knew. He wanted all of his children to be teachers. All five of us were teaching a combined total of 130 years and three are still teaching. I had to answer all the letters I received asking me if my father and I were in this story. I never wanted a young reader to believe we were. And I received at least over these 38 years 500 letters asking me this."*

*Jesse Stuart, "Split Cherry Tree," *Esquire*, Vol. 11 (Jan., 1939), pp. 52–53, 99–100; reprinted in *Scholastic*, Vol. 34 (March 18, 1939), pp. 27–29; *ibid.*, New York, Associated Educational Services Corp., 1967, pp. 3–14; supplementary teaching aids, pp. 15–20. Woodbridge, *Jesse Stuart Bibliography*, pp. 78–79, lists approximately 27 reprints including French and Israeli editions. During 1980–1981, the Jesse Stuart Foundation, which now manages most of Mr. Stuart's literary properties, granted four fee-permissions for reprinting "Split Cherry Tree," resulting in more than 30 reprints of the story since its first publication in 1939. The source of the author's comments on "Split Cherry Tree" is his unpublished manuscript, "Split Cherry Tree, by Jesse Stuart," in the Jesse Stuart Collection, W-Hollow, Greenup, Ky. Other information, such as his Edinburgh address during his year abroad as a Guggenheim Fellow, is from H. Edward Richardson, unpublished biography of Jesse Stuart, Chapter XI.

"I DON'T MIND staying after school," I says to Professor Herbert, "but I'd rather you'd whip me with a switch and let go home early. Pa will whip me anyway for getting home two hours late."

"You are too big to whip," says Professor Herbert, "and I have to punish you for climbing up that cherry tree. You boys knew better than that! The other five boys have paid their dollar each. You have been the only one who has not helped pay for the tree. Can't you borrow a dollar?"

"I can't," I says. "I'll have to take the punishment. I wish it would be quicker punishment. I wouldn't mind."

Professor Herbert stood and looked at me. He was a big man. He wore a gray suit of clothes. The suit matched his gray hair.

"You don't know my father," I says to Professor Herbert. "He might be called a little old-fashioned. He makes us mind him until we're twenty-one years old. He believes: 'If you spare the rod you spoil the child.' I'll never be able to make him understand about the cherry tree. I'm the first of my people to go to high school."

"You must take the punishment," says Professor Herbert. "You must stay two hours after school today and two hours after school tomorrow. I am allowing you twenty-five cents an hour. That is good money for a high school student. You can sweep the schoolhouse floor, wash the blackboards and clean windows. I'll pay the dollar for you."

I couldn't ask Professor Herbert to loan me a dollar. He never offered to loan it to me. I had to stay and help the janitor and work out my fine at a quarter an hour.

I thought as I swept the floor: "What will Pa do to me? What lie can I tell him when I go home? Why did we ever climb that cherry tree and break it down for anyway? Why did we run crazy over the hills away from the crowd? Why did we do all of this! Six of us climbed up in a little cherry tree after one little lizard! Why did the tree split and fall with us? It should have been a stronger tree! Why did Eif Crabtree just happen to be below us plowing and catch us in his cherry tree? Why wasn't he a better man than to charge us six dollars for the tree?"

It was six o'clock when I left the schoolhouse. I had six miles to walk home. It would be after seven when I got home. I had all my work to do when I got home. It took Pa and me both to do the work. Seven cows to milk. Nineteen head of cattle to feed, four mules, twenty-five hogs, firewood and stovewood to cut and water to draw from the well. He would be doing it when I got home. He would be mad and wondering what was keeping me!

I hurried home. I would run under the dark leafless trees. I would walk fast uphill. I would run down the hill. The ground was freezing. I had to hurry. I had to run and reached the long ridge that led to our cow pasture. I ran along this ridge. The wind dried the sweat on my face. I ran across the pasture to the house.

I threw down my books in the chipyard, I ran to the barn to spread fodder on the ground for the cattle. I didn't take time to change my clean school clothes for my old work clothes. I ran out to the barn. I saw Pa spreading fodder on the ground to the cattle. That was my job. I ran up to the fence. I says: "Leave that for me Pa. I'll do it. I'm just a little late."

"I see you are," says Pa. He turned and looked at me. His eyes danced fire. "What in th' world has kept you so. Why ain't you been here to help me with this work? Make a gentleman out'n one boy in th' family and this is what you get! Send you to high school and you get too onery fer th' buzzards to smell!"

I never said anything. I didn't want to tell why I was late from school. Pa stopped scattering the bundles of fodder. He looked at me. He says: "Why are you gettin' in here this time o' night? You tell me or I'll take a hickory withe to you right here on th' spot."

I says: "I had to stay after school." I couldn't lie to Pa. He'd go to school and find out why I had to stay. If I lied to him it would be too bad for me.

"Why did you haf to stay atter school?" says Pa.

I says: "Our Biology Class went on a field trip today. Six of us boys broke down a cherry tree. We had to give a dollar apiece to pay for the tree. I didn't have the dollar. Professor Herbert is making me work out my dollar. He gives me twenty-five cents an hour. I had to stay in this afternoon. I'll have to stay in tomorrow afternoon!"

"Are you telling me th' truth?" says Pa.

"I'm telling you the truth," I says. "Go and see for yourself."

"That's just what I'll do in th' mornin'," says Pa. "Jist whose cherry tree did you break down?"

"Eif Crabtree's cherry tree!"

"My God," says Pa, "what was you doing clear out in Eif Crabtree's place? He lives four miles from th' County High School. Don't they teach you no books at that high school? Do they jist let you get out and gad over th' hillsides? If that's all they do I'll keep you at home, Dave. I've got work here fer you to do!"

"Pa," I says, "Spring is just getting here. We take a subject in school where we have to have bugs, snakes, flowers, lizards, frogs and plants. It is Biology. It was a pretty day today. We went out to find a few of these. Six of us boys saw a lizard at the same time sunning on a cherry tree. We all went up the tree to get it. We broke the tree down. It split at the forks. Eif

Crabtree was plowing down below us. He ran up the hill and got our names. The other boys gave their dollar apiece. I didn't have mine. Professor Herbert put mine in for me. I have to work it out at school."

"Poor man's son, huh," says Pa. "I'll attend to that myself in th' mornin'. I'll take keer o' 'im. He ain't from this county nohow. I'll go down there in th' mornin' and see 'im. Lettin' you leave your books and galavant all over th' hills. What kind of a damn school is it nohow! Didn't do that, my son, when I's a little shaver in school. All fared alike too."

"Pa please don't go down there," I says. "Just let me have fifty cents and pay the rest of my fine! I don't want you to go down there! I don't want you to start anything with Professor Herbert!"

"Ashamed of your old Pap are you, Dave," says Pa, "atter th' way I've worked to raise you! Tryin' to send you to school so you can make a better livin' than I've made.

"I'll straighten this thing out myself! I'll take keer o' Professor Herbert myself! He ain't got no right to keep you in and let the other boys off jist because they've got th' money! I'm a poor man. A bullet will go in a Professor same as it will any man. It will go in a rich man same as it will a poor man. Now you get into this work before I take one o' these withes and cut the shirt off'n your back!"

I thought once I'd run through the woods above the barn just as hard as I could go. I thought I'd leave high school and home forever! Pa could not catch me! I'd get away! I couldn't go back to school with him. He'd have a gun and maybe he'd shoot Professor Herbert. It was hard to tell what he would do. I could tell Pa that school had changed in the hills from the way it was when he was a boy but he wouldn't understand. I could tell him we studied frogs, birds, snakes, lizards, flowers, insects. But Pa wouldn't understand. If I did run away from home it wouldn't matter to Pa. He would see Professor Herbert anyway. He would think that high school and Professor Herbert had run me away from home. There was no need to run away. I'd just have to stay, finish foddering the cattle and go to school with Pa the next morning.

I would take a bundle of fodder, remove the hickory witheband from around it and scatter it on rocks, clumps of greenbriars and brush so the cattle wouldn't tramp it under their feet. I would lean it up against the oak trees and the rocks in the pasture just above our pigpen on the hill. The fodder was cold and frosty where it had set out in the stacks. I would carry bundles of the fodder from the stack until I had spread out a bundle for each steer. Pa went to the barn to feed the mules and throw corn in the pen to the hogs.

The moon shone bright in the cold March sky. I finished my work by moonlight. Professor Herbert really didn't know how much work I had to do at home. If he had known he would not have kept me after school. He would have loaned me a dollar to have paid my part on the cherry tree. He had never lived in the hills. He didn't know the way the hill boys had to work so that they could go to school. Now he was teaching in a County High School where all the boys who attended were from hill farms.

After I'd finished doing my work I went to the house and ate my supper. Pa and Mom had eaten. My supper was getting cold. I heard Pa and Mom talking in the front room. Pa was telling Mom about me staying after school.

"I had to do all th' milkin' tonight, chop th' wood myself. It's too hard on me atter I've turned ground all day. I'm goin' to take a day off tomorrow and see if I can't remedy things a little. I'll go down to that high school tomorrow. I won't be a very good scholar fer Professor Herbert nohow. He won't keep me in atter school. I'll take a different kind of lesson down there and make 'im acquainted with it."

"Now Luster," says Mom, "you jist stay away from there. Don't cause a lot o' trouble. You can be jailed fer a trick like that. You'll get th' Law atter you. You'll jist do down there and show off and plague your own boy Dave to death in front o' all th' scholars!"

"Plague or no plague," says Pa, "he don't take into consideration what all I haf to do here, does he? I'll show 'im it ain't right to keep one boy in and let the rest go scot-free. My boy is good as th' rest, ain't he? A bullet will make a hole in a schoolteacher same as it will anybody else. He can't do me that way and get by with it. I'll plug 'im first. I aim to go down there bright and early in the mornin' and get all this straight! I aim to see about bug larnin' and this runnin' all over God's creation huntin' snakes, lizards, and frogs. Ransackin' th' country and goin' through cherry orchards and breakin' th' trees down atter lizards! Old Eif Crabtree ought to a-poured th' hot lead to 'em instead o' chargin' six dollars fer th' tree! He ought to a-got old Herbert th' first one!"

I ate my supper. I slipped upstairs and lit the lamp. I tried to forget the whole thing. I studied plane geometry. Then I studied my biology lesson. I could hardly study for thinking about Pa. "He'll go to school with me in the morning. He'll take a gun for Professor Herbert! What will Professor Herbert think of me! I'll tell him when Pa leaves that I couldn't help it. But Pa might shoot him. I hate to go with Pa. Maybe he'll cool off about it tonight and not go in the morning."

Pa got up at four o'clock. He built a fire in the stove. Then he built a fire in the fireplace. He got Mom up to get breakfast. Then he got me up to help feed and milk. By the time we had our work done at the barn, Mom had breakfast ready for us. We ate our breakfast. Daylight came and we could see the bare oak trees covered white with frost. The hills were white with frost. A cold wind was blowing. The sky was clear. The sun would soon come out and melt the frost. The afternoon would be warm with sunshine and the frozen ground would thaw. There would be mud on the hills again. Muddy water would then run down the little ditches on the hills.

"Now Dave," says Pa, "Let's get ready fer school. I aim to go with you this mornin' and look into bug-larnin', frog larnin', lizard and snake larnin' and breakin' down cherry trees! I don't like no sicha foolish way o' larnin' myself!"

Pa hadn't forgot. I'd have to take him to school with me. He would take me to school with him. We were going early. I was glad we were going early. If Pa pulled a gun on Professor Herbert there wouldn't be so many of my classmates there to see him.

I knew that Pa wouldn't be at home in the high school. He wore overalls, big boots, a blue shirt and a sheepskin coat and a slouched black hat gone to seed at the top. He put his gun in its holster. We started trudging toward the high school across the hill.

It was early when we got to the County High School. Professor Herbert had just got there. I just thought as we walked up the steps into the schoolhouse: "Maybe Pa will find out Professor Herbert is a good man. He just doesn't know him. Just like I felt toward the Lambert boys across the hill. I didn't like them until I'd seen them and talked to them. After I went to school with them and talked to them, I liked them and we were friends. It's a lot in knowing the other fellow."

"You're th' Professor here, ain't you?" says Pa.

"Yes," says Professor Herbert, "and you are Dave's father."

"Yes," says Pa, pulling out his gun and laying it on the seat in Professor Herbert's office. Professor Herbert's eyes got big behind his black-rimmed glasses when he saw Pa's gun. Color came into his pale cheeks.

"Jist a few things about this school I want to know," says Pa. "I'm tryin' to make a scholar out'n Dave. He's the only one out'n eleven youngins I've sent to high school. Here he comes in late and leaves me all th' work to do! He said you's all out bug huntin' yesterday and broke a cherry tree down. He had to stay two hours after school yesterday and work out money to pay on that cherry tree! Is that right?"

"Wwwwy," says Professor Herbert, "I guess it is."

He looked at Pa's gun.

"Well," says Pa, "this ain't no high school. It's a damn bug school, a lizard school, a snake school! It ain't no damn school nohow!"

"Why did you bring that gun," says Professor Herbert to Pa.

"You see that little hole," says Pa as he picked up the long blue forty-four and put his finger on the end of the barrel, "a bullet can come out'n that hole that will kill a schoolteacher same as it will kill any other man. It will kill a rich man same as a poor man. It will kill a man. But atter I come in and saw you, I know'd I wouldn't need it. This maul o' mine could do you up in a few minutes."

Pa stood there, big, hard, brown-skinned and mighty beside of Professor Herbert. I didn't know Pa was so much bigger and harder. I'd never seen Pa in a schoolhouse before. I'd seen Professor Herbert. He always looked big before to me. He didn't look big standing beside of Pa.

"I was only doing my duty," says Professor Herbert, "Mr. Sexton, and following the course of study the state provided us with."

"Course o' study," says Pa, "what study, bug study? Varmit study? Takin' youngins to th' woods. Boys and girls all out there together a-galavantin' in the brush and kickin' up their heels and their poor old Ma's and Pa's at home a-slavin' to keep 'em in school and give 'em a education! You know that's dangerous too puttin' a lot o' boys and girls out together like that! Some o' us Paps is liable to add a few to our families!"

Students are coming into the schoolhouse now.

Professor Herbert says: "Close the door, Dave, so others won't hear."

I walked over and closed the door. I was shaking like a leaf in the wind. I thought Pa was going to hit Professor Herbert every minute. He was doing all the talking. His face was getting red. The red color was coming through the brown weather-beaten skin on Pa's face.

"I was right with these students," says Professor Herbert. "I know what they got into and what they didn't. I didn't send one of the other teachers with them on this field trip. I went myself. Yes, I took the boys and girls together. Why not?"

"It jist don't look good to me," says Pa, "a-takin' all this swarm of youngins out to pilage th' whole deestrict. Breakin' down cherry trees. Keepin' boys in atter school."

"What else could I have done with Dave, Mr. Sexton?" says Professor Herbert. "The boys didn't have any business all climbing that cherry tree after one lizard. One boy could have gone up in the tree and got it. The farmer charged us six dollars. It was a little steep I think but we had it to pay. Must I make five boys pay and let your boy off? He said he didn't have the dollar and couldn't get it. So I put it in for him. I'm letting him work it out. He's not working for me. He's working for the school!"

"I jist don't know what you could a-done with 'im," says Pa, "only a-lar- ruped 'im with a withe! That's what he needed!"

"He's too big to whip," says Professor Herbert pointing at me. "He's a man in size."

"He's not too big fer me to whip," says Pa. "They ain't too big until they're over twenty-one! It jist didn't look fair to me! Work one and let th' rest out because they got th' money. I don't see what bugs has got to do with a high school! It don't look good to me nohow!"

Pa picked up his gun and put it back in its holster. The red color left Professor Herbert's face. He talked more to Pa. Pa softened a little. It looked funny to see Pa in the high school building. It was the first time he'd ever been there.

"We were not only hunting snakes, toads, flowers, butterflies, lizards," says Professor Herbert, "but, Mr. Sexton, I was hunting dry timothy grass to put in an incubator and raise some protozoa."

"I don't know what that is," says Pa. "Th' incubator is th' new-fangled way o' cheatin' th' hens and raisin' chickens. I ain't so sure about th' breed o' chickens you mentioned."

"You've heard of germs, Mr. Sexton, havn't you," says Professor Her- bert.

"Jist call me Luster if you don't mind," says Pa, very casual like.

"All right, Luster, you've heard of germs, haven't you?"

"Yes," says Pa, "but I don't believe in germs. I'm sixty-five years old and I ain't seen one yet!"

"You can't see them with your naked eye," says Professor Herbert. "Just keep that gun in the holster and stay with me in the high school today. I have a few things I want to show you. That scum on your teeth has germs in it."

"What," says Pa, "you mean to tell me I've got germs on my teeth!"

"Yes," says Professor Herbert. "The same kind as we might be able to find in a living black snake if we dissect it!"

"I don't mean to dispute your word," says Pa, "but damned if I believe it. I don't believe I have germs on my teeth!"

"Stay with me today and I'll show you. I want to take you through the school anyway! School has changed a lot in the hills since you went to school. I don't guess we had high schools in this county when you went to school!"

"No," says Pa, "jist readin', writin' and cipherin'. We didn't have all this bug larnin', frog larnin', and findin' germs on your teeth and in the middle o' black snakes! Th' world's changin'."

"It is," says Professor Herbert, "and we hope all for the better. Boys like your own there are going to help change it. He's your boy. He knows all of what I've told you. You stay with me today."

"I'll shore stay with you," says Pa. "I want to see th' germs off'n my teeth. I jist want to see a germ. I've never seen one in my life. 'Seein' is believin',' Pap allus told me."

Pa walks out of the office with Professor Herbert. I just hoped Professor Herbert didn't have Pa arrested for pulling his gun. Pa's gun has always been a friend to him when he goes to settle disputes.

The bell rang. School took up. I saw the students when they marched in the schoolhouse look at Pa. They would grin and punch each other. Pa just stood and watched them pass in at the schoolhouse door. Two long lines marched in the house. The boys and girls were clean and well-dressed. Pa stood over in the school yard under a leafless elm, in his sheepskin coat, his big boots laced in front with buckskin and his heavy socks stuck above his boot tops. Pa's overalls legs were baggy and wrinkled between his coat and boot tops. His blue work shirt showed at the collar. His big black hat showed his gray-streaked black hair. His face was hard and weather-tanned to the color of a ripe fodder blade. His hands were big and gnarled like the roots of the elm tree he stood beside.

When I went to my first class I saw Pa and Professor Herbert going around over the schoolhouse. I was in my geometry class when Pa and Professor Herbert came in the room. We were explaining our propositions on the blackboard. Professor Herbert and Pa just quietly came in and sat down for awhile. I heard Fred Wurts whisper to Glenn Armstrong: "Who is that old man? Lord, he's a rough looking scamp." Glenn whispered back: "I think he's Dave's Pap." The students in geometry looked at Pa. They must have wondered what he was doing in school. Before the class was over, Pa and Professor Herbert got up and went out. I saw them together down on the playground. Professor Herbert was explaining to Pa. I could see the prints of Pa's gun under his coat when he'd walk around.

At noon in the high school cafeteria Pa and Professor Herbert sat together at the little table where Professor Herbert always ate by himself. They ate together. The students watched the way Pa ate. He ate with his knife instead of his fork. A lot of the students felt sorry for me after they found out he was my father. They didn't have to feel sorry for me. I wasn't ashamed of Pa after I found out he wasn't going to shoot Professor Herbert. I was glad they had made friends. I wasn't ashamed of Pa. I wouldn't be as long as he behaved. He would find out about the high school as I had found out about the Lambert boys across the hill.

In the afternoon when we went to biology Pa was in the class. He was sitting on one of the high stools beside the microscope. We went ahead with our work just as if Pa wasn't in the class. I saw Pa take his knife and scrape tartar from one of his teeth. Professor Herbert put it on the lens and adjusted the microscope for Pa. He adjusted it and worked awhile. Then he says: "Now Luster, look! Put your eye right down to the light. Squint the other eye!"

Pa put his head down and did as Professor Herbert said: "I see 'im," says Pa. "I'll be damned. Who'd a ever thought that? Right on a body's teeth! Right in a body's mouth. You're right certain they ain't no fake to this, Professor Herbert?"

"No, Luster," says Professor Herbert. "It's there. That's the germ. Germs live in a world we cannot see with the naked eye. We must use the microscope. There are millions of them in our bodies. Some are harmful. Others are helpful."

Pa holds his face down and looks through the microscope. We stop and watch Pa. He sits upon the tall stool. His knees are against the table. His legs are long. His coat slips up behind when he bends over. The handle of his gun shows. Professor Herbert pulls his coat down quickly.

"Oh, yes," says Pa. He gets up and pulls his coat down. Pa's face gets a little red. He knows about his gun and he knows he doesn't have any use for it in high school.

"We have a big black snake over here we caught yesterday," says Professor Herbert. "We'll chloroform him and dissect him and show you he has germs in his body too."

"Don't do it," says Pa. "I believe you. I jist don't want to see you kill the black snake. I never kill one. They are good mousers and a lot o' help to us on the farm. I like black snakes. I jist hate to see people kill 'em. I don't allow 'em killed on my place."

The students look at Pa. They seem to like him better after he said that. Pa with a gun in his pocket but a tender heart beneath his ribs for snakes, but not for man! Pa won't whip a mule at home. He won't whip his cattle.

"Man can defend hisself," says Pa, "but cattle and mules can't. We have the drop on 'em. Ain't nothin' to a man that'll beat a good pullin' mule. He ain't got th' right kind o' a heart!"

Professor Herbert took Pa through the laboratory. He showed him the different kinds of work we were doing. He showed him our equipment. They stood and talked while we worked. Then they walked out together. They talked louder when they got out in the hall.

When our biology class was over I walked out of the room. It was our last class for the day. I would have to take my broom and sweep two hours to finish paying for the split cherry tree. I just wondered if Pa would want me to stay. He was standing in the hallway watching the students march out. He looked lost among us. He looked like a leaf turned brown on the tree among the treetop filled with growing leaves.

I got my broom and started to sweep. Professor Herbert walked up and says: "I'm going to let you do that some other time. You can go home with your father. He is waiting out there."

I laid my broom down, got my books, and went down the steps.

Pa says: "Ain't you got two hours o' sweepin' yet to do?"

I says: "Professor Herbert said I could do it some other time. He said for me to go home with you."

"No," says Pa. "You are goin' to do as he says. He's a good man. School has changed from my day and time. I'm a dead leaf, Dave. I'm behind. I don't belong here. If he'll let me I'll get a broom and we'll both sweep one hour. That pays your debt. I'll hep you pay it. I'll ast 'im and see if he won't let me hep you."

"I'm going to cancel the debt," says Professor Herbert. "I just wanted you to understand, Luster."

"I understand," says Pa, "and since I understand he must pay his debt fer th' tree and I'm goin' to hep 'im."

"Don't do that," says Professor Herbert. "It's all on me."

"We don't do things like that," says Pa. "We're just and honest people. We don't want somethin' fer nothin'. Professor Herbert, you're wrong now and I'm right. You'll haf to listen to me. I've larned a lot from you. My boy must go on. Th' world has left me. It changed while I've raised my family and plowed th' hills. I'm a just and honest man. I don't skip debts. I ain't larned 'em to do that. I ain't got much larnin' myself but I do know right from wrong atter I see through a thing."

Professor Herbert went home. Pa and I stayed and swept one hour. It looked funny to see Pa use a broom. He never used one at home. Mom used the broom. Pa used the plow. Pa did hard work. Pa says: "I can't sweep. Durned if I can. Look at th' streaks o' dirt I leave on th' floor! Seems like no work a-tall fer me. Brooms is too light 'r somethin'. I'll jist do th' best I can, Dave. I've been wrong about th' school."

I says: "Did you know Professor Herbert can get a warrant out for you for bringing your pistol to school and showing it in his office! They can rail-road you for that!"

"That's all made right," says Pa. "I've made that right. Professor Herbert ain't goin' to take it to court. He likes me. I like 'im. We jist had to get together. He had the remedies. He showed me. You must go on to school. I am as strong a man as ever come out'n th' hills fer my years and th' hard work I've done. But I'm behind, Dave. I'm a little man. Your hands will be softer than mine. Your clothes will be better. You'll allus look cleaner than your old Pap. Jist remember, Dave, to pay your debts and be honest. Jist be kind to animals and don't bother th' snakes. That's all I got agin th' school. Puttin' black snakes to sleep and cuttin' 'em open."

It was late when we got home. Stars were in the sky. The moon was up. The ground was frozen. Pa took his time going home. I couldn't run like I did the night before. It was ten o'clock before we got the work finished, our suppers eaten. Pa sat before the fire and told Mom he was going to take her and show her a germ some time. Mom hadn't seen one either. Pa told her about the high school and the fine man Professor Herbert was. He told Mom about the strange school across the hill and how different it was from the school in their day and time.

The Slipover Sweater

About the story:

"The Slipover Sweater" is a story of youth and a study in symbol. It deals with Shan Stringer's growth to a new, suddenly perceived awareness of the contrast between illusion and reality; for the high school senior has learned to penetrate the guise of infatuation and to discriminate between it and those more solid, enduring human passions clustering about those we come to cherish. Although many differences exist between the details of the story and the facts of life as Jesse Stuart encountered them, it should hardly come as a surprise to the reader that the author found—in Henry James's phrase—the "solidity of specification" in his own experience and that of his contemporaries in W-Hollow, the town of Greenup, and Greenup High School, that raw material out of which a literary artist shapes his fictional world.

When Jesse Stuart was growing up in W-Hollow, he often walked to Plum Grove School with his cousins, Grace, Glen, and Essie Hilton, who lived in the same hill country. He attended Greenup High School from 1922–1926, and frequently he and Grace shared the same mountain path to and from Greenup High until they graduated together in the Class of 1926. "I was the girl in 'The Slipover Sweater,'" she said. "You know, Jesse and I thought we belonged to each other when we were children. We went to Plum Grove School everyday, we played together down in the hollow, and we [practically] lived in an old cabin down there."

"Well, she is," the author agreed, "but I just don't talk about it." Just as is the Grace of the story, the real Grace Hilton of Greenup County was valedictorian of her class. Jo-Anne Burton was suggested to the author by his high school sweetheart Rose Bergmeier, "one of the finest girls that ever went to Greenup High School . . . as good as gold." As Shan Stringer dug gensing, May apple, and yellow root, dried these valuable roots by the kitchen stove, and sold them in Gadsen, so had Jesse Stuart—to Dave Darby's Banner Produce Company in Greenup. The local banker who loaned Shan Stringer the money for the sweater in the story was based "on May and Helen Cole's father," whom the author knew well.

The story was first published in *Woman's Home Companion* in January,

1949, and has since been reprinted six times, most recently in the textbook
Voices in Literature, Language and Composition 3 (1969).*

* * *

"Now if you don't get the sweater," Grace said as she followed me
up the narrow mountain path, "you mustn't feel too badly.
Everybody in Gadsen High School knows that you've made your letters.
Just because you don't wear them like the other boys. . . ."

Grace stopped walking before she finished the last sentence. And I knew
why. But I didn't say anything—not right then. I stopped a minute to look
down over the cliffs into the gorge where the mountain water swirled over
the rocks, singing a melancholy song without words. Grace walked over and
stood beside me. And I knew the sound of the roaring water did the same
thing to her that it did to me. We stood there watching this clear blue
mountain water hit and swirl over the giant water-beaten rocks, splashing
into spray as it had done for hundreds of years before we were born.

The large yellow-gold leaves sifted slowly down from the tall poplars.
And the leaves fell like big, soft, red raindrops from low bushy-topped sourwoods to ferny ground. Dark frostbitten oak leaves slithered down among
the lacework of tree branches to the leaf-carpeted ground. Two of these oak
leaves dropped onto Grace's ripe-wheat-colored hair. And a big yellow-gold
poplar leaf fell and stuck to my shirt. They were a little damp, for they fell
from a canopy of leaves where there was no sun.

Gold poplar leaves would look good in Jo-Anne Burton's chestnut-col-
ored hair, I thought. And how pretty the dark oak leaves would look on her
blouse. I was sorry she wasn't with me instead of Grace. I could see Jo-Anne
standing there with the red and yellow leaves falling on her.

I would say, "Gee, you look wonderful with those golden leaves in your
dark hair."

"Do you think so?" she would answer. And I could imagine her smile
and her even white teeth. She was always gay and laughing.

I didn't say anything to Grace but Grace knew how I felt about Jo-
Anne. Grace and I had gone to Plum Grove grade school together for eight

*Jesse Stuart, "The Slipover Sweater," *Woman's Home Companion,* Vol. 76 (Jan., 1949), pp.
25, 52, 54; collected in *Clearing in the Sky* (N.Y.: McGraw-Hill, 1950), pp. 76–90, reprinted in Jay
Cline and Ken Williams, *Voices in Literature, Language and Composition 3* (Boston: Ginn, 1969),
pp. 129–138. Other reprints are listed in Woodbridge, *Jesse Stuart Bibliography,* p. 77. The
material on Jesse Stuart's youth in W-Hollow with his Hilton cousins is in H. Edward Richardson, unpub. biography on Jesse Stuart, Chs. I-III. Also Grace Hilton Carter and her sister
Essie/H. E. Richarson, Interview, Greenbo Lodge, Greenup, Ky., Sept. 2, 1978; Jesse Stuart/
H. E. Richardson, Interview, W-Hollow, Greenup, Ky., Sept. 15, 1978, and Interview, Nov. 4,
1978.

years. I had carried her books from the time I could remember. And then we started walking five miles across the mountains to Gadsen High School together. When we started to Gadsen I was still carrying her books. I'd carried them down and up this mountain for three years. But I was not carrying her books this year and I wouldn't be again, for Gadsen was a bigger school than Plum Grove and there were many more girls. But there was only one for me and Grace knew who she was. She was the prettiest and the most popular girl in Gadsen High School. When she was a sophomore she was elected May Queen.

Grace knew why I wanted the slipover sweater. It wasn't just to show the letters and the three stripes on the sleeve I'd won playing football three years for the Gadsen Tigers. Grace knew that Roy Tomlinson had a slipover sweater and that he was trying to beat my time with Jo-Anne Burton. Grace had heard about Jo-Anne asking me one day why I didn't get a sweater.

"You've got a small waist and broad shoulders," Jo-Anne had said, "and you'd look wonderful in a slipover sweater!"

I didn't care about having a sweater until Jo-Anne had said this to me. Now I wanted it more than anything on earth. I wanted a good one, of the style, color, and brand the other boys had bought. Then I could have my G and the three stripes sewed on, as my teammates had done. They let their favorite girls wear their sweaters. Jo-Anne was wearing Roy Tomlinson's, and that hurt me.

Grace probably knew I was thinking of Jo-Anne now. And as she stood beside me, with the leaves falling onto her dress, I couldn't keep from thinking how they would look on Jo-Anne.

Why we had stopped at this high place every morning and evening for three years, I didn't know. But it was from here on the coldest days in winter, when the gorge below was a mass of ice, that we listened to the water singing its lonesome song beneath the ice. And here in early April we watched spring come back to the mountains.

We knew which trees leafed first. And even before the leaves came back we found trailing arbutus that had sprung up beside the cliffs and bloomed. Then came the percoon that sprang from the loamy coves where old logs had lain and rotted. It was the prettiest of all wildwood flowers and its season was short. Grace and I had taken bouquets of this to our high-school teachers before a sprig of green had come to the town below.

Grace shook the multicolored leaves from her hair and dress when we silently turned to move away. And I brushed the leaves from my shirtsleeves and trousers. We started up the mountain as we had done for the past three years—only I used to take Grace's arm. Now I walked in front and led the way. If there was a snake across the path, I took care of him. I just protected Grace as any boy would protect a girl he had once loved but had ceased to love since he had found another girl who meant more to him than anyone else in the world.

"If I had the money," Grace said after our long silence, "I'd let you have it, Shan, to buy your sweater."

"I'll get the money some way," I said.

Not another word was spoken while we climbed toward the ridge. But I did a lot of thinking. I was trying to figure out how I could buy that sweater. I was not going to hunt and trap wild animals any more and sell their skins just to get clothing for my own skin. Books had changed me since I'd gone to high school. I'd never have the teacher send me home because I had polecat scent on me. I'd always bought my schoolbooks and my clothes by hunting and trapping. But I'd not done it this year and I'd not do it again. I was determined about that. Books had made me want to do something in life—for my girl. And I knew now that I wanted to be a schoolteacher and teach math in Gadsen High School. And that's what I'd do.

When Grace started from the path across to her home, a big double-log house on Seaton Ridge, she said good-by. And I said good-by to her. These were the only words spoken. We used to linger a long time at this spot by a big oak tree. I looked over at the heart cut in the bark of the oak. Her initials and mine were cut side by side inside the heart. Now, if I'd had my knife, I would have gone over and shaved these initials and the heart from the oak bark. Now I hoped that she would find some boy she could love as much as I loved Jo-Anne.

When I first realized I had to get that sweater for Jo-Anne, I had thought about asking Pa for ten dollars. But I knew he wouldn't have it, for he raised light burley tobacco, like Grace's father, and it hadn't been a good season. Pa had not made enough to buy winter clothes for my four brothers and six sisters. And another thing, I'd never in my life asked him for money. I'd made my own way. I'd told my father I'd do this if he'd only let me go to high school. He wasn't much on education. But he agreed to this and I'd stick to my end of the bargain.

That night I thought about the people I knew. I wondered if I could borrow from one of them. I didn't like to borrow, but I'd do anything to get Jo-Anne to take off Roy Tomlinson's sweater and to put mine on in place of it. Most of the people I knew did not have the money, though.

At noon the next day the idea came to me: what are banks for? Their job is to lend money to needy people—and that's why I walked straight to the Citizens' State Bank at lunchtime. I was a citizen, a student at Gadsen High School, and I needed money to buy a sweater. If Mr. Cole asked me why I needed the money, I'd just tell him I wanted very much to buy myself a sweater so I could put my school letter on it and my three stripes—and be like the other high-school boys. I wouldn't mention Jo-Anne.

I stood nervously at the window. Mr. Cole was a big heavy man with blue eyes and a pleasant smile. "Something I can do for you?" he asked politely.

"Yes, sir," I stammered. "I'd like to have ten dollars."

"You want to borrow it?" he asked.

"Yes, sir." Now the worst was over and my voice was calmer.

"You go to high school, don't you?"

"Yes, sir."

"Thought I'd seen you around here," he said. "You're the star player on the Gadsen Tigers—you're Mick Stringer's boy."

"Yes, sir," I said.

"What's your first name?" He started making out a note for me.

"Shan," I said, "Shan Stringer."

He shoved the note forward for me to sign. And he didn't ask for anyone to go my security. If he had, I don't know who I could have got to sign. I wasn't old enough to borrow money at the bank. But it just seemed to me as if Mr. Cole read my mind. He knew I wanted the money badly. So he gave me nine dollars and seventy-five cents and took a quarter for interest.

"This note will be due in three months," he said. "This is October twenty-eighth. Come back January twenty-eighth. And if you can't pay it then, I'll let you renew for another three months. And then we'll expect all or partial payment."

"Thank you, Mr. Cole."

I hurried to Womack Brothers' store and bought the sweater. It had a red body with white sleeves—the Gadsen High colors. I would have Mom sew the white G on the front and the red stripes on the sleeves as soon as I got home. I was the happiest boy in the world. Gadsen High School had always been a fine place but now it was wonderful. I loved everybody but I worshiped Jo-Anne Burton.

That afternoon when Grace and I walked through the town and came to the mountain path, we talked more than we had in a long time. But I didn't mention what was in the package I was carrying. We stopped at our place on the cliffs and looked down at the swirling waters in the gorge. The dashing water did not sound melancholy to me. It was swift dance music like a reel from old Scotland. Even the trees above us with their arms interlaced were in love. All the world was in love because I had got what I wanted and I was in love.

The next morning Grace was waiting for me beside the old oak where we had cut our initials. Grace was all right, I thought. She was almost sure to be valedictorian of our class and she was good-looking too. But she didn't have the kind of beauty Jo-Anne had. Jo-Anne was not only beautiful—she was always happy, laughing, and showing her pretty teeth. She wasn't one of the best students in the class—her grades were not high at all. But she was friendly with everybody and as free as the wind. Her clothes were always pretty, and they fitted her much better than Grace's did. I loved the way she wore her clothes. I loved everything about Jo-Anne. She held my love as firmly as the mountain loam held the roots of the wild flowers and the big trees.

"Why are you taking that bundle back to school?" Grace asked.

"Oh, just to be carrying something," I said.

Grace laughed as though she thought I was very funny.

We got to school early. When I had a chance to speak to Jo-Anne alone, I told her what I had.

"Oh, Shan!" she exlaimed. "Oh, you're a darling!"

"Brand-new," I said. "You'll like it, Jo-Anne."

"Oh, I know I'll love it." she said. "I'll put it right on!"

I handed her the package and she hurried off. I was never happier in my life. When she came back she was smiling at me, her eyes dancing. She walked over to Roy Tomlinson and handed a package to him. Everybody standing around was looking at Jo-Anne in the new sweater with the three stripes on the sleeve—the only sweater in the school with three stripes. Was Jo-Anne proud! And I was proud!

"Do you like it on me?" she asked as she walked up to me.

"Do I like it?" I said. "I love it."

She smiled happily and I was glad that Roy could see now that I was the one Jo-Anne loved. And everybody knew now that I was in love with her. Roy would probably wonder, I was thinking, how I was able to buy that sweater. He had probably thought that he would be able to keep Jo-Anne with his sweater and his two stripes because I'd never be able to buy one for her. But Roy would never know how I got it—that would be a secret between Mr. Cole, the banker, and me.

While the girls were admiring the sweater and many of my teammates were looking on, I glanced over at Roy. He stood by not saying a word, just looking at the sweater that had replaced his. I hadn't expected him to react that way, but in a few minutes Grace came in and she was wearing Roy Tomlinson's sweater.

"Boy!" Jim Darby exclaimed. "Look at Grace! Doesn't that sweater look swell on her!"

"She isn't the same girl!" Ed Patton said.

I stared at Grace. I didn't realize a sweater could make such a difference. Her clothes had never become her. But this sweater did! There were many whispers and a lot of excitement as we flocked into the auditorium. I was watching Grace move through the crowd in her new sweater when Jo-Anne edged over close to me.

"You do like this sweater on me, don't you, Shan?" she asked.

"Sure do, Jo-Anne," I said. And I walked proudly beside her into the auditorium.

That afternoon after I had said good-by to Jo-Anne I looked around for Grace. She was just saying her good-by to Roy. When she turned toward me I could see that she was as proud of that sweater as she could be. And Roy stood there looking after us as we started toward the mountain together.

We stopped at the gorge but we didn't stay long. Grace did most of the talking and I did the listening but I didn't hear everything she said. I was wild with joy for I was thinking about Jo-Anne wearing my new red sweater.

At every football game Jo-Anne sat on the front bleacher and yelled for me. And Grace yelled for Roy Tomlinson. Once when I made an eighty-five-yard run for a touchdown Jo-Anne came up to me after the game and kissed me. I could outkick, outpass, and outrun Roy Tomlinson. And I didn't brag when I said it. He earned another stripe that season and so did I. Grace sewed Roy's third stripe on his sweater with pride. She kept the sweater clean as a pin. I'll have to admit she kept it cleaner than Jo-Anne kept mine.

When Grace was almost sure to be valedictorian, Roy Tomlinson could hardly stand the idea of our walking over the mountain together. He walked with us to the edge of Gadsen. But he never climbed the mountain and looked down at the gorge. He could just as well have come along. His going with her didn't bother me, not exactly. She did, of course, seem close to me—like a sister. As we walked along together I saw the trees along the ridge where we had had our playhouse and grapevine swings. I saw the coves where we had gathered bouquets of trailing arbutus and percoon. And those initials on the oak reminded me of the days when we were little.

It was in the basketball season, just before the regional tournament when I received a notice from the bank that my note was due. With the other little expenses I had at school even twenty-five cents wasn't easy to get.

If the interest is hard to get, I thought, what will I do about the principal? What if I have to take the sweater from Jo-Anne and sell it to make a payment on the principal?

But when my mother let me have fifty cents and I paid the interest I felt much better and didn't think about it again during the basketball season. Jo-Anne came to every game and she was always urging everybody else to come. She was as proud of me and the way I played as I was proud of her and the way she looked in my sweater.

Grace was never so talkative and gay and popular as Jo-Anne and I was always glad to hear anyone pay Grace compliments. I heard Harley Potters say one day, "You know, Grace Hinton is a beautiful girl. Think, she comes five miles to school and five miles home and makes the highest grades in her class. There's something to a girl that would go through all kinds of weather and do that."

I thought so too. All through the winters when snow was on the ground and the winds blew harshly on the mountain, she and I had walked back and forth to school. I walked in front and broke the path through new fallen snow. I had done that even when we went to Plum Grove. We had walked through the rain and sleet together and I couldn't remember a day that she had not been good-natured. And I knew she had the durability and the toughness of a storm-battered mountain oak. I didn't believe there was another girl in Gadsen High School who could have done what Grace had done. And now to the Gadsen boys and girls she was as pretty as a cove sapling. Yet I was sure I would never go back to Grace. I'd always love Jo-Anne.

I only hoped that Roy Tomlinson appreciated Grace. I got a little tired of looking at his sweater so often. Sometimes I wondered if I were jealous of him for making his third stripe. But I was sure I wasn't because I had four, and I had the most popular and beautiful girl in the world. I decided I was tired of looking at it just because Grace never wore anything else. I could hardly remember what Grace's clothes had looked like before.

When the heavy snows of January and February passed away in melted snow and ran down the gorge in deep foaming waters, I grew as melancholy as the song of this swollen little winter river. Jo-Anne didn't know what was worrying me. Sometimes I wished she would ask but she never did. And that hurt me too. If I didn't always smile at something she said, she acted impatient with me. I'm sure I could not have told her about the note due in

April, if she had asked. But I looked for some kind of sympathy because I thought I needed it and that she loved me so much she would want to cheer me up. Instead, she kept asking me if I didn't love her and if I did, why didn't I show it the way all the other boys did?

So I tried my best to cheer up. I didn't want to lose her but I did have to figure out some way to make money. I couldn't hunt now even if I'd change my mind about killing animals. Spring was on the way and animal pelts weren't good now.

One day Grace said to me, "What is the matter with you, Shan?" That was in late March as we were watching the blue melted snow waters roll down the gorge where the white dogwood sprays bent down to touch them. "I know something is bothering you."

"No, it isn't," I said. "I'm all right."

"If I can ever help you, I'll be glad to," she said. "Just let me know."

Her words made me feel better. I didn't want to tell her that I'd never been in debt before and that a debt worried me to death. So I didn't say anything.

After the snow had melted from the mountain, I grew more despondent. Neither the sight of Jo-Anne nor of Grace could cheer me. My grades went down and some of the teachers asked me what had happened to me. Everyone around me seemed happy, for April had come again. And Jo-Anne seemed gayer than ever. Several of my teammates had their eyes on her constantly and it only made me more despondent.

Grace coaxed me again one day to tell her what was wrong. "You always like spring on the mountain," she said.

Then I decided I had to tell somebody my trouble and she was the one to tell. "Grace," I confessed, "I need money—ten dollars!"

"I don't have it," Grace said quietly. "If I did, you could have it. But that doesn't help. Maybe I'll think of a way. . . ."

I didn't think she would, but it made me feel better—just to share my worry.

On April fifteenth something happened to me that the whole school witnessed. We were gathering for assembly period when Jo-Anne handed my sweater back to me!

"I'm tired of it," she said, without the pretty smile on her lips. "And I'm tired of your ways. You go around with your lower lip drooped as if the world had turned upside down and smashed you. You never have anything to say. You've just become a bore and everybody knows it." She left me standing there with my sweater in my hand.

I was stunned. I couldn't speak. My face grew hot and I felt everybody looking at me. When I looked up I saw Grace and Roy standing at the other side of the auditorium. They were looking in my direction and Grace suddenly started to talk to Roy and neither looked my way again. I don't know how I got through that day at school.

After school I didn't wait for Grace. I hurried out and away from them all. But just as I started up the mountain, Grace overtook me.

"I've thought of something, Shan. I know a way to get ten dollars."

I looked at her without speaking. I was still stunned.

"You know there's a big price at Dave Darby's store for roots and hides and poultry," she said, speaking quickly. "I noticed that sign yesterday. And you know the coves above the gorges are filled with ginseng, yellowroot, and May-apple root."

She waited for me to speak. I walked in silence for a while, thinking it was all too late now—thinking I'd sell my sweater for whatever I could get for it.

"When is the note due?" she asked.

"Ten more days," I said. "April twenty-eighth."

"We'll have it by then," she said.

We, I thought. I looked at her and thought of Jo-Anne. Jo-Anne was pretty and gay and popular but her face had changed in my mind. I began to wonder if all that gaiety was real—and what she had meant by "love." I was too puzzled to think anything out.

Grace and I walked along silently. We didn't stop at the gorge because Grace had suggested that we go into the cove. I just followed along and started to hunt ginseng after Grace had started.

I never saw anyone before who could find three-prong and four-prong ginseng like Grace. We found patches of yellowroot and May apple. We filled our lunch pails with these precious roots and I took them home, strung them the way Mom used to string apples and shuckbeans to dry, and hung them on nails driven on the wall above our stove.

We stopped every evening that week and gathered wild roots, and I brought them home to dry. On April twenty-seventh, one day before my note was due—and I had already received the notice—I took a small paper sack of dried May-apple roots, a small sack of yellowroot, and more than a pound of the precious ginseng roots to Dave Darby. When he was through weighing the roots he did some figuring. Then he said, "It all comes to sixteen dollars if you trade it out in the store."

"How much if I take cash?" I asked.

"Fifteen dollars," he said.

"Let me have the cash."

I went straight to Citizens' State Bank and paid off my note. And I had five dollars for Grace. I never felt better, not even when I was so much in love with Jo-Anne.

As I walked home with Grace I told her how much the roots had brought. "This is not your half," I said as I gave her the five dollars, "but we'll dig more until we get your share. I paid my note."

"Wonderful," she said, smiling at me.

I looked at Grace. Whatever had been wrong with me, I wondered. Why didn't I see before that she had beauty such as Jo-Anne could never have? Grace was as beautiful as our mountain was in April, prettier than a blossom of wild phlox or a mountain daisy. She was as solid as the jutted cliffs, I thought, and as durable as the mountain oaks.

"Now ask me if there is anything more I want from you," I said as I took her arm to help her up the mountain toward the gorge and the wild-root coves.

"What is it?" she asked quickly.

"Take off Roy Tomlinson's sweater," I said. "I'm awfully tired of looking at it."

"But what will I do without it?" she said. "It keeps me warm."

I didn't answer. I started to pull off mine. Then I felt her hand on my arm. "No, Shan," she said. "Keep it a while. I couldn't wear it yet."

We stood silently on the mountain path and looked at each other. "I couldn't wear it yet," she had said. And that was all the promise I needed. I knew how fine she was and I was proud that she would not discard Roy Tomlinson's sweater as Jo-Anne had done, without a word to him first.

I didn't know what she was thinking as we started down the path and she didn't know what I was thinking. I didn't ask her, she didn't ask me. But I was thinking that our high-school days would soon be over and I could build a house, if she'd want it there, right on Seaton Ridge on the path that leads from her family's house to mine.

New-Ground Corn

About the story:

Edgar Lee Masters wrote Jesse Stuart a letter on November 25, 1941, in which he distinguished between genius and talent. He said that the story "New-Ground Corn" had given him a definition of genius:

> Genius is a bend in the creek where bright water has gathered, and which mirrors the trees, the sky, and the banks. It just does that because it is there and the scenery is there. Talent is a fine mirror with a silver frame, with the name of the owner engraved on the back.

Masters concluded his letter simply: "I hope you will do lots of stories. They are out of the soil. . . . "*

Nearly thirty-seven years later, Mr. Stuart discussed the story in an interview that went like this:

RICHARDSON: One of your most fascinating stories is "New-Ground Corn." Remember, Pa and Shan hoed corn on a hot day in new ground. There's a deep green patch of corn "like a green wave in the sun." What is a corn balk?

STUART: It's between the rows. The space between the rows. . . .

R: Pa talks of the time long ago when Bill McKinley was president: 1897–1901.

S.: That's the way he measured time. Do you know who wrote that up? He wrote it first. I didn't know he'd written it. Thomas Wolfe. His father measured time that way. They was both Republicans. My daddy and Thomas' daddy was. . . .

*Edgar Lee Masters' letter to Jesse Stuart is in Mr. Stuart's correspondence folder labeled "Edgar Lee Masters," now in the Jesse Stuart Collection, University of Louisville, Louisville, Ky., in the Patterson Rare Book Room in the Ekstrom Library. Following excerpts are from Jesse Stuart/H. E. Richardson, Interview, W-Hollow, Greenup, Ky., Aug. 19, 1978, pub. in H. Edward Richardson, "*Men of the Mountains*: An interview with Jesse Stuart, *Adena*, Vol. 4, No 1 (Spring, 1979), pp. 12–15. The extended quotation in brackets is from Thomas D. Clark, *The Kentucky* (N.Y.: Farrar & Rinehart, 1942), p. 223.

"New-Ground Corn" was first published in *American Prefaces*, Vol. 5 (Feb., 1940), pp. 66–72, reprinted in *Men of the Mountains* (N.Y.: Dutton, 1941), pp. 65–79, subsequently reprinted (Lexington: Univ. Press of Ky., 1979), pp. 65–79.

R.: There is much lyrical style in that story. . . . You mention a stump, two piles and bull grass—

S.: It's a grass that grows along a creek; it grows up and has a broad blade, and cattle like it green and they'll eat it if it's cut for hay. It just grows in little patches.

R.: And we are to understand that it was planted by Pa? Why would he have planted bull grass?

S.: Probably he was the father of the child buried there.

R.: You mention Lucretia Hornbuckle and her sorrel pony, and Pa reflects upon when McKinley was president and they went to Six Hickories Church. Now all the hickories have gone to the sawmill.

S.: You've been to that cabin on the hill [Seaton Ridge]?

R.: Yes.

S.: That's where that church stood. . . . A church and a hotel—small one—

R.: A real settlement once there?

S.: Yeah . . . people'd come up there and drink the sulphur spring water, right down the valley below there. It was one of these health things. . . .

[Historian Thomas D. Clark writes that these "chalybeate watering places attracted swarms of low-country visitors each year . . . boats unloaded crowds of decrepit strangers who came to seek pleasure and physical restitution by the side of the sulphur-laden waters."]

R.: There's a pile of bones of a chimney, foundations. . . .

S.: They're all gone. . . . Dad's dead and she's gone. I just took the title and then wrote a story. . . .

R.: Did you father ever tell you such a story?

S.: He told *at* it.

R.: What do you mean?

S.: Well, he didn't come out.

R: You must have discerned something like this.

S.: I was just waiting for it. I jumped right on it.

R.: Pa says in the story that Lucretia is under the earth at Plum Grove. Do you think she might have died, but only in your father's imagination?

S.: No. The Hornbuckles were around here. Isn't that some name?

R.: Yes. Pa tells his son that the Hornbuckle women in this story are not for "a living." What does that mean, a suggestion of a wild girl?

S.: Not for work.

R.: But she liked to play, then?

S.: That's right. They had that type of girl. . . .

R.: At the end of the story, the son's off to see Daisy Hornbuckle.

S.: Well, boy, I never knew any Daisy Hornbuckle.

R.: Maybe a descendant of the Hornbuckles?

S.: Daisy Hornbuckle—it's a nice name, but I didn't know any. In other words it makes a good story, though.

R.: Why is she depicted as having brown eyes, wavy black hair, being big and robust, and "laughs, laughs like the wind"?

S.: Imagination, again. You see these girls . . . [laughter]

R.: How much of this is historical?

S.: Let's say 15 percent.

R.: What would you say would be the place, the setting of the story?

S.: Goose Creek right here. . . . I got Hornbuckle from up the road. You know, the way you go out to the [Greenbo] Park? The first river you cross, East Fork?

R.: Yes, toward Argillite—

S.: —Right on the side of there, down the road and on the right going out is a cemetery where the Hornbuckles and the Nichols are buried. . . . That's where I got the name.

R.: Why did you write the story?

S.: I don't know; it was just one I had to write. . . . It was written before 1940. It was just right for me to write. It's the type of thing I think I can do better than a lot of folks. . . . When you think about it . . . out here alive, somebody that might be kin to you; could have grown up and been a brother—well, that excites you. It did me. So I got right on it. We don't know about what all happened among our ancestors.

* * *

"THIS IS PURTY CORN," Pa says. "Shan, this is the way I like to see corn grow. Look at the stalks of this corn won't you! Big nearly as our hoe handles! It is the deepest green I've ever seen in a patch of corn. Looks like a green wave in the sun. And the blades lap in the rows and rustle when they touch each other. I don't believe we'll get to plow this corn again. Just haf to come in here with our hoes and chop it out!"

Pa bends over and pecks with his sprouting hoe. He cuts the soft tender sprouts from the stumps. He rakes the loose loamy new-ground silt from the balk around the tall sturdy stalks of corn. The corn is so heavy the guard roots cannot hold them stalks in place. The wind leans the heavy stalks of corn.

"It's gettin' hot and smothery to work in this corn now," I says. "We'll not be able to plow it again. We might come in here with our hoes and chop the weeds out. If we don't it will be mighty foul by corn-cuttin' time."

"Yes," says Pa, "these black locust sprouts will rake a body's legs and cut his hands all to pieces. He'll haf to get in here and cut corn when the dew has softened the ripe fodder blades. The dew will be on the sprout-leaves too. The dew will be on the crab-grass. A body will get wet to his waist. I can't help how hot it is—we'll haf to cut it out again with our hoes!"

"Funny," I says, "about this big rock-pile here in the middle of this new ground piece of corn. Funny about the two little rocks down there in that corn balk with the bull-grass growing between them. I can't understand why you didn't plow that little place. It makes un ugly spot in the cornfield! Funny about this good land in the middle of a new-ground. It is like a garden-spot."

Pa stops the click-click of his hoe. He takes a red bandanna from his hip overall pocket. He spreads the big red bandanna over his red face. He wipes the white drops of sweat that trickle down his graying beard. He pulls off his black hat. He wipes the sweat from his thinning black hair. He puts his hat back on his head, and his red bandanna in his hip pocket. Pa looks at the sun above the corn. He holds his hand up and feels the slow lazy wind above the corn.

"We can get too hot in this smothery corn," says Pa. "We'd better sit down and wind a minute. A fellow don't know how hot he can get down among this corn until he reaches up and feels the wind above him. It feels like ice atter a body digs through one of these long corn rows with his head down lookin' at this rich ground. Ah, Shan, I remember the day when I could stand anything! I can look at this ground and I can remember. You do not know—you do not remember. You were not in this world then. That was when Bill McKinley was President of the United States!"

Pa sits down on a stump in the corn-row. He takes his hat off and fans his face and head with one hand. He looks at the clumps of bull-grass in the corn-row. He looks at the giant rock-pile in the middle of the new-ground cornfield. He watches the corn blades slapping each other across the balks.

He hears the rustling of the corn-blades in the wind. Pa's face is red as a beet. It is tanned by the wind and the sun. Pa's face is hard as a brown sand-rock. His flesh is hard and his muscles are tough as hickory withes that you tie fodder bundles with in the fall time.

"Son," says Pa, "I ain't told you a lot in my day. I've give you good advice though. You'll haf to say I have. I can remember, Shan. I can remember lots of things. I can remember things I don't want to remember! They won't go away. They stay in my head. They come back to me in dreams. They come back to me when I see this new-ground corn. They come back to me when I see this rock-pile. You remember this place as our hunting ground don't you? You remember when we used to bring Black Boy into this hollow on rainy nights—how we used to get the minks, possums, polecats, and coons. Remember how Black Boy would tree a coon and how we'd build a fire up under the tree to keep the coon from coming down—how we'd sleep there all night and shoot the coon out'n the tree the next morning?"

"Yes I remember," I says. "I remember how you'd send me to the house to get more shells. I'd be afraid of this long dark hollow. I'd pray to myself a hant wouldn't jump out'n the place where the old Hylton house used to be and get me—yes, I remember—that too, is like a dream——"

"You didn't know then that there used to be a house here," says Pa—"well there was. About the time Bill McKinley was killed this house burnt down. I can remember where the apple trees used to stand in the yard—where the rose bushes stood by the palings. This stump I'm sittin' on—this stump——"

"What about it Pa?" I ask—"what about the stump?"

Pa pulls his bandanna from his hip pocket and he wipes more sweat. He lets his hoe handle lean against the stump. He fans with his hat in one hand. He wipes sweat with a red bandanna in his other hand. The corn is above his head. The wind is above the corn and it is nosing slowly through the corn. The sky that holds the sun is above the wind and the glimmer of heat is over the land. The corn is wilted and it is begging for a drink of water from the water-over-gravel color of sky. There is not any water to beg from the waterless sky but it is thirsty and it begs for water and the rain crow croaks for water at the cornfield's edge.

"I remember when this stump was a tree," says Pa. "God in Heaven only knows why it ain't rotted sooner. It's a black-locust stump and black-locust is slow to rot. You know that, Shan, by the black-locust fence posts we have put in the ground. When this stump was a shade tree in this yard, I used to be under it every Sunday before McKinley was killed. Yes, I was here. Time goes by so—I can count back the years—I can remember by Bill McKinley. I used to come here all the time. I'd ride my sorrel mare around that ridge. I'd have two pistols on my hips. I'd shoot all the way around that ridge just to be shooting. God knows why I'd do it. I'd just shoot to hear the crack of my pistol. Son, I could take a row of corn and hoe it through the new-ground in them days!

"I could tell you for days," says Pa, "all that used to happen here. Son, you think this has allus been a wilderness. Well it ain't allus been a wilderness. I used to take Lucretia Hornbuckle from this house—she rode a sorrel pony—I rode my sorrel mare. We'd go side by side up that pint where you can still see that dip in the ground. Only that is left now. That used to be the main road to the church. I'd go to church with Lucretia and of all the times—you never heard sicha shoutin' and house warmin' as we'd have in that house. That was called the Six Hickories Church House. Six big hickory trees stood in front of the house. I saw the cattle snake them away to the saw-mill years later. I stood there by the church the day the mighty cattle got down on their knees—straining to pull sicha mighty trees! While Old Brother Litteral was praying for the Lord to come down through the loft, we's on the outside seeing whose pistol would crack the loudest. We'd hold them in the air and shoot at the moon, Son, I hate to tell you this—but you're a grown man and I'm an old man and it comes back to me and I've got to tell it to somebody. It comes back like a dream comes to a man—when I see this rock-pile—when I see that patch of bull-grass and the two rocks at each end of it. I think that I can tell you now. You wanted to know why the corn was so tall here. There was a good garden here then. It is still rich where the old house used to be."

"Where did all the people come from to the Six Hickories Church?" I ask. "I didn't think there were many houses here then. You can go for miles now and can't find a house. It is a wilderness now."

"Shan," says Pa, "you can find old roads, can't you? You can find them on every ridge. You can find them running down the pints and across the hollows. You can see these great sinks in the land. They used to lead to houses. This land was covered with houses. Son, that's when people had to dig a livin' out'n the ground or they starved—not like it is now-a-days. We used to have old iron-furnaces in this county. People moved here to cut charcoal cord wood. The old men told me they used to see these hills ricked with cords of charcoal wood fir the furnaces. They saw as many as twenty yoke of oxen pulling cord wood and pig-iron—all hitched to one big wagon. Now you know about these roads—ah, the strength that has been spent on them! When the ore was dug from the hills, and the trees all cut into cord wood—the people didn't have no place to go. They just lived on in their little shacks. They piled the brush where they had cut the cord wood. They burnt it—plowed the land and dug a living from the land as we are doing still today, Shan."

"About Lucretia, Pa," I says—"I never——"

"Like a dream, Son," says Pa—"I never talk about her. She is gone. She went the way the timber went; the church house went; the iron ore went; she went the way our horses went and the houses went; the big yokes of oxen went; the merry crowds in the days of Bill McKinley went—Lucretia is gone. She went young. Now who knows all of this? No one knows about it but a few of us that time is withering on the stem. I've seen the wild game go. I've seen the timber go. I've seen the oxen go. I've seen the horses go. I've seen the surreys go. It seems like I am lost. And, I've seen the people go. The boys and the girls I used to know are under the dust and scattered somewhere among the four winds of the earth—beyond these dark hills. They never come back any more than the otter, mink, and coons come back!"

"But about Lucretia, Pa," I says—"you never told me about her."

"She was a woman for a good time," says Pa—"and I couldn't help lovin' her. I knowed it wasn't the best. Son, she wasn't a woman for a living—it was always a good time. I can see her ride today. I can see her pony goin' over the fences leadin' my sorrel mare—I remember how I used to follow. I can hear her laugh—that laugh has not died on this wind. That laugh still re-echoes on this hill. When I used to coon hunt here when you was a little boy—it seemed like I could hear laughing—I could hear it sound against these hills. I could hear her voice. I can't forget. I was warned but I was mad with life and fun. She wasn't a woman for a wife, Son—She wasn't a woman for a living but I just can't forget."

"Somewhere back in a tin-type album," I says, "I saw a tin-type turning yellow with age—a young man standing with his hands on the back of a chair and a young woman with flowing hair—sitting in the chair with her hands across her lap—and the dress—the full-bosom and the big sleeves—I remember and the combs in her hair. And the man with a black mustache, and the high collar and the black bow-tie—I remember——"

"Right where we are sittin', Son," says Pa. "That picture was taken under this tree. That picture was taken where you see this big new-ground corn—where the corn is tall and stalwart—where it grows from this dark loamy earth—I remember the day the man walked down that hill. He carried his camera with him and it was on a three-legged contraption. It was on Sunday when he came. And you see where that tall timber stands over there on that slope—that was in corn then. I'll tell you times change a lot. It took him two hours to take our pictures. 'Look at the birdie and smile,' he says. He had a cloth spread over his head. He had us get fixed this way and that. 'Don't move now,' he says and then he pulls a little rope. Honest it's funny to think about him. He was a little bird-like man with a long beard. He had tiny hands and bird-claw fingers. I paid three dollars for six pictures. I made fifty cents a day working for Bill Fultz. I plowed corn for him. I tell you there wasn't much money then. Pictures cost me six days work—harder work, Son, than hoein' in this new-ground corn."

The wind that blows through the corn and over the corn moves the thinning locks of graying black hair on Pa's head. The sweat trickles down his arm where he holds the hoe handle. It drips to the dry loamy ground and makes a little damp puddle. The wind smells of corn and pusley and careless and saw-briars. The wind smells of shoemakes and sourwood sprouts. It smells of pumpkin vines that run across the corn balks with big yellow blossoms and tiny green pumpkins setting on the vines. The wind smells of the bean vines that climb the corn stalks where Mom has planted her a patch of fall beans. And the wind smells of morning glories. It is a strange wind to smell but it is a good wind to smell and it makes one lazy. It makes one's nostrils open wide and it makes one inhale deeply and exhale slowly. The work and the wind give one an appetite so that he can't get enough to eat when he puts his feet under the table. He just eats and eats after he feels full and then he wishes he could eat more.

"Son, you remember," says Pa, "that I have warned you—ain't I?"

"Only about one woman," I says. "You told me not to go there. You heard I was going to see Daisy Hornbuckle twice a week."

"Yes," says Pa—"Lucretia was her Aunt, Son. That is why I warned you. That set of wimmen didn't make good wives. I don't know about 'em now. I heard she was as much like Lucretia as two peas in a pod. That is why I warned you. I have the years behind me. You have the years before you. I remember this spot. I wouldn't talk about it so but we are working today. I never dreamed I'd be hoeing corn here with a grown-up son. I never dreamed things would be changed in forty years and the old life would be replaced by things that are new. I never thought the church at Six Hickories would go and all the houses on this tract of land would go as time went on and on like wind over the corn. But things change and change. They just keep changing and you find that if you loved the things of yester-day you are lost today. I just often hear the pounding of the horses' hoofs on this ridge road. I can't hep it if the road is old and choked by briars. It's still a road to me. I can't hep it if the little trails that led from the main ridge road down these pints to the houses in the hollows and on the flats are just dips on the land today—I've run my horse over all of them and emptied my pistol over about every foot of these roads. Today, no one remembers. I remember—and I remember most of all, Lucretia!"

"Mom never dreams of all of this," I think, "when she comes to hoe her fall beans in the corn. She'll never dream of all of this when she comes and picks her apron full of beans—Mom with a slat bonnet on her head and drops of sweat standing like white blisters over her face and on her nose— Mom with her pipe in her mouth and blowing long streams of blue smoke to the wind. Mom will not know about this locust stump and where Pa and Lucretia had their pictures made. Mom will never know when she steps over the big yellow pumpkins ripe in the corn-balks after the frost has hit the corn and the blades have ripened into buff-colored fodder; no, Mom will never know. Mom has seen the tin-type in the album. Mom has seen the young man with the high white collar, the black bow-tie and the black mustache—the heavy head of hair parted on the side. But Mom doesn't know the rock-pile in this cornfield is a chimney that stood at a house where Pa used to come three times a week before McKinley was assassinated. She doesn't know about the two rocks and the clot of bull-grass growing between them. Mom would wonder then and she would ask questions. Something would come back to her that she would not like; though, the years have pressed upon her and her youth is done. Yet, there is something she hasn't known and she would like to know."

I do not ask Pa about the stones and the clot of bull-grass. He sits and stares as the sunlight falls upon us—as it twists and shifts through the green leaves on the oak at the edge of the field. Shadows are shifting now. Shadows are shifting over the green stalwart corn that will make us bread and feed our hogs, mules, and cattle for the winter. It grows from the dust of Pa's dreams. It grows from the earth he knew and played over when Bill McKinley was President of the United States—a time that I have lived because his coming measured time for Pa. Time then covered the earth like a yellowing wind and kissed the blades of corn where the bird-like man with the long beard carried the three-legged contraption down the road—where now is only a dip of land and where the tall trees grow on both sides to mark out the time and footprints of man—to cover it over with time and wind and leaves and the roots of trees. It is strange and something far back of the days of McKinley calls me—something back to the days of Grover Cleveland when Pa first rode this ridge road and emptied his pistol at the big snakes that sunned on the rocks. Something time has done to these hills that makes me weep. Time has not only covered the foot paths and the ridge roads where the cattle pulled the pig-iron and the charcoal cord wood but time has covered a civilization—time has left it and it will never be unearthed for only their footprints were left, the traces of the hoes and the axes—and these are gone.

"And that hump of earth covered by bull-grass," I think, "that hump of earth—that spot that Pa has left. If I had plowed this land—but Pa wouldn't let me plow it. He let me plow the rest of the land but he took the plow handles here. Pa skipped that little spot of land as if it were something sacred—and the two stones—and the tall corn that overshadows it—the talking of the corn blades that seem to whisper something ghost-like and strange about the love and the joy and the dreams of a civilization gone with the floating winds of time—I would like to know about it——"

"Son," says Pa—"this ain't gettin' the corn hoed, is it? Remember, we'll never be able to go over this corn again only with our hoes. It will be over the mule's back. It will be too tall to plow. The single tree will knock it down when the mule has to go around the stumps in the balks. Ah, just one more time with our hoes—and the pumpkin vines will cover the black loam here! Mule steps on one he'll squeeze the life out'n it——"

"Yes, Pa," I says——

"And, Son, you know the ways of man?" Pa asks.

"A few," I says—"I didn't know that a house had once stood here until you told me today. I didn't know that rock-pile was the bones of a chimney and the foundations of a house and that locust stump was a shade tree where you made that tin-type picture that is in the family album—I didn't know but that picture connects something back for me with the days of Bill McKinley—the dream I have of them. There are so many things I do not know——

"No," I says—"lots of things I don't know. I don't know why you have left that stump of earth with the two stones down there. I do not care to know. I know you have left them for a reason. I do not know that reason. I know you wanted to plow this hill and you plowed the mule slowly here. The mule acted as if he were dreaming and you followed between the handles of the cutter plow as if you were in a deep study as if something were calling you back—and now I can understand——"

"Son," says Pa, "that is sacred earth to me. I put rocks there. I've kept them there throughout these years; though the fire has run over that spot time again and again—the bull-grass has always marked it. Timber has been cut nigh it and coons caught from the tall trees over it—cattle have pawed hard down upon it when they strained behind their yokes—the mighty poplars and black oaks have crossed it—and now the corn grows around it—but that is sacred earth to me. The dust is the dust of you and me. That is the dust of my people. It is there under that bull-grass between the two rocks. You do not haf to talk about it. Let it pass over now as the wind blows over—remember I'm not as young as I used to be. I am not sorry about it. It just makes me remember. It is a dream. It is a love that has always lingered and I ain't a man to talk about love. I don't think you ever heard me sit around and talk about love. I always got sick of hearing a lot about love. But something about Lucretia that always lingers—and if she hadn't gone—if she hadn't gone—my life would have been different—and she wasn't a woman for a living. Son, that is why I warn you——"

"If Mom wonders about this spot of earth," I think—"she is bound to see it. I wonder if she sits on one of the stones and smokes her pipe when she comes to hoe her beans in the tall corn rows. I wonder if she ever thinks to cut the bull-grass—if she wonders why it stands in a row of corn. I wonder if she knew about it if she would lay a wisp of corn flowers and pumpkin blossoms there. I believe Mom would. But that is Pa's dream; something he has held all of these years; something buried by dirt and time and wind and leaves. I wonder if Mom would think of other hidden dreams as she picked the beans and looked at the big yellow pumpkins laying in the corn balks. And the dead bull-grass when the frosts come and the hump of earth barren to the winds—weighted by snows and soaked by rains and covered by the yellowish flowing of wind and time!"

"The shadders are creepin' upon us, Shan," says Pa—"We'd better get up and get to work. We'll never fill a corn crib for this winter settin' on stumps. I believe in the old way—one dream I've never lost—that is, Son, makin' your livin' by the sweat of your brow. I believe in diggin' it from the earth and not asking a red cent from any man. That is what I learned when I was a boy and I am too old to forget it now—that seems to be old too now-a-days! It's the only sure way I know. Look at the pumpkins to roll in the fodder shocks here this fall. Look at the beans there will be to pick. Look at the corn to cut and the big white ears of corn that will hang down two on a stalk like sticks of stove wood—all these to shuck and we'll come with the mules and the sled and haul big white piles of corn away from each fodder shock and big yellow heaps of pumpkins. Lord, atter we get all we want we'll have plenty for the cows and the fatten-hogs! And I love the smell of ripe corn and big fat pumpkins! I like to smell them when the frost hits the land! Everything is so purty then!"

Pa gets up slowly from the stump. He puts his hat back on his head. He pulls a wisp of home-made tobacco from his hip pocket. He twists a chew into his mouth of the bright burley leaf—he puts his bandanna into his hip pocket. He takes his hoe and starts to peck-peck the earth—to cut the sprouts and rake the rich loose loamy silt around the guard roots of the rank growing corn. The sprouts fall behind his hoe and they wilt in the lengthening shadows of the sinking sun. They fall with the underside of their soapy leaves upturned—milk-white in the shadows of approaching evening. I follow Pa with my row of corn, my hoe white-gleaming when I raise it from the earth. We move toward the far end of the field. The rain-crow is still croaking for rain but the cool of the evening has made the corn look fresh again. The wilt has gone from the stalks and the dew has dampened the corn. They do not look to the bright heavens and pray for rain as they prayed under the blistering heat of a fire-ball sun. The dew has quenched the thirsting blades and the lengthening shadows of approaching night have cooled their parching tongues.

"We'll make a couple of rounds," says Pa, "before we turn in to do up the work. This is a good time to work. It is cool now and a body can do twice as much work as he can in the heat of the sun. I like to work this time of day. I feel as fresh as the corn."

I do not speak to Pa. I dig behind him. I keep my row of corn up with him and the weeds from my row, above his row, fall at Pa's heels. I work hard to get my row to the end of the field.

"Where is Lucretia?" I ask Pa.

"Under the earth at Plum Grove," says Pa—"where a lot of my generation has gone—but she went too young—she died three months after I set the bull-grass down there between the two rocks! Just three months later!"

Silence. Shadows keep lengthening. Evening is coming on. Night will soon be here and the stars will come to the water-over-gravel colored sky. Night will come and the stars and the moon will look down on the tall new-ground corn. The stars will explode in the sky above the corn, beans, and pumpkins. Night will come and cover all. Night will come quickly as a dream—creep stealthily as a shadow—quietly as the footsteps of a fox.

"Two rounds," says Pa, "to yan end of the field and back. We can say then that we have done a good day's work. We can look at the clean corn below us and go home and be satisfied. I've always liked to see my work when the day is done. It puts something in me to see a clean cornfield."

We hoe the row to the end of the field.

"I'm quittin' Pa," I says. "I'm quittin' for today."

"Why, Son?" Pa asks. "Can't you stay with your old Pa? You ain't all pooped out, are you?"

"No," I says, "I can take it. I could work all night if the moon and stars put enough light on the earth until I could see to dig the crab-grass and cut the sprouts. I could work tonight and all day tomorrow—but I've made a promise."

"What kind of a promise?" Pa asks.

"To a girl," I says.

"Who?" asks Pa.

"Daisy Hornbuckle," I says.

"I've warned you," says Pa.

"I know," I says. "Just seems like I can't take warning. I've been warned by people of no blood kin to me. I just can't break away from her."

"I've never seen the girl," says Pa—"but I'll bet she has brown eyes."

"Yes," I says——

"And purty white teeth and every one sound as a silver dollar," says Pa.

"Yes," I says—"not a cavity in a tooth she says. And I believe her. I believe everything she says."

"And wavy black hair?" Pa asks.

"Yes," I says—"like love vines on a fence——"

"And she is big and robust?" Pa asks——

"Yes," I says——

"And she laughs, laughs—laughs like the wind?" Pa asks.

"Yes, I says—"how do you know all of this?"

"It runs in the blood, Son—" says Pa—"Her father—I remember him. Just looks like Lucretia and they looked like their mother. I'd know a Hornbuckle when I met one.

"Son," says Pa, "you will haf to live and learn. Don't come to me and say I didn't warn you. Your life is your own. No one owns your life and your life is all you really own or ever own. So it belongs to you."

I stand my hoe against a stump at the end of the field. I walk down across the clean corn rows. Pa stands and watches me as I leave the new-ground cornfield. He leans on his hoe handle and he looks at the heap of rocks and the hump of bull-grass, just below it. I look back to see him look at them and then he takes his eyes away to watch me go down the hollow.

"You are certainly my son," I hear him say to himself.

Eustacia

About the story:

In 1939 Edward J. O'Brien, distinguished editor of the yearbook of the American short story, *Best Short Stories*, dedicated his twenty-fifth annual volume jointly to Jesse Stuart and Richard Wright. One reviewer, writing for the Hartford, Connecticut, *Courant*, said, "Of the stories, 'Eustacia,' a straightforward character study by Jesse Stuart . . . seemed to me the best." Critics differ, of course, and May Cameron of the New York *Post* thought the story "a rambling, inconclusive narrative inexplicably told in the present tense. . . . " In making his selection from hundreds of short-story possibilities, Mr. O'Brien sought excellence based on "organic substance . . . in which the pulse of life is beating," and on the shaping talent of the writing in putting the "living substance into the most beautiful and satisfying form by skillful selection and arrangement." High among O'Brien's criteria was the *sense of life*, and that year, "The leaders in numbers of stories cited for outstanding merit [were] William Saroyan and Jesse Stuart, with eight each, [and] Morley Callaghan [with] six. . . . "

In recognizing Mr. Stuart's honor in having "Eustacia" reprinted in O'Brien's anthology, an editor of *Household* magazine wrote,

> Whenever I publish a story by Jesse Stuart, I receive letters from readers commenting on the accuracy of his observation and the effectiveness of his interpretation of the life of everyday folk in the Kentucky mountain country. . . . I am sure none of those who read ["Eustacia"] has forgotten its vivid picture of the girl seeking education and beauty against the opposition of the ignorant and prejudiced. It offers a stimulating commentary, incidentally, on American perseverance and American opportunity.

And just what is the significance of a writer's ability to depict the life around him? At the time Mr. Stuart's "Eustacia" appeared in *The Best Short Stories, 1939*, a reviewer for the Chicago *News* took time to remind readers that "Few cultures have arisen without a literature. Few literatures have flowered without self-respect. Lacking articulate self-respect a civilization vanishes and cities become green mounds. . . . But writers have always sought to tap what pools of self-respect a people possess. . . . The most stubborn resistance to returning man to his bestial state is being made by our culture builders, the writers." The same critic went on to praise the short-story genre, and among other writers represented in O'Brien's anthology, pointed to the culture builder Jesse Stuart, who gives each reader "a picture . . . of the Kentucky hill country."

The germ of the story and many of its details were true enough. Asked to comment on "Eustacia," Mr. Stuart said, "She was a high school girl at McKell and worked in my office. Like the story." However, he did not put everything into the story that was real, and he found it necessary to play down the meanness in the girl's family. "They shot people and asked questions later. They were a mean set of people. There was a streak of violence in the people and she was part of that streak." Shortly after "Eustacia" was published, Jesse Stuart told Wisconsin writer August Derleth, "I can't write about these people the way they really are; no one would believe it. . . . I've got to temper things down."*

* * *

"I'LL SHOW 'EM," says Theopolis Pratt, "that they can't put it over on me. I'll show 'em the state can't put a new road through here and take my bottom land and cut my trees. The first man that puts the ax in one of them trees 'll feel the buckshot in a slat of his ribs. The first man that sticks a road-scraper, a pick, mattock, or shovel in that bottom 'll get a dose of lead he can't carry."

Theopolis means what he says. If you could see the man he is. His great massive shoulders, his arms big as fence-posts, his muscles that bulge up and split his shirt-sleeves, his powerful bull neck, firm-set iron jaws, and his eyes blue as the Tygart waters that swirl past his door.

"I've been here, Mel, in these hills a long time," says Theopolis. "I've

---

*"Eustacia" was first published in *Household*, Vol. 38 (July, 1938), pp. 2–3, 12, 15, 18. Woodbridge in *Jesse Stuart Bibliography*, lists five reprints of this story, including Edward J. O'Brien's *Best Short Stories of 1939* (Boston: Houghton Mifflin, 1939), pp. 259–273. The review alluded to above was published in the Hartford, Conn., *Courant*, May 28, 1939, clipping in Jesse Stuart, Scrapbook #6, p. 89, M. S. U. May Cameron's review, titled "O'Brien's 25th Annual Volume," was published in her column "Book on Our Table," N. Y. *Post*, May 26, 1939, clipping in Jesse Stuart, Scrapbook #6, p. 90, M. S. U.; the list of leaders in numbers of stories receiving recognition for outstanding merit in O'Brien's anthology appeared in an anonymous review in the Milwaukee, Wisc., *Post*, June 10, 1939, p. 89, M. S. U. The quoted editorial was published in *Household*, Topeka, Kansas, Aug., 1939, clipping in Jesse Stuart, Scrapbook #6, p. 95, M. S. U. The commentary relating culture and literature appeared in a review in the Chicago *News*, June 7, 1939, clipping in Jesse Stuart, Scrapbook #6, p. 93, M. S. U. The source of Mr. Stuart's remarks on "Eustacia" is Jesse Stuart/ H. E. Richardson, Interview #41, W-Hollow, Greenup, Ky., Sept. 15, 1981. August Derleth quoted Jesse Stuart regarding the Kentuckian's need "to temper things down" in his short stories in Derleth's article, "He Visited Jesse Stuart," *News of Books and Authors* (May–June, 1939), clipping with photographs in Jesse Stuart, Scrapbook #6, p. 91, M. S. U.

seen people come and go. I've seen them whipped. I've seen them killed. I've seen one family run over another. But they don't run over the Pratts, do they? They won't run over the Pratts long as I can use my fists. When I can't use my fists and whip them I can use something else. I'll fight in the open long as I can. And when they outnumber old Theopolis I can take to the cliffs and pick 'em off. They'll have to put that road over my dead body. Put a brand new schoolhouse right in my door! They can't do it!"

"W'y, Theopolis," says Mel, "they'll put that road through there. The state is too powerful. They'll send out men to 'praise your land and take it. They'll pay you for it."

Mel, a big black-headed man, wheezes on his pipe. He is sitting with Theopolis under the apple tree by the country store where two roads meet. Theopolis is whittling a stick of wood with a hawk-bill knife. Mel Sperry is whittling with a fifteen-cent brown-handled barlow. The blue smoke swirls above them through the green branches of the tree.

"We don't lie about things," says Theopolis. "We come out flat-footed and get it over with. Pap was always that way. That's the Pratts. We boast a little. But we make our boasts good."

Theopolis blows out another wisp of smoke. "I've seen too much of that fangle-dangle education come here," he says, "too much for no good. Getting away from the abc's we's used to, Mel. W'y, all we had was writin', readin' and 'rithmetic. Good enough for anybody's youngins."

"Good enough for mine," says Mel. "No need for a new school. The old schoolhouse will do. No use spending a lot of the taxpayers' money for foolishness. Of course I'm not 'gainst education, you know. I'm just 'gainst these new things."

"I got seven children by my first wife, and five by my second," says Theopolis, "and all the first children are married off and gone. Got the second litter with me. Durned if I send my little girls to school if I don't want to. They are my children and I'll do as I please with 'em. When I go upon the hill to get wood or haul fodder I like to have my children right with me. W'y, that little one of mine's a Pratt up and down. I say to her: 'Sarah, you go fetch your Pap a drink.' She'll say: 'If you want a drink of water, get up and get it yourself.' I tell you she's my best girl. Just a little Pratt up and down." Theopolis would laugh a husky, strong laugh, like the wind in the fodder blades in January.

Sarah says: "Where you going, Pap?"

"Ah, Honey," says Theopolis, "just going out for a little walk. Going out to fish a little. Come along with me."

Sarah goes with her pa—Sarah, Fern, and Eustacia. They get their fishing poles and a can of bait. They go down beside the Tygart. The percoon blossoms now in the coves beside the Tygart, rich beds of this snow-white flower, Kentucky's prettiest springtime flower. The trailing arbutus vines on the rough shaggy cliffs. Elms and water birches are thin-leafed and the sycamores are budding leaves. The sycamores have white and brown trunks and the portions of their bodies are the color of a blue-bird's beak. They are pretty in the April wind.

"Fish when I please," says Theopolis, "don't my land run down to the creek? Who's going to stop me when I want a mess of fish? I tell you this country's getting too many people in it and too many of this too-many are busy-bodies." He sits on the bank and drops his hook and line into the water. The girls fish with him.

Theopolis leaves Eustacia, Fern, and Sarah at the house. He lights his pipe and walks across the bottom. "I've kept 'em out so far," he says to himself. "Not a shovel nor a mattock will they stick in this earth." Theopolis walks behind a blue stream of smoke, bluer than the wind of April. He walks over to the old tie yard by the railroad tracks. Three men are sitting on a tie pile. One is playing a guitar and all are singing. Theopolis walks up and he says:

"Boys, I like your music."

"The devil you do," says one. "You old buzzard, who told you to open your bill?"

"My bill is my own," says Theopolis, "and I'll open it and close it when I get good and ready. If you've got anything to say about it, why don't you say it!"

"I got a lot to say," the little mean-looking man says. "I'll show you what a man is." He makes for Theopolis. Wow! and Theopolis piles him on the ground with a left. Wow! over Theopolis's head the guitar is splintered in a hundred pieces.

"What is this, a fight?" says Theopolis. Down goes the man that used the guitar.

"Come on, you young sprouts," says Theopolis, "your old Theopolis Pratt's just started to fight."

"Oh, you have?" says the third young man as he pulls a thirty-eight in Theopolis's face. "You might be big as the side of a mountain to the other boys on the ground, but you're nothing to me. You're no bigger than an ant. Stand there or I'll blow your brains out."

You wouldn't shoot a man in a little friendly fight," says Theopolis, "when three young men are fighting an old codger like me." Before the man can speak, Theopolis goes into a tussle with the young man. The gun fires and shoots Theopolis across the wrist. The second time it fires, it shoots the young man through the heart. Theopolis says: "Didn't mean to kill the man. I ought to a-been at home—but just to think people won't let you 'tend to your own business any more."

He darts behind the tie piles with half-bricks hurled at him. Theopolis's arm is bleeding—and two young men are after him. Theopolis makes it home tired and sick.

"What's the matter, Papa?" says Fern.

"Nothing, Honey," says Theopolis gazing in the embers in the cook-stove and punching them with a poker. "I'm just hungry and want my supper."

They see the sheriff come and arrest their father and take him away. They put him under bond but death came in the meantime and took him out of his troubles. "Only thing in the world," says Mel Sperry, "that let Theopolis Pratt out'n all his trouble was when he cashed in his checks. Old moonshine licker was a friend to Theopolis, after all. It eat the lining out'n his stomach. He kicked the bucket in time. Left a good family, though. Never heard a ought 'gainst one of his girls in my life nor 'gainst his wife. I tell you moonshine ain't no friend to man but was a friend to Theopolis. Had one trial and it was a hung jury. Was getting ready for another trial and death settled it. Old Theopolis sleeps upon the hill now.

"No, he didn't leave anything for his wife and children. Was a poor man. He was one of the best neighbors I ever lived by in my life. It's a shame—and his wife with five children. Don't know how they'll make it. Nothing to go on. He's got a fine bunch of little girls."

Theopolis sleeps where his kin have slept for nearly two centuries. There are soldiers among them, tillers of the earth, fighters among them and lovers of peace. He sleeps while the scrapers turn loads of new dirt into the fills—while the plows trailed new furrows and blazed a new highway. He sleeps where the click of the pick and the shovel are listless as the fall of the autumn leaves to the earth.

"I don't want relief," says Sallie Pratt. "I want work." She gets work at two dollars a week in a kitchen. She has to sell her cows. She keeps the wolf from the door. Two dollars a week is a small sum. Relief has to come whether she wants to take it or not.

"I'll tell you Sallie Pratt is a good woman. Look how she hangs on to her children. Look how she works and what she works for and keeps her children together. She is in church every Sunday morning. You will find her there. She's a good religious woman. Two dollars a week don't go very far when a woman has five mouths to feed at home."

Even the new schoolhouse comes right across the Tygart on a hill. It is a brown-brick school building with sixteen acres of playground on a hill top where the water runs from all sides equally. The Tygart comes down from the Kentucky hills and faces the Ohio River. The schoolhouse stands here, a monument to the community.

When the sassafras leaves begin to turn on the Kentucky hills any one knows that summer is ended. Any one living in Kentucky knows when the farewell-summers begin to bloom it is time to start cutting corn and digging potatoes in Kentucky. This is what Professor Stringer sees when he returns in September to take his school. He is proud to be back with a young river of humanity.

It is in the algebra class that Professor Stringer notices a slender frail girl with blue eyes. She sits in the second seat in the first row from the wall. When he asks for daily work she always answers that she has done all of her assigned work. When he sends students to the board she always works her problem with accuracy. She has but a few words to say. When he gives an algebra test she never makes anything but A grades. Her name is Eustacia Pratt. One day Professor Stringer reads the grades for the algebra test. He says: "Eustacia Pratt, 90." She speaks up and says: "Didn't I make 100?" And he says: "No, Eustacia, you made 90."

When the class is over she comes up and says: "May I see my paper?"

Professor Stringer says: "Yes, if you'll go over there and dig it out of the waste-paper basket."

She goes over and finds her paper. She hands it to him and says, "Look at the problem you marked wrong."

Professor Stringer looks over the problem and finds he has made a mistake and graded the paper wrong. She has made 100.

He finds Eustacia so accurate that he lets her work in the office. She is a freshman. Once she says: "I have two sisters and they are as good or better in their books than I am. They'll be up here some day. They are in the grades now."

Professor Stringer lets Eustacia make out transcripts of grades and eligibility lists. He finds her to be one of the most reliable girls of a long list he has had to do office work before for him. She is only in her first year of high school and she looks so lean and frail and like she will fall every step she takes. "W'y, all the Pratts are smart," a student told him once. "Eustacia is just like the rest of them."

As the year goes on he becomes interested in the girl because of her remarkable ability to do things in books. She has an undaunted spirit and precocious intellect wrapped up in her tall frail body. Once he asks her about her father. Her face colors and she says: "My father is dead." That was all she would say.

And the year goes on. Eustacia's grades come into the office each six weeks. They are all A's. Once a group of girls come to school the first period and do not go to class. They loaf in the basement. Professor Stringer is told by a teacher that they are loafing in the basement. Eustacia is working in the office at this period. One of the girls says: "Professor Stringer, Eustacia told on us."

Eustacia walks in and says: "Did she say that I told on her? If she did I'll pull every hair out of her head."

When Professor Stringer goes home he tells his landlady about Eustacia Pratt wanting to fight. "W'y, she comes by it honest," says Mrs. Failford. "Haven't you never heard of old Theopolis Pratt? Dead and gone now but, honest, that man would fight a running sawmill."

The year has passed away as swiftly as it has come. Spring comes again to the hills. The school year is over and the year of A's, B's, C's, D's, and F's are recorded and put on dry files behind locks and keys. And the boys and girls go back to their homes on the farms.

Eustacia often comes to Professor Stringer's mind while he works during the summer on his own farm. He wonders about her people and the struggle her mother has to send her to school.

School starts the second year. Eustacia comes back to work in the office. She has grown a little. This year Professor Stringer teaches third-year English. He doesn't have Eustacia in his class as she takes second-year English. Eustacia is growing now. She is a tall girl and slender, taller than her mother. Her mother is making four dollars a week now. She has been given a double raise in salary.

The leaves swiftly turn brown again. The autumn winds and rains come. Leaves float like golden ships on some strange and far-off voyage down the Tygart. Eustacia walks home each afternoon beside the Tygart. She sees the cornfields and the giant beech trees beside the Tygart. She sees the brown autumn-cupped leaves floating down the swift dark waters of the Tygart. She thinks: "Every dead leaf is a golden ship going to some far and distant land. Some day I shall be going beyond these hills. I shall be a golden leaf on the Tygart. I shall go to college. I shall be a leaf floating on a swift stream of water away from the hills."

Spring passes and the second year of school sinks into the past as the sun sinks over a hill and is gone for ever. The boys graduate from the school and leave. Some go to college, others go to work. Boys go home from the school and start work between the handles of the plow. They start work with hoes chopping weeds from the corn and hoeing the cane and tobacco. They work under the skies that float above Kentucky's green hills. Professor Stringer goes back to his farm to follow the plow again.

Autumn comes again to the hills. The sassafras leaves start turning red in early September. The pigskin tumbles end over end through the air. The boys and girls are back. Eustacia is back in the office. She is taking English III. She asks Mr. Stringer for novels to read. He lets her have them. She can wade through a novel with the ease of a blowing wind where the bottom corn is cut. She is growing swiftly into womanhood now as a plant grows into maturity in its season.

Eustacia finds a rival in English III. Little fair-haired blue-eyed Freeda Blank watched Eustacia Pratt keenly. When objective tests are given, Freeda always captures the lead in her class by one or two points. Eustacia always comes second. The two girls lead the class by a good margin of points. Professor Stringer heard Eustacia say: "If I did like one or two in that class, I could make good grades, too." The next test he puts both girls in front seats. The grades are as usual; Freeda leads by one or two points. Eustacia just can't surpass her. Both girls made A's, but that isn't it. Eustacia just can't stand to be beaten.

Once Professor Stringer says to Eustacia in the office: "Why is it I never hear you speak of your father?"

"I loved my father," says Eustacia. "I love the name of him better than the name of any one I know. I love the memory of him. The three men he had the fight with, if I knew them, I'd like to take a club and go in on them. I'd like to whip them right." Her face flushed red and then the blood left her cheeks. They grew pale again.

N. Y. A. jobs are offered in the schools and Eustacia Pratt is an A student and her family has been on relief. She is past sixteen years and meets the qualifications. She gets paid for work the first time in her life. She continues work in the principal's office and makes six dollars a month now. How proud she is to make it!

The autumn again swiftly passes into winter, and the winter passes into spring. The trees get green again. The hills that overlook the Tygart are budding again as the white showers of spring streak their sleeping bare bodies and wash the bark clean. The oaks are budding and the maples, water-birches, sycamores, and elms. The apple trees start blooming and the percoon whitens the coves where the blue waters of the Tygart run swiftly down fern-infested channels.

Professor Stringer walked up the path by the Tygart. Where an apple tree stood in the front yard white with blossoms, and an orchard of blooming trees on a steep bank at the back of the house, he saw a group of children at play. He immediately recognized one as Eustacia Pratt. She came running out to the road.

"Come up, won't you? she says.

He walks up to her house. He is invited in by her mother, Mrs. Pratt. She is a small, lean woman, who looks unable to work. He wonders how a woman so lean and frail can do housework at four dollars a week and keep five children.

Spring passes again and the school has closed. Another part of the youthful river of humanity has flowed to its destiny. The teachers and the students go home. Professor Stringer goes away to school. He does not go back to the farm. It is books again and new methods in school work to take back to the students. A letter comes to him from Eustacia. The letter says:

"I got a job staying in a kitchen this summer at four dollars a week. The bedbugs nearly ate me up. I packed up and left. I got a better place to stay but with less pay. I only get two dollars a week."

Kentucky again, with the farewell-summers in bloom and the sassafras slowly turning on the bluffs. The pawpaws are turning along the fence-rows from green to golden. School has started again. The teachers are back in their places. Eustacia is back in the office. She has bloomed into womanhood now as a plant reaches full maturity.

"The future of a country depends upon women like Eustacia," thinks Professor Stringer. "They shall some day give birth to sons and daughters and they shall be the builders of our destiny. It is in the endurable flesh and blood, the honest flesh and blood that will do or die, that will work and sweat, and the fearless and the hopeful on which our destiny depends."

Eustacia takes English IV under Professor Stringer. He finds her gradually creeping up on Freeda Blank. That rivalry isn't over. Whether Freeda wants to be Eustacia's rival or not, she accepts her as one and proceeds. Eustacia now edges Freeda out by one or two points and leads her class. "I never saw such fight in a girl student. She's a tremendous fighter. That girl can do things. I admire her. I wish I had a school with a thousand students just as good as she is."

The autumn passes and winter comes, when the Kentucky hills are white with a blanket of snow. Birds chirrup plaintively in the bull-grass by the Tygart. Blue sheets of ice span the Tygart and the skates ring out a merry echo against the frozen hills.

The winter days recede and spring comes again, a glorious burst of spring in Kentucky. The deep velvety green comes again in April—blue skies and snow-white blooming percoon. There was a streak of heavy green foliage up the Tygart, where the trees along the water course leaf earlier than the sturdy oaks that grow on the hillsides. The blue swirling water of the Tygart runs swiftly down its green-lined banks.

"Eustacia," says Professor Stringer, "Mrs. Maxwell has checked your grades and finds that you have the second highest grades. Freeda Blank edged you out by the fraction of one honor-point. I've written to Benton College to get application blanks for you. You'll have to take a stiff entrance examination, too. Many try to enter that institution but few are chosen. It's a school where you can work the biggest portion of your way."

Eustacia smiles and says: "I'm not afraid of the examination. I'll need a little money. I'll work this summer. I've got the promise of four dollars a week cooking and doing housework for Mrs. Blair. I can just get some clothes with that money. But Uncle Jarvis Pratt says I can't go to college. He's been talking to Mom about it."

"What's he got to do with it? Is he your guardian?"

"No," says Eustacia, "but you'd better come over and talk to Mom about it. Uncle Jarvis says he wants to see you about it. He's just raising Cain!"

"I'll help you to raise a little money," says Professor Stringer. "I'll help you all I can. Instead of your Uncle Jarvis trying to keep you from going to college he ought to be trying to send you."

Eustacia fills in the application blanks. Mrs. Maxwell gives her the entrance examination. "W'y, she took the test in one-half the time the college allows. She waded through those questions with all the ease in the world. It was some test too! Eustacia Pratt is one of the best students in this school."

Before Eustacia hears from the examination Professor Stringer walks over again to see Eustacia's mother. "Mrs. Pratt, I want to know if you are Eustacia's guardian. Does her Uncle Jarvis Pratt have anything to do with her going to college or does he not? Eustacia tells me he doesn't want her to go."

"Mr. Stringer," says Mrs. Pratt, "I'm Eustacia's guardian. Her Uncle Jarvis has nothing at all to do with her. I would love to see her go to college. She's made up her mind to go and there's not much that can stop her. I'll just tell you the whole story why her Uncle Jarvis is trying to keep her from college. This house we are living in belonged to my husband

Theopolis Pratt before he died. It was mortgaged. When Theopolis died, his brother Jarvis took the mortgage on himself to pay. My husband had the place nearly paid for. Now with the mortgage and the interest that has accumulated on it, the whole thing amounts to something over five hundred dollars. Jarvis wants to get Eustacia a job in town in the shoe factory to start paying on this debt. Either in the shoe factory or working in somebody's house. It isn't fair to Eustacia, for she didn't make the debt. And Jarvis Pratt is not a poor man. He owns something like seventeen houses that he rents. We don't pay any rent here. We can hold this house until Sarah is twenty-one. She's eleven now. We can stay here ten years longer and Jarvis can't do anything about it nor can he make us pay the debt. He'll get this property in the end, anyway."

Professor Stringer walks up the hill where sleeps Eustacia's dead—the dust she is made of for many generations. "Theopolis is sleeping now. The green hair of April entwines above his sleeping dust. The crows fly over and caw-caw the dreams of a thousand years to the green hair of April. Ah, the secrecy of the green hair of April, what are the dreams it hides? The thousand water-bubbles of bursting dreams? The million dreams of humanity lost in the cobwebs of time, spun on the invisible stuff that dreams are made of! Theopolis is not dead. Theopolis, the fighter, the dreamer, the fisherman, the boozer, lives on. Thanks to him, sleeping under American skies on a Kentucky hill, for the blood he left in Eustacia's veins. Theopolis lives on in a new day."

"I'm going to tell you, young man," says Jarvis Pratt, "that you've got no business prying into my family affairs. You put the idear of college in that girl's head. You know she's too young to send off to Benton College. You stay out of the Pratt affairs!"

"She's too young to enter college, but yet she's old enough to get down on her knees and scrub out five hundred dollars for you at four dollars a week! She's too young to enter college, but old enough to start work in the factories! I know why you don't want her to enter college. I've just seen her mother. She told me the whole story. Eustacia Pratt is going to college if she passes the entrance examination."

"Now listen to me, young man," says Jarvis Pratt, puffing at his cigar, "I want you go get this right now. I've got friends in town. I can get her a job in some office. She can use a typewriter, can't she!"

"Yes," says Professor Stringer, "but not to compete with the graduates of the business college over there, and they are standing in a queue waiting for jobs. What chance has she? Her best bet is college and there is where she is going. You ought to be ashamed. You with a wrinkled face and white hair.

You with enough to do you the rest of your days. Life is before her. Her father is in the earth. You are his own brother. You ought to help to pay her way in college. You rent seventeen houses."

"What's the use sending a girl to college?" asks Jarvis Pratt, puffing his cigar again. "Just go and get married. Her old dad if he was alive wouldn't want her a-gallivanting off down there to college. He wouldn't have it either. I've kept them children in a home up there ever since he's been dead. They look to me like I was their father and they'll listen, too."

"This is one of the times they won't listen. And in the end you get the property that was three-fourths of the way paid for. So I can't see as you've helped them very much."

"Well," says Jarvis, "the Pratts have always got along, haven't they? Yes, and they never went to college. It's just a lot of foolishness. She'd better be at work than gallivanting there. She's learnt enough up there in the high school. Besides, the way I see this, it's none of your business. You are interfering with our private affairs."

"A high school principal has the right to interfere when he has seen the struggle of Eustacia Pratt for the last four years. Lots of times she just had bread and water to eat. Those children would go home and go to bed hungry. Yet she stands right at the head of her class."

Professor Stringer walks away. He leaves Jarvis blowing cigar smoke to the wind under a cluster of locust trees. He walks up the railroad to the post office. There he sees Eustacia. She is holding a letter in her hand. She runs to meet him. She says:

"I'm accepted. I'm accepted. I passed with a good grade. I'll get to college. I'm the first of my people. Uncle Jarvis can't stop me either. I didn't make the debt, and, besides, if I ever have to pay it I can pay it quicker teaching school than I can scrubbing floors."

Professor Stringer looks beyond the hills that have held Eustacia and her people. He sees Eustacia on the train. She is leaving now. She is going to a bigger dream. It is bigger than the school by the Tygart. He can see her on the street with many young women. They are not better-looking girls than Eustacia. Their eyes are not bluer. They are not any straighter. They certainly are not any stronger. Few will be better students! She is laughing on the streets now with her friends. She is living her dream of pride, joy, fulfillment. She feels the strength of her native Kentucky hills.

How to Thread a Needle

About the story:

Remarking on Jesse Stuart's "gift of observation," Robert Penn Warren recalled that, even in his youth, Stuart was "keen of eye, full of all sorts of curiosity . . . a compulsive writer, as though all the life he had absorbed was struggling to find a way out, and perhaps to achieve its meaning." When August Derleth visited Stuart in 1938, he saw the Kentuckian's home country and his people about whom he wrote. Derleth got to know Stuart, too, and when it was time to leave W-Hollow Derleth wrote that Stuart was

> A man who is clearly the product of his country: rugged and brawny, strong as the hills he loves, he belongs to Kentucky, and Kentucky belongs to him. The tremendous vitality and vigor of his writing, too, are essentially Jesse Stuart. He knows the people about whom he writes so thoroughly because he is one of them, not alone by virtue of his birth, but by his life among them, his sharing their lives. He knows them better than anyone else can know them, and his interpretation is faithful to life.

Of the action and characters in "How to Thread a Needle," the author's knowledge was, then, not unsurprisingly, firsthand. Talking at his home in W-Hollow, he said, "They were neighbors who lived on this farm for awhile." The setting of the story is "Carter County, up beyond Grayson, near Olive Hill. I talked with the man who told the story and watched his expressions." As he had long ago told Derleth, he kept a "reserve" of such stories. "To tell the truth," he later said, "material is necessary, but you've got to have the idea as well as the material." The idea of "How to Thread a Needle" is an age-old one—youth and its life-loving ideals find themselves in conflict with tradition and outmoded, even if somewhat understandable, values and emotions. Here a young man questions those suspect values and emotions and eventually rebels; but the garb of conflict in which they are clothed, though perhaps "queer" to many readers, remains, nevertheless, fresh and singularly original.*

*Robert Penn Warren, "Foreword," Jesse Stuart, *Head o' W-Hollow* (Lexington: Univ. Press of Ky., 1979 reprint), pp. ix–x. August Derleth, "He Visited Jesse Stuart," in *News of Books and Authors* (May–June, 1939), clipping in Jesse Stuart, Scrapbook #6, p. 91, M. S. U. "How to Thread a Needle" first appeared in *The Ohio University Review*, Vol. 9 (1967), pp. 16–30. Jesse Stuart's comments on this story are from Jesse Stuart/ H. E. Richardson, Interview #41, W-Hollow, Greenup, Ky., Sept. 15, 1981.

THERE STOOD Grandpa Baines before me with a rifle across his shoulder and a blanket rolled up like a hand-rolled cigarette under his left armpit. The June wind was blowing slowly across our front yard, rustling the dark-green slick-bellied leaves on the persimmon tree on the slope behind our house. And the wind rustled Grandpa's beard, just lifting it up enough to show little patches of pale skin on his face. Grandpa's beady black eyes were mean as our bull's eyes before Pa made us stop teasing him with our red bandannas.

"Where's your Pa, Son?" Grandpa asked before he said 'goodmorning.' "Is he a-goin' with us to help do something about this thing?"

"Oh, yes, Grandpa," I said. "He's in the house getting ready. He'll soon be out!"

Grandpa's thin lips were set way back in a little half-hole surrounded by mustache and chin whiskers. Back in his mouth were some partly-white natural teeth. And I don't know what made me have a thought like this, but a long time ago I climbed up an oak to a crow's nest where I looked down inside at the blue-white eggs. The black sticks in that nest always reminded me of Grandpa's beard, while the eggs reminded me of his teeth. His thin lips reminded me of a terrapin's hard bony lips. When Grandpa talked his words were as hard as his lips looked to be.

"We're goin' to get them boogers," he said. "We're goin' to stay until we do! We'll break this wild stuff up! Never in my eighty years and three months upon this earth, Jasper, have I heard of anything like it!"

Just then Pa came out of the house with his rifle across his shoulder.

"Cy, did you fetch your pistol?" Grandpa asked him.

"It's in the holster home under my arm," Pa told Grandpa. "Pap, I'm prepared for battle!"

Pa had his blanket rolled like a hand-rolled cigarette too, and tucked under his arm. Ma had tied my rolled blanket on either end so it couldn't come unrolled. I had my .22 rifle that had a heavy eight-sided barrel. I could hit a dime at twenty-five steps with my rifle. But I didn't take a pistol.

"Cy, who are our enemies that would belittle our sleeping dead?" Grandpa asked. His words were hard. They had come through the bearded opening to his mouth and from behind his hard terrapin lips. And when he asked Pa this question, he almost stood upon the toes of his stiff brogan shoes. His eyes deep in wrinkled sockets sparkled like fire-lit embers out in the clearing when the wind stirs the ashes and the sparks. "You think they are the Gullets, Zornes, or the Simpsons?"

"I don't know Pap," Pa said. "Maybe, we will find out today or tonight!"

"All right let's get goin'," Grandpa said.

Grandpa led the way stepping sprightly in the shoe-mouth deep lush grass across our yard while Pa followed him. I couldn't help but notice that Grandpa Baines wasn't as tall as Pa and I was taller than Pa. We went across the yard like stairsteps, only Grandpa was the bottom step and I was the top step, and this didn't seem right. The wind blew through the persimmon leaves and made a funny noise. The noise I thought was like what I used to think were the mingled whispers of the dead when the winds blew among the rose vines, shrubs, and flowers planted in our Homeland Graveyard over at Big Beechie in Darter County. That's where our people had come from to Greenwood County. Beechie Creek was our home and no matter where one of us died, our people took him back to be buried in Homeland. Grandpa said we should all be together in the end. And right now I thought I'd heard the whispers of the dead when we walked across our yard to Pa's old dilapidated car.

Mom hadn't wanted us to take our guns and go. She thought there might be a lot of shooting and more people planted under the ground never to sprout. But Grandpa Baines made a lot of decisions in our family. When we thought we were being attacked, Grandpa always planned our battle strategy. Since I had only one brother and we both wanted to go, but one had to stay with Ma, we had pulled straws to decide who would go and I got the longest straw. When we had something important to do and only one could go we always pulled straws to see who went and who stayed home. So, I went and he stayed. He said I was always the lucky one and I might get to see some action. Yes, I had one brother and five sisters. Our sisters were married and gone. My brother Willie was number six and I was number seven in our family. When I followed Grandpa and Pa across our yard, I saw Willie's face up against a window pane, but when I looked at the window he jerked his face back. He didn't want me to see him watching me. He didn't want me to think he was jealous of me because I got the long straw and he got the short one.

"Sit up here by me, Pap," Pa said. "Jasper you take the back seat."

Grandpa got up in the front seat beside Pa. And I got in the back seat just as Pa had told me.

"Now let's drive over and get Charlie and his boys," Grandpa said. "They will be ready and waiting. I told them to have their guns and bottles of drinking water ready. The battle might get hot and we might need water. I'm suspicy of drinkin' water from the wells and springs near our Homeland."

Pa had finally started our old jalopy and it was clattering like our mule-pulled mowing machine. We didn't have but a half mile to go after Uncle Charlie and two of his boys. He had four boys, all single and at home. Since they'd all want to go, they would have to pull straws too. Two of my cousins who got the longest straws would go and two who got the shortest straws would stay. Aunt Emerine had to have help at the house. Farm work was going on at our homes.

"Yes, right in crop time, right when the corn is growing and the wheat ripens and the terbacker needs our attention, we haf to take our guns and go," Grandpa said. "It's our old enemies at work! They couldn't whop our livin' and now they attack our dead!"

Our jalopy clattered over the bumpy road down to Uncle Charlie's place. And when Pa pulled up and stopped at the yard gate, there stood Uncle Charlie under an apple shade tree with his rifle across his shoulder and a blanket under his arm. And he had his holster around his waist and a big pistol in the holster. Uncle Charlie was about the size of Pa. We were tough-butted white oaks growing on rocky slopes. There were no softwood trees among us. Pa and Uncle Charlie looked enough alike to be twins. And they looked like Grandpa. They had the terrapin lips and the hawk eyes. They had clean shaven faces. Maybe they didn't think they were old enough to grow beards like Grandpa. And Pa and Uncle Charlie had most all their natural teeth. Pa and Uncle Charlie had the bowed pipe-stem legs, and the short muscled arms and the sharp pointed noses.

Two of Uncle Charlie's boys were standing beside him. They had their rifles and blankets and each had a basket in his hand.

"We are here, Pap, and we are ready," Uncle Charlie said to Grandpa.

Grandpa got out of the car where he walked around like a rooster.

"Trevis, you and Zeke got the long straws didn't you?" I said.

"Yes the longest and the next longest," Trevis said.

"Cief and Egbert 're takin' it hard over gettin' the short straws," Zeke said. "I've told Pa that I was born under the lucky star. I've always been lucky. I just hope that my luck holds out. Wouldn't surprise me if I don't get the first crack at one of them boogers who are fighting our dead."

"No, I'll get the first crack," Grandpa said. "I'm the head of this family."

"You're right, Pap," Pa said.

"You are right as right can be, Pap," Uncle Charlie said.

"Have my grandsons got the water?" Grandpa said.

"A bottle of water for each one of us in these baskets," Cousin Zeke said. "Each one will have a long-neck horsequart whisky bottle of water. Will it be enough?"

"Let us hope it is," Grandpa said. "We can't be bothered with too much water and grub. We can't fight well enough on full stummicks!"

"Pap, how do we ride?" Uncle Charlie asked.

"I'll ride between my sons in the front seat," Grandpa said. "We'll be first and second generations of the living. And my grandsons can ride in the back seat. Keep your rifle barrels pointed to the roof of the car!"

Up front there was Pa under the wheel and there was Grandpa with his rifle barrel stuck up to the roof of the jalopy. And there was Uncle Charlie with his rifle barrel up against the roof. Trevis was on one side of me with his basket while Zeke sat on the other and we held the barrels of our rifles against the roof of the jalopy. Pa started the motor and the black smoke rolled! It coughed, clattered and spit and we were off. We were crowded in the car.

"When you get to Gadsen stop at Porter Reffitt's Store," Grandpa said. "We got to get some rations so we can stay until we get this job done. We got to get grub that will keep. If you don't like what I get, you'll like it when you get hungry enough."

When Pa drove into the little town of Gadsen, he did what Grandpa told him. He pulled up before the Porter Reffitt Store and stopped.

"Stay in the car boys," Grandpa said. "I'll leave my gun. Take care of it, Charlie!"

"All right, Pap," Uncle Charlie said.

Grandpa squeezed out of the car. "Don't let anybody see your guns," he said. "We don't want anybody to know we're drivin' around armed. We don't want anybody to know where we are going. This is a secret, for we want to catch the boogers there!"

Grandpa went into the store while we waited. In about twenty minutes he came out with a large paper sack.

"Now in this paper sack I have seven small paper sacks," he said. "Each one of you will get a paper sack of ration, a pound of brick cheese, box of crackers, bar of candy, and an apple. And you'll have your horsequart of water."

"Not much grub, so go slow on it," Grandpa said as he got back into the car. "Your water and grub might have to last you three or four days."

When Grandpa was seated betwixt his sons, Pa and Uncle Charlie, he picked up his rifle and fondled it like my mother used to fondle one of us when we were small. After Grandpa had gently rubbed his rifle barrel he pointed the barrel up against the roof. Now Pa had finally started the motor and our old jalopy was spitting fire and belching a stream of black smoke down the hard-surfaced road where cars were going around us.

"I remember when there was no hard road here," Grandpa said. "I've fetched a big wagon load of tanbark over the road here with three yoke o' pullin' it. And back in them slower days we didn't have men cowardly enough to attack the dead! Even our enemies wouldn't attack our dead! They would attack our livin' but not our dead. My sons and grandsons, I don't know what has happened to our people."

"Pap, what is our aim on this trip?" Uncle Charlie asked.

"We will drive up a backroad from Grahan," Grandpa said. "There we will leave this old car. No one will see it there. We will climb up on the hill and go into our Homeland from the Beechie Creek side. This is the back-door where no one will see us. We'll about reach Homeland when the long shadows fall and the moon is comin' up!"

When the traffic was coming to meet us, a long line of traffic gathered behind us. When we didn't meet cars the long line behind us zoomed around us like flying bullets.

"My old car is about as far behind these new cars as it would be ahead of the old mule, hoss, and cattle teams," Pa said.

"But your car is not ahead of the old mule, hoss, and cattle teams," Grandpa said. "We ain't ahead of the people then because the mules, hosses, and cattle breathed air and they liked people and we liked them. They were alive. This car ain't alive. It's a dead thing that can't talk and eat and it can't breathe air. Somethin' has changed this world, Cy, and it ain't been the hosses, cattle, and mules that have caused people to attack our dead. Animals didn't cause us to have to take our guns and go!"

"You are right, Pap," Pa said. "Animals didn't go into our Homeland in the night and push the tombstones over! They didn't pile wood on top of the stones and set fire to the wood to turn the white and gray stones black!"

"Animals didn't knock the little lambs from the tops of the children's stones," Uncle Charlie said.

"No, the lowdown human boogers are cowards," Grandpa sighed.

"How are we to deal with a body we see shoving over a stone, Grandpa?" I asked.

"Cut 'im in two with bullets." Grandpa's words were hard and as fast as a handful of clean creek gravels thrown into the soft green leaves on the sweet gum tree. "He's a lowdown nothing that will turn over a stone! Shoot 'im first and we'll talk about what to do with him later. Let's get rid of the lowdown boogers!"

"Pa, how many of the stones were turned over?" I asked.

"About all of them," he said.

"We worked four days getting them back straight," Uncle Charlie said. "I never saw anything that looked as bad as our Homeland. Some of our stones had been scarred with rifle bullets too. The boogers might have guns!"

"That will be better," Grandpa said. "They can't say, if a trial ever gets to court, that we shot unarmed people in our graveyard turning over the gravestones of our ancestors! They will have to say we both had guns and we shot it out at close range!"

"Yes, their feet had skived up the grass and had uprooted the flowers when they had turned our headstones over," Uncle Charlie said. "I never saw the likes of it since I've been a living man upon this earth! I couldn't have believed unless I'd seen with my own eyes that our human kind could be low and vile. Why wouldn't they let our dead rest? Our people had come and they had lived their days upon this earth. They'd known their joys and sorrows and now they were taking rest and returning to the clay of which they were a part. They couldn't bother anybody and yet they were attacked!"

"There is no reason for it," Grandpa said. "There are people in the world that don't deserve to live! When you shoot at one be sure you have him lined up in your gun sights. Be sure you thread the needle! Never stop pouring the hot lead into him until he falls. Hear me?"

"Yes, Pap," Uncle Charlie said.

"Sure, Pap," Pa said.

"Yes, we had to haul sand, cement, and water," Grandpa said. "We had to make forms and fill them with concrete. And we lifted the big stones up and set them on new foundations. It took a long time and a lot of work to get our Homeland fixed again. And I would have sworn they'd 've never got my Pap's stone over again but they have! Only hot lead will stop these low-downers! We'll shoot 'em until our guns get hot! Hot lead is too good for the boogers!"

When Grandpa talked about what somebody had done to the stones with the names of our people and the dates of their births and deaths, his voice got higher and higher. His words got harder and bigger until they sounded like rocks as big as hens' eggs hitting the soft green leaves on the sweetgum tree.

"When Cy pulls up the old land road on the Beechie Valley side of our Homeland, be sure to get your rations and check your ammunition," Grandpa said.

"What about the chiggers out there in that grass, Grandpa?" Cousin Zeke asked.

"Forget about a thing as little as a chigger that gets under the skin and makes a little bump," Grandpa said. "You keep your eyes open and watch for a man. Ask no questions. Let 'im have it!"

"What about a copperhead, Grandpa?" I asked.

"Shoot one like you would a man that's come to insult our helpless dead," Grandpa said. "Honest, we've got men folks sleeping in Homeland that I don't see how the ground holds them when the boogers come to do their dirt!"

When Pa left the hardroad, there must have been a hundred cars behind us. When we drove onto the old sideroad, we all were sitting up as straight as ramrods with our guns pointing up so if one went off it would blow a hole in the top of the car. The cars sped like flying bullets and some of the hands waved to us and somebody shouted: "Watch about driving so fast! You might burn it up!"

"If I had hold of that jay-bird I'd burn *him* up," Pa said. "It makes me awful mad to have somebody a-hollerin' at me on the highway! I don't like these smart boys!"

"We didn't have 'em, Cy, when we had the hosses, mules, and cattle," Grandpa said.

"Yes, Pap, I know," Pa said. "I barely remember them days!"

Pa drove our old jalopy up over an unused road. The lapping of green tops overhead cut away the dim light of the rising moon.

"We'll soon be there," Pa said. "None of the people around Grahan will know we're here!"

"Yes, go easy on the rations and water but don't spare the ammunition," Grandpa said.

"Well, here is where we stop," Pa said. "No one will find the car here."

"Pa, how could you find such a good place to hide the car," I asked.

"We've not overlooked anything," he replied. "We figured our plans the last day we were here setting up the overturned stones!"

Well I was glad to get out of the car. My cousins and I were all big young men and we were strong as bulls and we had the shrewd cold eyes of the young hawks when they flew overhead at sixty miles an hour and looked down and discovered a ground-sparrow or a woodmouse in the hayfield. We had good eyes that could see in the dark. And we could thread a needle with a rifle bullet a hundred yards away. I had my horsequart of water and my rations of grub, my rifle, and my pockets filled with ammunition.

"All right leave 'er there Cy," Grandpa said. "Remember rations and ammunition. And let's crawl up the hill and go in from the backside. Now, I'll be up on the top side of Homeland where I can look down over the highway and guard the front. Charlie you can drop behind me on the East End and Cy you take the West End behind me. Jasper, you, Zeke and Trevis spread out on the lower side. Zeke take the West, Trevis take the East and Jasper you'll be in the middle. Lay down on your belly in the grass. Be careful about raising up for one of us might mistake you for one of them."

All the years Grandpa had lived hadn't slowed him down much more than the years had slowed Pa and Uncle Charlie. Grandpa hit the slope and went wiggling up the steep bank on his knees and elbows. He had his rifle, pistol, blanket, horsequart of water, and his rations. The long moon shadows had crept over the land. Grandpa went on to the top and Pa and Uncle Charlie followed him almost all the way. But they dropped back to the places Grandpa had told them to guard. And down on the lower side Zeke and Trevis went to the West and East and I stayed in the middle. Now the small new moon, like a bright hooked sickle, rode above the tops of the green timber. And there were hundreds of stars coming into the sky.

I unrolled my blanket on the soft cool grass and I stretched out on it with my rifle beside me. You're my friend if they come, I thought. But I hoped that they didn't come. I didn't want to shoot anybody. When they came in and shoved the tombstones over, they didn't do any harm to our sleeping dead. Grandpa and I didn't think alike. I didn't want to kill anybody. I'd heard a lot about our enemies but I didn't want to shoot one of them.

I looked to the east and there was Zeke on his blanket. And I looked to the west and there was Trevis sprawled on his blanket. The thin sickle moon and the stars looked down on us and down on the tombstones that looked like hounddog's teeth scattered over a dark mouth. Above me in the east was Uncle Charlie and above me in the west was Pa. And above all was Grandpa who was on top of the slope where he could look over on the highway to see the bright lights going toward the east and toward the west in two steady lines like yellow jackets ascending into the bright morning air and descending in another line, dropping down from the bright air to their castle in the ground.

While I lay here watching the thin moon go down behind the trees, I had a lot of thoughts. Then, I watched hundreds of stars come into the sky. I saw stars fall from heaven and when one fell I made my wish and my wish was for no one to come into our Homeland so I wouldn't have to shoot at him or to be shot by him. I was afraid of all the guns and all the ammunition we had. I had my pockets filled with cartridges. I wondered what was going on in everybody's mind. And I wondered about each person who was dead and buried in a grave, if he had gone on a long journey to another world and if he had met people, his loved ones, like Grandpa said he was going to meet when he went on his long journey. I had a lot of thoughts coming into my mind. I had thought I might want to go to sleep, but these thoughts came into my mind so that I couldn't go to sleep.

All around were my ancestors who had lived and died before I was born. Each had a big white stone to tell where he slept, the year he was born and the year he died. But the stone told so little about him. I wondered about the kinsmen each stone represented. And then I wondered why anybody would want to come onto this lonesome hillside, on a night in winter, spring, summer, and autumn and shove over a marker that marked the last place one of my kinsmen would ever sleep on this earth. Why were my kinsmen planted on this hill, I wondered. Why this part of earth? Why would people slip in and root their stones over? Was this called fun? Or were the people who did this cowards who wouldn't face and fight the living? Had they taken their vengeance out on the dead? I couldn't figure out why they had done it.

I dreamed of shooting and running in the night. I dreamed that the weather turned cold and I would have to have more cover. When I woke up at about two o'clock in the morning, I watched Grandpa raising his head up and then putting it down and up again like a lizard lying on a log in the summer sun. Grandpa was watching over the whole graveyard. I didn't see another head going up and down. Maybe they're asleep, I thought. Well, I laid back down and I rolled up in my blanket. Are there any copperheads in this graveyard? I thought.

When I woke, it was six o'clock by my wrist watch. Grandpa was up eating a piece of cheese and tipping his horsequart of water. I wondered if Grandpa wasn't missing the hot coffee that Grandma made for him each morning. I heard Pa snoring and Uncle Charlie was off his blanket on the dewy grass. Trevis was rolled up in his blanket. Zeke was lying on top of his blanket with his rifle beside him.

"They didn't come last night, Grandpa!" I said.

"No, the boogers didn't come," he said. "I wish they had!"

Then I sampled my breakfast of hard cheese, crackers and water while Grandpa and I talked up and down the slope. Maybe our words hit a few of the tombstones and they angled off in this and that direction until they woke Pa and Uncle Charlie. Then Cousin Trevis rose up and wiped his eyes. "Oh, Lord where am I?" he said. And we laughed until we woke Cousin Zeke.

"Pap, will we stay here all day?" Pa asked.

"You bet we will, Cy," he said. "We've got to get the scoundrels! They'll be back!"

Well everyone woke up and ate his breakfast of cheese and crackers and drank water from his horsequart.

"Go easy on the water," Grandpa said. "It will have to last today, maybe tonight, and tomorrow. Maybe even longer. We can't go out to buy more grub and let people around here know we're in our Homeland. The people who are turning these stones over may not live too far away!"

We didn't have water to shave and wash our hands and faces. We had to let our whiskers grow. We didn't bring razors and toilet articles with us. And Grandpa told us we couldn't use any part of the Homeland for a toilet. This was the only time we'd leave Homeland and then we could just cross the fence and not get too far away.

In the morning the sun came up and dried the dew. Little clouds rose up and ascended toward the heavens. Everywhere fluffy white clouds rose on the wind. Grasshoppers jumped from grave to grave and from stone to stone. Birds flew over with worms in their bills. They were taking breakfasts to their young.

"Cy, did you see a ghost last night?" Uncle Charlie asked Pa.

Then Uncle Charlie laughed loudly and Pa laughed because Uncle Charlie laughed. Cousin Trevis, Zeke, and I joined them but Grandpa didn't laugh. He didn't see anything funny about seeing a ghost in our Homeland. He was sitting up there perched above us where he could look over the highway and then down at us.

In midafternoon, I had more cheese and crackers and drank a little water to quench my thirst. A very hot sun beamed down upon us. Sweat drops dripped from Grandpa's beard and I saw them shining like silver beads in the glimmering sunlight. I watched two lizards mating on a corner fencepost. When a crow flew over it flapped its wings lazily in the air. It was carrying a young squirming blacksnake in its bill. What a lazy quiet forsaken place we have chosen for our kinfolks to be planted for eternity, I thought. And now I have to come and guard the place.

At three o'clock in the afternoon, I saw him coming toward me, his golden head just above the grass, his forked tongue out vibrating in the lazy heat. His short blunt body was down under the green wilted waves of grass but his head was like a periscope coming up from the sea. I couldn't stand to see a copperhead coming toward me. Maybe it wasn't the people who had turned the stones over as much as it was this copperhead that was my enemy. I knew a copperhead wouldn't get out of the way of forest fire. He'd strike at a ring of fire until it burned him to death and left his body a wisp of gray ashes on the dark burned-over land.

I didn't tell Grandpa, my Uncle, my Pa, or my cousins. I lined him up in my rifle sights. If he kept coming toward me, I knew what would happen when his body met mine. I threaded the needle with the sights and gently squeezed the trigger. The bullet drilled a hole through his neck just under his bony blunt head. He flopped over and squirmed on the grass. When my rifle went "sprink" everybody jumped.

"Don't get excited," I said. "It was a copperhead crawling toward me. But I got him."

Then everybody got up from his blanket and walked toward me and I led them down to the writhing snake. We watched the motions of his body grow less and less until he became very still.

"What was he doin' in here?" Grandpa asked.

"He lives in here," Uncle Charlie said. "Copperheads like old grave-yards. When a grave sinks and leaves a break in the ground he will slide down into the break. In the summer the place is cool. And when days get cool in early autumn the place is warm. And often copperheads hibernate in old graves.

"That's not good talk, Charlie," Grandpa said. "I don't like to hear it."

"But you know it's the truth, Pap!"

"Look out, Jasper, for tonight or tomorrow," Pa said. "That snake's mate will be looking for him. If it comes onto you in the night when you're sleeping, it will be too bad."

"Try to stay awake, Jap," Zeke said. "You'd better heed warning! Ain't he a dangerous looking thing!"

"I'd hate to be bitten by him," Uncle Charlie said. "I'd say if he'd 've bitten one of us, the one that got his fangs in his flesh would have been the next one planted here. I'd say there would have been a fresh mound of yellow dirt in Homeland!"

Cousin Zeke offered to take my place when night came on and the curved sickle moon came up and the stars came out. But I told him I'd stay for it had just as well be me that got the copperhead fangs and if I got them and died I'd just as well be the next one planted in Homeland. But I told him I didn't want to be planted in this lonesome place or anywhere else. I didn't mention that I didn't agree with what Grandpa was doing.

The moon didn't stay up too long. After it went down over the rim of leafy trees on the distant hill, more stars showed up in the sky. A whippoorwill sang over the hill the moon had gone over. And down in Beechie Valley this whippoorwill was answered by his mate. She sang him a beautiful love song. It sounded beautiful to me under the circumstances, where I had to eat cheese and crackers, never wash my hands and face, and never shave. Out in a graveyard sleeping on a blanket watching for our "enemies" and now watching for another enemy, a copperhead snake. Pa had told me the mate would come back as sure as our Creator had made little green apples on the trees, and I believed Pa.

I got in the middle of my blanket when I got chilly in the night. I pulled the edges of the blanket up over me and just let my head stick out. I had my rifle beside me, for I was more afraid of that copperhead's mate than I was of an enemy who would slyly enter Homeland and attack our sleeping dead by uprooting markers. "Sprink." I heard it. I jumped up. I guess I'd been asleep. And when I rose up with my blanket around me, five others rose up with blankets around them and Cousin Zeke was already up with his blanket around him. We looked like ghosts sitting up in Homeland with our blankets around us.

"I know I saw him," Cousin Zeke said. "I saw a man with a black mustache, white shirt, and bow tie! He wore a coat split up the back. He looked like a young man! I took a crack at him. He disappeared on the air soon as that bullet hit him!"

"Must have been Brother Dock," Uncle Charlie said.

"Yes, Brother Dock, who went of fever when he was young," Pa said. "He had the black mustache."

"And he was buried in the dark suit, the white shirt and black bow tie," Grandpa said. "And his funeral coat was slit up the back! Son, I'm sorry you shot at Dock!"

"But how was I to know, Grandpa?" Zeke said.

"Maybe too much sun on Zeke's head yesterday," Uncle Charlie said.

"Maybe too much strain," Pa said.

"Let's all lie back down and sleep off the creeps," Uncle Charlie said.

We agreed to what Uncle Charlie said and we took our positions again. But I couldn't go back to sleep. I knew that I felt something up against my blanket. With one hand I held to my rifle and with the other I struck a match. There he was the real old he-copperhead. I'd killed the she, I turned over away from him quickly and I struck another match and at close range I threaded the needle of my rifle sights and let him have it.

Well, when my rifle sprinked everybody jumped up once more with their blankets around them and they sure looked like ghosts.

"I didn't shoot a ghost," I said. "I got a big old he-copperhead! He's the old bull residenter. He's lived in Homeland a long time. If he'd put a fang in me I'd have been planted here! Come strike a match and take a long look."

Well that is what they did. Grandpa said he was the biggest copperhead he'd ever seen in his life. He was about two and a half feet long and bigger around than my wrist. He was the kind that could coil and jump twice the length of his body.

"Grandpa, I don't want to die," I said. "I don't want to die by a copperhead's fangs. Come daylight, I'm leaving here if I have to walk home."

"Now, Jasper," Pa said.

"Don't 'now Jasper' me, Pa," I said.

"Well, you've got the snake," Grandpa said. "You can lie down and sleep in peace to settle your nerves. Let's all lie down and sleep."

I looked at my watch. It was three in the morning. We agreed to lie down again but I thought the copperheads might keep coming. We hadn't been down thirty minutes until Trevis's rifle went 'sprink.'

"I know I saw 'im," Trevis said. "He was a short, stocky man, wearing a black suit, white shirt, and bow tie. His hair and his mustache were as white as wild plum blossoms."

"You saw Pap," Grandpa said. "Maybe Pap's disturbed!"

"Maybe you were dreaming, Trevis," Uncle Charlie said.

"No, Pap, I wasn't dreaming," Trevis said.

"Maybe Pap doesn't want us here," Grandpa said. "Looks like a bad omen."

Grandpa went back up the slope and took over his place. He didn't lie back on his blanket. He sat up with his blanket around him.

"Maybe you're a-seein' things, Trevis," Uncle Charlie said.

"I am seeing things, Pap," he said. "I saw a man. And I wasn't dreaming. I never saw this man before in my life. But I saw him tonight as plain as I ever saw a man in daylight."

"I am sure you saw my father, Trevis," Grandpa said. "I'm sorry you shot Pap!"

Maybe Uncle Dock and Great Grandpa had had enough rifle bullets. They didn't show up again in the morning hours. Light streaks began to break at five o'clock. Everybody sat up with his blanket around him. Then, a redbird rooster sang. And we talked to one another and Pa asked Uncle Charlie how he would like to have a good cup of coffee. So we began eating cheese and drinking water. Stars were still in the sky and Pa and Uncle Charlie smoked home-rolled cigars and blew the smoke up toward the morning stars. And I looked up to Grandpa and he was sitting up high smoking a cigar.

"Boys, I'm goin' to tell you," Grandpa said. "There's no use to stay here any longer. The boogers won't be back. The spirits of our dead have appeared to them same as they have to us. They don't want to be disturbed no longer."

"That will be all right, Pap," Uncle Charlie said. "My sons might start getting trigger happy if we stay another night."

"Get your belongings," Grandpa said. "Let's move out of here before it's good daylight."

*Stuart on June 28, 1955, in the "old" living room at his home in W-Hollow, Greenup, Kentucky. (*Maurice Kaplan photo)

The "Strange and Powerful" Characters of W-Hollow ✗✗✗

Part 4

Beyond the News in Still Hollow

About the story:

In a New York *Herald Tribune* review of Jesse Stuart's first collection of short stories, *Head o' W-Hollow*, Mark Van Doren wrote that "the stories in themselves are strange and powerful; a great deal happens in W-Hollow, even if the world has been ignorant of the fact." Entitled "The Good Speech of a Kentucky Hollow," the review continued, "The grammar of Mr. Stuart's people is particularly fascinating to me. 'Yes, I'd ruther have her as any doctor that's in Berryville. She's my sister and bad to fight, but I'd ruther have her by my side when I'm sick as anybody I know.' It is rather by such manipulations of word-order, grammar, and syntax than by apostrophes and misspellings that he succeeds in giving the flavor of a remote and special speech."

"Beyond the News in Still Hollow" is one of Jesse Stuart's rare stories set in a World War II atmosphere. Even so, his place and world overshadow every scene as Sheriff Enic Bradley seeks out Crooks Cornett in a remote, landlocked hollow among the Kentucky hill people, whom Jesse Stuart knows so well. As the sheriff's journey narrows into the isolated area of the Cornetts beyond Piney Point, he must leave his car "at the end of the WPA road," a car "built as high as cars were built in the late twenties, over rocks, stumps, and rutty roads," and borrow "a gallopin' mule . . . as easy a saddler as a body ever rid," in order to complete his journey

199

toward where "Ye'll haf to ast the rest of the way." There in a shack by a cliff he finds the house of the suspected draft dodger he seeks, a youth "who shied away to the far side of the room when he saw the stranger." The family's remoteness is dramatized in a dozen subtle ways, italicized by the people's very dialect, "Thar haint a house in seven miles o' here. We never hear any news, only what people tell us, and we're suspicy of strangers in Still Hollow."

Far from trying to escape the draft, when Crooks Cornett is made aware that the war has been going on for a year, he declares, "If I'd a-knowed hit I could a-been fightin' a year.... Do ye want me to go tonight?" The tradition of the family Bible with the name and origin of the paterfamilias, "Jarvis Cornett, Yorkshire, England, May 17th, 1797," draws a clear line of cultural history which deepens the authenticity. It is a story of rough-hewn familial dignity, of simple honesty and loyalty to one's native land rising with touching naïvety out of the circumstances of a forgotten people, of their individuality, of their strange ways, apparently emotionless reserve, simplicity, and pride.

The origin of the story is neighboring Lewis County, near Vanceburg, Kentucky, where Gus and Lena Voiers, longtime friends of the author, told Jesse Stuart this story of the draft, setting an atmosphere imminent with violence of the most destructive war in the history of the United States over against the mountain life of an isolated hollow, in Van Doren's phrase, "the life that has a symmetry of its own, together with an effect of completeness." Though the outer world may penetrate the world of Jesse Stuart and his people, it never dominates it. There "National politics take on the charm of folklore," Van Doren wrote; "hospitality is absolute; and the wind incessantly blows lovely speech from one lone farm to another."*

* * *

SHERIFF ENIC BRADLEY thought he knew Melton County, deep in the mountains of Kentucky, better than he knew the pages of the old McGuffey Fourth Reader which was his highest scholastic attain-

---

*Mark Van Doren, "The Good Speech of a Kentucky Hollow" (review), New York *Herald-Tribune*, May 3, 1936, clipping in Jesse Stuart Scrapbook #3, p. 7, M. S. U. On the same page with Van Doren's review is a photograph of Jesse Stuart standing in the midst of his snowy white Kentucky hills, hatless and distinctively clad in a dark serge overcoat, white scarf, and white handkerchief protruding from his upper front pocket. Jesse Stuart's "Beyond the News in Still Hollow" was originally published in *Esquire*, Vol. 20 (Dec., 1943), pp. 71, 257–258, 260, 262, 264, and reprinted in *My Land Has a Voice* (N.Y.: McGraw-Hill, 1966), pp. 28–38. Mr. Stuart's comments on the origin of "Beyond the News in Still Hollow" are from Jesse Stuart/H. E. Richardson, Interview #41, W-Hollow, Greenup, Ky., Sept. 15, 1981.

ment. He was born in Melton County, had lived in it all his life, had seen the WPA roads come to the county, government electricity to the county seat, and a WPA stone jailhouse. Before these new improvements came there wasn't an electric wire, a stone building, or a road a car could be driven over in the county. Not yet was there a telephone, a foot of railroad, or a foot of surfaced highway. Now he sat in his car at the end of the WPA road, baffled as he looked over the warrant. The name of the young man he was to arrest was Crooks Cornett. The post office where the young man got his mail was Piney Point. But someone had scribbled a note on the warrant, "You'll find him in Still Hollow." He knew county sheriffs and revenue men, those that returned, had many occasions to remember Still Hollow.

The road beyond the WPA road was a wagon road, filled with deep ruts and chuck holes. It was impossible for him to drive his car, though his car was built as high as cars were built in the late twenties, over rocks, stumps, and rutty roads. This wagon road was too much for his old car, and he made up his mind to lock the car and walk to the first house to inquire for Piney Point and Still Hollow. He had not walked a mile until he came to a shack beside the road, where he decided to inquire. Two children playing in the yard saw him first, dropped their playthings and ran into the shack as fast as they could to warn their parents a stranger was coming. When he reached the shack door he knocked.

The door opened enough for a man to stick his head out cautiously.

"Sheriff Bradley," the beardy-faced man greeted him, opening the door the rest of the way.

"Ollie Hendrix," Sheriff Bradley said, "I didn't know you lived here. I'm tryin' to find Piney Point and Still Hollow."

"I haint never been thar," Ollie said in his slow way. "Years ago it was a dangerous place. 'Spect, Sheriff, it's twenty-five miles to Still Hollow! Ye haint a-tryin' to walk thar, air ye?"

"I planned to," Sheriff Bradley said. "You don't have a good saddle horse I could hire for a couple of days?"

"Nope, but I got a gallopin' mule," Ollie said, laughing, showing his yellow, discolored, tobacco-stained teeth. "He's as easy a saddler as a body ever rid."

"I'd like to hire 'im," the sheriff said. "I'll pay you well for the mule. I'd like to pay you to watch my car too."

"Where is hit, Sheriff?"

"It's parked at the end of the WPA road."

"I'll do hit, Sheriff," Ollie said happily.

Ollie bridled and saddled his mule for the sheriff and helped him mount, for the mule was as wary of strangers as the mountaineers themselves.

"Follow this road until ye reach Blue Creek," Ollie directed the sheriff. "Follow Blue Creek until ye reach Rocky Branch. Ye'll haf to ast the rest of the way."

"Many thanks, Ollie," Sheriff Bradley said, riding away.

He galloped the mule where the road was suitable. Soon he and the mule were almost covered with mud. But he followed the road to Blue Creek; then he followed the Blue Creek road, which was impassable for any sort of wagons, until he reached Rocky Branch, where the road simmered down to a mule path. He rode wearily up Rocky Branch until he came to a shack that was crowded between the road and a high wall of cliffs. When he stopped his mule and laid the bridle rein over the gate post, children playing in the yard dropped their playthings and ran into the house. When he knocked on the door a beardy-faced man opened the door enough to stick his head out and say, "What do ye want, stranger?"

"How do you get to Still Hollow?"

"Ye haint a revooneer, air ye?"

"I'm goin' to visit Cornetts. They're my kinfolks."

"Right good people they are," the man said, holding the door. "Ye're 'bout eleven miles from thar. If ye ride fast ye'll make it by sundown. Follow Rocky Branch road to the ridge. One road turns right, one turns left. Take the road to the left."

"Thank you," Bradley said.

When the sheriff mounted his mule he saw the man looking from the door at him and his many children's faces peeping from behind the curtains of the only window in the shack. He rode away thinking these people were strangers to him, though he lived not more than twenty miles away.

Before sundown Sheriff Bradley asked a man walking along the path, carrying a pole of stovewood on his shoulder and an ax in his hand, if he could tell him where Cornetts lived.

"What do ye want?" the stranger asked.

"Just want to see my kinfolks."

"See that shack against that cliff," the man pointed with the handle of his ax.

"Thank you."

He rode to the shack and hitched his mule to the garden palings, walked over rocks laid down for a walk to the front door and knocked. A big man opened the door part of the way; he was barefooted, wore overalls and his face was unshaven.

"Do Cornetts live here?" Sheriff Bradley asked.

"They do," he said. "I'm Jarvis Cornett. What might yer name be?"

"Enic Bradley."

"Haint ye some sort o' law in this county?"

"I'm the sheriff."

"We don't make moonshine any more."

"I've come to see your son, Crooks."

Jarvis looked worried. "What's he done?" he asked.

"The Melton County Draft Board has sent him three notices."

"Come in, Mr. Bradley, and explain this thing to me," Jarvis Cornett said.

Sheriff Bradley walked into the shack, where there were four girls and four boys who looked at him suspiciously and didn't speak. Then a small wrinkled-faced woman came into the room smoking a long-stemmed pipe.

"What's the sheriff want, Jarvis?" she asked.

"It's something about Crooks," Jarvis told her.

"What's Crooks done?" she asked Sheriff Bradley.

"He's evaded the draft, Mrs. Cornett," Sheriff Bradley said.

"Which one of these boys is Crooks?"

"Crooks is out a-huntin' a mess of land turtles," she told Sheriff Bradley.

"What's land turtles?" Sheriff Bradley asked, rather hesitantly.

"Maybe ye call 'em terrapins."

"I didn't know they were good to eat," the sheriff said.

"Better 'n water turtles," Jarvis said.

"Mr. Cornett, did you get the cards notifying Crooks he was called?" Sheriff Bradley asked.

"We never go to the post office," Jarvis said. "We never git any letters. We don't take any kind of papers. No ust to. Not one here can read."

"Then you've never been to the post office?"

"When did ye go to Piney Point last, Ma?" he asked Mrs. Cornett.

"One of the youngins was over thar last Christmas," she said.

"The cards have been sent since then," the sheriff said.

"Who sent the cards?" Jarvis asked, looking at Sheriff Bradley suspiciously.

"The U.S. government," Sheriff Bradley said.

"What does the govern-mint want with Crooks?" Mrs. Cornett asked, looking directly at Bradley.

"Wants 'im for a soldier," Sheriff Bradley said.

"We haint at war again, air we?" Jarvis asked.

"You don't mean to tell me you don't know we are at war?"

"I didn't know hit. Who air we a-fightin' this time?"

"Germany and Japan."

He's trying to make me think he doesn't know, Sheriff Bradley thought; he knows this country is at war. He doesn't want his boy to go. Thinks we won't find him.

"When have you been to the county seat, Mr. Cornett?"

"Hit's been over two year."

"How do you live?" he asked.

"Raise what we eat, eat what we raise," he said.

"Don't you buy anything?"

"A few clothes and shoes."

"Where do you buy them?"

"At Bert Vaughn's General Store down the creek," he said. "Sometimes we don't go thar fer clothes and shoes. When roads air good the huckster wagon comes to the foot of the hill and we all go down and have our winter shoes fit on our feet."

"How do you make money to buy shoes?"

"Sell hides, chickens, eggs, young calves to the huckster man," he said. "Ye see the boys and me do a powerful lot of huntin'."

"And you never go to the county seat?"

"Let me tell ye, Sheriff Bradley," Jarvis said, pulling a tobacco leaf from his pocket and cramming it into his mouth, "I'm the only one of my fambly that's ever been out'n this county."

"You don't have a radio to get the news?"

"Heerd one play once," Jarvis said. "My youngins haint heerd a radio."

"And you didn't know that we'd been at war over a year?"

"Not until ye come fer Crooks and told us about it."

While they sat talking in the small room the door opened and a tall red-cheeked boy with long uncombed hair walked in. He carried a basket on his arm, filled with terrapins.

"Look, Pa, at the land turtles," he said before he noticed the stranger sitting among his people.

"They air fine-lookin' land turtles," Jarvis said to his son, who shied away to the far side of the room when he saw the stranger. One of his brothers whispered something to him.

"Sheriff Bradley has come all the way from the county seat to see ye," Jarvis told his son. "He says our country's at war and Uncle Sam wants ye fer a soldier."

"When does Uncle Sam want me?"

"Right now," Sheriff Bradley said.

"When did the war start?" the boy asked, knocking the terrapins back into the basket when they tried to crawl out.

"Over a year ago," Sheriff Bradley said.

"If I'd a-knowed hit I could a-been fightin' a year," Crooks said. "Do ye want me to go tonight?"

"In the mornin'," the sheriff said.

"Will Uncle Sam have ye if ye'r fifteen?" the boy second in size asked Sheriff Bradley. "I'd like to go with Crooks," he said. "Would ye keer if I'd go, Ma?"

"Not if Uncle Sam needs ye."

The sun had set, and twilight was brooding over Still Hollow.

"I'll have to spend the night with you, Mr. Cornett," Sheriff Bradley said. "My mule is tired and I can't get back tonight."

"Wouldn't think about lettin' ye go back tonight," Jarvis said. "We've got a bed fer ye, maybe hit's not as good as ye're ust to; we've got grub for ye; such as hit is. Did, take his mule to the stable and stall and feed 'im for the night."

"All right, Pa," Did said.

"Clean the land turtles," his father commanded. "Ye'd better be a-cookin' us a bite o' supper, Ma!"

The skinny mother left the front room at her husband's command. The children followed her into the kitchen while Sheriff Bradley and Jarvis Cornett talked as darkness engulfed the twilight. Jarvis lighted a pine torch and stuck it in a wooden holder on the mantel.

"Crooks won't sleep tonight," Jarvis told the sheriff. "He'll be a-thinkin' about leavin' in the mornin'."

"I thought he was dodging the draft," Sheriff Bradley said.

"Honest, we didn't know about the war until ye told us, Sheriff," Jarvis said. "Thar haint a house in seven miles o' here. We never hear any news, only what people tell us, and we're suspicy of strangers in Still Hollow."

While the men talked in the torch-lighted room, Enic Bradley observed the scanty furniture. There were two crudely made beds in the room, an old paintless dresser with a broken mirror, a small table made of puncheon boards. There were pictures of two old men with long beards and two wrinkled-faced old women. There was a picture of Jesus Christ and below it these words were framed, GOD BLESS OUR HOME. The walls were papered with newspapers turned yellow with age and punctured in many places, letting Enic see the rough log walls. Over the ceiling, newspapers were circled where the shack had leaked. And in one corner, a ladder was placed from the floor to a hole in the loft.

"Supper's ready, Jarvis," Mrs. Cornett announced.

"Let's eat, Sheriff," Jarvis said.

In the small kitchen there was a table covered with oil-cloth in the middle of the floor. There was a cookstove in one corner and a cupboard in the other. Pots and pans were hanging to nails over the newspapered walls. Pods of peppers and leather-britches beans hung from nails behind the stove.

"Welcome to our table," Jarvis said as they sat down.

Jarvis and Mrs. Cornett sat at one end of the table and the sheriff at the other. The boys sat on a bench on one side, the girls sat on a bench at the opposite side. There was a dish of land turtle fried brown in the middle of the table, a dish of corn pone cut in squares and stacked high on a plate; there was a dish of fried brown potatoes, mouse's-ear greens, and wild strawberries for a dessert.

"This will be my first land turtle," the sheriff said when Jarvis passed him the dish. "You don't have a ration book to buy meat, do you?" he continued.

"What's a ration book?" Mrs. Cornett asked.

"It's a book put out by the United States government that entitles you to buy your share of certain foods," Sheriff Bradley said.

"We manage to git along without that book," Jarvis said.

While they ate and the sheriff explained the ration books, the early summer wind blew in at the broken window panes and cooled the hot kitchen. The pine-torch flame that lighted the kitchen fluttered in the wind but did not go out. And above the sound of the wind and the voices around the table, Sheriff Bradley could hear the who-whos of the horned owl on the distant mountain. The sheriff ate many pieces of fried-brown turtle legs. He was eating a rare delicacy, he thought. He never knew they were good before he visited Cornetts.

Soon as they had finished supper, the men went into the front room while the girls and their mother remained in the kitchen. While the sheriff was telling Crooks Cornett about the war, he picked up the well-worn family Bible from the crude home-made table. When he turned to the flyleaf, he found a name written in beautiful English, "Jarvis Cornett, Yorkshire, England, May 17th, 1797."

"I see this Bible's come from England," Sheriff Bradley said to Jarvis.

"Hit was my great-grandpappy's Bible," Jarvis said. "Hit was handed down from him to his oldest son, who was my grandpappy, and my grandpappy gave it to my pappy, who was his oldest son, and my pappy gave it to me because I'm his oldest son. I'll give hit to Crooks, since he's my oldest son," Jarvis said.

"We ust to have a lot more books that come from England but used 'em to start fires with, since we couldn't read them."

"Then your people are of English descent?" Sheriff Bradley said.

"Yep, they all came from England long ago and settled in these mountains," Jarvis said, spitting ambeer into the open fireplace.

My people came from England too, Sheriff Bradley thought as he fondled the old Bible and laid it back on the table. We used to have a Bible like this that came from England. Nearly all of our neighbors did, but now most of them are gone. They were the last things we lost that we brought from England.

"Sheriff, you'll have a long ride tomorrow," Jarvis said. "Don't want to rush ye to the hay, but 'spect ye's better be a-hittin' hit since ye're tired."

"I'm ready to hit the hay," the sheriff said.

"Ye'll haf to sleep upstairs with Crooks, Sheriff," Mrs. Cornett said. "Hope ye haint got no objections."

"Mrs. Cornett, I'm so tired and sleepy I could sleep on the floor," Sheriff Bradley said.

"Then take Sheriff Bradley to bed, Crooks," Jarvis said softly.

Next morning at four o'clock Jarvis and Mrs. Cornett were out of bed. She got breakfast while he fed the mules. Sheriff Bradley, Crooks, and Did Cornett were awakened for breakfast. They sat down to a breakfast of hot biscuits, wild honey, roasted turtle eggs, butter and coffee.

"You've sure got good things to eat here," Sheriff Bradley said. "First time I've ever tried a roasted turtle egg."

"Glad ye like 'em, Sheriff," Mrs. Cornett said. It was the first time she had smiled.

"It'll be yer last breakfast fer a while with us, Son," Jarvis spoke across the torch-lighted table to Crooks. "Did can go with ye and ride one of the mules and lead yer mule back tomorrow. They air waitin' when ye air ready to go."

Soon as they finished breakfast Sheriff Bradley asked Jarvis what the care of his mule and his night's lodging would be.

"Ye insult me trying to offer me pay." Jarvis laughed. "Was glad to have ye and yer mule."

Crooks took a few personal belongings tied up in a pillowcase that his mother had packed for him. There wasn't a sign of emotion. There was only that deep, shy, sensitive look his mother gave him as he stood trying to say something to her. There was not a farewell kiss, as mountain people do but little kissing in parting.

Jarvis, his wife, and their children watched them mount their mules, ride away waving good-by. They watched them follow the narrow path single file until mules and riders had disappeared into the dawn of morning in a region where the war hadn't reached.

Woman in the House

About the story:

Of the book in which "Woman in the House" was first collected, *Head o' W-Hollow*, Jeannette Greenspan, writing for the Brooklyn *Citizen* (May 1, 1936), recognized Jesse Stuart as an authentic voice from a hitherto neglected and misunderstood hinterland." Up to that time, because of his *Man with a Bull-Tongue Plow* (1934) and other published poems, Stuart had been known mainly as a poet; and Greenspan observed of his style, "even when he is writing prose, Stuart is essentially a poet, and his stories become prose-poems." She further perceived that the farmers of W-Hollow "are not the poor white trash inevitably encountered in sectional Southern novels. They are respectable, hard-working sharecroppers, growing their corn and beans, believing in predestination, hating the sight of a Republican, bearing many children, and burying their dead in the cemetery on the hill. They are pipe-smoking women and hard-drinking men, fighting long winters, stubborn soil and venomous snakes." Yet, for every sturdy, life-affirming Powderjay and happy family-loving Uncle Fonse there is the counterbalance of a human current gone awry—a drunken Hankas, for example, about whom America, the heroine of "Woman in the House, is instantly alerted, "I knowed I was goin' to have trouble that night. The devil was in his broth a-brewin'." Greenspan wrote, "The . . . deliberate horror of 'Woman in the House' equal[s] the most macabre mood of William Faulkner."

Robert Penn Warren originally selected this story for publication in the July, 1935, issue of the *Southern Review*. Forty-four years later, when it was reprinted for the fifth time in 1979, Mr. Warren, acknowledging Jesse Stuart's "true literary talent," pointed to his fellow Kentuckian's wide-ranging effect—pathos, gruesomeness, comedy, and his gift of observation. Specifically, in this story, "A man has 'one of them old sour drunk man's frowns on his face.' A character . . . is 'drunk as the Devil wanted him to be.' When another man refuses a drink from religious scruples, Hankas says: 'I'll be dogged. Lord has saved him and he promised not to drink any more licker to the Lord. Wonder what the Lord wants fer nuthin'.' " Again, " 'Striking a match in a dark room of people is like turning the lights on in Hell to see what your next door neighbor is.' In fact, one of the pervasive effects—one

208

of the most difficult effects for a writer to achieve—is the sense of language speaking off the page, and that is a gift Jesse has, a gift based on years of astute listening and watching. It is a gift that goes far toward creating a world."*

* * *

THE moon was comin' up over that fringe of poplar trees last night when I saw Radburn and Hankas coming through the greenbriar thicket by the pig pen. I knowed jist what had happened when I saw them together. They had been over the hill to Mort Anderson's to get some of that old rotgut licker. I knowed I was goin' to have a time for the night. I saw them come through the patch of ragweeds this side of the pig pen. Radburn was holdin' to the apple-tree limbs. Hankas was talkin' with his hands. I could see them just as plain as day. The moon shined on them and if they had been rabbits I could have shot them both, it was so light. Not even a wind was blowin' to make a racket. It was the quietest night a body might nigh ever seed. The pigs thought I was comin' to slop them when they passed the pig pen. The pigs grunted a little bit. Then they went back to the old sow.

I heerd Hankas say to Radburn: "We gotta take the medicine back to Lake. He is cut purty bad. I could see the blood. It is all over my hand, see! People will think I cut Lake with a knife. God Almighty knows I didn't cut Lake with anything." Then Radburn said to Hankas: "Be quiet so America can't hear you. If she thinks there's trouble she'll be right into it. She's soon hit me as not. She's soon hit you. I know her. I have lived with her long enough to know her. When we first married and got into a racket she knocked me down the first lick she struck me right above the eye. She didn't have on no knucks neither. She done hit with her plain fist. I've lived with her thirty years now and I know she'll fight. Right when we was first married and my stepma Middie pulled a pistol on Pap, she walked right in and said, 'Give me that gun.' Then she struck her with her plain fist right above the eye—the same place as she allus hits 'em and God only knows how long Middie laid there."

"America allus wuz that way at home. When us kids was playin' about the place, she whipped all of us but me. I could whip America. I watched

*Jeannette Greenspan, "A Place under the Sun" (review of Jesse Stuart's *Head o' W-Hollow*), Brooklyn (New York) *Citizen*, May 1, 1936, clipping in Jesse Stuart, Scrapbook #3, p. 9, M. S. U. Robert Penn Warren, "Foreword," Jesse Stuart, *Head o' W-Hollow*, reprint (Lexington: Univ. Press of Ky., 1979), pp. ix–x. "Woman in the House" was orig. pub. *Southern Review*, Vol. 1 (July, 1935), pp. 139–150, reprinted in *Head o' W-Hollow* (1936), and (1979), pp. 54–66. Woodbridge, *Jesse Stuart Bibliography*, p. 86, lists two other reprints through 1979.

and never let her get the first lick. But ever time I whipped her, Pap throwed a fit and jumped all over me. I allus told Pap she'd whip the man she married if she ever got the first lick. She allus plugs a body right above the right eye."

"She is a hard woman to live with, but she is a good woman. Last winter I'd been a dead man if hit hadn't been for my wife. You know Lefty Penix, don't you, Hankas? Well, he come over here and we got holt of some bad licker. We must have went crazy. We got right over there by the corn crib and started to fight. I don't remember hit. But they said Lefty had the corn knife that we keep stickin' out there in the crib log to cut the cow corn with. He had that knife and was makin' for my throat. America saw him. And she come runnin' right through the snow shoe-mouth deep and hit Lefty right above the eye. He had long been sobered up before he come to his senses. Both of that man's eyes settled black around them for a week and a big door knob riz under Lefty's right eye. But my wife saved my life. If she hadn't run out there, I'd a been in hell right tonight."

I could see them comin' up closer to the house. There was Radburn, my man. He wore the same old dirty overalls that he'd been wearin' all week in the 'backer patch. They was all gluey and would stand alone in the green 'backer glue. His shirt was dirty and his beard was out all over his face. Just me here and I was ashamed of him. Beadie went home with the little Jurdan girl to stay all night; Fonse and Gilbert went to the square dance; Libbie and Win went to see Sister Mossy last week and they ain't got back yet. I was right here—well, Pap was here. But he's sick in there in the bed. He can't do nuthin'. Pap has one foot in the grave and the other foot ready to slide in. I knowed Hankas and Radburn was drinkin' that old rotgut they got over to Mort Anderson's. I knowed trouble was a-brewin'. Everytime Radburn gits a drink he thinks he can lick me. He gits to thinkin' about me knockin' him down and he wants to try hit over and show me he can lick me. Everytime he gits a drink of that old rotgut in him, hit is a fight here. I knowed what was goin' to happen.

Before they got up to the house I went in the back room and looked under Radburn's piller. I found his .32 automatic. The moon shined in at the back-room window and left a white place on the floor. I stepped out where I could take a good look at the .32. Hit looked right purty fer a pistol. I looked into the chamber and saw that hit was loaded. Then I said to myself: "Ready, Hankas. Don't care if you are my brother. Ready, Radburn. I don't care if you are my man. Hit won't be a fist above the eye this time. Hit'll be a bullet." They come up and opened the door. There was Hankas, my brother, and he's a big man. Some over two hundred that man is, and mean as a copper-head. I could see in the moonlight he had one of them old sour drunk man's frowns on his face. He looked like the devil. His arms come down nearly to his knees. They are hairy as a dog. His arms is nearly big as fence posts. He had on his old gluey 'backer clothes too. Hankas has a big blocky body without a pound of fat. He's solid as a rock. But he ain't got much of a head. Hit is a little hard for sich a big body. I know how us children used to laugh at him and call him "simlon head." He'd git so mad. He'd want to fight. He could whip everybody. Well, I said if I ever got a house o' my own, I'd whip him or I'd kill him before I'd let him run over me. Pap allus upheld for him at home, because Pap was afraid of him and Mother was too.

They come in the house. They hushed talkin' for a minute when they come in. Radburn struck a match and lit the lamp. I could see he was drunk as a biled owl. Hankas staggered over to the mantelpiece and helt onto hit long enough to fill his pipe with my best smokin' 'backer. He lit his pipe over the lamp and he looked at Radburn. Then he wiped his hands on his gluey overalls. Pon my word, I wouldn't be caught wearin' dirty clothes as them men had on. Hankas said to Radburn: "Call America. Reckon she's here. We got to git the turpentine and git back to Lake. He's cut purty bad. Look at the blood on your hands and on my hands. People will think we cut him. God knows we didn't. I like old Lake. He's a bully good fellar."

"Yes, and think about him layin' out there bleedin' in that ditch." I just stepped from the back room into where they was by the mantelpiece. I had the .32 in my bosom. I had my hand on hit. If they had started anythin' I aim to let 'em have hit right above the eye. I said, "Who got cut?" Radburn said: "W'y America, Lake Burdock got cut. He's out there bleedin' in the ditch." And I said: "Where did he git cut and when?" Hankas said: "Don't know how he got cut. He jist got cut's all we know about hit. He jist fell. He's cut on the hip—place big enough to lay your hand in." And I said: "This don' sound right. Somebody had to cut him. Let me see your knifes. Both of you drunk and you wouldn't know hit if you did cut him." Well, Hankas looked at Radburn and Radburn looked at Hankas. Then Radburn said, "Hankas, we'd better let her look at our knifes." They took their knifes out and they wasn't a drap of blood on 'em. I felt so good. I felt like gittin' down on my knees and prayin' to God Almighty. I didn't want 'em to have to go to the pen for knifin'. "Pon my word, Meck," Radburn said: "We didn't cut Lake. We didn't cut him. No." Then I said: "How in the world did he get cut?" Radburn said, "I don't know." Hankas said, "I don't know." There Hankas hung to the mantelpiece. The very Devil was in his eyes. I knowed I was goin' to have trouble that night. The Devil was in his broth a-brewin'. I said: "You ain't takin' no turpentine out'n there. You go bring that man to this house. Go now before he bleeds to death." And they went out the house. Radburn looked at Hankas and Hankas looked at Radburn. They never said a word to each other ner to me.

I walked the floor. I was so uneasy. I was more uneasy than I was the night Brother Tim and Candy got in that cuttin' scrape with the Tinsleys. Tim got his right eye cut out, and Candy got his juggle vein nicked a little and a couple of cuts to the holler. But he lived. One of the Tinsleys bled to death. The other lived but ain't been able to work none since. I was so uneasy that night. But I was just about that uneasy this time. I didn't know what had happened. God knows I didn't. Whippoorwills hollerin' up there on the hill and some leaves fell off the trees. I could hear them blowin' so lonesome. And I jist paced the floor. The moon shined right up there over the hog pen. I could see the moon then jist like I could see hit last night. I could see the rails on the hog pen jist as plain as I can see my hand before me now. I was so uneasy. The moon kept gettin' over further in the sky—out past the hog pen and round to the right near the Hoggens' Graveyard. I could see the tombstones over there on that pint. Hit made me so lonesome—jist like last night. I could see the tombstones and the moon. I could hear the whippoorwills hollerin' and the dead leaves a-rattlin' in the wind. I guess some tears come down my cheek. I thought I felt tears runnin' down my cheeks. I don't know.

Then I looked through the back-room winder and I seed two men comin' carryin' somethin'. Hit looked like a log. They was staggerin' up the cow path from that gate right down yander. I heerd Hankas say, "Let's put him down, Radburn, and open the gate." And I saw them throw the log-lookin' thing from their shoulders jist like they'd throw down a sack of corn. They opened the gate. Then they shouldered the man. Mercy, how I felt. I thought: "Now what if they bring him here and he dies from that cut. We'll go to the pen. What if he dies on our hands. People will think we kilt him and the Law will git us all fer killin' him. Merciful God, what if he's to die here. A dead man in the house. What would we do? What could we do?" But I saw Radburn and Hankas comin' wobblin' up the yaller bank down yander on this side of the gate. They wobbled like ducks. The moon shined down on them. It was light as day. And here they come carryin' that man. The lamp was lit up in the front room and the moonlight come in at the back-room winder.

They come right to the front door. Hankas was behind, carryin' Lake's shoulders. Radburn was in front, carryin' Lake's legs. Radburn shoved open the door and brought him in feet foremost. And he was bleedin' frum the seat of the pants. The blood jist poured on the floor like water from the raindrip. Hankas said: "Meck, git the turpentine quick. He's bleedin' purty bad." And I said: "You're so drunk you don't know what you're talkin' about. Turpentine ain't goin' to stop that blood. Hit takes chimney sut to stop blood. Stick your head up that fireplace there and git some chimney sut from behind the jam rock. Do hit quick. Put Lake on the bed first." They throwed Lake down on the bed hard enough to break all the slats. Lake was drunk as the Devil wanted him to be. Then I said: "Radburn, you pull his pants down so I can see where this man is cut. We got to do somethin' fer him." Radburn says, "You ain't no doctor, air you?" And I said to Radburn: "I may not be no doctor, but tell me nairy nuther woman that's delivered more babies in this country than I have, and I'll eat her blood raw. Who's cured more sick than I have among cattle and men? Who's cured more colic and fever than I have? Who does the people come to when they want help—even for drunken fits and blind billiards? I guess you remember that mule's front legs that had all the skin peeled off'n 'em like hit was bark the time he tried to jump the wire fence—who sewed that up? Never was a scar left. Who sewed up a duck's back that the hound pups tore the skin off in a three-cornered fleek? The duck lived, didn't hit? Take that man's pants down. I aim to look at that cut, and if I can I aim to sew hit up."

Radburn started undressin' Lake. I went into the kitchen and put a fire in the stove and put water in the teakettle. Then I started to huntin' fer some white thread and a darnin' needle. By the time the water het, I had the darnin' needle and the thread. Radburn had the clothes from off'n the cut. Hit looked like he had been whacked with a corn knife. And I said, "Radburn, let me look in Lake's overall pockets." I took his overalls—blood-soaked and dirty with green 'backer glue. I heerd somethin' rattle in the hip pocket. And my Lord, how hit did stink with that old rotgut whisky. And what did I find in the pocket on the seat of his britches? I found a broken bottle. "Here's what's cut him," I said, "a bottle. He's fell on hit. A rotgut bottle. If hit wasn't fer his wife, I wish hit had cut him in two. He's got as good a woman as ever the sun shined on and out cavortin' 'round like this. Drinkin' 'round and leavin' his family at home. I'll sew him up this time. But never again will I do hit." Radburn looked at Hankas. Hankas looked at Radburn. They never said a word. Hankas looked mean as the Devil out'n his black eyes. "Goin' sew him up, air ye?" he looked at me and said. And I said, "Yes, I'm goin' to sew him up if this darnin' needle don't break."

By this time the water was warm. I brought hit in from the kitchen.

Radburn helt the lamp. I swathed out the deep lash. Lake jist laid there
and moaned like a fat hog. Then I put the turpentine on. Hit jist keep
bleedin'. Hankas give me the chimney sut and you'd a laughed to a seen
Hankas atter he went up behind the jam rock. He was black as a piece of
wet chestnut burr. I daubed the chimney sut in the lash. I knowed hit
would leave a black stripe under the skin when hit healed over. But I didn't
care. I wanted to save him on account of his wife, Polly, and his five young
'uns. I used the chimney sut to stop the blood. I poured in the whole bottle
of turpentine to keep hit from gittin' sore. Then I pulled up the soft sides of
the cut and made Hankas hold them while I used the darnin' needle. Lake
flinched a little when the needle went through his skin. I took thirty-seven
stitches on that man. And when I got through, the stitches was jist as even
as if I'd been tuckin' up a skirt that was too long.

Hankas jist set and looked at me. The Devil was in his black eyes. I had
the pistol in my bosom. I jist wanted to git away so he couldn't git the first
lick. I kept my eyes on him all the time. I said: "Pull his pants back on him
and throw that glass out of this room, Radburn. Put Lake in the bed. And I
don't want any more rotgut whisky brought in this house tonight." Hankas
said: "Who's runnin' this house? You or Radburn?" And I said, "I'm runnin' my own house and them that don't like hit can git out." "Us go, Radburn," said Hankas. They staggered out. Hankas said when he left the
house, "Poor home, ain't hit, Radburn, when you ain't got a word to say in
your own house." Radburn didn't say a word. He turned and looked back
at me. Then they went out into the moonlight, around the corner of the
house, under the dark night-shade of the hickory tree—down over the hill
toward Reek Finney's house.

They left me in the house with Lake. He was drunk. I thought he would
sober up before they got back and want to know who cut him and what he
was doin' sewed up. But I had the pistol. I could shoot him if he started
anythin'. I went to the kitchen winder. I looked out. The moon was goin'
down over the cornfield where the boys had cut the early piece of corn. The
fodder shocks looked like wigwams between me and the moon. I could hear
the lonesome whippoorwill. I could hear the katydids out in the dead grass
by the cow lot. I could hear the pigs gruntin'. I could hear Lake's breath go
up and down and then sizzle like the wind goin' through the dead sticker-
weeds back of the smoke house on a windy day. And then I heerd the dogs
bark over at Reek Finney's house. I went to the back yard. I looked over at
Reek Finney's place. The house was dark and the moonlight showed on the
winder lights. Then I saw the winders lit up with lamplight. I knowed Hankas and Radburn was over there. Then I heerd them talkin' and cussin'

around. I heerd Hankas ask Reek if he wanted a drink and Reek said yes. Then I heerd them cussin' some more and runnin' the dogs over at Reek's house fer barkin' at them. I heerd Radburn say: "I'll git my knife out and straddle that dog's back and cut hits throat if hit don't shet up that barkin' in my ears. I've seed a lot of blood tonight and I wouldn't keer to see a little more."

Well, I didn't want Lake to sober up. I wanted him to stay drunk till mornin'. So I hunted fer the whisky jug that Radburn and Hankas brought in the house but didn't take out again. I found a gallon jug behind the door with a sea-grass string run through hits gill. I got the jug and I went to the right, over from where Pap was a-layin' and I opened Lake's mouth. I poured rotgut from the jug with the other hand. I guess I poured a pint down him. He guzzled hit down and licked his lips. Then I pulled the pistol from under the bosom of my dress. I looked at the little barrel. I said: "W'y this can't kill a man. I'd ruther trust my fist. The barrel is too little. Look at this little hole. Look at that big man Lake. Look how big Hankas is. Hit would take a bigger pistol than this to kill him. That barrel ain't as big as my middle finger and ain't much longer." So I took the pistol back to the bed and took the shells out'n hit and put hit under Radburn's piller.

I went and looked behind the meal barrel and got the double-barrel shotgun. Hit looked more like a gun to me. Long bright-blue barrels glistened in the lamplight. I brought the shell box from off'n the wall plate. They wan't but two shells in the box. One was loaded with number three shots and one with number fives. I put the shell loaded with number threes in the left-hand barrel for Hankas. I put the shell loaded with number fives in the right-hand barrel for Radburn. Then I pulled the trunk out and put hit slonch-ways across the corner of the room so I'd have more room to shoot from. I blowed out the lamp and I got behind the trunk. I pinted the double-barrel over the trunk and I cocked both triggers and turned the safety off.

The chickens had begin to crow fer midnight. I stayed right behind the trunk with the double-barrel in my hands ready to shoot. I seed the fire in Hankas's eyes. The Devil was in his eyes. I jist waited fer him to come back. I knowed he would want to start somethin'. Well, I heerd him comin'. I heerd him come up through the cornfield and cuss about the moon goin' down. I heerd him say he fell on the sharp edge of a cornstalk where the boys had cut the potato patch of corn. I heerd him cuss about the night gettin' so dark. Then they come to the door. Radburn opened the door. He struck a match and lit the lamp. Then he said: "Wonder where America is?" And then he hollered and hollered: "America, come here! America, come here! I want some buttermilk. I want fresh water. I want some clean clothes." I never said a word.

They went over to the bed where Lake was. They pulled them up a couple of chears and set down by the side of the bed. Radburn said, "Wonder if that'll get all right where America sewed up that place?" Hankas said: "Yes. I'd ruther have her as any doctor that's in Berryville. She's my sister and bad to fight, but I'd ruther have her by my side when I'm sick as anybody I know." "Cut on glass, wasn't he, Hankas?" "That's what America said." "Do you reckon she'd wear that if the Law gits us all before the court." "Yes, I believe she would." "Well, he's drunk, ain't he? Air you drunk? Am I drunk?" "Git that gallon of licker from behind the door, Hankas, and let's have a snip before we take our shoes off."

Hankas staggered over to the door. He got the jug by the sea-grass string. He took hit over to Radburn. There they set. They wuz jist so drunk they didn't know who hit was in the bed. Radburn put his arms around Hankas. Hankas put his arms around Radburn. Then Hankas said: "You have got a decent woman, Radburn, but she don't treat you right. Now she has left you." "Surely she ain't left me. What will I do about somebody to cook fer me?" "Yes, she's left you." "I'll see." Then Radburn called: "America, America, come here! I want a drink of water. My head is killin' me, America, come here." Pon my honor, hit was right laughable. Then he got down on his knees and looked under the beds. He looked behind the doors, I leveled the gun right on his head. When he moved, the gun barrels moved. I kept the gun right on him. I kept hit right on his temple. He never did git to the trunk. He went back and set down by Hankas. He said: "You're right, Hankas. She's gone. She's left me." Now I kept the gun pointed right at them.

Hankas said: "You got a good woman and you'll miss her some. But hit's the best thing for you. You can live right here by yourself and do your own cookin'. Lake can stay with you part of the time. I'll come to see you often. Jist let her go and the Devil take her. You don't need no woman nohow. You can do without a woman more than you can do with a woman. She runs the house. She's hit you with her fist and deadened you two or three times or more than that. She won't do to fool with. Now you can bring the pig pen out here behind the smoke house and keep the dogs in the back room there at night. You can put your cows in the mule pasture and the mules in the cow pasture. That will make hit closer to milk out there by the sand rocks. You can make hit all right and you'll be a lot safer right here with your children or without anybody."

Then they became silent. I kept the shotgun leveled about with their temples. The night out behind the winder was blacker than chimney sut. The whippoorwills kept hollerin'. The katydids kept hollerin' out behind the smoke house. I wasn't skeered a bit. I was jist lonesome. God, but I was lonesome. Three drunk men in the house. One of them a brother fer the Devil. I didn't like hit—all the stuff he was tellin' Radburn. I didn't want Radburn to run with him and I told Radburn he would git him in trouble. But Hankas jist come up and got him. He can do hit every time. Radburn 'll jist do anything Hankas says. He'll follow him any place. And when he gits that old rotgut whisky in him he'll do about anything else.

About four o'clock a chicken crowed and Radburn waked from a doze. He said: "Ain't that boy of Reek's a funny boy? Don't he like licker? W'y when I give him that bottle I had to pull it away from his lips. But poor boy, Hankas. They have to give him pizen to keep him alive. Hit's the God's truth. They feed that boy pizen. He ain't but ten years old and he weighs two hundred and ten pounds. He walks like a string-haltered hoss. Ever notice him? His face is red as a beet. He's marked with a turkey. Before he come to this world a turkey gobbler flogged his Mama out by the corn crib one mornin'. That's what the matter with him." "And you say that he has to take pizen medicine so he won't die?" "Yes, hit takes about all the money that old Reek can make to keep that boy alive. He has that boy that eats pizen and eleven more boys stouter than old Reek is. He has seven girls and they ain't much good." "Well, I'll be dogged." "Reek is a clever man as you's ever about the house of." "Reckon that boy got drunk on the licker you give him?" "W'y, yes, he got drunk and even old Reek had to hold to the cornstalks to git up the hill when he left us down there in the holler." "Well, I'll be dogged."

I kept the gun right level with their temples. They dozed off again. Lord, how I did pray for daylight. I never closed my eyes for a wink of sleep. I never put in sich a night in all my life. I watched the clock. I could see the minutes was creepin' up. I could hear the sparrows workin' in the box. Hankas riz up and said: "Radburn, we forgot somethin'. Give me the whisky quick. We have forgot Pap. We ain't offered Pap no whisky."

Radburn got up and walked over to Pap's bed with Hankas. Hankas helt the jug to Pap's lips and said, "Come on, Pap, and drink with us tonight." Pap waked from a doze and said, "I don't want no drink." "Come on and have one," Hankas said. "Ain't you goin' to drink with us?" "No, I ain't goin' to drink none of that stuff. Hit is a sin. The Lord has saved me and I promised the Lord I wouldn't drink no more licker. I aim to be good as my word." Then Hankas turned and said: "I'll be dogged. Lord has saved him and he promised not to drink any more licker to the Lord. Wonder what the Lord wants fer nuthin'. Well, I'll be dogged. My own Pap won't drink with me and him so nigh the grave." I kept the double-barrel leveled right on his head. I thought: "If you start anythin' here I'll get you with a gun this big. Hit will kill you. This ain't no toy .32. This is a gun that will kill." Hankas sat down. He dozed off to sleep again.

Of all the snorin' I ever heerd in my life hit was from them three drunk men. Of all the strange noises—fiddles, shotguns, mauls, hammers, drums, and axes—I could hear all kinds of noises. I prayed for daylight to come. The sparrows begin to chatter in their boxes. The pigs begin to grunt. The whippoorwill shet up. I could hear the quails hollerin' down in the crab grass. I knowed daylight wasn't fer away. I took the shells out'n the gun. I slipped out the back winder. I come around and opened the kitchen door and come through to the meal barrel. I put the gun behind the meal barrel. Then I come into the front room. I took Radburn by the shoulder and I said: "What's all this goin' on here? Run me out'n my house last night, didn't you?" And he said: "I don't remember if I did or didn't." "Well, you did." I says. "I stayed in the woods all night. The moon went down and hit was so dark I couldn't follow a path out and you was drunk and took the place." Hankas waked up and I said, "Brother Hankas, you tried to pour that old rotgut down your dyin' father's throat. You are a brute." "I didn't do nuthin' like that, did I?" And the tears jist streamed down his beardy face and dropped off the ends of his beard. He got up and sneaked out home. He couldn't look me in the face.

Lake waked up. He put his hand on his hip and hollered, "O Lord God, my hip! Whut is the matter with my hip?" I went out of the room. I guess Radburn must to 'a took his pants down and they both looked at his hip. When I come back in, Radburn looked at me and Lake looked at Radburn. Radburn got the express and hauled Lake home. Before Radburn left with Lake he sneaked up to me and he said, "I'm plagued to death over whut happened to Lake."

I never ast whut happened. I knowed whut happened and I wanted to make Radburn tell me, but he did feel too plagued. We both jist hoisted Lake in the spring wagon on a feathered tick and hauled him home to Polly. I felt a little uneasy about maybe a little piece of glass was left in the lash and hit might not heal. But in a few days Lake was walkin' around. I heerd my boy say that he was in the crick with Lake, and his body was allus dirty as a pig on the seat. Radburn looked at me. I looked at Radburn. We never said a word.

Death Has Two Good Eyes

About the story:

When Wisconsin author August Derleth visited Jesse Stuart following the Kentuckian's return from his Guggenheim year abroad, he found Stuart "in the heart of a Labor Day celebration in Greenup, just another Kentuckian from the hill county near the county seat: a strong, husky young man of my own age, sun-tanned, his hair cropped fairly close. Beyond his friendly eagerness, I saw the tremendous energy of the man, the driving force that made him put down on paper . . . [*Man with a Bull-Tongue Plow, Head o' W-Hollow,* and *Beyond Dark Hills*]." Together they watched "an old-time dance" on the street by the courthouse. Derleth observed Stuart's people—"farmers, villagers, Negroes, whites, all mixing together in open friendliness, with nothing of the race- and class-consciousness of western Kentucky. It was not the wild kind of square prevalent in provincial Wisconsin; it was slower, with a suggestion of dignity not quite lost." Within a short time Stuart introduced Derleth to "a heavy-set woman," with the comment, "She's one of my characters. . . ."

Stuart not only wrote about his Greenup County friends and neighbors, but he also wrote about his relatives, such as the Stuarts who still lived back in the Big Sandy region of Kentucky and across the state line in West Virginia. He wrote about his Grandfather Mitch Stuart, perhaps most notably in his poem published in the *American Mercury* (January, 1933), "Elegy for Mitch Stuart." He wrote about his Uncle Marion in "Word and the Flesh," and he wrote about his Uncle Joe in several stories including "Death Has Two Good Eyes," first published in *Esquire* in 1942.

It is a rollicking good story rich in local color and dialect, as Shan and Finn Powderjay go up into the West Virginia mountains to take up (with fists if necessary) for the wife and children of Uncle Mel Powderjay against their "blood-kin" half-cousins, the fruits of Uncle Mel's liaison with his "unlawful wedded wife." The surprise ending is richly Chaucerian, setting uproarious tragicomedy over against Dobie Powderjay's sagacious observation that "Love of two wimmen is too much fer any man's heart."

Underlining the basic authenticity of this comic story, the author said,

Let me tell you in actuality, the first time I ever went to my Uncle Joe Stuart's, I stayed all night. I was a college graduate, of course. I went there and all of my cousins, when they went to bed, put their pistols under the pillows. And damn, that was a funny feeling. . . . [Later,] we fought all over the place . . . over that thing . . . my uncle having those children by that other woman. . . . And I joined in to help out. . . . It's a factual ending. Isn't it a good one?*

* * *

"IT'S FUNNY WHEN YOU go to visit kinfolks you've never seen you have to carry a pistol," I said.

"But it's best to play safe," Finn said.

The Big Sandy train was screeching around the curves up the single-line track. Finn and I looked out the window at the Big Sandy River that wound between the Kentucky and West Virginia Mountains like a big silver-bellied cow-snake. We'd heard Pa talk about this river—how Grandpa had taken big trains of log rafts down the Big Sandy to the Ohio River to Cincinnati and Louisville.

We'd heard Pa tell about how the Kentucky boys used to shoot it out with the West Virginia boys across the Big Sandy River to test their pistols. Pa told how they'd make for cover when they heard a bullet wheeze about their heads or when a bullet plowed the dirt under their feet. Pa said if there wasn't a cliff close for them to git behind, they'd fall flat on the sand and empty their pistols at the men across the river. Said you couldn't tell whether you hit a man or not. Said sometimes you'd hear a fellow scream and then you'd see a crowd take for cover behind a cliff.

I thought about all this as we looked from our coach window at the engineer across the curve from us.

"Blanton, Blanton, all out for Blanton," the gray-headed conductor came through the coach yelling.

*August Derleth wrote about his 1938 visit to Jesse Stuart's home in his essay, "He Visited Jesse Stuart," in *News of Books and Authors* (May–June, 1939), clipping with photographs in Jesse Stuart, Scrapbook #6, p. 91, M. S. U. "Elegy for Mitch Stuart" was Stuart's first major publication drawing national attention, in *American Mercury*, Vol. 28 (Jan., 1933), pp. 30–32, reprinted in *Kentucky Is My Land* (Ashland, Ky.: Economy Printers, 1952), pp. 30–33. For my commentary on "Word and the Flesh," see *"About the story"* in this section. "Death Has Two Good Eyes" first appeared in *Esquire*, Vol. 18 (Dec., 1942), pp. 118–119, 227–228, reprinted in *Tales from the Plum Grove Hills* (1946), the source of the copy here being the Mockingbird ed., 1974, pp. 96–104. Mr. Stuart's comments on this story are from Jesse Stuart/H. E. Richardson, Interview, W-Hollow, Greenup, Ky., Sept. 16, 1978, and Interview #41, Sept. 15, 1981.

"That's our station," Finn said. "Wonder where we'll find Cousin Frank."

When Finn and I got off the train, we saw a big man riding a bare-backed mule. He was leading two mules that were saddled.

"He must be Cousin Frank," Finn said, pointing to the big beardy-faced man.

"Are you Frank Powderjay?" I asked.

"Shore am," he said.

"I'm your Cousin Shan Powderjay," I said. "This is your Cousin Finn Powderjay."

"Glad to meet you," Frank said. "I've heerd a lot about ye, boys, but this is my first time to lay my eyes on ye. Git on these mules; we've got to hurry home. We're a-havin' a lot of trouble at home."

I climbed on one mule; Finn reached me our suitcase. Then Finn ran from behind the other mule, slapped his hands on the mule's rump and leaped to the middle of the tiny cowboy saddle.

"Never seen a man mount a mule like that," Frank said. "Ye're more active than I thought ye'd be."

Finn's mule followed Frank's mule and my mule followed Finn's mule from the big crowd gathered around the tiny railroad station. Soon as we left the Big Sandy Valley, we were among the rugged hills on a road filled with chugholes and deep jolt-wagon ruts.

"What's the nature of the trouble we're going to have?" Finn asked Cousin Frank as our trotting mules leaped the chugholes and ruts.

"Ye'll see soon as ye git thar," Frank said. "I don't like to talk about it. We'll haf to fight our bloodkin. Much as we hate 'em, we respect 'em enough to put our pistols and knives aside to fight with fists, clubs, and rocks."

Finn turned and looked at me; I looked at him as our mules dashed up the narrow road behind Frank's mule. Soon we left the narrow wagon road for a mountain footpath between thickets of brush and briars. We wound around this mountain path until we reached the ridge path and then it was faster going. Our mules were wet with sweat—flecks of foam fell from between their legs and foamy slobbers dripped from their hanging lips.

"It's a right fur piece over here from the station," Frank said. "It's eleven miles by crossin' this mountain. Fifteen miles if we go around it."

Now Frank spurred his mule to a trot and our mules followed. I was getting a little sore riding on a small cowboy saddle. Finn was having a little trouble with the brush switching across his face since he was tall and was riding a long-legged mule.

"It's a shame that none of us have never seen none of ye before," Frank said. "I heerd ye's a mighty stuck-up people since ye boys went to high school. Heerd ye's eddicated and soft."

"Tell me more about that trouble you're having," Finn said.

"Wait till ye git home," Frank said. "Then ye'll see what it is. I don't like to think about it. I tell Ma that we ought to use guns and knives and git it over with. A body can't finish a piece of trouble with fists, rocks, and clubs."

"Will the other fellows fight?" Finn asked.

"Ye damned right they'll fight," Frank said.

When we reached a big double-log house down at the foot of the mountain, Frank rolled off his sweaty steaming mule. Finn jumped off his mule and threw our suitcase to the ground. And I rolled over the bony side of my mule. Soon as I hit the ground, I stretched my arms and legs and looked around for Uncle Melvin. But there wasn't anybody around but young men I took to be my first cousins.

"Where's Uncle Melvin?" I asked.

Everyone was silent.

"I want ye to meet my brothers," Frank said. "I want ye to meet some more of yer first cousins that ye have never seen."

Finn and I met Dobie, Erf, Tim, Gullet, Don and Van, our first cousins. They were husky, strong, tough-looking as tough-butted white-oak saplings. The palms of their hands were hard as brogan shoe-leather where they had been gripping mattock handles, double-bitted ax handles, saw handles, broad-ax handles, pitchforks and one-eyed sprouting hoes. Erf and Tim had heavy black beard on their faces. Don and Van were too young to shave; they had white fuzz on their faces that needed to be shaved.

"Come to the house and meet Ma," Frank said, sadly.

Seven of us followed Frank toward the house while Van took the mules to the barn. When we reached the house, we walked through the dog-trot between the two big log pens. Aunt Mallie met us at the door wringing her hands and crying.

"Ma, here's Finn and Shan," Frank said.

"Glad to know you, Aunt Mallie," I said, shaking her hand.

"Glad to know you," Finn said, shaking her hand quickly.

"Sorry ye boys come right in the midst of all this trouble," Aunt Mallie said, weeping again. "But I don't know of any time ye could come here lately when we weren't a-havin' trouble."

I looked at Aunt Mallie's wrinkled face and the gray wisps of hair stringing over her face. I didn't think she ought to look as old as she did.

"How's Brother Micky?" Aunt Mallie asked.

"He's getting along as well as common, Aunt Mallie," Finn said.

"I'd like to see 'im," she said, her face brightening some when she spoke of Pa. "It's been nigh twenty years since I seed 'im. I'll bet he's changed a lot."

"I don't know how he looked twenty years ago," Finn said. "That was before I was born."

"I don't think he's changed much," I said. "I believe you'd know 'im if you were to meet 'im in the big road."

"Where's Uncle Melvin?" Finn asked.

"Oh, Oh," Aunt Mallie screamed, "he's not here. Haint ye heerd about our troubles? Haint Micky told ye?"

No," Finn said.

"He's over the hill yander a-livin' with that old thing," Aunt Mallie screamed, then she dropped to her chair.

"Never mind, Ma," Frank said, "we're a-goin' to clean that place up today. We'll fetch Pa home."

"Be keerful, boys," Aunt Mallie warned between sobs. "They'll do anything to ye. They are liable to bushwhack ye, use knives 'r pistols 'r anything they can use to git ye with. Anybody that will try to pizen yer well-water will do anything."

"But we got two more to put into the fight today," Frank said. "I think Finn and Shan can hep us out. I think two more men can decide the fight. We've been too evenly matched before—seven of them and seven of us. Today, it will be nine of us and seven of them."

Finn looked at me; I looked at him.

"I hate fer Brother Micky's boys to come to see us and haf to fight the first day," Aunt Mallie said between sobs.

"Ah, we don't mind," Finn said.

We followed Frank to the woodyard. He called his brothers around him.

"Shan, I didn't know that you and Finn didn't know about Pa," Frank said. "But he's a-livin' with an old hag over that mountain yander. He's been a-goin' to see 'er the last twenty-five years. He got a fambly over thar too. We've got seven half brothers and two half sisters. Here lately he spends more time over thar than he does with Ma. That old frowsy-headed hag is younger than Ma. It's damned nigh a-puttin' Ma in 'er grave. We've got to do something about it. We aim to bring Pa back dead 'r alive."

I looked at my first cousins. Their beardy faces got red as Frank talked. They looked mean out of their eyes as snakes as they kicked the ground with the toe of their brogans. They twitched their nervous fingers.

"Cousin Finn and Shan, do ye mind dirtyin' yer hands and maybe gettin' yer noses mashed flat in a fight to hep yer Big Sandy cousins?" Frank asked us.

"When we came to see you," Finn said before I had time to speak, "your fight is our fight. We'll stay with you until the fight is finished."

"That's the speret," Erf said.

"What do ye say, fellars?" Erf said, spitting ambeer at his feet, wiping his beardy lips with his shirt-sleeve.

"Let me tell Cousin Shan and Finn a leetle about the way we fight," Frank said. "See the mountain yander. We'll climb the path to the ridge road. We'll scream like wildcats and cuss Pa's youngins by that old hag with every kind of a son-of-a-bitch we can lay our tongues to. They may be up thar on the mountain a-layin' fer us and jump from the bushes and grab us soon as we git upon the mountain. Seems like they've allus got spies up among the trees like crows a-watchin' everything we do down here! Now if ye hear war whoops and see 'im a-comin' from the bushes at ye, go right after 'em."

Frank walked in front down the path like he was going to a funeral. All of our first cousins looked that way as they went to battle their half brothers. Before we got to the end of the garden, Aunt Mallie opened the door.

"Frank, do be keerful." Aunt Mallie hollered. "I feel like somebody is a-goin' to die."

"Okay, Ma," Frank yelled.

"I believe they've got a spy a-sittin' up in one of these trees," Frank said as we started up the mountain. "Thought I heerd 'im give a signal whistle."

They must have had a spy someplace. Before we reached the mountain top, seven husky men met us.

"Ye would come to take the advantage o' us, ye sons-of-bitches," Frank snarled as he singled out the biggest of our half first cousins by unlawful wedlock.

"Where ye git yer hep?" he snarled back at Frank. "Hit'll jist be too goddamned bad fer yer strangers. We'll give 'em a double dose of all that we've been a-givin' ye."

"The hell ye will," Frank said.

Before Frank's words had left his mouth, Finn had met his man and up-ended him the first lick.

"Jesus Christ, ye've got a wallop fer a eddicated man," Cousin Erf told Finn.

"I've got the difference too," Finn said, "in case I have to have it. They'll never whip us."

Frank and his big half brother had tangled. They were clinched—arms around each other, and like logs tied together with big brown cables, they were rolling down the mountain side, cussing, biting—fighting—like old enemies. We were all fighting—nine men against six now for Finn had knocked one man out the first lick he struck. I wasn't mad at the man I was fighting until he stuck his broken discolored teeth into the fat of my ear. That made me a little sore and I fought him a little harder. But I thought Uncle Melvin wasn't worth all this fighting. I had never heard as much swearing in any fight I'd ever seen. I had never seen such fighting. Frank and his half brother were standing up pounding one another with big fence-maul fists. The blood was dripping from their ears where they had bitten each other and it was flying from their noses where they were pounding each other—but Frank was pushing him up the mountain.

"Get in there and fight," Finn screamed as he was getting hot under the collar. "Everybody fight! Come on, you first cousins! You are not fighting!"

Finn upended another man. He looked to be their youngest but it was another one out of the way. When our first cousins saw what Finn had done, they started fighting harder. If Uncle Melvin's boys by his unlawful wife had just known to have clinched Finn, he was easy to throw down. But long as he could stand up and maul with his long gorilla arms, he'd knock 'em out fast as he got to them. They didn't know how to fight Finn.

"Ye brought yer damned first cousins in here to hep ye," one shouted. "Ye couldn't whip us by yerselves. One is a prize fighter!"

"Yer a goddamned liar," Erf shouted as we drove them closer to the mountain ridgetop with two already on the ground—nine of us were fighting five now.

"I'll break the rule when ye foul us," one of Uncle Melvin's boys by his unlawful wife yelled as he whipped a pistol from his hip pocket.

"The hell you will," Finn said, whipping his pistol out covering him as he aimed his pistol at Frank who was about to get the best of his brother. "If you move, I'll let you have it."

"Don't kill 'im, Finn," I yelled. "Don't have trouble the rest of your days over Uncle Melvin."

"Drop that pistol or you die."

He dropped the pistol. Erf ran in and grabbed it. Finn put his pistol back in its holster and Erf stuck his captured pistol down in his hip pocket. Now we had them backed on the mountain ridgetop. We would soon be fighting more to our advantage for we would be backing them down the other side of the mountain toward the shack where they lived.

I don't believe I could have whipped my man if it hadn't been for Erf helping me. When Erf started to fight him, I thought it looked bad to have two men on one that was smaller than I was. I dropped out of the fight and just let Erf fight him. I sat on a stump and watched the fight as everybody tangled on the ridge road.

"Ye tried to pizen us," Frank said to the half brother that he was fightin'. "Ye passed our house when we's all out in the field at work and ye tried to throw a hunk of meat in our well. Ye missed the well and our dog got the meat. He was dead in three hours after he et it. This lick is fer that piece of meat ye throwed at our well."

Frank stood on his tiptoes and threw all the weight of his powerful shoulders against his fist. It connected with his half brother's beardy chin and he upended him. He lay sprawled on the ridge road with blood running from his nose, mouth and eyes.

"Think that old hag sent 'im to pizen Ma on our well-water," Frank said, "while we's out in the field."

Finn was about to get the best of his third man. He had clinched Finn because he was tired and Finn was pounding him with little short uppercuts to the chin and to his short-ribs.

"Oh, my God, ye brothers stop yer fightin'," a woman screamed just as I was getting ready to light my pipe. She came up the mountain path from the other side of the ridge, wringing her hands and screaming. "No ust to fight now. My poor Melvin is dead."

"Did ye pizen 'im?" Erf shouted.

"Oh, no, I loved 'im too much," she wept, wringing her bony calloused hands and then pushing the crow-wing black wisps of hair back from her face. "My true love is dead."

Everybody stopped fighting and started wiping blood from his face but her three boys that were sprawled cuckoo on the ground. Everybody was too dumbfounded to speak. I didn't light my pipe. I remembered that Aunt Mallie had a feeling that somebody would be dead before this fight was over.

"We're a-takin' Pa home dead 'r alive," Frank said. "Let's go git 'im, boys."

We followed Frank down the path toward the shack down in the valley. She followed behind us weeping and her boys followed her—helping one another down the mountain path and wiping blood from each other's faces. There wasn't any cold water to throw on their faces on the mountain top.

When we reached the three-room mountain shack, all the doors were open. Frank looked in at each door. He couldn't find Uncle Melvin. Then he went inside and looked but Uncle Melvin wasn't in the house.

"He's not in here, boys," Frank said.

"Wonder where the hell he is," Van said.

"God, I'd like to know," Erf said. "Wait till she comes and we'll find out."

"We ought to burn this goddamned shack," Dobie said.

"Hell no, the trouble will end if Pa is dead," Gullet said. "No ust to burn the shack. We don't want this bunch to come over the mountain to live offen us."

When Uncle Melvin's unlawful wedded wife walked down the path with her seven boys crippling along the path, their two sisters were following them.

"Where did they come from?" Don asked pointing to his half sisters.

"Must've taken to the brush when they saw us a-comin'." Erf said.

"Where's Pa?" Frank asked soon as she reached the yard.

"Out thar," she said, pointing.

"Out where?" Frank asked.

"The privy."

"Did he die out thar?"

"Yes, poor Milvin did," she said weeping. "He complained about his heart this mornin'. And when the boys went upon the mountain, he jist went outside. He stayed a leetle long and I went to see about 'im and found 'im dead."

"My God," Frank said as he walked toward the toilet that was built over a little creek.

"Love of two wimmen is too much fer any man's heart," Dobie said.

We followed Frank.

"He's here all right," Frank said.

"Ain't this awful," Erf said.

"Wonder what Ma'll think?" Van said.

"She jist won't think," Dobie said. "Ma'd rather have 'im on our side the mountain dead than to let that old Hag out thar have 'im alive on this side the mountain."

"It's a disgrace fer Pa to die in her privy," Gullet said.

"Death has two good eyes," Erf said. "He can find a man in the privy same as he can find 'im in a house 'r a cornfield."

"I'd've loved to've seen Uncle Melvin alive," Finn said.

"He'd a liked ye, Finn," Gullet said. "Ye're a fighter."

Frank stuck Uncle Melvin's legs out at the privy door. Erf took one leg, I took the other. Frank carried his head and shoulders through the door. Uncle Melvin was a big man with broad shoulders and a big white mustache. He looked like he was still alive but he wasn't for his big eyes had set under his ferny eyebrows that hung over his deep-set eyes. When Frank squeezed his shoulders through the door, Van took hold of one arm, Gullet got the other and Frank carried his head to keep it from sagging down on his limber neck.

When we left the house all the boys were weeping over their father. And his unlawful wedded wife was carrying on something awful. The two girls were weeping.

"Cry all ye damned please," Frank said, "he don't belong here. He's a-goin' back where he belongs. And ye be damned shore ye stay on this side the mountain when we bury 'im. We'll be prepared at the funeral with powder that is dry enough to burn."

He'll be a load to carry up this side of the mountain and down the other side, I thought as we moved along the path more slowly than the lazy mountain wind that fingered its way through the thickets of brush, briars, sprouts, and trees on the rugged mountain slopes.

We walked along the narrow path with Uncle Melvin while our first cousins bragged about what a fighter Finn was, said he took after the Powderjays while I must have taken after my mother's people.

Toes

About the story:

Out of that inexhaustible mine of human experience, the raw material out of which the artist creates his world of fiction and poetry, Jesse Stuart shaped this remarkable tale of psychological revelation—a story of infidelity, pregnancy, childbirth, jealousy, and hatred at times approaching violence, but with the advent of innocent new life evolving into tenderness and, if not into forgiveness, then into love, understanding, and acceptance of the blameless fruit of a man's philandering. "It takes a woman to feel and understand," Amanda Scout thinks as she narrates the strange sequence of events around her. "Man is fickle as the wind. The wind will blow the ragweed seeds over the earth. They will grow here and there. Man is not particular. He will leave his seed to grow here, or there, and in awfully poor soil, sometimes."

One reviewer observed that this story, told in the first person by Amanda Scout, reveals "points of view that show the whole world closer kin than we would ordinarily admit." Remarking on the author's convincing power in dealing with "one of the world's greatest domestic troubles—infidelity," another reviewer wrote, "Jesse Stuart is able to express the 'noble savage' sentiment, without overdoing it. He is never directly sentimental, but his sympathy, love and understanding of his forgotten race interpret them in a light that could not be achieved by one without his deep sensibilities." Writing in the New York *Times*, Edith H. Walton recognized that Stuart

> is one with the land, one with the people of whom he writes. One feels that he identifies himself with these Kentucky mountain folk whom he understands so luminously and shrewdly. Although he is fully conscious of their characteristic oddities, and savors the tang of their humor as any outsider would, he describes them without any tinge of patronage and with the deep insight of one who belongs in their midst.

As if to fill out the accuracy of Walton's observation, the author frankly discussed the story, revealing two sources—Mrs. Doris Johnson, who talked with him in his office when he was principal of McKell High School, and his own mother, Martha Hylton Stuart. Of the story in general and its facts he would say little more than, "That's in our family. It is related to my father, and that's enough. It is a story in family lore. . . . " In her review Edith Walton characterized the story as one of Stuart's "subtle psychological studies," and in "Toes"—as the author does in numerous other of his more serious pieces—"he achieves a moving lift and intensity that are purely lyric. He pictures dark, cold . . . fields sparkling under the moon; he voices, rhapsodically, his lament for the pain and uncertainty of living."*

* * *

PARSIE LIVES right across the road from me. She moved there last spring. Her man, Peg-Leg Jake Mullins, rented the place from old Bill Sizemore. I think Bill is wrong in the head to rent to Peg-Leg Jake. He's the laziest man in the world. When he was burnin' brush last March he went to sleep close to a brush pile on fire. The fire burnt the leaves out around the brush pile. The fire slipped up like a mouse in the kitchen safe and caught Peg-Leg's wooden leg on fire. It popped and burned like dry shoemake. It was locust wood. It burned right off his body before he could get the strap unbuckled. Peg-Leg hobbled in on a stick to the house. He went to plow one day. He went to sleep when the day got up. The peckerwoods drilled in his wooden leg for worms. That's the God's truth. Old Bill Sizemore must be wrong in the head to rent a farm to him. He'll run old Bill in debt instead of makin' money to pay the taxes on the place.

I could tell Parsie was goin' to have a baby. I knowed it all the time. I remember last Spring how my man Blue used to hunt with Peg-Leg and Timothy. Say, that Timothy Muscovite was a man I never did like. I never did like that name. Timothy is a big hairy man, with big hands and a face like a monkey. He looks funny beside of my man, Blue. My man looks more like somebody. I've got the only decent-lookin' man in this neighborhood. I'd like to see a woman who could love Peg-Leg or Timothy. Peg-Leg's got a fine fuzz on his face where he never shaves. I always say his face is poor as some old land that we got that won't bring weeds and sprouts. His face won't grow whiskers. He's not got a tooth in his head that I've ever seen.

*"Toes," *American Mercury*, Vol. 37 (Feb., 1936), pp. 152–159, reprinted in *Head o' W-Hollow* (1936) and *Fiction Parade* (April, 1936), pp. 711–717, also reprinted in *Head o' W-Hollow* (1979 ed.), pp. 232–244. Anon. rev., "The People of the Hollow," Raleigh, N.C., *Observer*, Aug. 2, 1936, clipping in Jesse Stuart, Scrapbook #3, p. 19, M. S. U. Anon. rev., "Head o' W-Hollow Symposium of Life in the Kentucky Hills; Volume Prepared by Jesse Stuart," Lexington, Ky., *Herald*, May 3, 1936, clipping in Jesse Stuart, Scrapbook #3, p. 15, M. S. U. Edith H. Walton, "Jesse Stuart's Kentucky Tales" (review), the New York *Times*, clipping in Jesse Stuart, Scrapbook #3, p. 13, M. S. U. Jesse Stuart/H. E. Richardson, Interview #41, W-Hollow, Greenup, Ky., Sept. 15, 1981.

His thin jaws just blab-blab and blubber when he talks like the wind goin' in and out of a bee smoker. Then he's just got one good leg and it's not any bigger than a hoe handle. I don't see how Parsie can stand him. Parsie's a right good-lookin' woman to have six brats.

I could see last May Parsie was goin' to have a baby. She went out and worked in the fields a little. That didn't matter. She couldn't hide it from a woman. She's as pretty a woman as there is in these parts of the country. Ain't but three families here. Just two women. Parsie and me. Timothy Muscovite is too ugly to ever get a woman. He lives by hisself over there in the old Hinton house on the ridge. Ain't nobody in this country knows where he come from. He's got money. We don't know where he got it. He's too ugly to ever get a woman. He don't look like a man. He looks like a brute that walks on its hind legs a-standin' up. Great big devil. Big hands and feet and hairy as a dog with a face like a monkey. We heard there use to be a big gamblin' man that strolled these parts when they built them tunnels on the E-K railroad. He won money from the workin' men every pay day. He rode a big black horse. We heard Timothy Muscovite waylaid him on the other side of the Barney tunnel and knocked him off his horse with a club and robbed him. The horse went to old Sweeter Hensley's place. I've heard Pap talk about it. I don't like for Blue to run with him, but he does. They fox-hunt together.

Parsie, Timothy, and Peg-Leg calls Blue, "Duck-Foot" Blue. I never did like that name. There's not anythin' I can do about it unless it would be take a pair of scissors or a butcher knife and cut Blue's toes apart. He's web-footed like a duck. His toes, the two next to his big toe on his right foot, are growed together; and the two next to his little toe on his left foot are growed together just about half way up. The two on his right foot are growed together plum out to the end. And people call Blue, "Duck-Foot" Blue Scout. They call me Mrs. Duck-Foot Blue Scout. Law, how I hate that name. If I'd cut Blue's toes apart now it wouldn't matter. He's already got that name. Then it might set up blood pizen. A body just can't tell about them things. Better to leave them as God made them. God marked the Scout family for a sin a way back yonder in the Scout line. A old man by the name of Jim Frailey got two of his toes mashed flat in the log woods. Blue's great-grandmother laughed at his toes. That was right before Blue's grandfather was born. When he was born, he come with two toes on each foot growed together. When he married and had children the seventh child had toes growed together on both feet. That was Blue's father. When Blue's father married, his seventh child was Blue. He's got toes just like his Pap and his Grandpap. It runs in the Scout family.

I never was to say jealous of Parsie. I know she's a better-lookin' woman than I am. I'm not a good-lookin' woman. I used to be when I was young. When I walked down the church aisle, men riz to their feet and watched me pass. But they don't anymore. Hoein' corn and bearin' babies for the man I love's took all that out of me long ago. So much housework to do. So many cows to milk and hogs to slop. So many chickens to feed. A big house to keep clean. It's a pine-log house and for God's sakes, women, don't ever let your man make you a pine-log house or move you into one. They're too bad for bedbugs. They've nearly et us up since we've been here. If I didn't scald twice a week all the beds, the slats and the cracks they'd eat us up. Then I keep my bed casters a-settin' in a tin can of coal oil. So it's work around here besides havin' a baby every couple of years. That takes some time out.

Parsie's had to work out. She don't go ahead like I do. She ain't worked like I have. I live right here across the road from her and know. She's never done it since she's lived over there in old Bill's house. She's never done the work I have. That's the reason she's held her shape. If she'd a worked like I have! But she ain't. I don't see for my life how she lives with that thin-lipped ugly Peg-Leg man of hers. Pon my word, if I was choosin' between the two men I'd ruther have old Monkey-faced Timothy Muscovite. He would provide for a woman and treat her halfway decent if he'd a been good-lookin' enough to a-got hisself a woman. He wouldn't a worked her like a horse nohow.

I used to stand up there by the drawbars and watch Parsie goin' out there to the sand bottom to hoe corn. She would be barefooted walkin' along the path dodgin' the saw briars. Peg-Leg would be in front with a mule hitched to a plow. He'd let the mule drag the plow along and skive up the grass and the saw briars. He was too lazy to lift the plow by the handles. He just let it drag. Parsie would walk behind with her hoe on her shoulder and her lap done up down to her petty-coat with pumpkin seed and bean seed that Parsie would stick in a hill of corn in the rich spots of ground around the old rotted stumps and rock piles. I used to watch her pass. I would say to myself, "If my hair was just black and pretty as hers I wouldn't begrudge everything I got includin' the old cow Gypsy. She's got the prettiest blue eyes. Just like two blue bird eggs. She has got the whitest skin and the longest fingers. Her teeth's white as chalk. She's pretty as a doll." Then I would say to myself, "I am a liar. Parsie is not pretty. She is not pretty as I am. My hair is light. My eyes are blue. My teeth are fairly good. I am prettier than Parsie. I have four children. I don't want to have the seventh if I can dodge it. But I can't. I am just twenty-six years old. I don't want a duck-footed youngin. I don't want a marked baby just over Blue's great-grandmother laughin' at a man's mashed toes. That's too much punishment for God to put on any person. It's not fair. I can't help what she done. Why should I suffer for her sin? I am not a ugly woman. I am prettier woman than Parsie. I am not a liar."

But I was a liar. Parsie is the prettiest woman I ever saw. I used to watch Blue when Parsie and Peg-Leg come over on Sundays to eat dinner with us. I used to watch Blue to see if I could catch him lookin' like a man looks at a woman he likes. I never could see a thing myself. I would fry the meat on the stove. Parsie would be in the kitchen helpin' me. We would talk and the meat would sizzle in the pan. I would keep my eye on Parsie. I would glance around to see if Blue was lookin' through the front-room door into the kitchen at Parsie. I never could catch him lookin' at her. I would be nice to Parsie because she was so good-lookin'. I was nice to her because I couldn't be as good-lookin' as she was. She didn't know she was good-lookin'. And just think her married to that thin-lipped toothless, peg-legged, no-count, good-for-nothing man of hers. She ought to a married Timothy. Just us three families in our neighborhood. Two women and three men. And somethin' ugly about all the men but mine and he had his toes growed together. I watched him around the other woman. We would cook dinner for the men layin' in the front room on the floor smokin' their pipes and talkin' about the crops. I could see the smoke goin' up toward the ceilin' in little blue clouds. And under my breath I hoped and prayed to God old Peg-Leg would get his hair filled full of bedbugs from the pine-wood floor. It's bad to do that, but I did. I don't deny it. I never liked that no-count man. I don't see how any woman could. I am a woman. I know about a woman. She wants a man all the other women like. She wants to walk right in and take him by the arm and say, "Look, woman. I got him. He's my man." And after she gets him, if some woman doesn't want him, then she wants to dump him and get her a man they all want. That's the way it is here. I knowed sure as God made the grass that Parsie would like to have a man like Blue. That made me want Blue more than ever. I had him, but I wanted more of him since I felt like Parsie wanted him. I couldn't help it.

Well, we used to eat Sunday dinners together. We borrowed meal and sugar and coffee from one another. We was the best neighbors you ever saw. But I always watched. I always thought if you had a man worth anythin' he was worth watchin' and worth havin'. So many men these days are no-account. Not worth powder and lead it takes to blow out their brains. I used to watch Parsie more than I do now. She is ready to bring a baby now. I've been listenin' for a call from Peg-Leg every night. I've been listenin' to hear him come out in the yard and stand under that bare walnut tree in their yard and say, "Oh, Amanda Scout, come over here quick to Parsie." And I've just been lookin' to see all six of their children come stealin' in over here carryin' them infernal bedbugs on their clothes to stay all night any time. I just think every night I'll see them comin'. Fall-time here. Leaves dead on the ground and a body so sad this time of year. All this trouble and all this weary. It worries me just to think about it. Parsie is soon to have her baby.

Last summer durin' crop-time when we's workin' so hard in the fields and would come in dog-tired and do up the work—I'd go to bed and I couldn't go to sleep for thinkin' somethin'. I didn't think it. I felt it. A woman feels like a dog that raises its bristles when it smells where another dog has been. That's just the way I felt. I just raised my bristles when I thought about Parsie. God knows I liked her in a way. God knows I hated her in a way. If it just hadn't been for Blue. I felt like she felt the same way toward Blue that I felt. My bristles would raise. I could just feel a feelin' comin' in all over my body that Parsie liked Blue same as I did. I just couldn't stand to think about it. God, I cried. God, I rolled and tumbled in the bed. I done everythin'. I couldn't forget.

Last summer Peg-Leg, Blue, and Timothy would take the hounds. They would leave me and Parsie here together and go fox-huntin'. Parsie would sleep in one bed with her little youngins and I would sleep in another with mine. I was filled with the very devil. I could see myself pullin' out Parsie's coal-black hair and throwin' it to the ground in handfuls like sheep wool. I could feel my fingers goin' into her eyes. Law, how I wanted to put my hands on her. But I was afraid. She's a stout woman with her hands. I thought about gettin' a scythe blade and whackin' her across the face. Then I thought that was not the way to do it. I could get a sickle and sickle her neck like I would a bunch of plantin' in the yard. But a better way still to do it was to get a garden hoe off the palings and just light in on her with a hoe and chop her good like choppin' weeds. I can fight with a hoe better anyhow. But here was all them little babies around her asleep. Pon my word, I just didn't have the heart to do it. I could just see my man Blue in her. I knowed it was Blue. I just felt it. God knows I did. God knows it's the truth. A woman just feels, that's all. She can't help it. Men never understand like a woman.

Parsie would lay in the bed and snore. Her babies would cry and wake her. When she would rouse up I'd snore just like I was dead asleep. But I couldn't sleep in the room with her knowin' she's goin' to have a baby. When she would go back to sleep I'd set up in the bed and look out at the winder. I'd see the summer moonlight in the green corn. I'd hear the whippoorwills so lonesome—my God, how lonesome the night would be. Then I'd hear the hounds bringin' the fox around the piney pint. I could hear old Skeeter, Blue's blue-tick hound, leadin' the pack. He's got a bark like beatin' in a rain barrel with a plow pint when he's leadin' the pack and when he's behind he squeals like a pig. I'd lay in the bed and listen and think. I couldn't help it. Why was I like I was? Maybe I just thought things. Then I'd think that I was crazy and I'd have to be sent to the asylum. I'd seen one man go there. They used to put him in the corn crib and feed him bread and water every day. A County man come out and found him. They hauled him off handcuffed in a spring wagon. The last words he said to me: "Put my shoes down by the fireplace. I'll not get any more shoes." I didn't have his shoes. I'd never seen his shoes. He was just ridin' past in the wagon. What a terrible thing it is to be crazy. It's not anything to laugh about. "Am I crazy as the man I saw in the wagon, barefooted with the hair as long on his face as it was on his head? What a terrible thing."

Then I would think: "No, I am not crazy. I just feel like somethin' is goin' to happen that I don't want to happen. The wind told me. God told me. I feel it." When we'd come in from work I'd pitch and tear in the bed till twelve o'clock many a night. Blue would be beside me snorin'. I'd think to myself: "Wonder if Parsie loves him. Wonder if she has ever told him that she loved him and them lips that trembles in snores—wonder if words come from between them to Parsie: 'Yes, I love you too.' That silent body of a man. It is like a child. It cries to get things. It gets them, then it is through. It is quiet like a child. A woman is not like a man. A woman feels things. A woman understands."

The days passed by last summer. We planted the corn. We plowed it the first time and chopped the weeds out of it. We plowed it the second time and the third time. It was soon over the mule's back. When it got that high we quit plowin' it. I'd lay in my bed at night and look at it. I'd look at the moonlight on the cornfield bright as day. I would think: "The night is pretty. The night was made for man and the fox. The night was made for silence. The stars in the sky. The silver-like dewdrops on the corn. The night is pretty, whoever made it and whatever it was made for. I like the night. I love the night."

I watched the moonlight flicker on the corn blades as the night wind blowed them this way and that way. And I thought: "The night is so pretty. The God that made the night made me. I am not pretty. I am such a fool. If I was ugly as a hill, I would be pretty. Quiet, ugly people are pretty. But I can't be quiet, as trustworthy as the earth. I am such a fool. Some women are such fools. I am one. But the reason I am a fool, I can't trust. If I could make myself believe that I trusted like a lot of women. But I can't. I just can't lie about it when I feel a thing. You can trust the earth, but not its seasons of drouth, rain, snow, and sleet. You can trust a huntin' dog, but not when she comes in her season. Women are a lot like a dog. They have their seasons." I could smell the wet weeds that bordered the corn—the rag-weeds and the pussley. The wind from them smelled awfully sour. God, I thought of women and their seasons.

And as the moon rolled along in the flyin' fleece clouds I thought about man and woman. If I could only have Blue just so I could hold him in my hand like he was a piece of money. If I only owned him like he was a quar-ter or a half of a dollar I wouldn't mind. But no woman can own a man like that. No man can quite own a woman like she was a pound of salt or a dime's worth of soda. There's somethin' else to a man or a woman besides that. And there's nothin' in the world—not even marriage vows, lovers' vows, God, churches or anythin' above the sun or under the sun that would keep man and woman from lovin' one another. (Just to show you what I am talkin' about, old Felix Harkreader fell in love with his sister. He may not a fell in love with her. He lived with her just the same. They had two children. Young Felix Harkreader lived with his sister and they had four children. That would make the children only havin' one Grandpa and one Grandma. They had a little money and they kept it in the family. They didn't marry off to bring any more into the family. The old Grandpa kept a little notebook with the names of women in it he'd met and lived with. If he found one and didn't like her he marked her name off the list. He carried one thousand dollars in a red handkerchief and five hundred dollars in a blue handkerchief. He used the white handkerchief for his nose. Two women heard about the thousand dollars he kept in a handkerchief. They thought it was the blue handkerchief. They had a date with him. One had him upstairs and stole the handkerchief. She thought she got a thousand. She got five hundred. He come home and laughed and said: "They thought they's gettin' my thousand, but they just got my five hundred. She's not any good anyway." So he marked both names from his notebook. You just can't trust people. You can't own them. I try to own Blue. I want him for my own.

Just as I expected. It was cold as blue blazes. I'd sent my children to school—all but my little ones. Parsie sent her children to school all but her two little ones. The cold November wind was blowin' across the cornfield where we worked last summer. It was a awful day. Wind blowed the rags out of the winders where the lights had been busted out by the hail last summer. I trembled when I saw Peg-Leg comin' across the road runnin' on that wooden leg. I knowed somethin' must be wrong or he wouldn't a got such a move on him. Wooden leg was sinkin' in the soft ground where it had got sharp on the end. He'd pull it out and run and it would sink up again. He said, "Oh, Amanda—come quick—It is Parsie. She is sick—come quick!" He took back toward the house. I let my work go and took out toward the house. I knowed what was up. I left my little children in the house. I was afraid they might get burnt up. I hollered to Blue. He was out at the barn. I told him to stay with my little youngins till I went over to Peg-Leg's and Parsie's a minute. Blue understood. He took to the house a-runnin' and left the mules' harness on the ground that he was punchin' holes in to brad up a little.

I was nearly out of breath when I got in the house. I put water in the teakettle and het it. God knows just how much there is to be done when a woman is havin' a baby and they ain't no doctor. But I've delivered a many a baby. I knowed just what to do. I done it. It was a lot of pain for Parsie. No woman wants the pain of bringin' a baby into the world. She has to go through a lot for the sake of a child that just grows up and spits in his mother's face and flies off like a wild quail. But they bring them just the same. Woman has her season. She was made to bear children. She is happier lots of times with her children and never happy unless she has them. But I'm tellin' you it's a lot of trouble and a lot of pain. Woman pays for her pleasure. I never saw a woman suffer like Parsie. I done the best I could. I hated to see her suffer so. Cattle suffer the pain of birth and dogs and horses suffer. But not any livin' bein' suffers like a woman. Men don't understand. Women soon forget and are ready to bring another baby into the world. They soon forget all about childbirth pain. I couldn't think for hearin' Parsie suffer.

When the baby come a wee thing of cry and a bundle of nerves, I didn't want to see it. But I had to see it. The water was hot. I poured in some cold water and made it lukewarm. I washed the baby. I just couldn't believe before I saw it that it would look like Peg-Leg Jake. I wanted to think that it would look like old Timothy Muscovite. Then I'd hate to see a little baby brought into the world and have to go through the world ugly as old Timothy—so ugly he looked like pictures of the Devil. I just didn't want to look at the baby at all. But I had to look at it. Before I washed it, I thought about Blue over at the house with my two little children. I thought that Blue was just a child. I was his mother and his wife. He was one of my children.

The baby cried. Parsie went off into a doze. She closed her eyes. Her lips

were blue. She was bad off. I could tell. She had been too long bringin' the
baby into the world. I had to wash the baby. I had to care for it. Peg-Leg
ran out of the room. I looked at the baby's ears to see if it had little lettuce-
leaf ears like Blue. I looked at its lips. I thought I could see cut in the upper
lip beneath the nose what we call the "trough" just like it was on Blue's lips.
I could see Blue's eyes in its head. Surely, I was dreamin', but I could see the
image of Blue in the baby more than in any child I bore for him. It was a
boy. It was Parsie's seventh child. And I thought: "Could it be Blue's baby?
It looks like him. No. It does not look like him. I am dreamin'. This is a
world full of trouble and dreams. It has some joys. Not many. I cried over
this before. I felt it. Is it a lie? Is it the truth? It doesn't matter. Parsie is
dyin'. She says: 'It ain't my baby. I never saw it before. Take it away. I
won't have it. Who give me that baby anyway—take it away or I'll scream.
Timothy brought it here. Timothy Muscovite, the ugly son of Satan. Take
it away.' And I saw Parsie. She wilted like a rose throwed in the fire. Her
eyes set in her head. She had never remembered. I was sorry that I hated
her and wanted to hook her white neck with a sickle and glomb her eyes
with my fingers and fight her with a hoe. I was sorry. But I have to wash
the baby. It feels like it is mine."

And then its toes! I thought. I'll look at its toes. I looked—My God—
Oh—God. The two little pink toes on the right foot next to the big toe was
growed together plum to the end. The two toes next to the little toe on the
left foot was growed together halfway up to the end. It is Blue's baby! Oh
my God! It was Blue Scout's baby. It is a Scout! I tore my hair. I screamed.
Parsie was Blue Scout's baby. It is a Scout! I tore my hair. I screamed. Parsie was quiet. She didn't hear me. She didn't bat a eye. I thought she was
playin' possum on me. I thought she understood. I dropped the baby down
on the cloth. It moved its little pink hands and wiggled its little toes like
toes and hands of young mice a body finds in the corn shocks in the spring.
The baby cries like a little pup. I couldn't help it. I ran out of the house. I
wanted to kill Parsie. Blue couldn't help it. It was not his fault. I ran to get
the hoe off the palings. I saw Peg-Leg Jake talkin' to Timothy Muscovite—
two of the ugliest-lookin' men I ever saw. I hated them both. Just to think
of woman and her child. Think of the mother dog when pups are born how
ill she is with the dogs. She makes up with them before her season starts
again. God made them that way. God made us all that way. I cannot understand. I took the hoe and run into the house. I thought I would kill Parsie. There she was in the bed. Her face was white as snow. Her eyes was set.
She wasn't getten her breath right. I just couldn't kill her. She was down. I
couldn't kill a person down not able to help herself. I don't care what she's

done. Here was blood in the room. I thought of that sour smell of weeds last summer when the wind blowed in across the fields into the open winder where I was sleepin'. That sour smell. I held to the hoe handle. I thought once I'd chop her head off right where her neck was the least to chop through. That was Blue's baby. Then I thought I wouldn't kill her, for she was goin' to die anyway. Her down there sufferin' so and me standin' up with a hoe to kill her like I'd kill a snake. That was not fair. I couldn't do that. So I walked over and raised the winder. I pitched the hoe out the winder. The dead leaves blowed in when I raised the winder. November winds and them as cold as all get-out.

I got the wash rag and I finished washin' the baby. I hated them toes. Just to think! The baby belonged to Blue. You are not foolin' me. God don't prank with people for the sins of their people. They carry the mark. Now if I lived to have my seventh child it would have duck-foot toes. It is a mark of Blue's people.

The children come in from school. Peg-Leg sent them all over to the house for Blue to keep. Blue never come about. He acted like a whipped dog. That is a man for you. He doesn't pay for his pleasure like a woman. If he could have only seen Parsie suffer like I saw her. Now her eyes set. Surely she was dyin' from childbirth. What a awful death. Only a woman can understand. Only a woman knows. I couldn't kill her with a hoe or a sickle. Poor woman was dyin'. I could hear breath come and go and sorty sizzle. She just looked up at the brown-ringed paper on the ceilin' where the rain had leaked through. Her eyes were about half open. She said: "I know it ain't mine. It ain't mine. It is Amanda's baby. It belongs to her. She will have it. I won't need it." And when she said that, I said: "Sure, the little thing is mine." I pulled it up and kissed it. The baby was Blue's. The baby was mine. I'd take it. It was Blue's child. I love Blue. All that is him is me. We are together. We are one. His child was mine. I held the baby in my arms. I couldn't love Parsie. I just felt for her. Her there on the couch a-dyin'.

The winds played around the house as night come on and the sun sunk down on the other side of the pasture. The bare limbs of the trees looked like they was growed into the white patches of the sky. I could see them betwixt me and the moon. The baby cried. I nursed it with peppermint tea that Peg-Leg found by the old Daugherty gate. I told him right where to find it. Women have got it there before for their babies. All the men in the country has come there to get it for their wives. I never told Peg-Leg about the baby's toes. I told him I wanted the baby if Parsie died. He told me I could have him. I told him I would raise him right and under the eyes of the Lord. Peg-Leg shed some tears. So did old Timothy. I felt sorry for him—him so ugly a-cryin' when he walked up with Peg-Leg Jake and saw Parsie on the couch.

I remember the moon that come up. It looked to me like it had a spot of blood on it. I saw blood maybe. It was on the bed. It was on the floor. It was on the moon. Blue was in the house with all the children. He didn't know Parsie was dyin'. Her breath got shorter and shorter. It kindly sizzled and she crossed her hands on her breast and she went out of the world. I had the baby in my arms. I saw her go. I can't forget. I called Peg-Leg. He come runnin' in. Timothy come in with him. I took the baby and walked out. I took it to the house. I started making clothes for it before its mother was laid out to bury. I was glad she died. I had to be glad. I didn't want to kill her with a hoe. The baby is mine. He is dear to me as my own. I call him Blue. He looks more like Blue than airy one of the children I have by him.

They buried Parsie back by the edge of the sand cornfield where she used to hoe corn before the baby was born. She is buried under that hickory at the fence corner. Timothy Muscovite has moved in the house with Peg-Leg. He loved little children so. They ain't afraid of him any more. I ain't said a word to Blue about the baby bein' hisn. I think he understands. I take care of the baby. It belongs to me. Man doesn't understand. It takes a woman to feel and understand. Man is fickle as the wind. The wind will blow the ragweed seeds over the earth. They will grow here and there. Man is not particular. He will leave his seed to grow here, or there, and in awfully poor soil, sometimes.

Old Op and the Devil

About the story:

Theopolis Akers made one of his early appearances in Jesse Stuart's novel *The Good Spirit of Laurel Ridge* (1953). Years before, when the author bought 252 acres of rugged land around Seaton Ridge above W-Hollow he also bought the house in which Old Op Acres was living. "I had a deed recorded in the county court records... but Old Op Acres had a deed for it in his heart." A self-sufficient master woodsman, Old Op told Jesse Stuart

> "stories about ghosts, hunting, fishing, and about turtles and snakes. He told me how he got tired once and sat down on a log. And when the log began to move with him, he discovered he had sat down on a big snake. Then he told me that every weed, flower, and tree was put on earth for a purpose and that the blossom, bark, and roots of these had medicinal purposes. He said the proper mixtures would cure any disease he knew about. He had remedies for everything. Old Op was a character.... The story about the devil is one of Op's many stories...."

When I asked Mr. Stuart about Old Op, our interview went like this:

RICHARDSON: Is Old Theopolis partially modeled on anyone who ever lived? Or is he totally imaginary?

STUART: No, he's not imaginary at all. He was modeled on a man, George Alexander.

R.: Did he live on your land?

S.: We bought our land from him. He lived up in the cabin [on Seaton Ridge]. He lived on this place all of his life.

R.: Was he really knowledgeable about all those aspects of nature?

S.: Everything I said about him.*

* * *

*"Old Op and the Devil" was orig. pub. with variations as a chapter in *The Good Spirit of Laurel Ridge* (N.Y.: McGraw-Hill, 1953), pp. 213–219, reprinted in *A Jesse Stuart Reader* (N.Y.: McGraw-Hill, 1963), pp. 172–177, and most recently in *Glenmary's Challenge*, Vol. 33, No. 4 (1970), pp. 14–15. Mr. Stuart's background information on Old Op is from his *"Author's Introduction," A Jessee Stuart Reader*, pp. 170–171. Other comments are from my interview with him, W-Hollow, Greenup, Ky., October 8, 1978. Stuart spells Op's surname both "Akers" and "Acres."

"L ET'S STOP here fer a few minutes, Alf." Op took the mattock from over his shoulder and held it on the ground beside him. "Somethin' happened to me here onct that I'll never ferget!"

"What was that, Op?" Alf was breathing heavily after climbing the steep slope from Sulphur Hollow to Laurel Ridge. They had added to the bulging sack some yellow root ("fer bellyache and sore mouth"), life everlasting ("good fer the asmie"), boneset, toe-each, and calamus.

"Right here is where I climbed on the Devil's back and rode 'im home," Op said.

"Oh, good Lord!" Alf stared at Op standing there with the coffee sack filled with herbs over his shoulder and the mattock in his hand. He looks like some sort of prehistoric man, Alf thought.

"I don't care whether ye believe it or not," Op told him. "I know I'm a-tellin' ye the truth. I climbed on the Devil's back right here one night and he took me home. I'll tell ye just how it happened.

"It was in October and I'd come out here a-possum-huntin' with old Jerry the night before," Op explained. "It might've been two nights before. I'd fetched along a quart of 'simmon brandy. It was a dark night when possums love to stir. There wasn't a wind to shake the dead leaves on the trees and skeer 'em. The air was hot-like and felt like rain. Jerry had treed one possum up a bull 'simmon tree. So I took an extra snort of brandy and scaled up the tree atter it. Throwed 'im down and Jerry sulled 'im. Out Laurel about another hundred yards and old Jerry treed one of the biggest possums I ever saw up a little pawpaw bush. All I had to do was shake 'im from the bush. I put 'im in the sack and I felt purty good atter gettin' that possum. Then I took a real big snort of brandy.

"The next thing I woke up right about here where we're a-standin' and I was flat on my back and my eye sockets were filled with water. But my clothes were dry. That's the reason I say I might've come out here a couple of nights before the Devil carried me home. I might've been here that long. I know it had poured rain some time atter I'd laid down or my eye sockets wouldn't have been full of water. And that's a sign that I'd never moved till I'd woke up. The wind on this ridge had dried my clothes atter the rain. Old Jerry was a-layin' beside me when I rose up and the water run down my face. The moon was shinin' and poor Jerry looked like a mud dauber, he was so thin in the middle. The possums were a-jumpin' around in the sack. I got up on my feet, wiped the water from my eyes with my shirttail and looked up at the thin little moon above Laurel Ridge. I didn't feel bad at all. I felt purty good. Old Jerry barked and ran circles all around me when I come alive agin. I picked up this very mattock I'm a-carryin' now, put the possum sack across my shoulder and hadn't walked five steps till I met somebody. I thought he was a fox hunter at first!

" 'Howdy, Op,' he said to me. 'Where do ye think ye're a-goin'?' 'I'm goin' home,' I told him. 'Ye've not been there for three days,' he said to me. 'How do ye know?' I ast him, suspicious-like. 'Ye've not been fox huntin' that long, have you, Plack?' I thought he was old Plack Rivercomb who hunts the fox here on Laurel Ridge. 'I'm not Plack Rivercomb,' he said to me. 'Op, look me over. I've never fox-hunted in my life. Several of the fox hunters are my boys and I'm with 'em a lot. Ye know, Op, I take keer of my own. Climb on my back and I'll give ye a lift. I'll take ye home.' I wasn't a bit skeered right then. I thought he was the speret of one of the big timber cutters that had gone on before. But when I looked him over right there in the moonlight, I knowed he wasn't the speret of a man."

"How did you know?" Alf asked amiably.

"Ye never saw the speret of man with a pair of horns above his ears that come out about two feet from the side of his head and bent back like ox-bows, did ye?" Op said. "I never saw such horns. How he managed to get through the brush with that pair of horns was a mystery to me. I'd thought when he first spoke to me he was wearing a dark suit of clothes that needed pressing, for the legs of his pants were like big, round, dark-black oaks. But when I looked him over more keerfully I saw he wasn't wearing a suit at all. His skin was somethin' like a bearskin, only the hair was longer. And when I looked at his feet I saw he had the cloven hoof. Whether he was wearin' steel shoes like the giant oxen on Laurel Ridge ust to wear I'll never know. But he was made in the image of man. He walked standin' up and not on his all fours. He had shoulders broader than my cabin door and a big un-shaven face somethin' like a bear's. He had a full set of teeth that looked like small white handspikes. He had mule ears he could twitch in the direction of any sound.

" 'What kind of a speret are ye?' I asked, lookin' 'im over. 'I've never seen ye before on Laurel Ridge.' "

" 'But I've been on Laurel Ridge many times before!' he said. 'I was on Laurel Ridge before ye were born. And I'll be here atter ye're gone. I'm a speret ye've heard more about than any other speret on Laurel Ridge. I'm the Devil. Get on my back, old Op, and let's get goin'.' 'No thank ye, I'll walk,' I said, nice and polite-like. 'No, I'll take ye home, Op,' he insisted. 'If ye don't ride on my back, ye'll be a sorry speret one of these days.' Then old Jerry, who had whined and barked inched a little closer to smell of this gi-ant Devil. Old Jerry must've thought he was another harmless speret like so many he'd seen when we hunted at night on Laurel Ridge. But the Devil kicked at Jerry with a mighty hoof that whistled as it cut the air, and if Jerry hadn't been quick on the dodge, he'd've kicked his head clean offen his shoulders! Jerry took off around Laurel Ridge a-runnin' and a-barkin' as I'd never heard 'im before. That's the only time he ever fersook me. And I've never held it against 'im.

" 'Get on my back, Op,' the Devil said, speakin' plain as I ever heard with a voice as big as the roar of waters in April down at Sandy Falls. 'I don't have time to fool too long with ye. I've got business to do. Ye know I'm a busy speret. I never sleep, I go day and night and have to be in a thousand places at once. I'm nowhere else tonight but right here. Ye're not a-gettin' my split personality. Ye're gettin' all the charm I can turn on one of my prospective subjects. I saw ye here sleepin' with puddles of dark rain water in yer eye sockets. Saw ye drinkin' my brew from the 'simmon. So I want to do somethin' fer one of my own.' 'But I have my mattock and my sack with two possums in it,' I said, thinkin' fast. 'That won't add too much to the load I'm able to carry on my broad shoulders,' he said. And he took my mattock in his hand big as a coal scoop, with hairy fingers big as sticks of stovewood. He took the possum sack in his other hand. I leaped upon his back like a squirrel. I took him by the horns and swung my weight up to his shoulders. Put a leg over each shoulder and a hand on each horn. And he started around Laurel Ridge with me."

"That's enough, Op," Alf said. "I don't want to hear any more."

Alf started walking around Laurel Ridge, and Op followed with the sack across his shoulder and the mattock in his hand.

"No matter what ye want to hear, I'm gonna finish. It happened right where we're a-walkin' now. This is the way we come."

"You carry these tales too far," Alf said, walking faster. "I've heard enough. It does something to me."

"What do ye think it did to me that night?" Op answered. "Don't ye think I was nervous? But I thought I'd better ride. I didn't want to take any chances. When a man's old body is planted back on this earth and his speret leaves the old clay temple and journeys on into the next world, he never knows where he's goin' to land. I had to play along with 'im, don't ye see, Alf?"

"I expect so," Alf murmured.

"Now right along here was where the Devil started trottin' with me." Op pointed at the path. "He jogged up and down so I thought he was a-tryin' to throw me off. But I locked my legs around his bull neck and gripped his big horns fer dear life while the fire streaked like lightnin' from his feet. That's the reason I've often wondered if he wore steel shoes like an oxen on his cloven hoofs. And while I held onto his horns and he trotted, there was a great rumblin' among the leaves still a-hangin' on the tough-butted white oaks. I thought all the leaves were fallin' from the trees. Then, suddenly, the Devil changed his pace. He started rackin' like one of the hosses I'd seen young men and wimmen ride around this ridge when I was a boy. 'How do you like yer ride?' said the Devil to me. 'I love the rackin',' I said. When I said this, he changed to a slow pace. And dark clouds started rollin' over Laurel Ridge and hidin' the moon and stars. It suddenly got dark as charcoal and all of Laurel Ridge began to tremble. I could feel it on the Devil's back. All of a sudden the lightnin' flashes cut the dark, thick air. They danced over the Devil's horns till I thought, onct, I'd have to let go.

" 'How do ye like it now?' the Devil ast me. 'I don't like it 't'all,' I said. And he laughed and it sounded like the thunder that was jarrin' Laurel Ridge to its foundations. I heard trees a-splinterin' on both sides of me as the Devil took off in a gallop. I thought he was a-runnin' to beat a great storm that was at our heels. I could hear the rain behind us but I couldn't look back to see. The fire was flyin' in all directions, rain fallin' behind, yet the Devil was gallopin' ahead of the storm. And I was a-ridin' as comfortably as I'd ever ridden anything in my life, with my legs locked around his bull neck and my hands ahold of his horns. He took me full speed right up in front of my cabin and stopped so suddenly his big feet skid twenty feet on the ground, and streaks of fire shot from them. Old Jerry ran from the cabin barkin' and growlin'.

" 'Get away from me, ye mongrel!' the Devil shouted as he kicked at 'im agin. 'Don't try to bite me! I'll kick yer head clean from yer shoulders.' 'If ye kick that dog, I'll dehorn ye,' I said. I would have done it too. I had my knife from my pocket and I'd 've really worked on one of his horns. 'Wonderful, Op,' the Devil said. 'That's the way I like to hear ye talk, especially to anyone who has done ye a favor. Allus be that grateful and ye'll be my favorite speret someday. I'll call ye home. I've got a great need fer ye. Get down offen my back, friend!' Well, right there I climbed down offen his back. Right in my own front yard.

"And the Devil gave me my mattock and my sack of possums. He smiled, a-showin' his full set of big white teeth. He looked down at me right kindly, and fer a minute I thought he was gonna pat my head. Good thing he didn't, he'd a probably crushed it. I didn't thank the Devil fer my ride. To hell with him, I thought, that's a friendship that can't do me no good. When I got my gate opened, I looked back to see if he was still standin' there grinnin' his big horse-whinny grin. But the Devil had gone. And with him had gone the thunder, lightnin', splinterin' of trees, and the great roar of the storm among the white-oak leaves. The sky was clear agin and the moon and stars were a-shinin'."

"That was some ride," Alf said, looking Op in the eye. "Don't guess you were able to do much sleeping after that."

"I turned the hungry possums loose, went into the cabin, shelled my rags off down to my shirttail and underwear," Op said. "I went to bed and slept like a log. Got up next mornin' and thought so much about my ride on the Devil's back that atter breakfast I walked back out Laurel Ridge to see how many trees the lightnin' had struck and what the storm had done. Not a tree was split by lightnin' and the 'simmons and pawpaws were all a-standin'. And I decided to myself the Devil was a big bluff. Jist a big wind. If I ever got on his back agin, I would shore dehorn 'im!"

Word and the Flesh

About the story:

In 1927 Jesse Stuart finished his freshman year at Lincoln Memorial University, Harrogate, Tennessee, and went home to northeastern Kentucky for the summer, where he worked for the American Rolling Mills (now known as Armco Steel) at nearby Ashland, Kentucky, to defray his college expenses. "I never had a scholarship and I didn't have any help from home. I had to finance myself." While living at Ashland that summer, he visited his Uncle Marion and his family near Ceredo-Kenova, West Virginia. A long-time U.S. marshal, his Uncle Marion was "about six feet four, had a steady cold blue eye, walrus mustache, and was a man without humor." In the Sunday morning paper, Stuart read a news article about a religious sect that planned to meet that very night. Those people would, they claimed, "take up a 'dead sister' and she would live again. She would walk and breathe."

"Uncle Marion," Stuart said, "I want to stay another night. . . . I like it so well here. I want to go and see them dig this woman up, to see her 'live again.' I want to see all this. Read this in your paper."

His uncle put on his "specs," read, then said, "They're crazy people. If I had a warrant to arrest them, I'd like to put all in the cooler. That's where they should be. They're not fit people to run loose among the decent people!"

The author recalled how "Uncle Marion looked straight at me with his cold blue eyes. I wondered if he might not think his nephew, who was a college student, wasn't a little crazy too. 'We'll be glad to have you stay over,' he said. 'I thought you were going to stay another night. One night is not enough. We'd like to have you stay a week, if you could and would. And if you want to see this crazy tomfoolery of ignorant crazy people, this will be all right, too. But I won't be with you—not unless I had warrants to arrest them.' "

It was the kind of local color Stuart was after. The rural cemetery he sought was not far for him to walk to, and after dinner that evening, he started out. "I journeyed on foot to the graveyard, which I didn't have any trouble finding. And here I found drama of its kind. I saw people the likes

247

of whom I never knew existed even in the colorful late 1920s. Here was an unusual story enacted before my eyes. ... "*

* * *

GROAN LEADS THE WAY along the cow path; his Disciples follow. The cow path is narrow, the pawpaw bushes are clustered on both sides of the path and they are wet with dew. Brother Sluss pulls a pawpaw leaf and licks off the sweet dew with his tongue. Brother Sluss is like a honeybee. The moon floats in the sky like a yellow pumpkin, dark yellowish like the insides of a pumpkin.

Groan and his Disciples, Brothers Sluss, Frazier, Shinliver, Littlejohn, Redfern, and Pigg, are headed for the Kale Nelson Graveyard. It is approximately one mile away, across Phil Hogan's cow pasture, Ben Lowden's pig lot, Cy Penix's corn patch, thence through the Veil Abraham's peach orchard to a flat where the ribs of an old house (the old Abraham's house) are bleached by the autumn sun and cooled by the autumn night wind. The robe Groan wears is similar to the robe Sunday-school cards picture Christ wearin' when He walked and talked with His Disciples. It has a low neck, loose flowin' sleeves. It is long and tied with a sash at the waist line. The loose sleeves catch on the pawpaw twigs along the path.

"Tell me more about the ten virgins, Brother Groan."

"I don't know about the ten virgins and I ain't discussin' the ten virgins. You know there was ten of them, don't you? And you know one of them was Virgin Mary, don't you?"

"Yes, I know that, Brother Groan. But tell me more about them."

"Brother Sluss, we have other things to talk about. Leave me be won't you. I want to talk with God. I want to feel the sperit. I want to show you what Faith will do tonight. Leave me alone. I am talkin' to God now. I am in God's presence. Leave me be, will you?" Brother Groan carries a bundle under one arm. He carries a walkin' staff in one hand. His loose sleeves are hard to get between the pawpaw twigs alongside the path.

There is silence. Brother Groan talks to God. They keep movin'. They come to the drawbars. One by one they slip between the drawbars, all but Brother Frazier. He is too thick to slip between the rails. He crawls under

---

*"Word and the Flesh" was first published in *Head o' W-Hollow* (N.Y.: Dutton, 1936), reprinted (Lexington: Univ. Press of Ky., 1979), pp. 129–149, also in Jesse Stuart, *Dawn of Remembered Spring* (N.Y.: McGraw-Hill, 1972), pp. 67–93. Although Jesse Stuart had been employed at Armco in the summer of 1926 as well, according to his Employment Department Record [and] Re-Employment Data folder at the American Rolling Mill Co., Ashland, Kentucky, Jesse Stuart worked in the steel mill the summer of 1927 from June 2nd to September 10th. The quotations are from Jesse Stuart's unpublished ms. "The (*sic*) Word and the Flesh, by Jesse Stuart," in the Jesse Stuart Collection, W-Hollow, Greenup, Ky.

the bottom rail. Now they are goin' through Ben Lowden's pig lot. The moon above them is pretty in the sky. It is still a yellow pumpkin moon— that darkish-yellow, the color of the insides of a ripe sun-cooked cornfield pumpkin. The dew on the crab grass in the pig lot sparkles in the yellow moonlight. The September wind slightly rustles the halfway dead pawpaw bushes. The crickets sing, the katydids sing, the whippoorwills quirt-quirt, and the owl who-whoos. Brother Groan mutters Unknown Tongue whispers to God.

"Brother Groan is goin' to show us the Faith tonight."

"Brother Groan is talkin' to God."

"No. That is the wind over there in Cy Penix's ripe corn. That is the wind in the corn blades talkin'. That is not Sweet Jesus talkin'."

"Be quiet, won't you. Brother Groan is tryin' to talk to God."

"I ain't said nothin'."

"No."

"It is the wind in the fodder blades, I tell you."

"The wind!"

"Didn't I say the wind?"

"Yes, you said the wind."

"Then why did you ask?"

"Because I thought that you said that Brother Sluss said that God whispered."

Brother Groan is first to mount the rail fence. His sleeve catches on one of the stakes-and-riders, but he gets over into Cy Penix's cornfield first. One by one his Disciples climb over the fence. Here is the ripe uncut corn in the yellowish wine-colored moonlight. The dead blades are whisperin' somethin'. Maybe it is: "The dead lie buried here, the dead of-ever-so-long-ago. But they lie buried here under the dead roots of this ripe corn."

The corn blades whisper to the wind. There is a sweet dew on these corn blades for Brother Sluss to lick off with his tongue, for Brother Sluss is like a honeybee. This dead fodder is buff-colored in the yellowish pumpkin-colored moonlight. Brother Sluss leads his Disciples through the field of dead corn. There is a ghostly chill of night piercin' the thin robe of Brother Groan's; and the overalls and the unbuttoned shirts of his Disciples.

There is a loneliness in the night, in the moonlight that covers the land and in the wind among the trees. There is somethin' lonely about dead leaves rakin' against one's clothes at night, for they seem to say: "The dead lie buried here, the dead of-ever-so-long-ago. But they lie buried here under the livin' roots of these autumn trees."

Lonely is the quirt-quirt of the whippoorwill, the song of the grasshop-

per, and the katydid. And there is somethin' lonely about dead fodder
blades the way they rake against the wind at night.

"Does God talk, Brother Littlejohn?"

"W'y yes, God talks. Ain't you got no Faith?"

"How do you know?"

"Because it is in the Word."

"Be quiet, please."

"It is the wind in the dead fodder."

"Are you sure that is all?"

"Yes."

"No."

"Why, no?"

"It is Brother Groan feelin' the sperit."

"How do you know?"

"I saw him jump up and down right out there before me."

"I saw him too jump up and down out there in the path. I saw his sleeve
catch on the brush. I saw him in the moonlight."

"He is feelin' the sperit then."

The peach orchard is not a new set of teeth. Too many of the teeth are
gone if each tree is a tooth. Many of them are snaggled teeth too. Brother
Groan walks under the peach trees too, and the good teeth and the bad
teeth chew at his robe. Brother Groan gets along. The dead leaves hangin'
to the peach trees are purple. One cannot tell tonight. But come tomorrow
afternoon when the sun is shinin' and look. There are half-dead leaves on
the trees and whole-dead leaves on the trees. The wind fingers with the
leaves. Brother Groan's sleeve has caught on the tooth of a peach tree.
Brother Sluss hurries to free him. The sleeve is free now. The Disciples move
on. Brother Groan is silent.

"Where are we goin', Brother Shinliver?"

"To the Kale Nelson Graveyard."

"What for?"

"Brother Groan is goin' to show us the Faith in the Word."

"How?"

"I don't know."

"By the Word?"

"No!"

"How?"

"I told you once I didn't know."

"Is that you talkin', Brother Redfern?"

"No."

"I thought I heard somebody."

"That was the wind you heard."

"Yes—that was the wind."

"Yes, that was the wind in the peach-tree leaves."

"Ain't we about there?"

"About where?"

"Kale Nelson Graveyard?"

"Right up there!"

"Right up where?"

"Right up there—see them white tombstones! That is the Kale Nelson Graveyard."

The moon is high above the Kale Nelson Graveyard and the wind is down close to the earth on this high flat. The dead weeds rattle. The dead grass is whisperin' somethin'. Maybe it is: "The dead lie buried here. The dead of-ever-so-long-ago. They lie buried here under our roots. We know the dead lie buried here." The loose leaves rustle in the wind. The moon is still as a pumpkin floatin' in the pretty night sky. The moon is still the color of the insides of a pumpkin.

Across the bones of the old house, Groan and his Disciples go. The myrtle is vined around the old logs. There is a pile of stones here, a pile of stones over there. Here is the butt of an old field-stone chimney. There is a gatepost half-rotted. Ramble rose vines climb halfway the rotted post. Here is a bushy-top yard tree with hitchin' rings stapled in the sides. Here is a patch of blackberry briars. The wind blows through the blackberry briars and the blackberry briars scratch the wind. You ought to hear this wind whistle when it is scratched by the briars. If the wind dies, it cannot be buried here where the dead weeds whisper: "The dead lie under our roots, here in the Kale Nelson Graveyard." If Brother Groan dies, he can be buried here. Brother Groan is the kind of dead, when he does die, a grave can hold. Listen: Brother Groan is goin' to speak now: "Gather around me, ye men of the Faith. Gather around me, ye men of God. Gather around me here. I want to show you there is power in The Word. Gather around me and let your voices speak in the Unknown Tongue to God."

Here on the myrtle-mantled logs of the old Abraham's house men are groanin'—men cryin' to God. They are pleadin' to God. They are mutterin' quarter-words, half-words, and whole words to God. It is in the Unknown Tongue. Brother Sluss is on the ground now. He rolls out into the graveyard. He breaks down the dead weeds that just awhile ago whispered to the wind that the dead lay under their roots. Brother Sluss smashes weeds half-dead like a barrel of salt rollin' over them. Brother Sluss is a barrel-bellied man. He rolls like a barrel. Brother Littlejohn's pants have slipped below his buttocks. Brother Shinliver is holdin' to a tombstone and jerkin'. Brother Groan is cryin' to God. He faces the yellow moon and he cries to God. Brother Frazier is pattin' the ground with his shovel hands and cryin' to God. "Come around me, men, come around me, you men of Faith, and listen to the Word. I aim to show you what the Faith in the Word will do. It will lift mountains. It will put life back into the dead bodies on this hill here tonight. Here are the dead beneath these weeds and the dead leaves. And one of these dead shall breathe the breath of life before mornin'. Brother Sluss, get up off the ground and go right out there to that chimney butt, look under the jam rock where the pot-hooks used to swing and bring me that coal pick, that corn scoop, and that long-handled shovel."

"Where did you say to go, Brother Groan?"

"Out there and look in the butt of that chimney."

"Out there by the blackberry briars, Brother Groan? I'm worked up with the sperit."

"What are you goin' to do, Brother Groan?"

"Through me, Brother Redfern, God is goin' to give new life to a dead woman this very night."

"Who, Brother Groan?"

"My dead wife."

"Your wife!"

"Yes, my dead wife. What do you think I brought this bundle of clothes along for? They are the old clothes she left in the shack when she died. She is goin' to walk off this hill tonight with me. She is goin' to live again through the Faith in the Word. It will put new life into the dead. It will lift mountains. You see, Brother Sluss come here with me a year ago today when my wife was buried here on this hill. You remember my wife, don't you, Brother Sluss?"

"Yes, I remember your wife. I was by her bedside prayin' when she died. I heard her last breath sizzle. I heard her say, 'I see the blessed Saviour.' Then she was gone. I followed Joe Mangle's mules that pulled her here that muddy September day last year. When your wife died, I thought I'd have to die too. I just couldn't hardly stand it. You had a good woman."

"That cold rainy day was the day I waited till they had all gone off'n the hill but the grave-diggers and when they was throwin' over her some of the last dirt I watched them from behind the butt of that old chimney there in the blackberry vines—I was scrounched down there in that hole where the pot-hooks used to swing. And when one of the grave diggers said: 'Boys, since we're so nearly done and the weather's so rainy and cold, what's you fellars say let's slip down yander behind the bank and take a drink of licker? Looks purty bad to drink here over this woman's dead body and her a woman of God's, but a little licker won't go a bit bad now.' And they all throwed their shovels and picks down and took off over the bank. While they was down over the bank I slipped out beside the grave and took a long-handled shovel, a corn scoop and a coal pick—I had this in mind when I hid if they ever left their tools. I wanted to see them throw the dirt in and I didn't want them to see me. I hid the tools in the butt of the chimney where I was hidin'. And I said to myself, 'I'll come back here a year from to-day and I'll put new breath in her through the Faith in the Word.' So, I got the tools. I hid them right here. I stayed with them. The boys couldn't find their tools and they argued how funny it was their tools disappeared so suddenly, said it was such a strange thing. Some men accused the other men of not bringin' their tools. They throwed in the rest of the dirt on my dead wife; then they swaggered full of licker off'n the hill. A red leaf stuck to the long-handle shovel handle. I think it was a leaf blowed off'n that sweet-gum tree right over there. There was death in that leaf same as there was death in my wife. Dead leaves are on the ground tonight not red with death so much as they was red with death last September in the rain when my wife was buried here."

"Brother Groan, I knowed your wife. She was a fine woman, wasn't she?"

"Yes. My wife was a very fine woman."

"Brother Groan, I knowed your wife since you spoke about her. Your wife had a harelip, didn't she? She was marked with a rabbit, wasn't she?"

"Yes, Brother Redfern, my wife had a harelip. But she wasn't marked with no rabbit. God put it there for the sins of her people. And my wife wouldn't let no Doctor sew it up. My wife would say in church, 'God put this harelip on me for the sins of my people and I shall wear it for God.' My wife was a good woman."

"Brother Groan, I remember the woman with the harelip. And she was your wife! Well, I saw her five summers ago, a tall woman slim as a bean pole with a harelip. I saw her in Puddle, West Virginia. She was in God's house and she said the words you said that she always said about her lip. And one thing she said has always stuck with me. It was somethin' like this: 'A man swimmed out in the river with his two sons. He was a good swimmer and they tried to follow him. He led the way for them. One went under the water and never come up again. The father started back with his other son toward the river bank and under he went too to never come up again. 'My God Almighty,' the father cried out, 'my sons are lost. They went the wrong way too far and I led them. I led them into this danger.' And your wife fairly preached there that night. And the sperit of God was there in that house."

"Brother Groan, I was in Venom, Kentucky, two summers ago and I saw your wife. She was in God's house there. She had a harelip I remember and all her teeth nearly showed in front. They looked like awful long teeth. I remember when she was talkin' to God she had a awful hard time sayin' her words to God. She got up and said the words you said she said about her lip to the people, then she pulled her sleeve up and showed where she was marked on the arm by the belly of a sow. There was a patch of black sow-belly skin on her arm and thin sow-belly hairs scattered all over it. And there was three small sows' teats about the size of a gilt sow's teats. And your wife said: 'People, God has marked me because my people have sinned against God and I am to carry the marks of my sinnin' people. I aim to carry the marks too. No Doctor can cut the one off'n my arm or sew the one up on my lip.' Brother Groan, your wife was a good woman."

"Yes, Brother Littlejohn, my wife was a good woman."

"Brother Groan, I remember your wife. I saw her in God's house. It has been three years ago this September. I saw her at a tent meetin' at Beaverleg, Ohio. And I'll die rememberin' one good thing I heard your wife get up and say. She said: 'Women, if I had a man mean as the very Devil which I ain't got, I would get up and cook for him at the blackest midnight. I would get a good warm meal for him if I had the grub to cook for him. Why? Because where he is goin' after he leaves this world there he won't have no sweet wife to cook for him.' Yes, I remember your wife sayin' these words. She had a hard time speakin' her testimony to God, for her words was not plain. I remember your wife and the half words she said. It was September in a hayfield near Beaverleg, Ohio, where the tent of God was. Your wife was a good woman, wasn't she?"

"Yes, my wife was a good woman, Brother Pigg. She was a good woman. You are goin' to see my wife again. She is goin' to walk off this hill with me. You bring the corn scoop here and shovel down through the loose dirt on top of the grave far down as you can shovel and lift out with the short-handle corn scoop. Here is the place. Start right here. Here is the place my wife was buried a year ago today. Yes, my wife was a good woman."

"Did you say to begin here, Brother Groan?"

"Yes, begin right there."

"Right at her feet?"

"I don't like to do this—mess with the dead."

"Ain't you got no Faith?"

"Faith in what?"

"Faith in the Word?"

"Yes, I got Faith in the Word."

"Dig then!"

"Well."

The moist September grave dirt is scooped out like loose corn out of a
wagon bed. When the scoops of dirt hit the dirt pile, they are like so many
dish rags hittin' the kitchen floor. Dirt hits the dead weeds and the dead
leaves on the ground in little thuds. The big moon is yellow above the dead
dirty grass and the white tombstones and the rain-cloud gray tombstones.
The Disciples are silent now except for the wet dirt piece-meal in the
ground. Brother Fain Groan is whisperin' to God.

"I need the long-handle shovel!"

"Here is the shovel, Brother Pigg. Leave me dig a little while, Brother
Pigg. Ain't you about fagged out?"

"Brother Littlejohn, I believe I will let you spell me a little."

"You have sure scooped this down some, Brother Pigg."

"I raised enough sweat. Closed in down here and the wind don't hit you
right."

"Wind can't hit a body down in this hole, can it?"

"No."

"Boys, I'll know my wife by her lip. Thank God, I ain't ashamed of it
neither. She told the people she wasn't ashamed of it. And I ain't ashamed
of it neither, thank God. God don't heal this old clay temple of ours only
through the Faith in the Word. I'll put breath back in my dead wife's body
and she'll become my livin' wife again. My wife—you have seen my wife
and you'll know my wife when she is risen from the grave, Brother Sluss,
and breathes the breath of life again."

Brother Groan walks out among the graves. His face is turned toward
the stars. He whispers unknown syllables to the wind. The wind whispers
unknown syllables to the weeds and to the dead leaves.

"I thought I heard a voice."

"A voice!"

"Yes."

"Ah!"

"The voice of God."

"No."

"It was the voice of the wind."

"Yes."

"The wind."

"The wind in the dead grass."

"Well then, did you hear the voice?"

"No."

"What did you hear?"

"I heard the wind in the grass."

"The wind!"

"Yes. The wind. The wind."

"You are gettin' way down there, Brother Littlejohn. Let me spell you a little while with that shovel."

"All right, Brother Redfern. The ground is gettin' hard here. Bring the coal pick down with you."

"Did you know there is a slip on one side of this grave? There is a hole down in this grave like a water seep. That is what made the shovelin' easy. That is why we are gettin' along fast."

"Is it?"

"Yes."

"Throw me down the pick, Brother Pigg. I have found some white tangled roots down here. Wait! I may be able to pull them out with my hand. A root this big down this far in the ground. I don't see any close trees. It must have come from that wild-cherry standin' over there on this side of the blackberry patch."

"Can you yank them roots out with your hands or do you want the coal pick? The ax end of the coal pick will cut them."

"Wait! I'm stung. The root flew up and hit my arm. Wait! Stung again. Wait! Here it comes. May be a snake! My God Almighty, but I'm stung. It can't be a snake though—a snake this deep down!"

"I'll see if it is a root. If it is a wild-cherry root it is a chubby wild-cherry root nearly big as a two-year-old baby's thigh. My God, but it has stung me. It jumped and stung me. I am bit by a snake and you are bit by a snake. Yes. It is a snake. Strike a match! Watch—it is goin' to strike again. Watch out. There! See it strike. It is a rusty-mouth grave copperhead. My God!"

"Come out of the grave, Brother Redfern. You have been bit by a rusty-mouth grave copperhead."

"Let us have Faith in the Word."

"Give me your pocketknife, Brother Littlejohn."

"What for?"

"To cut out the bite and suck the blood."

"Ain't you got no Faith in the Word?"

"Yes, but I know what to do for a copperhead bite. We ain't no business here messin' with the dead nohow. It is against the Word to prank with the dead. Don't the Word say, 'Let the dead rest. Bury the dead and let them rest'? Give me that knife."

"Brother Redfern, I'll cut your arm on the copperhead bite and suck your blood and you cut my arm on the copperhead bites and suck my blood."

"All right."

"God, ain't this awful out here this night."

"Brother Pigg is bit. Brother Redfern is bit."

"Go down in the grave, Brother Shinliver."

"Are you afraid to go? We're bit and we can't go back. We're goin' to get sick in a few minutes."

"I thought I heard a voice."

"You did."

"Yes. Is it God's voice?"

"No. It is the voice of Brother Groan."

"See him! He has opened the bundle of clothes he brought. He is holdin' up a woman's dress he brought in the bundle of clothes he carried up here on the hill tonight. He brought them clothes to dress his wife in when we get her dug out'n the grave."

"New clothes?"

"I'll ask and see."

"No—the clothes she used to wear. The dress Brother Groan liked to see her wear. The dress she looked so pretty in. Here is the hat she wore. It is a high-crowned black hat with a goose plume on the side. And here are the shoes she wore last. They are peaked-toe, patent-leather, low-heeled, button shoes. The clothes are right here for the woman soon as she comes out of the grave and the breath of life goes into her lungs."

"I have hit the wood, men. It is the box. I'll have to shovel the dirt from around the box so we can lift it out. I need hand holts. Wait till I clear some of the dirt away with my hands. I'm stung—stung like a red wasper stings right in the calf of the leg. Its teeth are hung in my pants leg. Get me out, men—get me out quick—It is another copperhead."

"Heave him out of the grave, men. See it. It is a copperhead. Its fangs are hung in his pants leg. Hit it with a shovel handle. Cut it with a knife. Kill it!"

"Cut the calf of my leg, Brother Littlejohn, with your pocketknife and suck the blood, for I can't get to my leg to suck the blood out and the blood won't come out fast enough unless it is sucked out."

"All right."

"Strike a match. It is a she-copperhead. Its head ain't as copper as the he-copperhead's. I thought it must be a she, for the old rusty-mouthed one was the he-copperhead."

"Ain't you got no Faith in the Word, Brother Shinliver?"

"Yes, but Brother Littlejohn, we ain't got no business messin' with the dead. The Word says, 'We must bury the dead and bury them so deep and leave them alone.' Don't the Word say that? I don't want my leg rottin' off. Cut my leg and suck the blood."

"All right."

"I got that copperhead."

"Strike a match."

"See how gray the belly is turned up. It looks like a poplar root."

"Are you afraid of that grave, Brother Littlejohn?"

"No, I ain't afraid of that grave."

"Get down and shovel awhile then."

"You want the coal pick?"

"Yes, the coal pick."

"God—God I'm stung. The first pop out'n the box and I'm stung right on the soft part of the jaw. The sting was like the sting of a red wasper."

"You stung, Brother Littlejohn!"

"Stung! Yes! My God! Take it off! Take it off! Its fangs are fastened in my flesh. Take it off, men. Take it off!"

"Yank him out'n the hole, men. All right. Come, Brother Frazier."

"Cut that snake off with your pocketknife. Cut it through the middle and it'll let loose. I've heard they wouldn't let loose till it thundered, but cut its guts out with a knife and it'll let loose, I'll bet you a dollar."

"Wait, I'll get it. Got it. Feel its fangs leavin' your jaw?"

"No. My jaw is numb."

"Cut his jaw, Brother Frazier, and suck the blood."

"All right."

"You're hit awful close the eye."

"Makes no difference. Cut the bite and suck the blood."

"Let me down in that grave. I'll take that coffin out by myself. I ain't afraid of no copperhead—no grave copperhead can faze me."

And Brother Frazier, short and stocky two-hundred-and-fifty-pounder goes down into the grave. He is a mountain of a man. He lifts one end of the box, coffin and dead woman—he lifts it from the gluey earth. He lifts one end out and puts it upon the grave. The other end of the box rests down in the hole.

Brother Pigg and Brother Redfern are gettin' mighty sick. They were bitten by the first copperhead, the rusty-mouthed grave he-copperhead. Brother Redfern and Brother Pigg are down under the hill by the wire fence. They are wallowin' on the weeds. They are sick enough to die. They have a very high fever, the arm of each man is swollen and numb. They do not know they are wallowin' on the weeds in the graveyard; they know no more than the dead beneath them.

Brother Groan comes up with the button shoes, the dress with the white dot, the black high-crowned hat with the white goose plume. Brother Fain Groan does not have a screwdriver to take the coffin out of the box and the woman out of the coffin that the mountain of a man Brother Frazier lifted out of the grave hole alone. Brother Fain Groan grabs the coal pick. The box boards fly off one by one—these water-soaked coffin box boards. They are all off. Here is the color of an autumn-seasoned beech-stump coffin, rather slim and long the coffin is—but Sister Groan was tall and slender as a bean pole, remember—Brother Groan doesn't have a screwdriver and he puts the sharp end of the coal pick under the coffin lid and he heaves once—only a screak like the tearin' off of old clapboards pinned down with rusty square-wire nails. Another heave and another heave, still another and another—off comes the lid.

"My God Almighty. My wife. My God! My wife! Oh my God, but it is my wife. Perfectly natural too! My God! Oh my God Almighty! My wife!" Brother Groan just wilts over like a tobacco leaf in the sun. He wilts beside his dead wife. She wilted one year ago. The whole night and the copperheads is nothin' to him now. The night is neither dark nor light to him. He knows no more than the dead woman beside him.

"That's Groan's wife all right. See that lip, Brother Sluss."

"Yes, that is Brother Groan's wife all right. Strike a match. See that arm where it is crossed on her breast. That is Brother Groan's wife all right, Brother Frazier."

"She looks like a rotten black-oak stump since the wind hit her on the face, don't she?"

"She looked like a seasoned autumn-beech stump before the wind hit her face didn't she?"

"Yes, she did."

"But she looks like a black-oak stump now."

"No. She looks like a wet piece of chestnut bark."

"Ain't it funny the things the wind can do. Change the looks of a person. Talk with God. Whisper around in the corn like Brother Groan whispers to God."

"What is it that smells like wild onions in a cow pasture?"

"No, that smell to me is like the sour insides of a dead persimmon tree."

"Let's get away from here. Shake Brother Groan. Get him up and let's go."

"Brother Groan won't wake. See how hard I pull his coat collar. He don't breathe. His heart has quit beatin'. Feel! Brother Groan, get up and let's leave here! He's dead sure as the world. Brother Groan is dead! His breath is gone! Let's get out of here!"

"I tell you it don't pay to tamper with the dead."

"The Word says the dead shall be at rest. They shall be buried deep enough not to be bothered by men plowin' and jolt wagons goin' over the tops of them and the cows pickin' the grass from over them. The Word says the dead shall rest."

"I think I ruptured a kidney liftin' that box out awhile ago by myself. No, it don't pay to tamper with the dead."

Brother Frazier and Brother Sluss walk away from the grave. Brother Frazier walks like a bear. He is short, broad man. He has to squeeze between some of the tall tombstones. Brother Sluss does not have any trouble. Here is Brother Littlejohn wallowin' in the graveyard. He tries to get up and he falls back. He acts like a chicken that has lost its head, but Brother Littlejohn has not lost his head, his head is big and swollen. He does not know anymore than the dead beneath him. Here is Brother Shinliver. He lies with his swollen leg propped upon the grave. He, too, is dead, dead as the dead under the ground—dead as Brother Groan; dead as Brother Groan's wife. Brother Pigg and Brother Redfern are lyin' lifeless now; lyin' down beside the wire fence where one first comes into the graveyard. They were tryin' to get home. They couldn't get through four strands of barb wire stretched across the wind. They know no more than the grass beneath them; the dead beneath them. There is vomit all around them on the grass and the dead and the half-dead weeds and the dead leaves. Brother Sluss and Brother Frazier leave the graveyard. They are afraid. They leave the dead there and the sick there with the dead. They go down through the peach orchard, the corn patch, the pig lot and the cow pasture. They are crossin' the cow pasture now—down the path where the pawpaw bushes trim each side of the path. Brother Frazier says: "Brother Groan died beside of his dead wife. Or was that put-on do you suppose? Was he in a trance or was he dead?"

"No, Brother Groan is dead. His heart stopped beatin' and I suppose he is dead. I guess that kills the old clay temple when the heart stops beatin'."

"I don't believe Brother Groan had the right kind of Faith in the Word."

"Let your wife die—be dead a year. Go at midnight and dig her up and look at her and let the moon be shinin' down on them lip-uncovered front teeth of hers and see what it does to you. See if your heart beats. See the pure natural bloom on her face at first. Strike a match and see the wind turn it black right before your eyes while the match is still burnin' and you'd forget all about the Faith in the Word."

"Yes, I saw that. I got sick too. I tell you it don't pay to dig up the dead. The Word says the dead shall have their rest. The Word says the dead die to rest, that they shall be buried deep enough to get their rest without bein' bothered by cattle pickin' grass from over them, wagons makin' tracks over them, men walkin' over them. Then we go out and dig up Brother Groan's wife. It is the Word that filled that grave with copperheads. The copperheads was put in there for a purpose when Brother Groan hid in that chimney butt and hid them tools in there that he stole from the gravediggers. We have worked against the Word."

"I got awful sick there at the grave when the coffin was opened and I saw Groan's wife. Lord, I got sick when I saw that mark on her arm—looked plain-blank like the belly of a young sow. I saw the lip too—a three-cornered lip and it black as a last year's corn shuck. It had long white teeth beneath it and one could see the roots of her front teeth. And then her face was the color of a rotten stump. I saw the face turn black as the match stem burned up in the wind. Lord, I had to leave."

"It wasn't the looks that made me sick. It was that awful scent when the coffin was opened. I smelled somethin' like mushrooms growin' on an old log—a old sour log where the white-bellied water dogs sleep beneath the bark."

"Smelled like wild onions to me."

"I don't believe that Brother Groan had the right kind of Faith. I have never thought it since we was all supposed to meet down there at the Manse Wiffard Gap at that sycamore tree. We was to crucify Brother Groan that night. We was to tie him with a rope to a sycamore limb. And he said his sperit would ride to Heaven right before us on a big white cloud. We went down there and waited around nearly all the night and he never did come. I don't believe he had the right kind of Faith in the Word."

The sun is up. The bright rays of sun, semi-golden fall on the peach tree leaves semi-golden. The oak leaves swirl like clusters of blackbirds in the wind; oak leaves, red, golden, scarlet—semi-golden oak leaves the color of one that stuck to the shovel handle last September. There is fire in the new September day. The wind is crisp to breathe. The tombstones gleam in the sun; the wind has dried the dew off the weeds; the wind has dried and half-dried the vomit on the leaves and the grass and the vomit that still sticks to the lips of the four senseless yet livin' men that lie in the graveyard with the dead.

The neighborhood is astir. They hunt for Fain Groan, Wilkes Redfern, Roch Shinliver, Cy Pigg, Lucas Littlejohn; David Sluss and Elijah Frazier could tell where they are but they are ashamed. They slipped in at their back doors. They are in bed now sleepin' soundly as the dead.

People know here in the neighborhood that Fain Groan has a band of Disciples; that they meet out two and three times each week in the woods and in old houses; but they have always come in before daylight. The neighborhood is astir.

But Constable Ricks sees somethin' from his house. He sees somethin' goin' on up at the graveyard. He has seen plenty of buzzards and crows workin' on the carcasses of dead horses, but he has never seen such swarm in all his life as he now sees upon the hill at the graveyard. He sees crows sittin' up in the wild-cherry tree; enough of them sittin' upon the limbs to break them off. There are the guard crows even. The ground is black with crows. He hears the crows caw-cawin' to each other and to the buzzards tryin' to fight them back. But they are turkey buzzards and they won't be whipped by cornfield crows. They bluff their wing feathers and their neck feathers right out and like fightin' game roosters take right after the crows. The crows give back when they see the turkey buzzards comin'. They don't give back until then. Crows fly from the ground up in the wild-cherry tree and then back to the ground. They change about crow habit, some guard while others eat.

Constable Ricks starts for the Kale Nelson Graveyard. He is ridin' a mule. He leaps the mule up the hill. He sees a pile of fresh dirt before he gets there, he see somethin' like a box on top of the ground, somethin' like a man, somethin' like a pile of clothes. Up to the graveyard and he sees. The crows fly up in a black cloud. The buzzards are very slow about it, but they fly up too. He ties the mule to a fence post. One buzzard alights on the back of the mule and scares him. Constable Ricks rides the mule back fast as the mule can gallop to Coroner Stone's house. He calls Coroner Stone from the corn patch. He jumps on the mule behind Constable Ricks. They gallop the mule back to the graveyard. Here are all the crows and buzzards back and more are comin'.

When they scare the crows and the buzzards off Brother Groan and Brother Groan's wife, they fly down at the lower end of the graveyard, they fly down to somethin' on the ground. Many as can find a place alight on the fence posts. Constable Ricks runs down there and shoos them away and strikes the air at them as they fly with the long-handle shovel he picks up back at the grave. He finds four men on the ground and he finds plenty of sun-dried vomit on the leaves and on the dead weeds. Wilkes Redfern, Roch Shinliver, Cy Pigg, Lucas Littlejohn are lyin' senseless on the ground. Constable Ricks thinks they are dead the way the crows are tryin' to get to them and the way the buzzards are fightin' back the crows from them. He goes up and feels over each heart to see if it is beatin'. All hearts are beatin'. The flesh of each man is cold. The warm September sun has not thoroughly thawed them after the cool night. "Found four men senseless but yet alive, Fred. Come down here. Let's take care of the livin' first." Constable Ricks picks up a clod of dirt and he throws it at the crows with intent to kill. The clod goes through the whole flock of crows and does not touch a feather.

Coroner Fred Stone stays with the dead and livin' at the graveyard while Constable Ricks jumps on the mule and gallops over the neighborhood to tell that he has found the missin' men. Coroner Stone finds the rusty-mouthed copperhead, the she-copperhead and the young copperhead. The snakes are dead, wilted and limber like a dead horse-weed in the sun. He knows the four men have been bitten by copperheads down under the hill by the wire fence where one first comes in the graveyard when walkin' up the path and not ridin' a mule or bringin' a team. He looks at the face of Brother Groan—it is black—black as a wilted pawpapw leaf. It has been picked on by the crows. But picked on is all. His face is old and tough. It is tough as crow meat. Brother Groan's wife's face is the color of a young blackberry sprout hit by a heavy October frost—wilted and soggy black. Her face has been picked on by the crows. Most of it is gone. Coroner Stone looks carefully at the dress with the white dot, the patent leather low-heeled button shoes, the black high-crowned hat with the white goose plume in the side. They are in Brother Groan's left arm; his arm is wound around them like the short stubby body of a copperhead and his dead fingers clutch them like the copperhead's fangs. Before the neighborhood gets back upon the hill and Constable Ricks comes with the spring wagon to haul the four senseless men home, Coroner Stone holds his inquest: "Fain Groan committed suicide when he dug his wife up and looked at her." He said, "I know he planned to dig her up because here are the old clothes I used to see her wear." That was Coroner Stone's duty.

When Constable Ricks comes upon the hill he arrests the dead man. He thinks that is his duty, for he doesn't know much about the Law. He arrests him on the charge of "Public Indecency." Then he says, "My duties have been faithfully performed within the 'sharp eyes' of the Law."

The neighborhood men put Fain Groan's wife back in the coffin and give her a second burial. They hang the copperheads on the fence wires, for they say it is a sign of rain to hang a dead snake on the fence. They throw the four men in the wagon, senseless but livin' men, throw them in like four barrels of salt, throw in Brother Groan with his loose flowing robe like he was a shock of fodder with loose stalks danglin' around the edges and they hurry them off the hill in the spring wagon.

Quinn Snodgrass claims the body of Fain Groan. Fidas Campbell claims him too. Quinn Snodgrass is the brother of Fain Groan's second wife; Fidas Campbell is the brother of Fain Groan's first wife. His third wife didn't have a brother to claim him as it is the custom to be buried by the first wife and that is in keepin' in accordance with the Word. But Quinn Snodgrass got the body of Fain Groan.

It was the first house beside the wagon road and the team pulled up and they carried his body in the house, though his dead body was still under arrest for Public Indecency. That day Quinn shaved the long beard from his face and cut his hair. He pulled the Christlike robe from his body and bathed his body in water heated in the wash kettle, put the moth-eaten minister's suit on him and prepared him for a nice clean burial. Out in the cow shed hammers and handsaws were kept busy all the time makin' his coffin. The next mornin' he was hauled in a jolt wagon with four boys a-sittin' on his coffin to Pine Hill Graveyard and buried beside of his second wife, Symanthia Snodgrass. He was still under arrest for Public Indecency for diggin' up his wife so the crows and the buzzards could expose her parts.

There was a quarrel between Beadie Redfern and Sibbie Frazier over Fain Groan's wife's clothes that were picked up at the grave upon the hill. Sibbie got the hat and shoes and Beadie got the dress. Men came and claimed the tools and thanked whoever found them. Tim Holmes claimed the long-handle shovel. Carlos Shelton claimed the corn scoop. Bridge Sombers claimed the coal pick. All testified they had been missin' since the day they buried Fain Groan's wife the first time, a year ago the day before.

It is tough now to see Cy Pigg and Wilkes Redfern tryin' to plow with one arm. Looks like they both would make a good plowin' team. Wilkes lost his left arm. Cy lost his right arm. It is horrible to watch Lucas Littlejohn tryin' to eat with just one jaw. One can see his teeth grind the food and watch some of it squirm out through the hole in his jaw if one wants to watch it. The doctors couldn't keep the flesh from rottin' and fallin' out though pokeberry roots and sweet milk did heal them. And there is Roch Shinliver, fast as mud, hobblin' around on a wooden leg. People knows his tracks by a big shoe track and a peg hole in the ground. His leg is all there— the bone is there—it has never been taken off where the flesh rotted from the copperhead bite and the muscles rotted and left the white bone.

Betwixt Life and Death

About the story:

"As authentic as a cornfield in August, as crude as a lean-jawed farmer sweating behind his plow, as fresh as a mountain stream, come Jesse Stuart's narratives of the Kentucky hill country," commenced Milton Rugoff's review of Jesse Stuart's second book of short stories, *Men of the Mountains*, in the New York *Herald-Tribune* on March 16, 1941. He praised the author's "Bluff, good-humored exaggeration characteristic of folk tales," such as that in " 'Betwixt Life and Death' wherein the Grayhouse family, in according with Grandpa's will and to the scandal of the county, keeps his body salted down in the attic for six months while they hold a weekly shindig downstairs. . . . "

Lewis Gannett wrote in his column "Books and Things" that Stuart's short stories are

> the dust and sweat, the laughter and anger of the people that he knows best . . . and they are told with the voice, in the old folk way. They begin when the tale begins and stop when it stops. Sometimes they are incidents, sometimes they are rounded stories. But through them all there is a strong sense of the bond between men and their earth—the remembering earth that bears them and covers them over. The apples haven't been shined for Madison Avenue trade—they smell like apples and the juice runs under the knife. . . . And after you have gone a little way in . . . "Betwixt Life and Death" it seems quite natural to you that Grandpa should have wanted his funeral that way. They kept him in the garret until spring, . . . but that was the way he wanted it and that was the way it was.

In an early interview with Jesse Stuart, Raymond Brewster observed, "Surprisingly unspoiled and never shallowly boastful, Stuart nonetheless is endowed with that supreme conceit of the artist that permits him to tell you such and such a story of his is better than Gorki! Or to matter-of-factly link his name with Shakespeare's, Burns' or Milton's in discussing some technical point of his art." Something of Jesse Stuart's open, ingenuous personality emerged in our interview on this story, an excerpt of which follows:

RICHARDSON: Let's look at "Betwixt Life and Death." Grandpa has made
 a will—

STUART: That's one of the best short stories I've ever written.

R.: [Nodding in agreement]. And there's a belated burial that takes place when "the wild roses bloom." Grandpa says, "There will surely be room up in the garret for my coffin until spring."

s.: You know when I came back from the Guggenheim Fellowship, I stopped in New York at the [Prince George] Hotel, and somebody sent me a clipping, whole page of a local paper, that told about my returning . . . and I turned that page over and there was an article that fascinated me. It was about a man . . . right across the Sandy River who they was holding for a funeral, and that was the story. . . . You know what I wish I'd done about that story? . . . Made it a novel and not a short story. . . . *Reader's Digest* published that story—later reprinted it, and paid me a good fee. I believe they paid me $500. . . .

R.: The place then is over at Alcorn across the Sandy River [west of here]? . . .

s.: [Nodding]. In the original short story [I think] I've got the man's real name. . . .

R.: Pa says when he starts to write a sentence on his will, "Betwixt life and death upon this footstool."

s.: Well, haven't you heard the old people call the earth a footstool?

R.: [Nodding slowly]. The earth is God's footstool. Where did you first hear that expression?

s.: I heard it all my life with my parents.*

* * *

"HEP ME IN AT THE DOOR, Lonnie," says Grandpa to Pa. "Don't be so slow about it. My breath is gone. It jest keeps gettin' shorter. I can't get enough wind to keep me goin'."

"I told you, Pap, about goin' out on a mornin' like this," says Pa. "It's

*"Betwixt Life and Death" first appeared in *Esquire*, Vol. 12 (Sept., 1939), pp. 40–41, 132, 134, 136, 138, 140–141, reprinted in *Men of the Mountains* (1941), and most recently in (Lexington: Univ. Press of Ky., 1979), pp. 205–225. The story has been reprinted two other times in *A Jesse Stuart Harvest* (N.Y.: Dell, 1965), Laurel-Leaf Library, pp. 210–227, and in abridged form in *Reader's Digest*, Vol. 40 (Jan., 1942), pp. 46–60, under the title "Sittin' Up for Grandpa." Milton Rugoff, "As Fresh as a Mountain Stream/Jesse Stuart writes Warmly of His Hill Neighbors," New York *Herald-Tribune*, March 16, 1941, clipping in Jesse Stuart, Scrapbook #7, p. 22, M. S. U. Lewis Gannett, "Books and Things" N.Y. *Herald-Tribune*, March 17, 1941, clipping in Jesse Stuart, Scrapbook #7, p. 30, M. S. U. Raymond Brewster, "An Appraisal of Jesse Stuart," Huntington, W. Va., *Herald-Advertiser*, 1936, clipping in Jesse Stuart, Scrapbook #3, p. 32, M. S. U. Jesse Stuart/H. E. Richardson, Interview, W-Hollow, Greenup, Ky., Sept. 2, 1978, pub. in *"Men of the Mountains*: An Interview with Jesse Stuart," *Adena*, Vol. 4, No. 1 (Spring,.1979), p. 20.

zero weather. Snow is on the ground. The frost is siftin' through the trees like corn meal through a sieve."

Pa took Grandpa by the arm. He hepped him up the steps. Icicles were hangin' to his beard. His beard was whiter than the icicles. It was white as the snow that lay on the January hills. Grandpa's hands were shriveled like a sleepin' black snake is shriveled under the dead winter leaves.

"Take me to the bed, Lonnie," says Grandpa to Pa. "I'm blind as a bat. Think it was th' sun shinin' on the snow that caused it. I looked at the hills for the last time. I looked too long. I'm goin' to leave 'em, Lonnie. It will be jest a matter of time. I'll pass to the Great Beyond before sundown."

"Maybe not, Pap," says Pa. He led Grandpa to the feather bed in the front room.

"Here, Pap, is the bed," says Pa, "now lay down and take a nap and you will be all right!"

"Yes," says Grandpa, "I'll be all right, Lonnie. I'm goin' to take a long nap. I'm goin' to take a long trip. I've got a lot I want to tell you. Bring you up a chear and sit down. I want to talk to you. I've jest finished the deed. I've worked on it all last year. I've jest got it finished in time."

Grandpa grunted as he talked. His long white beard fell down across his vest. His shriveled hands looked blue. Grandpa laid and looked at the ceilin'. He talked fast as his breath would let him talk.

"I got my deed writ out before you got your corn gathered, Lonnie," says Grandpa. "I'll tell you, Lonnie, you can't get no place in this world and let your corn stand out and take the weather until January. A good farmer has his corn in the crib before Christmas. Never but once in my life did I miss gettin' my corn in before Christmas! Your Ma was sick then. I had to wait on her and do all the work. I's just eighty then. You're a young man with health in your body, yet you let your corn stand out in the shocks and the mice eat it. You're a young man at sixty-five!"

"Pap, you ain't had no business being out on a cold day like this," says Pa. "Out without socks on your feet and your shirt opened at the collar!"

"I've done it all my life, Son," says Grandpa, "cut timber that way when the weather was twenty degrees below zero. It ain't hurt me yet. If the good Master had seen fit to let me live four more years I would a-been on His footstool five-score years. He calls for me to come home. I am goin' Lonnie, before th' winter sun sets in the cloudy sky!"

It hurt me to hear Grandpa say this. He'd lived with us since I could remember. Wind blowin' over our house top made a wild sound. Just seemed like it was the lonesomest sound I ever heard. Frost flyin' through the bare treetops and the sun shinin' and the hills looked like big mountains of shinin' silver.

"I'm deedin' you the home place, Lonnie," says Grandpa. "I'm deedin' Jim, Mart, Steave, Cy, Ambrose, and Alf a farm apiece. I didn't have a farm for Liz and Nance. Their men can take care of them. I want the name of Grayhouse to go on. I'm deedin' all my children's children a hundred dollars a piece. I don't want them to save it nohow! I don't want 'em buyin' cattle, sheep, and hogs with it. I am makin' it plain in my will that I want them to buy clothes with it. I want them to come dressed to my funeral! I've got the dresses marked in the 'Wish Book' that I want my granddaughters to buy! I've deeded you boys my saddle horses. No better in the land, Lonnie. I want you to ride to the funeral on these horses. I want the saddles shined. I want the bridles shined. I want the horses to look like they did when I took care of 'em!"

"Will we have time to do this, Pap?" says Pa. "Can we get Jim here from Oklahoma? He's down with the fever you know!"

"I want you to wait until he gets well," says Grandpa. "Keep me here at th' house until the girls can buy their dresses and the boys buy their suits o' clothes! Set a day and bury me. Let it be in the spring when the wild roses begin to bloom in the fence rows! I've never dressed fine enough while I lived. You boys never did. I want my grandsons and granddaughters to dress while they live. I want them to look like they've just come out'n a bandbox."

"I'll try to carry out your plans, Pap," says Pa. The tears streamed from Pa's eyes. Pa wiped his beardy face with his hands.

"Try to carry them out," says Grandpa—"you must carry them out. I am dyin' now. I want you to say you will carry them out!"

"I'll carry them out," says Pa. "I'll do just as you say!"

"Put me in the coffin that I've made," says Grandpa. "Put me up in the garret of this house. I want to stay here long as I can. I was born and raised in this house. I was married in this house. I raised my family here and I will die here before the sun sets today. There will surely be room up in the garret for my coffin until spring! Keep me until Jim gets over the fever and can get here from Oklahoma. I know it is a fur piece he has to come. Be sure to give him plenty of time."

"I'll do it, Pap," says Pa. "I'll do just as you say."

"Have a settin' up a night a week and let the young people come here and have a good time," says Grandpa. "I didn't have enough of a good time when I was a little shaver. Pap worked us too blasted hard. I want my grandchildren to have a good time. That's about all I can think of, Lonnie, just now. I hear the death bells! Have a good time, take care of the horses, and hold to the land. I've got it fixed so it can't leave the name of Grayhouse. Let the children enjoy themselves—I'm goin'—on my long trip!"

That's the last Grandpa said. He went to sleep. Died just so easy. I watched Grandpa die. Pa stood by and saw the last breath leave 'im. Grandpa was layin' across the feather bed in the front room. Pa wiped the tears from his eyes. He walked out'n the room. "I can't stand it," says Pa— "just to think Pap changed that way in his old days. I wonder if he was in his right mind."

"Yes, Grandpa was in his right mind," I says. "You know he was in his right mind. He worked until last year. The last thing he did was cut the brush from the fence rows. It took him a year to make the deed. He had so much writin' and so much figurin' to do with all his land, horses, and cattle. He had so many to give it to. Grandpa just sees what he's missed in life. He's missed a good time and a lot of fine clothes. I'll take my hundred dollars and buy clothes. I'll dress fit to kill. I'll get me a girl and I'll do some sparkin'. Worked here all the time and I never go anyplace!"

"It'll be all right I guess," says Pa. "Pap jest never teached us like that. He used to make us work. He used to say, 'If you spare the rod you'll spile the child.' He ust to get us out'n bed at night and whop us. W'y he's done more work than any man I know among these Kentucky hills. He's got the land bound up until we can't sell it. We haf to deed it to a male heir by the name of Grayhouse."

"Now you know he's in his right mind," I says, "'r he wouldn't a done that."

"Son, get on the mule," says Pa, "and go over the deestrict and norate that Pap is dead. When they come tonight we'll read parts of his will and explain to the people that we'll put him away now and bury him later in the spring. We'll bury him when the girls have time to buy their fine clothes and Brother Jim gets over the fever and can get back here from Oklahoma. Th' other children can get to th' funeral anytime."

"All right, Pa," I says, "I'd better tell Ma to come home from Sister Rachel's. I'll tell her Grandpa is dead."

It was a cold time. I saw the sun goin' down like a fadin' ball of fire over the hills beyond Little Sandy River. "Just as Grandpa said," I thought. "Said he would be a dead man before the sun got down."

I remembered hearing Grandpa say, "When a child is born it is a sunrise. The sun goes up over the sky through the long day. That is a lifetime. Then the sun sets. Man is dead. His work is done."

The wind nearly took me out'n the saddle. The frost flew into my face. It made tears come to my eyes. The wind stung my face. I felt the sting of cold chillin' th' blood in my veins. I rode to every house in the deestrict. I told them to come tonight to the settin' up. When I told Ma that Grandpa was dead she wouldn't believe me.

"W'y he et two eggs for his breakfast, seven biscuits, milk gravy and bacon like he's done for the past thirty years," says Ma. "He drunk two cups of strong black coffee without sugar or cream in 'em." Ma hurried home. Sister Rachel come with her.

When people come to our house through the flying night frost they would say before they got beside the fire to warm, "W'y I'm surprised about the death of Doug Grayhouse. I've been seein' him goin' over the farm every day. It is a big surprise."

They would ask what Grandpa had done with all his money, his land, and his fine saddle horses. Pa would tell them he willed it to his children and his money to forty-nine grandchildren. He would tell them he didn't have enough to will to his thirty-six great grandchildren or his five great-great grandchildren.

The first night we sung a few songs. Brother Combs preached a few words. The neighbor men dressed Grandpa—put him in his weddin' suit and put him in the wild cherry coffin he had made. It had been seasonin' fifteen years up in the garret. Pa, Brother Raymond, Uncle Cy, and Uncle Alf carried it down from the garret. Grandpa was laid away in his coffin.

"It bothers me to know," says Pa, "how I'm goin' to keep Pap up there. It is all right to keep him up there now in this cold spell. But what will happen when th' spell breaks?"

"I'll tell you how they kept my Pap for forty days," says Washington Nelson. "They put his coffin in a big box and put salt around it. Had about a foot layer of salt all around the coffin. It preserved Pap all summer!"

"Then that would preserve Pap until spring wouldn't it, Wash?" says Pa.

"Oh yes," says Wash. "Ain't no danger o' nothin' when you got a foot of salt around the coffin. You could keep 'im five years up there in the garret like that."

"Then tomorrow we'll make a big box and put Pap's coffin in it," says Uncle Cy. "We'll haul out about ten barrels o' salt from town and put around 'im. That will keep 'im until spring."

The crowd didn't do a lot of laughin' and talkin' until we got Grandpa carried up in the garret. Then the women went to talkin' to one another like nothin' had ever happened. They shook hands and talked about knittin' socks, piecin' quilts, and plaitin' rugs. The men talked about farmin'.

Oh, sometimes someone would say: "Doug Grayhouse was a good man. He'll be missed in th' deestrict."

"The Lord kept Doug Grayhouse here for a long time. Must a-had a purpose in mind when He done it."

Just the old people would say things like these. The young people acted just like Grandpa wanted them to act. They had a good time. There was a lot of sparkin' goin' on among us. Gracie Thombs come. I liked her looks a lot. Cousin Willie Grayhouse, Uncle Cy's boy, watched her too. I could tell that he liked Gracie. He tried to set next to her. I got the closest. It pleased Gracie a lot to watch both of us tryin' to get the closest to her.

January was a cold month. Snow laid on the hills. The wind whipped through the lonesome oak tops. It made the sound of a mournful turtle dove. When I heard the wind in the oak tops above the house, it made me feel sad. When I heard the wind in the pine tops I wanted to cry. It made me think of Grandpa. I'd think about Grandpa up in the garret with all that salt around 'im. I'd wonder if Grandpa was a spirit, flyin' about the house like a night owl. I thought he might be a screech owl in one of the oak trees in our barn lot—sittin' there in the cold with his feathers all ruffled up. I'd think Grandpa might be a spirit, you couldn't see—that he might be goin' through the big rooms of the house my Great Grandpa built. When I heard the wind I was scared to death. I couldn't help it. It brought Grandpa back to me. I was afraid to go upstairs to bed and to think that Grandpa was only a floor above me. One night I dreamed he come to my bed and patted me on the head. I choked until I couldn't speak to him.

Pa would get Grandpa's will and read a little bit of it every day. Pa would put the will in the trunk after he read awhile in it. Pa would wipe tears from his eyes. "I'll tell you, time changed Pap a lot," Pa would say. "I never thought a man could change so after he reached ninety. Every time Pa started to write a sentence in the will he would say: 'Betwixt Life and death, upon this footstool.' Then Pap would go on and bring out what he wanted to say. He wants the young people to come here once a week until he's buried. He wants them to play *Skip To My Lou*. He wants 'em to even have dances! He wants them to drink if they feel like drinkin'. Pap's will even sounds crazy in places! I will do just what I told Pap. I told him on his death bed that I'd see that what he wanted was carried out. I don't like to do it. But I'm afraid Pap will come back to me and haunt me if I break my promise. I look for him every mornin' when I get up to build a fire at four o'clock. Pap allus got up when I got up to build a fire. 'Early to bed,' he allus said, 'early to rise, makes a man healthy, wealthy and wise.' "

"Yes," says Ma, "we want to do everything your Pap wanted. If we don't, this house will be haunted eternally. Doors will fly open. There will be knockin' on the walls. A red dog will run over top the roof. There will be noises like somebody ripping off the shingles. Do everything Pap Grayhouse wanted you to do. I don't want to spend the rest of my years in misery. I'm scared to death now to think that I live and work beneath 'im. It's hard for me to believe he's up in the garret awaitin' burial when the wild roses begin to bloom in the fence rows!"

Pa got a letter from Uncle Jim's boy John. He said he was glad to get his hundred dollars that Grandpa had willed him. Said he would strut out in new clothes now. Said he would show the girls in Oklahoma a good time.

"If Cousin John can show the girls in Oklahoma a good time," I thought, "then I can show the girls in Kentucky a good time. I'll show one a good time. I'll show Gracie Thombs a good time. If Cousin Willie Grayhouse hadn't got a hundred dollars too! If Grandpa had just left him out'n the will! But Grandpa hadn't! I'd just haf to fight it out with 'im. I'd get Gracie Thombs!"

We had the settin' up every Friday night. That's the night Grandpa said for us to have it in his will. He said if we had it on Saturday night, we could only stay up until twelve. After that was Sunday and we broke the Sabbath. Said for us to have it every Friday night and stay up all night if we wanted to. Grandpa said we wouldn't do much work on Saturday anyway since it was so close to Sunday. Said since he'd grown older and a little wiser, that he believed people ought to take Saturdays off anyway. Said too much work and not enough play made "Jack a dull boy." Then, think of Pa thinkin' Grandpa was not in his right mind when he wrote his will! It hurt me to think Pa had said these words. Pa just hadn't lived as long as Grandpa! If Pa ever lived that long he might agree with Grandpa's will. My young days would be over then. I wouldn't care about dressin' in good clothes, sparkin' girls, and dancin' all night.

We had four settin' ups in January. Gracie was there every time. We played *Skip To My Lou*. I skipped with Gracie. Cousin Willie got mad. He'd break in everytime he had a chance. "I'm as good a-lookin' as you," I thought. "I'm as old as you. Why ain't I got the same chance as you to get Gracie? She smiles at me more than she does you. She skips with me more. Why don't you take Murtie Perkins and let me have Gracie Thombs? Murtie loves you. You won't pay her any mind. People are talkin' about the way we're fightin' over Gracie, and Grandpa a corpse up in the garret!"

We had four times as many young people at the last settin' up we had in January as we did the first one. Young people heard about what Grandpa had said in his will fur and near. They come in droves. Some of them didn't know Grandpa and they didn't know us. They didn't have anyplace to go among the hills in the winter time and they just come to the settin' up. They joined in our games. They had a good time. The winter nights didn't get too dark for them. The roads didn't get too muddy or too long and the snow didn't get too deep. The young people come.

It was in February that I fell deeper in love with Gracie Thombs. I begin to think I couldn't do without her. I could shet my eyes and see her standin' before me. I could see her purty brown curly hair. I could see her blue eyes. I could hear her laugh. I could feel the touch of her hand like I felt when we were skippin'. I was in love with Gracie Thombs. Cousin Willie's Ma told my Ma that her boy Willie was wild about Gracie. Said she wished there was some way to stop the settin' ups. Said they'd become a nuisance and the whole country was talkin' about them. Said they was talkin' about the way the young people were actin'. Ma told Pa about what Aunt Emma had said.

"I can't hep it," says Pa. "I can't hep how much the people talk. They will just haf to talk. I've got to do what I told Pap I would do. He is up in the garret. Maybe, Pap hears every word I'm sayin'. I hope Pap does. I can't go against a promise I made 'im on his death bed. I'll do what I promised Pap I would do no matter if I don't believe in the foolish idears Pap got in his head after he passed ninety. I'll do what I promised if it does go against the grain. I don't want Pap's spirit to follow me and haunt me in this house the rest of my days. I don't want to ride one of Pap's fine saddle horses to Pap's funeral either. I know the other boys won't. It will look funny to see seven of us boys on seven thoroughbred horses ridin' to our father's funeral but we'll haf to do it."

At the settin' ups in February we had a few dances. We had Willie Sizemore's jug band. We stayed up nearly all night long. What a time we had! I wanted to see Friday come all week. Pa worked us so in the fields. "Children you can frolic on Friday night but remember you are under my thumb durin' the week. Now forget about Friday night. Bend down on your hoe handles. Bend down on your ax handles. Bend down on your mattock handles. Spend a little elbow grease! You're drivin' me crazy talkin' about Friday night!"

Just like January, we had a cold February. The heavy snow laid on the ground. Just seemed like it loved the ground so much it would not leave. The deep snow and the cold wind held back the old people. They wouldn't come to the settin' up. A lot of them thought Grandpa was out'n his mind when he made his will. "W'y old Doug Grayhouse was a fine man. He was a Christian man. What got into him in his old days—after he passed ninety that he wanted the young people of the hills to leave the plow and come in every Friday night and kick up their heels at a shindig under his dead body! Peared like he wanted to be where he could hear their love makin'. Peared like he wanted to be where he could hear the old dance tunes and the clickin' of their brogan heels on the puncheon floor! You can't tell about people! That's the strangest thing I ever heard of here among the hills! Wants to wait until the wild roses bloom in the fence rows before they bury him. Wants to wait until Jim gets over with the fever in Oklahoma."

It was the last of February when we heard from Uncle Jim. "I'm out'n bed now," he said in his letter, "but my hair has all come out. I hate to come home without hair on my head. I know it will come back in a few months' time. I hope I'll have hair on my head by the first of June! Don't bury Pap before I get there. I ain't seen Pap for forty years. I want to see him no matter if he is a corpse. It will be a great day for me. I'll get to see all my brothers and my sisters and all of their children. It will be like a family reunion."

We had to get the corn ground turned in March. The snow melted and left the hills and we had worlds of work to do. The snow had laid on the ground too long. We had our terbacker beds to turn and sow. March nearly worked us to death. We had corn ground to get ready. Stalks and sprouts to turn under so they'd be mellowed for the corn roots. We had fences to mend so we could turn the sheep and cattle in the pastures. We had sassafras sprouts to cut out'n the young wheat before they got so tall they'd shade the wheat. Everybody worked along the Little Sandy. All the boys and girls in the deestrict were workin' but they found time to come to the settin' ups. They come in from the fields tired and they went away rested.

April came and we had the fences mended. We had the sheep in the pastures. We had the cows on the grass. We had the thoroughbred horses on grass. We had the sprouts cut from the wheat. We had most of the corn ground turned. We had the terbacker ground ready. We's just gettin' along fine with the work. The birds come back to build in the boxes Grandpa had fixed for 'em. When I'd see the wrens comin' back to the coffee sacks filled with rags in the smoke house, I'd think of Grandpa. He'd fixed the rag sacks for them and a lot of tin cans and water buckets he'd hung up for them to build in. The wrens and the martins would fly about the house and barn. They'd light on the comb of the house. I wondered if Grandpa could hear their footprints above him on the clapboard roof. I had a lot of thoughts like this. Pa must a thought a lot too. He'd stand and watch these birds buildin' their nests. Grandpa loved the birds. The birds loved him. They'd fly down from the top of the house and barn and eat bread from his hands.

The oak trees leafed out. The wild rose vines leafed along the fence rows. Great masses of 'em leafed along the roads that led over the place. I wished Grandpa could just be back for a day in the spring and walk over his farm here among the Kentucky hills. I know he'd like it! I could just see him now walkin' along lookin' at the oaks when the buds started swellin' and sap come back to their veins. I could see him lookin' at the wild rose stems along the fence rows. I could see him take his mattock and cut the sprouts from the fence rows and leave the wild rose stems stand.

"It takes clean fence rows to make a purty farm," Grandpa used to say. "Wild roses look good along the fence rows in June."

I'll tell you I was glad to see spring come back. I was glad to see the creeks fill with blue waters from the high hills. I was glad to see the little lambs taggin' after their mammies. I was glad to see the horses run and kick up their heels. Grandpa used to like to watch them. "That is the young life in a horse that makes him kick up his heels," Grandpa used to say. "He will slow down soon enough. It all comes betwixt life and death."

I was just glad that spring had come. I wasn't scared like I was last winter. Ma wasn't scared half as bad to hear a wind rustlin' among the tender leaves on the oak trees as she was to hear a winter wind moan through the bare limbs on the oaks and whistle among the corn stubble in January.

I could see Gracie Thombs pass our house now. She was barefooted goin' to the store. I'd see her takin' a basket of eggs to the store. She was so purty. She was just like the spring. It made me love Grandpa more than I ever did. Just think if it hadn't been for Grandpa's will I'd never got to a-been with Gracie every Friday night! The young couples almost doubled in April. They heard about the big settin' ups we's havin'. They flocked from every hollow among the hills. "If th' crowd keeps multiplyin'," says Pa, "I don't know where we're goin' to put 'em. It's two months yet before we can bury Pap accordin' to the last words in his will. Pap's got that will worked out wonderfully well. He didn't spend the last year of his life for nothin'."

It was in May. The wild rose buds had started to swell. The corn was peepin' through the ground on the high hill slopes. The lambs were gettin' big enough to eat grass. We had started settin' terbacker plants. "The time is gettin' near," says Pa, "that we bury Pap. I hate to see my father go under the green grassy ground. I guess the ground will be good as the garret. But seems like when we have put him under the ground we have lost him. When we have him in the garret, it seems like he is closer to us. But I'll be glad to see Pap put under the ground. The crowds at the settin' up are gettin' too big. It's the talk of this county and the wind forever blowin' among the tree tops and keepin' your Ma scared to death. It is a great worry to me. I didn't know what all was in that will when I made the promises to Pap on his death bed last January."

It was in May when all of Grandpa's grandchildren got their hundred dollar checks to buy their fine clothes. I'll never forget when I got mine. Grandpa said in the will: "Don't write the checks out to my grandchildren until May. I want their clothes to look good at my funeral." He went on and said a lot more about how to take care of the clothes before the funeral and atter the funeral, he would advise us to take care of our clothes, yet he didn't care if we plowed in our new suits since they belonged to us, we could do as we pleased with them.

When Ma opened the "Wish Book" she turned the pages where Grandpa had turned the corners down. In his will Grandpa said: "In the 'Wish Book' you will find the dresses I want my granddaughters to wear at my funeral. They are the prettiest dresses I have found in the whole book. They are plenty long and decent." Ma read what it said about these dresses and that they should be worn at night to parties and dances.

"I can't understand," says Ma, "what got into your Grandpa's head. Have you to wear dresses that girls wear to dances at his funeral. But they are long and purty and I guess they are all right. You will haf to dress like your Grandpa requested in his will."

The girls ordered their dresses. The boys ordered their suits. I got me a gray suit with a blue pin stripe runnin' up and down it. I'll tell you it was a beauty. I got a pair of shoes, socks, striped neckties and a dozen shirts. I spent every cent of my hundred dollars for clothes just like Grandpa requested.

"When Cousin Willie thinks he'll out-dress me for the funeral," I thought, "he'll be mistaken. I'll show him who'll look the best to Gracie on Grandpa's funeral day!"

We'd had the second settin' up on the second Friday of May. There was some crowd. The house was so full part of us had to dance in the yard! We tied lanterns up among the oak limbs and went on like we'd done since last January. The Sizemore band played and we danced on a platform built o' planks. I danced with Gracie. I forgot Grandpa was up in the garret. I forgot how scared I was last winter when the snow was heavy on the ground and the wind made such a lonesome sounds among the oaks. The wind made purty rustlin' sounds now among the green leaves on the oaks. I forgot about thinking Grandpa's spirit might be in a screech owl that roosted in the oaks in our barnlot. I forgot what Grandpa had said about the wild roses in the fence rows. I forgot everything about Grandpa when I danced with Gracie. If it just wasn't for Cousin Willie Grayhouse, everything would have been all right.

Maybe Cousin Willie didn't like me. Maybe he hated me more than I hated him. I didn't know. I didn't care. I had my mind made up if he fooled with me I'd beat the face off'n him. I told him that one night at the settin' up when he jumped in and danced with Gracie. He had the impudence to say: "The time will come when we'll fight this thing out. We'll fight to a finish. One of us has to conquer the other. The one who whops gets Gracie."

"Cousin Willie," I says, "I'll take you up on that. I'll fight you tonight. I'll beat your damned head into the ground."

"I don't want to dirty my new suit of clothes tonight," says Cousin Willie. "It's the first time I ever wore a long suit of clothes, I don't want to ruin 'em on you."

"I've got on my first suit of clothes," I says. "It's the first time I've ever wore long clothes. But I'll ruin my suit to beat you up."

"I've got more sense than to fight tonight," says Cousin Willie. "Wait until I'm in my old work clothes. Then we'll just see who gets Gracie."

I took a swing at Willie. The crowd come in and stopped us. I would a hit Willie right there. I couldn't hep if it was at the settin' up. I couldn't hep it if Grandpa was right above us. My blood was riled and I'd a-fit Cousin Willie Grayhouse all over the hill. I was in love with Gracie. I'd got so I didn't care who knowed it. I was a little bashful at first. But that wore away. Now I had my new suit of clothes and I wasn't goin' to be out-done by a first cousin. I didn't like Willie. He had the same blood in his veins that I had but that didn't make no difference. I'd taken enough off'n him. I wasn't goin' to take any more.

"I believe there's drinkin' goin' on at the settin' ups," says Pa, one mornin' at the breakfast table. "There's a lot of glass laying around all over this yard. It looks like broken bottles to me. If I find bottles of licker out there I don't know what I'll do!"

I thought Pa might pour the whisky out. I told the boys about it. We worked out a way. We tied the horse quarts of whisky up in the oak trees by the necks. Pa would never find them then. When we wanted a quart one of the boys went up the trees and cut the string and brought back the quart. One night Pa and Ma were out watchin' us dance. They stood under the oak. They heard the wind blowin' the bottles together.

"Listen, Gurtie," says Pa, "that's the funniest sound I ever heard made by the rustlin' o' leaves in th' wind. It may be Pap's spirit over here. He might be sorry for the rope he's given these youngins. They've whopped the older folks from the settin' ups!"

Ma never said a word. She just looked at Pa. Then she watched us dance. The platform was so full we barely had room to dance. It looked like we's goin' to haf to build another platform.

It was on the first day of June when Pa got a letter from Uncle Jim. "I'll be home June 10th for the funeral," Uncle Jim wrote in his letter, "have everything ready. My children have their clothes. They can hardly wait to come. I dread ridin' a thoroughbred saddle horse to Pap's funeral. Pap must not have been in his right mind when he put sicha foolishness in his will. That don't sound like the Pap I had. He used to make me read the Bible two hours every Sunday before he'd let me go to the river to swim."

"Wait until he reads Pap's will," says Pa, "he'll find that Pap changed his mind atter he passed ninety. He'll be surprised at Pap's will. He'll see what a time I have had to see that Pap's will was carried out as Pap wanted it done. I'll never see that another will is fulfilled. It's had me worried to death. From last January until this June has put ten years on top my head. I'm ten years an older man."

We had our last settin' up the first Friday in June. I'll tell you the house was full and the yard was full. We had our dances goin' and all kinds of games. We had our bottles up among the green leaves of the fruitful oaks. I danced every dance with Gracie. Cousin Willie was so mad at me he could bite a spike nail in two. He acted like he wanted to fight me all night. Our settin' up didn't end until the moon went down in the mornin' and the roosters had started crowin'. I just wondered what Grandpa thought about the good times we's havin' now. I believe if Grandpa knowed how much better our good times was a-gettin' he wouldn't a-been buried until summer was over—maybe not until snow fell again. I was havin' the best time I'd ever had in my life. But it was time for the funeral now. Our good times must come to an end. Three more days and Grandpa would be under the ground. I'll never forget takin' Gracie home Saturday mornin' atter th' last settin' up. I come back along the fence row just as the sun was gettin' up— while the dew was still on the weeds. I never saw wild roses purtier in my life. I never saw the place as purty. Terbacker was lookin' so good in the long curved rows around the high hill slopes. The corn was gettin' up to a mule's knees.

"Grandpa picked a purty time to be buried," I thought. "He couldn't have picked a purtier time in Kentucky!"

I wish you could have seen the crowd at Grandpa's funeral. It was like a homecomin'. I met my first cousins in Oklahoma. I'd never seen them before. Pa shook hands with all his brothers. I saw my sisters among the twenty-seven granddaughters of Grandpa's. All the girls were dressed in long dresses that swept the ground. They wore white slippers and golden slippers. The dresses didn't have any back in 'em. I'll tell you they looked good.

"It's a funny idear of Pap's," says Uncle Jim, "about the girls wearin' sicha dresses to his funeral. I guess if he wanted it—we haf to abide by his will."

"Yes," says Pa, "his will has been properly carried out and we can't afford to break it now."

The girls didn't have nary two dresses the same color. Grandpa's twenty-two grandsons were dressed fit to kill. "I wish Grandpa," I says, "could be here and see us now. He would be proud of his blood kin. He would see us dressed fit to see the President of the United States."

The grave had been dug two days before. The wagon and the mules were waitin' to haul Grandpa to his last restin' place. We hadn't carried him down from the garret. It was a crazy thought, I guess, but I thought: "What if Grandpa is not in the garret. Wouldn't it be a joke. What if Grandpa had come to life and got out and slipped away? What if Grandpa had become young again?"

Pa, Uncle Jim, Uncle Cy, and Uncle Alf went up in the garret and let him down with ropes to the upstairs. They took the coffin out'n the box of salt and carried it downstairs. Pa looked a little shaky when he started to take the screws out'n the coffin. When he raised the lid he says: "Pap's just as natural as he was the day we put him in here."

We marched past and looked at Grandpa for our last time.

"Looks just like he did before I went to Oklahoma," says Uncle Jim. Uncle Jim had his hat off. I couldn't keep from looking at his head. I'd told Gracie about Uncle Jim losin' his hair when he had the fever. I saw her lookin' at Uncle Jim's head too. The hair had sorty come back.

You should have seen us as we went to the graveyard. The mules and wagon were in front with Grandpa. Pa and all his brothers were on Grandpa's thoroughbred horses. They rode up next to the wagon. The horses pranced and twisted and stood on their hind feet. Then all of Grandpa's granddaughters and grandsons come next. Then the rest of the kinsfolks. Then there was a whole army of young couples that had been comin' to the settin' ups. It was the biggest funeral we ever had at Oak's Chapel. Brother Combs preached Grandpa's funeral in the chapel. Sister Reeves played the organ and we sung a lot of songs. I was with Gracie. Cousin Willie sat right over from us. He looked at us all the time Brother Combs preached the funeral. I thought he was goin' to try something just by the way he looked.

It was when they carried Grandpa out'n the church house, many of Grandpa's friends carried wreaths of flowers to put on his grave. There were many wreaths of wild roses. . . . When they started to put them down by the side of the grave one rolled off'n the pile. I picked it up and put it back on the stack. Cousin Willie reached down and fixed it on the stack another way. It was right in front of all of our people and a lot of our neighbors. Then Willie looked hard at me. He was just mad because I was with Gracie. I tried to punch him in the nose and Uncle George held me. Uncle Jim grabbed Cousin Willie. "You can't fight here, boys," says Uncle George.

We stood and looked at one another all the time they's lowerin' Grandpa in the grave. Before they got him down, while Uncle George and Uncle Jim were watchin' Grandpa lowered with the check lines, I lunged at Cousin Willie and give him a haymaker on the chin. He sprawled on the ground in his new suit of clothes. He got up and come at me again. The second haymaker I handed him, he stayed on the ground.

"Stop that fight, George," says Pa. He come runnin' over.

"Ain't no fight to it," I says, "I hit Cousin Willie and he hit the ground."

"It's awful," says Uncle Cy, "you boys fightin' at Pap's funeral. I'd be ashamed."

Cousin Willie was down on the ground moanin' and goin' on. Cousin Willie was cussin'. He wouldn't a-done it but he's out'n his head.

"Let 'em fight," says Uncle Ambrose. "It's a good sign that the Grayhouse blood ain't losin' it's color."

"Come on, Gracie," I says, "let's go home."

I took Gracie by the arm. Aunt Emma was fannin' Cousin Willie when I left. The crowd was divided. Part o' 'em was standin' around Cousin Willie while the rest o' 'em watched th' men lower Grandpa into the grave.

Yoked for Life

About the story:

Of his Uncle Jesse Hilton, a frequent model for Jesse Stuart's Uncle Jeff stories, the author wrote that his relative

> came to spend a few days with us. He stayed twenty years. Uncle Jeff had been married and was the father of a large family. Now that his wife was dead, his children married, he had no place to go. My mother, who was his sister, took him in, gave him a room, bed, and food, and washed and mended his clothes. Since we needed a farm hand, Uncle Jeff worked for us. . . . After Uncle Jeff came to live with us, a sort of rivalry built up between him and my father about who had the most knowledge of land and farming.

Man and character, Uncle Jeff "took to drink." He is described in another story, "A Stall for Uncle Jeff," as weighing "Two hundred and seventy pounds!" and "when he took to drinking in earnest he was more trouble than a cold-collared mule in February." Often Jesse Stuart and his brother, James, "had to go fetch Uncle Jeff. . . . " The author also had an Uncle Jesse *Stuart*, his father's brother, who was a model for such stories as "Uncle Jeff," which appeared in *Head o' W-Hollow*. But Uncle Jesse *Hilton* was the model for such stories as "Uncle Jeff and the Family Pride," "Uncle Jeff Had a Way," and "Uncle Jeff Had a Fault." He was also quite a yarn spinner, as Pa acknowledges in "Yoked for Life," and is the narrator of this powerful story of strange characters, which deals so memorably with submerged horror and superstition, and an even stranger fate.*

*Jesse Stuart wrote of his Uncle Jesse Hilton in his *"Author's Introduction"* to "Uncle Jeff Had a Way," *A Jesse Stuart Reader* (N.Y.: McGraw-Hill, 1963), pp. 32–33. Jesse Stuart, "A Stall for Uncle Jeff," *Esquire*, Vol. 19 (Feb., 1943), pp. 60–61, 105, reprinted in *God's Oddling* (N.Y.: McGraw-Hill, 1960), pp. 98–108; quotations here are from pp. 98–99. The author's Uncle Jesse *Stuart*, his father's brother, however, is the model for such stories as "Uncle Jeff," *Head o' W-Hollow* (Lexington: Univ. Press, of Ky.), reprinted ed., pp. 93–104, and should not be confused with the model Uncle Jesse *Hilton*. "Uncle Jeff and the Family Pride" was first published in *Esquire*, Vol. 44 (Dec., 1955), pp. 119, 187–188, 190, reprinted in *My Land Has a Voice* (N.Y.: McGraw-Hill, 1966), pp. 219–232. "Uncle Jeff Had a Way," Southwest Review, Vol. 43 (Autumn, 1958), pp. 313–319, reprinted in *Best Articles and Stories*, Vol. 3 (May, 1959), pp. 4–8, and in *A Jesse Stuart Reader*, pp. 32–44. "Uncle Jeff Had a fault" appeared in *Southwest Review*, Vol. 59 (Summer, 1974), pp. 254–261. Jesse Stuart's short story "Yoked for Life" was originally published in *University Review*, Vol. 30 (1964), pp. 264–272, and reprinted in *My Land Has a Voice*, pp. 13–27.

"**B**UT YOU must not shudder and quiver when we talk about the living things of God's creation," Uncle Jeff said. "I know the subject of snakes is not a very polite one. And I know people don't want to hear about 'em. But why I brought up the subject of snakes is that it fits into a defect in our human society."

I didn't know what Uncle Jeff's line of thought for the evening conversation was going to be. But I knew when he got to talking about a favorite subject it was hard to get him stopped. He liked to talk, and when he started telling one of his favorite stories he wouldn't stop. Well, he might have stopped if we had got up and left the room.

"Now you take old Seymour Pratt," Uncle Jeff said. "He's our neighbor and friend. How many wives do you think he's had?"

"Well, I can remember three," Sister Mary said.

"I remember four of Seymour's wives," I said.

"I'm older than you, Shan," Sister Sophia said. "I remember five."

"I remember Seymour's wife Bertha," Pa said. "I'm not nearly as old as Jeff. Bertha made six wives."

"He had one more," Uncle Jeff said. "Tillie Pruitt was his first wife."

"What happened to all of his wives?" Brother Finn asked. Now my brother Finn was nine years younger than I was. "I didn't know Seymour Pratt had so many wives. What did he do with all of 'em?"

"Uncle Jeff, what has this got do with snakes?" Sister Glenna asked.

"It's got a lot to do with snakes," Uncle Jeff said.

"Stop interrupting your Uncle Jeff," Mom said. "Let him continue with his story. When Brother Jeff talks, he always has something to say."

When Mom said this, Pa turned his head and smiled. And often when Uncle Jeff was talking at his best to us on the long winter evenings before the fire, he had had a little nip from his bottle. And Uncle Jeff's nipping was another story which he never told. But this was why he was living with us. He had been married and was the father of eight children. They were all married now and had homes of their own. And his wife, Aunt Mettie, was dead. But before her death, she and Uncle Jeff had lived apart for twenty years. They were never divorced, but they were separated. She stayed in their old home, and Uncle Jeff came to live with us.

"Now you asked about old Seymour's wives," Uncle Jeff continued. "Three are dead, and four are living. I guess old Seymour and his seventh wife, Hattie Sprouse Pratt, are having some awful battles. I hear they've been in court, but Judge Rivercomb shamed old Seymour and told him he'd had enough wife trouble and to settle down and behave himself. Now, old Seymour's troubles have caused me to think of the snakes. And right now I'm thinking of the copperhead."

"Oh, Jeff," Mom said, "one bit me once and I lived. And one bit you once and you lived. Why bring up the copperhead?"

"Because the copperhead is the meanest snake, the most dangerous and deadly of all snakes we have in these parts," Uncle Jeff said. "Remember, Mollie, when the copperhead bit you, you disturbed him, didn't you? You reached your hand under a tobacco stalk to pull the grass away and you put your hand right on him. He was under the cool leaves away from the summer sun, taking his afternoon nap. You scared him, and he bit your hand. Once I was plowing tobacco and stepped on one beside a rock in the tobacco balk. And he jumped up from his sleep and grabbed my leg. But we lived, Mollie! And I like to think we lived for a purpose. See, we look at any kind of snake as being something evil. And we think there is more evil in the copperhead, because he's the meanest of all snakes."

"I agree with you, Jeff," my father said.

My father seldom agreed with Uncle Jeff on anything. And maybe the reason was, he could never tell a story like Uncle Jeff. We liked to hear Uncle Jeff talk, but not about snakes. Uncle Jeff was a big man. He weighed three hundred seven pounds. He was six feet two, and there were no bulges on his powerful body. He was a muscular man with arms as big as small fence posts, legs at the calves as big as gate posts, and hands as big as shovels. His big head sat almost squarely on his shoulders, and a stranger had to look twice to see if he had any neck. He had a kind face and big blue eyes. His head was bald on top and there was a rim of white hair around the base of his head. He had to have shirts, shoes, gloves, pants made for himself. The only ready-made clothes he could buy to fit him were a necktie and a hat. We had to make a special chair for him to sit on, and once one of our beds broke down with him in it asleep.

A person who had never seen Uncle Jeff before might have thought he was as mean among men as the copperhead snake was among snakes. But Uncle Jeff didn't hunt. He wouldn't kill anything. He wouldn't even kill a poisonous copperhead. Once in the field I saw him shoo one away.

"Why did you do that, Uncle Jeff?" I asked.

"It was put here for a purpose," he said. "Besides, the copperhead has his own enemies."

"Who are his enemies?" I asked Uncle Jeff.

"The blacksnake and the terrapin," he replied. "And man isn't exactly friendly to the copperhead."

I didn't know a blacksnake and a terrapin could kill a copperhead until Uncle Jeff told me.

"Now the copperheads wed for life," Uncle Jeff said, looking up at the ceiling. "Oh, I'm not sure whether a pair might separate or not. I suppose they do. But when the old he-copperhead gets killed, the old she-copperhead becomes a widow. And if the old she-copperhead gets squeezed to death by a blacksnake, or chewed to death by a stud terrapin, then the old he-copperhead becomes a widower. The love life is all over for them. See, our Creator put them here to point the way of deep and abiding love for our human family."

"Now, Jeff, you're going too far," Pa said.

"Mick, let Jeff tell his story," Mom said. "He has more to tell. If you give Jeff time, he will prove the point."

"Yes, I have more to tell, and I will prove my point," Uncle Jeff continued. "And . . ."

"But I don't believe copperheads love like that," Pa interrupted.

"Just listen until I finish, Mick," Uncle Jeff said.

"Yes, let Uncle Jeff go on," I said.

"We do want to know about snake-love," he said. My oldest sister, Sophia, was old enough to be having dates now. She could hardly keep from laughing at Uncle Jeff.

"Now back in Elliott County a young couple got married," Uncle Jeff said. "You remember John Porter and Ann Cox."

"Yes, Jeff, I do," Mom interrupted him. "I know what you're going to tell now. Go ahead and tell us."

"Well, John Porter was our fourth cousin and Ann Cox was some distant cousin to us—eighth, ninth, or maybe a tenth cousin," Uncle Jeff said. "Before they married back in them days, it was always customary to have the house built so they could move in. So the parents of the young couple cut trees to make logs for the walls. They rove clapboards from tall straight oaks to make a roof. They split chestnut puncheons for the floor. They built the house in about a week. And after the belling, John and Ann went straight to their new house. One of their parents had given them a feather bed, pillows, and quilts—and the other's parents had given them a stove! You know how it used to be, Mollie. The parents of the bride and groom gave them the base necessities to go to housekeeping on. Their parents gave them a cow for milk and hens to lay eggs. See, in them days people had to dig a living from the ground or starve, and it wasn't easy to live farming the steep Elliott County hills.

"Well, John and Ann were a nice-looking couple," Uncle Jeff said. "John was a tall, powerful man and handy with an ax, and Ann was a medium-size buxom woman with real blue eyes. I'll never forget her eyes as long as I live. I was a sapling of a boy then, and I thought she was the prettiest young woman in Elliott County. They were married in April and moved into their new house just after the wedding and after we belled them there that night. I remember the house wasn't finished but it didn't matter, for they were in a hurry to move into their new home. And back in them days, people weren't afraid of a few cracks between the logs—especially in April when the wind was warm and fresh. And of course they had planned to have the cracks chinked and mud daubed over the chinking before the cold autumn nights.

"Well, John cleared the ground, planted a crop of corn, tobacco, and wheat the first spring," Uncle Jeff continued with his story while we listened eagerly to every word he said. He spoke words we could catch and hold just like somebody putting rocks into a bucket. They were there, and they were solid things. No one could write down what Uncle Jeff said as well as he could tell it. "April, May, and June passed. There was consistent love between them, John and Ann. I remember seeing them ride all hugged up in a little hug-me-tight buggy to Bruin to the store. They traded eggs for groceries. And they had some money to spend. Their corn grew tall and their wheat grew up, and ripened until a high slope looked like a sheet of gold. Their tobacco grew tall and the leaves were broad and dark. John was a good farmer. And Ann helped him some in the fields. She helped him until their first child was on the way.

"Now August came, and if you don't know it, I do know, that August is a bad month for snakes. The old hot sun beamed down in Elliott County in August, and every living thing and just about everybody hunted shade. The minnows in the mountain streams found a shady pool of water, the ground-hogs went back into their dirt holes where it was cool. They stirred early in the morning before the sun was up, or in the late afternoon when the sun went down. And the squirrels stirred early and late too, and slept in their nests in the shade or deep in holes in the hollow trees when the sun was up. The snakes found cool places to coil and sleep too, and they stirred mostly at night when it was cool. They foraged for food at night in the dense dark woods and weed fields.

"One August night when the weather was very hot and the wind didn't come through the cracks and windows in John and Ann's house, John thought he heard a noise like a broom swishing over the puncheon floor.

" 'Ann, do you hear something?' John whispered.

" 'Yes, I'm awake listening to it, John,' she whispered. 'Couldn't be somebody here, could it?'

" 'I'll see,' he whispered.

"Since John kept a kerosene lamp on a chair beside his bed, and a box of matches by the lamp, he struck a match and lit the lamp. 'Ann, Ann,' he said, 'don't look!' But Ann did look at the big copperhead crawling slowly over the puncheon floor toward the bed.

" 'I told you not to look, Ann,' he said. 'See, when a pregnant woman looks at a snake, the snake will go blind.'

"The snake stopped suddenly after Ann looked at him, held his head in the air, and moved it around and around like he was addled. Then John got out of bed and shined the lamplight in the snake's eyes, and sure enough, he was blind. His once beady black eyes in their lidless sockets were like clots of phlegm.

" 'Sorry, darling,' he said to Ann, 'but you blinded him.'

" 'But you plan to kill him anyway, John,' she said.

" 'No, I planned to shoo him out with the broom,' John told her. 'I'm afraid to kill a snake. I let the snakes kill each other.'

" 'John, that's crazy talk,' she told him. 'You are a big strong he-man! You've got too much sense to think like that.'

" 'Haven't you heard, darling, that the copperhead is filled with the damned souls of evil men? There is more evil in that snake than you might think. Since you have blinded him, I will have to shoot the snake. Stop your ears with your finger, darling.'

"John lifted the squirrel rifle down from the joist where he kept it hanging above the bed. He took aim at the copperhead's neck when it stopped moving. He fired and the snake went limp on the floor. The bullet almost severed its neck and passed on through the green chestnut puncheon floor and went into the ground under the house.

" 'I never saw a snake bleed like that one,' John told Ann. And if you don't know this, when a snake bleeds a lot, it's not exactly the snake's blood that pours forth," Uncle Jeff said. "That blood is supposed to be the blood of all the damned that has become a part of the snake. John Porter knew this.

"So, that night John took the snake over to Clem Worthington's shack," Uncle Jeff continued. "Clem, an old man whose wife was dead, now lived alone. Many people thought he was a Wise One. He read the stars, coffee cups, studied nature; and he read Hosea, the Prophet, until he had begun to think he was a prophet. He told the people he was a prophet and they believed him. And to tell you the truth," Uncle Jeff said, with a sigh, "it was old Clem that first put me on to the constancy of snake-love. And it was old Clem who said the snake was more sacred than people thought and that the Creator put him here for a purpose, or he wouldn't be on this earth. Well, what he had said made sense to me. I can see old Clem yet in his little two-room house with weeds growing high as the porch was tall. He sat in a little room with his books around him, and he took long walks the four seasons of the year. He observed 'the Creator's handiwork' and he tried to figure things out to his own satisfaction, and for his people. He called us his people, and I guess we were. Old Clem has long gone to his reward. He sleeps on an Elliott County hill without a marker to show where he lies. Well, I went back there, and I couldn't find his grave. And this reminds me of a truth he said once, that man wasn't as immortal as a grain of sand. He said a grain of sand went on forever, but man disappeared from the earth. And poor old Clem, by dying, has proved his point.

"But the night John shot the copperhead, he took him to old Clem and told him how Ann, who was with child, looked at the snake and how its eyes turned to clots of phlegm, as she looked, and how he shot it instead of shooing it out with a broom as he had planned. He told old Clem that he was scared after the way it bled.

" 'You had better be scared,' old Clem told him. 'You and Ann are in for serious trouble. I could mention a half dozen evil men, cutthroats, murderers, and robbers, who might be hidin' in this snake.'

"John Porter, who was young, big, and powerful, and unafraid of man or animal, now stood before old Clem, shaking like an oak leaf in the night wind.

" 'Rufus Johnson, who knocked old Jerry Bruck in the head for his money, was in that snake,' old Clem told John. 'Old Mary Howes, who tolled Flem Berry to the rock cliff where Tom and Boz Bean were waiting to murder him, was in that snake. Old Fose Jones, so mean to an animal he'd beat his mule's eye out with a stick—I'm sure he was there too. Thurmond Turnipseed, who killed four men for the love of killing, was surely in him. Erf Springhill, who shot his own father, was there. It was their blood, John, that spilled when you shot the snake,' old Clem told John. 'You've unleased all this evil upon us. The copperhead holds the evil, and should be left for other snakes to kill.'

" 'I told Ann that,' he told the wise old Clem. 'She didn't believe.'

" 'She will believe,' old Clem told him. 'She might be killed and you might be killed with her, since you are yoked together by the Creator's Divine Law.'

" 'What will I do with this dead copperhead?' John asked old Clem.

" 'It won't matter now,' he told him. 'As you ride back, throw him off in the weeds. All the evil he held has gone into his mate. She will take up the fight.'

" 'You may be the wisest of all men around here,' John told old Clem before he left, 'but I can hardly believe all this. How can evil go from evil back to evil?'

" 'You will see,' old Clem warned him. 'Throw the dead snake away. It isn't as much as a grain of sand now. It won't go back to a little grain of sand, but it will go back to loam, and nothing will grow from that loam for three years. It will kill everything close to it. Take that evil carcass out of here, John.'

"John took the snake and threw it in a weed patch beside the path as he rode his mule back home."

"Jeff, you're making all this up," Pa said. "It's the wildest story I ever heard. No man in his right senses will believe that stuff."

"No, Brother Jeff isn't making it up," Mom said. "I know the story. I left Elliott County when I was twelve years old. Everybody up there used to know this story."

"All right, if I am making up a bunch of lies I'll stop my story, Mick," Uncle Jeff said. "I don't like to speak before an unbeliever."

"Go on with the story, Uncle Jeff," I said. "I believe you, Uncle Jeff, because I want to believe you. I want to hear all the story."

"Yes, Uncle Jeff, tell the rest of it," Sophia said.

But Uncle Jeff sat there for a minute. Brother Finn begged him to tell the rest of it. Mary begged him to go on, and then Glenna, our baby sister, wanted to hear all of the story. We liked to hear Uncle Jeff tell stories. We'd seen copperheads, and I had killed them. But now I wondered whether I would ever cut one's head off with a hoe again, and unleash all that powerful evil. I had killed them because I was afraid of a copperhead. But now I thought of all the evil I might have unleashed as I thought back; each time I had killed a copperhead something dreadful had happened in our neighborhood. About the time I'd killed one, a man was stabbed to death. And at another time, a neighbor's barn burned with all his livestock in it. I thought the evil men were sealed up in a copperhead like poison was sealed in a bottle.

"Now, what started all of this was old Seymour Pratt and his seven wives," Uncle Jeff said. "I said that the copperhead snake was put on this earth for a purpose and that purpose for mankind might be to teach constant love. See, there is the frivolous love like old Seymour has, or he wouldn't have had seven wives. Now when the copperhead takes his bride, it is a lifetime proposition with him! Now Mick, if you won't interrupt me again, I'll continue . . . "

"All right, Jeff, you win," Pa said. "The children want to hear that crazy stuff, and I don't think it will contaminate their minds to listen to you. But my mind is closed to it."

"Contaminate their minds?" Uncle Jeff repeated in a surprised tone of voice. "It should help them. All of your children, Mick, my little nieces and nephews gathered around their old uncle listening to his voice now, will be proud someday they had the opportunity to listen. They will be choosing mates someday. Let's hope your sons won't be Seymour Pratts when they and your daughters choose mates for all eternity."

Pa shook his head disgustedly and leaned back in his chair.

"The news of Ann's blinding the snake and John's shooting it and its bleeding and his going to wise old Clem in the night with the dead snake was norated all over that community the next day," Uncle Jeff said. "John told the story to Bill Wilcox, and when he went to Bruin to Jeff Harper's store Bill told the story to old Jeff, which was like putting it in the Elliott County *News*. And that very night when John and Ann went to bed, John lit the lamp.

" 'John, I can't sleep with the light on,' Ann said. 'I like to lie in the dark and feel the night wind come through the cracks, and then I can sleep.'

" 'Darling, something else might come through the cracks,' John said.

" 'What are you talking about?' she asked.

" 'The mate to that snake I shot last night,' he replied.

" 'John, who told you that?' Ann asked. 'That old bag of wind you call wise old Clem?'

" 'Yes, old Clem told me,' he said. 'When I left here last night with the dead snake you were asleep,' he said. " 'Old Clem told me the mate might take revenge. And now, since the snake bled like it did, it was carrying the souls of the damned and the evil. No fewer than seven, according to what old Clem said. He even named them last night.'

" 'John, are you losing your mind?'

" 'I hope not.'

" 'Well, I can't sleep with that light on,' she said, 'besides we have to be rested to do the work ahead of us tomorrow.'

" 'If we don't keep the lamp burning, that copperhead's mate might come back to undo us. She will take her revenge, for I killed her mate, and copperheads wed for life.'

" 'I'm going to blow the lamp out so I can sleep,' Ann told John. 'I'm not afraid, because all that crazy talk goes in at one ear and comes out at the other.'

" 'You are taking a chance,' John told her. 'And since you and I are yoked by the Creator's Divine Law, I am in danger with you.'

"Ann blew out the lamp and she went to sleep in the dark while John lay on the bed and tossed, so he told me the next day when I went out there to borrow a hoe. What I wanted to find out was about his killing the snake. He told me the story and he said he felt tired to go to work in the tobacco, pulling suckers from the stalks. He said he'd not had enough sleep. And he told me how Ann had got up that morning laughing. And at the breakfast table she had said to him, " 'Well, the mate of the constant lovers didn't get us last night, did she?'

"And John told me his wife accused him of being 'teched in the head.' 'But I told Ann the mate could still come back on the second or the third night. And she laughed more than at any time since we've been married. And she even said her looking at the copperhead hadn't blinded him, but that this was a season called 'dog days,' and all snakes went blind in dog days and regained their sight after the season was over.' I remember every word John told me that morning.

"Well, this was the last time, Mick, I ever talked to John Porter, my fourth cousin," Uncle Jeff said. "Next time I saw John Porter, he was lying beside Ann, and they were dressed in their wedding clothes, side by side in a big double coffin Pap and the other men made for them. Not just the two of them, but there was a third one, too. Their unborn went with its mother, Ann. It was on the third night that the old she-copperhead followed her mate. She crawled through the crack of the cabin and found her mate's bloodstain on the puncheon floor. Then she sought revenge. She crawled up in the bed with John and Ann, and she must have bit one and then the other. Birdie Crump went over to help John sucker his tobacco, the next morning, since they were exchanging work. And Birdie knew John got up early. Well, he waited around outside, from six until seven. He watched the flue from the cookstove for smoke, too. There was no fire in the stove. Ann was not up getting breakfast. So Birdie knocked on the door and no one answered. In those days, every man kept his hunting gun handy by his bed, but no one ever locked a door. It was a disgrace and showed a man's cowardice. Then Birdie just eased the door open and went in. He saw John and Ann still in bed. He spoke to them, but there was no answer. And he walked back to the bed and looked at their pale silent faces. They weren't breathing. And just as he was about to touch John's forehead to see if he were really dead, the old she-copperhead poked her head right up between them from under the cover. Birdie said, 'I jumped three steps backward in one hop. I took off to notify the neighbors.' I remember when Birdie came and told Pop, he was short of breath from running and he was scared—a scared man," Jeff continued. He shook his head sadly. I thought he was going to cry.

"When Coroner Waterfield went to the cabin, the old she-copperhead had gone. She had come to the cabin with all her evil intent, and she had done her duty. John had been bitten four times, and Ann had been bitten six. They had been bitten early in the night when they were asleep and the dose of poison injected in them was so much they were dead before morning. Well, we had a big funeral! You remember the funeral, don't you, Mollie?"

"Yes, I was a little girl, nine or ten, but I went to that funeral," Mom said. "That was the first and only time I ever saw a man and his wife buried in the same coffin."

"Now, Mick, what do you think of that?" Uncle Jeff asked Pa. "Do you believe copperheads are yoked for life? Do you believe in the constancy of their love?"

"Jeff, it doesn't matter what I believe," Pa told him quickly. "I keep a good sharp hoe for the copperheads. I think a man's greatest problem of staying married to the woman he loves is her relatives. I wonder if the copperhead snakes have relatives that are as big pests as we have among the relatives in our human family?"

Pa got up from his chair and rubbed his sleepy eyes. "I believe I'll turn in after that one, Jeff," he said. "You've really told one tonight."

"Mick, you don't appreciate Brother Jeff," Mom said.

"I'm sure glad it's wintertime, and the copperheads have hibernated," I said. "If it was summertime I'd light the lamp upstairs and keep it lit all night, too."

"Yes, they're put here for a purpose just like old Clem used to tell us," Uncle Jeff sighed as he got up from his special chair Pa had made for him, so he wouldn't break all Mom's chairs down. "The Creator had in mind a purpose for every loving thing. And I believe the copperhead was put here to point the way to the constant and abiding love."

"What about Seymour Pratt, Uncle Jeff?" I asked. "Since he's had seven wives, will he join the six evil men and one woman in that old she-copperhead?"

"Son, I can't judge," Uncle Jeff sighed.

"I'm never sure of many things," Pa said, "but I'm sure of one thing. If old Seymour is confined with the six evil men and one woman in the belly of that old copperhead, evil or no evil—not one of the six men would have a chance, for old Seymour will get old Mary! You can bet on that! I know him. Come on, and let's everybody get in bed before Jeff spins another one."

The Human Comedy 🌂🌂🌂

Part 5

Hair

About the story:

"Hair," the story of Jersey Harkreader's pursuit and marriage of Lima Whitehall, is a masterpiece of comedy; the first-person narrator of Plum Grove speaks in a rhythmic Appalachian dialect as purely rendered as that of Mark Twain's Hannibal, Missouri. "They were kindly rich people," Jersey says, or "They think they're better'n everybody else in the whole wide world—have to watch about getting rain in their noses." About mountain religion Jersey admits that he saws the fiddle, plays set-back, dances, and may not have his name "on the Lamb's Book of Life," but he will not be denied the earthly pleasures of the mountain church: "I just up and go to see and to be seen—that's what we all go for. It is a place to go and about the only place we got to go."

The story "Hair" has been thrice honored. In reviewing Edward J. O'Brien's *The Best Short Stories, 1937*, Ralph Thompson mentioned "Hair" before all other stories in his column in the N.Y. *Times*, noting that the editor's purpose was "to make a representative cross-section of contemporary American life as it is being interpreted by our best short-story writers." Other distinguished selections that year included William Faulkner's "Fool about a Horse," Katherine Anne Porter's "The Old Order," and Ernest Hemingway's "The Snows of Kilimanjaro." Further, O'Brien pointed to Jesse Stuart as the author who had "published the greatest number of first-rank stories during the year—seven in all," with Kay Boyle, William Saroyan, and Morley Callaghan having six each, and Faulkner having four. When O'Brien published his *50 Best American Short Stories: 1915–1939*, arranged chronologically, the collection included Jesse Stuart's "Hair" as well as such pieces as Thomas Wolfe's "Only the Dead Know Brooklyn," Ring Lardner's "Haircut," and Dorothy Parker's "Telephone Call," inspiring one reviewer to summarize, "Here they are—the cream of the crop. The American short story has come of Age." Again, "Hair" appeared in Stuart's splendid 1941 collection *Men of the Mountains* and was one of the reasons the author received that year the award of the American Institute of Arts and Letters, along with an expense-paid trip to New York City to receive the $500 award at Carnegie Hall in a ceremony presided over by Stephen Vincent Benét.

Lewis Gannett wrote, "The story called 'Hair' . . . is as old, in its central situation, as any of Boccaccio's, but the story is fresh and new."

Teacher-writer Harry Harrison Kroll, who had been Stuart's creative writing teacher at Lincoln Memorial University, wrote to the author on May 3, 1943, that he had read "Hair" aloud to his short-story classes every year. Kroll had earlier located the heart of that story's ebullience, so he thought, when he wrote to Stuart: "Your chief strength all along has been some kind of glorious hell-roaring boyishness and masculinity, a gusty satisfaction in sheer living that has hurtled you through to amazing success" (June 25, 1942).

Those qualities inhere in the droll and obsessed narrator of "Hair"—a youth subject to crazed jealousy, amoral finagling, and self-conscious arrogance but hell-bent determined to get the woman he loves. Stuart balances his intense narrative with sensuous imagery and, thus, sustains his evocation of the Plum Grove hill people and their ways.*

* * *

IF YOU'VE NEVER been to Plum Grove then you wouldn't know about that road. It's an awful road, with big ruts and mudholes where the coal wagons with them nar-rimmed wheels cut down. There is a

---

*H. Edward Richardson, "Foreword," *Men of the Mountains*, reprinted (Lexington, Ky.: Univ. Press of Kentucky, 1979), pp. 8–9. "Hair" was originally published in the *American Mercury*, Vol. 38 (July, 1936), pp. 311–320. It was reprinted in Richard Croom Beatty, William Perry Fidler, eds., *Contemporary Southern Prose* (N.Y.: D. C. Heath, 1940), pp. 537–551, Edward J. O'Brien, *50 Best American Short Stories, 1915–1939* (Boston, Houghton Mifflin, 1939), pp. 716–733, and has been reprinted four other times, most recently in *Men of the Mountains* (Lexington: Univ. Press of Ky., 1979), pp. 248–265. Ralph Thompson, "Books and the Times," the New York *Times*, May 26, 1937, clipping in Jesse Stuart, Scrapbook #3, p. 33, M. S. U. "T. W. T." in "25 Years of Short Stories," Charleston, S.C., *News*, July 9, 1939, clipping in

lot of haw bushes along this road. It goes up and down two yaller banks. From Lima Whitehall's house in the gap it's every bit of a mile and a half to Plum Grove. We live just across the hill from Lima's house. I used to go up to her house and get with her folks and we would walk over to Plum Grove to church.

Lima Whitehall just went with one boy. I tried to court her a little, but she wouldn't look at me. One night I goes up to her and I takes off my hat and says: "Lima, how about seeing you home?" And Lima says: "Not as long as Rister is livin'." Lord, but she loved Rister James. You ought to see Rister James—tall with a warty face and ferret eyes, but he had the prettiest head of black curly hair you ever saw on a boy's head. I've heard the girls say: "Wish I had Rister's hair. Shame such an ugly boy has to have that pretty head of hair and a girl ain't got it. Have to curl my hair with a hot poker. Burnt it up about, already. Shame a girl don't have that head of hair."

Well, they don't say that about my hair. My hair is just so curly I don't know which end of it grows in my head until I comb it. I've prayed for straight hair—or hair of a different color. But it don't do no good to pray. My hair ain't that pretty gold hair, or light gold hair. It's just about the color of a weaned jersey calf's hair. I'll swear it is. People even call me Jersey.

There was a widder down in the Hollow and she loved Rister. Was a time, though, when she wouldn't look at him. She was from one of those proud families. You've seen them. Think they're better'n everybody else in the whole wide world—have to watch about getting rain in their noses. That's the kind of people they were in that family. And when a poor boy marries one of them girls he's got to step. They are somebody around here and they boss their men. So Rister James went with the woman I loved, Lima Whitehall, when he could have gone with Widder Ollie Spriggs. Widder Ollie wasn't but seventeen years old and just had one baby. Rister was nineteen and I was eighteen. Lima was seventeen. If Rister would have gone with Widder Ollie it would have made things come out right for me. God

Jesse Stuart, Scrapbook #6, p. 96, M. S. U. "Stuart Receives Literary Award," Portsmouth, Ohio, *Times*, clipping in Jesse Stuart, Scrapbook #7, p. 27, M. S. U. Lewis Gannett, "Books and Things," N.Y. *Herald-Tribune*, Mar. 17, 1941, clipping in Jesse Stuart, Scrapbook #7, p. 30, M. S. U. For Harry Harrison Kroll's letters to Jesse Stuart, see H. Edward Richardson, "*Men of the Mountains*: An Interview with Jesse Stuart," *Adena*, Vol. 4, No. 1 (Spring, 1979), p. 9. According to my interview with Mr. Stuart on this story, #42, W-Hollow, Greenup, Ky., Sept. 17, 1981, "Hair" was "a Plum Grove story . . . based on fact. . . . I considered it a local story . . . all of it." Its original locale was Plum Grove and the model for Lima Whitehall's house was the log house of the author's Grandfather Mitch Stuart on Shacklerun Road, although it had been sold out of the family by that time.

knows I didn't want Widder Ollie and she didn't want me. I wanted Lima. I told her I did. She wanted Rister. She told me she did.

Widder Ollie was a pretty girl—one of them women that just makes a good armful—small, slim as a rail, with hair pretty as the sunlight and teeth like peeled cabbage stalks. She'd have made a man a pretty wife. She might not have made a good wife—that's what Effie Spriggs told me. Effie is John Spriggs' mother and Ollie married John when she was fifteen. Effie said Ollie broke a whole set of plates, twelve of 'em, on John's head over nothing in God Almighty's world. And he just had too much honor in his bones to hit a woman with his fist. He just stood there and let her break them. And when she got through, John was kind of addled but he got out of the house and came home to his mother Effie, who is Widder Effie here in the Hollow. (She tried to pizen her man, but he found the pizen in his coffee and left her.) Widder Ollie went to live with Widder Effie later. They had plenty—a big pretty farm down in the Hollow, fat barns, and plenty of milk cows. They were kindly rich people with heads so high you couldn't reach them with a ten-foot pole.

Widder Ollie, as I said, wouldn't look at Rister at first. She laughed at him when he used to hoe corn for her pappie for twenty-five cents a day. She made fun of poor old Rister's snaggled-toothed mother and said she looked like a witch. She laughed at Rister's pappie and said he looked like old Lonsey Fannin. That was an old bald-headed horse-doctor who used to go from place to place pulling the eye-teeth out of blind horses, saying they would get their sight back. And she said all the children in the James family looked like varmints. She'd laugh and laugh at 'em and just hold her head high. Then suddenly she was after Rister to marry him. But that's the way—pride leads a woman to a fall. And after she gets up, with a little of the pride knocked out of her, she's a different woman.

But I didn't blame Rister for not wanting her when he could get Lima. Lima was the sweetest little black-headed armload you ever put your two eyes on. I was in the market for Lima the first time I ever saw her. And I guess that was when we were babies. But I didn't know how to get her. I think I was a durn sight better-looking boy than Rister. It's funny how a woman will take to an uglier feller that way and just hold on to his coat-tails whether or not. Hang on just as long as she can. I always thought the reason Lima did that was because she knew Widder Ollie wanted Rister. And if there'd a been another girl around in the district in the market for a man *she* would have wanted Rister because Lima wanted him and Widder Ollie wanted him.

But nobody was after me. I was left out in the cold—just because of my hair, Mom always told me. Mom said I was a good-looking boy all but the color of my hair, and women wouldn't take to that kind of hair. Of course, it don't matter how ugly a man is, his Mom always thinks he's the best-looking boy in the district.

I used to go down past Lima's house last June when the roses were in bloom, and the flags. Them blue and yaller flags just sets a yard off and makes it a pretty thing. Now Rister never saw anything pretty in flowers. He never saw anything pretty in a woman's voice or the things she said, or the shape of her hands. He would watch a woman's legs—and go with them far as he could. He was that kind of a feller. I knew it all the time. I'd pass Whitehall's house. It would be on a Wednesday when Mom would run out of sugar or salt and I'd have to get the mule and go to the store and get it. Rister would be down to see Lima on a weekday. Now God knows, when a man is farming he don't have no time to play around with a woman like a lovesick kitten. He's got to strike while the iron is hot. If he don't he won't get much farming done. When I saw Rister and Lima I reined my mule up to the palings. And I started talking to them as if I didn't care what they were doing. But I did care. I says: "How you getting along with your crop, Rister?"

"Oh, pretty well," he says. "Nothing extra. Terbacker's getting a little weedy on me. Too wet to hoe in it today. Ground will ball up in your hand. Too wet to stir the ground when it is like that."

Well, I knew he was lying. But I never said anything. I know when ground is wet and when ground ain't wet. I'd been out working in it all morning. It was in good shape to work. Rister used to be a good worker. But you know how a man is when he gets lovesick after a woman. Take the best man in the world to work and let him get his mind on a woman and he goes hog-wild. That was the way with Rister.

While I was there looking over the palings, Lima went right up into his arms. He kissed her right there before me. Mom always says a woman that would kiss around in front of people was a little loose with herself. Well, I would have told Mom she lied about Lima if she'd said that about her to my face. I just didn't want to believe anything bad about Lima. I wanted her for my wife. But, men, how would you like to look over the palings from a mule's back and see your dream-wife in the arms of a man bad after women—right out among the pretty roses and flags—and her right up in his arms, her arms around his neck, and his arms around her waist pulling her up to him tight enough to break her in two. And he would say to her: "Oo love me, oo bitsy baby boopy-poopy oo." And she would say: "I love U, U bitsy 'itsy boopy-poopy oo. I love my 'ittle 'itsy 'itsy bitsy turley-headed boopy-poopy oo." God, it made me sick as a horse. It's all right when *you're* loving a woman. It don't look bad to *you*. But when you see somebody else gumsuck around, then you want to get the hell out of the way and in a hurry. It's a sickening thing.

I reined my mule away and I never let him stop till I was a mile beyond the house. I went on to the store and got the sugar. That was Wednesday night and Prayer-Meeting night at Plum Grove, so I had to hurry back and do up the work and go to Prayer Meeting.

I'm a Methodist—I go to church—but God knows they won't have my name on the Lamb's Book of Life because I saw the fiddle, play set-back, and dance at the square dances. Some of them even say terbacker is a filthy weed and none of it will be seen in heaven. Some won't even raise it on their farms. But I go to church even if they won't have me until I quit these things. I just up and go to see and to be seen—that's what we all go for. It is a place to go and about the only place we got to go.

I hurried and got my work done. I put the mule up and fed him. I helped milk the cows. I slopped the hogs, got in stove-wood and kindling. I drew up water from the well—got everything done around the house and I set out to church. Well, when I got down to Whitehall's place, there was Lima and Rister. They were getting ready to go. I gave them a head start and followed after. But I hadn't more than walked out in the big road until here come Widder Ollie and that baby of hers. He was just big enough to walk a little and talk a lot. We started down the road. I said to Ollie: "Rister and Lima's just on ahead of us."

And Ollie says: "They're on ahead? C'mon, let's catch up with them. Take my baby boy, you carry him awhile."

So I took her baby and started in a run with her to catch up with Lima and Rister. You know, a woman will do anything when she loves a man. I could tell Widder Ollie loved Rister. She was all nervous and excited. She had her mind set on getting Rister. And when a woman has her mind set on getting a man she can about get him. That made me think if she could get Rister I'd have a chance to get Lima. That was the only reason I'd be carrying a widder's baby around. I had heard that baby was the meanest young'n in the world. Now I believed it. It had been spiled by them two women—its mother and its grandmother. He would kick me in the ribs and say: "Get up, hossy! Get up there! Whoa back, Barnie." And when he would say "Whoa back" he would glomb me in the eyes with his fingers like he was trying to stop a horse. Then he would say: "Get up, hossy, or I'll bust you one in the snoot." And then he started kicking me in the ribs again. I was sweating, carrying that load of a young'n and keeping up with Widder Ollie. I felt like pulling him off my back and burning up the seat of his pants with my hand.

We saw them—Rister had his left arm around Lima's back and she had her right arm around his back. They were climbing up the first hill, that little yaller hill on this side of the haw bushes. It was light as day. The moon had come up and it lit the fields like a big lamp. Pon my word and honor I couldn't remember in all my life a prettier night than that one. You ought to have seen my corn in the moonlight. We had to pass it. I was glad for the girls to go by it and see what a clean farmer I was and what a weedy farmer Rister was. Not a weed in any of my corn. Pretty and clean in the moonlight and waving free as the wind. Lord, I felt like a man with religion to see my corn all out of the weeds and my terbacker clean as a hound dog's tooth—my land all paid for—not a debt in the world—didn't owe a man a penny. Raised what I et and et what I raised. All I needed was a wife like Lima. She'd never want for anything. And I thought: "What if this baby on my back was mine and Lima's? I'd carry him the rest of my days. I'd let him grow to be a man a-straddle of my back. But if I had my way now, I'd bust his little tail with my hand."

We got right up behind Rister and Lima. And they looked around. Widder Ollie had me by the arm. I had her baby on my back yet. God, it hurt me. But I held the baby while Lima won the battle. You know women are dangerous soldiers. They fight with funny weapons. The tongue is a dangerous cannon when a woman aims it right. We just laughed and talked. We just giggled before Rister and Lima got to giggling at us. I was afraid they'd laugh at me for carrying the baby. They went on up the next hill—us right behind them. We went past the haw bushes and on to church. We just laughed and laughed and went on crazy. That baby on my back, a-making a lot of noise. We went up the hill at the church and the boys said: "Look at that pack mule, won't you?"

Well, to tell the truth I'd ruther be called a pack mule as to be called Jersey. So I just let them whoop and holler to see me with Widder Ollie and carrying her baby. Everybody out on the ground laughed and hollered enough to disturb the Methodist Church. Church was going on inside. But there was more people out in the yard than there was inside. They could see more on the outside than they could hear going on inside. I just wagged the baby right in the church house. Everybody looked around and craned their necks.

Rister and Lima acted like they were ashamed of us. Tried to sidle out of the way and get us in front so they could dodge us. But we stayed right with them. They set down on a seat. We set right beside them as if we were all together. People looked around. I had Widder Ollie's boy in my lap. He tried to hit the end of my nose. I had a time with him. I could see the girls whisper to one another. They watched us more than they did the preacher. He was telling them about widders and orphans. He was preaching a sermon on that. Rister would flinch every now and then. He wanted to be on another seat. But he couldn't very well move. So he just set there and took it. And I took it from that young'n. But I thought: "There'll be the time when I come back to this church house with a different woman. I'll come right here and marry her. It will be different from what they see tonight."

We set right there and listened through that sermon. Boys would come to the winder and point to me from the outside—being with a widder woman who hadn't been divorced from her man very long. Boys around home thinks it's kindly strange to go with a widder woman—but I don't think so. They say a body is in adultery. But when two can't go on loving each other and start breaking plates—twelve at a crack—it's time they were getting apart. Especially when two has to go through life tied together when the mother-in-law tied the knot. I just felt sorry for Widder Ollie. She had always loved Rister and would have married him to begin with if it hadn't been for that mother of hers telling her so many times that she got to believing it that she was better than any man in the Hollow.

Well, they got us in front coming out of the church house. I thought we'd better take advantage of getting out first. So we took the lead going back. Boys just giggled and hollered at me when I come out of the house with the baby on my back. I didn't care. I was seeing ahead. So we just went out the road. The moon was pretty on the fields. A thousand thoughts came into my mind. I didn't want Rister to have Lima. I loved Lima. God, I loved her. Widder Ollie said to me going home: "Don't think it has done much good for both of us tonight. We'll have to think of something different. I love that boy till it hurts. I could love him forever. I can't get him: Lima don't love him. She holds him because I want him. That is the way of women. You want what you can't get. When you get what you want you don't want it. I have always loved Rister. But my people wanted me to marry John. I married him. My mother married him. Life is not worthwhile without Rister. And here you've been out carrying my baby around and letting people talk about you so you could help me get Rister and you could get Lima."

That was right. Life was not fair. The night was so pretty. The moon above my clean corn. My house on the hill where I would take Lima. I needed a wife. I wanted the woman I loved. I loved Lima Whitehall. And when we passed her home I wouldn't look across the palings at the roses. I remembered the week-day I passed and saw Rister out there with her. I just took Widder Ollie on home. And when we got to the gate I said: "Widder Ollie, I am Rister kissing you. You are Lima kissing me. You are Lima for one time in your life. I am Rister one time in my life. Shut your eyes and let's kiss. Let's just pretend." So we did.

Then I started on the long walk home up the branch. I had to pass Lima's house. Moonlight fell on the corn. Wind blew through the ragweeds along the path. Whippoor-wills hollered so lonely that they must have been in love with somebody they couldn't get. I went in Lima's yard to draw me a drink of water. And right by the well-gum stood Rister and Lima. They weren't a-saying a word. They didn't see me; I didn't let myself be known; I just stepped back into the moonshade of one of the yard trees. I just stood there and watched. Lima went into the house after kissing and kissing Rister. When Lima left, Rister stood at the well-gum. He looked down at the ground. He kicked the toe of his shoe against the ground. There was something funny about the way he was acting. He kept his eye on the upstairs winder in that house. It had one of them pole ladders—we call them chicken ladders—just one straight pole with little tiny steps nailed across it. It was setting up back of the house—from the ground to the winder.

Then, suddenly, Rister let out one of the funniest catcalls you ever heard. It would make the hair stand up on your head. It wasn't a blue yodel, but it was something like a part of that yodel Jimmie Ridgers used to give. He done it someway down in his throat. It started out like the nip-nip-nipping of scissor-blades, then it clanked like tin cans, then like a foghorn, way up there high, then it went like a bumblebee, then it rattled like a rattlesnake, and ended up like that little hissing noise a black snake makes when it warns you. I never heard anything like it. If it hadn't been for me knowing where it had come from I'd set sail off of that hill and swore it was a speret that made the noise. Rister gave the catcall once—held his head high in the air—no answer. So he gave it again. And from upstairs came the answer—a soft catcall like from a she-cat. So he takes right out in front of me and runs up the ladder like a tom and pops in at the winder.

I thought I'd go home and get the gun and come back and when he came down that ladder I'd fill his behind so full of shot it would look like a strainer. Then again I thought I'd go over and pull the ladder down and make him go down the front way. God, I was mad! But I didn't do neither one. The whole thing made me so sick I just crawled out of the moonshade and sneaked over the hill home. I didn't know what to do. It just made me sick—sick at life. I just couldn't stand it. I couldn't bear to think of Lima in the dark upstairs with Rister.

I thought about taking the gun and going back and blowing Rister's brains out when he came back through that upstairs winder. I could have done it—God knows I could have done it. But they'd have got out the bloodhounds and trailed me home. Lima would have known who did it. I thought there must be a way for me to get Lima yet, and for her to come to her senses. But then I thought they are up in that dark room together. Lord, it hurt me. Pains shot through and through me. Life wasn't worth the pain one got out of it. I had something for her—a farm, a little money, clean crops, and plenty of food for cold days when the crows fly over the empty fields hunting last year's corn-grains. Rister didn't have nothing to take a woman to but his father's house, and den her with his own father's young'ns.

I went upstairs and got the gun from the rack I put a shell into its bright blue barrel. Just one shell for Rister. I would kill him. Then I put the gun down. I would not kill Rister. I could see his blood and brains all over the wall. Old Sol Whitehall would run out in his nightshirt. He would kill Lima if he knew. And I wouldn't get Lima. It is better not to let a man know everything—it is better to live in silence and hold a few things than to lose your head and get a lot of people killed. I put the gun back, took the shell out of it, and set it back on the rack. I went to bed. But I couldn't sleep. I could see Lima and Rister in a settee in the front yard, kissing. I could hear that catcall. I memorized it. I said it over and over in bed. It came to me—every funny noise in it. I called it out, several times. It made the hair stand up on my head. It waked Pa up and he said: "I've been hearing something funny in this house or my ears are fooling me. Funniest thing I ever heard. Like a pheasant drumming on a brushpile. Goes something like a rattlesnake too. I can't go to sleep." But Pa went back to sleep. I kept my mouth shet. I just laid there the rest of the night and thought about Rister and Lima.

I didn't eat much breakfast the next morning. I went out and got the Barnie mule and I started plowing my terbacker. I couldn't get Lima off my mind. I prayed to God. I did everything I knew to do. And it all came to me like a flash. It just worked out like that.

So I waited. I just waited about ten hours. I plowed all day, worked hard in the fields. After I'd fed the mule, et my supper, done up the rest of the work, I slipped back up the path that I had come over the night before.

All the lights in the Whitehall house were out. The ladder was up at the winder at the back of the house. Everything was quiet. The old house slept in the moonlight. The hollyhocks shone in the moonlight. Old Buck came around and growled once or twice. But he knew me when I patted his head. He walked away contented. Brown, he was, in the moonlight—like a wadded-up brown carpet thrown among the flowers.

I held my head in the air, threw my chin to the stars, and gave that catcall—just as good as Rister gave it. Lima answered me from upstairs. The dog started barking at the strange sounds. My cap pulled low over my funny-colored hair I climbed the ladder and went in through the winder. The dog barked below. I was afraid. If Sol Whitehall found me there he would kill me. But I had to do this thing. I just had to.

Lima said: "Oo bitsy 'itsy boopy-poopy oo. My turley-headed baby boy."

I kept away from the streak of moonlight in the room.... Well, no use to tell you all. A man's past belongs to himself. His future belongs to the woman he marries. That's the way I look at it. That's the way I feel about it. This is a world where you have to go after what you get or you don't get it. Lima would not stand and say: "Here I am. Come and get me." No. She couldn't say it long as she was free—free without a care in the world. If she was like Widder Ollie, she'd be glad to find a nice young man like me even if I did have hair the color of a jersey calf and so curly you couldn't tell which end grew in my head. I know that much about women.

When my hat come off in the moonlight upstairs Lima just screamed to the top of her voice. Screamed like she had been stabbed. I made for the winder. She hollered: "That hair! That hair!" She knew who I was. I went out of that winder like a bird. I heard Sol getting out the bed. I landed on soft ground right in the hollyhock bed, as God would have it. I took down over the bank—circled up in the orchard through the grass so they couldn't track me. I hadn't got two-hundred feet when I heard Sol's gun and felt the shot sprinkling all around me in the sassafras like a thin rain falls on the green summer leaves.

I went on to bed that night. I dreamed of Lima. I loved her. I didn't care about Rister and his past with Lima. The way I looked at it, that belonged to them. A girl has the same right to her past that a boy has to his. And when a man loves, nothing matters. You just love them and you can't help it. You'll go to them in spite of the world—no matter what a man has done or a woman has done. That's the way I look at it. Be good to one another in a world where there's a lot of talking about one another, a lot of tears, laughter, work, and love—where you are a part of the world and all that is in it and the world is a part of you. I dreamed about Lima that night. She was in my arms. I kissed her. She was in the trees I'd seen in the moonlight. She was in the wild flowers I saw—the flowers on the yaller bank. She was in my corn and my terbacker. She was in the wind that blows. She was my wife. She wasn't Rister's. She was mine. I loved.

Well, August ended, and September came along with the changing leaves. Then October when all the world turned brown and dead leaves flew through the air. The wind whistled lonesome over the brown fields. The crows flew high through the crisp autumn air.

The months dragged by. We went to church, but I barely ever spoke to Lima or to Rister. I went with Widder Ollie sometimes. People were talking about Lima. People understood. A woman, with her crooked finger over the paling fence, said: "That poor Lima Whitehall was raised under a decent roof, and in the House of the Lord, a church-going girl with as good a father and mother as ever God put breath in. And look how she's turned out. You just can't tell about girls nowadays. They'll fool you—especially when they run around with a low-down boy like Rister James. Curly-headed thing—everybody's crazy about his hair. Look at that bumpy face and them ferret eyes and you'll get a stomachful, won't you?"

And the woman driving home from town with an express and buggy said: "You are right, Miss Fairchild. It's them low-down James people. That boy. He ought to be tarred and feathered, bringing a poor girl to her ruint. She's a ruint girl. Never can stand in the church choir anymore with the other girls and play the organ and sing at church. Her good times are over. That James boy won't marry her now. They say he's got to dodging her. Poor thing."

So I went to Widder Ollie and I said: "Everybody's down on old Rister now. You ought to go talk to him. He's down and out. Now is when he needs help. You know what they are accusing him of. I guess it's the truth. Wait till after I see the baby and I might take Lima and the baby. Be glad to get them. If I do, you can grab Rister."

"I'll do it," said Widder Ollie. "I'll spin my net for him like a spider. I'll get the fly. I love that boy. I love him. He's got the prettiest hair you nigh ever see on any boy's head."

The land was blanketed in snow. The cold winds blew. Winter was here. We heard the people talk: "W'y, old Sol Whitehall's going to march that young man Rister right down there at the pint of his gun and make him marry Lima. It's going to be a shotgun wedding. Something is going to happen."

The talk was all over the neighborhood. Everybody in the district knew about Lima. It is too bad when a girl gets in trouble and everybody knows about it. Around home she can never get a man. She's never respected again. For the man it don't matter much. He can go right back to the church choir and sing when they play the organ. Nothing is ever said about the man.

"I won't marry her," said Rister, "and old Sol can't gun me into it. I'll die first. I'll go away to the coal mines and dig coal till it is all over. I'll go where Widder Ollie's pappie is—up in West Virginia."

So Widder Ollie goes to West Virginia after Rister has been there awhile. She leaves her boy with her mother and she goes to stay awhile with her pappie. I thought that was the right move. It just looked like everything was coming nicely to my hands. I had worked hard. I had prayed hard. I had waited. It was time to get something. But what a mess. What a risk to run over a woman. How she had suffered. How I had suffered. The lonely nights I'd gone out to the woods—nights in winter when the snow dusted the earth—when the trees shook their bare tops in the wind and the song of the wind in the trees was long and lonesome and made a body want to cry— lonely nights when a body wondered if life was worth living—white hills in the moonlight—the barns with shaggy cows standing around them and sparrows mating in the eaves. Life is strange. Lima there, and the Lord knew what she'd do the way people were talking in the district. I was just waiting to see. It would soon be time.

The winter left. Birds were coming back from the South—robins had come back. And Rister was gone. Rister was at the mines—had a job—making more money than he'd ever made in his life. He wasn't working for twenty-five cents a day no more. He was working on the mine's tipple for three dollars a day. He was wearing good clothes. He was courting Widder Ollie right up a tree. And he had her up the tree-a-barking at her like a hound-dog trees a possum.

The days went swiftly. April was here—green in the hills and the plow again in the furrows. Mom was there that ninth of April. She was with Lima. Doctor so far away and hard for poor people to get. Lima came through all right. She had the baby. Mom came home the next morning—I was waiting to see. She said: "It's got that funny-colored hair—that jersey hair with two crowns on its head. But it ain't no Harkreader. It's the first time I ever saw any other person but a Harkreader have hair like that."

I never said a word. I was so happy I couldn't say a word. I had the almanac marked and it had come out just right. So I up and went down to Whitehall's to see the baby. I went in by the bed. I reached over and picked up that baby. It was my baby. I knew it. It was like lifting forty farms in my hands. I kissed it. It was a boy. I never lifted a little baby before or never saw a pretty one in my life. But this baby was pretty as a doll. I loved it. I said: "I'll go to the store and get its dresses right now, Lima."

And she said: "W'y, what are you talking about?"

"Look at its hair," I said. "Only a Harkreader has that kind of hair. You know that."

Fire popped in her eyes—then tears to quench the fire. They flowed like water. "When you get out of bed," I said, "we'll go to church and get married. We'll go right out there where we went to school and where we played together. We'll forget about Rister."

She started out of the bed. I put her back. When a girl is down and out—a girl you love—a girl who is good and who loves as life lets a woman and a man love—I could shed tears. I could cuss. I could cry. But what I did was to run out and chop up that settee. I dug up the green sprouts of the flags and the roses. My daddy-in-law, old Sol Whitehall, ran around the house on me and yelled: "What the devil are you doing? Am I crazy to see you in my yard digging up my flowers?"

And I said: "You are crazy, for I am not here, and you are not Sol Whitehall. You are somebody else."

I dumped the flower roots over the palings. I left Sol standing there, looking at the wind.

I ran toward the store. I said to myself: "I got her! I'll plow more furrows. Clear more ground. Plant more corn. I'll do twice as much work. I got her! And I am going to get my boy some dresses. Hell's fire! He's greater to look at than my farm!"

I got him the dresses. I ran back and told the preacher to be ready soon. She must be mine. And when I got back with the dresses my pappie-in-law said: "And that scoundrel—married. Rister married to Widder Ollie Spriggs. Damn him to hell! God damn his soul to hell and let it burn with the chaff!"

But let them talk. Let them talk. They'll never know.

We went to the church. We were married there. Made Lima feel better to be married there. I could have been married in a barn. Would have suited me.

You ought to see my boy now. Takes after me—long jersey-colored hair. He's my image. He don't look like his Ma—not the least. He's up and going about.

Rister's back home now. He works for Widder Ollie and her mother. They all live in the house together. Everything came out just fine. We went to church together the other night, all of us. Rister and Widder Ollie walked behind. We went into the church house carrying our babies. I know people thought I was carrying Rister's baby, and that he was carrying the one I ought to carry. The Widder Ollie's brat was digging Rister in the ribs and saying, "Get up, hossy. Get up, hossy, or I'll hit you on the snoot."

And he'd have done it too, if Rister hadn't stepped up a little faster. That kid is twice as big as he was the night I carried him. Ollie says he won't walk a step when she takes him any place. Makes Rister carry him everywhere. People look at us and grin. They crane their necks back over the seats to look at us all together again. Ollie understands. Lima understands. Rister don't understand so well.

And we go back across the hills shining in moonlight. Summer is here again. Corn is tall on the hills. Then I hold my head in the air, throw my chin to the stars, and I give that strange catcall once more. Rister looks a little funny. He understands now better than he did.

Hot-Collared Mule

About the story:

This is the story of two peculiar mules and a vaunting horse trader. Rock was a mule who would not work until he was hot, so the story aptly opens in a breathless frenzy as Pa and his son are running the mule in a circle, the older man "running stiff-legged like a cold buck rabbit in the wintertime," his face "red as a sliced beet." When the mule is heated up, Pa starts his complicated horse-trading technique, putting the planned victim Cyrus Broadfoot "on the fence" with a challenge, whittling "big shavings from a poplar stick," then "laying his stick and knife down so he could pull his galluses out and let them fly back like he always did when he was trading." His son narrates the story. The comic highpoint of "Hot-Collared Mule" is achieved when Rye, the newly acquired mule, begins to back up in his harness, and the horse-trading braggart Pa receives his comeuppance.

When I mentioned this story to Mr. Stuart, bedfast since a 1978 stroke, he began to laugh at it all over again. Mrs. Stuart interrupted our conversation to say that she vividly "remembered them talking about it. . . . Mr. Mick Stuart had the hot-collared mule; they traded one for the other." Jesse Stuart interrupted Mrs. Stuart and his own laughter to say, "I was with him!" Then Mrs. Stuart continued while the author laughed, "Your father tricked a man into a trade—Wash Nelson, I think—and then your father found *he* was tricked and had to pour water on that mule to cool him down—"

The author agreed, "That's right," lying in his bed, laughing.

Mrs. Stuart said, "I remember Jesse just laughed and laughed, and I said, after a week or ten days had passed, 'Jesse, if you don't write that you never will.' And so he wrote it. He really got into his stories, laughed at them, and enjoyed them. . . . "*

* * *

*Jesse Stuart, "Hot-Collared Mule," originally published as "Rock and Rye," *Columbia*, Vol. 25 (July, 1946), pp. 5, 24, reprinted as "Hot-Collared Mule" in *Clearing in the Sky and Other Stories* (N.Y.: McGraw-Hill, 1950), pp. 243–255, and *Save Every Lamb* (N.Y.: McGraw-Hill, 1964), pp. 216–226. Jesse Stuart/H. E. Richardson, Interview and conversation, with Mrs. Jesse [Naomi Deane] Stuart, W-Hollow, Greenup, Ky., Sept. 17, 1981.

"KEEP THAT MULE A-GOIN'," Pa hollered as I passed by where he was sitting on a log under the shade fanning himself with sourwood leaves. "Run 'im until he's hot as blue blazes!"

I couldn't answer Pa. My tongue was out of my mouth and I was getting my breath hard. If you have never owned a cold-collared mule then you wouldn't understand what a job it is to run one long enough to get him hot so he'll work in the harness. What you do when you run him is put a collar on him and run along behind and slap him across the back with the lines when he begins to slow down.

The bad thing for Pa and me was, we had a mule we couldn't ride or work until we got his collar hot. Pa had tried to ride him. Pa went over his head when he bucked and came down belly-flat on the hard road in front of the mule, knocking all the wind out of him. When I had him galloping, he stopped suddenly with me. I bounced up in the air like a rubber ball. It was done so quickly I couldn't come down to the ground on my feet. I came down a-sittin' in the middle of the road. And I sat there seeing stars. Of all the trading Pa had done, he'd never got a mule like Rock.

"He's a-gettin' warmed up," I grunted to Pa as I passed him on the second lap.

"Fetch 'im around agin and I'll take 'im," Pa said. "Just be keerful and don't do any hollerin'."

If I had wanted to holler at Rock I couldn't, for I was so short of breath. I was running Rock up a logging-road to the turn of the hill; there we turned right up a cowpath that wound up the hill and connected with another logging-road which ran parallel to the one below and then turned perpendicular down the hill and connected with the first road. The circle of narrow road looked cool, for it was bordered by culled trees whose clouds of green leaves sagged in wilted pods. These leaves were so thick they not only obscured the sun but they kept out the little August breeze that idly swayed the wilted pods of leaves. It was a close smothery warmth down under the trees that heated up a man faster than it did a cold-collared mule.

"All right, Pa," I grunted as I came in on my last lap. "It's your time now."

"Hit'll be the last time one of us has to run this mule," Pa said as he took the lines.

I dropped down on the log where Pa was sitting and picked up the sourwood fan. Sweat ran from my face like little streams pour from the face of a hill after an April shower. I'd run Rock three laps around the circle. Now Pa would run him two. Pa couldn't run as well as I could, for he was older and his legs were stiffer and his breath came harder. While I sat fanning, I watched him go out of sight, running stiff-legged like a cold buck rabbit in the wintertime. The twist of burley leaf was jumping up and down in his hip pocket as he made the turn to climb the hill.

"Hit's a hard way to git a mule to work," Pa grunted as he passed me going into his second lap.

I was fanning fast as I could fan. I had cooled down some, but my clothes were as wet as if I had jumped into the river.

When Pa came around on his second lap, I didn't think he'd make it. But he did. His face was red as a sliced beet, and his clothes were as wet as mine were. But a sweaty foam had gathered under Rock's flanks and his shoulders were wet around his collar.

"He's in shape to work now," Pa said as he dropped to the ground. "I'll wind a minute before we hitch 'im to the drag."

But Pa didn't wind very long. He sat there long enough to catch his second wind. We couldn't wait until Rock's shoulders cooled. We threw the gears over his back, hitched a trace chain to the singletree, and let him draw the log chain to the dead oak that Pa had chopped down for us to haul to the woodyard.

"When Cyrus sees my mule pull a log like this," Pa said as he wrapped the log chain around the log, "he'll swap that good mule o' his 'n and give me ten 'r fifteen dollars to boot! See, this log's heavier than Rock. He'll be a-pullin' more than his weight on the ground," he went on as he fastened the log chain around the drag. "I'm a-goin' to ast 'im twenty-five dollars to boot. Then, maybe, I'll drop to fifteen dollars. Remember, I'm through runnin' a cold-collared mule. My ticker ain't good enough fer it and my legs won't stand."

"It's some job for a young man," I said.

"All right, Rock," Pa said, slapping him with a line. "Git down and pull!"

Rock squatted, braced his feet, and pulled, shaking the big log from where it had indented the hard earth. Then, without Pa's telling him, Rock pulled again, and the big log started sliding along while sparks flew from his steel shoes.

"If he wuzn't cold-collared I wouldn't trade 'im fer any animal I ever laid eyes on," Pa said, holding the lines up from the briars.

I walked behind Pa as he drove Rock toward our woodyard.

Maybe our timing was just right. We pulled into our woodyard under the sour-apple tree just as Cyrus Broadfoot rode his harnessed mule up and stopped.

"That's some log, Mick," he said.

"Well, it's purty good-sized," Pa said. "But Rock's pulled a lot bigger logs than this 'n. I'll pull 'im agin any mule of his pounds. Do you want to pull your mule agin 'im?"

"Not necessarily, Mick," Cyrus said, dismounting his mule.

"I thought if you wanted to hitch yer mule to my mule's singletree, we'd let 'em pull agin each other," Pa said as he unhitched the log chain from the drag. "If yer mule pulls mine backwards," Pa went on, "I'll give you my mule. If my mule pulls your mule backwards, then ye give me yer mule! That's fair enough!"

That was the way Pa always started a trade. He would always put the other fellow on the fence. He'd set a price, give or take. And he'd trade at sight unseen. That's how we'd got old Rock. He'd traded with Herb Coloney. Herb told Pa he had a mule that could pull his weight on the ground. That was enough. Pa traded him a two-year-old Jersey bull and got ten dollars to boot right there. Now he was going after Cyrus.

"I don't keer much about tradin' that way, Mick," Cyrus said, pulling a big knife from his pocket with one hand as he picked up a stick with the other.

"Yer mule's bigger 'n mine," Pa said.

"I know that," Cyrus said, whittling a big shaving. "But he ain't as old."

"How old is yer mule?" Pa asked.

"Rye's a-comin' five in the spring," Cyrus said, his words muffled as the sound of his voice was strained through his big mustache.

"Rock ain't but four," Pa bragged. "He ain't shed his colt's teeth yet."

Then Pa picked up a stick, pulled his knife from his pocket, and began to whittle. While Pa whittled big shavings from a poplar stick, Cyrus opened Rock's mouth and looked at his teeth.

"He's still got his colt's teeth all right," Cyrus said. "Don't ye want to look in my Rye's mouth, Mick?"

"I'll take your word fer his age, Cyrus," Pa said, whittling away. "Ye've allus been a good neighbor and a truthful man!"

Pa's words didn't please Cyrus. Maybe Cyrus was thinking about the last time he had traded with Pa. Pa had said these same words and patted Cyrus on the back when he sold three steers for a hundred and forty-three dollars. Cyrus kept them all that winter, put them on grass next spring and summer, and sold them late in the fall for a hundred forty-four dollars. He knew Pa was a good trader, the best among the hills.

"Jist how much boot are you a-goin' to ast me, Mick?" Cyrus asked.

"Tell you what I'll do, Cyrus," Pa said, laying his stick and knife down so he could pull his galluses out and let them fly back like he always did when he was trading. "Since it's you, I'll take twenty-five dollars to boot and trade."

"That's a lot of boot, Mick," he said.

"Won't take a cent less," Pa said.

"I won't give you a penny," Cyrus said, whittling a long shaving.

"I'll tell you what us do," Pa said. "Let's split the difference!"

"Okay," Cyrus said.

Cyrus pulled a ten-dollar bill, two ones, and a fifty-cent piece from a Bull Durham tobacco sack he was carryi.ng in the little watch pocket on the bib of his overalls.

"Jist a minute," Pa said, before he took the money. "That means we're trading harness too!"

"Right," Cyrus said.

Then Pa took the money. I knew Pa had got a barg'in on the harness. Rock's harness was wrapped and tied in many places with groundhog-hide strings.

"You got a pullin' mule," Pa said as Cyrus picked up the rope lines to drive Rock away. "He's the only mule in these parts that can pull his weight on the ground."

Then Pa looked at me and winked. I knew what Pa meant, for Cyrus didn't know how we had to run old Rock to get up steam. In a cold collar he wouldn't pull the hat off a man's head.

"I'm satisfied, Mick," were Cyrus's last words as he drove Rock up the hollow.

I wasn't sorry to see Rock go.

"Now we've got a mule," Pa said. "We'll hitch 'im to the express wagon and take that load of melons to town."

With all the confidence of a strutting turkey gobbler, Pa drove Rye to our express wagon. He was proud of his trade, and I was too. I never wanted to see another mule that I had to run to get steamed up like I had to run Rock. I never wanted to see another cold-collared mule.

Our express wagon was loaded with watermelons and parked under the shade of a white oak in our backyard. When Mom saw Pa backing the new mule between the shafts she came out at the door.

"I told ye, Sall, I'd have a new mule to take these melons to Greenup," Pa bragged. "I really set Cyrus on fire in that trade! I really give 'im a good burnin'. One he'll never forget!"

"I guess it's all right to do that, Mick," Mom said. "Men do such things. But one of these days you're goin' to get a good swindlin'."

"Not me," Pa said, laying the lines down and pulling at his galluses. "I've made you a good livin', ain't I?"

"Yes," Mom agreed by nodding her head.

"And I've done hit mostly by tradin', ain't I?" Pa went on bragging as I hitched the trace chains to the singletree.

"Yes, by cheating people," Mom said. "I feel bad about Cyrus Broadfoot's six little children. Never have a pair of shoes on their feet all winter!"

Then Mom turned around and went back into the house.

"Funny how softhearted wimmen are," Pa said as he fastened a chain through the loop while I fastened the other. "If wimmen had to make a livin' and men stay in the house, wouldn't that be funny? Could ye imagine yer Mom out a-mule-swappin'?"

Pa laughed at his own joke as he climbed upon the express seat and I climbed up beside him. With a light tap from the line, Rye moved the loaded express wagon across the yard and down the road toward Greenup. Pa sat straight as a young poplar with his whip across his shoulder and a chew of burley leaf under his sun-tanned beardy jaw.

As we drove down the sandy jolt-wagon road, I never heard such bragging as Pa did. He talked about the trades he had made in his lifetime, how he had cheated people from the time he began mule trading. That was when he was sixteen. He would tell about cheating people, then he would laugh. And when he spoke of how he had traded a cold-collared mule to Cyrus, he would bend over, slap his knees with his hands, and laugh until people walking along the road would stop and look at us.

"When old Cyrus starts runnin' Rock . . ." Pa would never be able to finish what he started out to say for laughing. He laughed until I had to take the lines and drive so he would have both hands free to slap his knees.

"Old Cyrus will get hot under the collar," Pa went on. "I can just see old Cyrus a-takin' off behind old Rock. . . ."

The tears rolled from Pa's eyes down his sunburnt face.

"Wonder if he'll know what's the matter with . . ." and Pa got down on the load of melons and rolled around like he was crazy.

At first it was a little funny, but after I thought about what Mom had told him I couldn't laugh any more. And I was ashamed of him the way he rolled over the watermelons, laughing. The people we passed would stop and look at him like he was out of his head. I'd never seen a man in my life enjoy a barg'in like Pa was enjoying his trade with Cyrus.

And Pa had made a barg'in, for Rye pulled the load easily and smoothly along the jolt-wagon road until we reached the turnpike. Now we were on the road to Greenup, where we would soon sell our melons. When we reached the turnpike where there were more people traveling, Pa got back on the seat beside of me, put a cigar between his beardy lips, and took the lines. He would never chew burley when we got near town. He would always light up a cigar, though Pa enjoyed a chew more than he did a smoke. He thought he looked more important with a cigar in his mouth.

Rye had pulled steadily along for three miles or more, and now I noticed there was foaming sweat dripping from his flanks and oozing from beneath his collar and dark shades of sweat on his sleek, currycombed and brushed brown hair over his ribs. Pa didn't notice the sweat on Rye. He just sat upon the high springboard seat with a whip over his shoulder that he carried for an ornament, a cigar in his mouth to make him look important, and looked down at everybody we passed.

"Pa, you'd better let Rye take it a little easy," I said. "He's gettin' pretty warm!"

"A mule can stand an awful lot of heat," Pa said, driving on.

But when we reached the Lottie Bates Hill, Rye braced his feet and wouldn't move a step.

"Wonder what's wrong with Rye?" Pa asked me.

"I don't know," I said.

"He needs a little ticklin' with the whip," Pa laughed, pulling it from over his shoulder and tapping Rye on the back.

Then Rye started going backwards, shoving the express wagon zigzagging from one side of the road to the other.

"Slap on the brakes," Pa shouted to me.

I put on the brakes as quickly as I could and stopped the wagon. People passing us along the road started laughing. And Pa was really embarrassed. His sun-tanned face began to change color into a pawpaw-leaf crimson.

"He's a mule that goes backwards," a man said, laughing.

"Somethin's wrong with the harness," Pa said. "Here, take these lines. I'm gettin' down to see what's wrong."

I held the lines while he started to examine the backband and the trace chains. When Pa put his hand on the back-band, Rye kicked up with both hind feet and squealed.

"What's the matter with that mule?" Pa said, jumpin' back in a hurry while the strangers walking home with loads on their backs stood at a safe distance and laughed. "He acts like he's crazy. I'm sure it's his harness hurtin' 'im or a blue-tailed fly on his belly."

"See if the bridle bit is cutting his tongue," I said.

When Pa started to open his mouth to look, Rye lunged forward with both front feet in the air and tried to hit Pa, but he side-stepped just in time.

"That mule's dangerous," Pa wailed. "Git this near town when we can see the smoke from the chimneys, then he acts up like this!"

The words weren't out of Pa's mouth when Rye lunged forward and I pulled back on the lines. Then he started going backwards and the express wagon started rolling down a little hill. The endboard came out and the melons rolled like apples from the wagon bed, down the hill into Town Branch.

"There goes our melons," Pa moaned.

Twenty people, who had stopped to enjoy our trouble, all made a run for the melons that were broken and ruined. While all of them but one old beardy-faced man ran for the melons, Rye jumped forward again, veered to one side, and broke the shafts from the express.

"Hold 'im," Pa shouted.

"I'm doing my best," I said, rearing back on the lines until I brought the mule under control.

And now it worried me not so much that the people were eating our melons, but that I was providing entertainment for them while they ate. They could hardly eat our melons for laughing at us. But Pa puffed harder on his cigar and there was a worried look on his face.

"Say, stranger," the old man with the beardy face said as he slowly approached Pa, "I don't want to butt into yer affairs. But I'm an old mule skinner. I ust to drive a mule team when they had the furnaces back in this county. I drove mules fer forty-three years and hauled cordwood," he went on talking, "and I can tell ye what's the matter with that mule. I've seen four 'r five like 'im in my lifetime!"

"Hit must be his harness that's a hurtin' 'im, Dad," Pa apologized for Rye.

"Nope, that ain't it, stranger," the man said. "He's a hot-collared mule!"

"Never heard of a hot-collared mule," Pa said, throwing up both hands. "I've heard of a cold-collared mule!"

"Well, that's what he is, stranger," the old man said. "Somebody's give ye a good burnin'. He's sold ye a hot-collared mule. And this one is a dangerous animal!"

I looked at Pa and he looked at me.

"And I can prove to ye he's hot-collared," the old man said.

"How can ye do it?" Pa said, turning around to face the old man.

"Take this bucket and go down to the crick and get a bucket of cool water and throw hit over his shoulders," the old man said, as he emptied his groceries so Pa could use it. "Ye'll see that he'll pull when he gits cool shoulders!"

"I'll try anything," Pa said. "I'd like to git my express wagon back home."

Thirty-five or forty people who had now gathered to eat our water-melons looked strangely at Pa when they saw him dip a bucket of water from the creek. They watched Pa carry the water up to the road and throw it on Rye's shoulder, while the mule stood perfectly still as if he enjoyed it.

"It'll take more water," the old man said.

While the people laughed at Pa carrying water to put on a mule's shoulders like he was trying to put out a fire, I thought of what Pa had said about Cyrus's having to run old Rock to get up steam. And the people with watermelon smeared on their faces laughed at Pa more than he had laughed at Cyrus. But after Pa had carried the tenth bucket of water the old man said, "That's enough now, stranger. Ye've put the fire out!"

And when the old man smiled I could see his discolored teeth through his thin dingy-white mustache.

"Now try to drive 'im, young man," the old man said to me.

"Get up, Rye," I said, touching his back lightly with the lines.

The mule moved gently away, pulling the express wagon with the broken shafts which made it zigzag from one side of the road to the other. And when I stopped the mule, Pa came up and said, "It's a new wrinkle on my horn. I never heard of a hot-collared mule but we've got one, Adger. We'll haf to wire up these shafts someway until we can git home. I'll haf to do some more swappin'. Yer mom was right."

Rain on Tanyard Hollow

About the story:

In 1956 Jesse Stuart dedicated his fifth collection of short stories, *Plowshare in Heaven*, "To Oscar Sammons/classmate and friend/and storyteller." They had been classmates in Greenup High School, graduating in 1926, and in the 1930s both married and established homes in Greenup County. At Oscar and Ann Sammons' home on the Ohio River, they often gathered with other young couples to share each other's society and to tell stories. "One evening," Jesse Stuart wrote,

> I told a very serious story which involved nature and superstition, and man's winning against both. It involved a man's praying for something and getting more than he asked for. It was a story that had happened in our neighborhood to a family I had worked for when I was an itinerant farm worker. I knew the family and its problems. I had never thought of this as being a story. I didn't add anything to this story and I didn't subtract anything. When I finished with this story, everybody laughed hilariously and applauded me. "Go write it," Oscar shouted. I did, and the story sold the first trip to a magazine. ... Had it not been for my telling it to this circle of friends in a little white house on the Ohio River bank it would never have been written.

When questioned about the source of the story, how it evolved from his W-Hollow world—for the actual Tanyard Hollow is a kind of geographical tributary of the factual W-Hollow—Mr. Stuart was even more specific: "The neighbor in the story was Bunion Thacker, who really did kill snakes and hang them on the fences to bring rain. It was told to me by Dan Uhlen, a black man who had one leg shorter than the other. All ... details are authentic. He prayed for a storm to move boulders and he got it. His prayers were answered. The measure was heaped. ... "*

*   *   *

*Jesse Stuart, "Dedication," *Plowshare in Heaven* (N.Y.: Mc-Graw-Hill, 1958). Jesse Stuart, "Author's Introduction" to "Rain on Tanyard Hollow," *A Jesse Stuart Reader* (N.Y.: McGraw-Hill, 1963), pp. 59–61. Jesse Stuart/H. E. Richardson, Interview #41, W-Hollow, Greenup, Ky., Sept. 15, 1981. The story first appeared in *Esquire*, Vol. 15 (April, 1941), pp. 55, 160–163, and has been reprinted three times since through 1979, first in *Tales from the Plum Grove Hills* (1946), Mockingbird ed. (1974), pp. 115–124, and in the *Jesse Stuart Reader* (1963), pp. 61–73.

"Don't kill that snake, Sweeter," Mammie said. "Leave it alone among the strawberry vines and it'll ketch the groundmoles that's eatin' the roots of the strawberry plants."

Mammie raised up from pickin' strawberries and stood with one hand in her apron pocket. Draps of sweat the size of white soup-beans stood all over her sun-tanned face and shined like dewdrops on the sun. Mammie looked hard at Pappie but it didn't do any good.

"Kill that snake," Pappie shouted. "It must a thought my knuckle was a mole. It ain't goin' to rain nohow unless I kill a few more blacksnakes and hang 'em on the fence."

Pappie stood over the blacksnake. It was guiled and a-gettin' ready to strike at 'im again. It looked like the twisted root of a black-oak tree rolled-up among the half-dead strawberry plants. It must a knowed Pappie was goin' to kill it the way it was fightin' him back. It kept drawin' its long black-oak-root body up tighter so it could strike harder at Pappie. It stuck its forked tongue out at him.

"You would fight me back," Pappie shouted as he raised a big flat rock above his head high as his arms would reach. "You would get me foul and bite me. That's just what you've done. Now I'm goin' to kill you and hang you on the fence and make it rain."

Pappie let the big rock fall on the blacksnake. The rock's sharp edge cut the snake in two in many places. Its tail quivered against the ground and rattled the dried-up leaves on the strawberry plants. Its red blood oozed out on the dry-as-gunpowder dust. Mammie stood and looked at the pieces of snake writhin' on the ground.

"Old Adam fit with rocks," Pappie said. "They air still good things to fight with."

Pappie stood with his big hands on his hips. He looked at the dyin' blacksnake and laughed.

"That blacksnake didn't hurt your hand when it bit you," Mammie said. "Sweeter, you air a hardhearted man. You've kilt a lot of snakes and hung 'em on the fence to make it rain. They air still hangin' here. I aint heard a rain-crow croakin' yet ner felt a drap of rain. The corn is burnt up. You know it has. The corn ain't goin' to git no taller. It's tasselin' and it's bumblebee corn. If you's to drap any ashes from your cigar on this strawberry patch it would set the plants on fire. They look green but they air dry as powder. Where is your rain?"

"I don't know, Lizzie," Pappie said. "You tell me where the rain is."

"It's in the sky," Mammie said, "and you won't get it unless you pray fer it to fall. It's about too late fer prayer too. And the Lord wouldn't listen to a prayer from you."

When Mammie said this she looked hard at Pappie. Pappie stood there and looked at Mammie. What she said to him about the Lord not listenin' to his prayer made Pappie wilt. His blue eyes looked down at Mammie. The hot dry wind that moved across the strawberry patch and rustled the strawberry plants, moved the beard on Pappie's face as he stood in the strawberry patch with his big brogan shoes planted like two gray stumps. His long lean body looked like a dead snag where the birds come to light and the beard and the long hair that stuck down below the rim of his gone-to-seed straw hat looked like sour-vines wrapped around the snag.

"Don't stand there, Sweeter, like a skeery-crow and look at me with your cold blue-water eyes," Mammie said. "You know you air a hardhearted man and the Lord won't listen to your prayer. Look at the harmless black-snakes you've kilt and have hangin' on the fence and you aint got rain yet. Sweeter, I'm lettin' the rest of these strawberries dry on the stems. I'm leavin' the strawberry patch."

Mammie slammed her bucket against the ground. She pulled her pipe from her pocket. She dipped the light-burley terbacker crumbs from her apron pocket as she walked toward the ridgetop rustlin' the dyin' strawberry plants with her long peaked-toed shoes. By the time Mammie reached the dead white-oak snag that stood on the ridgetop and marked our strawberry patch for all the crows in the country, Mammie had her pipe lit and there was a cloud of smoke followin' her as she went over the hill toward the house.

"Tracey, your Mammie talked awful pert to me."

"Yep, she did, Pappie."

"She talked like the Lord couldn't hear my prayer."

When Pappie talked about what Mammie said about the Lord not payin' any attention to his prayers, his beardy lips quivered. I could tell Pappie didn't like it. He felt insulted. He thought if the Lord listened to prayers, he ought to listen to one of his prayers.

"I'm just hard on snakes, Tracey," Pappie said. "I don't like snakes. My knuckle burned like a hornet stung me when that dad-durned blacksnake hid among the strawberry plants and bit me. It didn't come out in the open and bite me. Your Mammie got mad because I kilt that snake. I know the baby-handed moles air bad to nose under the roots of the strawberry plants and eat their white-hair roots and the blacksnakes eat the moles. But that ain't no excuse fer a blacksnake's bitin' me on the knuckle."

"I don't blame you, Pappie," I said.

When I said this, Pappie looked at me and his face lost the cloud that was hangin' over it. The light on Pappie's face was like the mornin' sun-shine on the land.

"It's a dry time, Tracey," Pappie said as he kicked the dry strawberry plants with his big brogan shoe. The leaves that looked green fell from the stems and broke into tiny pieces. Little clouds of dust rose from among the strawberry plants where Pappie kicked.

"We don't have half a strawberry crop," I said. "And if we don't get rain we won't have a third of a corn crop."

"You air right, Tracey," Pappie answered. "We'll get rain. If it takes prayers we'll get rain. Why won't the Lord listen to me same as he will listen to Lizzie? Why won't the Lord answer my prayer same as he will answer any other man's prayer in Tanyard Hollow?"

When Pappie said this he fell to his knees among the scorched strawberry plants. Pappie come down against the dry plants with his big fire-shovel hands and at the same time he turned his face toward the high heat-glimmerin' sky. Dust flew up in tiny clouds as Pappie beat the ground.

"Lord, will you listen to my prayer?" Pappie shouted. "I don't keer who hears me astin' you fer rain. We need it, Lord! The strawberries have shriveled on the vines and the corn is turnin' yaller. It's bumblebee corn, Lord. Give us rain, Lord. I've kilt the blacksnakes and hung 'em on the fence and the rain don't fall. Never a croak from the rain-crow ner a drap of rain. The blacksnake on the fence is a false image, Lord."

Pappie beat his hands harder on the ground. He jerked up strawberry plants with his hands and tossed them back on the ground. He dug up the hard dry ground and sifted it among the strawberry plants around him. He never looked at the ground. His face was turned toward the high clouds. The sun was beamin' down on Pappie and he couldn't look at the sun with his eyes open.

"Send rain, Lord, that will wash gully-ditches in this strawberry patch big enough to bury a mule in," Pappie shouted. "Let it fall in great sheets. Wash Tanyard Hollow clean."

I didn't bother with Pappie's prayer but I thought that was too much rain. Better to let the strawberry plants burn to death than to wash them out by the roots and take all the topsoil down Tanyard Hollow too. Can't grow strawberry in Tanyard Hollow unless you've got good topsoil of dead-leaf loam on the south hill slopes.

"Give us enough rain, Lord," Pappie shouted, "to make the weak have fears and the strong tremble. Wash rocks from these hillsides that four span of mules can't pull on a jolt-wagon. Wash trees out by the roots that five yoke of cattle can't pull. Skeer everybody nearly to death. Show them Your might, Lord. Put water up in the houses—a mighty river! Put a river of yaller water out'n Tanyard Hollow that is flowin' faster than a hound dog can run. Make the people take to the high hill slopes and let their feet sink into the mud instead of specklin' their shoes and bare feet with dust!"

Pappie prayed so hard that white foam fell from his lips. It was dry foam the kind that comes from the work cattle's mouths when I feed them corn nubbins. The big flakes of white foam fell upon the green-withered strawberry plants.

"Send the thunder rollin' like tater wagons across the sky over Tanyard Hollow," Pappie prayed. "Let the Hollow grow dark. Let the chicken think that night has come and fly up in the apple trees to roost. Let the people think the end of time has come. Make the Hollow so dark a body can't see his hand before him. Let long tongues of lightnin' cut through the darkness across the Hollow and split the biggest oaks in Tanyard Hollow from the tip-tops to their butts like you'd split them with a big clapboard fro. Let pieces of hail fall big enough if ten pieces hit a man on the head they'll knock 'im cuckoo. Let him be knocked cold in one of the biggest rains that Tanyard Hollow ever had. Let the rain wash the dead-leaf loam from around the roots of the trees and let the twisted black-oak roots lie like ten million black snakes quiled at the butts of the big oaks. Lord, give us a rain in Tanyard Hollow to end this drouth! Give us a rain that we'll long remember! I'm through with the brazen images of black snakes! Amen."

Pappie got up and wiped the dry foam from his lips with his big hand.

"I ast the Lord fer a lot," Pappie said. "I meant every word I prayed to Him. I want to see one of the awfulest storms hit Tanyard Hollow that ever hit it since the beginnin' of Time. That goes way back yander. I ast fer an awful lot, and I hope by askin' fer a lot, I'll get a few things."

"Pappie, I don't want to wish you any bad luck," I said, "but I hope you don't get all you ast fer. If you get all you ast fer, there won't be anythin' left in Tanyard Hollow. We'll just haf to move out. The topsoil will all be washed away, the dirt washed from around the roots of the trees and they'll look like bundles of blacksnakes. The big oaks will split from their tip-tops to their butts—right down through the hearts with forked tongues of lightnin'. Trees will be rooted up and rocks washed from the hillsides that a jolt-wagon can't hold up. There won't be any corn left on the hillsides and the strawberry patch will be ruint."

"Tracey, I've ast the Lord fer it," Pappie answered, "and if the Lord is good enough to give it to me, I'll abide by what He sends. I won't be low-lifed enough to grumble about somethin' I've prayed fer. I meant every word I said. I hope I can get part of all I ast fer."

"It's time fer beans," I said. "I can step on the head of my shadder."

Pappie left the strawberry patch. I followed him as he went down the hill. He pulled a cigar from his shirt pocket and took a match from his hatband where he kept his matches so he could keep them dry. He put the cigar in his mouth . . . struck a match on a big rock beside the path and lit his cigar.

"When I was prayin' fer the rain to wash the rocks from the hillsides," Pappie said, "this is one of the rocks I had in mind. It's allus been in my way when I plowed here."

"If we get a rain that will wash this rock from this hillside," I said, "there won't be any of us left and not much of Tanyard Hollow left."

"You'd be surprised at what can happen," Pappie said. "You can turn a double-barrel shotgun loose into a covey of quails and it's sight at 'em that'll come out alive."

Sweat run off at the ends of Pappie's beard. It dripped on the dusty path. Sweat got in my eyes and dripped from my nose. It was so hot it just seemed that I was roastin' before a big wood fire. It looked like fall-time the way the grass was dyin'. Trees were dyin' in the woods. Oak leaves were turnin' brown.

Pappie took the lead down the hill. It was so steep that we had to hold to sassafras sprouts and let ourselves down the hill. The footpath wound down the hill like a long crooked snake crawlin' on the sand. When we got to the bottom of the hill, Pappie was wet with sweat as if he'd swum a river. I was as wet as sweat could make me and my eyes were smartin' with sweat like I had a dozen sour-gnats in my eyes.

"Whooie," Pappie sighed as he reached the foot of the mountain and he rubbed his big hand over his beard and slung a stream of sweat on the sandy path. "It's too hot fer a body to want to live. I hope the Lord will answer my prayer."

"I hope Mammie has dinner ready."

Mammie didn't have dinner ready. She was cookin' over the hot kitchen stove. Aunt Rett and Aunt Beadie were helpin' Mammie.

"Lord, I hope we'll soon get rain," Mammie said to Aunt Rett. She stood beside the stove and slung sweat from her forehead with her index finger. Where Mammie slung the sweat in the floor was a long wet streak with little wet spots from the middle of the floor to the wall.

"It's goin' to rain," I said.

"Why is it goin' to rain?" Mammie ast.

"Because Pappie got down in the strawberry patch and prayed fer the Lord to send rain and wash this Hollow out," I said.

Mammie started laughin'. Aunt Rett and Aunt Beadie laughed. They stopped cookin' and all laughed together like three women standin' at the organ singin'.

"We'll get rain," Mammie said, "because Sweeter has prayed fer rain. We'll have a washout in Tanyard Hollow fer Sweeter prayed fer a washout in Tanyard Hollow. We'll get what Sweeter prayed fer."

They begin to sing, "We'll get rain in Tanyard Hollow fer Sweeter prayed fer it."

"Just about like his hangin' the snakes over the rail fence to get rain," Mammie cackled like a pullet. "That's the way we'll get rain."

Uncle Mort Shepherd and Uncle Luster Hix sat in the front room and laughed at Pappie's prayin' fer rain. They thought it was very funny. They'd come down out'n the mountains and were livin' with us until they could find farms to rent. Uncle Mort and Aunt Rett had seven children stayin' with us and Uncle Luster and Aunt Beadie had eight children. We had a big houseful. They's Mammie's people and they didn't think Pappie had any faith. They didn't think the Lord would answer his prayer. I felt like the Lord would answer his prayer, fer Pappie was a man of much misery. Seemed like all of Mammie's people worked against 'im. They'd sit in the house and eat at Pappie's table and talk about gettin' a house and movin' out but they never done it. They'd nearly et us out'n house and home. When they come to our house it was like locust year. Just so much noise when all their youngins got to fightin' you couldn't hear your ears pop.

"It's goin' to rain this afternoon," Pappie said. "There's comin a cloudbust. If you ain't got the Faith you'd better get it."

Uncle Luster got up from the rockin' chear and went to the door. He looked at the yaller-of-an-egg sun in the clear sky. Uncle Luster started laughin'. Uncle Mort got up from his chear and knocked out his pipe on the jam-rock. He looked at the sun in the clear sky and he started laughin'.

Uncle Mort and Uncle Luster hadn't more than got back to the two rockin' chears and started restin' easy until dinner was ready, when all at once there was a jar of thunder across the sky over Tanyard Hollow. It was like a big tater wagon rollin' across the sky. Mammie drapped her fork on the kitchen floor when she heard it. Aunt Rett nearly fell to her knees. Aunt Beadie set a skillet of fried taters back on the stove. Her face got white. She acted like she was skeered.

"Thunderin' when the sky is clear," Aunt Beadie said.

Then the thunder started. Pappie was pleased but his face got white. I could tell he was skeered. He thought he was goin' to get what he'd ast the Lord to send. The thunder got so loud and it was so close that it jarred the house. 'Peared like Tanyard Hollow was a big pocket filled with hot air down among the hills and the thunder started roarin' in this pocket. It started gettin' dark. Chickens flew up in the apple trees to roost.

When Mammie saw the chickens goin' to roost at noon, she fell to her knees on the hard kitchen floor and started prayin'. Mammie thought the end of time had come. The chickens hadn't more than got on the roost until the long tongues of lightnin' started lappin' across the Hollow. When the lightnin' started splittin' the giant oak trees from their tip-tops to their butts it sounded louder than both barrels of a double-barreled shotgun.

"Just what I ast the Lord to send," Pappie shouted. Mammie jumped up and lit the lamps with a pine torch that she lit from the kitchen stove. I looked at Pappie's face. His eyes were big and they looked pleased. All Aunt Beadie's youngins were gathered around her and Uncle Luster. They were screamin'. They were screamin' louder than the chickens were cacklin' at the splittin' oak trees on the high hillsides. Uncle Mort and Aunt Rett got their youngins around them and Uncle Mort started to pray. All six of us got close to Mammie. I didn't. I stuck to Pappie. I thought about how hard he'd prayed fer a good rain to break the long spring drouth. Now the rain would soon be delivered.

Mammie, Aunt Rett, and Aunt Beadie let the dinner burn on the stove. I was hungry and I could smell the bread burnin'. I didn't try to get to the kitchen. I saw the yaller water comin' from the kitchen to the front room. The front room was big and we had a big bed in each corner. When I looked through the winder and saw the big sycamores in the yard end up like you'd pull up horseweeds by the roots and throw 'em down, I turned around and saw Aunt Beadie and Uncle Luster make fer one of the beds in the corner of the room. Their youngins followed them. They were screamin' and prayin'. Uncle Mort and Aunt Rett and all their youngins made fer the bed in the other corner of the room. Mammie and my sisters and brothers made for the stairs. Mammie was prayin' as she run. I stayed at the foot of the stairs with Pappie. When he prayed in the strawberry patch, I thought he was astin' the Lord fer too much rain but I didn't say anythin'. I didn't interfere with his prayer.

The water got higher in our house. A rock too big fer a jolt-wagon to haul smashed through the door and rolled across the floor and stopped. If it had rolled another time it would have knocked the big log wall out'n our house. Uncle Mort waded the water from the bed to the stairs and carried Aunt Rett and their youngins to the stairs. When he turned one loose on the stairs he run up the stairs like a drownded chicken. Uncle Luster ferried Aunt Beadie and their youngins to the stairs and turned them loose. Pappie had to take to the stairs. I followed Pappie.

"If we get out'n this house alive," Uncle Mort prayed, "we'll stay out'n it, Lord."

Uncle Luster prayed a long prayer and ast the Lord to save his wife and family. He promised the Lord if He would save them that he would leave Tanyard forever. I never heard so much prayin' in a churchhouse at any of the big revivals at Plum Grove as I heard up our upstairs. Sometimes you couldn't hear the prayers fer the lightnin' strikin' the big oaks. You could hear trees fallin' every place.

"The Lord has answered my prayers," Pappie shouted.

"Pray for the cloudbust to stop," Mammie shouted. "Get down on your knees, Sweeter, and pray."

"Listen, Lizzie," Pappie shouted above the roar of the water and the thunder and the splittin' of the big oaks on the high slopes, "I ain't two-faced enough to ast the Lord fer somethin' like a lot of people and atter I git it—turn around and ast the Lord to take it away. You said the Lord wouldn't answer my prayer. You've been prayin'! Why ain't the Lord answered your prayers? You ain't got the Faith. You just think you have."

When the lightnin' flashed in at our upstairs scuttlehole we had fer a winder, I could see Uncle Mort huddled with his family and Uncle Luster holdin' his family in a little circle. Mammie had all of us, but Pappie and me, over in the upstairs corner. I looked out at the scuttlehole and saw the water surgin' down Left Fork of Tanyard Hollow and down the Right Fork of Tanyard Hollow and meetin' right at our house. That' the only reason our house had stood. One swift river had kilt the other one when they met on this spot. I thought about what Pappie said.

I could see cornfields comin' off'n the slopes. I could see trees with limbs and roots on them bobbin' up and down and goin' down Tanyard Hollow faster than a hound dog could run. It was a sight to see. From my scuttle-hole I told 'em what I saw until I saw a blue sky comin' over the high rim of rock cliffs in the head of Tanyard Hollow. That was the end of the storm. I never saw so many happy people when I told them about the patch of blue sky that I saw.

"This is like a dream," Uncle Mort said.

"It's more like a nightmare to me," Uncle Luster said.

"It's neither," Pappie said. "It's the fulfillment of a prayer."

"Why do you pray fer destruction, Sweeter?" Mammie ast.

"To show you the Lord will answer my prayer atter the way you talked to me in the strawberry patch," Pappie said. "And I want your brother Mort and your brother-in-law Luster to remember their promises to the Lord."

The storm was over. It was light again. The chickens flew down from the apple trees. The big yard sycamore shade trees went with the storm but the apple trees stood. There was mud two feet deep on our floor. It was all over the bedclothes. There were five big rocks on our house we couldn't move. We'd haf to take the floor up and dig holes and bury the rocks under the floor. Trees were split all over Tanyard Hollow hillside slopes. Great oak trees were splintered clean to the tops. Our corn had washed from the hill slopes. There wasn't much left but mud, washed-out trees, rocks, and waste. Roots of the black-oak trees where the dead-leaf loam had washed away, looked like bundles of clean washed black snakes. The big rock upon the steep hillside that bothered Pappie when he was plowin' had washed in front of our door.

"I promised the Lord," Uncle Mort said, "if we got through this storm alive, I'd take my family and get out'n here and I meant it."

"Amen," Pappie shouted.

"Sorry we can't stay and hep you clean the place up," Uncle Luster said, "but I'm takin' my wife and youngins and gettin' out'n this Hollow."

They didn't stay and hep us bury the rocks under the floor. They got their belongin's and started wadin' the mud barefooted down Tanyard Hollow. They's glad to get goin'. Pappie looked pleased when he saw them pullin' their bare feet out'n the mud and puttin' 'em down again. Pappie didn't grumble about what he had lost. The fence where he had the black-snakes hangin' washed down Tanyard Hollow. There wasn't a fence rail 'r a black snake left. The strawberry patch was gutted with gully-ditches big enough to bury a mule. Half of the plants had washed away.

"It wasn't the brazen images of snakes," Pappie said, "that done all of this. Tanyard Hollow is washed clean of most of its topsoil and lost a lot of its trees. But it got rid of a lot of its rubbish and it's a more fitten place to live."

Hurdie's Night Out

About the story:

Pedike Mullins and Hurdie Howard's mountain valley world is one in which "a good sermon" is a social event, love is "a little sparkin'," "Old Lizzie" is a Model-T Ford, and "O.K." is "K.O." To start a car is "to crank her tail," smokes are "home rolled chicken-bill" cigarettes, and a car is morally suspect by the good people of the valley community. On the way to church they say, "One of them old cars" has "been the ruination of many a good girl." Like a gaited horse, Old Lizzie can "rack" or "lope," and rattles along "pantin' and a-blowin' like a mad boar hog in the red brush." At the Vine Grove Church grounds moonshine is sold in fifty-cent "horse-quarts" among the "Devil's Crowd" hanging about outside "the winders." Fundamentalist Brother Baggs admonishes the young people, "Come in the house tonight with the Lord's flock. Don't stay out in the dark with the Devil's rams." What follows in "Hurdie's Night Out" is pure mountain hilarity, typical of a Jesse Stuart short story, and the movement is anything but slow-paced.

Of this story Jesse Stuart said, "I just wanted to write a story I remembered from youth . . . a friend who had a tin Lizzie who went a-courting. It is not a family story, but it is right out of my memory. . . ."*

* * *

"**W**HAT DO you say, Pedike?" Hurdie asked me. "You want to hear a good sermon tonight?"

"I've worked all week in the corn, Hurdie," I said. "I don't mind if I do. Might be a chance of doin' a little sparkin'."

"You're right, Pedike," Hurdie said. "We'll get in the old Lizzie. Might be old and run-down but the girls like to ride in it! Better to ride than to walk through the mud."

We walked out to the shed. Hurdie took the broom and swept the chickens' droppings from his Lizzie. I took a coffee sack out of the corncrib. I dipped the sack into the water barrel by the drainpipe and wiped the manure-stain spots off the doors.

*Jesse Stuart, "Hurdie's Night Out," *Arizona Quarterly*, Vol. 30, No. 3 (Autumn, 1974), pp. 239–252. The source of Mr. Stuart's comment on the story "Hurdie's Night Out" is Jesse Stuart/H. E. Richardson, Interview #42, W-Hollow, Greenup, Ky., Sept. 17, 1981.

"You ought'n to keep the car here," I said to Hurdie. "Chickens roostin' upon the poles above it! Too much trouble to wash it every time you drive out."

"Pedike," Hurdie said to me, "I've not got no other place for it unless we let it rust to pieces out in the weather. Just have to drive it in the entry shed, that's all. We ought to wring the chickens' necks. Plenty of trees for them to roost in around here. Afraid of the owls, I guess. All try to get in this shed. Even on cold nights they roost on the cows' backbones with their toes in their good warm fur. Chickens have got more sense than we think."

We put the K-O on the Lizzie. We swept her out with the broom. We wiped her seat and her sides with a coffee sack and rubbed off the stains very well. The girls couldn't see these in the dark. Now, we wouldn't get our good suits all mussed-up.

"Crank her tail, Pedike," said Hurdie. "Crank, while I give 'er the juice."

Around and around I spun her just like turnin' a cider mill. I said, "Give 'er more spark, John-Henry."

Hurdie pulled down the spark. The engine's heart started flutterin' like a turkey buzzard's. The old Lizzie started rackin' like an old broke-down Jenny—actin' like somethin' tryin' to tear outen the barn!

"K-O, Pedike," Hurdie said. He was sittin' up high on the front seat actin' like he owned the valley. "Get in and let's be off."

Right down the road like a bat out of the barn loft. Right up the lane— just missed Pert Newsom's cows.

"Watch out where you fools 're a-takin' that thing," Pert Newsom shouted. "It's not got eyes, you know!"

"Eye it yourself and be-damned, you old codger," I yelled as we passed him up like a bullet.

"He thinks, Pedike, that he owns all the road," Hurdie said.

"For heaven sakes, Hurdie, don't go around these curves on two wheels," I said.

Steam was poppin' up from the radiator in a big white stream. Moon was comin' up over the mountains. People walking along the road were goin' to hear Brother Baggs preach the gospel. They ran to both sides of the road to let us pass. Old Liz was gettin' her breath now in big quick chug-chugs.

"Pa says that Brother Baggs is a deep man," I said. "He says he's the deepest man Vine Grove Church has ever had. Pa likes 'im."

"He's goin' to bring the price of terbacker up," Hurdie said, "the way everybody's gettin' saved and goin' out and cuttin' his green terbacker down. If our pas don't get saved we'll get a wallopin' big price for our ter-backer this fall. Won't be none left in the country but ours."

"No danger of my pa gettin' saved," Hurdie said. "Pa's too fat to waller in the floor and jerk. Pa has heart trouble nohow."

"Look! Two girls," I said. "Slow 'er down and ast 'em if they want to ride."

"K-O," said Hurdie.

Old Lizzie was all warmed up and rearin' to go and it was just like stop-pin' a stiff-mouth pair of mules. Hurdie put on the brakes. We came to a stop. Old Liz was pantin' and chuggin' and jerkin' all over.

"How about a lift, girls?" Hurdie said. "Goin' to church, aren't you?" Hurdie talked real loud.

"Yes," one of the girls said. She giggled.

"My ma said for me to never get in a car with strangers," said the other. She giggled.

"Come on girls, and climb in," Hurdie said. "We're goin' right your way. We're not strangers. We're a couple of nice boys goin' to hear Brother Baggs preach the Gospel. I'm Hurdie Howard. My pal here is Pedike Mul-lins. Safe in this car as you are at home with your mammies."

"Come on, we're takin' the chance," I said. "Can't see you well in the dark nohow. Plenty of girls at Vine Grove Church 'll be glad to ride with us. You know you want to ride."

"Don't be bashful, girls," Hurdie said. "Climb in and let's get goin'."

The girls whispered to each other. Hurdie punched me in the ribs and puffed his home rolled chicken-bill cigarette. Old Lizzie was tired as she'd been rackin' like a turned-to-the-barn Jenny. People passed us walking while we talked to the girls. Moon up, and stars out too. Pas and mas were afraid to stumble in the dark. I heard one say, "One of them old cars. Been the ruination of many a good girl. Wild boys in that one there. They're a-drinkin' too! They come nigh as a pea hittin' us back yander. Now pickin' up poor girls that don't know of sin."

"Sin, hell," said Hurdie as he blew smoke up toward the moon.

"We're goin' to ride," said one of the girls.

She climbed upon the runnin' board. She twisted and giggled.

"Have to get between us, Sister, and you'll have to flop your tail on Pe-dike's lap," said Hurdie.

"Suits me fine if you're not too heavy," I said.

"Heavy, hell," said Hurdie. "Climb on in and let's get started here. Old Liz is a-rarin' to go! We're late now! Church will be started, singin' will be over, and I like good singin'."

One girl got between us in our one-seater. I couldn't see 'er very well in the dark. She put her arm up around Hurdie's shoulder! My girl got into her lap. She put her arm around my neck. I put both my arms around her waist and drew her tight up against me.

"What's your name, Honey?" I asked.

"Prudie Martin," she said.

"Enzie Martin's girl?" I asked.

She said, "Yes, Honey, that's who I am. I know your pa, old Jeff Mullins."

"Right you are, Honey," said I.

"My name is Dollie Weaver," Hurdie's girl said. "Payson Weaver's girl. I know your pa, Crum Howard."

"You guessed it, Sister," Hurdie said as he puffed his sugarsack rolled cigarette and stepped on the gas. He let the reins loose and our old one-seated rackin' Lizzie took up the lane a-shakin' all over.

"Let 'er go," I said to Hurdie. "Give 'er enough rope to hang 'erself, by-hell!"

"What do you say, Babies?" Hurdie asked. "You want to be aired out in our old Lizzie?"

"Suits us," Dollie said. "I like to go fast."

"I'll let 'er lope then," Hurdie said. "This rackin's about jarred me to pieces."

There was no top on Old Lizzie. The wind from the cornfields hit our faces. I could smell the green terbacker as we passed it. I could see terbacker and corn in the moonlight.

"Sweetie-pie," said I, "ain't love grand?"

I tightened my arms around her. She put her other arm around my neck and held me with both arms like a man holds to a log with both arms to keep from drownin'.

Right around the lane. The people walking left the road and took to the bushes. Around the curve and up the first part of the hill ... Old Lizzie pantin' and a-blowin' like a mad boar hog in the red brush.

"More juice, so we can take the big hill in high," I said to Hurdie.

"Who's drivin', me or you, Pedike?" Hurdie asked me. "Guess I know how to take this hill in high as many times as Old Lizzie has climbed it with me."

"Lizzie's not as young as she used to be," I said. "You ought to have some respect for old age."

"That's what my pa always says if we butt-in when he's talkin'," said my sweetie-pie.

Right up the hill . . . zzzzzzzzzzzz . . . bbbbbbbb . . . tic-tic-tic . . . chuci-chuci-chuci-chuci, I was sure every stick on the road as big as a stick of stovewood was blown from under our exhaust pipe fifty yards over in the greenbriars and persimmon sprouts.

"I know how to climb this hill," Hurdie said as we rolled right up in front of the church where everybody was lookin' at us. There was a big crowd in front of the church and a big crowd in the church. A lot of people with their heads stuck out the winders were a-doin' a lot of talkin'.

"Where are you tryin' to get," I said to my sweetie-pie as she tried to dodge me. "Ride here with a feller then don't want to go in this house with 'im. You've not got a boy friend here lookin' for you, have you?"

"Oh, no," said Prudie. "I was just straightenin' out my legs. I've been cramped up in the car too long."

"A damn good thing," I said.

"Church is ready, boys," Brother Baggs said as he stood in the front door and waved his long arms. "Come in the house tonight with the Lord's flock. Don't stay out here in the dark with the Devil's rams. Be good children tonight. Come on, all of you."

"That means us too," said Hurdie.

Boys were lying down wallerin' on the grass. People still had their heads stuck out the church winders like a bunch of yahoos.

"Come on, children," said Reverend Baggs, "the singin' is ready to begin now. Come inside tonight and be children the Lord would have you to be. The Devil wants you out here wallerin' on the grass."

Prudie took my arm. She held onto it now. She knew I was not standin' for any damned foolishness. I might have wanted her to turn loose my arm when I saw her face better in the lamp light. She might be as ugly as home-made sin. I picked 'er up and took a chance. Dollie had Hurdie by the arm holdin' onto him like a leech when it grabs you by the leg in a frog pond. There's not but two ways to get a leech loose. Whack 'im with a knife or chew homemade terbacker and spit ambeer spittle on him. Then he lets go all holds on you. He drops down like a beef shot between the eyes with a high-powered rifle.

My sweetie-pie, Prudie, and I walked in front now. We walked up to the door. Joe Finnie's boy, Steve, stopped me and said, "Say, Pedike, how about a couple of horse-quarts? Just fifty cents apiece!"

Dollie said, "Here at the Lord's house?"

"He turned the water into wine, didn't He," said little Steve Finnie. He stood back in the dark by the door.

"Who made it?" I asked. "My pap make it?"

"That's enough," he said. "You know what happened to Waymore Stevens drinkin' a horse-quart of your pap's moonshine. He was ridin' on the Old Line Special and ast the conductor when the train was goin' to get outen the Barney Tunnel. It's not out of the Barney Tunnel yet for him. In the poorhouse now blind as a bat. I want to keep my eyes. They're not so pretty, but damned useful."

We went into the house. We got one of the seats on the left side of the Vine Grove Church. The seat was just big enough for four. Really, it was just big enough for three, but we all crowded in. There was a winder by us with good cool air comin' in and swarm of lightning bugs and millers flying around the lamps. I had Prudie's left hand in my left hand. She had her right arm up around my shoulder. I had my right hand free to use at the winder if one of the Devil's crowd started anything with me. Dollie and Hurdie were all hugged-up a-holdin' hands and lookin' at one another's eyes. We were lucky to get such pretty girls. We took a chance and won like shootin' a seven, that's all. Pretty eyes and hair and with skin as white as a dove. That was my sweetie-pie, Prudie.

"We'll start worship tonight," said Brother Baggs, "by singin' 'We'll Feast on the Mountain.' Glory to His name, Brothers and Sisters! Glad to see this house packed tonight. Know you've come out here to get the real old-time salvation that the preachers nowadays are afraid to preach. Glory to God, I say, Amen!"

Brother Baggs looked up at the ceilin'. He was a tall man in a blue shirt open at the collar and a long black coat.

"Amen," said one of the Devil's crowd near my winder. "Amen. Brother Ben, shot a goose and killed a big fat hen!" A rock hit the wall above the organ. It fell back on the pulpit.

"Pay no attention to the Devil with his rock throwers. Remember what David did to Goliath with one of God's rocks. That's what we'll do to them before mornin'. We'll run the Devil from the hills. It's the Devil causin' all this. He's out there among his boozers, gun toters, and whoremongers."

The music from the organ was so pretty it made me sorry for every time I had cussed the mule in the cornfield yesterday. And I'd cussed every time the plow hit a stump, too. Plowin' in new ground is rough, you know. Everybody was singin' in the church now. Brother Baggs stood upon the pulpit and waved his big hands.

He said, "Glory to God, Brothers and Sisters, ain't that sweet? What will Heaven be like when we all get there and get rid of the old Devil and his angels. That Happy Land! Oh, won't you come, Brothers, and come right up here and be saved tonight? Won't you come?"

Brother Baggs jumped up and down and jerked as the organ played and everybody sang. I saw one boy in the choir, Bundie Billie, with a black bow tie that worked up and down on his Adam's apple as he sang.

People jumped from their seats. They ran up the aisles and clapped their hands and shouted, "Glory to God! Glory to God! There won't be any sorrow there. Won't Heaven be sweet, Brother! Won't Heaven be sweet, Sister!"

Seats went over. The stovepipe went down. People shouted on. They jerked and stretched out on the floor! Shouters tramped over and on them lying there on the floor. People were talkin' in unknown tongues.

"Won't Heaven be sweet, Sisters! Won't Heaven be sweet, Brothers!

"There'll be no spittoons in Heaven for the vile terbacker weed. W'y' wouldn't touch that stuff for anything on earth!"

"Give us faster music," shouted Brother Baggs. "Faster music for the Spirit!"

"They're gettin' riled, aren't they," I said to Prudie.

"Gettin' riled with the Spirit," said Hurdie. "Uncle Ted jined 'em last week and cut all his green terbacker down. Had the prettiest crop you have ever seen. Don't know what he'll do this winter with ten children! I asked him about it. All he said was, 'God will provide someway.' I'm keepin' my terbacker. Need gas for Old Lizzie and another suit o' clothes."

"Wow," somebody hit my hand layin' in the winder.

"What the hell," I said, lookin' out in the moonlight.

"I'll show you what the hell," said a beardy prowler of the Devil with eyes that shone like a possum's eyes after dark. "You come out here and I'll run this clean through your damned heart." I could see his big knife blade shining in the moonlight.

"Oh, it's Warhorse," said Prudie. "He's followed me here. I'll bet Tim is with 'im, Dollie."

"Let 'im be here," said Dollie. "I don't care. I love Hurdie so much already!"

"Thought you didn't have a date," I said. "Your Warhorse is out there with a knife as big as a scythe blade and my gun is at home. If I had my gun I'd shoot the hell outen him from this winder. I'd shoot him in the guts. I might miss his head. The low-down, sneakin' son-of-a-bitch. I'd leave 'im for the buzzards and the crows to pick his bones clean."

"Come on out and do it, you dull-eyed bastard, you. We'll take that other pretty man you got in there and ride 'im on a rail if it warn't for mussin' up that purty suit. You two low-down cotton-eyes hellions!"

"Let's get 'em," I said to Hurdie. "Let's get a club and go atter 'em.

Let's don't take them words off'n nobody."

"Hell, no," said Hurdie. "We've got the girls, haven't we? We can't do nothin'. They got the drop on us."

"Come on out," said Warhorse. "We might come in and get you! You purtie things! Must be from town all dressed up in your blue serge suits and pretty bow ties."

"Come on," said Hurdie. "We double-dare you! Come right in and get us! You ain't men enough, you sons-of-bitches! Dollie belongs to me. There's nobody takin' 'er neither."

"Prudie belongs to me," I said in a loud voice. "Not anybody gettin' her neither. You'll have to burn the house to get us out of here. We're happy as two old coons on a holler log, ain't we, Sweetie-pie?"

"We sure are," Prudie said, holdin' my hand tighter and squeezin' my neck like a lump of sugar.

"By God, we'll burn the damn house," said Warhorse. "We'll burn it to the ground. We'll smoke you bastards out of there. Set fire to your tails and you'll come."

"They won't burn nothin'," said Hurdie. "They're a couple of damn blowguns! They're tryin' to bluff us. Take it easy, Pedike, and watch he don't stab you through the winder."

Brother Baggs was jumpin' high now and kickin' his feet together twice before he came down on the floor. People were wild—hollerin' and rollin' on the floor and playin' the organ and singin' "Glory to God." Brother Baggs had his eyes closed and he was jumpin' up and down.

"I can see Heaven plain as day," Brother Baggs shouted. "I can see rows of little children with harps. I can hear the death bells. I can see the pearly gates, children."

"Got rid of 'em didn't we," said Hurdie. "Why do they want to come around after the girls took us? They don't want them ugly sons-of-bitches!"

"We're through with 'em," said Dollie. "They don't have a car. We have to walk every place with 'em. They get drunk on us, don't they Prudie?"

"They sure do," said Prudie. "I met old Warhorse at a dance and I've not been able to shake 'em loose since. He won't act decent with me nor let nobody else go with me."

"Well, Sweetie-pie," said I, "he'll act decent and by God he'll let me go with you. He can't tell the one I love what to do."

"I smell somethin' burnin'," said Hurdie. "It smells like coal ile and rags!"

"You just think you do," said Dollie. "I know they said they'd burn the house down or get us out."

"Hell, my nose is like a hound-dog's nose," said Hurdie. "I smell somethin' burnin'."

Shoutin' was gettin' faster now. Nearly everybody was shoutin'. The people not shoutin' were young couples back in the house all loved-up. The organ was playin' and people singin' "God's A-goin' to Set This World on Fire Some of These Days." Brother Baggs was so hoarse he couldn't shout. He was just cryin' and foamin' at the mouth.

'My God," said Dollie, "look yander! Whole front of the house is on fire! Look, won't you, Prudie!"

"I said," said Hurdie, "I smelt rags and coal ile burnin'. Them crazy yahoos were settin' this house on fire then. Look at that fire, won't you! Let's get outen here!"

"Fire, fire, fire, God's fire. God's a-goin' to set this world on fire," shouted Brother Baggs with his eyes closed.

"Fire, hell," said a man runnin'. "It's not God's fire. It's man's fire. Somebody iled the house and set it. Thought I smelt that ile. What is this world a-comin' to nohow!"

The congregation was hollerin'! They were mad and shoutin'. They poured out th' door and winders! Men dragged the jerkin' mourners off the floor.

"Get God's people out from the Devil's fire," said a man.

Men grabbed men who were senseless on the floor. They dragged them through the crowd. Women were screamin' and hollerin' for their children. Lord, I held onto Prudie. Hurdie held to Dollie.

"Don't that beat all," said Hurdie. "Watch that fire climb the walls! It will soon get the organ and the pulpit!"

One man grabbed the Bible from the stand. Young men rolled the organ up the aisle. Big yaller flames were leapin' high now. And the light from the fire shone on people's sweaty faces.

"Let's get out," I said. "Let's get Old Liz and get away from here. Let's hide among the fleein' crowd."

"Haf to, or get stabbed," said Hurdie. "Come, let's get goin'! Let's hide among the people."

I grabbed my sweetie-pie, Prudie. We joined the fleein' throng.

"To the car," said Hurdie.

Hurdie had Dollie. People against us were shoutin' and cryin'! Glory to God. Glory to God. Selah! Selah! Selah! Fire of the Devil. Fire of the Devil's angels."

We squeezed through the door.

"Warhorse and Tim's waitin' some place," said Dollie.

"Hid and goin' to stab us," I said. "Let's get among as many people as we can."

We came out of the house like a swarm of bees and were in the middle of the swarm too. The house was a-blazin' well now. No way to put it out. No well of water on this hilltop and no water buckets. People were on the grass wallerin' and shoutin' and groanin': "Glory to God! Glory to God!" People held to the fence posts and jerked. Men lost their pants and shouted in the yard in their shirttails: "Glory to God! Glory to God! I can see Heaven, Sweet Heaven."

We made it to the car. "Thank the Lord," said Hurdie. "They didn't know Old Lizzie belonged to me or I wouldn't a-had 'er. She'd a-been torn to pieces and scattered among the persimmon sprouts."

Hurdie jumped in and turned on the juice and spark. I twisted Old Lizzie's tail. While I twisted 'er tail, Dollie and Prudie climbed in.

zzzzzzz — sssssssss — chic — chic — chic — chic — chug — chug — chug — chug — chug—chug—chug.

I jumped on the runnin' board. Hurdie let 'er out from a rack to a lope.

"Careful, Hurdie," said Dollie, "don't kill one of us!"

"We don't want to get killed," I said. "And look comin'! I'd ruther kill than to be killed, by God."

"I see 'em," said Prudie. "Look at that big knife shinin' in the firelight and that big club."

"Too late now, boys," said Hurdie. "We're safe unless our Lizzie goes flooey. We'll soon be safe on yan side of Jurdan."

zzzzzzzz—sssssssss—zzzzzzzz.

Around the curve. Flashlights and lanterns were goin' to the weeds. Down past the young boys in front of the old people runnin' from the burnin' house. Now we passed the last lone boy in front runnin' like a turkey and leadin' the fleein' crowd.

The moon was shinin' down on the hills, the cornfields, and th' terbacker patches. Back in the distance we could see the flames of our church reachin' up to the sky and the stars. We could hear the shouts of men and women. We could hear the children screamin'.

"Fleein' from th' wrath to come," said Hurdie.

Lord, I squeezed Sweetie-pie in my arms now. She put both her arms around my neck. She kissed me a thousand times. Dollie had 'er arms around Hurdie but he had his hands on the throttle and his eyes on the rail and Old Lizzie was a-ballin' the jack. Around the lane and the road was clear. The screams grew fainter and fainter as we raced through the moonlight.

"Old Warhorse will kill me, Honey, when he sees me again," Sweetie-pie Prudie said.

"He's not goin' to see you again," I said. "My little tater-bug, you're one of my choosin'. I could a-picked the world over and not a-found another as much to my likin' as you. You'll be tomorrow night where you are tonight—right in my arms!"

"You're so sweet, Sugar," said Prudie. She squeezed me tighter and kissed me faster.

"You'd as well be in my arms too, Sugar," said Hurdie as he drove slowly in order to light another home rolled chicken-bill cigarette. "Picked you up in the dark. Loved you as soon as I put my two peepers on you in the lamp light of the old Vine Grove Church. It's in a heap of ashes by now. We got the dope on the birds that set the fire, too. All four of us. We can swear it."

"You just made me think," I said to Hurdie. "We can get rid of them birds and get 'em clean outen the country."

"I've been thinkin' that already," said Hurdie. "I've thought this ever since we left the church. We'll send them yahoos to the pen. Let 'em use their clubs and knives there. We don't want to take no chances fightin' them and get killed now. We'll have our wives to take care of."

"Believe to my soul Old Lizzie got saved tonight the way she's jerkin'," I said.

"Sweet Heaven," says my little sweetie-pie, Prudie, who was all curled-up like a blacksnake in my arms.

Sparks and fire were flyin' from Hurdie's cigarette. The moon, stars, sky, and wind above and the dirt and grass below were great. And Old Lizzie was goin' like a bat outen the corncrib for home. And she was shakin', jerkin', and rattlin' mightily.

Love in the Spring

About the story:

In May, 1969, Whit Burnett wrote Jesse Stuart in regard to Burnett's forth-coming collection *This Is My Best in the Third Quarter of the Century,* assuring Stuart that he should be represented by a short story. "Anybody who has done more than three hundred of them and still can come up with new ones, like ["]Love in the Spring,["] which sparkle and also warm the heart, doesn't need to be a poet and a biographer as well." He went on to write that he liked many of the stories in Jesse Stuart's new book *Come Gentle Spring* (1969), but

> it seems to me the one that would stand out like a jewel for its humor, uni-versality and its bounce and rhythm is "Love in the Spring," which did more to my sensibilities than any of the others, although many are unique for other qualities. . . . For this particular book, where I'm both short on short stories and short on humor that is honest to God humor, I would like very much to include the youth, the ugly guy and the neighbor's philosophy of love and human frailty. It would shine out without competition from anyone.

Whit Burnett went on to request "a little comment on this story as at least one of your best," and here in part is what Stuart wrote for the editor and his readers:

> ["] Love in the Spring ["] is out of my world which is part of the hill and mountain country of Eastern Kentucky which is a part of Appalachia, which is an important segment of America, the only one which has a defi-nite culture of its own. My outlying area is larger than England, Scotland, Wales, the South and North Irelands combined—but with a population only comparable to the City of London.
> My world has become much larger than the physical world of W-Hol-low into which I was born. . . . The four seasons are balanced and diver-sified in my world—descriptions are varied and exciting the full length of the year and always exciting for this writer, a son of this segment of Ameri-can earth. But the original humanity here is more exciting than the physical aspects, seasonal beauty and winter's depressive moods. Each man and woman is one or more stories, poems and novels. There are too many

for one writer to write. Out of this comes this episode, ["] Love in the Spring, ["] which was a short story created by the characters. All I had to do was record and with help select it for you.

Since I was born into W-Hollow, the center of my world, where I still live a mile from where I was born, at the age of six or seven I began writing of my world—and I have never stopped. I have written of my friends and relatives (I have no enemies for I am one of them), in poems, stories and novels. I have written of three generations where my characters are akin to each other and to me.

My world has now become so large, my green and dark hills of W-Hollow can no longer hold my friends and relatives. They have gone out to all America and to countries in the world where I have and haven't been. (I've been in seventy-four.) ["] Love in the Spring, ["] I believe, is a gay, humorous leaf from the Family Tree.*

* * *

It was last April when I met Effie. It was over at the Put-Off Ford at the Baptis foot-washing. Effie is a Slab Baptis. She was there having her feet washed. And I can't forget that day in April. It is always work in the spring. Fence to fix. Plowing to do. Cattle to tend to. Seems like everything is to do in the spring on the place. Planting crops is the big job. We don't have no place to go only to church and we don't feel like going there only on Sunday. That is the day we have off and we don't have that day off until we've milked seven cows and slopped the hogs and got in wood and got up water for the day. I can't forget that Sunday in last spring when I met Effie. I just packed in the last load of wood and Mom says to me: "Elster, you are going to fall for a woman sometime so hard that it's going to hurt you. Run around and talk about Mort Anderson being in love and how silly he is. Wait till you fall in love once. The love bug is going to bite you right over the heart."

I went to the baptizing with a clean white starched shirt on and a blue necktie and blue serge pants and black slippers. I looked about as good in them as I can look. I felt good just to get off to the foot-washing. I remember that row of elms along Little Sandy River had just started to leaf out. The rest of the hills just had a few sycamores and poplars down along the creeks that had leafed a little. It was a pretty morning. And down by the

*Jesse Stuart, "Love in the Spring," orig. pub. in *Come Gentle Spring* (N.Y.: McGraw-Hill, 1969), pp. 55–69. Reprinted in Whit Burnett, ed., *This is My Best in the Third Quarter of the Century* (N.Y.: Garden City, Doubleday, 1970), pp. 575–578, and in Martin Levin, ed., *Love Stories* (N.Y.: N.Y. *Times* Book Co., 1975), pp. 360–370. Mr. Stuart mailed me a copy of his letter received from Whit Burnett in New York City, dated May 23, 1969, and included in Mr. Stuart's letter to me from W-Hollow, Greenup, Ky., June 23, 1969. Also included in his letter was an original copy of "*This Is My Best* by Jesse Stuart," his manuscript for submission to Whit Burnett, from which Mr. Stuart's comments above are taken.

ford I never saw as many people in my life gathered at that one place. And I've seen a lot of baptizings there. Horses hitched to the trees with ropes and bridle reins. Wagons here and there with washing-tubs of grub in them and chears where whole families rid miles in them to the foot-washing. And horses eating yaller corn out'n the wagon beds of a lot of the wagons. I just walked down where they's singing "Where the Healing Waters Flow." It was soft music and I wished I was a child of the Lord's then. Good people—the Baptis is—we live neighbors to them. Ain't no better people to help you out in a time of sickness or weedy crops in the spring. Come right in and help you out. Now on this bank and washing feet. I walked down along the edge of the river where the horseweeds had been tromped down. I just wanted to look the crowd over. A whole row up and a whole row down. The row standing up was a-washing the feet of them on the ground. Just setting there on the ground as unconcerned and washing feet. Then they would sing another verse of "Where the Healing Waters Flow."

I looked up in front of me. I couldn't believe my eyes. I saw the prettiest woman I ever saw in my life. She was prettier than a speckled pup. Honest I never saw anything like her. Eyes that just looked at you and melted like yellow butter on hot corn bread—blue kind of eyes—and a face that was smooth as silk and cheeks the color of the peeling on a roman beauty apple in September. Her hair was the color of golden corn silks in August hanging from the shooting corn. Hair pretty and curly waving in the wind. I never saw a woman so pretty in my life. Her hands didn't look to me like no hands that had held to the hoe handle like my mother's hands and my sisters'. Her hands were pretty and soft. Her teeth were white as a bubble of foam in the Sandy River. She was an angel among the sinners trying to come clean. My heart beat faster when I saw her. Some man had his back to me. He was washing her foot. He had an old chipped washpan and a big towel and a bar of home-made soap made from oaktree ashes. He'd put it on her foot like he was putting axle grease on a wagon hub. Then he would smear it with his hands and rub. Then he would take the towel and dry her foot till it would look pink as a wild crab-apple blossom. I just stood there and looked at her. She looked at me. He saw her looking and he looked around. Of all the big ugly devils I ever saw in my life it was this fellow, Jonas Pratt's boy, Tawa Pratt. Lived down on Little Sandy on that big farm in the bend by the grove of cedars. When he turned around and saw me looking he said: "Ain't you a Baptis?"

And I said: "No I ain't no Slab Baptis. I'm a Methodist and I go to Plum Grove to church."

"Go on about your business then," he said, "and leave us Baptis alone. This ain't no side show. We are here worshipping the Lord."

I could see he just didn't want me to see the girl. He didn't like me. I didn't like him. I don't care if he was worshiping the Lord. And I says to him: "If that's the way you feel about it, all right. But I want to know the name of the girl here with you and where she lives."

That burnt him up. His lips just spread out and he showed them big yaller horse-teeth in front. I just thinks to myself: "What woman could kiss that awful mouth behind them big horse-teeth?" He looked at me with them black polecat eyes and his hair was right down over his eyes. He was a sorry-looking devil.

The girl says to me: "I'm Effie Long. I live up on Duck Puddle." I never said a word, I'd go to Duck Puddle. That's just down on Little Sandy four miles and up a hollow that comes into Little Sandy not far from the riffles. I knowed right then and there I'd see that woman again. I said to myself as I walked back from the riverbank over through horseweeds: "That's my wife if I can get her. Pretty as an angel right out of Heaven."

I thought of what Mom told me. I would fall for a skirt. I did like the looks of that woman. I went home. I remember it like it was just one hour ago. The daisies looked good to me. First time flowers ever did look good to me. I pulled off the top of a sweet William and smelt it. It smelt sweet as sugar.

"The love bug's got me right over the heart," I said to Mom soon as I got in at the door. "I saw my wife at the foot washing—over there among the Baptis today at the Put-Off Ford."

And Mom she says: "Elster, you ain't fell for no Slab Baptis, have you? No Slab Baptis woman can ever come under this Methodist roof until she's been converted into the Methodist faith. That bunch all running around and drinking licker. Won't see no licker in heaven nor no spittoons for that old terbacker."

That's how women are. Right half of the time. When a man is in love, what does he care for spittoons in heaven and bad licker or good licker? What does he care who a Methodist is or a Slab Baptis is? He wants his woman. That's the way I felt. Mom married Pop fifty years ago and she don't know what it is to be young and be in love. I just never said a word.

A week hadn't passed till I heard about church down on Duck Puddle. Slab Baptis holding a pertracted meeting down there. I put on a white starched shirt, a blue necktie and blue serge pants and my black slippers and I went down there. It was a awful walk through the brush and over them ridges. But I followed the fox hunters' path for more than two miles across through the brush. I walked across the rocks at the riffle and hit the big wagon road up to the church. Meeting was a-going on when I got there. I had to stop and ask four or five times before I found the place. A pretty place after a body gets there but a devil of a time getting to it. I never went inside the house till I peeped in at the winders and looked over the house to see if I could see Effie. I looked and looked. And one time when I looked with my eyes up agin the winderpanes and the Slab Baptis preacher said: "A lot of pilferers on the outside of the house tonight. The devil in sheep's clothing is out there. Methodists are snooping around." When I heard this I slipped back in the dark. I'm a Methodist and couldn't be nothing else. Methodist church is good enough for Pa and Mom and Grandpa and Grandma and it's good enough for me. Even if they don't want me, for I bet on chicken fights and play cards once in a while.

I slipped back to the winder. I had looked every place but the amen corner. I looked up there and saw the angel I had seen over at the ford. She was in a mighty good place to be. Me a Methodist and out in the dark. I picked up courage and just walked up and bolted in at the door. I found a empty seat and I saw Effie start looking at me. I started looking at her. And I looked up there and saw old Tawa too. He was in the amen corner. He started showing them teeth soon as he saw me. And I thinks to myself: "Old boy, one of these days I'm going to get me a rock and knock them ugly teeth down your throat. Running around here with a set of horse-teeth in your mouth."

The crowd looked at me. A lot of them had seen me at the Methodist church. A lot of them had seen me at the foot-washing. They all knowed I was a Methodist. They know the Harkreaders are all Methodist—every last devil of them!

I just waited till church was out. I was going to take Effie home. And I had my mind made up. If that horse-toothed thing of a Tawa should come around me and started anything, it would just be too bad. I was going to use my fists long as they would stand it. I got bad bones in my little fingers. And after my fists I was going to knife it with him and after that if he whopped me I was going to use the balance of power. I carried it right in my pocket. The prettiest little .22 you ever saw in your life—could put five balls between your eyes before you could say "Jack Robinson." I don't go into no strange territory unless I go prepared for the worst. That's the way we got to do here. I don't care if we are Baptis and Methodist.

The preacher was saying: "Men and women, since you got to work in your crops tomorrow and I got to work in mine, we'll call the meeting till tomorrow night at seven. All of you be here and bring your songbooks. Sing "Almost Persuaded," folks, and all who wants to come up and jine us just come right on." I never saw so many people fall at the altar.

Church was out and the people already saved—the young people went home and the old people stayed to pray with the people at the "mourner's bench." They was just a-going on something awful. A lot of them were sheep that had left the Methodist flock too. A bunch that wanted to stay in our church and drink licker and play cards and we just wouldn't have it in Plum Grove. Effie come right down the aisle and I said: "Honey, how about seeing you home tonight?" I know my face got red when she said: "All right." Here was old Tawa right behind her with that crazy grin showing that big set of yellow horse-teeth. I thought if he wanted anything he could get it on this night. I didn't speak to him. No use to hide it. He didn't like me and I didn't like him.

I got Effie by the arm, and I held it like a leech. We didn't speak. We just walked out of the house and past a bunch of boys at the door waiting for their girls and the other fellow's girl. People just looked at us. Boys lit their cigarettes and pipes and the old men started spitting their ambeer. A lot of the women lit up their pipes too—old long-stemmed clay pipes. Something you don't see around our church at Plum Grove among them already saved. If they done it they went home or out behind the brush.

I hadn't got out from under the oak trees by the church house till I had Effie by the hand. And I said: "Honey, I can't eat, drink, work, nor sleep for thinking about you." And I reached down and got her by the little soft hand, and she looked up at me and said: "Ain't that funny? I feel the same way about you. I have felt that way ever since I saw you at the foot-washing. I can't forget you. I keep thinking about you. When I saw you tonight I was thinking about you." I just squeezed her hand a little harder and I said: "Was you, Honey?" Then we went on out the path without speaking.

We went out past the Duck Puddle graveyard. White tombstones gleaming there in the moonlight. Lord, it was a sad thing to think about. I wondered what had become of old Tawa. It was a little dark even if the moon was shining. I didn't care though. I had Effie. I didn't blame him for loving her, but I just didn't want him to get her.

I guess we went through twenty pairs of drawbars before we come to Effie's place. It was a little log house upon the side of the bank, pretty with flowers in the yard. I'd always thought flowers was for the womenfolks. I told Effie I'd never liked flowers till I met her. I told her everything like that. We just went up to her door. I said a lot about the crops. Before I started to leave we was standing out at the well-gum. The moon came upon her old log house there among all them roses and flowers. It was a mighty pretty place. Effie said: "Guess I'd better get in the house and get to bed. Got to work tomorrow." And I said: "Where, Honey?" "In the terbacker field," she said. And then I said: "W'y, you don't work in no terbacker field and stay as white as you are." She said: "That's all you know about it, El-ster. I use stocking legs on my arms and a sunbonnet." And I says: "Honey, I love you. I want to marry you." I just pulled her up to me and kissed her there in the moonlight. Soon I left her there and run over the hill like a dog. Tears come into my eyes. Just to think about that. I used to laugh at such stuff. Now, I had six or seven miles to walk home and blue Monday and the plow before me the next day. But seeing Effie was worth a dozen trips like this. When a man is in love he just don't care.

I went to bed that night—must have been morning. It was after the roosters crowed for midnight. Lord, but I was tired. I just could see Effie. I could pull her up to me and kiss her. I could see her eyes, I could see her teeth. I could see her log house in the moonlight. I just couldn't forget it all.

I got up and et my breakfast. Drunk two cups of black coffee and went out to milk the cows. I'd just stop at the barn and look off into the wind. Pa come up to me and he said: "Elster, what in the devil and Tom Walker's got into you here lately—just go around with your head up in the air dreaming. W'y, you even stop when you are shaving your face. If I didn't see you the other day shave half of your face and put the razor up I'm a liar." I never said anything, for it was the truth. I just couldn't help it for thinking about Effie.

I went out to plow corn. I took the mule and the double-shovel plow and went down the path by the barn. I didn't pay any attention but I started the plow on the wrong side of the field and was plowing up the corn. I couldn't think about anything but Effie and how I run away and left her that night with my eyes filled with tears. Then I thought: "W'y, I must be crazy to act like this. I'm forgetting everything. I'm not happy as I was. I can't laugh like I did. She didn't say she would marry me. That's it. That's what's the matter." I just couldn't get back to see Effie that week. I had too much to do. Too much corn to plow and seven cows to milk.

Well, I went out to work Tuesday morning. I couldn't work. I thought I'd go up and see Uncle Tid Porter. He lives right on the bank above us. He gives us boys a lot of advice. Uncle Tid was in the woodyard whacking off a few sticks of stovewood. I walked up and I said: "Uncle Tid, I'm in love with a girl. I can't sleep. I can't work. I can't do anything. I'm going crazy."

You ought to have seen Uncle Tid sling his ax again the ground and laugh. You know Uncle Tid is a pretty good doctor when we can't get one from town. He uses the yarb remedies and he does pretty well. Used to be the only doctor in this section. Now, he gives us advice along with spring tonics of slipper-elm bark, shoe-make bark and ginsang and snakeroot. "Well," said Uncle Tid, shaking his long thin chin whiskers stained with a little terbacker juice—his blue-walled eye squinted a little—"when did you meet this girl and where is she from?"

"I met her last month at the Slab Baptis foot-washing at the Put-Off Ford. She's from Duck Puddle. She's a beauty, too, Uncle Tid. W'y, Uncle Tid, to tell you the truth, I never loved a flower till I met her. Now I notice them. See the wild rose in bloom in the woods. I noticed them this morning. She is with me everywhere I go. I can't sleep. I can't eat."

"It's love in the spring," said Uncle Tid. "Love in the spring is so uncertain I wouldn't trust it. Don't be too sure of yourself and jump in and try to marry. Wait a while. Just go out and watch life in the spring. Go to the house and put the mule in the pasture. Take the afternoon off and go to the pond and watch the frogs. Go find some blacksnakes in love and watch them. Watch the terrapins and the turtles. Everything is in love now. Listen to the songs of the birds. Listen how they sing to each other. It is time to be in love. All the earth is in love now. And love is so uncertain in the spring."

I just got on the mule and went back home. I took the harness off old Barnie and put it on the stall in the barn and I slapped him with the bridle and made him skiddoo to the pasture. I laid up the drawbars and I made for the pond. There's a lot of bull-grass there and about a foot of water. It's a regular frog and water-snake hangout. Lord, of all the noise! I slipped up by the pond. They all hushed. I never heard another noise only I heard some plump-plumps into the water. I saw that I'd scared them. So I laid down on my belly behind a bunch of bull-grass out of sight from the frogs. It wasn't two minutes before they all started singing. The old frogs didn't do much singing. They's been in love and out again or they'd just took on some other kind of love after so many springs. The little frogs made up for lost time. They'd get up on a log and jump off and chase each other. I crawled up to the edge of the pond and watched them. If you don't believe young frogs love in the spring when they are doing all of that hollering you just go around the pond and see for yourself.

When I got up to leave there, I heard the birds singing. They sung their love songs to each other and it seemed like I could understand some of the words. But the prettiest thing I saw was two snakes entwined upon the bank in the sun. They were blacksnakes and very much in love. If it had been before I met Effie I would have picked me up a rock and killed them because Pa says they kill all the birds and young rabbits. I saw two turtles out in the pond on a log. They were bathing in the sun, I just watched them a while. No wonder I fell in love with Effie, pretty a girl as she is. No wonder I dream of her at night and plan a house to take her to. My mother's bread don't taste as good to me as it used to taste. My bed at home don't look as good as it used to look and home and Mom and Pa don't seem the same. I just can't help feeling that way. I dream of the way Effie is going to bake my bread and fix my bed and clean my shirts and patch my pants. Life is great; and to be in love, love is so much greater. It's about one of the greatest things in the world—to be in love till you can cry. I just went to bed thinking about the house I had in mind and it was altogether different to the house here where we live. Just to see Effie with a blue dress and a little white apron on, lifting big white fluffy biscuits out of the pan—white biscuits with brown tops—and good hot gravy made out of milk—and butter yaller as a daisy eye—and steam off my coffee hot as hell and strong as love!

I just thought: "Well, I'm going to tell Pa and Ma that I am leaving them. That I am going to marry that little Slab Baptis and hunt me a home and help to replenish the earth with a good stock. A body can look at her and tell that she is a good stock and I ain't of such bad stock."

I went to the house. I never got the mule back out of the pasture. I was through. Of course I knowed Pa would hate to see me go and it would break Mom's heart when I told her. Mom is a shouting Methodist and it would kill her to see me marry one of them Slab Baptis that drink licker and bet on chicken fights and play cards. But no use to lie to Mom about it. I would go today and fix everything up. Frogs could fall in love and the birds and snakes and terrapins and lizards—well, why didn't I have the same right? And if Pa put his jib in I would tell him to stay out of my love affair and Uncle Tid Porter too. It may be love in the spring but I loved in the spring.

I'll never forget going into the house. Mom was making biscuit dough. I heard Pa telling her I put the mule up and knocked off for half day. Pa didn't like it and he was worried. "Well," I says to Mom, "I got news for you." And Mom says: "What kind of news, Elster?" And I says: "I am going to leave you. Going to get married."

"Who are you going to marry?" says Pa—his neck and face red as a hen's comb in the spring.

"I am going to marry Effie Long—that little girl I met over at the foot-washing last month," I said to Pa.

"One of them Slab Baptis?" said Pa.

"Yes, one of them Slab Baptis," I said.

"And you been raised under a roof like this one," Mom said, "under a Methodist roof—and then go and marry a Slab Baptis—one that has a religion that believes in drinking and playing poker and betting on rooster fights and spitting at cracks in the crib floor. Then you going to marry one of them kind. Remember, Elster, if you get burnt you got to set on the blister. You are brought up to believe a certain way it is hard to break away from. Elster, your people have been Methodist for nearly a hundred years. And you go marry that infidel. Don't you ever let her darken my door. You can come back when you want to but you be sure you keep her away."

The tears come from Mom's eyes. Pa put his hands up over his eyes. And I said to Mom: "Home here ain't the same any more since I met Effie. Life ain't the same, I tell you. My bed ain't the same upstairs and the good biscuits ain't the same."

"Your Ma's bread is the same. Good as it was twenty years ago. Best cook in the country. Then you talk about the bread and even your bed upstairs. Son, I'm not going to stand for anything like that. You can get out of this house if that is the way you feel about things around here. Get your clothes and go." Pa said it and his voice kinda quivered.

I went upstairs and got my clothes. It didn't take me long, for I don't have many. Lord, it burned me up to think about the whole thing. Life with Effie and I'd never come home to see the boys and Mom and Pa. I'd stay away till they would be glad to see me. That's what I'd do. They'd have to send to Duck Puddle to get me.

I put my clothes into the newspaper and got my work clothes—my heavy shoes and my Sunday shoes and my .22 pistol. I thought it might come in handy about a home of my own. I went down through the front room. Mom was crying. "Ain't you going to eat a bite before you leave?" Mom said. And I said: "Nope, I don't believe I care for anything to eat."

"Take a piece of hot corn bread and butter it and eat a piece of smoked ham as you go."

I took it. Lord, but it tasted good. I had et Mom's cooking for eighteen years and it was good. But I went out of the house. I wasn't going to wait till fall. Couldn't plant any ground that late. I was going to marry early enough to rent some ground and get out a late crop and pray for a late fall so they would ripen. I could make it all right.

I walked out into the sunlight. It was a pretty day in May. I never felt so good in all my life. Had my clothes under my arm and going to get my sweet Effie—sweeter than the wild red rose. I went down past the barn and I said farewell to the milk cows, Boss, Fern, Star, Daisy, Little Bitty, Roan, and Blacky. I waved my hands to them and to Pete and Barnie in the pasture—mules I'd worked many a day. Barnie nickered at me. He walked along the pasture fence far as he could follow me. I'd been his master ever since he was a colt. Now he would get another master. I said good-by to the trees, the barn, to everything. I was going to a new country.

Sky was pretty above me. The birds never sung any sweeter for me. The wind had music in it. Flowers bloomed so pretty by the road, whole hillsides covered with wild roses. Well, when I got to the riffles the sun was getting pretty low on tother hill. I knowed it would soon be time for them to come from the fields. I'd just get in there a little after suppertime. Lord, but I was hungry. I got across the rocks at the riffle all right, and I went right up the creek till I come to the church house. I was moving fast to get there before dark. A little moon in the sky already.

I crossed the ditch by the church and took out toward the first pair of bars. If I ever go over a road once I never forget it. I soon came to the second pair of bars. The moon was a little bigger in the sky. One of them quarter moons. And a dry moon at that. One edge kinda turned up. Darkness had come at last but here was the house. Light in the front room. So I goes up and looks in. There was old Tawa. He was setting on the couch beside of my Effie. I knocked on the door. Effie come to the door. I said: "How are you Honey?" and I just closed her in my arms. Old Tawa showed them big horse-teeth with that funny grin—them polecat eyes just a-snapping.

"Come here, Mart Long," Tawa hollered.

"Come where?" said a voice from upstairs. I heard him getting out of the bed. Sounded like the whole loft was coming in. Must 'a' been a big feller. "What are you coming here for?" said Tawa.

"If it's any your business," I said, "I'm coming here to marry Effie. That's why I've come."

"You ain't getting Effie," said Tawa. "She belongs to me. I'm one of her kind. I am a Slab Baptis. I ain't no damned infidental."

I thought I'd take my .22 out and blow his lights out. Calling me a infidental. I never did like the Methodists so much as I did now. And I said: "Who in the hell are you calling a infidental? You polecat you. I'll clean this floor with you." I started to turn Effie loose and get him. Just then in stepped Sourwood Long, Effie's pap.

"There's that infidental Methodist," said Tawa to Sourwood.

And Sourwood said: "W'y, he just looks like the rest of us. Got eyes like us and a mouth and talks. W'y, he's like the rest of us only I don't want Effie marrying you until you repent and get into our church."

"I have come after Effie right now," I said. "Besides, I am a Methodist. I don't intend to repent neither. Why can't she get into the Methodist church? What's wrong with us?"

"And what's wrong with us?" said Sourwood. Black beard covering his face. His arms were big as fence posts and hairy as a briar thicket around a old fence row. He kept them folded upon his big hairy chest. He didn't have many teeth. Had a lot of snags in his mouth—a big nose and he was dark as a wet piece of chestnut bark.

"Nothing ain't wrong with us," said Tawa. "We are the only people right. You know we got a lot of them Methodists in our church when the pertracted meeting was going on. Left your church for ours."

"You got a lot that couldn't stay in our church," I said. I was ready to fight. I still had Effie in my arms. I hadn't turned her loose yet.

"You ain't going to marry Effie. I wouldn't have one of you fellers in my house for dinner let alone in my family to put up with you a lifetime. Get out of here right now."

Another voice from upstairs. "Sourwood, what's going on down there?"

"Malinda, what are you doing up there? A Methodist has come to get Effie. Come on down here."

"Better let a Methodist have her than that thing down there. That Tawa. Get 'em both out of here. Get 'em out quick."

I never saw Effie's mother. I don't know how it was done. It was done so quick. Old Tawa must 'a' come around the back side of the house and upon the front porch and hit me over the head with something. I remember I waked up out in the yard. My clothes were under my head for a piller. The moon was in the sky. It just seemed like I'd been asleep and had slept a little too long. Seemed like a dream. Lights all out of the house just like nothing had ever happened. They's all in bed, I guess. Don't know what ever become of Tawa. Have never seen him from that day to this. I can hardly tell you how I got home. I was about half crazy from that lick. I remember I was so hungry. I remember, too, the chickens were crowing for the daylight. I didn't have my .22 on me. It was gone.

Mom was getting breakfast. I went in and I said: "Mom, your biscuits are all right. Lord, I can eat twenty-two this morning. I'm so hungry."

"Where's your wife?" Mom said.

"I took another notion," I said. "I remembered what you said. I didn't want one of them infidentals after we've been Methodists so long. I thought it over and changed my mind."

"I thought you would," said Mom. "A boy with your raising and get into a mix-up like that. Couldn't bring her home. You'll do better marrying one of your own kind. I'm making you some good strong coffee."

"Good strong coffee is what I need. Strong as love but not love in the spring. Love in the fall. Coffee hot as hell too."

Lord, but Mom did look good to me in that apron. She just looked the best I ever saw her. And her biscuits tasted right too. "Mom, you are the best girl I've ever had," I said and I kinda give Mom a bear hug and she says to this day I cracked a couple of her ribs. She says she can hardly get her breath at times ever since I hugged her.

This has been a day in September. Uncle Tid Porter was down today.

He said to me: "Now is the kind of weather to fall in love—now while the chill winds blow and the leaves fly—now while the frost has come. The spring is the time to marry and go on a gay carousal like the frog. Like the snakes and the flowers and all living things. Spring is the time to marry—not the time to fall in love. Love in the spring is fickle as the wind."

"I have often wondered what has become of Tawa," I said to Uncle Tid, "the fellow that loved the girl I loved last spring—w'y, he's the ugliest human being I ever saw for to love as pretty a woman as Effie——"

"She's married him, I guess," said Uncle Tid. "That's the way of a woman. They do the unexpected thing—not knowing which way the wind will blow and if there will be snow or rain tomorrow. That's what a man likes—he likes the unexpected thing."

The wind blows outside. The wind is cool. Pa is out at the barn putting a roof over the fattening hog pen. Mom is still complaining of her ribs: "I never heard of that but once before in my life. A teacher come to this deestrict to teach school and he hugged one of Mort Giggin's girls—it was Ester, I believe—and he broke three of her ribs. I tell you he never got another school in this deestrict."

Stuart at work at one of his desks (he has one in every room) at W-Hollow during the 1970s.

Epiphany 🎆🎆🎆

Part 6

Walk in the Moon Shadows

About the story:

Jesse Stuart's "Walk in the Moon Shadows," Ruel E. Foster writes, is "a story filled with the cool magic of an April night and a strange quest.... The brief opening lines suggest the mystery and the magic of the story as Shan questions his mother." In reality, the author's mother, Martha Hylton Stuart, "was great" on talking with her family about her strange beliefs concerning what could be seen in and about W-Hollow at certain special times when conditions were favorable. "And all kinds of stories," the author said, "went on about that ridge out there and what they saw on that ridge . . . the people and the lights. Had me almost scared to go out there at night.... I expected all the time to run into some of them. All those people who had lived and were gone...." The man remembered and embroidered with his imagination what the boy never forgot, and as the characters in the story wait in the still, cool April night for what they may see and hear, the reader discovers, as does the boy Shan, that these strange goings on have more to do with imminent new life than with what may live from the past. As in this story, Jesse Stuart's mother looms large in his work—in his poetry, too, as well as in his prose. Consider these poems as they serve to illuminate the heroine of "Walk in the Moon Shadows":

#48
I shall not speak soft words with stilted phrase
To one who has worked all her live-long days

In furrowed fields and in the open spaces,
But I shall sing of her in plowman's phrase.
The blood that flows in her now flows in me,
Like sap, two seasons, flows in the same tree.
And I am proud to have her blood in me.
I pray for more her solidness in me,
I pray for more of her philosophy,
I want a heart as free as hers to give,
I want a love like hers to see men live
And women live—her love to help the sick.
I want her meekness—never wanting praise,
And for this rugged mother of the hills—
I sing for her in rugged plowman phrase.

#50

The hills are dear to you, my mountain mother.
Corn-fields are dear to you—green in the sun,
The touch of wind is dear to you, my mother,
The rock ribs of the hills are dear to you.
White rain that falls on leaves is dear to you.
The lightning-storm will make no fear to you.
One of the elements, you surely are,
With power to love, a child, a stone, a star,
A will to work—one unafraid of life—
One that loves life and gave her seven life.
An autumn tree, my mother, now you are.
The gold of age is hanging to your boughs.
And unafraid you stand to meet new life,
*Beneath white glistening beauty of a star.**

* * *

"WHERE ARE we goin', Mom?" I said, looking up at my tall mother. "Where can we go when the moon is up and the lightning bugs are above the meadows?"

Mom didn't answer me. She was braiding Sophia's hair. Sophia was my oldest sister, twelve years old, with blue eyes, blond hair, and tight lips. Sophia didn't ask Mom any questions. She stood still, never moving her head while Mom finished braiding her hair. Mom had dressed Sophia in a white dress, and she wore a sash of red ribbon instead of a belt to her dress. The sash was tied in a big bowknot. Sophia was dressed like Mom dressed her when we went to Plum Grove's Children's Day once a year.

*Ruel E. Foster, *Jesse Stuart* (N.Y.: Twayne, 1968), p. 79. Jesse Stuart/H. E. Richardson, Interview, W-Hollow, Greenup, Ky., Sept. 15, 1978. The two poems are from Jesse Stuart, *Man with a Bull-Tongue Plow* (N.Y.: Dutton, 1934), pp. 26–27. Jesse Stuart's "Walk in the Moon Shadows" was first published in the *Southwest Review*, Vol. 40 (Summer, 1955), pp. 230–235, reprinted in *Plowshare in Heaven* (N.Y.: McGraw-Hill, 1958), pp. 25–35.

Mom had scrubbed me from head to foot. She had used more soap and water than she had ever used before. There couldn't have been a speck of dirt on me anyplace. Mom gave me the same kind of scrubbing she gave Sophia. That was the reason I asked her where we were going. Mom had combed my hair, parting it in a straight line, using the long comb for a straightedge to get the part straight.

Mom had dressed me the way she always had before Children's Day. She put on me a little pair of pants that came to my knees and buttoned to my shirt. Mom made all of the clothes that we wore.

"There's no use to go, Sal," my father said. He was sitting in a rocking chair in the room where Mom was getting us ready. Now and then he would turn his head slowly and watch Mom for a minute. Then he would turn his head back and face the empty fireplace. "You're dressin' the children for nothin'. They won't be there when you go. They never have been at home."

"Just because we've gone before, Mick, and they weren't at home, is not any sign they won't be there on an evening as pretty as this one," Mom said. "I'll keep on tryin' until I catch them at home!"

"Where are we goin', Mom?" I asked again.

"I'll tell you later, Shan," she said.

"Sal, we've been there several times since we've been married and we've never found them at home," my father said.

"Where are we goin', Mom?" I asked. Sophia remained silent, pressing her lips tighter than a turtle's. "Who are these people we are goin' to see?"

"Never mind, Shan," Mom said. "I must go in the other room and dress."

"Who are they, Pa?" I asked, turning to him when Mom left the room.

"Just people you don't know," he replied. "But your mother and I know them. And when we go to visit them, they're never there."

"Where do they live?" I asked as Sophia made a face at me.

"Up on a high hill," he told me.

Then I thought we might be going to see Sinnetts. They had two boys, Morris and Everett. If we went there, I'd have somebody to play with. Then I thought we might be going to see Welches. They had three boys, Jimmie, Walter, and Ernest. If we went there, I'd have somebody to play with. But Sinnetts lived upon a little bank above Academy Branch and Welches lived in the saddle between the Buzzard Roost Hills and the John Collins Knolls. I thought we might be going to see Alf and Annie Dysard. They lived on a low Plum Grove hill and had a son, Jack, and I could play with him. I didn't have a brother to play with.

When Mom came from the back room, she was dressed as fine as I had ever seen her dress. Mom's black hair was combed and laid in a big knot on the back of her head. Her hair was held there with combs that sparkled in the half-darkness when she walked to the far corner of the big room away from the kerosene lamp. She was wearing a blue dress trimmed in white frilly laces. She had worn this dress before to our Fourth of July celebration in Blakesburg. My mother was beautiful. Pa looked at her and he didn't turn away and look at the empty fireplace this time. He kept on looking at Mom.

"I'll take the children with me, Mick," she said. "You'd better go with us, Mick!"

"I've gone there too many times already," he said. "I've been disappointed too many times. Sal, they're never at home. Not when we go. So I say, what is the use to go? If they can't be at home, if we can never see them, why go and try to look them up? I don't see any use of pestering friends who try to dodge us."

"I want our children to see them," Mom said. "Come, Sophia! Come, Shan!"

"We're going to Sinnetts, Welches, or Dysards," I said happily. "I'll have somebody to play with."

Sophia made another face at me. She was trying to get me to keep still.

"Do you know where we're goin', Sophia?" I asked.

She didn't answer me.

"You'd better go too, Mick," Mom said as she walked toward the front door of the big room with Sophia and me following her. "Mick, I think you want to go but you're afraid."

"I'm not afraid to go either," Pa said. "We've never had better neighbors. As friendly a people as we ever lived by. What would they have against me now? That's where you're wrong, Sal. I'm not afraid. I just don't see any use of trying to catch them at home. I'll stay here this time and let you go."

We walked down the field-stone rock walk in front of our big log house. Mom in front and Sophia and I behind. When we came to the winding jolt-wagon road that went up the hollow, I watched to see which way Mom would go. If she went up the hollow, we would be going to Sinnetts. If she went down the hollow we would be going in the direction of Dysards and Welches. Mom turned down the hollow on the jolt-wagon road.

"Not to Sinnetts but to Welches or Dysards," I said. "I'll get to play with Jimmie, Walter, and Ernest. Maybe I'll get to play with Jack."

Mom didn't say a word and Sophia didn't make a face to keep me from talking. Mom took big steps down the road and Sophia hurried to keep up with her and I had to run. Sophia was three years older than I was and she was taller. She could take longer steps. And I looked up at the moon in the high blue sky. It was a big moon the color of a ripe pumpkin I had helped my father gather from the new-ground cornfield and lay on a sled and haul home with our mule. There were a few dim stars in the sky but over the meadows, down where there were long moon shadows from the tall trees, thousands of lightning bugs lighted their ways, going here, there, and nowhere. Upon Press Moore's high hill where Pa had found a wild bee tree, and cut his initial on the bark, a whippoorwill began singing a lonesome song. Somewhere behind us, I heard another whippoorwill start singing too.

Less than a quarter-mile down the hollow, an old road turned right. This road was not used except by hunters. And when we came to this road, Mom turned right.

"Mom, where are we goin'?" I said. "We don't go to Welches or Dysards that way. We can't go anywhere on that road. Not anybody lives on it."

"That's what a lot of people think," Mom said. "But I know people do live on it."

"Do they have any boys?" I asked as I followed Mom over the old road, marked by gullies where the jolt wagons once loaded with coal had rolled along, pulled by oxen and mules in years gone by. I'd never seen the oxen and mules pulling the big coal wagons but Pa had told me about it when he had gone this way in the autumn to shoot rabbits and he had taken me along to carry them.

"No, they don't have any boys," Mom said.

"Then why did you want me to go, Mom?" I asked.

"Shan, I want you to meet them and to remember," Mom replied. "You might see something you will never see again."

"What's that, Mom?" I asked as Sophia walked very close to Mom, and she was as silent as one of the tall trees with the moon shadows.

"Some old friends," Mom said.

Mom wouldn't tell us where we were going. If Sophia knew where we were going she wouldn't tell me. Sophia pretended that she knew. But I never believed that she did because she was afraid of the dark woods on each side of the dim moonlighted wagon road. I watched Sophia step from lighted spot to lighted spot along the road, dodging the deep ruts and the dark long shadows. But the shadows and the ruts didn't bother Mom. She walked proudly and she was as straight as an upright tree. She wasn't afraid of dark shadows and deep ruts. Mom could step over the deep ruts easily.

My mother wasn't afraid of anything at night. She loved the night because I had heard her say she did so many times. I'd heard her talk about old roads beneath the moon and stars, roads where people had walked, ridden horseback, and driven horses hitched to express wagons, surreys, hug-me-tights, and rubber-tied buggies. I'd heard her say she loved the lonesome songs of the whippoorwills and she loved the summer season when the lightning bugs made millions of lights on our meadows up and down the hollow. Mom often sat alone in our front yard and watched them at night. But Pa wouldn't do it. He'd sit whittling, making ax handles of hickory, butter paddles of buckeye, hoe handles of sassafras, and window boxes of yellow locust for her wild flowers. Pa always wanted to make his time count. I knew he would make a window box for Mom while she had taken us on this visit.

"Mom, where in the world are we goin'?" I asked.

I had to run to keep up with her as we climbed gradually up the hill on this deserted road that wound among the tall trees.

"Keep quiet, Shan," Mom said. "We'll soon be there."

Then Sophia turned around and put her fingers over her lips. She told me to keep quiet without using words.

In many places we ran into pockets of darkness under the trees. The moonlight couldn't filter through the dense green leaves rustled by the late April winds. I wondered where Mom was taking us. Soon after we had staggered and stumbled along, I looked ahead and saw a vast opening beyond the trees. It was like leaving the night and walking into the day to leave the woods and walk into a vast space where only waist-high bushes grew.

"We'll soon be there," Mom said, breathing a little harder.

We followed Mom along the ridge road until she came to a stop. In front of us was an old house and around it were a few blooming apple trees. The apple blossoms were very white in the moonlight and more lightning bugs than we had seen above our meadows played over these old fields.

"This is the place," Mom said.

"People don't live there, do they, Mom?" I said. "Half the windowpanes are out, planks are gone from the gable end, and the doors are wide open!"

I could see the windowpanes still in the windows because they shone brightly in the moonlight. And there were deep dark holes where the panes were out.

"Yes, people live there," Mom whispered. "Be quiet, Shan."

"Mom," I whispered, "are we goin' in?"

"No, we'll just wait out here," she said softly.

"Are there any boys here for me to play with?" I said.

"No," she replied very softly as she took a few steps forward. She reached one of the big apple trees that looked like a low white cloud. Mom sat down on a gnarled root beneath the tree. Sophia sat down beside her. And I sat down on the grass.

"I don't guess anyone's at home," Mom said. "We'll wait for them."

"Who are they, Mom?" I asked in a whisper, for I was beginning to get afraid.

"Our neighbors and friends," she said.

"Looks like they'd hang some curtains to their windows, plow the garden, and cut the grass in the yard," I said. "Looks like they'd nail the planks back on the house and put panes back in the windows. Pa wouldn't let us live in a house like that."

Mom didn't say anything. She looked toward the front door as if she expected to see somebody walk in or come out.

"Who are they, Mom?" I asked again. I wanted to know.

"Dot and Ted Byrnes," she said. "That is the old Garthee house. Dot used to be Dot Garthee . . . the prettiest girl among these hills. She and Ted and Mick and I used to be young together. None of us were married then. Many a time we rode down the road we have just walked up in a two-horse surrey together. Many people have seen them at night on this ridge in a two-horse surrey. Old Alec told me he did. Jim Pennix saw them one Sunday morning in the hug-me-tight driving early toward Blakesburg. That's the way they used to go to church every Sunday morning."

"But why don't they ever visit us, Mom?" I asked.

"Because they're not here any longer," she said.

"You mean they're dead?"

"Yes, in 1917, the flu epidemic," Mom said. "They left this world only hours apart."

"I'm afraid of this place, Mom," I said.

"Shhh, be quiet!" she said. "They won't hurt you. If they come in or go out of that house, I'll call to them. I want you children to see them. And I want them to see my children."

"Is that the reason we are all dressed up like we were goin' to Children's Day?" I asked.

Mom didn't answer me. She never took her eyes off the front door. Sophia sat closer to Mom and I got up closer to Sophia. We sat there silently and no one spoke. The April wind shook down a few apple blossoms from the branches above us. And when I saw a white blossom zigzag down toward us, I shivered.

"Mom, I don't believe we're goin' to see them," I said. "I don't believe they're comin' home."

"But they might be in the house," she said. "Dot's great-grandfather,

Jim Garthee, built that house. Her grandfather, John, and her father, Jake, lived in that house and raised their families. The well in that yard is ninety feet deep and cut through solid rock. I remember this house when there was a lot of life here. I've had many good times here visiting Dot. Dot was the last Garthee ever to live here. Now she's gone."

"Mom, they're not comin' out," I said. "They don't want to see us. Let's go back home."

Mom wouldn't answer. She sat silently and waited for Ted and Dot Byrnes. I stopped looking at the old house there under the blooming trees. I looked away over the fields where the night wind rustled the leafy tops of the bushes and there were little dots of light everywhere. These fields were covered with lightning bugs. I didn't want to think about Dot and Ted Byrnes. I didn't want to see them and I didn't want to think about them. I wanted to go home and get away from this place. The whippoorwills were singing lonesome songs on the ridges and their singing and the falling apple blossoms made me have strange feelings. I knew Sophia was scared too. I sat close enough to her to feel her shaking. Sophia would do what Mom told her to and she would never ask Mom a question.

"When I come back here another life comes back," Mom's words were softer than the April winds. "I can see the buggies filled with young people and the surreys with families going for visits or Sunday drives. I can see young men and women on horseback riding along this ridge. People used to stop here and drink cold water from that well and sit under the shade of the apple trees."

"Did you use to ride horseback here, Mom?" I asked.

"Yes, Dot and I used to ride her father's horses from one end of this ridge to the other," Mom said, looking away from me toward the house. "I'd love to see Dot and Ted. I know they'll never leave here no matter what happened to 'em. If Dot knew I was here with my family waiting, I think she'd come up and speak to us."

"Look, the moon is going over the ridge and it will soon be dark in the woods," I said. "How'll we get home?"

"Don't worry about that," Mom said. "We'll get back all right. Let's wait a while longer. Ted and Dot might be out somewhere on the ridge. And we'll get to see them when they come back."

"Do you want to see them, Sophia?" I said.

Sophia didn't answer me. She shook more than the leaves and blossoms in the wind above us.

"I wonder if Dot will be wearing one of the pretty dresses she used to wear," Mom said. "I think I can remember every dress she wore. Dot was always so pretty in her nice clothes. She knew the colors to wear and she was beautiful."

"Mom, I'm getting cold sitting here in this April wind," I said. "I want to go home."

"Just a few more minutes," Mom said, in a louder voice. "Maybe they'll hear us and come out."

"Could we go in the house and find them?" I asked.

"No, we'd better not try that," Mom said. "Your father and I did that once just before you were born. We didn't find them. I think it's better to let them come to us. But let's watch and see if anyone goes in or out."

While Mom watched the house the moon went down behind the ridge. I knew it must be midnight, for roosters crowed at faraway farmhouses.

"I wish we could have seen 'em," Mom sighed as she got up to leave.

Sophia jumped up and hugged close to Mom.

Mom walked slowly along the ridge and we followed her. We couldn't see the moon now and it was very dark. But we could see better than we thought after we followed the winding road into the deep woods again. We saw Pa coming toward us.

"Sophia, why did we ever come out here to the old Garthee house?" I said.

Then Sophia walked close to me. She whispered in my ear as Mom walked on with Pa. "Shan, Mom is going to have a baby. She did this before you were born. Pa said she did before I was born."

I couldn't answer Sophia as we ran in the darkness to catch up. A baby brother, I thought as I ran. I will have somebody to play with me now.

Another April

About the story:

After examining Jesse Stuart's new book, *Tales from the Plum Grove Hills*, in which "Another April" is the lead story, Donald Davidson, distinguished teacher, writer, and critic, modestly wrote his former student, "I can't set up much claim, really, to being your teacher. All I did, mainly, was to say, 'Flap your wings and fly,' and more or less push you out of the nest. *And you flew*! Well, at least I didn't tell you *not* to fly; and that is something." He expressed pride in his former pupil for succeeding

> in your own way, which asks no odds of anybody, and which comes from a kind of knowledge and belief that are sadly lacking in many writers nowadays. So much of what I read, here and there, leaves me with the impression that the authors have been buying literary vitamins to try to make up for their lack of either knowledge or beliefs. But all you need to do is to let your bucket down into the old Kentucky well, the well that never runs dry, and up comes the stuff of life again; plenty of it; and the vitamins don't need to be added.

Regarding *Tales from the Plum Grove Hills*, Davidson wrote, "And your opening story. 'Another April' is unbeatable. You have wrought better than you may realize in that story. It belongs at the top." Davidson later included "Another April" in the third edition of his widely known text *American Composition and Rhetoric*.

And it was also accepted and reprinted in Whit Burnett's 1942 collection of outstanding short stories, *This Is My Best*. Here Stuart wrote of why he had selected the story for the volume, and this in part is what he said:

> It is very strange how a man whose life has been filled with hard work and the associations of many human beings would in his declining days start talking to a terrapin. Maybe there is an understanding between an old man and an old terrapin when each knows his time to be alive is very limited. This sort of a thing haunts me when a ruthless dynamic sort of a human being, who has been as tough as the tough-butted white oaks on the rugged mountain slopes, is calmed enough by the passing of time to sit and talk with a wrinkled-neck terrapin, who is and has been quite willing to live half-buried in the dry dirt under the smokehouse floor during the cold winter months and to eat tomatoes in the garden during the summer. Maybe it

is because I am partial to this material—the reason I like this story—the reason why I am willing to put it forward as representative of my best work. Furthermore there is something to man's associations with earth and the living creatures upon the earth and his fight with the elements—his cutting trees, plowing the rugged soil for a scanty livelihood—these are enduring things . . . as solid and substantial as stone.

It took me less than two hours to write this short story. . . . I knew every detail in this story, "Another April," before I sat down at the typewriter. Two days after I had written this story, I sat down and added another paragraph. Strange that the editor of *Harper's Magazine*, Frederick Allen, asked that this paragraph be removed. I wrote him to remove it—that made the story published just the way I wrote it. The story wrote itself. My mind was only a medium to put it on paper. This is one of Nature's own stories, that Nature and Life have worked out together, dealing with three generations of people and a terrapin. . . .

"Another April" retains its power to reveal an essential meaning of life, initiated by the commonplace coming together of a boy and his mother, an old man, and an ancient turtle with "1847" carved into its shell, illuminating a sustaining bond between Nature and humankind.*

* * *

"Now, PAP, you won't get cold," Mom said as she put a heavy wool cap over his head.

"Huh, what did ye say?" Grandpa asked, holding his big hand cupped over his ear to catch the sound.

"Wait until I get your gloves," Mom said, hollering real loud in Grandpa's ear. Mom had forgotten about his gloves until he raised his big bare hand above his ear to catch the sound of Mom's voice.

"Don't get 'em," Grandpa said, "I won't ketch cold."

Mom didn't pay any attention to what Grandpa said. She went on to

*Jesse Stuart's "Another April" first appeared in *Harper's Magazine*, Vol. 185 (Aug., 1942), pp. 256–260. It was reprinted in Whit Burnett, ed., *This Is My Best* (N.Y.: Dial, 1942), pp. 408–414, and in Donald Davidson, *American Composition and Rhetoric*, 3rd ed. (N.Y.: Scribner's, 1953), pp. 383–391, and in the 4th ed. (1959), pp. 375–381. The story was collected in Jesse Stuart, *Tales from the Plum Grove Hills* (N.Y.: Dutton, 1946), pp. 13–21, reprinted in the Mockingbird ed. (N.Y.: Ballantine Bks., 1974), pp. 1–7. Through 1979 the story had been reprinted eleven other times in the United States and abroad.

Donald Davidson, letter from Nashville, Tenn., to Jesse Stuart, W-Hollow, Greenup, Ky., Oct. 15, 1946, in the Jesse Stuart Collection, University of Louisville, Louisville, Ky. Jesse Stuart, "Jesse Stuart: Why he selected 'Another April,' " pub. in Whit Burnett, ed. *This Is My Best* (N.Y.: Dial, 1942), p. 407; however, my source is an inscribed clipping in Jesse Stuart's letter to me dated June 23, 1969, now in my correspondence file with Mr. Stuart. In filling out Jesse Stuart's reflections on such ancient, carved-shell terrapins as that in "Another April," cf. his pp. 273–274 of *The Year of My Rebirth* (N.Y.: McGraw-Hill, 1956).

get the gloves anyway. Grandpa turned toward me. He saw that I was looking at him.

"Yer Ma's a-puttin' enough clothes on me to kill a man," Grandpa said,
then he laughed a coarse laugh like March wind among the pine tops at his
own words. I started laughing but not at Grandpa's words. He thought I
was laughing at them and we both laughed together. It pleased Grandpa to
think that I had laughed with him over something funny that he had said.
But I was laughing at the way he was dressed. He looked like a picture of
Santa Claus. But Grandpa's cheeks were not cherry-red like Santa Claus'
cheeks. They were covered with white thin beard—and above his eyes were
long white eyebrows almost as white as percoon petals and very much
longer.

Grandpa was wearing a heavy wool suit that hung loosely about his big
body but fitted him tightly round the waist where he was as big and as
round as a flour barrel. His pant legs were as big 'round his pipestem legs as
emptied meal sacks. And his big shoes, with his heavy wool socks dropping
down over their tops, looked like sled runners. Grandpa wore a heavy wool
shirt and over his wool shirt he wore a heavy wool sweater and then his coat
over the top of all this. Over his coat he wore a heavy overcoat and about
his neck he wore a wool scarf.

The way Mom had dressed Grandpa you'd think there was a heavy
snow on the ground but there wasn't. April was here instead and the sun
was shining on the green hills where the wild plums and the wild crab
apples were in bloom enough to make you think there were big snowdrifts
sprinkled over the green hills. When I looked at Grandpa and then looked
out at the window at the sunshine and the green grass I laughed more.
Grandpa laughed with me.

"I'm a-goin' to see my old friend," Grandpa said just as Mom came
down the stairs with his gloves.

"Who is he, Grandpa?" I asked, but Grandpa just looked at my mouth
working. He didn't know what I was saying. And he hated to ask me the
second time.

Mom put the big wool gloves on Grandpa's hands. He stood there just
like I had to do years ago, and let Mom put his gloves on. If Mom didn't
get his fingers back in the glove-fingers exactly right Grandpa quarreled at
Mom. And when Mom fixed his fingers exactly right in his gloves the way
he wanted them Grandpa was pleased.

"I'll be a-goin' to see 'im," Grandpa said to Mom. "I know he'll still be
there."

Mom opened our front door for Grandpa and he stepped out slowly, supporting himself with his big cane in one hand. With the other hand he held to the door facing. Mom let him out of the house just like she used to let me out in the spring. And when Grandpa left the house I wanted to go with him, but Mom wouldn't let me go. I wondered if he would get away from the house—get out of Mom's sight—and pull off his shoes and go barefooted and wade the creeks like I used to do when Mom let me out. Since Mom wouldn't let me go with Grandpa, I watched him as he walked slowly down the path in front of our house. Mom stood there watching Grandpa too. I think she was afraid that he would fall. But Mom was fooled; Grandpa toddled along the path better than my baby brother could.

"He used to be a powerful man," Mom said more to herself than she did to me. "He was a timber cutter. No man could cut more timber than my father; no man in the timber woods could sink an ax deeper into a log than my father. And no man could lift the end of a bigger saw log than Pop could."

"Who is Grandpa goin' to see, Mom?" I asked.

"He's not goin' to see anybody," Mom said.

"I heard 'im say that he was goin' to see an old friend," I told her.

"Oh, he was just a-talkin'," Mom said.

I watched Grandpa stop under the pine tree in our front yard. He set his cane against the pine tree trunk, pulled off his gloves and put them in his pocket. Then Grandpa stooped over slowly, as slowly as the wind bends down a sapling, and picked up a pine cone in his big soft fingers. Grandpa stood fondling the pine cone in his hand. Then, one by one, he pulled the little chips from the pine cone—tearing it to pieces like he was hunting for something in it—and after he had torn it to pieces he threw the pine-cone stem on the ground. Then he pulled pine needles from a low-hanging pine bough and he felt of each pine needle between his fingers. He played with them a long time before he started down the path.

"What's Grandpa doin'?" I asked Mom.

But Mom didn't answer me.

"How long has Grandpa been with us?" I asked Mom.

"Before you's born," she said. "Pap has been with us eleven years. He was eighty when he quit cuttin' timber and farmin'; now he's ninety-one."

I had heard her say that when she was a girl he'd walk out on the snow and ice barefooted and carry wood in the house and put it on the fire. He had shoes but he wouldn't bother to put them on. And I heard her say that he would cut timber on the coldest days without socks on his feet but with his feet stuck down in cold brogan shoes and he worked stripped above the waist so his arms would have freedom when he swung his double-bitted ax. I had heard her tell how he'd sweat and how the sweat in his beard would be icicles by the time he got home from work on the cold winter days. Now Mom wouldn't let him get out of the house for she wanted him to live a long time.

As I watched Grandpa go down the path toward the hog pen he stopped to examine every little thing along his path. Once he waved his cane at a butterfly as it zigzagged over his head, its polka-dot wings fanning the blue April air. Grandpa would stand when a puff of wind came along, and hold his face against the wind and let the wind play with his white whiskers. I thought maybe his face was hot under his beard and he was letting the wind cool his face. When he reached the hog pen he called the hogs down to the fence. They came running and grunting to Grandpa just like they were talking to him. I knew that Grandpa couldn't hear them trying to talk to him but he could see their mouths working and he knew they were trying to say something. He leaned his cane against the hog pen, reached over the fence, and patted the hogs' heads. Grandpa didn't miss patting one of our seven hogs.

As he toddled up the little path alongside the hog pen he stopped under a blooming dogwood. He pulled a white blossom from a bough that swayed over the path above his head, and he leaned his big bundled body against the dogwood while he tore each petal from the blossom and examined it carefully. There wasn't anything his dim blue eyes missed. He stopped under a redbud tree before he reached the garden to break a tiny spray of redbud blossoms. He took each blossom from the spray and examined it carefully.

"Gee, it's funny to watch Grandpa," I said to Mom, then I laughed.

"Poor Pap," Mom said. "He's seen a lot of Aprils come and go. He's seen more Aprils than he will ever see again."

I don't think Grandpa missed a thing on the little circle he took before he reached the house. He played with a bumblebee that was bending a windflower blossom that grew near our corncrib beside a big bluff. But Grandpa didn't try to catch the bumblebee in his big bare hand. I wondered if he would and if the bumblebee would sting him, and if he would holler. Grandpa even pulled a butterfly cocoon from a blackberry briar that grew beside his path. I saw him try to tear it into shreds but he couldn't. There wasn't any butterfly in it, for I'd seen it before. I wondered if the butterfly with the polka-dot wings, that Grandpa waved his cane at when he first left the house, had come from this cocoon. I laughed when Grandpa couldn't tear the cocoon apart.

"I'll bet I can tear that cocoon apart for Grandpa if you'd let me go help him," I said to Mom.

"You leave your Grandpa alone," Mom said. "Let 'im enjoy April."

Then I knew that this was the first time Mom had let Grandpa out of the house all winter. I knew that Grandpa loved the sunshine and the fresh April air that blew from the redbud and dogwood blossoms. He loved the bumblebees, the hogs, the pine cones, and pine needles. Grandpa didn't miss a thing along his walk. And every day from now on until just before frost Grandpa would take this little walk. He'd stop along and look at everything as he had done summers before. But each year he didn't take as long a walk as he had taken the year before. Now this spring he didn't go down to the lower end of the hog pen as he had done last year. And when I could first remember Grandpa going on his walks he used to go out of sight. He'd go all over the farm. And he'd come to the house and take me on his knee and tell me about all what he had seen. Now Grandpa wasn't getting out of sight. I could see him from the window along all of his walk.

Grandpa didn't come back into the house at the front door. He tottled around back of the house toward the smokehouse and I ran through the living room to the dining room so I could look out the window and watch him.

"Where's Grandpa goin?" I asked Mom.

"Now never mind," Mom said. "Leave Grandpa alone. Don't go out there and disturb him."

"I won't bother 'im, Mom," I said. "I just want to watch 'im."

"All right," Mom said.

But Mom wanted to be sure that I didn't bother him so she followed me into the dining room. Maybe she wanted to see what Grandpa was going to do. She stood by the window and we watched Grandpa as he walked down beside our smokehouse where a tall sassafras tree's thin leaves fluttered in the blue April wind. Above the smokehouse and the tall sassafras was a blue April sky—so high you couldn't see the sky-roof. It was just blue space and little white clouds floated upon this blue.

When Grandpa reached the smokehouse he leaned his cane against the sassafras tree. He let himself down slowly to his knees as he looked carefully at the ground. Grandpa was looking at something and I wondered what it was. I just didn't think or I would have known.

"There you are, my good old friend," Grandpa said.

"Who is his friend, Mom?" I asked.

Mom didn't say anything. Then I saw.

"He's playin' with that old terrapin, Mom," I said.

"I know he is," Mom said.

"The terrapin doesn't mind if Grandpa strokes his head with his hand," I said.

"I know it," Mom said.

"But the old terrapin won't let me do it," I said. "Why does he let Grandpa?"

"The terrapin knows your Grandpa."

"He ought to know me," I said, "but when I try to stroke his head with my hand, he closes up in his shell."

Mom didn't say anything. She stood by the window watching Grandpa and listening to Grandpa talk to the terrapin.

"My old friend, how do you like the sunshine?" Grandpa asked the terrapin.

The terrapin turned his fleshless face to one side like a hen does when she looks at you in the sunlight. He was trying to talk to Grandpa; maybe the terrapin could understand what Grandpa was saying.

"Old fellow, it's been a hard winter," Grandpa said. "How have you fared under the smokehouse floor?"

"Does the terrapin know what Grandpa is sayin'?" I asked Mom.

"I don't know," she said.

"I'm awfully glad to see you, old fellow," Grandpa said.

He didn't offer to bite Grandpa's big soft hand as he stroked his head.

"Looks like the terrapin would bite Grandpa," I said.

"That terrapin has spent the winters under that smokehouse for fifteen years," Mom said. "Pap has been acquainted with him for eleven years. He's been talkin' to that terrapin every spring."

"How does Grandpa know the terrapin is old?" I asked Mom.

"It's got 1847 cut on its shell," Mom said. "We know he's ninety-five years old. He's older than that. We don't know how old he was when that date was cut on his back."

"Who cut 1847 on his back, Mom?"

"I don't know, child," she said, "but I'd say whoever cut that date on his back has long been under the ground."

Then I wondered how a terrapin could get that old and what kind of a looking person he was who cut the date on the terrapin's back. I wondered where it happened—if it happened near where our house stood. I wondered who lived here on this land then, what kind of a house they lived in, and if they had a sassafras with tiny thin April leaves on its top growing in their yard, and if the person that cut the date on the terrapin's back was buried at Plum Grove, if he had farmed these hills where we lived today and cut timber like Grandpa had—and if he had seen the Aprils pass like Grandpa had seen them and if he enjoyed them like Grandpa was enjoying this April. I wondered if he had looked at the dogwood blossoms, the redbud blossoms, and talked to this same terrapin.

"Are you well, old fellow?" Grandpa asked the terrapin.

The terrapin just looked at Grandpa.

"I'm well as common for a man of my age," Grandpa said.

"Did the terrapin ask Grandpa if he was well?" I asked Mom.

"I don't know," Mom said. "I can't talk to a terrapin."

"But Grandpa can."

"Yes."

"Wait until tomatoes get ripe and we'll go to the garden together," Grandpa said.

"Does a terrapin eat tomatoes?" I asked Mom.

"Yes, that terrapin has been eatin' tomatoes from our garden for fifteen years," Mom said. "When Mick was tossin' the terrapins out of the tomato patch, he picked up this one and found the date cut on his back. He put him back in the patch and told him to help himself. He lives from our garden every year. We don't bother him and don't allow anybody else to bother him. He spends his winters under our smokehouse floor buried in the dry ground."

"Gee, Grandpa looks like the terrapin," I said.

Mom didn't say anything; tears came to her eyes. She wiped them from her eyes with the corner of her apron.

"I'll be back to see you," Grandpa said. "I'm a-gettin' a little chilly; I'll be gettin' back to the house."

The terrapin twisted his wrinkled neck without moving his big body, poking his head deeper into the April wind as Grandpa pulled his bundled body up by holding to the sassafras tree trunk.

"Good-by, old friend!"

The terrapin poked his head deeper into the wind, holding one eye on Grandpa, for I could see his eye shining in the sinking sunlight.

Grandpa got his cane that was leaned against the sassafras tree trunk and hobbled slowly toward the house. The terrapin looked at him with first one eye and then the other.

Dawn of Remembered Spring

About the story:

The home of the Jesse Stuarts spans Shinglemill Hollow and is so located that Shinglemill Creek flows under the house near the point where it debouches into the last prong of W-Creek at the head of W-Hollow. When asked to comment on "Dawn of Remembered Spring," the author, who as the result of a 1978 stroke says, "My world is the bed now," pointed toward the front of the house and W-Creek. "Here's the stream right here . . . along the front of the house. No road there then." A field led over to the creek, perhaps forty yards from the house. That was where young Jesse Stuart waded up and down W-Creek killing water moccasins in an act of vengeance, and that was where the neighbors saw the copperheads together in the spring. "I thought they were fighting," the author said. And further, "That was a factual situation. The little boy's real name was Charlie Deer. The family is buried up at Three-Mile Cemetery," which is located near the eastern entrance to W-Hollow from Highway 1. One difference: "The little boy in fact did not die [of snakebite]."

The poem which follows, when read in conjunction with "Dawn of Remembered Spring," may reveal anew something of that strange, many-leveled harmony existing between humankind and a fellow creature that, of all the citizens of the animal kingdom, lives closest to the earth.

Copperhead Speaks of Love and Enemies

I am earth's cold phlegmatic Copperhead
With venomed fangs as sharp as sawbriar jaggers;
My body's short; my head is copperish-red;
I strike an enemy so hard he staggers!
And everything that walks or crawls or flies
Is mortal enemy to our Great Clan;
I have fought fire, hail stones and wind that sighs;
I've killed a horse, cow, fox, blacksnake and man!

The rockcliff is our rendezvous for love
Since it's more secret than the briary coves;
We lie entwined in our spring hours of love
Where neither rustling weed nor briar moves.
Unlike Blacksnake's our great spring love is over
When Lady Copperhead lays young in loam;
Unlike old Whirley Pratt, we have one lover
And secret places of the earth are home.

I love recesses by cool autumn streams
Where bullgrass is the color of my skin
And I can rest to do my warring dreams
Molested only by grass-seething wind.
The brambled mountain graveyard is my place
To hibernate before I shall go blind;
Deep in a sunken grave, I leave no trace,
*Dreaming of spring within the earth's warm rind**

* * *

"**B**E CAREFUL SHAN," Mom said. "I'm afraid if you wade that creek that a water moccasin will bite you."

"All right, Mom."

"You know what happened to Roy Deer last Sunday!"

"Yes, Mom."

"He's nigh at the point of death," she said. "I'm going over there now to see him. His leg's swelled hard as a rock and it's turned black as black-oak bark. They're not looking for Roy to live until midnight tonight."

"All water moccasins ought to be killed, hadn't they, Mom?"

"Yes, they're pizen things, but you can't kill them," Mom said. "They're in all these creeks around here. There's so many of them we can't kill 'em all."

Mom stood at the foot-log that crossed the creek in front of our house. Her white apron was starched stiff; I heard it rustle when Mom put her hand in the little pocket in the right upper corner to get tobacco crumbs for

---

*"Dawn of Remembered Spring" first appeared in *Harper's Baazar*, Vol. 76 (June, 1942), pp. 74–92, and has been reprinted eight times since through 1979, most recently in the Mockingbird ed. of *Tales from the Plum Grove Hills* (N.Y.: Ballantine Bks., 1974), pp. 157–163, and also in Jesse Stuart, *Dawn of Remembered Spring* (N.Y.: McGraw-Hill, 1972), pp. 3–11. Mr. Stuart commented on the original locale and other aspects of "Dawn of Remembered Spring" in Jesse Stuart/H. E. Richardson, Interview #42, W-Hollow, Greenup, Ky., Sept. 17, 1981. Jesse Stuart, "Copperhead Speaks of Love and Enemies," originally published in Jesse Stuart, *Album of Destiny* (N.Y.: Dutton, 1944), p. 19, reprinted in his collection of short stories *Dawn of Remembered Spring* (N.Y.: McGraw-Hill, 1972), p. 176.

her pipe. Mom wore her slat bonnet that shaded her sun-tanned face—a bonnet with strings that came under her chin and tied in a bowknot.

"I feel uneasy," Mom said as she filled her long-stemmed clay-stone pipe with bright burley crumbs, tamped them down with her index finger, and struck a match on the rough bark of an apple tree that grew on the creek bank by the foot-log.

"Don't feel uneasy about me," I said.

"But I do," Mom said. "Your Pa out groundhog huntin' and I'll be away at Deer's—nobody at home but you, and so many pizen snakes around this house."

Mom blew a cloud of smoke from her pipe. She walked across the foot-log, her long clean dress sweeping the weed stubble where Pa had mown the weeds along the path with a scythe so we could leave the house without getting our legs wet by the dew-covered weeds.

When Mom walked out of sight around the turn of the pasture hill and the trail of smoke that she left behind her had disappeared into the light blue April air, I crossed the garden fence at the wild-plum thicket.

Everybody gone, I thought. I am left alone. I'll do as I please. A water moccasin bit Roy Deer but a water moccasin will never bite me. I'll get me a club from this wild-plum thicket and I'll wade up the creek killing water moccasins.

There was a dead wild-plum sprout standing among the thicket of living sprouts. It was about the size of a tobacco stick. I stepped out of my path into the wild-plum thicket. Barefooted, I walked among the wild-plum thorns. I uprooted the dead wild-plum sprout. There was a bulge on it where roots had once been; now the roots had rotted in the earth. It was like a maul with this big bulge on the end of it. It would be good to hit water moccasins with.

The mules played in the pasture. It was Sunday, their day of rest. And the mules knew it. This was Sunday and it was my day of rest. It was my one day of freedom, too, when Mom and Pa were gone and I was left alone. I would like to be a man now, I thought; I'd love to plow the mules, run a farm, and kill snakes. A water moccasin bit Roy Deer but one would never bite me.

The bright sunlight of April played over the green Kentucky hills. Sunlight fell onto the creek of blue water that twisted like a crawling snake around the high bluffs and between the high rocks. In many places, dwarf willows, horseweeds, ironweeds, and wild grapevines shut away the sunlight, and the creek waters stood in quiet cool puddles. These little puddles under the shade of weeds, vines, and willows were the places where the water moccasins lived.

I rolled my overall legs above my knees so I wouldn't wet them and Mom wouldn't know I'd been wading in the creek. I started wading up the creek toward the head of the Hollow. I carried my wild-plum club across my shoulder, with both hands gripped tightly around the small end of it. I was ready to maul the first water moccasin I saw.

"One of you old water moccasins bit Roy Deer," I said bravely, clinching my grip tighter around my club, "but you won't bite me."

As I waded the cool creek waters, my bare feet touched gravel on the creek bottom. When I touched a water-soaked stick on the bottom of the creek bed, I'd think it was a snake and I'd jump. I'd wade into the banks of quicksand. I'd sink into the sand above my kness. It was hard to pull my legs out of this quicksand and when I pulled them out they'd be covered with thin quicky mud that the next puddle of water would wash away.

"A water moccasin," I said to myself. I was scared to look at him. He was wrapped around a willow that was bent over the creek. He was sleeping in the sun. I slipped toward him quietly—step by step—with my club drawn over my shoulder. Soon as I got close enough to reach him, I came over my shoulder with the club. I hit the water moccasin a powerful blow that mashed its head flat against the willow. It fell dead into the water. I picked it up by the tail and threw it upon the bank.

"One gone," I said to myself.

The water was warm around my feet and legs. The sharp-edged gravels hurt the bottoms of my feet but the soft sand soothed them. Butterflies swarmed over my head and around me—alighting on the wild pink phlox that grew in clusters along the creek bank. Wild honeybees, bumblebees, and butterflies worked on the elder blossoms, the shoemake blossoms, the beet-red finger-long blossoms of the ironweed, and the whitish pink-covered smartweed blossoms. Birds sang among the willows and flew up and down the creek with four-winged snakefeeders in their bills.

This is what I like to do, I thought. I love to kill snakes. I'm not afraid of snakes. I laughed to think how afraid of snakes Mom was—how she stuck a potato-digger tine through a big rusty-golden copperhead's skin just enough to pin him to the earth and hold him so he couldn't get under our floor. He fought the potato-digger handle until Pa came home from work and killed him. Where the snake had thrown poison over the ground, it killed the weeds, and weeds didn't grow on this spot again for four years.

Once when Mom was making my bed upstairs, she heard a noise of something running behind the paper that was pasted over the cracks between the logs; the paper split and a house snake six feet long fell onto the floor with a mouse in his mouth. Mom killed him with a bed slat. She called me once to bring her a goose-neck hoe upstairs quickly. I ran upstairs and killed two cow-snakes restin' on the wall plate. And Pa killed twenty-eight copperheads out of a two-acre oat field in the Hollow above the house one spring season.

"Snakes—snakes," Mom used to say, "are goin' to run us out'n this Hollow."

"It's because these woods haven't been burnt out in years," Pa'd always answer. "Back when I's a boy the old people burnt the woods out every spring to kill the snakes. Got so anymore there isn't enough good timber for a board tree and people have had to quit burning up the good timber. Snakes are about to take the woods again."

I thought about the snakes Pa had killed in the cornfield and the tobacco patch and how nearly copperheads had come to biting me and how I'd always seen the snake in time to cut his head off with a hoe or get out of his way. I thought of the times I had heard a rattlesnake's warning and how I'd run when I hadn't seen the snake. As I thought this—plop—a big water moccasin fell from the creek bank into a puddle of water.

"I'll get you," I said. "You can't fool me! You can't stand muddy water."

With my wild-plum club, I stirred the water until it was muddy. I waited for the water moccasin to stick his head above the water. Where wild ferns dipped down from the bank's edge and touched the water, I saw the snake's head rise slowly above the water—watchin' me with his lidless eyes. I swung sideways with my club like batting at a ball. I couldn't swing over my shoulder, for there were willow limbs above my head.

I surely got him, I thought. I waited to see. Soon something like milk spread over the water. "I got 'im." I raked in the water with my club and lifted from the bottom of the creek bed a water moccasin long as my club. It was longer than I was tall. I threw him upon the bank and moved slowly up the creek—looking on every drift, stump, log, and sunny spot. I looked for a snake's head along the edges of the creek bank where ferns dipped over and touched the water.

I waded up the creek all day killing water moccasins. If one was asleep, on the bank, I slipped upon him quietly as a cat. I mauled him with the big end of my wild-plum club. I killed him in his sleep. He never knew what struck him. If a brush caught the end of my club and caused me to miss and let the snake get into a puddle of water, I muddied the water and waited for him to stick his head above the water. When he did, I got him. Not one water moccasin got away from me. It was four o'clock when I stepped from the creek onto the bank. I'd killed fifty-three water moccasins.

Water moccasins are not half as dangerous as turtles, I thought. A water moccasin can't bite you under the water, for he gets his mouth full of water. A turtle can bite you under water and when one bites you he won't let loose until it thunders, unless you cut his head off. I'd been afraid of turtles all day because I didn't have a knife in my pocket to cut one's head off if it grabbed my foot and held it.

When I left the creek, I was afraid of the snakes I'd killed. I didn't throw my club away. I gripped the club until my hands hurt. I looked below my path, above my path, and in front of me. When I saw a stick on the ground, I thought it was a snake. I eased up to it quietly as a cat trying to catch a bird. I was ready to hit it with my club.

What will Mom think when I tell her I've killed fifty-three water moccasins. I thought. A water moccasin bit Roy Deer but one's not going to bite me. I paid the snakes back for biting him. It was good enough for them. Roy wasn't bothering the water moccasin that bit him. He was just crossing the creek at the foot-log and it jumped from the grass and bit him.

Shadows lengthened from the tall trees. The Hollow was deep and the creek flowed softly in the cool recesses of evening shadows. There was one patch of sunlight. It was upon the steep broom sedge-covered bluff above the path.

"Snakes," I cried, "snakes a-fightin' and they're not water moccasins! They're copperheads!"

They were wrapped around each other. Their lidless eyes looked into each other's eyes. Their hard lips touched each other's lips. They did not move. They did not pay any attention to me. They looked at one another.

I'll kill 'em, I thought, if they don't kill one another in this fight.

I stood in the path with my club ready. I had heard snakes fought each other but I'd never seen them fight.

"What're you lookin' at, Shan?" Uncle Alf Skinner asked. He walked up the path with a cane in his hand.

"Snakes a-fightin'."

"Snakes a-fightin'?"

"Yes."

"I never saw it in my life."

"I'll kill 'em both if they don't finish the fight," I said. "I'll club 'em to death."

"Snakes a-fightin', Shan," he shouted, "you are too young to know! It's snakes in love! Don't kill 'em—just keep your eye on 'em until I bring Martha over here! She's never seen snakes in love!"

Uncle Alf ran around the turn of the hill. He brought Aunt Martha back with him. She was carrying a basket of greens on her arm and the case knife that she'd been cutting greens with in her hand.

"See 'em, Martha," Uncle Alf said. "Look up there in that broom sedge!"

"I'll declare," she said. "I've lived all my life and I never saw this. I've wondered about snakes!"

She stood with a smile on her wrinkled lips. Uncle Alf stood with a wide smile on his deep-lined face. I looked at them and wondered why they looked at these copperheads and smiled. Uncle Alf looked at Aunt Martha. They smiled at each other.

"Shan, Shan!" I heard Mom calling.

"I'm here," I shouted.

"Where've you been?" she asked as she turned around the bend of the hill with a switch in her hand.

"Be quiet, Sal," Uncle Alf said. "Come here and look for yourself!"

"What is it?" Mom asked.

"Snakes in love," Uncle Alf said.

Mom was mad. "Shan, I feel like limbing you," she said. "I've hunted every place for you! Where've you been?"

"Killin' snakes," I answered.

"Roy Deer is dead," she said. "That's how dangerous it is to fool with snakes."

"I paid the snakes back for him," I said. "I've killed fifty-three water moccasins!"

"Look, Sal!"

"Yes, Alf, I see," Mom said.

Mom threw her switch on the ground. Her eyes were wide apart. The frown left her face.

"It's the first time I ever saw anything like this. Shan, you go tell your Pa to come and look at this."

I was glad to do anything for Mom. I was afraid of her switch. When I brought Pa back to the sunny bank where the copperheads were loving, Art and Sadie Baker were there and Tom and Ethel Riggs—and there were a lot of strangers there. They were looking at the copperheads wrapped around each other with their eyes looking into each other's eyes and their hard lips touching each other's lips.

"You hurry to the house, Shan," Pa said, "and cut your stove wood for tonight."

"I'd like to kill these copperheads," I said.

"Why?" Pa asked.

"Fightin'," I said.

Uncle Alf and Aunt Martha laughed as I walked down the path carrying my club. It was something—I didn't know what; all the crowd watching the snakes were smiling. Their faces were made over new. The snakes had done something to them. Their wrinkled faces were as bright as the spring sunlight on the bluff; their eyes were shiny as the creek was in the noonday sunlight. And they laughed and talked to one another. I heard their laughter grow fainter as I walked down the path toward the house. Their laughter was louder than the wild honeybees I had heard swarming over the shoemake, alderberry, and wild phlox blossoms along the creek.

Clearing in the Sky

About the author:

Speaking to The Club in the Senior Room of Nassau Inn at Princeton University, Jesse Stuart concluded, "I write of what has actually happened, and in the only way I can—the way that comes naturally to me." In "My Father Is an Educated Man," the author wrote, "My father can take a handful of new-ground dirt in his hand, smell of it, then sift it between his fingers and tell whether to plant the land in corn, tobacco, cane or potatoes. He has an intuition that I cannot explain." In "Clearing in the Sky," the author's father is the story's undisguised hero, as Stuart himself is clearly the narrator, following his father up "a pretty little footpath under the high canopy of hickory, walnut, and oak leaves" to a clearing of fertile land "of leaf-rot loam," where his father tells him, " . . . something goes back. Something I cannot explain. You go back to the places you knew and loved." In his bio-critical study *Jesse Stuart*, Ruel E. Foster writes that this story "becomes a kind of hymn to the agrarian world," as the author's father, once again working in the new-ground earth, "is renewing his youth in the fertile, primeval soil. . . . " Mitchell Stuart says, "This is real land. It's the land that God left."

The W-hollow locale of the story, Jesse Stuart said, lies "about midway between here [the Jesse Stuart house] and Bud Adams' [place]. Dad went up in there . . . and that garden can be found right now. There's wire around it . . . fenced to keep the cattle off it . . . nailed to a piece of wood, nailed to the tree [so the tree would not grow around the wire]."

Consider these poems as they serve to illuminate the father of the poet, the hero of "Clearing in the Sky":

For M. S. #51

I've seen him go among his corn at night
After his day was done—By lantern light
He went, unless it was light of the moon,
And a bright moon was up—He's broken soon;
Lines are grooved on his face at fifty-two.
The work he does would get the best of you.

And now his love is wind among the corn;
His love is whispering, talking, green corn blades.
His love is cornfields when the summer fades,
Oak leaves to red and fodder blades to brown.
His love is autumn raining dead leaves down
And going out on autumn morns to salt the stock.
He loves his mules and whispering corn at night—
Buff-colored corn in full autumn moonlight.

54

This man has gone through mud and rain and sleet
And drank of whiskey, applejack and gin,
Lived in log shacks when winter winds blew in,
When seasons failed, had half enough to eat.
But did he shrink from this? And did he fear?
"I'll bet I'll get good cropping this next year!"
With spirit such as this he met the years.
There are no lands for him to conquer now,
To clear of brush, to wield the cutter plow,
There are no fields of game for him to squander,
No trails left for this pioneer to follow
Through hazel thicket, pawpaw bank and hollow.
There is no place for his wild blood to wander.
He can't adjust himself to paths through air,
And people and new houses everywhere.*

*　　*　　*

"THIS IS THE WAY, JESS," said my father, pointing with his cane across the deep valley below us. "I want to show you something you've not seen for many years!"

"Isn't it too hot for you to do much walking?" I wiped the streams of sweat from my face to keep them from stinging my eyes.

---

*For Jesse Stuart's appearance at Princeton University referred to here, see "Mountain Writer Gives Autobiographical Talk," Princeton, N.J., *Princetonian*, April 17, 1937, clipping in Jesse Stuart, Scrapbook #3, p. 35, M. S. U. Jesse Stuart, "My Father Is an Educated Man," *Tales from the Plum Grove Hills* (N.Y.: Dutton, 1946), reprinted (N.Y.: Ballantine Bks., 1974), Mockingbird ed., p. 29. "Clearing in the Sky" was first published in *Household*, Vol. 49 (March, 1949), pp. 8–9, 63, 65, reprinted in *Clearing in the Sky and Other Stories* (N.Y.: McGraw-Hill, 1950), pp. 32–40; the quotations here are from pp. 34, 37, and 40. Ruel E. Foster, *Jesse Stuart* (N.Y.: Twayne, 1968), p. 88. Jesse Stuart provided information on the locale of "Clearing in the Sky" in our interview, W-Hollow, Greenup, Ky., Sept. 15, 1978. Poem #51 is from Jesse Stuart, *Man with a Bull-Tongue Plow* (N.Y.: Dutton, 1934), p. 28; Poem #54, is from the same work, p. 29.

In addition to the reprints of "Clearing in the Sky" indicated above, Woodbridge, *Jesse Stuart Bibliography*, lists eight others, including editions in South Africa, Denmark, and Korea.

I didn't want to go with him. I had just finished walking a half mile up-hill from my home to his. I had carried a basket of dishes to Mom. There were two slips in the road and I couldn't drive my car. And I knew how hot it was. It was 97 in the shade. I knew from that January until April my father had gone to eight different doctors. One of the doctors had told him not to walk the length of a city block. He told my father to get a taxi to take him home. But my father walked home five miles across the mountain and told Mom what the doctor had said. Forty years ago a doctor had told him the same thing. And he had lived to raise a family of five children. He had done as much hard work in those years as any man.

I could not protest to him now. He had made up his mind. When he made up his mind to do a thing, he would do it if he had to crawl. He didn't care if it was 97 in the shade or 16 below zero. I wiped more sweat from my face as I followed him down the little path between the pasture and the meadow.

Suddenly he stopped at the edge of the meadow, took his pocketknife from his pocket, and cut a wisp of alfalfa. He held it up between him and the sun.

"Look at this, Jess!" he bragged. "Did you ever see better alfalfa grow out of the earth?"

"It's the best looking hay I've seen any place," I said. "I've not seen better looking alfalfa even in the Little Sandy River bottoms!"

"When I bought this little farm everybody around here said I'd end up with my family at the county poor farm if I tried to make a living here," he bragged again. "It took me thirty years to improve these old worn-out acres to make them do this!"

As I stood looking at his meadow of alfalfa, down in the saddle between two hills, I remembered how, down through the years, he had hauled leaves from the woods and spread them over this field in the autumn and then plowed them under and let them rot. All that would grow on this ground when he bought it were scrubby pines and saw-briars. The pines didn't grow waist-high. There wasn't enough strength in the ground to push them any higher. And the saw-briars didn't grow knee-high. In addition to this, the land was filled with gullies. But he cut the scrubby pines and turned their tops uphill to stop the erosion. And he mowed the saw-briars with a scythe and forked them into the gullies on top the pines. Then he plowed the land. He sowed a cover crop and turned it under. Then he sowed a second, a third, and a fourth cover crop. In a few years he had the land producing good crops of corn, wheat, potatoes, and tobacco.

"But this is not what I want to show you, Jess," he said as he threw the wisp of alfalfa to the ground. "Come on. Follow me!"

I followed him through the pasture gate. Then down a little narrow cattle path into the deep hollow.

"Where are we going?" I asked when he started to walk a log across the creek toward a steep, timbered bluff.

"Not up or down the hollow," he laughed. "But there." He pointed toward a wooded mountaintop. "That's the way we are goin'!"

"But there's not even a path leading up there," I said.

"There's a path up there now," he said. "I've made one."

I followed him across the foot log he had made by chopping down a white-oak, felling it over the deep-channeled stream. It was a foot log a flash flood couldn't carry away because its top branches rested on the far side of the channel behind a big tree. He hadn't chopped the white-oak all the way off at the trunk. He had left a little of the tree to hold it at the stump. His doctor had told him not to use an ax. But he had cut this white-oak to make a foot log across the stream so he could reach the rugged mountain slope.

Now I followed my father up the winding footpath under the tall hickory trees, a place where I used to come with him when I was a little boy to hunt for squirrels. We would shoot squirrels from the tall scaly-bark hickories and black walnuts with our long rifles. But that had been nearly thirty years ago. And through the years, from time to time, I had walked over this rugged mountain slope and there was never a path on it until my father had made this one. It was a pretty little footpath under the high canopy of hickory, walnut, and oak leaves. We couldn't see the sky above our heads. Our eyes could not find an opening among the leaves.

In front of me walked the little man who once walked so fast I had to run to follow him. But it wasn't that way now. Time had slowed him. The passing of the years and much hard labor had bent his shoulders. His right shoulder, the one he used to carry his loads, sagged three inches below the left one. His breath didn't come as easy as it used to come. For he stopped twice, and leaned on his cane to rest, before we reached the top of the first bluff. Then we came to a flat where the ground wasn't so steep.

"I like these woods, Jess," my father said. "Remember when we used to come here to hunt for squirrels? Remember when we sat beneath these hickories and the squirrels threw green hickory shells down at us? The morning wind just at the break of day in August was so good to breathe. I can't forget those days. And in October when the rabbits were ripe and the frosts had come and the hickory leaves had turned yellow and when the October winds blew they rustled the big leaves from the trees and they fell like yellow rain drops to the ground! Remember," he said, looking at me with his pale blue eyes, "how our hounds, Rags and Scout, would make the rabbits circle! Those were good days, Jess! That's why I remember this mountain."

"Is that what you wanted to show me?" I asked.

"Oh, no, no," he said as he began to climb the second bluff that lifted abruptly from the flat toward the sky. The pines on top of the mountain above us looked as if the fingers of their long boughs were fondling the substance of a white cloud. Whatever my father wanted me to see was on top of the highest point on my farm. And with the exception of the last three years, I had been over this point many times. I had never seen anything extraordinary upon this high point of rugged land. I had seen the beauty of many wild flowers, a few rock cliffs, and many species of hard and soft-wood trees.

"Why do you take the path straight up the point?" I asked. "Look at these other paths! What are they doing here?"

Within the distance of a few yards, several paths left the main path and circled around the slope, gradually climbing the mountain.

"All paths go to the same place," he answered.

"Then why take the steep one?" I asked.

"I'll explain later," he spoke with half-breaths.

He rested a minute to catch his second wind while I managed to stand on the path by holding to a little sapling, because it was too steep for my feet to hold unless I braced myself.

Then my father started to move slowly up the path again, supporting himself with his cane. I followed at his heels. Just a few steps in front of him a fox squirrel crossed the path and ran up a hickory tree.

"See that, Jess!" he shouted.

"Yes, I did," I answered.

"That brings back something to me," he said. "Brings back the old days to see a fox squirrel. But this won't bring back as much as something I'm goin' to show you."

My curiosity was aroused. I thought he had found a new kind of wild grass, or an unfamiliar herb, or a new kind of tree. For I remembered the time he found a coffee tree in our woods. It is, as far as I know, the only one of its kind growing in our county.

Only twice did my father stop to wipe the sweat from his eyes as he climbed the second steep bluff toward the fingers of the pines. We reached the limbless trunks of these tall straight pines whose branches reached toward the blue depth of sky, for the white cloud was now gone. I saw a clearing, a small clearing of not more than three-fourths of an acre in the heart of this wilderness right on the mountaintop.

"Now, you're comin' to something, Son," he said as he pushed down the top wire so he could cross the fence. "This is something I want you to see!"

"Who did this?" I asked. "Who cleared this land and fenced it? Fenced it against what?"

"Stray cattle if they ever get out of the pasture," he answered me curtly. "I cleared this land. And I fenced it!"

"But why did you ever climb to this mountaintop and do this?" I asked him. "Look at the fertile land we have in the valley!"

"Fertile," he laughed as he reached down and picked up a double handful of leaf-rot loam. "This is the land, Son! This is it. I've tried all kinds of land!"

Then he smelled of the dirt. He whiffed and whiffed the smell of this wild dirt into his nostrils.

"Just like fresh air," he said as he let the dirt run between his fingers. "It's pleasant to touch, too," he added.

"But, Dad——" I said.

"I know what you think," he interrupted. "Your mother thinks the same thing. She wonders why I ever climbed to this mountaintop to raise my potatoes, yams, and tomatoes! But, Jess," he almost whispered, "anything grown in new ground like this has a better flavor. Wait until my tomatoes are ripe! You'll never taste sweeter tomatoes in your life!"

"They'll soon be ripe, too," I said as I looked at the dozen or more rows of tomatoes on the lower side of the patch.

Then above the tomatoes were a half-dozen rows of yams. Above the yams were, perhaps, three dozen rows of potatoes.

"I don't see a weed in this patch," I laughed. "Won't they grow here?"

"I won't let 'em," he said. "Now this is what I've been wanting you to see!"

"This is the cleanest patch I've ever seen," I bragged. "But I still don't see why you climbed to the top of this mountain to clear this patch. And you did all this against your doctor's orders!"

"Which one?" he asked, laughing.

Then he sat down on a big oak stump and I sat down on a small black-gum stump near him. This was the only place on the mountain where the sun could shine to the ground. And on the lower side of the clearing there was a rim of shadow over the rows of dark stalwart plants loaded with green tomatoes.

"What is the reason for your planting this patch up here?" I asked.

"Twenty times in my life," he said, "a doctor has told me to go home and be with my family as long as I could. Told me not to work. Not to do anything but to live and enjoy the few days I had left me. If the doctors have been right," he said, winking at me, "I have cheated death many times! Now, I've reached the years the Good Book allows to man in his lifetime upon this earth! Threescore years and ten!"

He got up from the stump and wiped the raindrops of sweat from his red-wrinkled face with his big blue bandanna.

"And something else, Jess," he said, motioning for me to follow him to the upper edge of the clearing, "you won't understand until you reach threescore and ten! After these years your time is borrowed. And when you live on that kind of time, then something goes back. Something I cannot explain. You go to the places you knew and loved. See this steep hill slope." He pointed down from the upper rim of the clearing toward the deep valley below. "Your mother and I, when she was nineteen and I was twenty-two, cleared this mountain slope together. We raised corn, beans, and pumpkins here," he continued, his voice rising with excitement—he talked with his hands, too. "Those were the days. This wasn't land one had to build up. It was already here as God had made it and all we had to do was clear the trees and burn the brush. I plowed this mountain with cattle the first time it was ever plowed. And we raised more than a barrel of corn to the shock. That's why I came back up here. I went back to our youth. And this was the only land left like that was.

"And, Jess," he bragged, "regardless of my threescore years and ten, I plowed it. Plowed it with a mule! I have, with just a little help, done all the work. It's like the land your mother and I used to farm here when I brought my gun to the field and took home a mess of fox squirrels every evening!"

I looked at the vast mountain slope below where my mother and father had farmed. And I could remember, years later, when they farmed this land. It was on this steep slope that my father once made me a little wooden plow. That was when I was six years old and they brought me to the field to thin corn. I lost my little plow in a furrow and I cried and cried until he made me another plow. But I never loved the second plow as I did the first one.

Now, to look at the mountain slope, grown up with tall trees, many of them big enough to have sawed into lumber at the mill, it was hard to believe that my father and mother had cleared this mountain slope and had farmed it for many years. For many of the trees were sixty feet tall and the wild vines had matted their tops together.

"And, Jess," he almost whispered, "the doctors told me to sit still and to take life easy. I couldn't do it. I had to work. I had to go back. I had to smell this rich loam again. This land is not like the land I had to build to grow alfalfa. This is real land. It's the land that God left. I had to come back and dig in it. I had to smell it, sift it through my fingers again. And I wanted to taste yams, tomatoes, and potatoes grown in this land."

From this mountaintop I looked far in every direction over the rugged hills my father and mother had cleared and farmed in corn, tobacco, and cane. The one slope they hadn't cleared was the one from which my father had cleared his last, small patch.

I followed him from his clearing in the sky, down a new path, toward the deep valley below.

"But why do you have so many paths coming from the flat up the steep second bluff?" I asked, since he had promised that he would explain this to me later.

"Oh, yes," he said. "Early last spring, I couldn't climb straight up the steep path. That was when the doctor didn't give me a week to live. I made a longer, easier path so I wouldn't have to do so much climbing. Then, as I got better," he explained, "I made another path that was a little steeper. And as I continued to get better, I made steeper paths. That was one way of knowing I was getting better all the time!"

I followed him down the path, that wound this way and that, three times the length of the path we had climbed.

Thanksgiving Hunter

About the story:

"I killed for two things," the author said, discussing hunting as a youth in W-Hollow:

> I killed for our table—squirrels, groundhogs, even 'possums. Mom would cook them. We didn't have enough money to buy meats . . . and then I sold hides. . . . That's how I bought books. . . . But I got *acquainted* with all these animals I killed and I just couldn't kill them any more. I quit killing. I thought of the day they would disappear from the face of the earth. . . . W-Hollow is their only stronghold here in the county. They can always get something to eat here.

Although the Stuarts had once been known as a "tough set," the author reflected aloud, "I've been a non-killer . . . and have reverence for life." Even as a youth he took a lot of kidding, and "My dad couldn't understand. He taught us all how to shoot the gun. I'd leave home when they'd kill hogs . . . they always wanted me to shoot the hogs because I was a good shot with a rifle. I wouldn't do it." Questioned about "Thanksgiving Hunter" and the concluding action of the story, when the narrator could not bring himself to shoot the doves, the author replied, "No, I couldn't shoot the doves."

From the time Mark van Doren praised Jesse Stuart's *Man with a Bull-Tongue Plow* (1934) and hailed him as "a modern American Robert Burns," his poetry has been nearly as widely read and anthologized as his prose. His poems are as steeped in the many sensitive facets of life as his prose, and the following two may serve thematically to introduce "Thanksgiving Hunter" and one literary artist's view of that moment of self-revelation when even one who has eaten his kill decides never to kill again:

#426

The season killing starts today—guns speak
With tongues of fire and smoke in every hollow—
The wounded rabbit runs for a water seap—
The hunters and the yelping hound-dogs follow.
Hot guns speak under the red autumn sun;

The hot guns speak—the red-oak leaves are flying!
The shots ripped out the wounded rabbit's guts.
The rabbit falls on dead leaves—bleeding, dying.
The rabbit dies under the autumn sun.
The hunter slings its guts upon the ground.
He sacks his game—the rabbit chase is done.
The hounds eat guts and lick blood from the ground.
Mad guns speak on under the autumn sun.
More guts are ripped before the day is done.

#428

The slaughtering guns now roar on every side
Out on the rain-damped fields in gray November;
The frightened covey breaks its family pride,
Each seeks a shelter in the barren timber.
There is no shelter in the barren timber;
There is no shelter in the sunless sky;
The LAW has set the appointed time November
For coveys of these timid birds to die.
They die from number threes that rent their bodies
The wounded seek refuge in the tall weeds
Where they would rather bleed and die alone
Than be hit with the barrel of the gun.
And now these timid birds must bleed and die
In a red wreckage on the gray December sky*

* * *

"HOLD YOUR RIFLE like this," Uncle Wash said, changing the position of my rifle. "When I throw this marble into the air, follow it with your bead; at the right time gently squeeze the trigger!"

Uncle Wash threw the marble high into the air and I lined my sights with the tiny moving marble, gently squeezing the trigger, timing the speed of my object until it slowed in the air ready to drop to earth again. Just as it reached its height, my rifle cracked and the marble was broken into tiny pieces.

Uncle Wash was a tall man with a hard leathery face, dark discolored

*Dick Perry quotes Jesse Stuart in the former's *Reflections of Jesse Stuart on a Land of Many Moods* (N.Y.: McGraw-Hill, 1971), pp. 95–96, the source here. Further quotations of Mr. Stuart are from Jesse Stuart/H. E. Richardson, Interview #11, W-Hollow, Greenup, Ky., Oct. 7, 1978. Mark Van Doren's often-quoted review of Stuart's *Man with a Bull-Tongue Plow* (N.Y.: Dutton, 1934) appeared in the New York *Herald-Tribune Books*, Vol. 12, June 12, 1934, p. 31. Poem #426 is from *Man with a Bull-Tongue Plow*, p. 217; Poem #428 is from the same work, p. 218. "Thanksgiving Hunter" was first published in *Household*, Vol. 43 (Nov., 1943), pp. 1, 26–27, reprinted in *Tales from the Plum Grove Hills* (1946) and (1974), pp. 45–50. Woodbridge, *Jesse Stuart Bibliography*, lists through 1979 a total of fifteen other reprints, pp. 80–81.

teeth and blue eyes that had a faraway look in them. He hunted the year round; he violated all the hunting laws. He knew every path, creek, river, and rock cliff within a radius of ten miles. Since he was a great hunter, he wanted to make a great hunter out of me. And tomorrow, Thanksgiving Day, would be the day for Uncle Wash to take me on my first hunt.

Uncle Wash woke me long before daylight.

"Oil your double-barrel," he said. "Oil it just like I've showed you."

I had to clean the barrels with an oily rag tied to a long string with a knot in the end. I dropped the heavy knot down the barrel and pulled the oily rag through the barrel. I did this many times to each barrel. Then I rubbed a meat-rind over both barrels and shined them with a dry rag. After this was done I polished the gunstock.

"Love the feel of your gun," Uncle Wash had often told me. "There's nothing like the feel of a gun. Know how far it will shoot. Know your gun better than you know your own self; know it and love it."

Before the sun had melted the frost from the multicolored trees and from the fields of stubble and dead grasses, we had cleaned our guns, had eaten breakfasts, and were on our way. Uncle Wash, Dave Pratt, Steve Blevins walked ahead of me along the path and talked about the great hunts they had taken and the game they had killed. And while they talked, words that Uncle Wash had told me about loving the feel of a gun kept going through my head. Maybe it is because Uncle Wash speaks of a gun like it was a living person is why he is such a good marksman, I thought.

"This is the dove country," Uncle Wash said soon as we had reached the cattle barn on the west side of our farm. "Doves are feeding here. They nest in these pines and feed around this barn fall and winter. Plenty of wheat grains, rye grains, and timothy seed here for doves."

Uncle Wash is right about the doves, I thought. I had seen them fly in pairs all summer long into the pine grove that covered the knoll east of our barn. I had heard their mournful songs. I had seen them in early April carrying straws in their bills to build their nests; I had seen them flying through the blue spring air after each other; I had seen them in the summer carrying food in their bills for their tiny young. I had heard their young ones crying for more food from the nests among the pines when the winds didn't sough among the pine boughs to drown their sounds. And when the leaves started turning brown I had seen whole flocks of doves, young and old ones, fly down from the tall pines to our barnyard to pick up the wasted grain. I had seen them often and been so close to them that they were no longer afraid of me.

"Doves are fat now," Uncle Wash said to Dave Pratt.

"Doves are wonderful to eat," Dave said.

And then I remembered when I had watched them in the spring and summer, I had never thought about killing and eating them. I had thought of them as birds that lived in the tops of pine trees and that hunted their food from the earth. I remembered their mournful songs that had often made me feel lonely when I worked in the cornfield near the barn. I had thought of them as flying over the deep hollows in pairs in the bright sunlight air chasing each other as they flew toward their nests in pines.

"Now we must get good shooting into this flock of doves," Uncle Wash said to us, "before they get wild. They've not been shot among this season."

Then Uncle Wash, to show his skill in hunting, sent us in different directions so that when the doves flew up from our barn lot, they would have to fly over one of our guns. He gave us orders to close in toward the barn and when the doves saw us, they would take to the air and we would do our shooting.

"And if they get away," Uncle Wash said, "follow them up and talk to them in their own language."

Each of us went his separate way. I walked toward the pine grove, carrying my gun just as Uncle Wash had instructed me. I was ready to start shooting as soon as I heard the flutter of dove wings. I walked over the frosted white grass and the wheat stubble until I came to the fringe of pine woods. And when I walked slowly over the needles of pines that covered the autumn earth, I heard the flutter of many wings and the barking of guns. The doves didn't come my way. I saw many fall from the bright autumn air to the brown crab-grass-colored earth.

I saw these hunters pick up the doves they had killed and cram their limp, lifeless, bleeding bodies with tousled feathers into their brown hunting coats. They picked them up as fast as they could, trying to watch the way the doves went.

"Which way did they go, Wash?" Dave asked soon as he had picked up his kill.

"That way," Uncle Wash pointed to the low hill on the west.

"Let's be after 'em, men," Steve said.

The seasoned hunters hurried after their prey while I stood under a tall pine and kicked the toe of my brogan shoe against the brown pine needles that had carpeted the ground. I saw these men hurry over the hill, cross the ravine and climb the hill over which the doves had flown.

I watched them reach the summit of the hill, stop and call to the doves in tones not unlike the doves' own calling. I saw them with guns poised against the sky. Soon they had disappeared the way the doves had gone.

I sat down on the edge of a lichened rock that emerged from the rugged hill. I laid my double-barrel down beside me, and sunlight fingered through the pine boughs above me in pencil-sized streaks of light. And when one of these shifting pencil-sized streaks of light touched my gun barrels, they shone brightly in the light. My gun was cleaned and oiled and the little pine needles stuck to its meat-rind-greased barrels. Over my head the wind soughed lonely among the pine needles. And from under these pines I could see the vast open fields where the corn stubble stood knee high, where the wheat stubble would have shown plainly had it not been for the great growth of crab grass after we had cut the wheat; crab grass that had been blighted by autumn frost and shone brilliantly brown in the sun.

Even the air was cool to breathe into the lungs; I could feel it deep down when I breathed and it tasted of the green pine boughs that flavored it as it seethed through their thick tops. This was a clean cool autumn earth that both men and birds loved. And as I sat on the lichened rock with pine needles at my feet, with the soughing pine boughs above me, I thought the doves had chosen a fine place to find food, to nest and raise their young. But while I sat looking at the earth about me, I heard the thunder of the seasoned hunters' guns beyond the low ridge. I knew that they had talked to the doves until they had got close enough to shoot again.

As I sat on the rock, listening to the guns in the distance, I thought Uncle Wash might be right after all. It was better to shoot and kill with a gun than to kill with one's hands or with a club. I remembered the time I went over the hill to see how our young corn was growing after we had plowed it the last time. And while I stood looking over the corn whose long ears were in tender blisters, I watched a groundhog come from the edge of the woods, ride down a stalk of corn, and start eating a blister-ear. I found a dead sassafras stick near me, tiptoed quietly behind the groundhog and hit him over the head. I didn't finish him with that lick. It took many licks.

When I left the cornfield, I left the groundhog dead beside his ear of corn. I couldn't forget killing the groundhog over an ear of corn and leaving him dead, his gray-furred clean body to waste on the lonely hill.

I can't disappoint Uncle Wash, I thought. He has trained me to shoot. He says that I will make a great hunter. He wants me to hunt like my father, cousins, and uncles. He says that I will be the greatest marksman among them.

I thought about the way my people had hunted and how they had loved their guns. I thought about how Uncle Wash had taken care of his gun, how he had treated it like a living thing and how he had told me to love the feel of it. And now my gun lay beside me with pine needles sticking to it. If Uncle Wash were near he would make me pick the gun up, brush away the pine needles and wipe the gun barrels with my handkerchief. If I had lost my handkerchief, as I had seen Uncle Wash often do, he would make me pull out my shirttail to wipe my gun with it. Uncle Wash didn't object to wearing dirty clothes or to wiping his face with a dirty bandanna; he didn't mind living in a dirty house—but never, never would he allow a speck of rust or dirt on his gun.

It was comfortable to sit on the rock since the sun was directly above me. It warmed me with a glow of autumn. I felt the sun's rays against my face and the sun was good to feel. But the good fresh autumn air was no longer cool as the frost that covered the autumn grass that morning, nor could I feel it go deep into my lungs; the autumn air was warmer and it was flavored more with the scent of pines.

Now that the shooting had long been over near our cattle barn, I heard the lazy murmur of the woodcock in the pine woods near by. Uncle Wash said woodcocks were game birds and he killed them wherever he found them. Once I thought I would follow the sound and kill the woodcock. I picked up my gun but laid it aside again. I wanted to kill something to show Uncle Wash. I didn't want him to be disappointed in me.

Instead of trying to find a rabbit sitting behind a broomsedge cluster or in a briar thicket as Uncle Wash had trained me to do, I felt relaxed and lazy in the autumn sun that had now penetrated the pine boughs from directly overhead. I looked over the brown vast autumn earth about me where I had worked when everything was green and growing, where birds sang in the spring air as they built their nests. I looked at the tops of barren trees and thought how a few months ago they were waving clouds of green. And now it was a sad world, dying world. There was so much death in the world that I had known: flowers were dead, leaves were dead, and the frosted grass was lifeless in the wind. Everything was dead and dying but a few wild birds and rabbits. I had almost grown to the rock where I sat but I didn't want to stir. I wanted to glimpse the life about me before it was all covered with winter snows. I hated to think of killing in this autumn world. When I picked up my gun, I didn't feel life in it—I felt death.

I didn't hear the old hunters' guns now but I knew that, wherever they were, they were hunting for something to shoot. I thought they would return to the barn if the doves came back, as they surely would, for the pine grove where I sat was one place in this autumn world that was a home to the doves. And while I sat on the rock, I thought I would practice the dove whistle that Uncle Wash had taught me. I thought a dove would come close and I would shoot the dove so that I could go home with something in my hunting coat.

As I sat whistling a dove call, I heard the distant thunder of their guns beyond the low ridge. Then I knew they were coming back toward the cattle barn.

And, as I sat whistling my dove calls, I heard a dove answer me. I called gently to the dove. Again it answered. This time it was closer to me. I picked up my gun from the rock and gently brushed the pine needles from its stock and barrels. And as I did this, I called pensively to the dove and it answered plaintively.

I aimed my gun soon as I saw the dove walking toward me. When it walked toward my gun so unafraid, I thought it was a pet dove. I lowered my gun; laid it across my lap. Never had a dove come this close to me. When I called again, it answered at my feet. Then it fanned its wings and flew upon the rock beside me trying to reach the sound of my voice. It called, but I didn't answer. I looked at the dove when it turned its head to one side to try to see me. Its eye was gone, with the mark of a shot across its face. Then it turned the other side of its head toward me to try to see. The other eye was gone.

As I looked at the dove the shooting grew louder; the old hunters were getting closer. I heard the fanning of dove wings above the pines. And I heard doves batting their wings against the pine boughs. And the dove beside me called to them. It knew the sounds of their wings. Maybe it knows each dove by the sound of his wings, I thought. And then the dove spoke beside me. I was afraid to answer. I could have reached out my hand and picked this dove up from the rock. Though it was blind, I couldn't kill it, and yet I knew it would have a hard time to live.

When the dove beside me called again, I heard an answer from a pine bough near by. The dove beside me spoke and the dove in the pine bough answered. Soon they were talking to each other as the guns grew louder. Suddenly, the blind dove fluttered through the tree-tops, chirruping its plaintive melancholy notes, toward the sound of its mate's voice. I heard its wings batting the wind-shaken pine boughs as it ascended, struggling, toward the beckoning voice.

This Is the Place

About the story:

"This Is the Place," first published in *Esquire* in December, 1936, is a story about the immortality of those who love the land. Although the keystone of the story is Jesse Stuart's W-Hollow, its supporting arch is all America; and the scope of the story, as its conclusion declares with a choric triumph of spiritual affirmation, transcends the physical world of W-Hollow or any-place, achieving a universal amplitude.

My interview with Mr. Stuart concerning this story went like this:

STUART: I wrote that story and sold it while I was in Peabody College [in the summer of 1936]. . . . I'd been playing a little machine down there [in Nashville]. You'd play a nickel on it and . . . I'd been winning all the time . . . and they couldn't defeat me. When you talk to James [the author's brother], ask him about it.

RICHARDSON: The Uncle Mel Shelton, the main character here, is—

S.: Uncle Martin Hilton.

R.: Your uncle tells about his desire to have everybody buried—Sheltons and Powderjays (Hiltons and Stuarts) buried in the same place so on Resurrection Day, they'd all get up and know each other.

S.: Yeah. He had it all worked out. . . . I wrote that for Dr. [Alfred Leland] Crabb. He wanted a paper from his students in education, and he wanted each of us to give our philosophy of education. I told him "I don't have any, and I can't give it, but I've got an uncle who read the *History of the Decline and Fall of the Roman Empire* and let the weeds take his corn." He said, "He sounds great to me; write about him." Uncle Martin Hilton did that. He'd read a book and let the weeds take the corn. He was a great reader. . . .

R.: There is a powerful lyric throughout this story, that life cannot die. It is a beautiful passage:

But we speak not all—the ghosts of us light as the wind and the wind with the identity of us stamped invisible—laugh to the wind . . . in the April sky—we laugh and speak to each other on the same old mountain paths. We cannot die. You cannot take a club and kill us. You might beat off our husk but the real of us is here—it will not die—not even when the smell of sum-mer—the ripened corn and the heading cane with its white-dotted stems . . . the luscious sweet tang of scented wind from the growing summer and the creepy night of the sheepbells tinkling on the hills will mingle with the ooze of night wind in the green weeds and the foxglove on the bluffs . . . we who have been dead so long and sleeping on the hill. . . .

s.: [After a pause]. Well, it was read in class, and they all liked it. The class cried. . . .

r.: [Silence].

s.: . . . I sent it to *Esquire* and I didn't more than get it off than I got a letter back that had a $200 check. I told James, oh, boy, we'll have food until tomorrow. And you ask James about this because you won't believe it . . . that little machine you put a nickel in and beat it everytime and got our meals . . . I'd get food for both of us with a nickel. It was 1936. . . .

Tennessee reviewer George Scarbrough wrote of "This Is the Place" as "a tender, understanding story of the beauty and the ending of life, of the timeless faith of man that not all of himself will perish."*

* * *

UNCLE MEL'S BREATH IS a little shorter than it used to be. He is puff-ing, puffing like wind rattling the dead leaves on the January white-oaks. He moves along the path, pulling his gigantic frame, his muscu-lar two hundred pounds of muscled clay—his bald head with its fringe of graying hair—glistening in the sunlight—his arms at the old magnificent swing—like the pendulum of a clock, that old faded blue shirt, his faded blue overalls that always look clean on Uncle Mel, with one suspender over his shoulder—the other swinging loose—his giant hands flexibly attached to his huge hairy arms—lumbering along over the narrow path—squeezing be-tween the trees with his broad shoulders, under a Kentucky sun, under the Kentucky skies—and on the hills that gave him birth, clay for his gigantic frame—and food to nourish his strong body and give him his great strength to throw the green crossties on the wagon and lift one end of the small saw-logs

*Jesse Stuart, "This Is the Place," originally published in *Esquire*, Vol. 6 (Dec., 1936), pp. 54–55, 300, 302, 305–306; collected in *Men of the Mountains* (N.Y.: Dutton, 1941), pp. 315–331, reprinted (Lexington: Univ. Press of Ky., 1979), pp. 315–331. Jesse Stuart/H. E. Richardson, Interview, W-Hollow, Greenup, Ky., Sept. 2, 1978. George Scarbrough, "Fine, Enduring Work" (review), Chattanooga, Tenn., *Times*, Mar. 23, 1941, clipping with photograph of Stuart smoking a pipe in Jesse Stuart, Scrapbook #7, p. 10, M. S. U.

Uncle Mel walks down the hill—down the path past the strawberry patch. He takes the lead—his eyes, black as midnight, gleam brightly in the sun. They flash at the trees that Uncle Mel has seen so often—the tough-butted white-oak trees on the steep banks below the strawberry patch—the land too rough and too steep for Uncle Mel to clean of brush, briars, and sprouts for strawberry land. "Well, if I could recall the years," says Uncle Mel, "recall the years and had a new pair of legs. I'm like the apple on the tree. I'm getting ripe. There's a few soft specks in me. When the apple gets ripe it's likely to fall." Uncle Mel walks on out the path—out past the old logs left at the edge of the strawberry patch to burn on April nights and May nights and fill the heavens with smoke to ward off the frost that kills the strawberries. Ah yes—you are not fooling Uncle Mel. He always has strawberries. Uncle Mel knows how to handle the frost that kills the young berry in the blossom. In front of us is the little knoll with the grove of tough-butted white-oak trees—with thousands of sagging branches that sway with the wind-seeded Johnson-grass where men would love to roll and drink a keg of cool beer.

"This is the place," says Uncle Mel, "right here. You see this is a real place for all of us to be buried. Here is a good place for us to be reunited in the end—reunited for the long sleep." Uncle Mel stands beneath a branch-entangled white-oak tree. The sun is high now. Uncle Mel is looking at the sun. "You see the sun comes over from the east. It goes down quietly in the west. It does not leave a path. It goes the path of wind and sky. That is the way we are in the end. The sprouts will grow on our farms. We'll go over as the sun—come to a quiet setting on this little knoll. There'll not be any path in the end. The sprouts will come up here—they will cover this hill unless countless generations of our kin are born in this hollow and live here—that these hills are to breed Sheltons and Powderjays forever and take back their dust in the end."

We are the blood of hill people. We have always been hill people—back, back, back, back, for so many, many, many long years that the hills have become a part of us, in our brain and the dirt of the hills is the clay of us—the mood of the wind in the pinetops and the saw-briars are the mood of us—the freedom of the woods, the wind and the skies—quietly, quietly, quietly, with little change. We have come the paths of the rocks, the eternal rocks, and the clouds that float above our land—and the trees that grow upon it. We have come a long path down—long, long, long. The hills have claimed our dust—Cold Harbor has claimed it, Virginia has claimed it, Gettysburg has claimed it, Big Sandy has claimed plenty of it—enough for a fertile acre—Antietam has claimed it and the hills of West Virginia and

North Carolina—France has claimed it, and Flanders and Bull Run. There has not been a lot that we have owned to hold our dust—we are lone sleepers under the skies that float above the backbones of hills—under the skies that float across America—Kentucky holds our dust, bushels of it—her trees have grown from the strength of it and her wild flowers have blossomed from it.

"Yes," says Uncle Mel, "we could all get along here very well I think. Your Pa being a Republican—that will be all right then. We can sleep under the same cover." And then I could say to Uncle Mel: "It will be the first time the Sheltons and the Powderjays ever agreed on politics. It will be when we are all sleeping together in this silent city that we have planned—where we perhaps will not have the croaking frog to tell us spring is here and the crow building in the pines. Lord—Lord—Lord—I have heard Republican and Democrat—until I am sick of it all—down from 1854 the taut lines have been drawn—it will soon be the hundredth year if the two parties last that long. What does it matter? It should not matter in a graveyard—it should not matter when we are dust—when we have at last come under one cover on a land that is our own at last."

"I used to have a funny notion about where I would take my rest," says Uncle Mel. "I never said anything about it. I used to think I'd like to dig my bed down in the ridge of rock that is the line between your Pa's place and mine—where that pizen vine is and them initials cut all over the rock at that little sand gap—then I thought the sides of that rock would crumble off and I'd be in there and they'd crumble right down to me—expose me. Then I thought that rock would be too hard to sleep on. I've thought a lot about my bed here lately and I believe this is the right place for all of us."

"The Powderjays are about all gone, Uncle Mel," I say, "they sleep other places and under different skies—they sleep on the river from whence they came—the Big Sandy. You know why we got to this country—why we came to the hollow years ago—and we have lived here ever since in this small world. There are not many of us to come to this knoll—my brothers ought to be here. Don't you think we should bring their dust back from the low-hills on the other side to this west side? Grandpa don't own that land any longer over there—it is in the hands of strangers now—only a few rusted wires keep the cattle off the ground where they sleep."

"Just them two boys dead—let me see—isn't that right? Not one of my eight dead, not Jan's seven, nor Jake's nine—and let me see—one of Mammie's fifteen died when she was a little thing—buried on Trip Creek—all ought to be brought back—all of them ought to be brought into one family instead of sleeping on so many hills that other men own—not that it matters—for the dust of them will sprout wild flowers and trees and corn, my son. But that dust will rise you know and we need to be on the same hill where it will be a family reunion in the flesh—we can be together and then we will be able to tell who is right in this world and who is wrong. We can have a lot to talk about then—a lot my son, a lot."

Uncle Mel stands under the white-oak tree. He looks up through the tangled branches moving in the wind—his bald head gleams—shines where the sun plays through the openings between the branches and leaves bright criss-crosses of sunlight on his head. Uncle Mel moves his hands when he talks—a giant man standing in the rays of the setting sun, Uncle Mel speaks: "Never was in the whole Shelton race of people where a man killed a man. We have had fights but we have never killed a man. See the prints of boot-heels on my temples! That's where they stomped me when I was a boy—old Jim Fonson's boy—stomped me—got me down. Thought they had me killed. I got up and I followed them. They went on laughing. The other fellow who helped do it was Ron Green. Two of them on me. Busted a bottle over my head and left me. I was drunk. They were not near as drunk as I was. I never forget it. They've stayed out of my way all of these years. That happened when we were boys. I could break either one of them in two. We have killed in wars—but never a fight—man to man. Pap got knocked out once for an hour or two. Went in a coal bank to get a man. It was dark in there and Pap walking in against the dark—the man could see Pap for he was against the light. So, he took Pap in the head with the coal pick. Got the scars on his head yet. He never went in any more coal banks to get a man."

Uncle Mel stands and he looks over the fields. The wind blows with a scent of sweet smells from the cane heading in the sun and the tasseling corn. It is good wind to breathe, Uncle Mel breathes it and he talks: "No, my son—the Sheltons have loved books. They have been book people, my son. W'y my Grandpa, old Percy Shelton, used to have a big room of books—big stacks of them and he read and preached all the time. Before he died when he was past four-score year and five he walked five miles and preached four hours. The old men said it was the best sermon he ever preached. He was a dead man the next day. When a man started anything in his church—he went back and got him. He had order and he preached. He was a officer in the Union Army, my son—and his son, your Grandpa, turned against his own father for the South. And when he cast his first vote, my son—Grandpa was there with a withe—and he made Pap haul his coat— Pap hauled his coat and he said: 'You can lick me Pap but I'll vote the way I see fit.' And he saw fit, my son, to vote the Democrat ticket—the only way to vote, my son. It stands for the poor people—it is the right ticket, my son. That is why I say your Pa is wrong. You can't tell him that for the Powder-jays took after the old man Powderjay who fit in the Union Army. That ruint the whole family on down even among you boys—my own sister's boys.

"I can see the silent city here—the grass among the ridges—the old rose bushes that will grow here among the lichen stones. That will be forever—oh so many, many years—that will be so many years that there is no need for any one to count—the oaks will have grown taller and their branches spread more as to keep out the sun and the myrtle will blossom with tiny blue blos-soms—it will climb over the mounds and around the roots of the trees—the lichen stones where the Powderjays and the Sheltons will have at last come to dust—all joined under the same cover—the Kentucky earth—sleeping, sleeping, sleeping—where there is no noise save the tinkling of the sheepbells on the hills, the love calls of the whippoorwills, the katydids—and the wind blowing through the seeded grasses. The Blue and the Gray will have at last come together—quietly in the dust side by side—and who will remember then among the generations unborn where the Democrats among us sleep and where the Republicans sleep? And who will remember then about the dreams of two families—about the great strong man Uncle Mel—his strength of muscle and his clearness of mind—his old fields where he had in corn where timber grows tomorrow? Saw-briars trail over the thin banks of ster-ile earth—ah, then, who will remember the millions of dreams of those who sleep in the silent city and whose blood goes on and on—blood that is Amer-ican—cradled in the laps of American hills, under American rocks and American skies. And shall they who pass by laugh and say: 'There's the dust of yesterday—old dust sleeping with cornfield stones to take their names and numbers—old, old, old—ancient dust—dust of America—sleeping—wonder if they await a day when they'll pop from their graves like young rabbits from a nest!' "

If Uncle Mel could just hear them and answer he would say: "You damned right we'll come popping out 'n here. The whole dad-durn push of us. That's why I walked out on that summer day—or was it spring—what does it matter now—that's why I told that college boy of my sister's that day that we ought to all be buried together—that boy got a lot of sour pudding stuck in his head at college. Got to doubting until I got hold of him and showed him some light. I says to him: 'W'y look at the butterfly in spring how it wakes up in heaven. Comes from the tomb—the stout cocoon. Look at the flowers how they bloom in spring and the great magnificent earth—how it has its seasons and how it works right on the dot. Bound to have order back of that.' So I took my watch and I says: 'Son look at this watch. You see it don't you. See how it runs and keeps time to the second. If there wasn't somebody back of that watch in Switzerland—a God of that watch— its Creator—how in the hell could it keep time, son? Now how can the time of this world click like it does—got to have a Creator son—got to have a Master.' And you can laugh all you want to laugh but when that old trumpet blows you'll never see such strings of Sheltons and Powderjays coming from under the cover—all right here together under these trees where it will be cool and the blossoms of the myrtle will be sweet to smell. I hope resurrection will be in June. That's the month I've always loved.

"And to think, here on this hill—this little hill where life goes on quietly and undisturbed save by the wind, the sheepbells, the whippoorwills, and the katydids—I shall sleep beside of my brothers, my sisters, my mother and father, and all my uncles on Mom's side of the house—the big Shelton uncles and all their children. It will cover the knoll already—the generations already living if they were all dead—and there are the generations unborn to be brought here in the hollow to this silent city—where there is not a silent city nor has there ever been as far as we know and can trace—it might have been in the dim years past—but we do not know—we do not find their shin bones working out of the earth nor their elbows—it is a land that gives birth to men who live and die here and are hauled away to some other place to sleep where there is more noise.

"It does not matter so much about dust," says Uncle Mel, holding to the twig of a white-oak. "Our dust sleeps during a winter waiting for the trumpet just like this oak tree will sleep during this winter when the sleet covers its bark. We'll sleep just like one night. Then we'll all wake up and be our natural selves again— Now our dust doesn't matter. I never could see why people cried and went on so over a man when he died. Let him lose a leg in the lumber woods and have that leg buried they never thought about crying. Just went on and buried that leg and forgot about it. One of his arms the same way—both arms and both legs. You'd never hear a lot of crying and going on. But let the man die—the whole of him—and then you'd hear them crying and going on. What I never could understand why we grieve over the whole and never say 'scat' about one of the parts. It never matters about our dust so we all get close and can be together and give the old-timers a surprise when we all get out 'n the bed."

"And what do we do while we are waiting—while our dust is sleeping the long night," I say to Uncle Mel, "in the narrow confines of our small world—in the village of this silent city of Powderjays and Sheltons with our in-laws plus that have come to sleep beside their wives." "My son," says

Uncle Mel, "we shall go on living in the same way we lived here—only we'll be light as the wind. We shall be as we have been—have the same color of hair, shapes of noses, the same voice—we shall run with our old company—I expect to have my farm here and do the things as I have always done. How can that which is the real Mel Shelton die? It can't die. You can't take a hammer and beat it to death even if you beat my head off. The real Mel Shelton will be here. You can't kill it. It was not born to die—only the husk that encloses it was born to die. We are going to bring all these husks right here and crib them."

"Then I shall have the dust of my brothers brought here," I says to Uncle Mel, "though I hate to disturb them after they have slept these years on the low hill beyond the hollow. And I shall have their dust planted on the hill that will enclose our dead—the hill that overlooks the cane patches and the corn fields—beneath our skies at home—among my blood kin—not among the strangers on another hill—away from the rest of us." And then I think: "Wonder if we shall know when spring comes, Uncle Mel? Wonder if we can tell if it going to rain by our rheumatics bothering us a little and our hair standing on its end? Ah—wonder, wonder—and if we can feel the roots of the white-oaks as they expand by the new rich dust we give them—that strength that belonged to the big Sheltons and the tall Powderjays—that which was American dust—gathered from the thin earth of Kentucky clay banks beneath her wind and her suns—blest by Kentucky's fruitful crop years and her lean years—Democrat dust and Republican dust—Methodist dust and Baptist dust—ah, the long years, the lean years—all in a night of peaceful sleep—maybe, we shall welcome after a hundred years of living and loving life and the earth—the wind, the sun, the moon, and the trees on the Kentucky hills—and Uncle Mel says we shall not die. Uncle Mel will not die. He is a Shelton and the Sheltons often have their way—wonder, ah wonder if even about Death and the silent city where no man speaks—but where we sleep—sleep, night and the winds of destiny that speak not to us but pass over us and mourn through the warm nights of spring when the whippoorwills call—ah too, of another generation—speak of love, of life and of living. But we speak not at all—the ghosts of us light as the wind and the wind with the identity of us stamped invisible—laugh to the wind and walk through the corn fields at night when a pretty moon is in the April sky—we laugh and speak to each other on the same old mountain paths. We cannot die. You cannot take a club and kill us. You might beat off our husk but the real of us is here—it will not die—not even when the smell of summer— the ripened corn and the heading cane with its white-dotted stems—all of the smell shall pass over it—the luscious sweet tang of scented wind from the growing summer and the creepy night of sheepbells tinkling on the hills will mingle with the ooze of night wind in the green weeds and the foxglove on the bluffs—ah not when the winds of autumn sigh for those gone and forgotten—sigh for us with the mixture of wind in the dead grass and the hanging leaves—we who have been dead so long and sleeping on the hill, cold, cold, cold—sleeping on the hill, where the snake creeps by and the lizard crawls on the tough-butted white-oaks and the old blue demijohns that hold the clusters of odorless sweet Williams and percoon blossoms shriveled to tiny wisps—and the wild Indian turnip's white blossoms—ah, the lizard crawls and the lizard never speaks. We never know of expanded roots and whispering trees and grass and roses—and the roots of myrtle never whisper to us or hold a fragrant bunch of myrtle blossoms to our noses—we who have loved life, fought, kissed, played, worked, loved, and hated—we who have been a stream of life—a constant flowing river toward the sunset—we who have tramped the hills and had no home and died and were buried among the ribs and thighs of hills—and now we have a home—a bed for a long rest in the end while hither thither on the roads of destiny—blown by the strange winds of time."

"We must go, my son," says Uncle Mel, "the sun is going down in the west. It will be time for me to get home and do up the feeding. Got four hogs to feed and a couple of cows to milk." And we start toward the house—down the hill among the black-oak stumps—the graveyard of a gigantic forest, long dead and forgotten. Peach trees with well pruned tops and healthy coats of bark, row crookedly the rugged hill to the west. "My trees—see them—I believe in fine orchards and clean corn fields." And then Uncle Mel's garden with the rows of palings and the jars that hang on the palings—the goose-neck hoes that lean against the palings—"My garden is clean. I keep it clean. I work it clean as I read a book clean—one that I love—I read my Bible clean."

Ah, I could tell Uncle Mel what I once heard a preacher say: "Ah that old man—that old bald headed Shelton—he's an infidel. Fixes the Bible to suit himself. Twists it around him with a lot of crazy beliefs. He's standing in the way of many with his set idears on the Bible. He says we are wrong. He never comes to church. I have seen him out sauntering through the woods at night—ah, strange man that he is."

"And son," says Uncle Mel, "remember this, my son. Live, live your life till you will not fear whatever that is to come. Live so that you can look any man in the face. Be as solid as a hill. Pay your debts when you can—if you can't tell your creditor you cannot. And remember my son, there is not a substitute for sweat. There is not a substitute for honesty—live, live and tend the earth and know the spring, the summer, fall-time, and the winter. Know the seasons and when to plant as your people before you. Live by the square. Die by the square. Remember, my son, shrouds are pocketless."

Ten thousand stars are in the sky—a blue sky above the clouds of fluttering leaves that whisper to themselves and to each other—and beneath the clouds of leaves there is darkness. "Do you need a lantern," says Uncle Mel, "going up the holler? We stayed over there too long. Here I am after dark doing my work up." "I can make it all right, Uncle," I says. "Eyes of the owl—can see at night—could feel my way up that hollow." And I know Uncle Mel I think as I stumble up the hollow. "Late doing up his work. W'y he takes spells and reads a book clean before he cleans the corn. He keeps the weeds out 'n the book instead of the corn. Haven't I seen his corn get mighty weedy—then out of a clear sky he would come and work from daylight till dark—work until it was clean as a hound dog's tooth—ah, that is Uncle Mel."

"Shrouds are pocketless," Keeps drumming in my head—over and over again as the leaves whisper to each other and to the wind, "Shrouds are pocketless." And the wind moans through the leaves above my head—wind that is blowing across Kentucky and sweeping on to some destiny—or not to a destiny at all—winds of the broad America—that strike her rugged, hiss and moan with the jagged hills piercing the side of the wind—ah, the great expanse of America under the cold blue American heavens illuminated with millions of stars that shine upon an earth that is both cruel and kind—an earth that is American—an earth that is mine and that has given me the flesh I have on my bones—an earth, the rugged, jutted, cruel earth, kind earth, that will give me a knoll to sleep in—a silent city that will hold the dust of my kin under the same cover—in the same great bed—under the roots of the white-oak trees—ah, an earth that is mine forever where the winds will sweep over me and utter strange sounds that I shall not hear while I'm asleep beside of Mom and Pa and Uncle Mel and all of my kin that walks the hills today and generations of kin unborn—ah, that we are American—forever, American. And Uncle Mel would say: "W'y sure we'll pop out'n the graves Americans and Democrats and Republicans—Baptists and Methodists."

The boys carry Uncle Mel off the hill—Lon and Will, shoulder him and carry him to the foot of the hill and to the house. "I tried to keep him from going to the field this morning," says Aunt Vie, "but you know how your Uncle Mel is. He just tore up the place and said the crabgrass was taking the corn. He was out at daylight this morning with his hoe. He's been staying in and taking care of the garden and doing the work around the house.

But he had to get out—so I saw them carrying him off the hill this morning at ten. It scared the life out'n me. He's been such a strong man——"

The Sheltons have been a strong race of people. But the strong have to die same as the rest of the weak—all have to bow to the inevitable—strong as Uncle Mel must bow. "Yes," says Lon, "I was working right behind him. He had the lead row of corn when he fell. He fell hard as a tree, I heard him lumber on the ground. I turned and I saw him. I hollered to Will—and he come and got an arm under each leg and I got him by each arm. I tell you Pap is heavy. He was a load from that hilltop. We had a time walking down hill with him—down the path to the house. He has never spoken since—fell at work this morning at ten. You can go in and see him—he's in there on the cot."

"What did the doctor say?" I says, the tears streaming from my eyes—and I thought: "The mountains of fine men must slumber to some destiny—ah whither wind that moans above the seeded grass—ah wither is your destiny? Where is the home of man—the long, long home and the journey thereto?" "The doctor says," says Lon, "for us to call Den, Mack, Jake, and the girls. He says it is a stroke. And he won't say much more."

I do not want to see him now—my Uncle lying there on the couch in quiet sleep—he who was a mountain of a man when we walked to the top of the hill and surveyed the bed—he who wished for a new set of legs and many more lives to live on earth—how could I stand to see those hands—those giant hands that felt the ax, the maul, the cross-cut saw, the plow handles, and the wedge and hoe—how could I stand to see them silent—those great hands where streams of blood once rushed in channels—hands that cleared the fields and built the houses and farmed the land, dug the coal from the groins of the hills—those powerful shoulders still now and the eyes that scanned the strawberry fields withered and dull in their sockets—great dynamic wells of energy that ceased to flow—his words—his millions of words that shaped his dreams—ah, I couldn't stand to see him now—his silent lips and quiet hands. "These hills will call for him," I thought, "or they'll rebuild his kind. His fields will want him back—his mules and his hounds. The birds he fed will miss him at the well-gum and the quails that come down off the hill and ate with his chickens. His trees will miss him—his peach orchard to the west of the house and the apple orchard will miss him—and his bees—And we shall think of him tomorrow and our kin might remember him awhile until they pass quietly too—and generations unborn will probably hear of Uncle Mel. Whither, ah whither the winds of destiny? And where is the home of man—that long, long home—that faraway somewhere and the long journey thereto?"

That stream of life has journeyed long under the spacious skies of America—over the mountains and among them. It has flowed—a river through the beauty of the green slopes of spring—the lilting beauty of the poplar leaves and the poplar and beech—it was a surging stream of spring, of clean blue mountain water—and the summer where it flowed, through growing fields of grain and the ripened fields of golden wheat—over the hills and through the vales of smelly flowers—it has come a long way to its home— that great river of life—and it flowed through autumn—the winds of autumn mixed with the sweetened odors of dying leaves and shriveling petals—under the naked trees and over the rifts—multi-colored carpets—whither, ah whither strong river to your destiny? To what dark winter is a portion of the waters left? And the great swirl of water keeps moving—ah, even through the night the great stream of life keeps moving on through a channel strong to bear the surge of wild waters, strong surging waters against the wind, time and tomorrow.

Yes, the green leaves will come in the spring and the grass spring anew. Life will come back to these hills in spring. Winter is for the long sleep and the dream and forgetting the season past. Life will come back to the flowers of spring and they will bloom anew in a spring paradise. Life cannot die. You cannot take a stick and beat it to death. The butterfly will awake from the cocoon—and find himself in a heaven of green clouds—in a flowery paradise—to loiter in the wind and find the smelly flowers. "Ah whither, oh whither, oh man, and to what destiny? Is it the roots of the tree, the blades of grass, the leaves of the grapevine? Is it cold, cold, cold lying on the hill forever beneath the cold millions of stars that are forever American—sleeping, sleeping, sleeping, oh man where the winds of destiny moan over the seeded grass and whisper words you cannot hear or understand—something about the corn and the sweat of man and maybe the substitute for sweat, the substitute for the clay that made him—ah, man is strange and into what river and to what destiny? To what great sea of destiny does the river of man flow? You can't kill me. I won't die. You could take a club and beat me to death. You could beat off my husk and bury it under the white-oaks— yet the real part of me would still be here. It will not die."

Ah spring and hence the many, many years—long, long, long years of bright blue lilting winds of April stirring the early tender thin-green on the trees and the bright pollinated wind of summer and fluxions of yellow sunlight on the blackberry briars—ah spring and hence the many, many years— the long, long, years—the dead specks of autumn leaves blown on the strange silver winds of time—neither here, nor there, nor anywhere—autumn saw-briars whose leaves turn multi-colored in the sun and the naked stems of the briars that cut and scar across the ancient mounds—the carpet of dead leaves there above the myrtle and among the lichened stones—ah, whither that fertile husk—that off-bearing of the great river—ah whither to what destiny? And why does the green sprig of acacia speak to the wind, and what does it speak—about the breaking of the cocoon? Or that of man?—whispers to the wind strange words while the winds sweep over to their destiny without muttering the strange syllables, the sounds of words.

Whispers the sassafras sprout maybe, or the lizard on the old blue demijohn: "The Sheltons and the Powderjays sleep here. Under the seeded grass, the lichen stones—the myrtle vines they rest. All come home at last—no more for them the distant hills, the Big Sandy, Gettysburg, Cold Harbor, Flanders, Virginia, France. They have come to sleep under the tough-butted white-oak roots in the hollow where once there was no graveyard at all. They made the graveyard here—planned it. Took the dust from this hollow—used it for a space of time. Then, like good neighbors they brought what they had borrowed back and gave it to the neighbor they borrowed it from—Sheltons and the Powderjays and their in-laws and next of kin—all sleeping here—tall Powderjays and mountain-of-men Sheltons. See the pieces of broken dishes and the bottles on their graves—the cornfield stones, and the white stones that give their names and numbers here——"

The seeded grass waves in the wind. The oak leaves flutter dryly in the summer heat—maybe it is in June. The oak leaves whisper, see—say so many foolish things. But that will not matter in years hence—if you could only see us Powderjays and Sheltons breaking from our silent city—here on this hill where it is a good place to drink a keg o' beer—here on this seeded grass beneath these white-oak trees— Ah, Uncle Mel—big as he ever was right back—still a Democrat and Pa still a Republican and Ma and Grandpa Shelton and the balance of the Sheltons—and the thin tall Powderjays coming to life again after their brains have grown brittle and their blood ceased to flow through old veins—back again and rested and ready for another life—a longer life—for anything beneath a hundred years is not time enough for a Powderjay—to live, and love, and fight, and curse—and clear the land and build the houses and the bridges—the railroads and turnpikes and fight the nation's battles—under the skies that are American.

If you could see all of us Republicans, Democrats, Methodists, Forty-Gallon Baptists, Hard-shelled Baptists, Free-willed Baptists, Primitive Baptists, Regular Baptists, United Baptists, Missionary Baptists, Union Baptists, Independent Baptists—all of us out'n the graves a shaking hands and asking the other how he is after the long night o' sleep and how much land he expects to tend this year—How he likes this part o' life called sleep and how glad he is that he's born into this world—so full o' surprises, and life and death—how great it all is—and how much fun it will be to live it all over again—to fight, to love, to live and die—and pay debts and make debts and buy land—the freedom of the earth, and wind and skies—all under the skies American—the expanse of eternal skies upon the earth—all all, all, flesh and blood and sleep and graves and all, American.

Alphabetical List of Stuart's Separately Published Works

Album of destiny (*1944*) / Andy finds a way (*1961*) / Autumn lovesong (*1971*) / Beyond dark hills (*1938*) / Clearing in the sky & other stories (*1950*) / Come back to the farm (*1971*) / Come gentle spring (*1969*) / Come to my tomorrowland (*1971*) / Dandelion on the Acropolis (*1978*) / Daughter of the legend (*1965*) / Dawn of remembered spring (*1972*) / Foretaste of glory (*1946*) / God's oddling (*1960*) / The good spirit of Laurel Ridge (*1953*) / Harvest of youth (*1930*) / Head o' W-Hollow (*1936*) / Hie to the hunters (*1950*) / Hold April (*1962*) / Honest confession of a literary sin (*1977*) / Huey the engineer (*1960*) / A Jesse Stuart harvest (*1965*) / A Jesse Stuart reader (*1963*) / Kentucky is my land (*1952*) / The Kingdom Within (*1979*) / The land beyond the river (*1973*) / Land of the honey-colored wind (*1982*) / Man with a bull-tongue plow (*1934*) / Men of the mountains (*1941*) / Mr. Gallion's school (*1967*) / Mongrel mettle (*1944*) / My land has a voice (*1966*) / My world (*1975*) / Old Ben (*1970*) / Outlooks through literature (*1964*) / A penny's worth of character (*1954*) / The place we live (*1976*) / Plowshare in heaven (*1958*) / Red Mule (*1955*) / A ride with Huey, the engineer (*1966*) / The rightful owner (*1960*) / Save every lamb (*1964*) / Seven by Jesse (*1970*) / The seasons of Jesse Stuart (*1976*) / Short stories for discussion (*1965*) / Tales from the Plum Grove hills (*1946*) / Taps for Private Tussie (*1943*) / Thirty-two votes before breakfast (*1974*) / The thread that runs so true (*1949*) / Tim (*1939*) / To teach, to love (*1970*) / Trees of heaven (*1940*) / Up the hollow from Lynchburg (*1975*) / The world of Jesse Stuart (*1975*) / The year of my rebirth (*1956*)